PENGUIN

BRIGHT

G. H. Morris was born in Leeds in 1939. He started work in the pharmaceutical industry, eventually founding and building up his own highly successful business. He comes to writing, therefore, from a background of science and commerce. He now writes full-time, lives in Leeds and is married with three children, two dogs, a horse and a cat. His novel *Doves and Silk Handkerchiefs*, which forms the first part of this trilogy, was awarded the 1986 Constable Trophy for the most outstanding first novel from the North of England.

G. H. MORRIS

———————

BRIGHTSIDE

DOVES AND SILK HANDKERCHIEFS

GRANDMOTHER, GRANDMOTHER,
COME AND SEE

THE BRIGHTSIDE DINOSAUR

PENGUIN BOOKS

PENGUIN BOOKS

Published by the Penguin Group
Penguin Books Ltd, 27 Wrights Lane, London w8 5TZ, England
Penguin Books USA Inc., 375 Hudson Street, New York, New York 10014, USA
Penguin Books Australia Ltd, Ringwood, Victoria, Australia
Penguin Books Canada Ltd, 10 Alcorn Avenue, Toronto, Ontario, Canada M4V 3B2
Penguin Books (NZ) Ltd, 182–190 Wairau Road, Auckland 10, New Zealand

Penguin Books Ltd, Registered Offices: Harmondsworth, Middlesex, England

Doves and Silk Handkerchiefs first published by Constable 1987
Grandmother, Grandmother, Come and See first published by Constable 1989
The Brightside Dinosaur first published by Constable 1991
Published in one volume, under the title *Brightside*, by Penguin Books 1992
1 3 5 7 9 10 8 6 4 2

Printed in England by Clays Ltd, St Ives plc
Set in 10/12 pt Monophoto Baskerville

CONTENTS

Genealogy

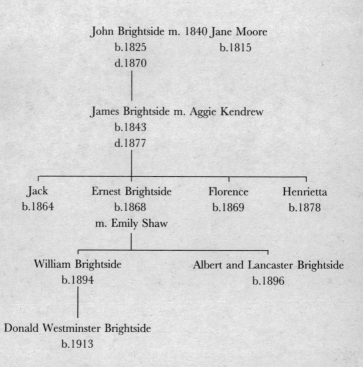

John Brightside m. 1840 Jane Moore
b.1825   b.1815
d.1870

James Brightside m. Aggie Kendrew
b.1843
d.1877

Jack   Ernest Brightside   Florence   Henrietta
b.1864   b.1868   b.1869   b.1878
              m. Emily Shaw

William Brightside   Albert and Lancaster Brightside
b.1894   b.1896

Donald Westminster Brightside
b.1913

DOVES AND
SILK HANDKERCHIEFS

To my father

I

My great-great-grandmother, Jane Brightside, and her first encounters with flying man

My great-great-grandmother, who had been born on the day of the battle of Waterloo, slowly climbed the slope of Hunger Hill. A body of immense durability; climbing the contour of the hill the old woman assumed the powerful posture of a quadruped. A slow engine, she lugged a string of invisible coal tubs, mooching through the incline. Despite the years of pulling below ground her frame had never naturally succumbed to tortuous perversion, but now on Hunger Hill geometry fixed her, bent into the dark and angular landscape. Gravity plotted her journey along the well-worn path. She gazed beyond into the yawning sky where touches of salmon flashed from the east. Below and behind her the few terraced houses stood awake and small in the near dawn, and below them the telltale squeak of the winding machine cycled in the new century and still below that, imperceptible to all but those who have spent a lifetime hearing it, came the tap-tappings from those who hewed the coal.

It was nigh on sixty years since she had been down a pit. Sixty years since John Brightside, by the eerie gloom of his candle, had first seen her ample buttocks running the tubs and sworn there and then that she should be his wife. Sixty years since his mate had teased the young John unmercifully. 'She'll be too much for thee, young lad,' he grinned. 'Suck thee in, boots and all.' But young John had been struck with a passion for the older woman which none could comprehend and which only the marriage bed might fulfil. And so it did. Every night for thirty years his passion for Jane Brightside was fulfilled. And each day for nearly thirty years the passion was sustained by the image of Jane's buttocks under her grubby skirts running the tubs. 'She's ugly as the devil hisself,' his brothers had taunted, but it made little difference, for the engine of the fever which drove him came not from her face but from that part of her anatomy which lay hidden and

3

wrapped in grimy sackcloth. 'She's an arse on her like an 'oss,' they then offered when they learned of the true centre of his passion; but John only smiled a knowing smile and from that night forbade the woman destined to be his wife ever to descend the pit again – never to bend her magnificent buttocks towards another man.

'Nivver, nivver, nivver,' snorted the youthful Brightside as he nestled between the woman's thighs and where he remained for nigh on thirty years until the day the roof fell and the pit prop split open his head like a ripe coconut. And for the sixty years, since the day of her marriage, during John's lifetime and since, Jane had, each dawn, collected plant material for her medicines and potions. Within easy reach of the village, on the hills, in the hedgerows and by the river bank, she was able to find biting stonecrop and woodvine, dead-tongue and monkshood, always filling her basket with a colourful selection of flowers, leaves and roots. In the churchyard from among the gravestones, she could even find deadly nightshade with its purple bells, an extract of which she sold to the apothecaries in Leeds and Wakefield. She would collect sun-spurge for warts (the juice of which is said by Dr Livingstone to kill zebras) and buckthorn as a purgative, yarrow for nosebleeds and inflammation, and out of which she made a beer, which tasted most foul but was so strong in alcohol content that even the hard drinkers were rendered insensible by no more than a pint or two.

Now approaching the stone wall which encircled the summit of Hunger Hill, like a crown on the brow of a proud medieval king she could see the yellow blaze of stonecrop which grew from the gaps in the stone. It was said that the Romans had built the original wall but succeeding generations had refurbished and replaced it until now the dry sandstone walls with its outpourings of golden moss and yellow stars told only of all too few days of the present summer. She looked again to the east where the sun now rising shone through a coal dust haze casting blood-red shadows on the rock. The crevices, out of which grew the worm-killing plant, were intensely dark and secretive, hiding green stems which trailed from the narrow cold into sunlight. 'Birds bread,' her father had called it, but she had never once seen a bird of any description feed upon it. She could see now, as she prised specimens from the cracks in the stone, the sun

4

rising above the river below. Down at Bottom Boat the red ball was kicked about above the gently waving poplars which lined the banks. Jane let her eyes scan the sky around and upwards; she was looking for men. Flying men. Or machines perhaps. Flying machines. Ever since that morning during the summer of last year she had been searching the skies for flying men. She had been in Kettle Flatt, a hollow piece of scrubby land, perhaps a crater sometime formed by a small meteorite, when out of the sky again fell an object. It fell right out of the sun along with the sparrows, the thrushes and the sedge warblers. It was then that she had met Duncan D'Arcy and Lady Annabelle Kerr; they too had tumbled drunk and downside up, together with the object, from the sky. Each clutched a bottle of champagne and they both fizzed and giggled. 'What is this place?' he'd asked. 'Ardsley,' she replied, stupefied by the glamorous finery – he in silk, she in chiffon and lace. 'Where you come from?' Jane finally had the courage to ask. 'Alexandra Palace, dear,' he'd replied. 'Air race you know.' Jane blinked uncomprehendingly. 'Never seen one of these before?' he inquired. 'No, don't suppose you have,' he answered himself, swigging from the bottle. 'Mark my words, madam, one day soon flying machines will fill the air.' His silk waistcoat glistened in a golden sun so that she had to shield her eyes from the explosive sheen. 'Common as the railway engine soon – you'll see,' he said and he offered his bottle of champagne. She gulped and spluttered her first and only ever swig of the fruity drink. The bubbles went up her nose, causing her to sneeze. She handed the bottle back after wiping the neck with a coarse dirty hand. He didn't seem to mind but went on, 'Perhaps you could direct us to a hostelry. We can have the airship collected later.' Jane looked at the broken basket and heap of crumpled material which billowed over the undulating ground. This she presumed to be the thing which the man referred to as an airship. Then, remembering her manners she offered a curtsy and withdrew a bottle of yarrow beer from among the blossoms in her basket. Duncan accepted her gift and much to her amazement drank almost the lot down without pausing for breath. 'Sorry Annie,' he said guiltily to his companion when he finally passed it. 'Saved you a little.' And he offered the lady the last drops of Jane's beer. The lady gulped the beer,

5

belched and then all three laughed heartily. Since that day Jane's world had not been the same.

Literally, the world had changed. If machines could fly, then which was up and where was down. The sky sometimes appeared to be upside down. How strange, she thought. One could float all the way from Castleford to Leeds in a contraption. Travel in a medium without obstacles. What freedom, she rejoiced. Did it matter which way up the sky was if there were no obstacles? She scanned the expansive, now fully awake and very blue sky, again, looking for men, one way up or another.

Although we called it a village the few streets which constituted our settlement and housed our small community was by definition a hamlet. There was no church but we had an alehouse. It was, at the turn of the century, like any other of a hundred or so similar communities scattered like stardust across the West Yorkshire coalfield. The family house built from heavy grey stone sat in the middle of a terrace of identical dwellings, sombre even rough but never brooding. The house was too small to overpower a man. Men and women then were masters of the piles of stick and stone which made a home. People poured out of the matchwood doors, growing organically from the buildings. The terrace was ours, people exuded from the brick like the yellow starry stonecrop creeping from the Roman wall on Hunger Hill. Jane's son, James Brightside, and my paternal great-grandfather had been the first to live in the house. The coal owner who sank the shaft and built the houses for the colliers to live in, stood in the rain and said to him and his new wife 'Tha rent's three shillin' a week. Choose an 'ouse; there's nowt between 'em. One's same as t'other. But tha can choose. They're mostly empty yonder.'

So James Brightside, with his new wife, Aggie, chose the one with the fewest and the shallowest puddles outside the front door and settled into the dark inside to watch the bouncing rain. But soon the house began to fill, first with children, then with his mother after the death of John Brightside, then with lodgers as many as seven or eight at a time. The downstairs parlour and the upstairs two bedrooms began to creak with the weight of colliers black and grimy, but each a five-pointed star like the stonecrop flowers in the wall.

Eventually into the house too, came the grandchildren, among them my father but more of them later. Suffice it to say that the smoky terrace and its occupants was like a train load of bright-eyed Indians hauled across continents and so excited they were too at the prospect of their cramped and chattering journey.

Returning from her walk on Hunger Hill, great-great-grand-mother entered the parlour through the door which led directly from the street. The uneven hollows in which the puddles had formed when James Brightside came to the house were long gone, replaced by a grassed lawn on which the youngsters played cricket (aspiring to be a Rhodes or Lord Hawke), a game peculiar in that the eleven was made up by dogs who fielded at the boundaries. Her granddaughter, my father's aunt Henrietta, stoked a roaring fire. Summer it was, but in the collier's home the boiling of water to wash the dirt from the menfolk was as constant as the sun in the heavens. All down the terrace, water was boiling atop the roaring coal fires. That selfsame coal which they had hewed perhaps a week before was now heating the water to bathe the soot from their bodies and the ache from their limbs, preparing them for another day on which they could limp to the pit. It was a constant passage of energy from the coal to the water to the collier to the pick and back to the coal. In most homes the colliers would bathe once or at most twice a week, the rest of the week a sort of strip wash would suffice, but in our house Jane's command was law. 'The mucky beggars get a full tin bath after each shift – medicated too,' she instructed all. And out would come the potions and the lotions, left on the mantelshelf, above the roaring fire for the men to administer to their tubsful of steaming water, while the women disappeared to the Lord knows where. It was a matter of endless debate amongst the men as to where on earth the women got to when they were left at home to bathe. The earth closets, the alehouse, a walk to the church in the next village, but no one knew for sure. They just disappeared and then quite magically reappeared as the last man was belting the trousers into which he'd just climbed, hair still wet and uncombed, but clean and smelling sweetly as the flowers in great-great-grandmother's basket.

At this time, at the turn of the century, our house breathed a little more easily as the population within contracted. As well as

7

great-great-grandmother it had housed my grandfather, Ernest – it was his name that was scrawled into the blue rent book which stood upright upon the mantelshelf behind a ticking clock; his wife, Emily and his youngest sister, the Henrietta to whom I have already referred. Then there was my father, now aged six, and his twin brothers, Albert and Lancaster, who were his juniors by a couple of years. The three children slept together with their parents in the larger bedroom while Henrietta and her grandmother slept next to them in the smaller room. Two lodgers, Mr Pettit and Mr Junkin, slept in wide winged chairs flying in the night-time parlour below, but always out of their cockpits and off to the colliery before the rest of the occupants had stirred and leaving behind them for the children to ponder the curious smell of sleep absorbed into the fabric of their makeshift beds.

Henrietta stoked the fire holding the long metal poker at such a distance from the heat to enrich only her air of absentmindedness. The reality of her situation, twenty-two and unmarried, ensured a vacancy filled inwardly with dreams of men. But not only that; there was something more. Henrietta was a poet, locked in like a bookworm, tight between pages she ate her own silence. Her grandmother startled her as she came in.

'Where's the children?' she asked.

'Playing cricket on the common,' Henrietta answered. 'Didn't you see them as you came in?'

'No.'

'They're out there somewhere,' she shrugged and turned her attention again to the boiling of water.

'Mr Pettit and Mr Junkin will be home soon, luv,' she heard her grandmother saying.

'I know, grandmother,' she said irritably. 'I can't hurry the water. It'll boil when it wants to.'

The old woman ignoring Henrietta's irritation asked, 'Did you see the stones today?'

At first she didn't answer, then she said, looking into the fire, 'Yes, I watched them awhile.'

The old woman waited for more, then, when it was apparent that nothing more would be added she spoke again, looking to the pen and ink which sat upon the mantelshelf above her granddaughter's stooped and long back.

'Did you write?'

'No, not yet.'

In the silence that followed Jane went into the back scullery, a tiny room beyond the parlour, where she stored her flowers and concocted her potions. She quietly unloaded her basket, twining stalks and hanging bundles from the low ceiling to dry. Some roots she placed directly into bottles and storage jars, replacing them carefully in their correct place among the tiers of shelving. She waited patiently for her granddaughter to talk, when she did Henrietta said, 'The river's in flood. The stones are covered again. I saw two small fishes playing hide among them. They were stickleback I think.' The old woman allowed the flesh about her face to creep into a smile while her eyes remained fixed on the task she was performing. 'Then you'll have much to write about,' she said at last with satisfaction.

'Yes, I suppose,' Henrietta answered poking absent-mindedly at the coals. She was preparing a journal, a kind of natural history of a group of stones down by Bottom Boat. She had for three years now been writing this history of the stones. Noting the imperceptible changes. The weathering of rock. The growth of lichen. An evolution Mr Darwin might have called it. Many would have chided her for even thinking of that name, but the idea of imperceptible change appealed to her. Not much to note in a lifetime perhaps, but just sufficient to make it all worthwhile. Nothing to disturb the living but enough to surprise the long, long dead. Her thoughts were broken by a tapping coming from the fire just above the glowing coals. The noise familiar to both women but more so to Jane because of her great advantage in years brought the latter quickly back into the parlour.

'It's Mrs Gill,' she said. 'Pass it on girl,' and immediately Henrietta went to the opposite wall and started to tap on it with the still hot poker. The tapping had been a signal from their nextdoor neighbour Mrs Gill to make them aware that a stranger had entered the village. She in turn would have heard it from the Hendersons and so it was that news travelled in the terrace, by way of Yorkshire range and interconnecting walls.

The two women together with all others who had received the warning draped their heads in black shawls and hurried to the front of the house. A chorus of curious, sometimes frightened women greeted the stranger as he walked to the common, herding unsure children before him. He was very tall and thin, wearing a faded frock coat and tight trousers which rode up at the ankles. On his head adding fearful height he wore a battered stove-pipe hat. His long white beard gave him a patriarchal look, although Henrietta was sure that he was a man of fewer years than the beard might suggest, certainly no more than forty she guessed. To her grandmother, however, the stranger looked like an etching she had once seen of Noah. In each hand he gripped a large suitcase, the weight of which sagged his shoulders, seemingly lengthening his already long arms. The spring in the stride of his spidery legs confirmed to Henrietta that she had been correct. This was no Noah, here indeed was a young and handsome stranger. Disguised maybe, but definitely Adonis. The man bounced along, knees well ahead of shoulders held back by oppressive weights. Arms in their turn lagged some way behind the shoulders as they dragged the cases along. Staring at the line of waiting women, he made directly for Jane whose face probably offered the best of a welcome among a score of black looks.

'Robber,' he said from amid shining white teeth.

'Cell. Robber?' He seemed to ask.

'There's no jail here, luv,' Jane replied helpfully.

'Shail?' he repeated searching the sky for meaning and finding an answer in that place which somehow links our brains to a vast beyond. 'No. Robber goods.' He made the last world rhyme with moods.

'I think he's a salesman,' Henrietta advised her grandmother.

'Yes,' said the stranger, catching her words and raising a bony finger to point at my great-aunt. 'Sell. Robber.'

'You'd better come in,' Jane said moving aside, at which a great intake of breath could be heard from among the chorus.

'Witch,' they said. Only a witch, or something worse could speak to and befriend strangers in such a way.

Once inside the parlour the man deposited his cases on the pegged carpet, which the women were constantly making and replacing from old rags, and immediately flailed his arms windmill fashion.

'Leeds. Strong,' he said indicating that he had walked at least ten miles, and flexing his arms at the elbows.

'Robber?' He nodded to Jane.

'What is this robber, luv?' she asked, as if speaking to a child.

'What is?' asked the man and immediately went down on one long knee to open a case from which seemed to coil dozens of black snakes. Both women gave short piercing screams, which brought faces to the window and open door. The neighbours saw only an open case out of which had poured a few pneumatic bicycle tyres, the last of which was still cycling unaided about the parlour. The remainder languished against the various bits of furniture where they had come to rest. The stranger handed a card to Henrietta. A neat hand had written in ink an explanation for the stranger's visit. She read aloud, in a weak voice.

'My name is Elyahou. I am from Transylvania. I wish to sell you rubber goods. I have bands, stamps, mackintoshes, golf balls and cycle tyres. False limbs and doormats are my speciality. Also pneumatic playsuits for the children, these may be hired for one penny each per day. Ideal for birthday parties and other celebrations.'

Elyahou grinned, recognizing the concluding words.

'You wan'?' he inquired.

Henrietta shook her head, withdrawing from the man's thrusting face. 'Mackintosh?' said the man pulling a dirty grey waterproof from the case. She shook her head again. Anxious faces were pressed up to the door. Could these hussies succumb and hand over money to a stranger?

'What was that about stamps?' Jane asked her granddaughter.

'Stamps, yes,' said the man still on one knee and already rummaging in the second case. 'You wan'?' he asked with a trader's desperation and now banging a large rubber stamp soaked in ink on to clean paper held to the ruffling pegged carpet.

The two women and everyone outside too strained forward, trying to read what had appeared by magic on the virgin paper.

ELYAHOU TSIBLITZ
RUBBER GOODS
SHIPS YARD, LEEDS

The man looked round at all the black shawled heads.

'Elyahou Tsiblitz, robber goods,' he shouted from the floor, and reading from the paper, stressing again the double 'o' sound and grinning widely.

'Can I have one of those with my own words on't?' Jane asked.

Elyahou shrugged, not understanding.

'Write,' she instructed her granddaughter. Henrietta took her pen with the ink bottle from the mantelshelf, tugged the paper from the man's hand and seated herself at the table, pen poised.

'Henrietta Brightside,' the old woman dictated. Henrietta unsure, at first, eventually wrote in large, neat, capital letters, looking eagerly to her grandmother for the next line. 'Child of charm, poetry and love,' she continued, a small grin playing at her mouth. Then seeing Henrietta's reticence she added, 'C'mon, girl. Get it writ. This is my present to thee. So tha'll do as tha's telled.' Henrietta wrote obligingly, handing the paper to her grandmother after blotting it carefully.

'How much?' Jane asked, thrusting the paper back at Elyahou.

'Two pennies,' he said, understanding the universality of the old woman's request.

'There now,' she said poking her hand deep into her pinafore and producing two bright new pennies. 'You bring that to me next time you pass, and don't be long mind.' Elyahou nodded brightly. The chorus outside winced, as the shiny pennies were passed across from one hand to the other, and just as three breathless children pushed their way through the door. No, not more, the neighbours seemed to be daring them. Not now. Not in front of the children.

'You wan' suit?' Elyahou asked delving deeper within the second case. 'Here, for childs,' he added pulling out the pneumatic suits which on his card had been advocated for birthdays. My father and the twins were struck dumb as he pulled himself up to his full height, almost touching the ceiling, and his agile arms quickly dressed each child in a suit of smelly rubber. When finally all three stood before the whole mournful female content of the terrace, bedecked in their suits, which seemed to hang in tatters from their thin bodies, the stranger clapped his hands once like a prestidigitator would do before performing a wondrous piece of magic. 'Hi!' he shouted, and pulled a valve on Albert's suit. The inrushing air caused him to be transformed into a round ballooning chicken. 'Hi!' shouted the man again and hey presto, my father became an overfed sheep and with a final monosyllabic ejaculation and a great inrush of air Lancaster floated to the roof bedecked in the costume of a bee.

The wondrous cries of 'Oh!' from his audience ensured once and for all that Elyahou would have a market, albeit a small one, in our village. Within moments he had sold out of pneumatic tyres and doormats. Even a false arm had been sold to Mrs Henderson but the Lord knows why. Mr Junkin returned home amidst the commotion to purchase a new set of rubber teeth, and Elyahou himself freely admitted that he had never sold so much knicker elastic in a single session (albeit said in a strange tongue which none present could understand). Over a thousand yards of it had gone to the women of the terrace. Mr Pettit who had a way with numbers and who knew about such things worked out that if put together it would have wound four times round the whole terrace and when stretched at least six times. 'Some knickers,' my grandfather was heard to say, raising his brows when told of it.

Amidst those bizarre and joyous moments my father and his brother Albert danced and sang in their inflatable costumes and above it all Lancaster buzzed tearfully about the room. Great-great-grandmother, who was forever, at that time, searching the sky for flying men, never would have dreamed even in her wildest fantasies that the first person she should see actually in flight would have been her great-grandson, Lancaster.

2

The *History of the Stones* and how my great-aunt Henrietta came to lose her virginity

It was more than a year before Elyahou Tsiblitz visited our village again. The neighbours had long scoffed that great-great-grand-mother had seen the last of her twopence and even she, a most ardent believer in man's inherent goodness, was beginning to think that she had been cheated and that Henrietta's present would never arrive. So it was, with a mixture of anger and relief, that she greeted the news of the stranger's second coming. A minute before Mrs Gill had put her poker to use at the Yorkshire range my father and his twin brothers had rustled breathless into the house to inform those present that the rubber man (for so they had dubbed him) had entered the village. This gave both Hen-rietta and her grandmother valuable seconds in which to prepare their respective faces. The former, beneath her shawled head, assumed the disinterested gaze of one whose heart pounds the true nature of longing while the older woman, overcoming her initial feelings of anger, assumed an approving smile and air of relief. They both walked slowly to the already open door, to greet, in their different ways, the man who had first brought both a bizarre new technology and the wonder of flight to our home. The masks which each had assumed were quickly dispelled, however, when they caught sight of him. The frock coat and the stove-pipe hat were unmistakably those of Elyahou but no more did he bounce his cases along at the ends of long rubbery arms. Instead the same cases were strapped to a cart which was towed behind a giant tricycle. The flapping shoes at the end of his long legs created great circles, driving the contraption with the three spoked wheels on to the common.

He looked as if he might have belonged to a travelling circus. Despite the fact that the long white beard no longer grew from his jowls and had now been replaced by a brown Wild Bill Hickock style moustache, Henrietta felt her Adonis looked older. Her heart ceased its racing, her face registered disappointment.

'Where's his beard?' her grandmother asked with a frown as the man cycled to their door.

'Don't know,' Henrietta replied, wondering if the question deserved an answer at all.

'Where's your beard, Elyahou?' the old woman piped as he dismounted, smiling through his pearly white teeth.

'Beard. Gone,' he said, indicating the world beyond the village with a large hand.

'It makes you look younger,' she said, now smiling approvingly again as the neighbours began to close around the stranger and her front door. He shrugged, not having understood, and went to the cart at the back of the tricycle. He started to unfasten a suitcase. 'Robber!' he shouted to the village at large. 'Robber goods.' Rubber boots spilled out on to the ground.

'Oo, I'll have one of them,' said Mrs Henderson, who it seemed would buy anything from the rubber man.

'You'll need a pair, luv,' a neighbour reminded her.

'What, two?' she asked.

'Yes, they're boots, luv. For't feet.'

'Oh. Are they?' she replied, pulling a face as if deciding she wouldn't have one after all.

Elyahou removed a card from the case and gave it to Henrietta, prompting, with his eyes and a gentle movement with his hand at her arm, for her to read it. It bore the same neat writing which the first card had shown. She cleared her throat and read aloud, with some embarrassment.

'My name is Elyahou. I'm sorry I didn't come sooner, but I have been travelling in Europe. I apologize for keeping you waiting. God bless you all when wearing my rubber boots.'

When she had finished reading he took back the card from between her limp fingers and replaced it with the long awaited present from her grandmother.

'Indelible,' he said. 'No go,' he then added, shaking both his head and his raised index finger. The latter was moved back and forth in very small motions as if he were trying to warn her of the permanence of some imaginary markings. Henrietta nodded understandingly and with excitement turned back into the house, eager to try out her new present. Throughout the next hour or so during which the second bazaar was held with just as much enthusiasm as for the first, stampings were heard to come from the parlour indicating to all that it had certainly been a twopence well spent. My great-great-grandmother spent most of the rest of the day carrying her justified smile between neighbours and loudly clanking the loose change which often accumulated in the depth of her pinafore pocket.

Before the sale got under way the children pestered both their parents and the rubber man to try out the inflatable suits. To show no favouritism Elyahou asked the children to draw the costumes from a sack. There were a dozen in all, one for each child who craved the excitement of dressing up and very soon, using the same dexterity he had shown on the previous occasion Elyahou had dressed them all, inflated their costumes and had them bouncing around the common in joyous mimicry of a well-stocked menagerie. All except Lancaster, that is, who had again got the bee. Tearfully, the twin ascended heavenwards, my great-great-grandmother wondering if perhaps he might never come down, particularly when, after a while he sailed right over the houses. He came eventually to land much to her relief, but not his own, in the ash pits. It's a strange thing, but on each occasion that the costumes were donned in our village my Uncle Lancaster always had the bee. He was the only villager always to fly in a costume at the times of the Transylvanian's visits, and with one notable exception, the only one ever to fly for real. Eventually he joined the flying corps and later the Royal Air Force, and by some peculiar twist of fate, just a little creepy really, he died piloting the bomber which bore his name, but that's another story.

After the dressing up the boot sale got under way. I write boot sale for Elyahou had little else to sell. Nevertheless, within the hour his stock had been exhausted and every collier had a new pair of rubber boots purchased by some lady on his behalf. Even Mrs Henderson, changing her mind yet again, had bought an odd right boot for herself, sharing the expense of a pair with Mrs Colley whose husband had lost a leg in a pit accident the previous summer.

Before taking his leave the rubber man shook my great-great-grandmother warmly by the hand and said, 'Present, yes?' Henrietta watched as he took from under his stove-pipe hat a cloth cap which he had been wearing beneath and handed it to the old lady. It was of a soft brown material and had an expensive satin lining. The old lady with rough but honest grace and insisting that exchange was no robbery, slipped the man an assortment of medicaments from her store in the scullery. When Elyahou had gone and the neighbours had returned to their own homes, Henrietta said, 'It's beautiful, grandmother. It's from America,' and she pointed to the silk label inside which read, 'Wizak Hatters, Paterson, New Jersey'.

After supper that evening and after each of the menfolk had bemoaned the fact that rubber boots would be of no use in a pit, where a dropped implement would almost certainly break the toes, the old woman handed the cap to Ernest explaining that it was a present from the strange Transylvanian.

'By, it's a grand cap is this, grandmother,' Ernest said, stroking the satin lining. 'Hello,' he then said, 'it's already got somebody's name on't' – bending the cap closer to the light at the window so that he could read out, 'Gaetano Bresci.'

'Give it 'ere, Ernest,' said Mr Pettit who knew about caps.

'Bresci,' he read finally: 'Isn't that t' bugger who murdered King of Italy?'

'Who? Humberto?' said my grandfather. 'Don't be daft, Bill.'

'Ay. Shot him stone dead last year,' said Bill who knew a thing or two. 'I'll not kid thee.'

'Give it back,' said my grandfather, grabbing it from his lodger's hands and fitting it to his head before it could be dispatched back to Milan. 'Fits a treat,' he said, and didn't remove the cap for a week. In fact nobody was quite sure how it came to be removed. He just came up out of that dark stinking hole in the ground one day minus cap, and with a pale ring around his hairline. 'Can't understand it,' he muttered. ''Ad it on't 'ead this morning when I went down.'

When James and Aggie Brightside first went inside our house and closed the door on the teeming rain and over-filled puddles, a quiet descended upon the stone interior which James later described as darkness. Not the darkness of the pit, which heaven knows is dark enough, but a silence and darkness living in the very fabric of the house he had said. It was as if there was no air in the house, just dark and quiet stone. Now, I have already said that the quiet was soon dispelled, that the insemination of children and others into the home brought a tumbling joy to the house and so it did. The stones at last breathed. Yet, through some as yet undisclosed agent an appreciation of the early solitude of the first inhabitants was passed from one Brightside to the next. Ernest's elder brother Jack felt it and it finally drove him from the house; from the pit even, to take up farming on the far side of Wakefield. Henrietta too, knew of it, indeed one might say enjoyed it. In the next generation the manifestation had already visited my uncle Lancaster by the time of his fourth birthday and certainly I can vouch for and attest the description given by my great-grandfather. I too have felt the depth of darkness in the stone. If not careful one could drown in it. That it is passed from one generation of Brightside to the next is confirmed by the simple fact that no lodger or visitor ever spoke of having experienced it, and indeed that the manifestation did not travel backwards through the generations is strongly suggested by the fact that great-great-grandmother had no experience of it either. Old Dr Cartwright who had known all the Brightsides well put it down to melancholia, which he had known to run in families, but putting a name to it really didn't seem to explain the phenomenon. After all, nobody seemed to experience melancholia outside of the house and indeed Jack, who was farming on the far side of Wakefield and his mother who still lived with him, had not suffered an attack since leaving our village. Henrietta, who was probably the cleverest Brightside who ever lived, put it down to history. History isn't that nonsense about long ago, she said. It's not about the kings of England, every one of whom Mr Pettit knew by heart in chronological order, nor is it about battles and governments and dates and laws. No, history is about people. Not *the* people as some colliers now found it fashionable to talk of, not the amorphous mass of unwashed heroes. No, she said, history was about a life. Each life was a history. And not just people but things too. The stones which built the house had a history. They too had a life. Some of us can sense the history of the stones, the quiet, the darkness; others can't. That's what's passed on, she said. It's not melancholia, it's just an ability to appreciate the living history of others, of objects as well as people. All this came to her when she was eighteen years old. She had been sitting on the grass alone, by the river at Bottom Boat. It had been summer, the flies and wasps whispering by the water. With her long legs drawn up and tucked beneath her chin she closed her eyes and thought of hearing the grass grow. She adjusted her straw hat, shielding her eyes from the strong sun, and watched the ichneumon wasps carrying spiders across the shimmering water and contemplated their grizzly end. She thought of how the wasp would deposit its eggs in the spider's body. How the larvae would grow, eating the spider from the inside but keeping it alive for as long as possible by eating the non-essential organs first. God is neither good nor evil, she said to herself, just clever. They are just two more different kinds of life, entwined but different. Not all spiders end up that way. Some, most even, have a different life, a different history. She then averted her gaze from the dazzle of the water to a group of stones half submerged by the bank. Moss green below, stone grey above, she thought how perhaps at one time they may have formed part of a way across the river, but then she dismissed the idea as being presumptuous. How should she know? What way? Where to? Whose boot on the stone? It was nonsense to guess. Like all of history, guesswork and lies, she thought. But the stones could be observed now. She watched them so hard they seemed to float out of the still water. She could observe them for as long as she lived, two different lives entwined again. She could describe them, record their subtle changes through the seasons. But how would the stone affect her? She supposed the very act of recording the stones would bring changes in her life. But was that enough? Was there more? she wondered. Again she closed her eyes hearing grass grow. Suddenly, a very familiar feeling came over her. It wasn't pleasurable, but neither was it unpleasant. It was the feeling she sometimes got in the house – the feeling old Dr Cartwright said was melancholia. She could feel the cold and the dark and the terrible solitude. She knew now what it was, this feeling; she knew now what it was which afflicted the family so. The Brightsides knew what it was to feel like stone – wasp and spider entwined as one, the living spider being slowly absorbed into the wasp. She was sure now, eyes tightly shut listening to the grass, that she was experiencing a quality of being different to human or even animal. Henrietta was being slowly absorbed into the stone, and here was the empty feeling of stoniness, and although she knew not to, for she was an extremely clever girl, she felt sorry for the lonely stones and started to cry. Stop it, she told herself, sniffling into the hem of her dress, such ideas will one day lead you to feelings for the spider and the ichneumon wasp and to question the intelligence of God. Stop it.

The morning after the episode with the cap which Elyahou had given to my great-great-grandmother, Henrietta sat at the table in the parlour writing up her journal and stamping the back of each written page with her name in indelible ink. The furious stamping heard during most of the period of the boot sale on the previous day had been Henrietta catching up and stamping the many hundreds of pages already written. The base of the stamp was about two inches square. It was supported by a polished thick wooden handle about four inches long. It bulged at the end forming a black rounded knot through which a long nail was sunk, holding the stem firmly to the base. Henrietta found that she could grip the handle, the phallic nature of which was not lost on the woman, very comfortably within her fist. She wandered off again into a distant dreamy land.

'C'mon girl. We'll be late,' said her grandmother.

Henrietta gripped the stem even more firmly and crushed the rubber to the paper on the table.

'I'm ready, grandmother,' she muttered. 'I've been waiting on you.'

'Hush, child,' the old woman tutted. 'C'mon. Mr Fox shan't wait for long.' Mr Fox ran a horse and carriage service from Kippax to Wakefield.

'Are you walking all the way into Kippax with me?' her grandmother asked.

'Yes. It's on my way. I can go that road to Bottom Boat.'

'To see the stones?'

'Yes.' Her grandmother nodded approvingly.

'Has thee a message for tha mother?' she asked Henrietta.

'No.' Henrietta shrugged. Why should she have a message for her mother?

'What of your brother, Jack?'

'No.' Why should she have a message for him either?

'How long will you be gone, grandmother?' she asked.

'A few days, girl,' the old woman answered. Henrietta smiled contemplating the luxury of not only a bed to herself but actually having a room to herself for several nights. It had never happened before. Until she was sixteen she had always slept with her sister Florence as well as the old woman. Before that she could vaguely remember sleeping in her mother's bedroom. But now her bedmate was going off to visit mother and Jack at the other side of Wakefield she could barely contain her joy. A bed alone. Then, as if she had read her mind, the old woman said, 'Don't go messin up my bed, mind. I want it neat and tidy when I get back.'

The two women walked the few miles to Kippax and Henrietta waved the old lady off in Mr Fox's carriage crammed full with trippers to Wakefield. She then made a detour to Bottom Boat, watched the stones a while, sketched them a little and made a few notes about a new species of lichen she had found growing on one of them, then returned home in good time to prepare the hot water for the menfolk, coming off shift.

That night Henrietta saw her brother Ernest and his family off to bed first. They climbed the stairs which led directly into the small bedroom shared by herself and her grandmother. She heard the interconnecting door close and watched the ceiling which told her when by the sounds of steadily filling chamberpots and the coiling of springs, the occupants were eventually settled for the night. Henrietta wanted no disturbance on this night, she wished to savour the peace of being alone in a room of her own. She lingered awhile talking with Bill Pettit and Mr Junkin, who recently had been joined by a third lodger, John Tregus, from Cornwall. As those above settled into moonful slumbers Mr Pettit who never would leave his knowledge alone, but who always had to unstack it and rearrange it in his head for fear that he might lose some of it, brought up again the subject of Ernest's new cap.

'I know it's that anarchist chap, 'cos I read that 'e come over to Italy from Paterson specially to kill the king. Now what do you suppose that travelling man has to do with Bresci?'

Mr Junkin, because of miner's asthma was too breathless to reply. He just stared with vacant eyes into the glowing embers and spat a thick gobbet black as printer's ink over the coals. 'Gerout an' walk,' he said at last and turned to smile at Henrietta; then removing the rubber teeth he'd bought from Elyahou the previous summer he poured himself another mug of cold tea from the pot on the table. Tregus quietly accepted a refill too from the wheezing miner.

'I'll tell thee,' Pettit went on. ''E's a Jew. Must be with a name like Elyahou Tsiblitz. All them Jews are anarchists. Go about shooting people and blowing them up. Pound to a penny the man's an anarchist.'

Mr Tregus who was temporarily lodging in the area and was attempting to set up some education classes at the mission hall said, 'Now hold on, Mr Pettit, all anarchists don't go about shooting people and causing mayhem. Anarchy's not about violence, you know; on the contrary it's about peace and freedom.'

'Give over,' Pettit scoffed. 'They do nowt but kill kings and princes. Not to mention the odd working man who happens to be about when the bomb goes off.'

Tregus shook his large head. 'No, Mr Pettit, all they are after is the same thing that you want; freedom from tyranny. The only difference is that you would like to see a government of working-class men to replace the capitalists in parliament, whereas they don't want a government at all.'

'How can you not have a government, Mr Tregus?' Henrietta asked.

'The anarchists believe that if men were truly free then there would be no need for government. They believe that freedom would bring trust and self-help.'

'Like the cooperatives you mean,' she asked to the accompaniment of another crack of Junkin's black spittle upon the fire.

'Yes,' Tregus answered, 'like a huge cooperative movement all across the country. There'd be no bosses, no royalty, just people working in harmony. Doing what they want to do both to benefit themselves and others.'

'And how does tha' suppose they'll bring that about?' Pettit asked, derisively.

'By the overthrow of the state,' Tregus answered, undeterred by the man's scorn. 'By inviting the revolution of working people through their unions,' he went on. 'Maybe a solid general strike would bring down the capitalists. It would cease their trade, destroy their economic base. Then the working class could take over the factories and the mines.'

''E's an anarchist Jew, I tell thee,' Pettit responded. 'I met a Jew once,' Junkin said without averting his gaze from where his spittle sizzled on the coals, and surprising everybody with his intervention. ''E told me that one day the Jews would go back to Palestine and live in communes without government.' Tregus looked thoughtful a moment, then said, 'The Jews live here in communes, Mr Junkin; that's what our friend here mistakes for anarchy. If you had been chased from one country to another, never allowed to settle, wouldn't you look to your own kind for help? Wouldn't you seek cooperation to protect you from the threat of expulsion? Don't be too disparaging of the Jews, they have a thing or two to teach us about trust and cooperation.'

Mr Pettit for once could find nothing in his head to offer by way of response. He too stared at Junkin's rapidly shrinking phlegm, caught on the flickering coals.

''E's an anarchist Jew I tell thee,' he repeated, eventually.

When sure that all was quiet upstairs Henrietta lit her candle (Ernest forbade the use of oil lamps considering them both dangerous and a waste of good money), wished the lodgers a good night and mounted the narrow steps to her room. She carefully closed the door, changed into her nightdress, snuffed the flame and spread carelessly across the entire width of the bed, long legs feeling for the endless limits of her comfort. With the pleasure principle so expanded too in her mind she soon drifted into a magnificent and open sleep. She was unsure how much later it was that she was awakened into a pitch blackness and an inability to cry out. The crude hand which tightly held her mouth and jaw made that impossible. The naked male presence, which now pressed upon her smelled pleasantly of grandmother's baskets. Perhaps because she had not moved her legs, spreadeagled still, as they had been when she fell asleep, it was quite easy for an unseen hand to ride up her nightdress and stroke the inside of her thigh. The visitor, sensing the passing of her initial fear relaxed his grip of her mouth and she immediately kissed him gently about the face. She could now feel that she was becoming very wet and with still spread legs writhed her buttocks slowly. The man was now kissing her ample breasts, occasionally gnawing on her nipples. Suddenly, with a pain that made her all but scream out the man had entered her and was quietly thrusting deeper. She bit hard

23

upon his shoulder, in pain as much as with passion, but after the initial burning sensation she settled more comfortably to contemplate the thing which moved inside her. He now moaned softly, the first noise he had made since entering her room and it was sufficient to bring her to realize her situation. His moans seemed to bring from her the last entrails of sleep. Fully awake she knew she was being raped. Now, as I have said before, Great-Aunt Henrietta was a clever one. Crying out she knew would put both herself and others perhaps in mortal danger, so she lay there writhing, absorbing the thrusts of both man and thing into her long, strong thighs. But she was actually writhing towards the small table at the side of the bed and on which she had placed her indelible stamper. She supposed that if she could identify the man's nakedness it would at least give the police a good chance of catching her assailant. So, gripping the handle as she would have wished to have held the thrusting object within her, given the chance, she stamped the man's right buttock with the words. 'Henrietta Brightside. Child of charm, poetry and love.' The touch of the rubber upon his bottom made the man only thrust the harder, which Henrietta hadn't expected and quite enjoyed. So she stamped his left buttock too with the same pleasant result. After the man had received perhaps twenty or so indelible stampings about his arse, my great-aunt must have been quite satisfied that the man could be identified, if he ever again dropped his trousers before anyone that is, but thought as the moanings continued that this whole episode really had to end. With great vision, she must have thought, she turned the stamper the other way up in her hands, holding it now by the square base, and in the pitch blackness carefully chose her aim and thrust as hard as she could. The wooden phallus then entered the man's anus with the most remarkable result. He ejaculated amidst terrible thrustings and choked screams muzzled by a pillow in which his head was now buried. These final thrustings however were something other than Henrietta had expected for they brought about her the most beautiful sensations of both mind and body which seemed to continue long after her assailant had ejaculated and ejaculated again. Finally coming to her senses amid the man's third ejaculation she realized that she was still wildly thrusting the handle of the stamper between the man's buttocks. She withdrew the object as gently as she could, continuing all the while to kiss the man deeply in the mouth until passion and pain subsiding like an ebbing tide they both fell asleep, he first, she within moments.

When she awoke at dawn her assailant had left. She could hear her brother Ernest together with the three lodgers downstairs chatting over their breakfast. At first she thought of summoning her brother upstairs but eventually rejected the idea, for what if the companion who so recently had warmed her bed were he. She then thought of informing the police but quickly dismissed that notion too. Although the man might be identified quite easily (if he were ever to bare himself in public that is) how on earth should they ever set about facilitating that identification. Besides, the stamp bore her name which might, if the story got about, bring odium upon her. It then struck her that she had quite contentedly, if exhaustedly, fallen asleep in this man's arms, and indeed, he in hers. Perhaps, here, in its effects at least, was something other than a normal rape. Very suddenly, then, she was overcome by a terrible longing; the emptiness which she felt she must fulfil was not unlike that which Dr Cartwright had diagnosed as melancholia and which she defined as history. She felt that she was being absorbed once more, not into stone but this time into flesh. It was as if this person had taken something of hers and she were being invited to go out and find it. But where should she begin to seek? she wondered.

3

Three philosophies of the coalfield

When the John Brightside who nestled between my great-great-grandmother's legs said, 'Tha'll nivver go down t'pit again', he meant it and she knew he meant it too. Although older and a good deal bigger than the boy, she respected him for what he would become – a hewer of coal and master of a home. She wasn't too happy to spend all her time above ground where in the cold light of day people might dwell upon her ugliness but on the other hand she praised the Lord for her marriage and for sending her such a handsome and virile young man. And as her respect grew so too did her understanding of how to make something better of the hard life led by the pitman and his wife. Firstly, she said, they must limit their family to a single child. She knew this to be an awful risk for she was well aware of how the life of a babe might slip away through contracting measles or whooping cough or one of the many other diseases which ransacked the coalfield. But she also knew that with tender care and time to devote to just the one child the risk was worth taking. The problem was, however, that her young husband seemed to spend most of his time above ground nestled into her sumptuous thighs, and as her vow to do for him was to be the cornerstone of their better life you can see poor Jane's dilemma. What to do? she said. What to do? And then it came to her, the language of flowers, the secrets of plants and herbs. Some of it she knew from her childhood. More, she had to learn from old women, hags who lived alone, eking out a living from the sale of their potions and medicaments. So each morning Jane would swallow a draught of foul-smelling brew to keep away the babies, and each night they would nestle secure in the knowledge that the long slow hours of dark lovemaking would surely produce no progeny. Having a single child produced other economic advantages besides having only one extra mouth to feed. It provided room for more lodgers for example. At times they would have as many as a dozen men sleeping in the parlour below, each paying her twelve shillings a week for his board with food. All laundry was contracted out and they saw to their own hot water for bathing, not therefore disturbing the time she needed to devote to young James when he came along.

From the rents alone she was able to save three to four pounds a week. This meant that John only need work four shifts a week bringing in another pound and saving strength for older age and more nestling in her thighs. There were few pitmen who were able to live like that. Few families who were able to save money.

Then of course, she had the money from the sale of her potions, her female mixture as she called it. The fact that it didn't work for many, calling into question her own fertility, or that of her husband, didn't seem to reduce the sales any. Then there were other mixtures; for diarrhoea, for warts, an eye lotion for those miners with the terrible rotating eyeballs syndrome, and of course her bathing lotions for aches and pains. All this money too was profit, which the thrifty lady saved. Next, she laid down a few simple rules of the house, which applied as much to her lodgers as it did to her husband. No drinking. No smoking. No gambling. Jane had never been a great churchgoer but she could see how drink destroyed so many homes in the village. She wouldn't preach against the demon to others but if her home were to remain decent and economically productive, then the men would not fritter away their wages on beer and tobacco, although she did allow the occasional mug of yarrow beer purchased from herself at cost. 'Tha's just playin' into the coal owners' hands,' some prospective lodgers would say. 'They'd love a guaranteed, sober workforce. Good clean units of production, but tha'll work out the coal quicker that way missus. Then wot? When there's no coal?'

'If tha think that, then there's no lodgin' here,' she would say and slam the door in their startled faces. But after all the planning and the loving and the saving, after all that brewing and book-work, infusing and cleaning, cooking and healing, the sky fell. Her John's skull – he was still only forty-five years old – was cracked open like a coconut. No more nestling in her beautiful thighs.

So it was in the summer of 1870, with Jack, Ernest and Flo already brightening the dark stone that Jane came from her village to the house of her only child, James Brightside, with a horse and cart and carrying in a small case the accumulation of her thriftiness. Aggie said, 'Let me take your case, mother,' but Jane hung on, went upstairs alone, and put the case upon her bed and no other comprehending soul has set eyes upon it, from that day to this.

It was soon after their marriage that John and Jane Brightside attended a meeting at the Greyhound (for so their local alehouse was named) to hear a Durham miner speak about self-help in the coalfields. The alehouse was an unsuitable venue for the meeting as the man was teetotal but the Greyhound was the only building in the village capable of housing the expected turnout. Besides, it was a Friday evening, and wages were to be paid as always at the pub. It was therefore with several colliers already roaring drunk that the Durham man took the floor. His eyes had an intensity which shone through the smoky fog. 'I'll make noo apologies for speakin' in an alehouse,' he said, 'but you should know that an ability to improve your circumstance and the drinkin' of this here ale are incompatible.'

'Stop the preaching and get on with what you have to say,' called Teddy Sloan, the landlord of the pub, amid supportive noises from the drunk.

Smoke billowed into the room from the stove-pipe near to the speaker, thickening the atmosphere and causing him to cough. He wiped the spittle from his mouth with his muffler and continued. 'How then are you to save your brass if you squander it on beer?' he challenged the rowdy element.

'Higher wages – that's what we want,' someone shouted.

'They'll come. They'll come,' he answered. 'But first we must put our oon house in order. What's the point in havin' higher wages if it only brings more drunkenness?'

'Piss off. You sound like the coal owners,' someone else shouted, applauded by Teddy Sloan.

The man put his hands in the air asking for quiet when another billow of acrid smoke enveloped both him and half his audience bringing forth enormous bouts of coughing. Taking advantage of the fact that many of his hecklers were now choking he weighed in, 'The first thing to do is build yourself a chapel. Your chapel. With your money.'

'I'm no churchgoer,' young John shouted.

'You don't have to be,' the man's eyes gleamed through the haze, 'just think what this meetin' would be like in a clean room, with real chairs and without the drunkards. Not havin' to shout. No one chokin'.'

Jane nodded approvingly to her husband.

'Just think what you might learn in a room full of people who are there only to learn too,' the man shouted dodging a pot of ale flying towards him. 'Next, you set up a cooperative store.'

'What's one of them?' came the question from his audience.

'Instead of buying your groceries and provisions from the coal owner's shop, you set up your own shop in competition. You sell goods cheaper than he does, then if there's a profit at the end of the day you share it out; you pay a dividend.'

'Rubbish, we haven't the brass to build a store,' a thin young man said in a wheezy voice.

'Then do it from your home.'

'The coal owner's home you mean. If I sold goods in competition with the grocery me and my mother would be on the street,' the man replied.

'Then put the store outside the village, where he has no property,' answered the Durham man.

'It won't work.'

'It will work,' he shouted, eyes still glinting through the smoke. 'If you unite; if you stick together; if you cooperate, it will work.' He dodged another flying drink, the beer splattering his shirt and muffler. 'And there's another thing,' he went on, undeterred, 'home ownership. Own your own homes. Get out of the colliery-owned houses.'

'And good riddance,' someone shouted.

'Build your own,' the man went on. 'Those of you with the skills can build your own. Others form clubs, take out mortgages with the building societies through your clubs. But whatever you do save your brass. You'll need it.'

'Rubbish. Higher wages is what's needed.'

'Ay, higher wages,' echoed the landlord, and someone threw a mug of ale directly in the man's face. Amid great laughter another billow of smoke wafted into the room enveloping all in a choking fog.

'C'mon lads,' shouted the landlord. 'there's a free pint. This one's on me.' There was a great unseen commotion as men disappeared with their pots and tankards into the acrid cloud. So it was that the meeting broke up, the Durham miner was howled down and my great-great-grandparents left the Greyhound with pandemonium filling their ears. 'It wasn't right, luv,' Jane Brightside said. 'They ridiculed that poor man yet he was speakin' good sense.' Her husband shrugged his boyish shoulders, unsure of what to think.

When John Brightside lay dead, the pit prop and his bust head like a bat and ball in the narrow roadway, his colleagues said the pit wasn't safe. The coal owners had insisted on the use of too few props for too long; something now had to be done. As their shadows stooped and flickered on the black coal walls, they huddled about their dead comrade and decided to invite a speaker from the Miners' National Union to talk about safety. So it was soon after the death of my great-great-grandfather and thirty years after the Durham miner had spoken at the Greyhound, Alexander Macdonald, the miners' leader, came to speak to an attentive audience at the mission hall which had been built in the next village. The wooden pews in the chapel accommodated a quiet group which included James Brightside and his mother. Macdonald first spoke at length of the needs for improvement in safety standards and inspection methods within the mining industry, but soon he was chiding his audience for their indifference and sloth, for very few of the men present and even fewer of those absent had ever belonged to a union. In the clean and cold chapel the men stamped their feet inside large boots trying to circulate a little embarrassed blood.

'We must organize to control the means of production,' he told them. 'To own the mines. They are your mines; we must eventually wrestle them from the coal owners.'

'How can we do that?' asked someone from the centre of the congregation. 'We can be imprisoned for striking, let alone stealing the pit.'

'Yes, friend,' Macdonald answered amid light laughter. 'But it isn't stealing, is it, if we can get a sufficient number of working-class people into parliament. If we can vote in a sufficient number of radicals and liberals who are sympathetic to our cause then we can change things through law.'

'Pie in the sky, man,' came the response.

Macdonald looked severely at the cynic. 'I tell you it can be done,' he said. 'It will be so, if you can organize your union properly. A well-organized union makes you less dependent on the bosses,' he shouted. 'Don't you see that?'

'Tell us,' shouted out someone else. 'Will it bring higher wages?'

'Yes. We can organize for higher pay,' Macdonald answered. 'And shorter hours,' he added. 'And more than that, you can pay yourselves sick money instead of having to rely on the smart money of the bosses. We can find assistance money in times of unemployment, and widows' benefit. With your support we can provide for your orphans and even for your own funerals.'

'What about strike money?' It was an immigrant voice asking in broken English. Macdonald's face suddenly became very serious. 'Beware the strike, friend,' he advised. 'Strikes can be good for us, they can teach the bosses a lesson, bloody their noses a little; but remember too, they can cause your union a lot of damage. If we have to give out strike pay over a long period we could run dry. Nothing for the orphans and widows; nothing for the sick. Strike yes – if it's justified we'll back you; but beware, that's all I'm saying.' The immigrant nodded his understanding of what had been said and murmured quietly to the well-dressed youth seated beside him. Even my great-great-grandmother would never, had she noticed it, have associated his face thirty years on, with the features of Elyahou Tsiblitz, whose father that day had walked him all the way from Leeds to hear Alexander Macdonald speak.

After the meeting most of the men present queued for hours in the cold chapel, creating a crocodile below the blue windows. Then, stamping into its communal boots, our village plodded into the union. James Brightside, standing with his friend Sidall Junkin, said 'Good speaker, Sid.'

'Ay. Didn't 'ear much on what bugger 'ad to say, though. I were t'sittin' at back. Chap next me were nattering all while to his young lad in Polish or summat.' He coughed a lump of black phlegm into a clean white handkerchief, and looked hard at it. 'Got more bloody coal dust in me than there is in t'pit,' he commented wheezily.

Now at the head of the queue James turned to smile at the evening's speaker. Alexander Macdonald, sitting next to the lodge treasurer at a trestle table covered in green baize, nodded approvingly at the young Brightside. James never saw him again, but the Scotsman went away to secure the Mines Regulations Act a year or two afterwards, which brought greater safety to the pit, and then in 1875, he took his seat in parliament, sitting as a liberal; together with Tom Burt, the first trades unionists to do so.

4

James Brightside and how he learned the notion of continuity

During thirty years of marriage John Brightside expressed little interest in anything other than his wife's body. When Jane was sure that she had enough money saved to enable them to build a house, he rejected her suggestion of it. When one night she suggested they build a shop instead, or even a small factory at which she could concoct her potions on a larger scale, he just turned over and went to sleep. She nattered for a time but her suggestions were always met with the same dull silence, so she soon stopped asking and just put her money into a small suitcase. Sometimes she would open the case and count the money in front of him but he never was interested enough even to inquire how much they had, and eventually she stopped doing that too. Their life was a round of hot nights and cold, lifeless days, which lacked inspiration; even with a parlourful of dossing colliers there was no more than a candle of pale light and a splutter of uneducated but temperate chatter. You could have chucked a bucketful of water over the lot, and they would have been extinguished along with the naked wavering flame.

It was a ghostly world into which young James had been born; solitary, almost unknown to his father he grew up amid quiet, broken bachelors who had nothing but their grey trousers and black boots to their names. So it was that the boy picked out very early in life two things. One was the lonely, ephemeral existence of the lodging collier and the other was the love of his devoted mother; the mother who had decided that it would be her son and not her husband who would own his own home and escape the coal owners' clutches. Yet, incompatible with hopes even for her son were the words of the dosser who had spoken to him as a boy, words which forever flickered in his ears like a trapped butterfly beating its slow and useless wings.

'No, mother,' he said, 'I wouldn't thank thee for a house of my own. Property is theft.'

'But that's not what the Durham miner said the night tha father and I went to the Greyhound. He said build us own. Free thaselves from the tied homes.' She sounded disappointed. But James would hear nothing of his mother's pleadings and, aloof and proud, naïve, misunderstanding and married, he entered in the rain the sombre stone house that would become my family home. Into the darkness he built simple cupboards from bits of wood. Aggie pegged a carpet for the stone floor and they bought a table and chairs to sit on, and finally they acquired a bed. It wasn't much, but as James argued if poverty were to be eliminated then luxury too would have to go; if there were to be no more hunger then there could be no more avarice. When the day of reckoning came and the oppressive coal owners finally were overthrown, he should be ready for it. Ready to receive a mean equality, a parity of possession and position within the society beyond the revolution. James Brightside was, in effect, preparing to receive his liberty.

We were a godless lot living there at that time, which might explain why a chapel was built not in our village but not very far away in the next one to it. It might also explain why it took so long for an intense idealist such as my great-grandfather to become a union man. Strangely, living slap bang in the middle of a terrace of colliery-owned houses gave him no sense of community, or equality. Well, at least it did in some ways and not in others. Of course, the occupants saw one another through various hardships; if it became necessary, food was shared. They did for each other, like laundry and baby minding, that sort of thing, but the pitmen had their own social structure, their own pecking order. At the top of the ladder were the men, like James Brightside, who hewed the coal; below them, and receiving less pay, were the putters who ran the tubs and the ponyboys who looked after the ponies. Then at the surface, and often receiving less pay still were an assortment of banksmen and weighmen, blacksmiths and joiners, general labourers and sorters who picked out the stones and sized the coal. These were often older men, clapped-out hewers who could never go down to the coal face again and, because they were old and knackered, respect for them diminished. Unlike the respect shown to one's own father, which never wavered to the grave and beyond, the respect for one's elderly neighbours and workmates fell short like a diminishing light until there was no more than the black pain of age perceived as an abstraction. Looking at such people the future seemed black indeed. Now in that sense James felt no community; like his father he felt no continuity with these people. The generations proceeded and had preceded; but that's all they were, generations. Each huddled within the coal, black and bent, waxing and waning, then extinguished. To be a union man, you had to understand continuity, you had to have a clear sense of future communities, and how to fight for them and their liberation, even before their birth. The liberty which James would receive at the revolution would be a personal liberty; what all other liberated people would be doing was not his concern.

On the night that he went to the mission hall with his mother, the night he joined the union, the act was not performed with any particular political zeal. The talk of parliamentary revolution interested him but brought about no conversion from the narrow and selfish idealism which he felt. No, that was harnessed and given direction by something which happened at about the time Alexander Macdonald first took his parliamentary seat. That was the year the coal owners put the colliery on a three day week, because of the slump in trade. A shaft had been sunk, but the mine not much worked, at the foot of Hunger Hill; so for the sake of something to do my great-grandfather, together with Sidall Junkin, descended the shaft on one of the days when not working. They had no idea what they might expect to find but waded chest high in foul water through the narrow galleries, examining the walls of the dead mine in the pale glow of light from a couple of flickering candles.

Sid's wheezing, of which James was always aware, stopped suddenly and my great-grandfather turned to see the other, breath held and candle thrust out towards a crumbling wall.

'What've thee got there, Sid?'

'Dunno, come and see.' The reply resounded thinly in the empty arch above the water level.

'It's nowt but a sheep's bone,' James commented from his companion's side.

Sid wheezed a bit more then said, 'No. Sithee, James, it's too big for a sheep,' and chipped away the rock from about the bone with a small pick.

My great-grandfather settled the candles on a ledge by the side of the discovery and helped his friend chip away the surrounding rock. After a couple of hours they had revealed a bone about three feet long running parallel to the gallery floor.

'It must belong to a bloody elephant,' Sid informed James from his rattling chest.

'I think it's a pit prop that's become buried,' my great-grandfather confided.

'Nay, lad. Tha's not felt it,' Sid said with exasperation.

'Look, James, it's like stone – petrified.' He tapped the object with his hard pick to illustrate the point. The hollow noise echoed around the gallery. Sid started to cough. 'That's no pit prop,' he added managing to squeeze the words between splutters.

'C'mon, Sid,' James said with concern. 'Let's get thee out of 'ere. This water'll be the death of thee if we stay here much longer.'

The two men waded out but waded back the next day, chipping away yet more of the rock and revealing an even greater length of bone and a second similar bone running parallel to it.

Throughout the two years of short working on each of two days a week they descended the shaft and chipped away at the bones slowly revealing a skeleton about fifteen yards long. The bones which they had managed to expose of course did not constitute the whole animal for there was little more than two feet in height between the surface of the flood water and the roof of the gallery. But nonetheless for the full run of fifteen yards they had exposed two feet of bones in the vertical dimension. They also had of course excavated back from the wall of the gallery some ten feet in all, and taken the height up some, in which area they had been able to work quite easily and even walk about, albeit with the stoop of apes.

The whole box-like cavern which they had created was a mass of bones, all of which supported magnificently the freshly created ceiling. The two huge feet were easily identifiable as was the area which Sid would insist on calling the rib cage; the head too, along with a mouthful of enormous teeth, could be recognized easily.

Sid, sitting between two rib bones, his head poking into the cavern where the lungs might at one time have been situated, said 'I've never seen owt like it afore.'

'It's a bloody monster,' James replied.

'Do thee think we should tell?'

'Ay. We'll 'ave to tell someone.'

'Vicar?' Sid offered.

'No, he'll only preach on us.'

'Who then?'

James thought a while stooped in the same cavern in which the other man was sitting, their shadows licking the bones as the candles burned down.

'Dr Cartwright,' he said at last. 'He'll know what to do.'

Dr Cartwright was a small skinny man. The only hair to grow about his head was a sprouting of grey fluff which developed in his ears and curled about his hearing. He wore a squat silk hat and because of his extraordinary hair he appeared to have ear muffs beneath. When he had descended the shaft and waded through the foul smelling water he couldn't believe his eyes. He'd expected at best to see the remains of a bear or perhaps a rhinoceros but when confronted by the massive skeleton he said, 'My God, it's a dinosaur. Just look at those teeth.'

'A what?' asked James.

'A dinosaur.'

'What's one of them?'

'You know, a terrible lizard. They're extinct.'

'But where did it come from?'

'It didn't come from anywhere, James. It died there, where it is.'

'You mean it died down t'pit.'

The doctor smiled, wondering how he might explain the fossilized phenomenon.

'It's extinct,' he said.

'What's that?'

'It died millions of years ago, and so did all others like it.'

'No, that can't be, doctor,' said James, remembering what he'd learned from the little schooling he'd had. He'd been taught that the world had begun in the year 4004 BC. 'How can it have died millions of years ago?'

'The earth is many millions of years old, James.'

'Not 4004 BC?'

'No. Not 4004 BC.'

James looked stunned.

'A man called Mr Darwin wrote a book not many years ago showing how life evolves.'

'What's that?' James asked.

'One species develops from another. Higher forms evolve from lower forms.'

The other nodded, signifying some understanding. The doctor continued.

'The highest form so far developed is man and we came from apes.'

Watching the doctor stooped in the bony cavern, James found no difficulty in accepting that. He nodded.

'And this here's a lower form, that's now gone,' he said, looking about the cave.

'Yes. Good, you've got it.'

'So when God made the earth millions of years ago, there were no men around.'

'That's right. There were lower forms, still. Man eventually evolved.'

'And is this evolving still going on?'

'Yes.'

'Will there be millions more years of evolving, doctor?'

'Yes. Of course. But the most evolved form then will probably be as different from man as we are from this monster here.'

Suddenly in that dark cavern, he and Dr Cartwright bent like apes among the dinosaur bones, James had his first glimpse of continuity. He had an idea of what lay beyond the blackened old men of the village. He now understood what his father had not and was deeply moved by the revelation. He felt godless no more. In fact he had an overwhelming urge to kneel at the foot of the creator and thank Him for making him, James Brightside, a part of the grand design. So, the following Sunday, he took himself, and Aggie, and the children, Jack, Ernest and Flo, off to the chapel, and when the family returned to the house they found Dr Cartwright waiting. He first took Aggie upstairs to the bedroom and came down to confirm to James what the husband already suspected. His wife was pregnant. He then led James outside and told him that he had decided to inform a friend of his, a man at the Natural History Museum, about the dinosaur in the disused pit.

'What'll he do?' asked James.

'He may ask you to dig it out completely,' the doctor answered. 'I can't really say. Be grateful there's another on the way, James.' The doctor nodded towards the open door and to Aggie. He put his friendly hand upon my great-grandfather's shoulder, then he mounted his chestnut horse and rode off through the rain puddles.

Within seven days the man from the Natural History Museum had arrived together with Cartwright in a carriage. He wore a frock coat and carried a round knobbed cane. The monocle which occupied the space about his right eye flashed in the afternoon sun. 'Dr Cartwright suspects it may be the remains of an iguanodon,' the man said in a tongue James had not heard before. 'It's all very exciting.'

'Maybe,' said James. 'I wouldn't know about that, sir. But I'd like to get it out complete like.'

'Yes,' said the man from London, 'but it's hardly your dinosaur, is it now?'

'I found it. Me and Sidall Junkin like,' James said possessively.

'No, it can't be yours. Firstly the pit belongs to the coal owner.'

'But it's not used no more,' James interrupted.

'But it's still his land, isn't it,' said the man, adjusting his monocle. 'And secondly, once found, a thing like this would immediately pass to the crown. I'm sure Her Majesty however, would want it housed at the Natural History Museum, for all her subjects to see.'

'You mean I can't dig it out?' asked James a little bewildered by all this talk of the queen.

'Well, you can't keep it, that's out of the question.'

'Can I dig it?'

The man looked uneasy then said, squinting at the sun, 'That's up to the coal owner; I'm on my way to see him now.'

'Yessir,' answered my great-grandfather, and the carriage rattled through our village out of the denaturing sun, taking with it the doll-like figures of old Dr Cartwright and the man from the museum.

The next day the coal owner sent for my great-grandfather who walked a couple of miles to the big house. When he got there the coal owner was waiting for him in the drive; the collier never would have been allowed to actually enter the house. My great-grandfather, big fellow that he was, removed his cap and towered over the boss.

'Brightside, who give thee permission to go down my pit?'

'Didn't know was needed, Mr Thwaite,' my great-grandfather said, wringing out his cap with large hands.

Mr Thwaite looked to the rustling leaves in the trees which lined the approach to his house.

'Well, tha did and tha's done it.' He said aggressively.

'Yessir,' said my great-grandfather, still wringing his cap.

Summoning more aggression still he threatened, 'Brightside, I ought to take t'ouse away. Do owt like this again and I will, lad. Be sure on that.' He paused for my great-grandfather's quiet response.

'Yessir.'

The two men looked at one another amid the wind-stirred leaves. The trees seemed to echo the big man's lament. With courage he asked, 'Now I've started, Mr Thwaite, can I finish t'job? Get it all out?'

'No, tha can't. Cheeky bugger,' came the quiet reply. 'First, thee 'ad no permission to go on my land there. No permission to hew out that skeleton. Second, if the buggers from London want that thing they can get professionals in to do it, not soft buggers the likes of thee.'

'Yessir,' my great-grandfather said again.

'Now, clear off, Brightside,' said the coal owner, 'afore I set the dogs on thee.' He turned to go back to the big house.

'Mr Thwaite,' the collier called after him. 'Mr Thwaite, will I be able to help?' He touched the boss's arm.

The man turned and said venomously, 'Don't put tha hands on me lad. Understood?'

'Yessir. Sorry, sir.'

'Let's get it clear, Brightside,' the boss said. 'Stay out of that shaft. That dinosaur thing's nowt to do with thee. It's my dinosaur on my land. An' them buggers in London will have it only if they pay my price. Otherwise it stays just as it is, in t' bloody ground. Is that understood?'

'Yessir.'

'Now stay clear of it, Brightside,' he said and turned a second time. 'I'm warning you, stay clear.'

My great-grandfather, crestfallen amid the warm sad trees, walked slowly back to our soot-grimed village, the butterfly in his ear flapping its useless wings once more.

James Brightside's philosophy had changed. The encounter with the dinosaur bones, and the subsequent meetings with Dr Cartwright and Mr Thwaite, and even the attendance at chapel, had all helped to change his views. The narrow idealist who couldn't see a world beyond his own death was able now to look to his children's future in a time without him; even the little devil stirring in Aggie's belly, the one he didn't yet know would, with luck, have a time beyond his own. He was also beginning to contemplate a better world for himself, beyond his own grave. The idea of heaven was beginning to appeal, realizing a different kind of liberty.

The butterfly too was starting to break free, at first painfully beating its useless wings, then cracking its wax encasement with such a rush, and flying blue and gold and all colours into the sun. Not one, but many, fluttering their paired wings into the sun, and liberating my great-grandfather from his naïvety and misunderstanding. He knew now the message that the dossing collier was carrying. The property he had spoken of was not a house, or the useless baubles that went to fill it. No, the property he had meant was himself and his labour. It was the cruel use the bosses made of the colliers; stealing their labour and the fruits of that labour which constituted the theft.

'Two years of labour digging out that bloody skeleton, and not so much as a thank you,' he told Sidall Junkin.

'He's thieved it, Sid. Thieved it and going to sell it, and we won't see a penny of the price they pay in London. And why? Because it's his land and we're his slaves. That's why, Sid.'

'Maybe Union can do summat.'

'Union,' James puffed. 'Union's on its bloody knees. They won't do owt.'

'Alexander Macdonald, then.'

'Nay, lad. 'E's part of 'em, now. Lordin' it up in Parliament. 'E'll be 'avin' supper with that bugger with the eye glass. There must be some other way, Sid.'

He turned to his mother, Jane Brightside, and said, 'Mother, I was wrong. We'll get that house. We'll free ourselves from the bosses. I swear we'll do it. But first, I'll sort out that bastard Thwaite.' Now my great-great-grandmother had no idea what he meant by that last remark but taking Sidall with him, James left the house. The old woman was watching the remnants of Sidall's mucus tearing itself apart on the hot coals when she was roused by a deep explosion. She felt the vibrations from it push through her womb and knew then that her son was dead. My great-great-grandmother moved herself wearily into the street and headed for Hunger Hill. Halfway towards the old pit she met Sidall Junkin running and wheezing as hard as he could go, and coming to meet her.

'He's blown up the old pit, missus,' he shouted at her.

'Well, go and get him, lad,' she said quietly. 'Go on, go and see.'

'Yes, missus,' the man said, then ran back, arms and legs all over the shop.

She walked slowly to the pit head and waited. Eventually Sidall came out of the hole in the ground dragging a sack. Handing it to the woman, he said, 'It's all I could find, missus.' He was wheezing and spitting great black gobbets of muck. There were tears in his eyes and his clothes stank and hung heavy with the foul water.

After a time Sidall took the sack back from her and said, 'C'mon, there's nowt to do here. I'll take thee home.'

On the way back to the village they passed dozens of women, their heads covered in black shawls each bowed, passive and supportive. There were no tears, no words of regret, just a terrible silent agony conveyed through the spaces between them. Black, Sidall recalled it afterwards, just black and angular like the slagheaps reaching in the sky; stones at prayer to an awful God.

Once inside the house, Aggie took the children up to her bedroom and great-great-grandmother put some water on to boil. Then she mashed some tea. Sidall and she sat before the fire drinking from mugs and Sidall said, ''E's under a pile of stones, missus. All them bones have fell and crumbled into stone. It's not bones any more, missus, just rocks. You wouldn't believe that an animal could be so much rock. It's like it was sculpted out of stone then knocked down. All knocked down and broken, missus.'

My great-great-grandmother put her arms around her dead son's friend, kissed him on the cheek and went out of the house. By the time she had arrived back, Mr Thwaite was already in the parlour, lecturing to the assembled occupants.

'Condolences,' he said to Aggie and the children. 'It were a silly thing to do. Lost me a lot of money has this, a lot of money.' And he shook his head. 'Who's gonna pay the rent now,' he continued looking to each of the three children in turn. Then he said to Aggie, 'The orphans' fund and the widow's pension won't be enough to live on tha naws.'

'No matter, Mr Thwaite,' said my great-great-grandmother, standing by the door. 'Tha's earlier than I expected.'

'Ah condolences, Mrs Brightside,' he said to the older woman warmly and moving to greet her. 'I didn't see thee come in.'

'Condolences, my backside,' she said in a matter of fact way. 'Here's twenty-five pounds for tha trouble and a year's rent, Mr Thwaite.' The landlord looked surprised but took the money. 'Now I'd be obliged if tha'd leave us to grieve, Mr Thwaite,' she said, and showed him the door.

When the coal owner had gone, Sidall Junkin put his hand in his pocket and pulled out two stones which he held in his outstretched palm for everyone to see. 'Iguanodon teeth,' he said to a puzzled audience. 'They're all I could recognize.' The following day he parcelled them up and sent them to the Natural History Museum in London where they can be seen on exhibition to this day. 'I'll stay,' Sidall said, 'if tha wants me to. Sithee all right through the night.' Great-great-grandmother agreed, and Sidall Junkin stayed in the parlour, sleeping each night in a wide winged chair until the time he passed away. The next day they buried my great-grandfather. Sidall never did reveal what or how much was in the sack and nobody cared to look, but the contents made a strange noise when the sack was put into the coffin, and rattled emptily when James Brightside's mates lowered it into the ground.

5

Mr and Mrs Gill's five little boys

Nobody in the family ever inquired how my great-great-grand-mother came to be carrying such a huge sum of money in her pinafore pocket on the afternoon that her son died. Aggie supposed that it must have been part of the fortune which she was reputed to have brought to the house with her, but she had no idea where that money may have been stored for safe keeping. It could have been in some bank vaults in Leeds or Wakefield for all she knew. But Aggie was thankful, and Aggie cried with relief. At least for a time, she and the children were safe with a roof over their heads. The cruel irony in the timing of James's death had not escaped her mother-in-law's attention though. For how long was she now to carry the payment for her early sacrifices before it would be put to use and free her family? If she were a man it would be different, she'd perhaps buy materials and a little land and build a house; or maybe she'd join a club and pay a mortgage. Perhaps, even, she'd go right up to the door of one of the nobs, bold as brass, and offer them cash to clear out and leave the house to her, fine contents and all for there was enough. Enough to buy her family's liberty, big house and all. But she was a woman. Who'd accept the money from a woman like her without question? Where did it come from? How'd you earn it? It must be stolen, they'd say. Or ill-earned. Tha's taken a lot of strangers to tha bed for this lot, luv, they'd say. She couldn't stand that. Not with her only genuine memory of it, being with her John, nestled in there, a little cock-sparrow between her legs. She realized she'd have to wait for her grandsons. Perhaps Jack or Ernest would be master of his own home. She'd wait.

Time passed in the village. Slump in the pits was replaced by good times. The boys growing into young men, began to earn wages. The union crumbled, then picked itself up as money poured in. Jack married a farmer's daughter on the other side of Wakefield, inherited a smallholding when his newly acquired father-in-law was gored by a bull on a carpet of bluebells, and left the pit and the village. Aggie, unable to bear the dark stone any longer, soon followed her eldest son and settled contentedly to the milking of cows and the feeding of chickens, leaving the young Henrietta in the care of her grandmother.

Ernest got religion. Following the example set by his father in the months before he died Ernest grew to be a godfearing man of the chapel, and he saw to it that his siblings too spent each Sunday in the bosom of the Lord. Pictures appeared for the first time in the house. Moses and Ezekiel adorned the parlour. Christ, Job and Ruth shared the bedrooms. The Bible with its heavy brass clasp, sat at the centre of a newly purchased sideboard, together with photographs of Henrietta and Flo in clean white pinafore frocks. The young family was comforted by the community, entwined eventually within it and all sucked to the teat of Methodism; the chapel took hold and they, like ivy, scaled the walls. Not just the Brightsides but most of the people of the terrace and the other pitmen's families too. Even the pit managers and eventually the coal owner worshipped at the same chapel. The amalgam was finally set when capital and labour were heard harmoniously singing together in the pews. Mr Thwaite smiled each time the minister urged his congregants to work hard, to be temperate, to be obedient, for that way lay their salvation; and Ernest too smiled at the thought of his being saved. Via the church's teaching, like so many pitmen before him, but unlike any previous member of his family, Ernest learned obedience, punctuality, industry, discipline, self-denial, abasement; in a word he was methodized. His labour was sanctified and he maintained grace. His poverty was blessed and in staying poor he knew himself to be saved in the next world. It was a mean business and my great-great-grandmother saw right through it, right to its rotten heart. She despised these ranters, preaching their sermons of everlasting hellfire and terrorizing the children, and so was relieved when Flo, at least, fell from grace.

Flo like her grandmother, but unlike her young sister, Henrietta, was an ugly woman. She not only shared the large, square frame which gave her body the solidity of a brute but she also had the face of one who might have been modelled in clay by a child. It was the unfinished coarseness of her features which made her so ugly. It was she who, after her fall, would visit the public house each Saturday and following the prize given to the prettiest girl in the pub would be presented with the booby, invariably a short shrivelled black pudding. Thus was it unanimously confirmed by those unafraid to voice such opinions; Flo was the ugliest woman in the village. Now, I have already mentioned that along with Ernest most of the people who lived in our terrace had got religion, but there was one notable exception; the Gill family. Mrs Gill was a small dear woman who hardly deserved what the Lord had sent her; namely a crippled husband and their five little boys. Each of the five was built like a brick shithouse and inside they were twice as nasty. Mr Gill had been injured in an explosion years before when the oldest boy had been barely of an age to go down the pit. Since that time he had lain on a board upon the table in the parlour, his back broken in two places. There, he lived and slept, to be removed upon his board by two of his strapping lads only when it was necessary for the family to eat. The house reeked of the spoonfed old man's decaying excrement and once a week two of the boys could be seen at the village pump washing down the crumpled father and scrubbing his board with all the vitality of butchers at their block.

'Lord, deliver us from such evils,' Sidall Junkin at the window once said, seeing the boys delivering home their pitiful load after such an excursion.

'Amen to that,' my great-great-grandmother said. Although she had lost the two men most dear to her, at least death had come mercifully quick in both cases. There was not the slow dripping away of life as on the parlour table next door.

Yet out of their prostrate parent, and huddled about that table, the sons seemed to grow. Like giant fungi, shooting out of a confused mycelium, the boys blossomed. Blastospheres with much spores; spawning mischief as well as children.

On one particular Sunday, it was before Flo's fall from grace, indeed it was the morning of her twenty-fifth birthday, great-great-grandmother returned from a walk to Bottom Boat with a whole basket full of hemlock, to find the five Gill boys digging up the scullery floor with an assortment of pickaxes.

'We're looking for the money, missus,' said John, the eldest, by way of explanation.

'You won't find 'owt here,' she answered, and put some water to boil in a pan on the fire.

'Now tha doesn't want trouble, does thee?' threatened Charley who was barely fifteen but just as large as his brothers. He brandished a spade in her face.

'No I don't want no trouble. That's why I'm going to have some tea. Now boys does tha want tea,' she asked in a comforting voice.

'No, missus, we just want the money,' said John.

'What money? I have no money.'

'The money tha brought here with thee, missus,' Barney chipped in. He wore braces to hold his massive trousers over a rotund and spreading gut.

'Oh, those stories!' exclaimed my great-great-grandmother, appearing to be hurt by such a reminder. 'It's not true. There is no money, Barney. Just tittle-tattle. Now have some beer. Come on, sit at the table and I'll get you some of my yarrow beer.' She was very calm and the boys sat one by one watching and mistrusting her all the time. She went into the scullery and came out clutching six bottles of her own brew. She gave one bottle to each in turn, then stripped a few leaves and roots from the plants in the basket. She tossed these carelessly into the pan of boiling water.

'They say tha's a witch,' missus. Is that right what they say?' asked Charley, elbow on table and supporting his child's head in a big man's palm.

'No, child. I'm no witch,' she answered. 'Now drink tha beer.'

The boys looked to John for a lead. At the nod of that older head it would not have been beyond them to have beaten her with their implements but John was thinking, and took a long swig from his bottle; thankfully the others quickly followed the example of their brother. Meanwhile, the old woman chucked a handful of tea leaves into the boiling water.

'If it's not 'ere, where is it then?' John asked, his voice already becoming thick from the effects of the beer.

'It's nowhere, John,' said my great-great-grandmother consolingly. 'It isn't. Tha's mistaken lad. It's just a tale, I tell thee. There is no money.'

'Course there is,' Barney slurred angrily. 'Everybody knows it.'

'Now come on, boys, drink up,' she said calmly. 'Then we can have some tea and talk it over.'

'Over what?' asked the terribly stupid Benjamin.

'Over the tea, daft bugger,' Barney said, taking off his cap and hitting his brother with it.

'That's right, boys, let's get the beer down now,' she said, grateful for the diversion which Barney had set up. They all supped on the home brew until the bottles were empty. Their limbs had become decidedly more relaxed, their flabby jowls more shaky. My great-great-grandmother talked the whole while she was pouring the tea. She spoke of their father on his board, of how her only son had blown himself to bits in the disused pit, of their mother, and how good and kind a woman she was, and eventually she placed the tea in best china cups before the five drunken neighbours.

'Is thee not havin' any?' John asked suspiciously.

'Not yet,' she said. 'I'll have my yarrow beer first.' She smiled and put a bottle to her mouth.

Within moments of drinking down their tea my great-great-grand-mother was able to perceive the flabby jowls becoming more solid. No more shaking. The five fat faces were becoming rigid. Their stares became fixed. Inside, their brains were swimming. From with-out their heads were like the stone balls atop the pillars of the gates to the big house. The five fat faces were frozen. The old woman poked a long bony finger into the puffy cheeks of the eldest brother and when she removed it a white telltale depression remained in the flesh. A hand on the table twitched. She was unsure which of the ten it might have been.

'Now, tha great lumpkins,' she said quietly when certain that all were in a state of paralysis, 'tha've been given a little of the poison of Athens. Just enough for thee to be rendered harmless; not enough to cause any permanent damage, mind. But if I catch thee round here again I'll have thee put down like Socrates. Does tha hear? Like Socrates.'

Suddenly, changing her tone she walked around the table to where Charley was sitting. Into the rigid face with its frightened eyes she said, 'So, Charley, tha've heard I'm a witch. Well, 'tis true dear. I am a witch. My spells have thee paralysed rigid. Come round here, frightening an old woman again and she'll have thee put down. Does th' understand? I'm going to release thee soon, boys, does tha hear. Release thee from the spell, but next time I'll let the poison do its work, all the way, does thee hear? There'll be no release next time, boys; remember, no release. I'll turn thee to stone, forever.' She looked into the frightened eyes and smiled. Another hand began to twitch and tremble. Both Barney and Benjamin were drooling, the saliva trailing over their fat chins as if a snail had passed unseen from their clamped mouths. She went on: 'Before tha leaves, boys, there's another spell to cast. One of thee fine strapping lads will wed our Florence. I command it.' (Was this the one she had cast on young John Brightside fifty odd years before?) 'Now, which of thee shall it be, I wonder?' she went on.

The flabby jowls started to shake again indicating to her that the terrible effects of the hemlock were beginning to subside, though perhaps even in their drugged state the boys were showing some dissent, so horrible was the contemplation of marriage to our Flo.

'I'll count to ten,' she said quickly, and staring hard in turn at all five brothers, 'then tha'll be released from the spell and tha can all go home. Does tha hear?' She started to count slowly and on the count of ten sure enough the hands began to twitch, the feet began to stir. Soft moanings issued from their blubbery lips. 'Now, boys, let's be quick,' said my great-great-grandmother. 'Back to mother now,' and the eighty-year-old woman rushed each of the great big Gill boys unsteadily out of one door and in through the next. She then poured out the dregs of the poisoned tea, washed the pan out with clean water from the bucket and put fresh water on to boil, and all the while she could hear the awful retching and vomiting of the Gill boys next door at their father's table.

Even my great-great-grandmother, I think, must have been surprised at the effects of the spell she had cast on the Gill boys. Florence, however, was undoubtedly the most surprised of all. The poor girl found that she suddenly had not one suitor, but five. They courted her on the common, in the fields, by the river, on the slope of Hunger Hill, even at the pit itself, and they fought over her too. They had their way with her two and three at a time (mercifully, never five) in the winding engine shed and even in the grounds of the big house at the very spot where her father had received humiliation at the hands of Mr Thwaite, and great-great-grandmother double-dosed her morning and night with her female mixture. They paraded her at the public house where she regularly was awarded the black pudding but what should she care of that when she had five strapping lads snapping at her buttocks. Her grandmother, though, was worried. She feared that the spell had not taken hold and that all this multiple lovemaking was the boys' way of getting even with her. She feared that after a time, the boys would become tired of their game, and that Flo would be tossed aside, a shagged-out doll crumpled at the pit head. Thus it was with both surprise and relief that she learned of a proposal of marriage coming from the slow-witted Benjamin. Relief turned to consternation however when it became known that poor Benjamin had been beaten to within an inch of his life by John and the proposal withdrawn. John's counter-proposal, that he should be her husband, was met in the same easy manner by Flo.

'Tha'll do, John,' she said, and that was that.

Barney, however, protested loud and clear that because he was the biggest and the strongest he should have the woman for his wife and did he really have to beat the living daylights out of his four brothers just to prove his point. It was now that great-great-grandmother realized that the magic had taken hold after all, but not quite as she had intended. If she were not careful the potency of the spell was such that the magic would lay low all five potential suitors and the unfortunate Florence end up without a man at all. It was then that help arrived from an unexpected quarter. News of the predicament came at last to the ear of the prostrated father. From his position upon the parlour table the old man decreed that his sons must draw lots to settle the issue once and for all. So, grouped around their wizened and shrinking father, the boys drew straws from the old man's clasped hands, like hyphae from the fungal mass, the whole episode being witnessed by both Mrs Gill and Florence. The short straw was drawn by the quiet one, Arthur, who didn't say a word. He just walked out of the house with Flo on his arm, the brute of a girl giggling into the rain. The intent of marriage was announced immediately by Mrs Gill, and with the proclamation the spell was broken. The remaining four brothers sensing their release rushed into the street to congratulate the lucky Arthur. There are some days when it rains in our village, and the teeming water somehow washes all the coal dust out of the air. Not only can one breathe more easily without having to taste the grit in each breath but one can see more easily too. The light for a whole while after the rain had ceased becomes bright and sparkling like clarified ale; it was such a time when the five brothers hugged and kissed each other, there in the street and each kissed the bride-to-be too. 'It was a day,' Charley told me many years later,' when the Lord said, Let there be light.' Then he studied for a bit and added, thoughtfully, 'And tha could see for fucking miles.'

My great-great-grandmother watched the commotion from the parlour window, pleased that it was the quiet Arthur who had won the girl. She never forgot that he had been the only one not to frighten her that Sunday when she had returned with the hemlock. The others, however, steered clear of the old woman whenever they could and never again was she pestered with the matter of the missing fortune.

After their somewhat hasty wedding (everybody went to great lengths to insist that the bride was not pregnant), the couple emigrated to Australia. The remaining brothers went on to take their positions in the greatest pack of forwards ever to grace the Northern rugby union and to make my father's early years a delight, basking next door in reflected glory.

Henrietta wrote constantly in a profuse exchange of letters with her sister. She passed on the news of how she had come to start writing the history of the Stones, and how it continued, of Ernest's love of God, of grandmother's experience with the people from the airship, of Sidall Junkin's asthma and of the arrival of Mr Pettit and his mind full of wondrous facts. From New South Wales, Henrietta learned of the love of Flo's new husband, of how much better was the organization of labour in the antipodes, of the New Unionism and the love of her husband. She heard of pregnancy and abortion and of strikes. Then one day Mrs Gill came round and informed Henrietta of the death of the man who lived on the parlour table and how she ought to pass the news on to her son in Australia. She then told her how she would have her husband cremated and have the ashes divided into five portions, one for each of her sons.

'Can I bring it round and tha'll send it for me?'

'Yes of course,' said Henrietta. 'I'm sending them some dried fruit, anyway. I'll put it in the same parcel.'

Though why she was sending dried fruit to the land of sunshine, she had not got the remotest idea.

Henrietta duly wrote her letter, accepting responsibility for the sad duty of having to inform Arthur of the death of his father and how she thought it to be for the better, releasing the man from all his suffering. She also told of how she would be enclosing the old man's ashes in a parcel to be sent.

The next letter which she received from New South Wales thanked her very much for the parcel of dried fruit which had unfortunately been damaged during the sea voyage. 'No matter though,' wrote Flo, 'we were able to scrape the lot together and make a lovely fruit cake – Arthur's favourite.' She also wrote that she was pregnant again. Henrietta hiccuped, put her hand to her mouth and waited for the next letter. It was much shorter than normal explaining that they had only just received Henrietta's last piece of correspondence.

'Arthur's quite upset at having eaten up his dad,' it said. Among other things it also mentioned that Flo had aborted again. Her grandmother found the latter comment of extreme interest, and wondered at the marketability of cremated remains.

6

Earth closets, ash pits and John Tregus's backside

After deciding not to inform the police that a rapist was at large, a rapist with her name stamped at least twenty times indelibly on his bottom, Henrietta wondered what her next move ought to be. A clever girl such as she knew how impossible life would be if she were merely to resort to pulling off the breeches of each and every man who crossed her path. She sat upon her bed and reasoned that firstly her assailant might try to wash off the offending ink marks, that is, if he was aware of their presence. After all, they were not exactly in a place where he normally might see them. What if he thought in the pitch dark last night, that the constant slapping of his bottom was Henrietta's way of encouraging him to greater passion in his sexual romp. Oh Lord, she thought, it gets worse. He probably had no idea that he was being branded, perhaps he thought that he was merely egged on by a love-sick girl. Then she reasoned that if he didn't know of the branding of his rear he would eventually learn of it from somebody else, and that meant gossip. Fortunately, or unfortunately for she could look at it either way, there were few solitary men in the village (she assumed him to be from the village if not from the very house in which she lived); most of them bathed in groups. Mates would inquire and chatter, laugh and eventually gossip. She'd know soon enough, she smiled, darkly.

That evening after each of the menfolk had bathed and not yet combed his hair, Henrietta returned to the house with her sister-in-law, Emily. There was no embarrassed chatter, no embarrassed silence, nothing to suggest that a person had been discovered with incriminating evidence tattooed upon his buttocks. All appeared, as always, to be perfectly ordinary. The smell of grandma's baskets hung in the steamy air, Sidall Junkin spat upon the fire; the damp men started to comb their hair. As the neat parting appeared at the centre of Mr Pettit's head he said, 'Tregus would make a grand wife. He washed our backs a treat.' And Ernest followed with: 'He's a mucky beggar though, seldom takes a bath he says.'

'Why, Mr Tregus,' Emily said, 'whyever not?'

'Oh, I do sometimes, ma'am,' Tregus answered uncomfortably.

''Course I do sometimes. It's just that not working in the pit I don't get quite as dirty as the others.'

'So how often do you bathe, Mr Tregus?' Henrietta asked with a boldness that shocked the others.

'Now steady on lass,' Ernest objected with a hint of warning to his young sister.

'No it's all right, Ernest,' said the big Cornishman. 'Fair question.' He thought a moment, smiling at Henrietta, then continued, ''Bout once in six months, I suppose.'

'Six months,' the other men chorused.

'Bloody 'ell. We 'ave to 'ave one every day. Jane Brightside d'ave summat to say to thee,' Sidall complained and spat on the fire again.

'When do you leave?' Henrietta asked Tregus.

'Leave?'

'Yes. Go back to wherever it was you came from.'

'Oh, I see. Leave,' Tregus said. 'Long before I'm due my next bath, ma'am. Why I had one only last night, didn't I, lads?' He grinned, widely, Henrietta thought too widely, like a Cheshire cat.

A few days went by. Her grandmother returned from her visit to Wakefield. Henrietta still pondered how she might expose her attacker. She had for those few days even stopped visiting Bottom Boat so that she could spend more time in the village. She resorted to gossip. She would stop people in the street, call on others she'd not spoken to in ages, merely to engage them in conversation; but not once did she meet an irate wife or sweetheart, never did she come across a cheeky or knowing smile. As time went by it seemed more and more likely that Tregus was the only possible suspect. She had remembered the smell of grandmother's flowers when her attacker had entered the bedroom; the big hand over her mouth; the smell of bath potions on his massive nakedness. Had the Cornishman not admitted to taking a bath that very night and had he not refused to have another one, ever again in our house, making some flimsy excuse that he bathed only once in six months. Not likely.

54

Tregus was an educated man; it was his job to educate others. Was that the sort of person to take a bath only once in six months? And another thing. Was anybody likely to be able to sneak into the house past three lodgers in the parlour without waking at least one of them? At one time she thought it might be John or Charley Gill next door, but could either of those great big men possibly enter the house without commotion? No. It looked increasingly like one of the residents of the house. They had bathed together, all except Tregus, for four consecutive days now without a murmur reaching her ears. Besides, she knew, as if further proof were needed, that Junkin would have wheezed his way through the whole episode, Pettit would never have been able to keep his mouth shut, unstacking God knows what information upon her pillow, and her brother's wife would by now have spoken out having discovered something by the light of her small candle. But if it was Tregus how on earth was she to get him to expose himself? She decided that she would have to enlist the help of her nephew William, my father.

Now I'd better tell you about the earth closets. The earth closets were our toilets and they were at the back of the terrace of houses and their doors faced onto the back scullery of each house, about twenty yards distant. For some reason never explained they had been built in pairs. Ours adjoined that of the Gill family. Each pair was of a squarish brick structure, with two wooden doors. A thin brick wall separated each toilet, running from front to back, between the two doors. The toilet seat was made of wood and ran the length of the building running right through the dividing brick wall. It was about two and a half feet from the ground. The holes in the centre of the seat were perfectly circular which was all right if, like the Gills, you had perfectly circular bottoms. We Brightsides, however, were on the slender side, particularly the men. We found our earth closet seats less comfortable than the Gills did theirs. The earth closets were open to the elements, a blessing of doubtful value, for though the structure was ventilated in this way, defecation was a truly miserable affair when it rained or snowed.

In the interests of hygiene all the muck and excrement was raked out from the earth below the toilets on a daily basis. This was done from the back, the wall away from the scullery. In our house it was always Sidall Junkin who did this. He would go for a crap and rake out the accumulated excrement each morning at five, a chore he'd assumed since settling in to lodge following the death of his friend James Brightside. He would rake all the muck and excrement together then cover it with a bucketful of ashes from the fire. The area behind the earth closets was for this reason called the ash pits, and remained a smelly heap of mounds and craters until the midden man came in his midden wagon, at somewhat irregular intervals, to shovel and cart the lot off to God knows where. Nobody could ever understand why the midden man had entered his chosen profession and the children in particular stayed well away from him, watching from a safe distance as he shovelled the loathsome mess into his wagon. My father and the twins felt terribly sorry for the horse, a large blinkered beast whose white hair had been slowly turned grey-brown in the atmosphere of shit and dust. They used to dream of freeing the poor animal from its awful servility but nobody ever dared more than dream. The midden man was a powerful symbol of evil in our village and Albert, right up to his early twenties, was convinced that the stinking load was carted right off to be burned in a huge dump at the very centre of the earth. It was after one such emptying of the ash pits that Henrietta caught sight of my father playing around the earth closets and she there conceived her plan.

'William, dear. Come here a moment,' she called.

My father, ever ready to please, came running. 'Yes, Aunt Henrietta.'

'William, I wish you to help me in rather an unusual way,' she confided. My father, then nine years old, listened with obscene delight to the plan which his aunt had hatched. She wanted him to play a game. He was to hide in the space below the toilet at the Gill side (it was a good job he was small). Eventually someone would come and sit on our toilet seat and when William heard his aunt singing 'Ta-ra-ra-boom-de-ay' (a favourite among the children at the time), he should light his candle, directing the illumination upward and across and see if there was anything unusual about the sitter's bottom.

'Will it be you, Aunt Henrietta, sitting on the toilet?' William asked.

'It most certainly will not,' she said offensively and clipped her nephew about the ear.

'Who will it be then? Not great-grandmother.' He pulled a face.

'No, not at all. It will be a complete stranger, William.'

My father, who was quite unused to bottoms, then asked what might be so unusual about the sitter's bottom, and Henrietta, who now realized that she too had little experience of them, had to think hard for a time.

'William,' she said at last, 'it will be dirty.'

This, however, was like informing him that coal was black. To little boys all bottoms are dirty. The puzzlement on his face must have shown itself for she added, 'It will be quite black, I think, William.'

'Don't you know?' he asked.

'And it may have some words on it too.'

Now to my little father this was all too much and he burst out laughing.

'Be serious, William,' she chided, 'this is very important detective work.'

'But what will it say?' William asked, sniggering into his little grubby hand.

'I don't know,' his aunt responded, 'but you must promise me, William, that you will not try to read it. Promise me, William. Promise that you will not attempt to read the words.'

'I promise,' my father said, already enjoying the game immensely. 'But why are we doing this, Aunt Henrietta?' he asked.

'To help the police, William,' she answered putting her fingers to her lips and hushing him with her mellifluous eyes. After tea, his aunt directed William to take his place, match and candle in hand, below the toilet seats. And there he stayed while his ever so clever auntie busied herself in the garden which the Brightsides had cultivated on the land between the scullery and the earth closets. Soon Henrietta caught sight of John Tregus making his way to the toilet and William heard somebody enter the small building. He heard the door close and the lighting of a candle as the Cornishman settled down to read. From the garden came the coarse strains of his aunt's version of 'Ta-ra-ra-boom-de-ay'. William struck a match, lit his own candle and gingerly held out his arm to cast light upon the sitter's bottom. From below the candle the boy peered into the ring of gloom. Lying, as he was, spreadeagled along the width of the two toilets, he was able to make room to gawp at the stranger's magnificent equipment. He was quite unaware of the songstress in the garden, reaching a peak of discord; to my father 'Ta-ra-ra-boom-de-ay' was not a song – only a game; it could not be played badly. You sang it, that's all. Then he was aware of the door to the Gill's toilet being opened, and suddenly a deeper darkness fell upon him as a second bottom cut off the circle of pale light above his legs.

'Hello, what's this?' It was Charley Gill's voice. 'Who've we got down 'ere then?' He felt a thick hand clutching at his trousers. Now, as my father later explained it to me, if you're being chased by the fastest second row forward in the Northern rugby union you move quickly, and he did. But there was only one way to go and that was to follow his hand and the lighted candle upwards. There was a terrible yelling as the Cornishman's magnificent equipment singed at the end of the flame. A welcome circle of pale light appeared as Tregus's bottom was removed like a lid from an Arabian jar and my father came screaming like a harridan, upward through the toilet, and away from Charley's awesome clutches. Tregus too startled, or maybe too injured to stop him, allowed the boy to escape through the door and into the arms of his gardening aunt who was still offering her grating refrain to the whole village.

'Did you see it, William?' she asked, excitedly.

William merely shook his head, his frightened eyes darting wildly around him. Eventually he left this island haven for the full comfort of his mother in the rooms above the parlour, sobbing uncontrollably for ages, before joining the others below.

Tregus then hobbled by, watched from the closet doorway by a bemused Charley Gill.

'Good evening, Miss Brightside,' he said, ever the gentleman. My father's aunt merely nodded and turned to follow the wounded man into the house. For the remainder of the evening my father refused communication with his aunt who, mainly through the agency of her beautiful brown eyes, kept on asking for information.

Unable to contain himself or the pain any longer, Tregus asked Ernest to step outside where he explained to a bowl of stars that he had been badly burned by an unknown person in a place which he didn't care to name. Ernest was sensible enough to tell his grandmother who offered the lodger her tender care. She was after all by now eighty-six years old and reputed to be a witch. So the big man put himself at her mercy and she got to massage his magnificent equipment at least once a day for nearly a month.

'Is there anything strange about his bottom, grandmother?' Henrietta asked.

'Why, child, what an odd question to ask me,' the old woman answered. 'Whatever would tha be thinking? His bottom's burned, that's all.'

'But is there anything different about it, grandmother?'

'Yes, child,' she said. 'It's getting better, that's what's different.'

Mr Tregus gradually recovered, still unsure of how his rear end had come to receive its injuries. The imp which screamed upward and outward from the toilet had not been identified, and he cared not to discuss too deeply with those who might prompt him whether it was the work of child or spirit. For a time the earth closets, and in particular the structure shared by the Gills and the Brightsides, became forbidden territory to the children. The thing which lurked there, they reasoned, had probably been left by the midden man, who was assumed now to have an even greater propensity for evil than had ever before been imagined. Even Charley Gill grew to doubt whether the trouser leg he had grabbed that evening had any material content. Thus did the 'ghost of the earth closets' become absorbed into the folklore of our village. John Tregus remained with us for several months, setting up a programme for adult learning at the chapel in the next village. He managed to get started classes in History and Science which all the menfolk in our house attended on Tuesday and Wednesday nights respectively. Then, when he had handed over the running of the classes to local people, he left our house to do the same in some other area of the coalfield. Before he left he gave my father a shilling, the twins sixpence each, and shook hands in turn with each of the remaining members of the household. He urged Henrietta to continue to write her History of the Stones, for one day he was certain it would be an immensely important document. My great-great-grandmother thought him to be the finest gentleman she had ever met.

7

A mad way of looking at the mad, mad world

The one piece of furniture in our house which had not been either knocked together by the occupants or purchased for two and six-pence as a mass produced article, was great-great-grandmother's dressing table. It had been brought back from France at the time of the Napoleonic Wars by her father. A part of his plunder, al-though he preferred to call it compensation (for the loss of an eye and a foot). He gave it to Jane at the time of her marriage to John Brightside. It had been the only piece of furniture which she had loaded on to the cart and carried to her son's house at the time of her removal. James had had to winch it through the bed-room window at the time and he and Sidall Junkin had positioned it against the wall which adjoined the Gill house in the room in which his mother would eventually sleep. In those difficult moments during which the article was hauled into the house the oval mirror was unfortunately cracked diagonally, a fracture which remained always, splitting the image of the looker into a curious derangement from top right to lower left. One looked into that mirror and couldn't help but see the crazy side of one's nature; no matter how composed and sensible one felt a madman always stared back, mortal and deeply flawed.

The dressing table was not particularly large, nor was it very heavy, but it was different and so assumed a pride of place within the small cluttered bedroom. One had to walk around it to get from the top of the stairs to the adjoining door between the two bedrooms, always brushing the bed as one did so, much to the annoyance of both the walking and the sleeping. The article, however, was rarely moved, just on the odd occasion would it be trundled aside so that one might clean behind it. In the spring of 1902, Henrietta and her grandmother decided that it was about time that their room was redecorated and for the first time they should use anaglypta wall-paper for the hanging of which they would have to pull out the dressing table. Mirroring their every crazy thought and action they tugged the object alongside the bed, the two women eventually sprawling across the width of the mattress faces down and exhausted. When they had recovered they both went around the back of the piece of furniture to continue their decorating. They were surprised to find that a hole, large enough for a man to crawl through, had appeared in the wall adjoining the Gill house. It had been covered with a large slate at the neighbour's side.

'So that's how they came in,' my great-great-grandmother said.

'Who came in, grandmother?' Henrietta asked, feeling immediate discomfort at the revelation.

'Those five Gill boys, dear. The day they dug up the scullery floor. Do thee not remember?'

Henrietta vaguely remembered the occasion but it had been ten or eleven years ago and had made little sense to the young girl. 'Why did they do that?' she inquired.

'They were looking for treasure,' she told her. 'We must get it bricked again,' she then suggested.

Of course her grandmother's talk of the Gill boys gaining access to the house through their bedroom had given my great-aunt other ideas. It was not now so far fetched to think that Charley or John (the only two of the five still living at home) might have been her assailant. Good Lord, she thought, one must by now have seen the other, stamps and all. And she visualized the frantic rubbing and scrubbing away of the offending marks practised in clandestine brotherhood on each bath night. A practice accompanied no doubt by grandmother's potions, for she had also learned that Mrs Gill was an excellent customer of the old lady's medicaments. But to no avail she was sure; for indelible Elyahou Tsiblitz had said the ink was and indelible it proved to be. By way of testing the truthfulness of his view she had stamped a very small area of her upper arm with the word 'love'. Indeed she was certain nothing on earth could remove the cloying ink. She began now to contemplate the second plan which would involve her nephew William in dangerous detective work.

The four remaining brothers each formed part of a terrible eight-some playing professional rugby for the Castleford club. As I have already mentioned they were part of the greatest and biggest pack of forwards ever to step on to the turf. Now, in those days, there were no baths or changing rooms at the ground, so the men would change into their playing strip at home, walk or cycle to the ground (Wakefield had a hooker who ran the fifteen miles there and back with a bruising game between journeys), play up and return bloodied and muddied for a hot bath and a good meal. At the Gill house Saturday afternoons had become a ritual. All four boys, together with their mother, would after the game have a spanking meal, usually a sheep's head cooked in beer, which the woman would spend nearly all day preparing. Henrietta's plan was this. After the next home match when the boys had returned for their bath and the curtains had been drawn (always a sure sign that men were naked within) Henrietta would stuff a turpentine soaked rag under the scullery door and set it alight. William then, on her signal would approach from the front of the house shouting 'fire', and advising the occupants to leave immediately in fear of their lives. Meanwhile, Lancaster and Albert, both having been presented at the last Christmas with cameras from their great-grandmother, would be positioned at points suitable to photograph the ensuing flight and capture on film and forever any incriminating evidence about the backsides of the Gill boys. In the furore, Henrietta would then slip into the house and douse the fire with the contents of the tin bath.

Well, the day arrived, Castleford were playing the massive team from Batley and my father, who had been to the game and seen his heroes mete out a terrible pasting to the men in blue, followed the Gill boys home. He was questioning whether it was righteous or not to carry through the plan and deceive the objects of his devotion in such a way. Detective work or not, he felt as if he were becoming a traitor, and he knew, from his father's preaching, what happened to them. He soon realized, however, that things were not going entirely to plan for walking up ahead with the four Castleford men were three others dressed in blue jerseys. His aunt had not allowed for the Gills' hospitality. These three men, almost half the opposition pack who only minutes before had been the object of his derision and hatred, were now, arms about their hosts' big shoulders, on their way to the Gill house for a bath and share in the sheep's head. Treachery's a slippery thing, it can be passed like a rugby ball, my father thought. Here now were the Gills behaving like traitors and he suddenly felt guilt no longer for what he was about to do. It was in such a frame of mind that he entered the village behind the giant neighbours and their guests. When the last rugby player had been clapped through the door (there was always a reception committee to greet them) and the black curtains draped across the window, Henrietta went into action. She quickly set up the two tripods for the twin cameras. She gave each nephew their instructions and then covered them in a black cloth. With the late afternoon sun filtering the hazy air they looked like two beings from another planet set down on our common for a spot of gentle grazing.

Henrietta quickly went to the back of the house and gave my father the signal to go into action. 'Ta-ra-ra-boom-de-ay' wafted over the roof. My father, now feeling quite guiltless and sure of the direction in which treachery lay, started for the door and began to shout, 'Fire, fire!' He ran to the Gill house and beat upon the closed door with little fists. 'Get out, get out! Run for your lives!' The door burst open and seven naked men ran over my little father in a hasty retreat from the smoke which was billowing from the parlour. The four biggest forwards in the rugby union, plus three of the terrible Batley eight, poured like a blancmange in clogs over the pitiful William. Half a dozen dogs fielding at the boundary, including a long stop named Denton, then attacked the naked men in defence of the run-down child. The rugby players turned and fled with the dogs snapping at their heels. The cameras went off with loud bangs and a puff of smoke from each of the strange animals. Henrietta appeared in time to see seven backsides hurtling into the distance, smiled, went inside the Gill house and put out the fire. On coming out again, she gathered up the dazed William, pulled to her the strange animals now separating into twins and tripods, and cuddled them all the way into the Brightside home, watched by wide eyes set into the dirty faces of the human half of the village cricket team. That's how we come to have in our family photograph album two pictures, taken from slightly differing angles, of seven naked men haring across the common and each with a bottom as white as the day that he was born. What a disappointment for my father's aunt!

At her first glimpse of the developed photographs she went upstairs to her bedroom. She peered behind the dressing table, whose tulip wood and delicate marquetry had been covered in a wash of lime as part of the redecorating process, checking that the freshly bricked hole remained intact. Sitting on the bed before the cracked mirror, she started to cry. She watched tears rolling down her left cheek as far as the glittering scar, then disappearing only to reappear somewhere else, yet still down the same cheek. She adjusted her position on the bed, lifting her head and shoulders, in such a way that the crack ran through her chin. Now the tear drops seemed to flow right into it like a tributary to a river. She remained motionless, crying, watching the river which carried away her tears. The flaw on the right side cut right through her eye. She imagined it blurred her vision, as it was cutting her eye in two. How would the world look to such an eye, she wondered. The two eyes looked down to her left, down the glinting river watching the tears pool and flow. What a mad and frustrating world, she thought. Would she ever find her rapist? She watched herself watching the tears flowing down the river and out of the oval mirror, then looked back to the photograph upon her lap. Was it wrong to create such mayhem?

Or did the disorder exist anyway? Had she promoted the madness of the photograph, if indeed it were mad? Hadn't the selfsame seven naked men been naked moments before she lit the rags? Were they mad then? Was the situation then mad? No, she came to the conclusion that it was she who was mad. She lit the rags, that was an act of madness. Everything which followed, the men fleeing the fire, William being mown down, the dogs barking, the twins photographing the whole scene, even her entering the house to douse the flames (for which she was commended by an admiring Mrs Gill) were natural consequences of what she herself had set in train at the other side of the house – at the darker side she thought. And what of poor William? Her crazy schemes had put the boy in mortal danger now on two occasions. She would have to apologize to her nephew, she thought, and so went in search of my unfortunate father. Finding him on the common directly in front of our house, she drew him to one side, at the same time asking his flock of dirty friends to take themselves off to other fields.

'I am sorry, William,' she said.

'What for?'

'For putting you in such danger at the earth closet and again the

64

other day outside the Gills' house. I didn't realize that police work was so dangerous.'

'I don't want no more police work,' my father said in sudden panic.

'Don't worry, William,' his aunt consoled him. 'I shall not ask you again.'

With relief he said, 'I thought you were going to ask me. I don't like detective work, Aunt Henrietta.' He sobbed, and she tugged him to her bosom. 'Oh, William, please don't cry,' she said, biting her lip as the dirty flock of friends approached within a stone's throw of them.

'No,' he said, pulling himself from his aunt and composing himself with a large sniff, 'Don't tell anyone but I'm going to try thieving for a time.'

'Don't be silly, William. You'll soon be found out.'

'Not if I'm careful,' he answered.

'You'll be caught,' she stressed. 'The police can now detect the culprit from his fingerprints.'

'What's them?'

'It's true, William. The police now are able to identify the criminal by the fingerprints he leaves at the scene of his crime. I read it in the paper only last week.'

'Go on, you're kidding me,' my father answered.

'No, it's true. We each of us have a different print which can be shown up using a special powder. It's just like leaving a calling card. There'll be no more thieves running free, William.' Seeing the group of ragged friends advancing ever closer she added, 'You'd better tell them, too. Just in case they have any ideas.'

My father took to heart what his aunt had told him and steered clear of a life of crime, at least for the next five years. That was until the year in which Elyahou Tsiblitz paid his third visit to our village.

It was in those five years that the world beyond our village went absolutely crazy. President Roosevelt and our king exchanged messages by wireless, talking to one another over a distance of thousands of miles. An anarchist attempted to kill King Leopold of the Belgians. In London trains appeared which worked by electricity, then too the trams were electrified. Then in December 1903, as

Duncan D'Arcy had predicted to my great-great-grandmother, a heavier-than-air machine flew for the very first time. Two American brothers in Kitty Hawk, North Carolina, had flown at thirty miles per hour on a flight lasting fifty-nine seconds. Then the buses were motorized; in London horsedrawn vehicles were becoming fewer. A man called George Rogers attached himself to the Russian army and sent back film he made during the Russo-Japanese war. Grand Duke Sergius of Russia was assassinated in Moscow, then somebody tried to kill the king of Spain in Paris, on two separate occasions within a few days of each other. A bomb was thrown at the Sultan of Turkey in Constantinople. Female agitators were ejected from the House of Commons, and then subsequently interrupted political meetings at Northampton and Manchester. Lieutenant Lahn won the Gordon Bennet Cup, flying all the way from Paris to Whitby in a balloon. Several suffragettes were arrested at the House of Commons and imprisoned. An anarchist made an attempt on the life of Alfonso XIII on his wedding day. The bioscope and kinema opened up in London and quickly spread to the provinces.

In our village, however, nothing happened. The men still hewed coal with picks and shovels and still bought candles from Thwaite. Accidents still happened. The dead were brought up if possible; the injured lay uncomfortably at home drawing a benefit barely enough to keep them alive. Ernest still forbade the use of oil lamps at our house, and the occupants still lived dimly within the halo of a candle's power. Henrietta, the incident of the rape fairly gone from her mind, continued to describe the stones. In her bedroom, the cracked mirror continued to monitor the sanity of those who cared to look into it.

8

The rise and fall of Sidall Junkin and the fall and rise of the price of coal

It was back in the summer of 1873 that a great row broke out down at the pit head. Now ours was only a small pit employing fewer than two hundred men, so when trouble brewed it fermented quickly. And there was nothing like a bit of cheating on the part of the coal owner or his lackeys to get the brew started. A checkweighman by the name of Cotton who had been appointed by Thwaite had been caught on the fiddle. I'd better explain that the checkweighman, being the man responsible both for recording the tally of tubs filled against a hewer's name and for seeing that there is no underfilling of tubs (the fine imposed for such was to discount the whole of the tub) could afford no enemies. Nor, for that matter, could he afford to have friends, at least he ought not to have friends at the coal face. Impartiality was called for if the checkweighman was to survive.

Unfortunately Cotton had not the impartiality required for the job for he kept discounting tubs filled by our neighbours, the Hendersons. Worse still, it seems that on odd occasions he actually recorded tubs belonging to old man Henderson to the tally of Enoch Carpenter, himself a loathsome cheat and drinking partner of Cotton. Well, you can imagine the commotion that broke when suspicion finally turned to proof and Cotton was caught red-handed fiddling the tallies. He was spreadeagled and pinned to a door which had been brought from the joiner's shop, a pickaxe each through cuffs and trouser bottoms, while the men debated what should be done with him. Those who couldn't add up were quick to point to their certainty that they too had been cheated in the past, while those who were able to add but who were short on memory claimed likewise. It quickly got to the stage when all the hewers were claiming some shortfall in their cumulative tallies and clamouring for the blood of the unfortunate man spread upon the door. Sidall Junkin, who could both add up and had a good memory (a rarity on that day), calmed things a little when he pointed out that it was not possible for everyone to claim a shortfall in their tally. After all, if one loses then some other has to gain, just as Enoch Carpenter had gained one from Henderson. There was a general nodding of agreement with the logic of Sidall's argument followed by a quiet accusatory silence when the men realized that perhaps their neighbours, the very men who were now gesticulating vociferously by their sides, might be fiddling at their expense. This appeared a thought common to all at that moment and it was Enoch Carpenter, sensing the mood of the men and in need of friends if he were not to end up like Cotton, skewered to a board, who turned the situation to advantage.

'Seems like Cotton can't do the job. Seems to me he's been making mistakes ever since he started. Serves us right, I suppose for accepting a checkweighman appointed by Thwaite.'

'Ay, he's right,' shouted old man Henderson. 'We should appoint us own. Someone we can all trust. A tallyman's position's too important for us to leave it to't coal owner.'

These two statements helped relieve the tension which the men were feeling. The cheat and the cheated were in common agreement with the unfortunate Cotton between, no more than an idiot doing his best. Nobody had been fiddled, not deliberately at least. The men breathed more easily. They ceased to eye their neighbours with suspicion. Cotton was released from his wooden bed of torment.

'Wait a minute. What if we've all been cheated?' It was Sidall Junkin's wheezy voice again. 'What if Cotton has systematically deducted tubs from all of us?'

'But tha said there'd have to be gains,' James Brightside reminded him.

'Ay, perhaps the gains went to Thwaite. By not recording a tub and not awarding it to anyone's tally, who gains? It's still a tub full of coal, isn't it?'

'Thwaite,' came the chorused reply.

'Ay. Thwaite and that bugger Cotton,' Sidall shouted back. Now here was a man to be listened to. In a few moments he'd come forth with two first-class ideas. What did it matter that one contradicted the other? It was more important that one was viewed as an extension of the other. Sidall was seen to be thinking not just on his feet but on the move. These were the ideas of a man of action.

The unfortunate Cotton was again pinned to the board.

'Chuck bugger down t'shaft,' someone shouted from the crowd. 'No. There'll be no need for that,' Sidall wheezed holding his arms aloft and waiting for silence. 'We'll tek 'im to Thwaite, just as he is.'

'Ay,' they chorused amid laughter. 'Let's tek 'im to Thwaite.' With Cotton spread upon the door and his clothes in tatters, fifty men marched on the big house. They went through the gates where the giant boulders stood aloft the stone pillars and up the leafy lane which led to the coal owner's home. Thwaite was waiting, the door shut behind him.

'Thwaite,' shouted the young Henderson, 'we've come to sithee 'bout this.' He motioned toward the board above the many outstretched arms, on which Thwaite could just see the lifted head of a man trying to make himself known out of the agony and the anonymity of crucifixion.

'It's Mr Thwaite to thee, lad,' the coal owner said with courage, before the mass of men and ignoring the prone man's plight. 'What is that, anyroad?' he eventually asked, pointing up to the board with his cane. The ragged man was set down with the care a family of Moroccans would exercise when showing a rare carpet. The men were aware now of his asset value, but the boss only too well aware of Cotton's changing fortunes prodded the prone tallyman with his stick.

'Been caught cheating 'ave thee, lad?' he asked. He tut-tutted, shaking his head and not taking his eyes from the unfortunate Cotton. 'A checkweighman really has to be beyond that sort of behaviour, lad. He really has.' Looking at the men he asked, 'What's tha want me to do?'

'Tha set him on, he's been cheatin' for thee,' Henderson said.

'Nobody cheats for me, lad. I can do my own cheating, thanks very much,' Thwaite replied with a light laugh.

'He's been under-tallying, regular,' Henderson said.

'Incompetent, is he?' the coal owner said, prodding Cotton again. A booted foot swung out of the crowd and struck the man on the leg. The crowd was beginning to realize what a useless asset they really had.

'I'm sorry, lads,' Thwaite continued. 'It was my choice, I admit that. I'll be more careful next time.'

'There won't be a next time, Mr Thwaite,' James Brightside said. 'We'll choose us own tallyman from now on.'

'Now steady, Brightside. Don't go threatening.'

'No threats, Mr Thwaite. We choose us own. What have thee to say?'

'I'm sayin' nowt, lad,' the coal owner said, holding his ground, and looking grimly about the mass of men. An immediate call for strike action went up from all the men on hearing the coal owner's response. Now Thwaite was nobody if he wasn't the supreme general; he knew exactly when to withdraw.

'All right, Brightside, who's tha' tallyman?' he asked, surprising the others with the allowed space into which they'd tumbled.

'Sidall Junkin,' my great-grandfather responded quickly. Perhaps too quickly for the colliers hadn't had chance to discuss it between themselves.

The coal owner studied Sidall for a long time, then he said, 'Tha's not a church goer, Junkin.'

Sidall shook his head.

'Tha's never been to a union meeting 'as tha, Sid?' he then asked. Sidall again shook his head.

'Tha's not a big man. Tha's not slow but I wouldn't say tha was quick-witted either. Tha's a small wheezy man with black spit, Junkin. Take care tha' doesn't end up on a board like Cotton here. Start as checkweighman in't mornin',' the coal owner said decisively and went back into the house, closing the door behind him.

Cotton was released from the board halfway down the leafy lane, and he was kicked all the way back to the village. He had an extremely sore backside but no further injury befell him, that is not until he was maimed in a rock fall the following year.

Sidall, as instructed, assumed his new duty immediately and became a very popular and efficient checkweighman. Four years later at the time of James Brightside's death he was still the most trusted of the tallymen. When my great-grandfather was killed, crushed beneath the fallen fossilized bones of an iguanodon, the pit was still working a three-day week, but soon after that the pit resumed full working. Due to the drastic fall in coal prices though, rather than work more short time the men had accepted a scale of pay which was related to the price of coal. Wages fell. When Jack went into the pit at the age of thirteen, he received no more than ten shillings a week, half of what he would have earned five years before.

The death of his friend wounded Sidall deeply. The day that he died, after leaving my great-great-grandmother and before descending the shaft to look for James, he had grabbed an old sack which lay on the ground at the holeside. Then, in the rising rotten flood water he had swum to where he knew the dinosaur bones to be. He could see a small light in the distance and knew it must be the flame of his friend's candle. 'I'm coming, James,' he shouted. 'Hang on!' The words echoed above the shortening chamber as the waters rose up the walls of rock. When he arrived at the flickering candle, however, he saw that it was still perched in his friend's helmet like a ghostly feather in an alpine cap. In the dim light he was able to see how the cavern had collapsed; the tons of fossilized bones lying in a great cairn, he assumed, above his buried friend. He reached his arm out of the water to grasp the helmet and as he did so the flame died. What he felt then was not a helmet but something altogether more soft, like flock he thought. He grabbed at it and stuffed it in the sack. In the dark, feeling about with one hand, he found other things and stuffed them too into the sack. Something touched his face lightly for a moment, then was gone. 'James,' he said quietly. 'Is tha here, James?' There was no answer from the wet darkness, only the noise of the rising waters, lapping the rock.

Swimming for his life in the foul flood and lugging the sack of God knows what behind in the pitch black, he swore there and then to find a better way. There had to be a way beyond Thwaite to dig coal with dignity and in safety. A way to die in bed surrounded by children and not blasted to nothing in a foul pit, or spitting alone from a chair in the parlour. The day after they had buried the sack Sidall went to a lodge meeting at the mission hall in the next village. It was at a time when Union rolls were falling; there were five other union members present. Sidall spoke for the first time in public. He had no recollection afterwards of what he had said, only that he rambled on for at least an hour to an almost empty hall. He spoke of Thwaite and James Brightside. Of the iniquities of the wage scale and the need for strike action. Of the need for cooperation, not just amongst working colleagues but between lodges, between districts, even between areas. He was speaking of federation. And at the end of the evening he found that because he was a man to be trusted, a man with a job that demanded trust, he had been made lodge secretary. But he was secretary to a lodge whose numbers fell in a district whose numbers were falling even faster. At times there might be only himself and the treasurer at the meetings, but he stuck it out talking to himself, occasionally being rewarded with an audience of a half dozen or more who would listen docile and polite to his wheezy oratory. Soon he was delegated to the district committee of the Yorkshire Miner's Association and here his views received more than a polite hearing. He spoke to them of federation, of the strength in unity. Yes, they all agreed a national federation was needed, that would give them strength in their fight with the mine owners. In 1881 the Association refused any longer to accept the scale of pay related to the price of coal, and the following year the Yorkshire and Lancashire miners supported each other in their bargaining for the 10 per cent wage increase. It meant strikes here and there, but Thwaite paid up without a struggle. Sidall Junkin was a hero, and the price of coal fell even further.

Then came Sidall's entry into the economics arena. Mr Thwaite met with him at the mission hall to hear his views. Outside a blizzard wrapped itself silently about the chapel. Quiet white footprints were filled in almost as quickly as they had been made. Inside, excited and frequently spitting into his clean handkerchief, the tallyman explained his ideas.

'Coal output's increased steadily, Mr Thwaite, so has the number of men employed. Nobody cuts any more coal now than he did fifteen years since. That means only one thing, over-production.'

'Ay, or over-manning.'

Sidall ignored the remark. 'There's too much coal chasing the same market, Mr Thwaite. Tha can see that.'

'Ay,' Thwaite said stamping his feet beneath the table.

'Well, it must make sense to thee, a business man like thee, Mr Thwaite, to cut production.'

'Ay,' he said, and stamped his feet again.

Sidall watched the great sky without shedding huge blue flakes through the coloured window.

'What are thee suggesting, Junkin?' the coal owner prompted.

'The eight-hour day, Mr Thwaite. That's what I'm proposing.'

'Bugger off,' scolded Thwaite. 'Does tha think I'm a muggins or summat? Nivver! If tha wants to reduce production, and I don't think it would be too bad a thing mind, if we all agreed, tha can have a three-day week like afore.'

'And three days' wages?' inquired Sidall.

'Ay, of course. Tha didn't think I'd pay a full week's wage for three days' work did tha?'

Sidall shook his head.

'Tha wants it all, Junkin. Tha wants federation, tha wants more brass, shorter hours. There's nowt for thee, lad. With price of coal as it is, pot's empty.'

'But I'm givin' thee a way to raise the price of coal, Mr Thwaite. Tha must see.'

'And what about the competition, lad? What about all t'other pits? Does tha think all the coal owners will follow suit? Will they buggery! I'll tell thee what they'll do, Junkin. They'll bury me, and thee and tha men. They'll bury us, lad, and good riddance they'll say.'

'So what'll it be, Mr Thwaite?' Sidall asked. 'Will it come to lay offs?'

There was no guile in that question, he merely tossed it like a bone to a dog – to see what Thwaite would do with it.

'Come on, Junkin, tha knows I can't do that. We don't want anybody starving, do we?'

'No,' said Sidall. But for the life of him he couldn't think why Mr Thwaite cared that much for the men and their families. The dog hadn't even licked the bone.

'Tha'll have to accept a new scale in the end, Junkin. Either that or a three-day week. Now is there any more?' Sidall shook his head. 'Then I'll be off,' Thwaite said.

'Why don't tha stay, Mr Thwaite?' Sidall asked. 'It's snowing hard out there. No point in going home in a blizzard.'

'Nay, lad, I'm not soft.'

'Well, I think I'll curl up here,' Sidall wheezed.

'Do as tha please, lad,' Thwaite said. 'I said I'm not soft. I'll make my way back.' Then he stepped out into a cold, white and silent as the stars.

Thwaite was right though. The men had to accept a sliding scale, but before that Sidall Junkin was humiliated into accepting a 15 per cent reduction in wages. The men were locked out for six weeks until they capitulated, cold and hungry. The price of coal continued to fall. In her lifetime, Jane Brightside could not remember having seen so many starve, so many children going without shoes and breeches. The hero in the wide-winged chair was a hero no more. His eyes became sunken and black. His black spit became more tenacious, resisting for longer the flames of the fire. The men couldn't trust him any longer, not as their tallyman. Thwaite gave him a job picking out stones from the coal at the pit head. The job of secretary to the lodge went to young Oliver Henderson in whose term the price of coal began to rise; in whose term the Miners' Federation of Great Britain was founded, and in whose term 40 per cent increase in wages was awarded to all the miners. Such was Sidall's luck riding on the price of coal.

But the price of coal is a switchback and within a year of the massive pay awards prices again took a tumble. The Yorkshire miners pugnaciously declared their wages were as low as ever they were going to be. There'd be no reductions and no scales negotiated. The capitalists would have to control their selling prices without affecting labour.

One Sunday Jack and Ernest, now both employed as hewers, took a walk. From chapel they decided to walk up towards Leeds. Leaving the taste of grit far behind they walked slowly through the meandering lanes about the Thwaite house. The sun filtered through the trees in the green leafy lanes, right down to the tracks, dry and rutted from the constant passage of cart wheels. What little grass there was appeared worn but it was a lush full colour like it always was away from the villages in the summer. The pink and white hawthorn hedgerows which hemmed them in for much of their walk broke suddenly to a field of yellow corn. At a bend in the lane they again tasted coal grit. It was Jack who noticed it first, his brother soon after. Then beyond the field of corn they could see rising and brooding over the flat fields stacks of coal. In the sun they shone black and brittle. They quickly crossed the track in the field and approached the steeply rising heaps.

'There's no pit here,' Ernest said.

'No,' said his brother, surveying the mountainous landscape they were coming upon. 'It must be a stockpile.'

They wandered about the awesome black pyramids wondering who on earth could own such mountains of their labour. The area seemed to extend for ever, black and brilliant and, from some angles, blotting out the sun.

'Thwaite,' Jack said. 'Thwaite's bloody stockpile.'

'Nay, this isn't Thwaite's land.'

'Who then? It's got to be Thwaite's.'

Ernest marvelled at the amount of coal set down in the middle of waving fields of corn.

'There's more 'ere than there is in't pit,' he said.

'Look on tha labour, lad,' Jack advised. 'It's all here. As much as tha'll ever cut in tha life. Thee and me both, maybe all lads in terrace. Thwaite's got us tallied up and saved, lad. There it is. Tha's been saved on earth lad, even as it is in heaven.'

When they arrived back at the house and informed Sidall Junkin of what they had found, the sunken eyes seemed for a time to lift themselves from their sockets. The dullness went and a gleam touched off from his dark pupils.

'I knew it,' he said with an enthusiastic wheeze. 'I told that bugger Thwaite years since he was over-producing and he knew it too.'

'No wonder price of coal is falling,' Sidall went on. 'Go get Henderson, Ernest.'

My grandfather ran from the house to bring home their illustrious neighbour, whose fortunes as lodge secretary were on the wane. The price of coal was falling again.

'Oliver,' Sidall said after Ernest had explained their find, 'tha needs a miracle, lad. Make good use of it.'

''Ows tha mean, Sidall?'

'We'll do Thwaite's job for 'im. We'll curb his stocks.'

'How?'

'We'll take it back, that's what.'

'What! Thieve the stockpile?' Oliver said incredulously.

'Ay.'

'Where'd we keep it?'

'Down't pit, silly bugger, where else?'

Oliver stared at the ex-secretary open-mouthed.

'Now, don't look like that, lad,' he continued. 'I don't mean down our pit, I mean in disused pit. Tip it down shaft on Hunger Hill where James is.'

'And how do we get it there?' Oliver asked still unbelieving.

'Call men to't pit, Oliver. I'll tell 'em 'ow.'

Sidall Junkin was now fifty-three years old, clapped out, wheezing and picking over coals at the pit head, but the glint in his eye convinced the young secretary, who was after all seeking a miracle, that perhaps he should do as requested. He called the men together at the pit head. It was the largest attendance ever to gather in the history of the village. The hero of 1882 was back, for a time, in the hearts of the people.

'Tha'll get carts and tubs, anything that'll hold coal. See the agriculturalists, get them to lend their beasts. Horses, oxen, anything with four legs. You pit lads, bring up the ponies. We start tomorrow morning at four. Women and children too. Tha'll bring every bit of coal tha' can carry until that shaft's full. Are we agreed?'

'Ay,' the men concurred, more enthusiastic than they'd been for years. 'We'll fill bugger's shaft brimfull,' Sidall shouted to the mob as it broke to seek out means of transportation.

The following morning the whole village turned out even to the youngest child and at a trot a strange train of wagons and carts set off up the rutted lanes leading to the cache of coal. Any wagon which broke down was simply lifted over the hawthorn hedge and dumped in the adjacent field. Horses had been borrowed from farmers and gypsies; there were even a couple of racehorses stolen from a stud at Wakefield. As they filed past the Thwaite house, the men and women jeered loudly. Eventually the coal owner came down his leafy lane to watch the procession filing by and to acknowledge the jeers with a smile. Even in such numbers and with such purpose the colliers were a little nervous of saying too much in the presence of the master.

To avoid congestion a route had been planned so that the procession filed in a great circle, creating a merry-go-round of enormous diameter. If only somebody had thought to have brought a steam-driven organ the circus would have been complete.

When loaded the carts continued beyond the stacks of coal to meet up with another road and proceed that way round to Hunger Hill.

'We'll not make much impression on this lot, Sid. Not like this,' Ernest said, shovelling the coal aboard his flat-backed cart with the red and silver tailboard as fast as he could. Sidall observed that all about him men, women and children were breaking backs in a strenuous effort to load their wagons as quickly as possible, yet the mountain of coal remained untouched towering above the labouring villagers.

'Keep shovelling, lad. Keep shovelling. Summat'll happen. I know it, tha'll see,' said the wheezing ex-tallyman. With the early morning sun, and maybe fifty loads already making the return journey, two strangers arrived at the stockpile. Sidall had seen them before but couldn't recollect where it might have been.

'Mr Junkin,' said the older of the two. 'I bring greetings from the Leeds Branch of the Social Democratic Federation.' The man's accent was foreign, his words lost in the scraping of shovels. 'We have brought machines to help.'

'Machines? What machines?' Sidall shouted.

'We have brought new rubber-belted machinery to convey the coal from the mountains to the carts. Your men will only have to shovel the coal on to the belts, the machines will do the rest.' He then turned to the tall young man next to him and spoke furiously in a foreign tongue. The young man ran up through the cornfield and disappeared out of sight.

'I told thee summat would turn up.' Sidall winked at Ernest. Then turning to the foreigner he asked, 'Has tha got two?'

'Oh yes. We have one for here and one for the pit at Hunger Hill. When we have set up the conveying machine here, we shall join the train of carts and take the other across and set it working over there.'

Within minutes the tall young man had returned with several helpers in a cart. They unloaded about fifteen yards of shiny black belting which was wound on to an adjustable incline and positioned it at the lower end to the foot of the coal mountain where Ernest was shovelling. A steam engine was rigged up to drive the belt.

'There's a stream about twenty yards to our left,' the foreigner told Sidall. 'You must detail your people.' He threw several buckets down from the cart.

'You seem to have thought of everything,' Sid said, his eyes twinkling again.

'I didn't bring fuel,' the man said with a smile.

'No matter, we'll find us own,' Sidall smiled back broadly.

Ten minutes later coal was coming off the end of the belt and loading the carts at a speed greater than the dumbfounded colliers could ever have imagined.

'Here,' said the man from the Social Democratic Federation.

'I have room on my cart now. Please, you load me with coal and I join the train for Hunger Hill.'

In this way did the merry-go-round speed up. The carts and tubs were loaded after only a short pause then were on their way again, journeying at a trot to Hunger Hill and the disused pit. The first wagons were soon passing the gates to the Thwaite house for a second time and a bemused coal owner, whose sharp memory now recognized a second coming, began to wonder just what was going on beyond those gates. When he had acknowledged faces at a quickening turn for the third and fourth time he felt at last obliged to speak.

'What's going on Brightside?' he asked Jack as he passed again leading his gold-painted cart, pulled by a magnificent grey shire horse.

'It's a fair, Mr Thwaite. A fair, and a circus all in one,' said my jubilant relative.

'Any lions, or tigers?'

'No. No wild animals, Mr Thwaite. Just people. Enjoying thesselves.'

'Got a ring master, 'as tha?'

'Oh ay. Foreign chap. Don't know 'is name,' Jack chuckled, and led his horse past the entrance to the big house. ''E's ring master and organ grinder all in one.' Then under his breath Jack said, 'And tha's bloody monkey this time, Mr Thwaite.'

The men, women and children of the village, together with their horses and oxen and their friends from Leeds moved mountains in twenty-four hours. The new rubber-belted machinery spewed coal back into the disused shaft at such a rate that within the rounding of the day it was filled to the top. Not another cart or tub of coal could be squeezed in. At the other end, the stockpile had been reduced considerably, mountains of their labour, as Jack had called them, had disappeared, pushed back to where they had come from. The moon shone pale on the black and straggled heaps which were left when Sidall, Jack and Ernest left the site at the back of the train for the last time. The huge merry-go-round had ceased and with the retirement of the village it too had to be put to bed. The animals were tethered to graze on the common, carts and tubs left about to be eventually returned to their owners.

Not a soul turned into work on the following day. At midday Thwaite arrived at our house.

'Junkin,' he shouted, 'this is tha doin', I know.'

'Ay,' answered Sidall from the doorway and for all to hear he said, 'and I'm proud of it, Mr Thwaite.'

From among the nuzzling horses the coal owner yelled back, 'Well, Junkin, tha knows me to be a man who speaks my mind, and I won't allow a turn good or bad to go by without a comment.'

'No, Mr Thwaite. I can vouch for that.'

Thwaite looked about the common where great pats of soft clap mingled with the harder bulk of horse shit.

'I hope tha's going to get this cleaned up, Junkin,' Thwaite said un-expectedly.

'Oh, it'll get cleaned, Mr Thwaite.' Sidall's voice was jubilant.

'Good man,' Thwaite shouted. 'Well, as I was saying I can't let a good turn go by without an appreciative gesture.'

'What good turn?' Sidall asked, with sudden suspicion.

'Tha circus, yesterday, lad. That's what good turn. I like a circus, lad.'

Sidall suddenly found it difficult to converse with the coal owner. He couldn't understand Thwaite's game.

'Bags of excitement, Junkin. That's what I like. So I want to thank thee.'

'For what?'

'For fillin' t'old pit with coal.'

Sidall laughed. 'Tha's welcome, Mr Thwaite. I knew one day tha'd see sense of reducing stockpiles.'

'Oh, that's not reduced stockpile, lad.'

'No?'

'No. Tha's increased it.'

Sidall watched the horses nuzzling each other. Saw the ecstasy of a scratched mane or neck. ''Ow come, Mr Thwaite?' he said.

'Weren't my bloody coal, lad,' the coal owner shouted. 'Still. It'll come in one day and it's a nice monument to tha friend down yonder.'

9

Big twin, little twin, and my grandmother Emily Brightside and her game with Russian dolls

Emily Brightside cuddled the new-born baby to her breast. 'He's a heavy one,' she told her husband's grandmother as she cleaned the blood from his face with a bit of rag soaked in warm water.

'Ay, heavier than William was,' the old woman answered. The two women had been closeted together in the bedroom for twelve hours, no other soul being allowed anywhere near.

'We were going to call the baby Victoria if it had been a girl, name her after the queen like. Ernest said we should call a boy Albert out of respect for the old queen's dead husband.'

'So it'll be Albert then, will it?' the old woman asked.

'I suppose,' she answered, still wiping the rag over the infant's nose and mouth.

The crying of the child had brought Ernest and Henrietta to the bedroom door. 'Out,' said their grandmother, pointing to the staircase up which they had trodden.

'Tha'll come and see when all's clean and well,' and she herded them back down the rickety wooden stairs. 'Yes, it's another lad,' she shouted down in answer to a muted question. She noted the small cheer which broke from the assembly in the room below, as the news whizzed in their circle like a ball in a roulette wheel finally coming to rest in a favoured slot.

'Keep tha knees up, lass,' she recommended coming back into the bedroom, and taking the baby from the young woman. Suddenly she grabbed Emily's shoulder in an old and painful grip and said severely into her eyes, 'Now, Emily Brightside, tha must do something for me. Tha must give me one more push.'

'But I've just pushed all I can,' Emily answered, the clammy perspiration still clinging to her once white skin.

'Just one more, luv. For old Jane. Now come on,' the old woman coaxed, laying young Albert into his crib.

'Oh, I can't. No more,' Emily cried. Her matted hair stretched on the pillow like young eels.

'Yes, tha can, lass. Tha can.'

Suddenly Emily's back arched responding to a terrible pain within. Her face contorted squeezing and pushing; breath held tightly within her line of a mouth.

'Good lass. Good lass,' shouted the old woman. 'Tha can relax now.' And as she did so, Emily felt more of herself oozing away. A slithering from herself which she didn't expect, then a cry from somewhere down there in a space beyond.

'What is it?' she asked, raising her head a little from the pillow.

'It's another boy, luv,' the old woman answered.

'You mean I've got two, grandmother?'

'Ay, lass, it's twins.' She held up the bloodied baby for the mother to see.

''E's much smaller than Albert,' were Emily's first words on seeing him.

'Ay, he's tiny,' she answered, 'but perfect, mind.' She turned him about in her hands as a potter would a lump of clay.

'He's been livin' in the shadow of that great puddin' there,' she continued. 'Born in his shadow too.'

The mother lay back, bemused, on the bed. 'Whoever would have thought, two,' she said.

The old woman cleaned him, then swathed the baby in blankets and handed him to Emily.

'He's wizened like an old man, grandmother,' she commented. 'Small and wizened.'

'He'll fill out, given time, luv. Don't tha worry.'

'But he's so small.'

'No matter. What'll tha call him?'

'I don't know. We didn't expect more than one. We only thought Albert.' She glanced across to where the large baby slept contentedly.

'Tha'll think of something.'

'I suppose. I just want to sleep now. I feel like I've been in the Wars of the Roses.'

'Why not call them York and Lancaster?' my great-great-grandmother smiled, putting the afterbirth and blood-soaked newspapers into a sack.

As the old woman was washing her, Emily said, 'That's a good idea, grandmother. The big one can be Albert York and this little chap here can be Lancaster. I like that.'

Afterward, Ernest objected. 'But Emily, luv, it's coming the old duchess a bit, isn't it. York and Lancaster, I ask thee, it makes 'em sound like a couple of dukes.'

'And what about Albert?' she replied. 'Wasn't he a king?'

'A consort, lass.'

'Same difference,' she snorted and dismissed the subject forever. Thus did my two uncles become christened Albert York Brightside and Lancaster Brightside at the church in the next village.

The twins grew in their early years much as my great-great-grandmother had predicted, one in the shadow of the other. Identical in all but size they would sit side by side in their little and tiny sailor suits, Albert (York was soon dropped from the nomenclature) a bigger version of the same thing as Lancaster, and Lancaster a small edition of the same thing as Albert. Old Dr Cartwright put it in a less sinister way; he wouldn't hear of this talk of shadows. Two Russian dolls he called them, the very same yet one fitting snugly inside the other. Because nobody in the family had actually seen a set of Russian dolls and therefore had no idea what he was talking about, old Dr Cartwright made a present of some on the occasion of the twins' fourth birthday. The present consisted of a set of six wooden dolls brightly painted in yellow, red and black traditional costume. They screwed apart at their centres, one fitting snugly into the other, until the largest having eaten all the others stood stolidly alone but reflecting in all but size the exact appearance of the others.

Emily was both fascinated and horrified by the toy. The idea that Albert might one day gobble up his brother in such a manner caused the hairs to prickle at her neck. But just as horrifying was the realization that, although Albert might be represented by the largest doll, there was no way in which Lancaster could be considered number two. She estimated in fact that her smaller twin was only number four. Thus she named each doll in descending order of size, York, Devonshire, Westminster, Lancaster, Cornwall and Rutland; she had however to commit the sixsome to memory, for she didn't wish at any time to arouse Lancaster's curiosity and cause her youngest little son notions of inferiority. Nor, of course did she wish her youngest big son to see himself as in any way superior. Nonetheless with the scale committed to memory she lived for the day when she might rename her son Devonshire. She then realized that Lancaster could not just jump a position. If there was any catching up to do he would first of all have to become Westminster. She was sure that Ernest would have something to say about that. Still it was a battle to be fought if and when the time came.

One area in which biological proportions were most certainly distorted however was the one which most Victorian mothers would have missed, that being the relative size of the boys' penises. My great-great-grandmother, however, who was definitely not Victorian but born in the reign of George III, schooled at the time of George IV, and had seen things which would have made sailors blush in the years of William, knew exactly what she was looking at. While Emily would smack small hands for messing with their parts, Jane looked on, allowing the stretching to continue and was delighted to note that Lancaster was capable of elasticating his white worm just as far as his brother's and if anything Lancaster's penis was thicker than that of Albert. Thus, with considerable satisfaction the old woman was able to assess that the boys were boys each like their forebears. For she had seen them all. They would both have their wives and their children like John and like James, like Jack and Ernest, all of whom were well endowed, for like I say, she had seen them all. (Though none would quite match John Tregus's, she would soon find out.)

Anyway, the day that Dr Cartwright delivered the Russian dolls and on which Emily had mentally named them, a curious thing happened. The twins had been put to bed, together with their older brother, William. An hour later the remaining occupants of the house, who were chatting in the parlour below, were disturbed by a terrible shrieking from the room above. Ernest ran to the stairs and was halfway up when he was confronted by Lancaster, quite beside himself and hollering uncontrollably at the top. Each adult in turn tried to comfort the inconsolable child. His mother tried tender kisses while his aunt attempted to read him a tale from the *Arabian Nights*, but each failed in their attempts at consolation. His father promised a visit to the rugby football game and his great-grand-mother promised money but again each was rejected with renewed bouts of shrieking. Finally, Mr Pettit, who admitted to knowing the psychology of children, produced the six wooden dolls which Dr Cartwright had brought for his birthday (three of them belonged to Albert but nobody ever could decide which three belonged to whom). The adults held their breath as the bellowing ceased, on a sudden inspiration, from the child. It seemed so long before he expelled any air that his poor mother expressed concern that he would choke, but Pettit's idea had certainly worked. The boy coughed only once, grinned broadly at the lodger, and took up the dolls. Soon he had them lined up on the floor, re-enacting the battles at Magersfontein, Elandslaagte and Colenso, and sensibly utilizing the relative sizes to indicate the measure of battalion, catastrophe and victor, like any seasoned wargamer.

'Whatever caused you such distress, Lancaster?' his Aunt Henrietta asked.

'Dark' was all that he would say, occupied as he was with blasting his mother's Cornwall from the face of the parlour floor.

'What was dark, dear?' his mother asked. 'Was it a night dream?'

'No. It was dark in there.'

'Where, in the room.'

'No. Shut up, in there,' he answered.

His mother gave a short gasp and explained later to Henrietta her fears for Lancaster being swallowed by the magnum Albert.

'What nonsense,' Henrietta scolded. 'It's only the stones.'

'Melancholia, you mean, like your mother and your Jack.'

'Not melancholia, Emily, history. He has the Brightside ability to sense the history of the stones.'

'Sometimes, Henrietta, I think tha's quite mad. Thee and that book, God forgive thee.'

'Then you would rather it was your son who was mad.'

'I don't understand. What do tha mean by that?'

'Quite simply, that you would prefer Dr Cartwright's definition.'

'Melancholia, tha mean?'

'Yes.'

'Yes, I would that. At least I understand Dr Cartwright and I think he knows us Brightsides.'

'Emily, do you realize that melancholia is a kind of madness too?'

Her sister-in-law looked shocked. 'Never,' she said.

'Oh yes,' Henrietta responded. 'You either accept that madness runs in the family, afflicting us at random, here and there, including now apparently your Lancaster, or you can put it down to some special ability that we have, a sensitivity not given to many. As one afflicted, I know which explanation I prefer.'

Emily turned away but she never again suggested that her sister-in-law was mad, nor did she ever again imagine her son to be suffering from melancholia.

During the next couple of years the twins grew steadily. These were the two years in which Elyahou Tsiblitz first visited our house, revealing his magical inflatable costumes to the children of the village. And in these years, the relative sizes of the twins still, in Emily's mind, reflected a four-doll span. Nothing had yet happened to make her call upon a change of name. Both boys showed considerable talent in art producing many sketches and paintings in the period. They would draw the pit and the pitmen's houses, the terrace and the winding engine shed, dogs and the common, hills and slagheaps; all met their steady gaze. Sketches were often executed with the piece of coal found at their very feet. Then they would draw their relatives and friends, and finally each other, and it was in their portraits of one another that Emily found relief and the knowledge that she had after all been a good mother. None of her fears of inferiority and superiority for the boys had been picked up. They saw nothing but themselves in the portraits they produced. Albert's portrait of Lancaster and Lancaster's portrait of Albert were the same. Each would take up the same central area of a white sheet of paper, that is until the day they drew each other naked. It was a great surprise to his mother to see the feelings of inferiority expressed by Albert in his painting of Lancaster. And when she compared it to little Lancaster's painting of Albert she gasped: 'Goodness, whoever would have thought', and the only thing she could find to say to the hitherto unprotected larger twin was, 'Now, Albert dear, you mustn't be jealous', but to Mrs Henderson she confided one day, 'Best not interfere too much. Children have a way of sorting their own problems. In fact sometimes we put problems on them which they haven't got.'

'Amen to that,' said my great-great-grandmother who was party to the conversation and promptly went out and bought two cameras with a small part of her hidden fortune. She gave one to each of the twins for Christmas, explaining that it was a way of encouraging their talent to grow in a new area. Of the two it was Lancaster who allowed his interest in film to expand and proliferate, indeed finding true expression eventually in that most novel and revealing of twentieth-century art forms, the cinema, about which more later. Albert, though, was grateful for his camera too, and as he grew continued to use it more in tandem with his blossoming talent as a painter.

It was soon after the incident of the fire at the Gill house that Albert became seriously ill. After a morning photographing his great-grandmother at the Roman wall on Hunger Hill, the rains came unexpectedly to mar their session. Albert caught a chill which developed into a nasty cough and all the old woman's potions were regrettably insufficient to prevent the development of pneumonia. At the height of the fever, spots appeared. Old Dr Cartwright diagnosed measles too and told Emily that the crisis was near. The house held its breath. Henrietta talked to the stones in the dark. The old lady with whom she slept thought she was praying and asked her what prayer it was.

'No prayer, grandmother,' she said in the pitch dark. 'Just a conversation with the house. Albert lives here too. The house will look after him.'

'That's a good lass,' answered her grandmother who knew nothing of it but believed it all.

Meanwhile Emily sat by the bed watching her son growing smaller. When the crisis came, young Lancaster was ushered to the bedroom to sit with his mother and watch the beads of perspiration scatter about the pallid skin of his dying brother. Emily looked to the smaller twin wondering how he had managed to avoid the illnesses which now so afflicted the one between the sheets; how had he managed to remain so healthy? Albert stirred and flickered his eyelids, attracting Emily back to the shrinking twin with the deathly pale mask.

'Will he be all right, mother?' Lancaster asked quietly.

'God will judge,' his mother answered.

Lancaster went downstairs again to sit with the others and await the outcome of the crisis. Old Dr Cartwright visited again and sat awhile with Emily at the bedside.

'He's shrinking, Doctor,' she said, 'just fading away.'

'No, Mrs Brightside,' he answered. 'Fading perhaps, time will tell, but shrinking's impossible.'

'I tell thee he's smaller than he was a week since,' said my grandmother.

Cartwright shook his head, 'But that's not possible.'

'We'll see,' she answered, closed her eyes and slept.

She was awakened by a quiet voice asking her for water. Struggling excitedly in the darkness to light a candle, she eventually cast the pale light on her son. His eyes were open, the perspiration had ceased. Feeling his forehead with her palm, she noted how his temperature had fallen. The crisis was over, the fever had passed.

'Can I have some water, mother,' Albert repeated and sat up in the bed. Jubilantly his mother poured water into his mouth from the spout of a stone invalid cup, calling all the while for the members of her family to come upstairs and witness the miracle of resurrection.

'Great God!' Ernest's voice broke and cried, as he knelt at the foot of the bed to pray.

My grandmother looked from the now smiling Albert to little Lancaster.

'Lord, look how he's shrunk,' she said, comparing the two. 'Nay, lass,' said my grandfather, hands still clasped in prayer. 'Albert's not lost 'owt. It's Lancaster who's gained it all during the last week or two.'

Could it be true? Emily stared again at the twins. Had Lancaster at last caught up? She compared the thickness of their arms, their thighs, noted the width of shoulders; even the size of their heads and feet seemed the same. Sure enough it was true. Albert hadn't shrunk after all, it had been Lancaster's growth spurt which had indeed confused her. Lancaster had swiftly moved to Westminster and on to Devonshire without her noticing. She pulled Lancaster to her, kissing him about the face and mentally renamed the dolls in order, Lancaster, York, Devonshire, Westminster, Cornwall and Rutland. In racing parlance, Lancaster had won by a nose except that, with their drawings in mind, Emily knew it to be not a nose but some other part of his anatomy which represented the winning margin. It seemed so much easier than renaming her children; and when I was born, my grandmother on first seeing me said, 'Goodness, he's a number four like Lancaster.' My father was quite uncertain of the meaning of this cryptic comment, and totally puzzled when Emily convinced my mother that I should be named Westminster, a name which in a mining community is not easily borne with pride. Emily, the quiet one, who before the birth of her twins wouldn't have had the nerve to blow out a candle, was now as fully self-possessed as all the other Brightside women, and won her way. Thankfully, though, at school, I became known as Big Ben, much to the confusion of all, for I was never more than five feet three inches tall, and forever a genuine number four.

Elyahou as purveyor of ladies' fashion, and Bill Pettit shows his knowledge of the turf

The only difference between a man and a motor is one of the imagination. If you take a man, extend some wheels and a means of driving them, you have a motor, or a man motor, or even a man with a fashionable if rather expensive suit, which also happens to get him along much more rapidly. It is the imaginations of the men who developed the wheel and the engine which make the difference. Such were Henrietta's thoughts when she next saw Elyahou Tsiblitz. It was the first time a motor had been seen in the village and there was the Transylvanian astride an eight-horsepower Rover coupé looking terribly dashing in his mufti tweeds and breeches. The tall hat had been replaced by a fashionable light coloured cap not unlike the one he had presented to her grandmother six years before. And there's another thing, she thought, the way in which these motors were going to change our habits. Why, Mrs Agar at the end house was only now banging on the wall with her poker, far too late to avert a catastrophe Henrietta was afraid. A shawled representative from each house was already in the doorway having been alerted by the dreadful chugging noise of the engine as it sped by each door. Some other means would have to be found by which the villagers could warn of the approach of strangers, thought Henrietta. Speed would have to be deployed in dealing with the coming world, she thought, hurtling her gaze to the angular peaks of Hunger Hill and beyond. Yorkshire ranges and adjoining walls in Henrietta's mind were clearly things of the past already.

The women and children were already crowding around the vehicle touching and stroking the dark red-painted bodywork here and there and making it impossible for the motorist to dismount. From his seat in front of the cab and open to the elements Elyahou flashed his smile at Henrietta. She allowed her brown eyes to soften in response. The wild and bushy tash had gone. Elyahou had grown a pencil-thin moustache rather like that of her brother Ernest but, unlike the latter whose hair was always short and neatly parted at the centre, the Transylvanian's jet-black shock of hair remained long. It lopped across both ears without parting emphasizing that this man was still essentially a foreigner, no matter how English all else might seem.

He was still unable to dismount. The older children, remembering that wonderful day when they had bounced about the common in ballooning animal suits, were clamouring for more, their thin arms like sticks penning him into the enclosure, in front of the red cab. The younger ones, who knew only of that day by the close following of folk tales put about by important siblings, waited hushed and expectant and fiddled with the shiny lamps, bonnet and radiator.

'Please, Mr Rubber Man,' a very young one was heard to begin to ask from a position in front of the radiator. Catching sight of the child directly before him Elyahou opened his mouth wide in an expression of mock wonderment. The child stared up into the rubber man's gaping chasm; he could see it to be filled with silver and gold teeth and beyond he could discern the flesh pink tonsils guarding the black hole out of which the true magic was bound to come. It was like the beginning of a new world. The orifice remained open wide for what seemed an eternity flashing its metallic bits in the sun, then suddenly it said: 'You want inflatable suits?'

As the cheers erupted Henrietta was as surprised and excited as any present; the words had been uttered in perfect English. Elyahou could speak; it was indeed a wondrous new world, she thought, and smiled at the tall busy man who had at last been allowed down from the motor and who was rummaging in the cab for the inflatable clothing.

'Youngest first,' he said, kneeling on the seat and poking his head on its long neck over his backside, so that he could see out of the cab. 'Line up, line up.'

The women lined up the children in order of age and, deft as ever before and in no time at all, Elyahou had half a dozen younger ones in rubber costume for the first time. Lion, tiger, sheep, horse and elephant were joyfully bouncing about the common while the fat child in the fat chicken could only succeed in rolling tamely on the grass. Some of the older ones took this as an opportunity to leave the line, deciding that a game of football with the unfortunate poultry was better even than the experience of dressing up. This was quite fortunate for my two uncles who otherwise would have been costumeless, being not among the twelve youngest any longer. My great-great-grandmother came down from a trip to the Roman wall just in time to see Lancaster yet again going up in the bee outfit. Emily who had not witnessed the flight of her son before asked, 'My goodness, wherever will he come down?' Then when it was apparent that nobody cared to answer, slung her eyes heavenward and shouted advisedly, 'Flap your arms, dear. Doggy-paddle' – as if she were advising him on how to swim. This Lancaster did but it only succeeded in taking him higher up and over the roof of the terrace and out of view of the congregation below, and from the worried eyes of his mother. Lancaster, however, was quite unafraid, this being the third occasion on which he'd donned the same costume. He was quite getting the hang of it.

'It's not fair, he always gets to fly and I never do,' said Albert, enviously watching his brother sail over the houses.

'Never mind, dear,' said his mother, 'you look wonderful in your Zebra suit. Now go and join the others on the common.' And off he bounced carefully bobbing his way among the footballers and avoiding getting mixed up in the match which was shaping up on the grass.

As the sun poured out of the sky that day the women watched and laughed at the children and commended yet again the Transylvanian for bringing another enchanted afternoon to their dusty and dirty village. Laughter then turned to fits of uncontrollable giggling when Mrs Henderson insisted on trying to play 'God save the King' on the rubber bulb of the trumpet-shaped horn which clung to the side of the motor.

'Ladies,' shouted Elyahou, after this musical interlude, 'shall we have the sale?'

As they all chorused in the affirmative, my great-great-grandmother said to Henrietta, 'I see his language has improved.' Then she shouted above the general clamour, 'Who's been giving thee lessons, then?' Catching sight of the old woman, the strange rubber man pushed his way through the crowd, shook her warmly by the hand and said, 'I learned in Turkey.'

'Oh, tha's been travelling again?' she asked.

'Yes. I went to Moscow, and then to Paris and to Turkey, and to America.' He counted the countries off on the fingers of his right hand then, as he touched his thumb with left forefinger, he added, 'Then I come back to my favourite place. But I learn my English from the Sultan himself in Constantinople.'

'Oh, tha's a waffbag,' said the old woman flirtatiously. The rubber man turned away, held up his hands to the crowd of women calling for silence then said, 'I am sorry that I haven't been here for six years but I have been travelling abroad. Russia, France, Turkey. Then America. I have seen something of the world to come. The motor, the aeroplane, cinema and telegraph. The world of new materials. Cheap goods at a price we can all afford. I shall bring that new world. But always, like now, I shall bring you rubber.' He was silent for a moment and the crowd hushed expectantly. He could hear the creaking sound of the winding wheel caught in a gentle breeze. 'I have brought you waspee-waisties,' he shouted.

An anticlimactic murmur rippled through the crowd.

'What's waspee-waisties?' Mrs Henderson asked squeezing the horn and frightening the life out of Mrs Gill. Amid laughter he took a single piece of corsetry from a box and wriggled it over his slender hips.

'Waspee-waistie,' he shouted triumphantly to the sniggering crowd. Then he produced a large pad of sketches which he held high for all to see which illustrated how the garment would look on the figure of a woman. 'See how it nips in the waist, like real ladies,' he said indicating the waspish effect of the strong elastic. 'No strings. No difficult threading. No help needed. You just climb into it, ladies. I have all sizes.'

Interest was slow at first, reservations were apparent. Eyes wavered from the man in the corset to the children bouncing in the sunshine beyond. The women could hear the low excited noises of brand new experience. Lancaster reappeared and hovered above them, buzzing in his solitude. Pink clouds nuzzled into the azure sky behind him.

'Come, ladies, please do not be embarrassed,' Elyahou coaxed.

'They are only two shillings and threepence each. Now won't that be a small price to pay to be a lady? Here, you can try them on first. Take, take.' He started to throw boxes into the crowd.

'I'd like to try one,' my great-great-grandmother said.

'Me too,' said Mrs Henderson.

He threw to each one a box containing the largest-sized waspee-waistie. The two women retreated to their respective homes to draw curtains across their bedroom windows. Meanwhile the crowd below warmed and grew more enthusiastic, accepting at last the invitations to a free try on. Soon every upstairs window in the terrace displayed a curtain shielding a lady's modesty. From some houses came whoops of delight, from other cries of pain. In our house the cracked mirror thrust back fractured images of the consumers' madness. Nearly seven bob was going to be spent on undergarments which covered neither this nor that and which uncomfortably strangled the viscera into the bargain.

With all the curtains drawn against him, Elyahou from his perch at the steering wheel in front of the cab contemplated things away from the terrace. Firstly he studied the diversion on the common. The children were occupied, not with nature's bits of stick and stone but with manufactured goods. Playthings created specifically for the purpose. Why shouldn't adults too have such things, he wondered. What prevented it? His gaze was drawn to the winding engine, the black wheel in a red sun spinning nothing but dirt and danger. Why not put toys down the pit? Sophisticated toys like machines to dig the coal. What was the resistance to it? Why did those men risk their lives every day and break their backs in boredom, when they could have toys to both entertain them and to work for them? Who resisted, the capitalists or the workers? Surely it was in the coal owners' interests to have a happy workforce; poor, yes, but happy. Misery couldn't lead to efficiency, surely they knew that? What of the pitmen? Were they afraid that once introduced the machines would take over, oust them from their jobs? They had allowed conveyancing machinery to be installed without loss of labour. So why such resistance to machines for digging out the coal? What part of the system made them so frightened, he wondered. On each occasion that he had such thoughts Elyahou came back to the same place. The system. Both capital and labour were caught up in it. Equally the coal owner and the pitmen were enmeshed in a game which ensured the perpetuity of their relative positions both socially and economically. There was fear here too. The fear of winning. The fear that somehow the winner might suddenly become the loser, never the reverse, mind. And in such circumstances best change nothing. It was a conservative view shared by most and bred by years of system. Best not meddle, radicalism might upset something, bust summat they couldn't put together again; then what of all this tender flesh and blood held in God's great hands. Winners? What did God care for winners, anyroad? Greed was a sin. Jesus Christ, those radicals and socialists poking their noses in where it didn't belong. Jesus Christ, they might bust summat. Jesus Christ, didn't they know that He might drop them, drop them from His big hands right through those hot cracks in the floor of the pit; right through to Australia.

The drawing back of curtains turned his gaze to smiling women at their windows. He'd devoted his life to change. He, a Transylvanian, now speaking an excellent English learned from the Turks, had no fear of those cracks; no fear of falling. The system could be prised apart. Men and women would be made to see a better world, made to be unafraid. Even as they smiled down at him from their small windows, even as the sun shone blood-red through the dusty haze on both himself and the bouncing children, on the joyful kicking, screaming children, on Lancaster alienated aloft and heralding the dawn of a new age, even as all this warmth and vitality filtered through his very skin, he could sense the fear which had seeped into the stone terrace of colliers' homes. But he and others, including the ugly old woman built like a horse, would change all that. There would be no fear in the coming world.

The women began to leak out from the doorways on to the grass, each with a waist a little slimmer than before. While each lady checked in her florin and pennies, Henrietta herded the ballooning animals back towards the motor. The now crimson sun was setting for the night and the children were stripped of their clothes. The unusual combination of the smells of rubber and sweat brought forth threats of soap and water from their mothers and when the last red rays had finally touched the Roman wall on Hunger Hill, turning the starry stonecrop blaze orange and the crevices secret violet, Lancaster fell like a stone out of the dark sky. He bounced for a moment then he too was stripped of his costume and taken indoors by a mother intent upon scrubbing memories from his sweating pores.

Jane and Henrietta Brightside remained outside to the last. Before leaving, the rubber man withdrew a long heavy package from the back of his motor.

'Be careful, it's very heavy,' he said, but still hanging on to the newspaper wrapped parcel he then asked, 'Do you still have the cap?'

'Ay,' the old woman answered.

'But, grandmother, Ernest lost the hat.'

'Nay, lass. You must be mistook.' The grandmother flashed her eyes angrily at Henrietta. The Transylvanian looked from one woman to the other letting his smile come to rest eventually upon the face of the old woman and indicating in this manner that it must be she who knew the truth of it. 'Good,' he said softly, 'I am pleased you still have it. Some things have too much value to be destroyed. They should be kept forever.'

'It's only a hat,' Henrietta said.

Elyahou now smiled at my great-aunt but the nature of the smile had changed. The smile said, 'Maybe one day you'll understand,' then he said, 'Even some hats can be valuable.' My great-great-grandmother nodded, and Elyahou said again, 'Be careful, this is very heavy,' as he handed the parcel across to her laying it length-ways in her cradling arms. 'Some things also are too beautiful, to be destroyed,' he added. Then he handed Henrietta a smaller packet similarly wrapped in newspaper. The three of them stood in silence for a while, as the darkness fell about them, then he cranked the motor; the engine fired and the man clambered into the driving seat of his car.

'I must go now,' he said, looking to the glow of candles lighting up the rooms in the houses behind the women.

'Why don't they put the motorist's seat inside the cab?' my great-great-grandmother shouted up at him.

Elyahou looked at the substantial piece of coach work behind him. It was true, the machine had been designed along the lines of a horse-drawn carriage. He shrugged, 'Perhaps it was thought that only servants would drive the motor.'

'Then why not have two cabs?' the old woman suggested, 'with a dividing wall like the earth closets. Doesn't the motorist, even if he is a servant, deserve a little comfort away from the wet and snow?'

The Transylvanian shrugged his shoulders again. 'Progress even when it's fast is very slow,' he said smiling.

'Tha'll tell them,' she shouted up to him. 'Tell them about the comfort of poor folk. Tell 'em it's the same as their own. When they learn it's the same needs we've got then they'll start changing the world. Not till, mind. I'll sithee again, rubber man.' She turned into the house, sagging beneath the weight of her present. Henrietta, left alone with the foreigner, blushed into the colder night air.

'How was your present?' he asked out at her face haloed by light from the window behind.

'My present?'

'Yes. The stamper,' he explained.

'Oh, that. It was nice,' she answered, embarrassed, into the dark. 'It was nice of grandmother to have bought it for me, I mean.'

'Did you use it much?'

'I stamped what was mine,' she answered.

He shrugged again. 'Perhaps we'll meet some other time.'

'Yes, perhaps.'

'I must go now.' He squeezed the bulb of his horn. The motor honked as it drew away from the house and down past the lighted windows of the terrace. Henrietta waved goodbye and turned through the open doorway and into the parlour.

'Come in and close t'door, lass,' my great-great-grandmother said, 'It's turning chilly.'

'What've you got?' Emily asked of Henrietta excitedly.

'Grandmother first,' Henrietta challenged.

'Nay, lass. C'mon.'

'Yes, Aunt Henrietta, c'mon,' chorused William. 'Open it.'

My father's aunt slowly untied the brown string wrapped around the object in the newspaper while her three nephews hovered around her at the table. Several pages of the *Leeds Mercury* were removed to reveal a hexagonal polished wooden object.

'What's that?' asked William breathing at his aunt's neck.

'I don't know, William,' she answered irritably. She turned the object in her hands noting the circular base which was covered in green baize material. 'Now yours, grandmother,' she ordered, looking to the old woman. My great-great-grandmother also took her time untying the string. She too eventually had discarded several sheets of the *Mercury*, before revealing a scrolled and decorative ornament of shiny golden appearance. The object was like a very elaborate candlestick, quite wide at the base, narrowing towards the centre and finally bulging out into the head of a mace in the upper section. The whole thing was surmounted by the small figure of a man with a cane.

'This must be the base for it,' William said, picking up the hexagonal object which had been given to Henrietta. 'Yes,' said Emily. 'Set the ornament down on it, grandmother.' On to the plinth, which William held firm at the centre of the table, my great-great-grandmother plonked the ornament.

'It's lovely,' said Emily.

'It's a bit rich for our table, perhaps it would be best on the sideboard,' Henrietta suggested. Her grandmother agreed so the boys, moving the bible to one side, transferred the heavy object to stand on its base between the family photographs on the sideboard.

'Bloody 'ell!' exclaimed Bill Pettit who knew all there was to know about horse racing. 'It's the Ascot Gold Cup.' He had just come through the door with the other menfolk. Each blackened with grimy coal dust and clinging to an empty snap-box, they froze at the doorway immobilized by the radiant splendour of the object on the sideboard. It was as if they had been caught in the presence of angels.

'Where did you get that, lass?' Ernest asked of his wife in a soft voice which indicated that he was slowly breaking free of the captive rays. Emily looked to the old woman. Taking their cue from her, all other eyes turned upon my great-great-grandmother.

'It were given me,' she said defensively.

'But it's the bloody Ascot Gold Cup,' Mr Pettit repeated, the incredulity in his voice rising beyond the weight of knowledge in his head.

My grandfather turned to his lodger and asked, 'Are you sure, Bill?'

It was always a mistake to question Bill Pettit's knowledge in such a manner for, while erudition came forth full chapter and verse, it was always accompanied by the restacking of much superfluous information like the taking apart of a Babbage machine.

'Ay. It were stolen at Ascot during the very race only two weeks since. The White Knight won from Beppo with Halsey up. Trained by Mr Sadler and owned by Colonel Kirkwood.' At this point, mercifully he stopped to consult a small book which he produced from his grimy waistcoat pocket. William wondered how Mr Pettit was able to read anything from it at all as the lodger smudged his licked thumbs through the blackened pages. 'I won myself three shillings and twopence on the race,' he continued, putting the book away and addressing himself again to his audience. Then before anyone could stop him he'd launched into reciting the previous winners of the race, starting at 1807, giving mounts and jockeys and breaking only to describe owners' colours where he knew them.

Shouting above the recitation to make herself heard my great-great-grandmother said, 'Mr Pettit, I didn't know you were a betting man.' This was uttered with such indignation that it completely upset the lodger who then had to start restacking his knowledge all over again. Taking advantage of the moment's silence, Ernest weighed in. 'For the Lord's sake shut up, Bill, and let's get back to the matter in hand.'

Sidall Junkin, also taking advantage of the broken recitation, spat upon the fire, and this indeed returned a kind of normality to the room. My great-great-grandmother, however, still with indignation, said, 'If tha'd been lodging at my house when my husband lived, tha wouldn't have been wastin' tha money on horses. I've put up with tha foul language and said nowt too long, Mr Pettit, but wastin' tha wage on horses is really too much. I'll hold my tongue no more.'

'Now, grandmother,' said Ernest patiently, stepping in to rescue his lodger.

'I shouldn't take too high a moral position with me, Mrs Brightside,' the lodger said, ignoring Ernest's help. 'A bet now and then hurt no man, but tha's got stolen property there.'

'How can tha be so sure of that?' Ernest asked. 'How can tha be certain it's what tha says it is?'

''Cos I seen it described in the papers, that's how,' said Bill who was not going to lose the opportunity of displaying his talents. He shut his eyes and quoted the gold cup as having scrollwork at the base and being surmounted by a small figurine depicting a man in a tailcoat and leaning upon a stick. All eyes turned to the shining

99

object on the sideboard to confirm the true description being quoted at them by the man with the shuttered lids.

'Where did tha get it, grandmother?' Ernest asked, the hint of a threat in his voice.

'It were a present' was all that the old woman would say.

'She got it from the rubber man,' William blurted to his father.

'Oh that explains it,' said Mr Pettit who had at last opened his eyes. 'Expect that Jew stole it.'

'Maybe,' Ernest said rubbing his chin. 'We'll 'ave to go to t'police.'

'Tha won't,' said his grandmother. 'It's my present.'

'Now, grandmother,' Ernest cajoled, 'tha can't go keepin' a thing like that. It weren't his to give you.'

'I'll bet it's worth a bob or two,' piped up the bright-eyed William, whose pupils reflected the gleam of the object over which he leaned. 'Why don't we take it to Leeds and have it melted down?'

'Ay, it's worth a fortune. A fortune,' wheezed Sidall. He spat on the coals again and shook his head sadly as the sputum sizzled.

'What a dishonest suggestion, William,' his Aunt Henrietta scolded. 'Put it out of your mind immediately.'

'Nay, tha's not melting it, lad,' my great-great-grandmother said. 'If tha wants a fortune, I've an honest one for thee. No one's doin' owt with it. I were given it to keep and that I mean to do. Keep it safe.'

'Now, grandmother, tha can't do that,' Ernest insisted.

'And as for thee, William, may the Lord forgive thee. In the morning we go straight for the law, tell them what we know, and leave it to them. No one in this house will have a bad conscience over the Ascot Gold Cup. Now let's get on with us baths and us dinners. Then it's an early night for all of us.'

Ernest had spoken with authority, even his grandmother was quietened. The women and boys left the house, the men set about their bathing and the Ascot Gold Cup shone like nothing had ever shone before into the gloomy parlour of our house.

Outside the old woman and Emily walked with the twins up towards the big house while William and his Aunt Henrietta strolled in the other direction towards Hunger Hill.

'What did great-grandmother mean by that?' asked William.

'By what?' his aunt responded.

'She said that she had an honest fortune for me.'

'Oh that,' Henrietta said, putting her hand on William's shoulder as they walked along. 'Grandmother was supposed to have brought a fortune with her when she came to the house.'

'And did she?'

Henrietta shrugged. 'Maybe.'

'Did anyone see it?' William asked.

'I think my mother might have seen it. She told me that the money was kept in a suitcase.'

'Where does she keep it then?'

Henrietta shrugged again. 'Nobody knows. The Gills once dug up the scullery floor looking for it, but they didn't find anything. I expect they've looked other places too.' William laughed. 'Do you think it's true? Is there a fortune somewhere?'

'There's probably some money, somewhere.' She smiled at her nephew. 'Maybe not a fortune, just a bit put aside.'

'She must have something,' William said. 'She's always buying things for people. That costs, doesn't it?'

'I suppose,' Henrietta answered.

They walked on a little way in silence. The angry peak of Hunger Hill loomed above them from the dark mauve sky. She watched the twinkling of a star an instant, then said. 'It seems like today never happened. That motor, those silly suits, the rubber man, that golden thing on the sideboard. Nothing's changed here since I was a child, since my grandmother was a child.' She wriggled her bottom, suddenly aware of the discomfort about her body. 'Except waspee-waistie, I suppose.'

William giggled. He'd been embarrassed watching much of the sale, being now far too old to qualify for a rubber suit, yet just too young for a job at the pit.

'Does it make you feel any different?' he asked.

'No. I don't think so, except that it's uncomfortable now I think of it.' She smiled.

'Seems silly, paying good money to make yourself uncomfortable,' he said.

'There's a silly world coming, William. I think we must learn to laugh at it if we are to cope.'

'As silly as the dinosaur world down there with grandfather?' William nodded at the disused pit.

'Oh much more silly than that,' his aunt advised him. She looked again at the dark peak above them. 'I didn't know my father,' she told him, 'he died before I was born; but I'm sure that he would have been amazed at what we saw in the village today. But somehow we just take it all in our stride. Even grandmother saw it all as inevitable,' she added remembering the old woman's last comments to Elyahou. 'I think we should turn now and head back.'

Together they turned about and walked a while in the mauve silence.

'Why for me?' It was the boy who spoke.

'What for you, William?'

'Why should she have a fortune for me?'

Henrietta was silent a long time, trying to remember. Then she said, 'I think she was going to give the money to my father the day he died.'

'And then?'

'Well he died in that accident. Then she must have waited for Jack and your father to grow to manhood.'

'And then what?'

'Well, perhaps she didn't like what she saw or maybe they rejected her offer; I don't know.'

'So, I'm next.'

'Yes. After your father you are next. Maybe soon she'll surprise you with a suitcase.'

He watched her white face moving along in the dark a while, and then said, 'I don't believe it. I don't believe any of it; there's no fortune. It's just stories like the ghost of the closets. People like us don't have fortunes.'

In silence and with tears in his eyes my father, who very soon would enter that gaping hole in the ground which beckons all the young men in a pit village, made his way home.

When they arrived back all the family were together and the table set for a meal. In the golden glow of the racing cup they ate heartily; the men washed and relaxed, the women fidgety in their new foundation garments. Ernest's promise of an early night for all was kept and by ten o'clock the house slept. The following morning everyone awoke to hear Bill Pettit shouting, 'Bloody 'ell. Someone's stolen the Ascot Gold Cup.' He was probably right but thankfully his wondrous mind could add nothing of substance to the comment. Worse still, however, was the fact that someone had stolen our William also; at least, that's how his mother put it.

Sidall Junkin gets a new set of teeth

Whatever motivated my father to steal the Ascot Gold Cup for the second time was never revealed. He had crept downstairs in the middle of the night and obviously with an expert stealth, stuffed the object into a sack and left the house with the swag slung over his shoulder, and because of his small stature he looked every bit the chimney sweep boy. It wasn't true as most thought that he awakened nobody, for Sidall Junkin said that when the cup was put into the sack it was as if several candles had been snuffed at once. Sidall, however, thought that what he had witnessed had been no more than a dream, and he'd gone back to sleep in his wide-winged chair, eyes more firmly closed than usual.

Bill Pettit and my great-great-grandmother were certain that William meant to take the cup to Leeds to have it melted down exactly as he'd suggested the previous evening, but could offer no motive other than greed for such action. Henrietta plainly saw his motive as being material salvation. The boy was obviously terrified of having to go into the pit and the opportunity to gain easy money to forestall such a happening had tempted him to the crime. Ernest, on first realizing that William had not been stolen, as the boy's mother would insist, but had in fact done a bunk with the booty, dropped to his knees and prayed for all; unaccountably and particularly did he single out the twins for special mention. They, however, with memories of the previous day fresh in their minds refused to believe that the rubber man had become a robber man and would only accept that the object which had stood upon our sideboard as wondrous as anything from another planet, had been but a harmless present. They thought that the adult world about them had gone mad and sadly now it appeared that even the youthful world of their brother was beginning to crack a little. Perhaps it was an inevitable response to the approach of adulthood they reasoned most soundly.

'You can't go to the law now,' Emily pleaded with her husband.

'Emily's right,' Henrietta agreed. 'What could we say, Ernest?'

'The Ascot Gold Cup's been stolen?' Bill Pettit posed it to himself as a question then shook his head. 'They'd say we know that, it was in all the papers.'

'Good God!' Emily said, horror dawning on her face. 'If the police pick him up in Leeds with that thing, they'd think he'd stolen it originally.'

''Im and us,' Sidall piped up from his chair.

'Bloody 'ell!' Bill Pettit exclaimed. 'We'd better get 'im afore they do. Ernest, get off tha bloody knees and let's get after 'im.'

My grandfather in a state of shock was helped up from the floor by Bill and Emily, dusted down, and sent into the street to air his addled brain. 'Prayin' all over the shop isn't going to help at this time,' his wife told him as she pushed him through the doorway.

In the house, all agreed that the boy had most likely set off to walk to Leeds and Bill Pettit was dispatched immediately to the pit head to get a horse and cart. Henrietta explained, 'He won't be walking too quickly with that sack.' They all concurred that Henrietta was probably correct, the weight of the cup would hold him back. When Bill had returned with the cart they all piled excitedly on. It had a gaily painted tailboard and sides in rich silver and red and was pulled by a black horse with a sad white face and blinkers.

'Wouldn't it be best if I went alone with Sidall or Ernest? It'd be a bit quicker,' Bill suggested, but he was shouted down unanimously. Everyone wanted a ride.

Great-great-grandmother who was sitting up front with Bill said, 'It'd be a lot quicker if we had one of them motors.'

'And where would we get one of them?' Bill asked.

'From the rubber man,' she answered folding her arms into her ample lap. Bill pulled a wry face but thought it best to say nothing. Ernest was tugged aboard still in a daze and lay with his head cradled in his wife's lap, murmuring softly to himself. Then with a self-assured 'Giddyup!' Bill cracked his whip and the cart, dragged by the sad horse set off across the common to link up with the road to Leeds.

'We're 'avin a day off,' Bill shouted when the neighbours came out to investigate the commotion caused by my family. 'There'll be no sick pay,' shouted the young Henderson. 'Bugger sick pay,' shouted back Bill as the cart wheels gathered a little speed and the sun peeped from the early morning mist.

Once out of the narrow, rutted lanes the horse was able to travel at a fair old lick and within two hours of setting off was trotting over the River Aire at Leeds Bridge. They then carried on into the main, wide, cobbled thoroughfare of the city. Briggate was a thriving street bustling with coaches and horse-drawn trams, there were also a fair number of motorized vehicles jostling for position. Men in suits as dark as their pavement shadows were everywhere, thronging the street with their billycocks and canes. A few ladies flitted about in satins and dark lace like silhouetted butterflies in the sun.

Just beyond the bridge, my family fell upon the public conveniences. Here, at the lower end of Briggate, Bill called the horse to a halt and with much relief, and amid great jubilation, the excited contingent descended from street level to use the underground toilets. It was the first time that both the twins and Sidall Junkin had seen a water closet and each occupied a cubicle for longer than he should to flush and reflush the white porcelain bowls, and great-great-grandmother finally had to draw them to order when Albert had climbed to perch at the top of an interconnecting wall there to view the newspaper-reading public at its duty. Eventually the cubicles emptied, chains swinging madly after one last communal and noisy flush. 'Why can't we have water closets instead of those smelly earth closets?' Albert asked, ascending the steps to the street and feeling the weight of the old woman's hand about his ear.

'They'll come,' she told him. 'Wait and see, lad.'

'Put thee out of a job, when they do,' Bill told Sidall Junkin at the top of the steps. Sidall eyed his fellow lodger humourlessly, moved the rubber teeth around in his mouth, and spat his black spit on to the cobbled street. 'Tha wants to think on, Bill. I'm a good bit older than thee. When I'm gone it'll be tha turn to clean closets.'

As the group was remounting the cart and arguing busily which direction they should take to start looking for William (even Ernest had recovered sufficiently to present an opinion) fate took a hand and solved the problem for them; William came to them. He suddenly stepped out from behind a horse-drawn tram looking dirty enough to have already swept three chimneys.

'There's William,' said Lancaster, pointing across the street as he was being hauled on to the cart. He had said it so conversationally that at first nobody paid attention to the remark.

'Where's William?' his mother suddenly asked realizing at last that the object of the twin's twisting gesticulations was the very thing they were seeking.

'There, there,' answered Lancaster, picking up some of his mother's excitement.

'Where?' the others chorused.

Dangling in mid-air, neither on the cart nor on the street, the twin shouted, pointing awkwardly.

'Behind me. Across the street, it's William.'

All eyes turned and at the same time the hands which had been bringing the twin aboard, relaxed their grip and Lancaster fell to the ground. I only mention this because it seems to me that my uncle Lancaster's life was full of nasty tumbles from the air, culminating of course in that final terrible fall during the Battle of Britain. Then, within seconds, feet were landing heavily on the cobbles all about him as the occupants of the cart jumped down to give chase to the errant William. He was caught up with outside Stead and Simpsons' shoe shop, above which was the largest piece of advertising that anyone had ever seen. It read in letters each two feet high, and taking up all of the space between the top of the doorway and the roof of the building:

MACDONALDS TEETH MACDONALDS
HIGH CLASS TEETH ENGLISH AND AMERICAN
ARTIFICIAL TEETH TEETH ARTIFICIAL TEETH
WITHOUT PLATES PAINLESS SYSTEM
MACDONALDS (ENTRANCE KIRKGATE) MACDONALDS

Leaving the squirming child in the hands of his parents and the sack securely in Bill Pettit's grasp, Sidall Junkin made his way round the corner to Kirkgate and to Macdonald's emporium, to reappear minutes later at the cart displaying a dazzling new smile. Mr Junkin's mouth appeared to be overfilled, Albert thought, as if he'd stuffed too much food into it. Nor could the boy help wondering how many different pairs of teeth he'd had to try on before settling for the ones now offering the big new smile. Worse still, Albert concerned himself with the notion that they might be second-hand.

Meanwhile Bill Pettit, mounted aloft, had his head thrust deep within the coal sack trying to establish that the trophy was still there without of course drawing the attention of an as yet unconcerned public. William, sitting dejectedly at the back of the cart, was receiving alternate kisses and chastisements from his mother. Ernest, however, told him only once that he would be dealt with when they got home, then proceeded to sulk.

'It's here,' Bill Pettit said finally, lifting his head from the sack like a satisfied horse. 'Shall we take it to the police?'

'No,' said my great-great-grandmother, gathering the sack up from the lodger's lap and dumping it in her own.

'But be reasonable, Mrs Brightside,' Bill said. 'Look, did tha ever ask thissen' why the rubber man should have stolen the Ascot Gold Cup only to give it to the likes of us?' she asked him.

Even with his marvellous knowledge, Bill Pettit couldn't answer that. 'I don't know,' he sighed.

'No. And neither would the police,' she answered. 'In short, they'd never believe the tale. Why should anybody go to the lengths of stealing a valuable trophy only to give it away to strangers?'

'Grandmother's right,' Ernest said. 'We'll 'ave to think on it.'

'Well at least while we're in Leeds we can call on't bugger and 'ave it out with 'im,' Bill said.

'That's a good idea,' Ernest conceded. 'What's address?'

'I know,' Henrietta offered. 'It was on his stamper that first time he came to our house. You remember, grandmother?'

'I'm sayin' nowt,' the old woman said, clutching the sack even closer to her.

Henrietta thought a moment with eyes tight shut, as the others nudged her memory with unhelpful suggestions.

'Ship's Yard,' she suddenly shrieked, opening her beautiful brown eyes wide as they would stretch. 'That was it, Ship's Yard.'

'Right,' said Bill dismounting. 'I'll go and get a bobby.'

Sidall Junkin snorted and tried uncomprehendingly to say something. His gutta-percha smile flashed in the sun as he too dismounted. After a couple of minutes they both returned.

'There is no bloody Ship's Yard,' Bill told them angrily.

'Well I'm certain that was the address,' Henrietta said. She felt disappointment.

'Ay. Well, it's false,' Bill went on. 'Bugger's given us a wrong 'un.'

'He's given us the Gold Cup, hasn't he?' my great-great-grand-mother reminded him.

''E's still leadin' us a right dance,' the lodger said, climbing back aboard and helping up Sidall Junkin.

'I'll bet 'e's not given us his right bloody name either.'

'Ay, whoever heard such a name. Elyahou Tsiblitz,' said Ernest.

'I'll bet he's not even a Jew,' the old woman mused.

'Ay, that's right,' said Bill. 'That'd be bloody typical of 'em,' and with that he gave a loud 'Giddyup!' and headed off up Briggate and away from the public convenience.

The journey back to the village was memorable for only two things. One was that it rained heavily for most of the way, the weather turning about half an hour out from Leeds. Secondly, and probably because of the wretched rain, Sidall Junkin suffered a very severe attack of asthma. It was so severe that, as my father told me years later for he was sitting next to him in the back of the cart, he feared that the poor man would die there and then. Unable to find his breath for what seemed like minutes but could have only been seconds at a time, the man with the new smile turned purple in the face, threshing about his arms and legs, searching for an airway. The huddled soaking mass of people in the back of the cart did what little they could for the ailing man but their discomfort was com-pounded by the knowledge that whatever they did it was not going to be enough. As Ernest said he just wanted to rip a hole in the man's neck to let him breathe. In short, they were all frightened for him, as they clapped him heartily on the back and at one time poked their fingers in his throat. Sidall's condition seemed to have improved a little by the time the cart had arrived back at the house, at least sufficiently for him to slip back into his jaws the new set of teeth which had been removed during the worst of the asthma attack. He was helped into the house and then upstairs to the bed shared between Henrietta and my great-great-grandmother, they both having insisted that he sleep there for the night. Then the old lady sent Lancaster to get old Dr Cartwright. After examining his patient the doctor proclaimed that the lodger was about to die at any moment, shook his head sadly and said that there was no more that he could do. My great-great-grandmother sent for a cooked ham which Albert brought from Mr Doyle who kept pigs. The experienced old woman well-trained in the rituals devised to attend the dying organized the making of sandwiches while she set out the Ascot Gold Cup once more upon the sideboard. She then sent the boys and the men for a walk. After an hour or two, Sidall appeared at the foot of the rickety stairs. He looked very much better.

'By, that ham smells good, Mrs Brightside,' he said.

'Now, Sid,' said my great-great-grandmother, 'the ham's for the wake. Go back to bed, lad, and get on with tha dyin'.'

But Sid's face registered a terrible hunger. So my great-great-grandmother sliced him a plateful of best boiled ham while he rummaged in his waistcoat pockets, finally producing his new teeth which he inserted once more into his jaws. With his plate of ham he turned smiling to the stairs, trying to wish a goodnight to the ladies through teeth which fitted his mouth to overflowing. That was the last anyone saw of him alive. In the morning Ernest shouted, 'Quick, quick! Sidall Junkin's dead.' Then the house fell into silence and even when Bill Pettit shouted, 'Bloody 'ell, the Ascot Gold Cup's been stolen!' – for the second time in twenty-four hours – it didn't seem to matter. Both statements were true of course. Dr Cartwright came and examined the body and said that it was probably Sidall's new teeth that had finally killed him. They were far too big for his mouth, he said. The man must have choked on his evening meal for the doctor drew attention to the half-eaten sandwich still on the plate in the bed, and to the tell-tale crumbs which spotted about the corpse's mouth. Then with a final wretched search for the over-burden of proof, he prised his bony finger into the gap between the teeth and ripped out the dentures with a powerful tug. Half-mastic-ated bread formed a glutinous mass which kept them together still biting hard on the doctor's outspread hand. As the teeth came out there was a great expulsion of trapped air and the face caved in to the customary lugubrious countenance of Sidall Junkin. Albert thought how Mr Junkin had not stopped smiling since he'd bought the teeth despite the asthma attack. 'He must have died happy,' he told the doctor.

It was also true that the cup had been stolen for the third time, but nobody had stolen William. Nobody had gone but for Sidall

Junkin, and nobody seemed to care that the trophy might have gone with him.

At the funeral service in the church in the next village Jane Brightside, who was now ninety-two years of age, listened to the ranters awhile then stood up and shouted back, 'Thee and tha kind sicken me. Tha fright the children, tha fright the grown men but tha'll not fright me. If tha must preach, preach on a new world, not that old sad place in your minds. God fell out the sky and showed me a new world at Kettle Flatt. God's come to our house three times now, the last time in a motor, who knows what wonders will be next.'

'That's not God, it's Mammon. The devil of covetousness,' the ranter raved back.

'Nonsense. It's the god of convenience,' she shouted at him. 'What is this better world tha talks of if it's not going to be convenient?' She looked about her at the congregants. 'Isn't it convenient to make tha lives here on earth easier to bear? Machines and motors may cost now, but if tha'll show tha wants them and tha know how to use them, the Lord'll make them cheaper for us. Design is not an art, it's an inevitability once tha tell Him what tha want. Design is a sign of the coming world. Design is a symbol of what tha' can have. Don't kick God backwards. God's an engineer and a sign of what's to come. He's been to our house.' She walked out unsteadily on the arm of her granddaughter. The neighbours thought the old woman had gone mad, but at her age you might expect it they said. It's been a long innings. The two women walked home, away from the funeral service, watching the dark peak of Hunger Hill, and each resolved not to think of Elyahou Tsiblitz again.

12

Of Lancaster's two passions, flight and the cinema

Soon after Sidall Junkin's death, a shelf was erected in the parlour. It was put up specifically to house the family library. All but Ernest's bible that is, which remained dark, brooding and closed with a brass clasp, occupying the spot which once had been reserved for the Ascot Gold Cup upon our sideboard. The books on the shelf were not many but included the family photograph albums and of course Henrietta's *History of the Stones* which was now running into many volumes. She still, almost every day, visited Bottom Boat looking for changes, and incredibly was still able to find the imperceptible moves which caused her book to evolve. But these changes only reflected her solitude and the isolation of not only herself but of the village, this place nestled at the foot of Hunger Hill and bounded to the west by the big house. But now even Henrietta was becoming anxious for more rapid changes; she had a plan for the stones but the time was not yet right to put it into operation.

Then there was H. G. Wells's *First Men in the Moon* and the same author's *The War of the Worlds*, and a book about fly fishing between the pages of which were tiny scales which glinted gold and silver blue when turned in the light. There was the *Colliery Manager's Handbook* dated 1906 and a slim volume by Henry M. Stanley, the famous explorer, entitled *Through Ukwere to Useguhha*. Nobody knew where this book had come from and it remained unread until I was well into my teens. There was also a volume of beautifully printed reproductions of *100 Favourite Paintings*. This marvellous book in full colour had been given recently to the twins by their great-grandmother as a birthday present and to encourage their steadily developing artistic talents. In fact at the time of the erection of the new shelf Albert was busily copying Gainsborough's *Blue Boy* on to a canvas the exact dimensions of the original. This information was of course given beneath each reproduction in the book together with the gallery at which the painting might be seen. It would be several months before the copy could be completed but the boy's dedication and remarkable talent were given wholehearted encouragement by all members of the household, especially his twin, who was beginning to be left a little way behind in his ability to paint. Not that Lancaster lacked talent, it was rather that he was turning that well of ability more in the direction of photography. Also, more dreamy than his brother, Lancaster nurtured at odd moments his notions of flight. At the age of twelve he managed to convince my great-great-grandmother that her first and, as it would turn out, her only visit to the nation's capital city should be to view the International Balloon Race. Through the sole agency of the rubber suit Lancaster had become obsessed with the notion of flight, and yet to date he had never seen an air device in the flesh so to speak. The old woman had the advantage of him, for at least she was able to see, just for a few seconds before it almost tumbled on top of her, the airship of Duncan D'Arcy and Lady Annabelle Kerr that morning at Kettle Flatt. Without hesitation, the old woman agreed to take my uncle to London. Why shouldn't he too experience the wonderment which she had then felt?

So it was that the strange pair set out in their best clothes taking Mr Fox's now grimy carriage to the station at Wakefield, and there to meet a train which would carry them on to London. Unfortunately, the train was delayed at Grantham because of repairs being carried out on the line, thus when they did finally arrive at the capital the race was already under way. Unaware of where they were or of how they should get to Fulham where the race was to have started, they wandered uncertainly into the Euston Road, whereupon their eyes were immediately directed upwards primarily because every other living soul they could see were cricking their necks in an effort to view the sky beyond the high buildings. The sight which met their gaze was totally beyond even the imaginings of the old woman and her charge. As Duncan D'Arcy had predicted my great-great-grandmother was at last seeing her sky full of flying men. Dozens of balloons were tossing silently above the metropolis. The steep-sided buildings only accentuated the height at which the lofty airships anchored into their spaces, for without wind they hung about like fish in deep waters giving no hint of their journey. Like the blue sea, the sky too teemed with life, and up there beyond the spires and towers built by the earthly Londoners, small men in baskets were waving; raising glasses to their glinting eyes and waving. After several minutes of sheer wonderment and with a pain in the back of her aged neck my great-great-grandmother hailed a horse-drawn cab. Then, with heads resting upon real leather cushions and with eyes slung heavenward, my two relatives scanned the skies all the way to Fulham, and all the time they were followed by the colourful balloons which now drifted on a sudden breeze, like so many ideas, across their lines of vision.

At the park it was apparent that several competitors had not yet managed to inflate their craft and therefore that Lancaster would have ample opportunity to inspect some airships at close range. Paying off the cabman they set off to view a small red, white and blue striped balloon which had caught their attention and which was slowly inflating in a flat area guarded at the back by a clump of dense trees. They were suddenly stopped in their tracks by somebody shouting. It was not the voice which was familiar, but the words immediately attracted the old woman's attention. 'Hey, yarrow beer!' the message repeated again. My great-great-grandmother turned to see the instantly recognizable Duncan D'Arcy. 'Hey there, Ardsley,' he shouted, changing his coding in the hope that both the drink and the place combined would touch off the old woman's memory. He needn't have bothered, of course, Jane Brightside had never forgotten him. He ran through the crowd from behind her waving his arms about in an alarming manner.

'I thought you'd be here,' she said to him, though it had been more in hope than certain knowledge.

'No flowers, madam? No basket of yarrow beer?' he remarked.

'No champagne?' she challenged back, and he laughed.

Lancaster gawped at the man's velvet jacket and the lace cuffs of his shirt, which ruffled through the sleeves.

'No,' he answered her, 'not any more. It's not a game any more. We sail these things for real now.' He glanced towards heaven.

'Yes, I see,' she said. 'Tha was right. The skies are fillin'. It'll soon be like fish in t'sea.'

He smiled, then looking at Lancaster, he said, 'And who have we here, madam?'

'My name's not yarrow beer, nor is it Ardsley, by the way. It's

Jane Brightside, and this 'ere's my great-grandson Lancaster Bright-side. Say 'ello to the gentleman, Lancaster.' She nudged my uncle.

'Pleesetomeetcha,' said Lancaster, awkwardly offering his hand. As the balloonist took my uncle's hand in his firm and large grip, the old woman said, ''E's mad about flyin'.'

'Oh, did you ever fly in a balloon, young man?' Lancaster shook his head, shyly looking at the ground. Then stirred by a sudden attack of vocabulary he blurted out, 'No. But I will. One day I'll win the Gordon Bennet trophy.'

'Yes, and so will I,' said Duncan D'Arcy. 'Perhaps we'll do it together.' Then he laughed that same hearty laugh Jane had heard when he'd downed the yarrow beer.

Lancaster's eyes brightened as he warmed to the big stranger. 'Did you enter in the race before?' he found the courage to ask.

'Oh yes, I was in the first race, a couple of years back. Set off from Paris and came down in the English channel. Had to swim the last five miles.' He laughed again, slapping the boy on the shoulder.

'Lahm won that one,' mumbled Lancaster.

'What, boy?' said Duncan D'Arcy, bending down closer to my uncle's face and turning his ear to the boy's mouth. His moustache was stiff and waxed.

'Frank P. Lahm won, sir,' Lancaster shouted.

'Know your stuff, eh,' said the balloonist stretching back up to his full height and poking a long finger into the ear which he'd so recently offered to my uncle.

'Flew 402 miles and came down on Fylingdales Moor.' Lancaster confidently continued to air his knowledge.

'Quite right, young man. Had to leg it in to Whitby and didn't know for days that he was the winner. What a place to come down, though. Whoever would wish to set anything down on that blasted heath, beats me.' He laughed again, even more heartily than before. 'Tell you what,' he went on, 'how would you like a ride in my air-ship?'

'What? You mean go up in it?' Lancaster asked excitedly.

'Not only that – not just go up and down – have a bit of a ride, what.' Lancaster was so excited he could scarcely contain his joy. 'Yes, yes,' he shouted, dancing round the gentleman. 'Would you, please, please?'

As Lancaster, now ignored, continued to jig on the grass, the man asked my great-great-grandmother, 'And you, madam? Would you do me the honour?'

'But I'm ninety-three years old' was all that she could say as he took her by the hand.

'Then you shall be the oldest person ever to have flown in a machine. It'll be a record worth having.' He laughed again. 'Tell you what. I'll take you home, back to Ardsley or wherever it is that you come from.'

'Oh please, great-grandmother. Can we? Will thee?' pleaded Lancaster.

'Of course we shall,' Duncan D'Arcy answered for the old woman, and led her by the arm to the red, white and blue striped balloon which was now full of gas and which swayed like a large drunken sailor in the rising wind. The old woman was helped unsteadily up some steps and into the basket, then the boy and gentleman quickly followed. The balloonist shouted instructions to his team of helpers outside the basket. The wind was rising quickly and as Duncan D'Arcy discarded sandbags from the sides of the basket the men ran round untethering ropes. With one last heave, the man in the velvet jacket discarded another bit of ballast and within seconds, and without noticing how they had got there, Lancaster saw that they were above the trees.

The balloon quickly picked up speed and sailed over central and north London soon to be crossing open country.

'It's strange,' said the old woman. 'I thought it would be noisy up here, but it's silent as the grave.'

'There's no noise because we sail on the wind, madam. You see, in effect, there is no wind up here at all.'

Looking down from the silent basket to the even more silent farms and lanes Lancaster thought that the whole of England must be asleep. Then as if stealing his very thoughts Duncan D'Arcy said, 'It's been like that for thousands of years. But change is coming, look there's a motor car track,' he pointed excitedly. Sure enough, the boy could discern a trail of disturbed dust winding through an old lane as if a snake had gone by. Then a motor was actually seen puffing up a little dust as it throbbed its way home. They all waved and shouted as the motorist waved back.

'What time will we be home?' Lancaster asked.

'Oh,' said the balloonist, taking out his fob watch, and looking to the hazy sun, 'You'll be home before dark.'

'What! It were near four when we left,' said my great-great-grand-mother.

'Yes,' he said with a shrug. 'With this wind we'll be there in less than four hours. If we climb higher it'll be quicker still.'

'No. This is high enough, thank you,' said the old woman, and they all laughed.

While Duncan D'Arcy took out his maps and compass and read them on the floor of the basket my relatives continued to watch the sleepy land below where only the balloon's shadow seemed to move. Lazy farms with lazy hens and lazy cows came into view and disappeared just as quickly under the balloon's black shadow. Duncan D'Arcy, having taken his readings, stood up and leaned over the basket and with hands cupped shouted, 'Wake up, England!'

The wind picked up again hurtling the balloon with its strange band of occupants into the unknown. 'For God's sake wake up!' he then muttered to himself as he wrapped a blanket around my uncle. He then put another about the old woman and sat her on the basket's floor.

'We're asleep. We're all asleep,' he said to her on his haunches, and twirled one side of his moustache.

'What does tha mean?' the old woman quizzed him.

'I mean what I just said. What I just shouted. We have to wake up. This is not the magic land of Merlin any longer.'

'Less of the we. We're awake in our village,' she admonished.

He thought for a moment, twirling his moustaches now with both hands. 'I'm not so sure,' he said eventually. 'The government sleeps. Those with the money sleep. The working class sleep. We all slumber on. Why?'

The old woman shrugged, then yawned. 'All this talk of sleep is making me tired,' she said, and her shoulders sagged back to the walls of the basket.

'It's all too cosy,' he said. 'Amidst the greatest changes ever seen, nobody wants to change anything. That's a recipe for disaster if ever there was one.'

'Oh, just take us home, luv,' she said. 'I'm all done.' Then she fell asleep.

Lancaster, chin resting on the backs of his hands which in turn were supported by the side of the basket, was astonished by the silence. He had never before in his life heard nothing so clearly.

The balloonist stood up and, next to my uncle, hollered down through cupped hands again, 'You can't stop progress, you know. Governments can't reshackle us once we've tasted freedom,' and the land shouted back a mauve and green stillness deafening the two watchers above. By the time the balloon had been whisked into Yorkshire my great-great-grandmother was awake. Duncan D'Arcy offered round cucumber sandwiches and lemonade then, the short meal done with, by carefully manipulating the valve to let gas from the envelope which stretched like the great dome of a cathedral above, he controlled the descent of the contraption. About a mile from the house he allowed the basket to trail through a thick hedge almost tipping the three occupants to the ground. But the desired effect was achieved in that the balloon slowed to almost nothing and, hovering two feet from the ground, he pushed out his two passengers.

'Thanks for the ride,' shouted up my great-great-grandmother.

'See you again sometime,' said the balloonist and blew her a kiss from the back of his hand.

'Will tha not come in for some cocoa?' she asked him.

'Madam, I'm in a race remember,' he said allowing the basket to hover just above the ground, then he clumsily tipped a sandbag from the craft and the balloon soared away in silence towards Hunger Hill. He waved once, then was gone.

'By gum, grandmother,' Ernest said as they entered the parlour, 'them locomotives get faster all the time. I didn't expect thee home till after midnight.'

'Nay, Ernest. We didn't come on't train. God brung us home in 'is chariot.'

Ernest laughed, and Lancaster didn't enlighten him to the true means of their transportation. Not then at least, and my great-great-grandmother is still unofficially the oldest person ever to fly in a balloon. Duncan D'Arcy didn't win the race but landed on that blasted heath called Fylingdales Moor, and from all accounts was glad to do so, in winds approaching sixty miles an hour.

*

Some months later old Dr Cartwright came to our house. He'd been sent for to tend Ernest's leg which had been fractured in a roof fall at the pit. The doctor arrived in a blue forty horsepower Crossley motor with a shiny gold radiator, and my great-great-grandmother was pleased to see that it had a soft hood which protected the motorist from the worst of the weather. The old medic spent several minutes watching Albert painting and studied the half-finished portrait of the *Blue Boy* carefully; then he told Emily that her son had a rare talent which needed careful nurturing. He made it sound like a disease which had to be treated. He then flicked through one or two books on the new shelf and, thumbing through the slim volume by Mr Stanley, he informed Lancaster, 'It was Gordon Bennet who put up the money for Stanley's expedition in search of Livingstone, you know.' Lancaster stared at the old doctor blankly.

'Come now, Lancaster,' he said, 'I know how interested you are in aviatrix.'

It sounded like another disease. 'Flying, boy,' he bawled at my uncle. 'It's the same Gordon Bennet, lad.' He threw his two hands into a great circle describing a balloon.

'Yessir,' said Lancaster as the doctor replaced the book upon our library shelf. 'Livingstone reckons sun-spurge to be poison to zebras, you know,' the old doctor then told him. 'You are still interested, lad, aren't you? Still keen to have a go in a flying machine?' he went on in an alarmed voice.

'Yessir,' Lancaster said, nodding at the old man.

'Good boy. That's the spirit.' He smiled and put his hand on Lancaster's shoulder and eyed him paternally. 'Now, did you hear that Mr Cody had flown a heavier-than-air machine down at Swann Inn Plateau in Hampshire?'

Lancaster nodded although unsure of who Mr Cody might be and definitely uncertain of the Swann Inn whatever it was. Had this Mr Cody flown inside a pub he wondered.

'Yes. Flew at a height of thirty foot for twenty-seven seconds before crash landing,' the doctor droned on. 'Covered about one third of a mile distance. Mind you, it doesn't compare anything with what the Americans are doing. I see that Wilbur Wright was up in the air for over an hour only the other day. An hour, boy, in which he flew forty-six miles.'

Lancaster nodded again, watching the careful brushwork of his twin seated at the canvas. Deep blue pigment seemed to be everywhere; on his smock, on the palette, some on the floor, and on the canvas of course; but nowhere did it appear more than at the tip of his black horsehair brush. There it resided like fire would at the end of a burning poker, ready to spread his blue inspiration.

'Took a passenger up with him too. Even that damned Frenchman Delagrange has been up for half an hour,' the old man went on. As the doctor searched our ceiling in a kind of mock exasperation, Lancaster continued to eye his brother's brushwork, noting how he was folding the blue paint into the subject's satin suit. Then Lancaster, turning his back on the old doctor, picked up a brush and without comment smoothed some paint into the same fold on which his brother had worked. If there was any resentment on Albert's part it wasn't shown and Emily noted how her sons were working as one, like Russian dolls for a while, painting Gainsborough's *Blue Boy*.

During the next several months many things happened to bring changes to the lives in our house. My great-great-grandmother brought home a phonograph which she had purchased in Wakefield for five shillings. It was the first in our terrace and music was heard wafting across the common for the very first time. It seemed to cause the dogs more concern than the humans, for long after the colliers and their families had grown used to the strange noises the dogs would cease their playing and chewing each time the records played. Then they would slowly come forward to the front of our house, ears pricked and heads quizzically tilted, perhaps to hear the better. Pedlars then came selling everything from picture frames to three-piece suits with rich satin linings. You didn't have to pay for them either, not immediately that is, for the pedlar was quite prepared to allow payment to be made over a period of two or three years. All the men, including William and the twins, had them for Sunday best, and even at the outbreak of war they had still not been paid for. The *Blue Boy* was finished and framed in gold. Ernest hung it above the mantelshelf sideways, for the painting was too tall to hang in the vertical dimension. Surprisingly it looked just as well and Bill Pettit retitled it *The Sleeping Blue Boy*, and Emily called it *Little Blue*

Boy for she thought it just like the boy in the nursery rhyme. Occasionally a car would visit our village driven by a salesman, or a flashy relative, but Elyahou Tsiblitz was never among them.

Then at the start of the new year, 1909, my great-great-grandmother drew her pension for the very first time from the post office in Kippax. She put the five bob into her pinafore pocket and along with many others shouted 'God bless Lloyd George', then treated the family to a trip to the cinema in Leeds. Ernest, whose leg was mending nicely, stayed home with Bill Pettit, but everyone else piled into Mr Archibold's motor bus and for the sake of a penny each way saved their shoe leather. At the Assembly Rooms, right at the top of Briggate, they saw a half-dozen short films. There was a film of a boxing match, and of a horse race, and of some ladies shooting bows and arrows at Beddington in Kent. Then came a film of a train entering a station and everyone gasped as it almost ran them down; the film froze for five minutes then continued with pictures of the passengers alighting from the coaches and walking along the platform. This was followed by a short comedy about a man trying to open a door. Then came footage of Winston Churchill's wedding and more of the king opening the Franco-British exhibition. Then came the evening's main attraction, a very short film about fruit-picking in East Africa. It was while watching this last film that Henrietta learned that the stone balls atop the pillars at the gates to the big house were actually pineapples. So pleased was she to learn of it that she wrote it into her *History of the Stones*. It had been a typical programme for the cinema of the time, an Aladdin's cave full of magic. Nobody thought then of it being a little short in material content. What the heck, they were pictures and they moved. So what if the movement was too quick and jerky to be real – did that matter? One had seen East Africa and the king and they existed for sure and so too did pineapples.

From that night my family became regular cinema goers, travelling at least once a week to shows in Leeds and Wakefield. Always, initially, seeing the same sort of programme as they had seen the day my great-great-grandmother drew her first pension. Then one day they saw a film which was different and which changed their lives completely. The film was called *Rescued by Rover* and it had been made by Mr Cecil Hepworth at a cost of £7.13s.9d. The film is acknowledged to have been the first to tell a real story and, although made in 1904, it was just coincidence that my family saw it five years later and it happened to be their first experience of a story on celluloid too. Suddenly the anarchy of the real world, of their lives, was gone. Here was something else, each Brightside was embroiled in the lives, yes the mortal lives, of others and yet these lives were no more than an illusion which disappeared as soon as the noisy projector was switched off or the film ran itself out.

Ernest never would go to the shows. He thought them to be the work of the devil, illustrating in one thousand and one ways how we might abuse ourselves and others. He stayed home with Bill Pettit who thought the cinema, like roller-skating, to be no more than a passing craze.

But Bill didn't count on the greedy need the human race seemed to have discovered for seeing and being cast with those big seeing eyes right into the epicentre of these celluloid implosions. For that's what they were, little eruptions deep within oneself calling us to account for the misery and joy of others. We were all film stars now. To illustrate the true involvement she felt, when Ernest asked his sister which were the most memorable moments during a particular film, Henrietta answered, 'I'll never forget that poor woman's screams, Ernest. They pierced me to the very heart.'

'But I thought those films were silent,' said her brother in exasperation.

'Oh, they are, Ernest. They are silent, but for the piano, that is.'

'What piano?' he asked, opening wide his deep brown eyes.

'Oh, they've taken to having a piano player to drown the noise of the projector,' she said.

'Isn't that off-putting? I mean, doesn't it spoil the film for thee?'

'No,' she answered. 'Somehow the piano helps you to hear the players.'

'I give up, lass,' Ernest said, shrugging his shoulders. 'It beats me how tha can waste tha money on such things.'

'It's just a craze, I tell thee Miss Brightside,' Bill Pettit said.

'Oh, can you be sure of that?' she asked, rounding on the lodger. 'Can you be certain of that, as you are of all else, Mr Pettit?'

'Ay. I'll give it another year or two, like roller-skating,' he said with confidence.

Even as he spoke, two more cinemas were being opened in the city not ten miles away, and Lancaster listening, as only a youth could, to the conversation which had just passed in our parlour thought how the cinema was neither music, not photography, neither real nor yet unreal, and resolved to find in those silent pictures the source of his aunt's wonderment at a lady's scream.

A few days later a letter was delivered to the house. It wasn't from Australia, nor was it from Wakefield, but it had been franked in London. It was addressed to Master Lancaster Brightside. The twin opened it excitedly, wondering who on earth would write to him from London, and withdrew from the envelope a stiff white card, scrolled around with gold leaf. The golden copperplate printing invited Mrs Jane Brightside and Master Lancaster Brightside to be the guests of the Honourable Duncan D'Arcy and the Doncaster Aviation Committee at the First Aviation Meeting to be held in Great Britain at the Doncaster Racecourse. They were asked to join their hosts on any day they cared between 15 and 23 October 1909. In a short note which accompanied the card Duncan D'Arcy explained that Mr Samuel Cody, who had recently flown a distance of one mile, would be there along with several other well-known aviators. He also thought that England was at last perhaps waking up.

'Waking up, my arse', said Bill. 'With two-thirds of the population now slumbering at the picture shows, who's he trying to kid?'

As part of the minority not attending the cinema Bill knew what he was talking about. Bill Pettit knew that when they entered those dark and smoky places the patrons were encouraged to leave their real selves at the door. How else could one explain the good-natured way they would put up with sitting for hours on end on uncomfortable box-wood seats in a filthy, choking atmosphere? How else could one explain Henrietta's hearing voices which weren't there? And, what's more, they never on any occasion, when leaving the cinema, recollected their whole selves. No, a little bit went missing after each subsequent visit. It was like collecting their coats from a cloakroom each time to find that a little more had been cut from the hem. Bill could see it but they, unfortunately, could not. It wasn't only the folk in whose house he lodged either but it was his workmates too. He'd seen the eyes of colliers, glazed like ham, as they moved into a new persona. Dreamlike, they made love with imaginary women, slaughtered their enemies in a thousand different ways, rode horses, drove locomotives and cars, flew aeroplanes. And their wives were no better, idling through their days with a handsome cowboy or a rich Arabian prince. It seemed to Bill that, apart from Ernest and himself, the whole working class was drugged on the craze, for it hadn't escaped his attention that the one-third of the population not attending the cinema shows were the rising middle and upper classes. No, they have it all sorted out, he thought. They needed their hold on reality in order to govern. They'd got the worker both out of the pubs and into a comatose state in one move. Clever. It might even be a Jewish plot, for weren't the film makers Jews, and weren't the cinema owners all Jews? Weren't they feeding unreality to the host population in darkened places? Who knows what might happen in the dark where you can't see the face even of the one sitting beside you? But for poor Bill, progress was thundering along too quickly. The old stacks, housing his information, were too cumbersome. More input was needed even before the rearrangements were complete. Picture palaces appeared. Big posh cinemas opened with seats more comfortable than a pasha's throne. Places where you got a cup of best tea at the interval all thrown in for the sixpenny price of your seat, and that brought in the toffs. Poor Bill, those with the money had only been waiting for the opening of palaces where the entrance fee was one which they could afford. Now the whole country slumbered in celluloid dreams. What's more, my great-great-grandmother, seemingly with money to burn from her five bob pension, was able to move her family upmarket and treat them all to the luxury of the sixpenny picture palace every Thursday.

13

Pause for a photograph of my father

'It is in the nature of those with inquiring minds to discover more facts,' said old Dr Cartwright from the deep sanctuary of one of our wide-winged chairs. The small man appeared lost in the comfort, hands clasped before him by a roaring fire. 'How in heaven's name should I be able to diagnose the Brightside melancholia were it not that I recognize the facts? Fortunately, child, I am able to recognize a scientific fact when I see one, but that is my calling. So too, I think, it is with you.' He was talking to Henrietta and tapped the open volume of bound papers which perched precariously on his knees. 'In your study, you also are seeking scientific facts. And finding them, I might add. Yes, finding many.' He nodded his small head and tapped the book again with bony fingers before linking them once more in desperate prayer and staring again into the flames.

Was that true? Henrietta wondered. 'Am I?' she found herself asking. 'Almost certainly you are, my dear. Each day you observe, hoping that the stones and their environment will yield more of their mystery to you, don't you? Well, what is it that they yield and which you faithfully record?' Here again he tapped the open volume in his lap. 'I'll tell you. It is facts, child. Scientific facts.' The old doctor had just carefully read several pages of Henrietta's beautifully written-up observations with their accurate illustrations, each one meticulously labelled. Henrietta was shaking her head as he adjusted the reading glasses on the end of his long thin nose.

If it was scientific fact that she required, Henrietta was quite aware that all she must do was lift her head from the study of the stones. If it was facts that she was after then they were all about her at Bottom Boat. Her journal would then have been quite different. She would have recorded pilewort in flower, frogs spawning, the yellowhammer and the pied-wagtail in song, blackcurrant in leaf, different species of ladybird depositing their eggs on the gooseberry leaves, the brimstone moth on the wing and the foxglove flowering

She would have recorded hearing the cuckoo and the redpoll, she would have heard the grasshoppers singing in the night and drawn long ears of barley and oats, described grubs suspended by threads and counted the spots and hairs on each of their abdominal segments. Spindle tree, guelder rose, wild hop, eyebright, bellflower, sainfoin, milkwort, field madder, red clover and cocksfoot grass would all have been lovingly described. She would have rejoiced in the variation among the birds; stonechat, chiff-chaff, swallow, sand-martin, redstart, blackcap, landrail, tree pipit. For she had already discovered variation to be the engine which pulled evolution along, hence her fascination for the imperceptible change. But facts, for sure, did not lead to truth and truth was what she was after, although she was very unsure of how one did arrive at such a thing.

'But it is not science that I study, it is history,' she told Dr Cartwright as he slammed shut the book with his skinny knees.

'Historic facts then. You look for historic facts.' He beamed from his spectacles.

What on earth was one of those, she wondered. Was 1066 an historic fact? And if 1066 why not 1142 or 708 BC? Was everything historic fact? Yes, she could accept that every moment of her life was indeed an historic fact, but who chose which to highlight and why? If some anonymous biographer were to choose the historic facts in her life would they choose the day she first sat down to write her journal? Cartwright probably would. Or would they give equal weight to the thousands of other days she had sat by Bottom Boat? Would they choose the night of the rape, or one of all the other nights she had spent in her bed? Was it an historic fact that she was unmarried and did it matter? Who was it who made history – Cartwright's sort of historic fact history? Was it the people about whom the history was written, or was it the historian?' 'No. No. It's not that kind of history,' she said. 'I don't observe facts.'

'A history without facts. That's a funny kind of history.'

'I've told you, my journal is not about facts.'

'Then what is it about?' he asked, adjusting his eyeglasses again and heaving the book on to the table without rising from his comfortable perch.

'I think it must be about causes.'

'What sort of causes?'

'The why things happen kind of causes.'

'Is that not the domain of God?' the old man asked, shuffling in his chair.

'Not exclusively. If he knows then why should we not know too?' The doctor tut-tutted into the red glow of the fire as Henrietta continued. 'Take your diagnosis of melancholia for example. Simply calling it a name doesn't satisfy me. Not without an explanation of how it comes about.'

The old doctor suddenly looked alarmed. 'You're on dangerous ground here, my girl,' he said sternly.

'Yes. I know,' she answered. 'You too share that ground. I'm sure you see it too as a dangerous path.'

'Bless my soul, child, whatever are you talking about? I am a doctor, this is my ground. No, I'm as sure-footed here as a mountain goat in the Alps. But you, child, you are like a horse on the same terrain.'

'Don't be such a stuffed shirt,' she said to the old man who was becoming quite agitated and finding it difficult to settle on a permanent spot in the wide-winged chair. 'You give me a name which describes the condition, and hope that the name in itself will be explanation enough. Well it isn't. I want to know the cause of this condition.'

'I've told you, girl. It's in your family,' he said irritably.

'But neither is that an explanation.'

The doctor paused a while, searching the fire before him. 'Juices, physiological juices,' he exploded, looking into her soft brown eyes. 'Perhaps your family has some strange ferment which is passed in the generations. I can't say more. Would that satisfy you as a cause?' He cocked his head to one side like a bald cockatoo. Henrietta nodded. 'Perhaps.' Then as the doctor settled smugly back into his wide winged chair, hands clasped before him, he closed his eyes. 'But how can you be sure?' she asked, jolting his eyes open again. He again thought a few moments, then said, 'Why, bless my soul child, I have no idea.'

'Then can't you accept that this thing which afflicts the family and which you call melancholia may have an external cause? Will you not accept that the cause may reside here in the house, in the stone?'

'Nonsense, girl,' he interrupted her. 'What on earth could there be in the stone which would cause such a thing.'

'But you ask me to accept the cause as some juice which is passed to me at birth.'

'Yes, I do.'

'Then what about Lancaster?'

'What about Lancaster?'

'Who passed it to him at his birth?'

The old doctor looked shocked and, had I been there, I should have asked, Yes, and what about me? Who passed it to me? That would have added a bit of weight to my great aunt's argument; but by the time that I was born, Dr Cartwright was preparing a different set of answers to those he was about to give. Henrietta filled in the silence of the coming years.

'It wasn't his mother or his father, for neither Emily nor Ernest suffer from the melancholia. So who, doctor, who passed it?'

'I don't know child,' said the old man shaking his head. 'All I know is that it can't be the stone. For me to say so would be – unscientific. Science is only just beginning to understand the techniques for extracting chemical substances from living tissue. Perhaps when we have identified the offending material we may then see how it's passed, but it will call for much experiment over the years.'

'Experiment!' Henrietta pounced on the word excitedly. 'That's exactly what my journal is, Dr Cartwright. It's an experiment.'

He looked perplexed. 'And I suppose Bottom Boat is your laboratory,' he said kindly.

'Oh no. Not if a laboratory is a place where controlled experiments take place. I have no control over the river. The elements come and go as they please.'

'Then I fail to see the experiment,' he said dismissively.

'I am the experiment,' she assured him, tapping at her bosom. 'I and the stones both; we constitute an experiment. Our interaction is the experiment.'

'But, my dear girl, there is nothing of you in these journals.' He waved his hand towards our library. 'You describe the stones and their changing environment, beautifully I might add, but that's all you do. Like it or not, Henrietta, your journal is nothing other than a collection of facts.'

'Well, it seems that you see only facts, Doctor. I write the book, yet you don't see me. Between the pages, between the days of observation, I am there and I'm constantly changing, yet remain hidden. For you, it would appear, the facts obscure the book. The stones and I are entwined throughout, changing together. Don't you see?'

'Bless me, child,' he said, 'well no, I don't see.' He shook his old head slowly. Henrietta gazed for a long time, penetrating the thick lenses of the doctor's reading glasses.

'It seems that the facts get in the way,' she said at last, and with some frustration. 'I shall have to move the stones to another place where the experiment might yield up results which you can clearly see.'

'But what is it that you wish me to see, child?' he asked now with mild exasperation.

'The truth, doctor. The truth about me.'

The old man shifted uncomfortably, staring into the fire, the heat from which now flushed his face. Bless my soul, he thought, the woman is mad. She's quite mad, I'm sure.

In the days immediately prior to the Doncaster aviation meeting the rains came. They tumbled incessantly from a leaden sky and tasted of metal. From the parlour window Lancaster watched his father and Mr Pettit now joined by William stomping across the soggy common in the direction of the pit. He thought how small and vulnerable his brother appeared to be, tucked as he was between the two strapping colliers and gripping his wretched snap box in slender coiled fingers. The boy had to scuttle, half-running, in order to keep pace with the two long striding men. It appeared though that William had settled quite happily to life in the pit. He had a pony of which he was very fond and was always pleased to exhibit his blackened face on the common just to let the younger ones know that he was now a man and drawing real wages.

Albert, having completed the *Blue Boy*, had turned his attention to the *Mona Lisa* and, sitting at his candle-lit easel like a flower-bearing visitor to a shrine, he would lay his colour on to the canvas, pushing it this way and that with a certain brush. In dark Leonardo strokes it moved about the fabric, stopping only to draw a brief moment's admiration from his mother or his aunt Henrietta. From the window Lancaster watched with a sharp eye pushing the brush, with unseen movements of his head, in the direction it should move, and dreamed of meeting Samuel Cody.

The American's plane had by now stayed in the air for over an hour. It seemed almost every day that news reached Lancaster of some wondrous feat performed by the aviators, each one of course bettering the others. And only yesterday he'd learned that Lord Northcliffe, the newspaper proprietor, was to offer £1000 to the first Britisher to fly a British-made machine a distance of one mile. It was not only Duncan D'Arcy who was urging us to stir from our slumbers; here indeed was inducement of a more positive kind.

From behind Albert's shoulder at the easel, Henrietta quietly watched more candles flickering in the scullery beyond. There her grandmother was busily preparing tinctures and extracts in shiny buckets and bottling others already expressed into glass storage jars which dimly reflected the wavering smoky flames. Here, in our house, was another shrine, a vestry in which Jane Brightside played. The liquids' straw yellow, red, brown, bright yellow, rose and black shone dully in their glass containers. Henrietta thought of old Dr Cartwright's words about juices and ferments and realized that her grandmother had been extracting juices from living material for years. Plant material maybe but to extend her dispensary to cover expressions of animal tissue would not be beyond the old woman's wit or calling and, looking across the room from one shrine into the other, Henrietta thought how science, if it was about anything at all, was concerned with unknown principles. Like the unseen energy released at the burning of coal, so unseen agents accumulated and grew in the leaves and roots of grandmother's specimens. So too, according to Dr Cartwright, did juices (or perhaps even spirits, she thought) pass in the generations of men.

And did it matter that you called it melancholia or history as long as you were aware that something was passing unseen? Perhaps here was the great task for science and scientists, identification of unseen agents. Isn't that what the doctor had said? She supposed, pompous as he was, the old man really was a scientist; he knew the way ahead. But not her, she was convinced now more than ever that her mode was history. But for some reason this historian needed a laboratory in which to work. She needed to prove something by experiment.

Emily watched her son. As the rain poured into the lush grass of the common, she watched his boots putting in two steps to his father's one. The three figures receded towards the ridge of green, then to the dip which would take them down to the winding-engine shed. Above the rough wooden structure the wheel cycled wet and noisily. As Lancaster moved from her side Emily wondered how, now the bill was law, an eight-hour working day would affect their lives. Precious little, she concluded, and sniffed. It had been such a long fight, something Sidall Junkin had urged almost all his working days without success. And now they had it, too late for Sidall, it didn't seem much. Eight hours plus winding time. But the colliers claimed it as their greatest victory. It was, they said, a testament to the durability of the mineworker. For more than a generation they had been banging away at the doors at Westminster finally to have them flung open. A victory for the working man, Ernest had called it. More like a testament to the slothful in parliament, she thought, an illustration of the snail's pace progess of parliamentary processes. Meanwhile the Miners' Federation had become affiliated to the Labour Party and wages were not rising fast enough to account for the increased cost of living, not that they'd starve. The old woman in the scullery behind would see to it that they didn't starve.

Emily watched Lancaster setting his camera upon its tripod. She saw the young boy, now beyond the window, rain dripping from his cap, direct the lens towards the three disappearing figures. From the candle-lit room she peered hard into the metal-tasting rain, and watched the magnesium flare momentarily brighten the gloomy sky, and realized the truth of her man and boy captured forever, disappearing from view to the hidden pit beyond. Walking from view. Running from view by the window. My father running from the window to catch his father. My father two-stepping to meet me.

Lancaster knew the truth of that image. It was a black and white photograph for a National Photographic Museum one hundred years hence. It was an expression of now and then. Then past and then future. It was the advertiser's dream, timeless. Emily already knew it as shoe-blacking, in time it would become custard, oven cleaner, deodorant soap, cornflakes, brown sauce, and she would know it as all those things. Then after her death the image would continue to represent washing powders, frozen food, gadgets. The advertisers would of course use more modern images, the new, the chic, the trendy, but always they would return to the image that Lancaster captured that day on film. For they knew the truth of it.

But Lancaster put the photograph in the family album and promptly forgot about it. His mind was on free running passages. Kinema was in his blood and as his young heart pumped, the idea of film wound itself in his brain. Static images, backtracking staccato fashion, were not for him. There could be no settling of Lancaster's mind until cameras were turning in his hands. It was an urge to overcome the truth and head straight for the lie beyond.

Like any good storyteller (my father reckoned I inherited the ability from my uncle), he needed to relate the whole story. Nothing could be left to the imagination, the terrible focus of truth.

The next day Lancaster and my great-great-grandmother went to the Doncaster aviation meeting. It was the sixth day of the show and poured down. Along with 50,000 other drenched spectators they watched Samuel Cody swear the oath of allegiance before Doncaster's town clerk. The American was now British, a curious conversion but for the lure of Lord Northcliffe's £1000. The band then played 'God Save the King' and Duncan D'Arcy from beside my uncle raised three hearty cheers for Cody. The ex-American's biplane was housed in a great shed which Duncan D'Arcy called the Cathedral but the press, through some misunderstanding, thought D'Arcy was referring to the name of the plane.

'No,' shouted the balloonist to *The Times* aviation correspondent, 'The airplane is to be called Lancaster Brightside,' but it was too late. Cathedral had already been telegraphed around the world, and all settled for that version of the truth. Not only were the newspapers reporting events, they were promoting and now making the news. D'Arcy thought it a dangerous turn of events.

The biplane remained in the shed all day as two days previous its nose had been damaged when Cody crash-landed, so Lancaster unfortunately didn't see Cody fly. But Duncan D'Arcy went up in a small monoplane based on the Bleriot model, circled for ten minutes or so, and was warmly applauded by the wet and appreciative crowd. Back at home, Lancaster cried because of the lack of understanding among the stupid pressmen. His Aunt Henrietta told him that it really didn't matter for it wouldn't have been he who was famous, but the aviation machine, and that names were unimportant anyway.

14

Water comes to the house and the reordering of the Stones

When the snows came the Airedale Water Company sent a man. He called himself a dowser and carried a V-shaped willow twig. The sun came out but the thermometer registered temperatures below freezing all day. Henrietta, welcoming the sunshine, wrapped herself warmly and sat out in a deckchair. Her bottom pushed the canvas red, yellow and black broad stripes almost to the level of whiteness beneath her.

She watched the man cross and recross the common many times, divining the water and leaving thousands of black tracks in the crisp snow. The man whose hair was almost as white as the snow itself kept shaking his head when the willow twig refused to divulge the presence of what he had been sent to find.

'I don't think it works,' she said to him on one occasion when the line he walked took him close by her striped deckchair.

'Oh, it works all right,' he said. 'There isn't any water here, that's all.' His two eyes were close together and appeared high up on his forehead, although in reality the man had hardly any forehead at all. If she squinted slightly the two eyes came together giving him the appearance of a cyclops.

'But how?' – she pointed to the twig which he held lightly in both hands – 'how can a silly thing like that tell where the water is?'

He shook his head again, 'Dunno, miss. But it works. My father was a dowser and his father afore him. It runs in families tha naws. If there's water we allus finds it.'

She focused her attention behind the one-eyed man to the where-abouts of the Roman Wall which lay buried under a cap of snow on Hunger Hill.

'Doesn't the snow interfere?' she asked.

'No. It's only water under t'ground that matters.'

'And isn't there any here?' She looked back at him without refocusing her gaze, all the while amusing herself with the man's single eye.

'Don't look like,' he answered and took himself off from the strange squinting woman to see what he might discover below the ash-pits and spawning many more small dark prints on the way, all in a perfectly straight line.

A month later, with a deep layer of snow still covering the common, the Airedale Water Company sent six Irish labourers. They dug many holes out of the frozen ground in the common and a long channel which ran all the way down the terrace from Mrs Agar's house at one end to the Waltons' home at the other. Some days it snowed persistently, covering up whatever tracks there were on the common, but this didn't deter the navvies. They just continued to dig into the hard earth like burrowing animals tunnelling from one hole to another, linking everything together and bringing their tunnels to the walls of the houses themselves. Then they went away and left us with an inverted black and white maze about five feet deep. The children played soldiers in these trenches, heaving great rocks from one area to the next, and when the snows thawed, coating the playful military in slithery liquid earth, horse-drawn wagons arrived with miles and miles of cast-iron piping. The pipes were laid out on the grassy bits which remained between the trenches and when spring arrived the Airedale Water Company sent a dozen men to lay them in the prepared holes. Now, one of the men included in this batch of newcomers was black as the ace of spades and was called Mr Ndolo. He said that he was a prince from West Africa. It was the first time that anybody from our village had seen a black man and they were all a little afraid. However, on learning that Emily was the mother of twins he developed an irrational fear of his own. He claimed the village water pump to be contaminated as he had seen Emily, this mother of twins, drawing from it and refused absolutely to take its water. Furthermore, he told everyone what a good thing it was for them to be having water brought to their homes, not least because Emily could no longer pollute the general supply. My grandmother was very distressed when she heard this story and Bill Pettit told her that the black bugger didn't know what he was talking about and complained to the Airedale Water Company who had Mr Ndolo replaced by an Irish labourer. Eventually, the pipes were laid all the way to the river, via the little pumping station which had been quickly built, and right up to the houses in the other direction. Then after all the holes had been filled in, they sent the plumbers to us. They put tanks into the houses and fitted shiny gold taps into the walls above the sinks in the sculleries. Then they fitted waste-pipes and drainage, and one day in later summer Ernest turned the tap to great cheering in our house and out flowed turbid water which was of a pea-green colour and smelled of cucumbers.

The handle of the village pump was then removed. The authorities, after all these years, had decided that the water which came from it was unfit for human consumption. Mrs Henderson was greatly relieved for she believed Mr Ndolo's fear to be not without foundation. The water had not been quite the same since those twins had been born, she said. She was never heard to pass an opinion on the condition of her household water though. However, my own family had much to say about it.

In the first place it frequently changed colour. Its natural state seemed to be somewhere between the pea-green liquid, which had oozed out on that first tap's turning, and murky brown. On occasions, however, it appeared pale blue and, even more alarmingly, red. Then, they complained, it smelled strongly of cucumber but sometimes of violet and even geranium. The greatest complaint was reserved though for when the water was heated. At about the mid-point between room temperature and boiling terrible sulphurous fumes would fill the parlour, choking the occupants and encouraging giggles from the twins who put the smell down to their great-grandmother's frequent bouts of flatulence. The water also had a permanently bitter taste and it sometimes brought on debilitating attacks of diarrhoea.

'Drink more water. You must replace the fluid loss,' said old Dr Cartwright when brought out to attend Emily who had been smitten.

'Can't something be done to reactivate the old pump?' Ernest asked.

'Don't worry, you'll all get used to it eventually.'

'But what's in the water to cause such terrible diarrhoeas?'

'Algae,' the doctor answered without hesitation. 'And they will also be causing the smells, and the changes of colour too.'

Seeing the lack of comprehension in Ernest's face, the old man offered to bring over his microscope so that the family might understand something of the life with which their drinking water teemed. The following day he came back with the apparatus, placed a drop of water upon a glass slide, covered it and laid it upon the microscope's platform. He then lit a candle close by the mirror so that the light reflected upwards illuminating the water on the slide. He then focused the lens and invited Ernest to peer into the eyepiece.

'What's that?' said my grandfather, tearing his eye from the glass and registering a look of amazed horror.

'Euglena, I think,' said the doctor with his face all screwed up and looking back down the tube.

'But it's moving.'

'Yes, it would. It's alive.'

'You mean we swallow them things live?'

By now everybody was wanting to view the marvels which the microscope was bringing to life and eventually, after much twiddling, they were all given a glimpse of one or other of the darting animalcules which lived in our water supply. There were also long green sticks and worm-like things which, despite their shocking appearance, at least managed to stay in one place. By the time Dr Cartwright's biology lesson had finished my assembled family were mostly close to hysteria. Bill Pettit had also managed to commit to memory the new words: spirogyra, stigeoclonium, arthrospira, synura and gomphospheria. There were many others which had tripped lightly from the doctor's tongue which even Mr Pettit couldn't recall.

'Facts. They are all there,' the doctor said for Henrietta's benefit, pointing down the microscope tube. Then he went on speaking to Ernest. 'They should have been filtered out. Perhaps they're having trouble at the plant. I'll have a word with them.'

'I should hope tha will,' said Mr Pettit, none too keen on the words which had found their way into his head.

'No matter. As I've said before, you'll all get used to it. Give it a few more weeks.' Cartwright went on, 'At least there'll be no more hauling buckets of water all the way from the pump. You'll be glad of that, I expect.'

Henrietta nodded. Since the installation of the supply she had taken to filling the sink almost full with cold water, adding a few soap flakes and washing dishes for hours on end. And during these long hours of dish-washing she would ponder the stones, their history, science and meaning, while her arms to a level above the elbows slopped about in sudsy water.

Some of the time she contemplated her new laboratory. Where it should be and how she would move the stones from one place to the other. She was unsure of exactly when such a change would come about when an incident at Bottom Boat forced a decision from her.

She had, as usually was the case, been sitting on the bank watching the stones and drafting a few notes, when she caught sight of two dead fish floating on the current and being taken downstream. At first she imagined nothing unusual for she often saw and recorded dead fish, especially if their bodies were caught up among the stones, but gradually more appeared. Soon her eye was taken with dozens of dead fish floating along, their bloated sides turned pink and upward to the sky. The river water was slowly turning pink too. Minutes later there were thousands of dead fish choking the surface of the river from bank to bank, all carried on a foamy red tide.

Her first thought was that it was the untreated waste from the village, which she knew to be poured into the river about a mile upstream, that was polluting the water. But what could there be in their household waste to cause such devastation? As water toilets had not yet been fitted, the waste returned to the river consisted of dirty water, being mainly the washings from the villagers' baths and their dinner plates. Henrietta quickly walked upstream to the place where the village effluent was emptied into the river. The water here was almost blood red and beyond, further upstream and floating down to meet her, were more dead fish looking very pale in the crimson rush. The foam too was becoming heavy. Following the river around past the pumping station my great-aunt came eventually upon the source of the pollution. Simmonds's dye works. It was a small factory with a tall brick chimney which continually puffed out clouds of black smoke which smelled of marzipan. Henrietta went inside through a wooden door which bore the company's name in white lettering and demanded to see the owner. She was kept waiting for an hour then eventually a man in a straw hat arrived who explained that Mr Simmonds was in London but that he was the company chemist and would help if he could. Henrietta explained her concern at the red stuff which was being released into the river and killing all the fish. She also explained that since the introduction of the water supply she and her family had to drink water from the river.

The straw hat which was slightly too large for the man's head moved a little as he spoke, and he kept having to readjust it with the red thumb and index fingers of his big hand. There was a pink area on the brim which suggested that this was a regular manoeuvre, and the smallness of the rosy patch was testimony to the man's accuracy in hitting the same mark on each occasion.

'It's a chemical which takes the oxygen out of the water,' he explained, 'so the fish are unable to breathe. We humans take our oxygen from the air fortunately, so it won't affect us. Don't worry, your water will be perfectly safe for drinking.'

She thanked him for his assurances and he smiled swivelling his hat ever so slightly. We had red water for a while and two people living in our terrace died that week. Others vomited into their sinks and flushed away the sickness with gushings of cold water from their golden taps. Old Dr Cartwright thought the deaths due to food poisoning and blamed Mr Doyle's pigs for both the deceased had consumed pork in the day before they died. The diarrhoea in our house ceased for a while and Ernest believed, as he had been told by the doctor, that everyone was getting used to the water. Of course, nobody was, and had they at that time put a drop of water on one of Dr Cartwright's slides and presented it to the microscope, they would have seen that all the little animals had been stained red and that none of them were moving.

The episode with the dead fish and the pollution of the river water made Henrietta see that she must act quickly. The stones had to be moved. So her journal dated 30 August 1911 was headed 'THE REORDERING OF THE STONES' in large capital letters and described how William and Mr Pettit brought the stones to our house in a wheelbarrow in six journeys and dumped them on the common just outside our door. There were 147 of them altogether, far more than she had ever counted before, but as William explained they kept finding stones underneath those which had been visibly available. The next day, the day of the start of a month-long strike, and also the day on which Albert finished his painting of the *Mona Lisa*, my great-aunt went outside with two pots of paint, one red, the other yellow. She then proceeded to paint all 147 stones choosing at random those to be painted red and those to receive the yellow paint. Watched by scores of out-of-work colliers who had little else to do, she covered the stones on all sides in the coloured paints. She then dispatched a dozen men with an assortment of implements and the wheelbarrow to dig up from wherever they could find them as many stones as possible of a similar size to the ones which had been brought from Bottom Boat. When the first barrow load of stones arrived back at the common my great-aunt immediately painted them with pitch on all sides and left them to dry on the common. This she did with each succeeding load until she had about six hundred stones, all black as pitch; then she went indoors and wrote up her journal.

She tested her indelible stamper, the stamp from which was becoming slightly faded, on the back of Albert's recently finished canvas, which lay on the parlour table. This she did only once, breathed on the inked rubber, and stamped the pages of her journal.

The following morning a congregation of about thirty men appeared in groups about the two piles of coloured stones and wandered aimlessly among the strewn-out black ones. Henrietta, after breakfast, went outside and told the dumbfounded miners, who looked as if they had stumbled upon the Easter Island monuments, that they were going to build a wall. Thus were the stones reordered with my great-aunt supervising the placement of the red and yellow stones amongst the black ones as carefully as an Egyptian architect would have seen to the placing of blocks in the building of a pyramid. The wall abutted to the front of our house at both sides and formed an enclosure taking in a part of the common about ten yards long by five, the latter measurement being the width of our house. With her laboratory complete and the stones identified and trapped amongst their dark and anonymous neighbours Henrietta brought out her deckchair with the matching striped canvas. She placed this just in front of the gateway which had been left in the front wall and in line with the doorway to our house. She then invited Albert to come and paint her sitting outside her laboratory. She ordered Lancaster to come and photograph, and asked Dr Cartwright to come and see. From the far side of the common, the coloured stones shone out like jewels. Dr Cartwright, always concerned when in the presence of madness and genius and never easily able to distinguish between them, blessed his soul again and diagnosed mania. But the woman seems harmless, he thought, and did no more about it.

Elyahou Tsiblitz was soon to arrive outside our house. He was driving a 28 horsepower Lanchester car. It had a hard covered roof but no glass windows and within the coachwork was so splendid it looked as if it might have been built for royalty, for the padded cushions were puffed up in kingly red.

'It was,' explained the rubber man when asked, 'built for the Jam Sahib of Nawangar. He had six motors built for royal occasions by the Lanchester company. As I was supplying the tyres I asked if they could manufacture an extra one for me.'

He was standing in Henrietta's laboratory. Behind him the body of the vehicle was quite visible through the gap in the wall and my great-great-grandmother could pick out the Jam Sahib's coat of arms painted in black and gold on the two doors.

'Will tha come in for some tea?' she invited as a crowd began to collect about the motor. He nodded and followed her into the parlour where Ernest and Mr Pettit sat reading the newspaper in the wide-winged chairs. Beyond, in the scullery, Henrietta was deep in thought with her arms to the elbows thrust in the sink and covered in foamy bubbles. Mrs Gill, banging at the back boiler with her poker, caused the two men to look up from their reading.

'What's he doin' 'ere?' Ernest asked.

'I invited him,' said the old woman possessively.

'Gerrout.' Ernest nodded towards the doorway through which the two had just walked. 'We don't entertain thieves.'

'Ay. Go on, 'opit,' said Mr Pettit, imitating Ernest's movement of the head.

The Transylvanian looked towards the open door but remained where he was as the old woman held him stubbornly by the sleeve of his tweeds. He could see the top halves of many people as they stood about his motor.

'I'd better leave,' he said to my great-great-grandmother.

'Nivver,' she said. 'Ignore them. They've no understanding.'

'Yes. It's for that reason I'd better go,' he smiled.

'No.' She tugged at his sleeve. 'Tha'll stay.'

Bill Pettit stood up and approached Elyahou, 'Go on, clear out,' he said up at him, for he was a good six inches shorter than the tall rubber man. 'Tha's not wanted here.'

The old woman rounded on Bill. 'Mr Pettit sit thee down. If there's any leavin' to be done, it'll be thee that goes. Remember, tha's only a lodger here thissen.'

'Grandmother. Watch 'ow tha speaks to our lodgers,' Ernest warned.

'Ay, and tha watch how tha treats a guest, Ernest,' she countered. The two men feeling the embarrassment of a family affair nothing to do with them now looked at each other with neutral eyes.

'Sit down, Bill,' my grandfather said softly, still looking angrily at the visitor.

'Tha must tell us sometime 'ow tha came to pinch the Ascot Gold Cup though.'

The tall man shrugged and gave the old woman a look which suggested he had no idea what her grandson was talking about. He was spared further pressure to stay, however, when a chant went up from the children outside the door.

'We want the suits, we want the suits,' they chorused.

Then as Lancaster appeared with his twin in the freshly walled compound before the door, it changed to 'we want to fly, we want to fly'.

Elyahou went through the doorway and stood beyond talking to the now hushed and expectant children. 'There is no more flying suit. No more bee,' he explained. 'It was damaged by a stupid parent down near Barnsley only last week. The child went up over the roof and the man went pop.' He squinted into the imaginary sights of an imaginary rifle held in his hands. 'The child came down unhurt, thank God, but the suit is beyond repair. So, no more flying, I'm afraid.'

As the moans went up around him Elyahou shouted, 'But everything else is here,' and he ran to the motor. Out came the same old battered suitcases and as always the children were quickly dressed and soon bouncing around the common.

142

From his side my great-great-grandmother asked, 'What have tha to sell us today, then?'

'I've nothing today,' he said, spreading his hands and smiling into her disappointed face.

'I have made my fortune in car tyres, Michelin, Dunlop and now Tsiblitz. I need nothing more.'

'Then why didst tha come?'

'Courtesy.' He shrugged.

'Tha's a liar,' she smiled. 'Tha's got summat for me.' The smile developed into a small giggle.

He laughed as she touched the red bodywork on the motor and ran her tongue over her lined lips.

'Come on. Get tha tea,' she said, gently tugging him by the sleeve. Reluctantly he followed the old woman.

On re-entering the house they quickly passed through the frosty atmosphere in the parlour to the scullery where Henrietta was still dibbling in the sudsy water.

As the old woman filled the new black kettle with water from the tap and took it into the parlour to boil on the fire, Elyahou asked Henrietta what she was doing.

'Thinking,' she said, blushing deeply.

'With your hands?' he inquired with concern.

'I just find it helps me to think,' she said. 'Having my hands in water helps me to think,' she elaborated.

'I never heard anything like that before,' he said.

'No. Perhaps.' She smiled nervously. 'But it works.'

A few years later he happened to explain Henrietta's habit to a Cambridge philosopher called Ludwig Wittgenstein who tried it out as a means of thinking. Wittgenstein took up the habit and washed many a dirty pot, hours on end, thinking about thinking. Because he developed a contact dermatitis the philosopher then asked Elyahou if it would not be possible to make a glove out of his damned rubber so as to protect the hands of the washer-up. They sat down together and designed it there and then.

Left and right. Elyahou made yet another fortune as the inventor of the washing-up glove, but one rarely hears of the part Wittgenstein played in its development.

'Tha'll get nowt but chaps, lass,' her grandmother said, coming back to the small room and searching among the bottles shining out of the shelving.

'Here,' she said at last, plonking a fat bottle down on the tiny wooden drainer by the sink. 'Rub tha hands with glycerin and rose water, it'll sooth tha chaps.' Ignored by the granddaughter the old woman turned to Elyahou.

'I've been thinking 'bout tha motor,' she said.

'What about it?'

'It's a grand motor is that. Will tha sell it to me?'

The rubber man looked away to study the labels on the neat rows of glass bottles behind the old woman.

'Tha's not answered me,' she told him.

'You couldn't afford it,' he said still with disinterest.

''Ow should thee know?'

He looked back at her searching her gnarled face 'Did you sell the cup?' he asked. A moment's panic crossed his face. 'I didn't believe you'd sell the cup.'

'The cup's safe enough, don't tha worry,' she assured him. 'How much for the car, rubber man?'

'Three thousand three hundred pounds,' he said still searching her face.

'Don't go away,' she said and went as quickly as she could from the house. Not that Elyahou had any thoughts of leaving, imprisoned in the scullery as he was by the hostile stares from the men in the parlour. For the while he felt safe where he was. It was a place for women. The men, he knew, would not transgress. He watched them reading their newspapers an instant then turned his gaze back into the scullery.

'What do you do in the house all day?' he asked Henrietta, his hands thrust deeply into his trouser pockets. She half turned towards him at the sink.

'Oh, I write my journal, boil the water; sometimes I cook. We take it in turns, Emily, Grandmother and I. Emily always bakes the bread though. I wash the dishes, but I enjoy it, now we have water to the house.'

Then, as if to prove the point, she sloshed her arms even deeper into the cold suds.

'Did you never think of work, going into service or something like that?' he asked. His hands were still thrust into his trouser pockets and she could see by the way he made unseen bulges with them that he was holding up his trousers with tight fists. Turning her head back to the sink she thought for the first time in a long time of the rape. She thought too of grandmother's baskets, sniffing the perfumed air in the small room.

'Ernest wanted me to go into service but when I started to write my journal grandmother forbade it. She said I should be free to concentrate on my writing.'

'She is an enlightened woman, your grandmother,' he said. She turned her head again towards Elyahou and noted how his trousers were too long for his legs. Although the Transylvanian had very long legs, his trousers seemed to have been built for a giant of even greater proportions. She allowed her eyes to lift slowly from his shoes to the area about his crotch where they lingered awhile. Elyahou, suddenly uncomfortable, hitched the trousers up about his waist by means of the hidden bulges at which the woman was staring. She smiled.

'Is it true that you have made your fortune selling motor car tyres?' she asked now with her back to him.

'Yes, I have a factory making tyres in Berlin.'

'Are you rich, then?'

He shuffled a little then said, 'Reluctantly, yes I am rich.'

'Whyever reluctantly, Mr Tsiblitz?' she asked, busily scrubbing a plate for the umpteenth time.

'Because, as a socialist I always believed the working class to need the fruits of technology, and I always thought that I might provide some of that harvest.'

'And so you did,' she turned and told him.

'But I did not intend to make myself wealthy. I did not intend to become a capitalist; employing labour, accumulating profit and all it entails.'

'And have you become a capitalist?'

'Yes. Well, no.' He struggled with his thoughts. 'I suppose I still think like a socialist.' He hitched his trousers again.

'Mr Pettit thinks you are an anarchist,' she smiled.

'That too. I used to believe in anarchy. No more government, the human race attaining its natural moral state without political masters. I still do really. I still think that way, but I've been overrun by success. I wanted to give rubber to the people and they gave me money in return. Perhaps I should give it all away.'

My great-aunt turned from the sink drying her long slender fingers on a towel.

'Grandmother has been trying to give away a fortune for years. It breaks the old woman's heart that no member of the family will take it from her.' She unstoppered the fat bottle which her grandmother had left on the drainer and poured the viscous liquid into her palm causing an effusion of roses into the atmosphere.

'How come a woman like your grandmother has a fortune to give away?' Henrietta rubbed the emollient between her palms, wringing her hands in the process. It made the soft intimate noise of flesh being squeezed into something other and looking again to the visitor's crotch she noted how a third bulge had suddenly appeared between the other two.

'As you said, she's an enlightened woman,' Henrietta answered, while undoing Elyahou's fly buttons. Hardly daring to breath the man pressed his back up against the shelves of bottles out of view of the men in the parlour. He could hear the turning of the pages of newspaper as my great-aunt proceeded to reveal his stiffly erect penis from among the folds of his large trousers. Stroking him lengthily with her glycerin and rose-water hands, she was on this occasion at least going to send him away with a cock smelling of roses. His own small responses following the movements of her hands caused a trembling to be set up in the wooden shelving which was immediately transmitted to the rows of bottles which rattled brittly against one another. This caused the whole of my great-great-grandmother's stock to sing at such a high frequency that the dogs on the common started to bark and howl in tune to the quiet masturbation which was happening in our scullery.

'Must be another stranger coming,' said Mr Pettit looking up from his newspaper and lending an ear to the cacophony on the common.

How true, Elyahou thought, while ejaculating into Henrietta's saponified palms, and unaware of the strange vibrations which were eddying through the coloured liquids above his head. In embarrassed silence the rubber man quickly made himself decent and, unperturbed by the dangers beyond, scurried from the room at the earliest opportunity leaving Henrietta with her arms thrust once more into sudsy water, although on this occasion she was washing herself rather than the dishes. My great-aunt hadn't felt so good in years. 'Next time I'll bite it off,' she said softly to the accompaniment of a bottle of red liquid falling from the top shelf and being dashed to smithereens on the stone floor.

''Ey up!' said Mr Pettit from behind his newspaper and, as Elyahou ran from the house, 'There goes another one.'

Ernest smiled, but didn't move from his seat. His sister would clear the mess.

15

Jane Brightside buys a motor and how the stones came alive

In the popular imagination the typical collier is a rugby-playing, beer-swilling mountain of a man who can withstand, because of his job, all that brute nature has to throw at him. We tend to think that all of them will have been spawned by the Adam and Eve who shared our earth closet; Mr and Mrs Gill. Nothing could be further from the truth. In our village at any one time the majority of the men were knackered. Like Sidall Junkin, they were asthmatic and breathless, or, like old man Gill, they lived with their broken backs, thighs, necks, arms and all. There were few who didn't suffer rheumatism or rupture and, because of the cramped conditions in which they worked, the constant scraping of knees, hips and elbows caused the joints to fester. The most pitiful of all though were those with the terrible rotating eyeballs. Unable to fix their gaze on anything for very long their eyeballs would swing wildly in their sockets sometimes causing their eyes to disappear completely, and giving them a ghoulish appearance, setting up panic and fear in friend and stranger alike. When my great-great-grandmother returned to greet Elyahou, her deep pinafore pocket stuffed full and clanking with coin of the realm, she knew exactly the use to which she would put the Jam Sahib's motor car. She would take the crippled and the unfit and unwell for trips into better areas. She would take them for a day away from the grit and smoke; she would see to it that they breathed more easily, that their pains were eased.

'I'll take them to Burnsall Fell where I once went as a lass and show them a river that's clear, and air that doesn't need rain to wash it clean,' she told the Transylvanian as he watched the inflated animals playing cricket on the common. He had taken himself off to watch the children in an attempt to recover from Henrietta's attentions.

'You can have the motor. Have it for nothing,' he said without humour.

'Nay, lad, tha must tek payment for it.'

'But I don't want to. I have enough,' he protested.

She would not hear of it and, remembering the words of the granddaughter, he felt an obligation to put an end to the breaking of an old woman's heart, and with some reluctance but an over-whelming sense of duty, he went to the motor and took one of the battered suitcases from the back seat. He knelt on one long knee at the woman's feet exactly as he had done on his very first visit to our house, and opened the case. Standing above him, she let cascade from her pinafore a noisy assortment of guineas, florins, half-guineas and pennies. As the coins tumbled past his face, and pulling apart the sides of the case in such a manner as to create more space while it filled ever higher with my great-great-grandmother's fortune, he felt himself becoming locked into a charade from which he could see no escape.

'Tha's earned it,' she smiled at him. Although that was about the last thing he wished to hear, he smiled back.

'You must let me give you something now,' he said when the metallic cascade had finally ceased and he'd closed the lid on the pile of cash.

'I knew tha would,' she grinned expectantly.

Elyahou stood up, put the case back into the motor and opened the second case from which he took a wooden tube. He removed a rag plug from one end and started to extract a scrolled canvas.

'Is it a map?' she asked not able to hide her excitement. 'Buried Treasure!'

Elyahou shook his head and continued to extract the object. When the scroll was finally free of the container in which it had been rolled, he handed it to my great-great-grandmother. Unravel-ling it between her wrinkled hands, she had no difficulty in recogniz-ing it for what it was.

After all she had been looking at a steadily developing copy of it for several months. It was the *Mona Lisa*. Taking the wooden tube from the man, she asked him to wait a moment and went into the house. As Ernest and Mr Pettit were still occupied with their news-papers the old woman had no difficulty in exchanging unseen Albert's copy of the gift which Elyahou had just made to her. Returning to the Transylvanian she then told the only downright lie of her long life. She said, 'No thanks, Ernest thinks I shouldn't keep it,' and, putting the copy into the container, handed it back. Elyahou shrugged, told her that he understood and arranged immediately in his mind for it to be returned to the Louvre. They must have been pleased to receive their precious Leonardo back in one piece but they must have wondered why it had been returned with my great-aunt's name on the back. Perhaps they knew it to be a fake (although I should stress that it was a very good one) but thought it hardly worth making too much fuss as the good citizens of Paris would be none the wiser if they covered it with glass, housed the painting in poor light and gave prayers at the cathedral of Notre Dame. The citizens proved to be very thankful indeed.

The original hung in a rough pine frame above our sideboard until the next time the pedlar came to our village when Ernest bought a fine golden frame for it. It fitted a treat and he hung it back on the wall centred against the bible with the brass clasp which remained darkly shut immediately beneath.

When the men in our house learned of the family's new acquisition they were very angry. My great-great-grandmother didn't let on that she had paid for the motor but allowed them to think that it had been given her as a present, like she had been given Bresci's hat and the Ascot Gold Cup. Naturally, though, they thought that it had been stolen. Mr Pettit made inquiries first in his head then with the police. No, the Jam Sahib of Nawangar had not reported the theft of a motor. A detective was sent from Leeds to look at the vehicle and take fingerprints, and my great-great-grandmother took him for a spin around the neighbouring villages. She sounded the throaty horn as they passed by the Thwaite house just as the coal owner was taking a walk along his leafy lane. The old capitalist didn't see who was driving it but thought what a magnificent machine had just passed by his gate with the pineapple balls. The detective went back to his inspector to report that the old woman believed that she had received a gift from God and he couldn't see, at this moment in time, any reason to doubt her.

William, though he approved absolutely of the use to which the old woman was to put the motor, was nagged by thoughts of her having squandered the family fortune. Perhaps it was because of something which his aunt Henrietta had said that he disbelieved the old woman, but he felt certain that the motor had not been given to her. He therefore decided to confront Jane Brightside alone.

'Don't worry, there's more,' she told him, when he'd informed her that he understood the fortune one day to be his. 'And anyroad tha's had tha chance with the Gold Cup. Great softee, tha could've hung on to that. Had it melted any time tha liked.'

'I would had tha not come lookin' for me,' my father accused.

'Nay,' she said, 'tha wouldn't William; tha's too honest, lad.' Then she started to laugh, great loud raucous laughter. She laughed and she laughed, tears streaming down her face and her mouth open wide like a barking dog. In mid-laugh she suddenly stopped. Her old gnarled face seemed to collapse in on itself; her mouth closed then the rough dry lips parted as if she were about to say something. She might have been about to say that the real *Mona Lisa*, not Albert's *Mona Lisa* but Leonardo's *Mona Lisa*, was hanging above the sideboard. Or she might have revealed the whereabouts of the Ascot Gold Cup or of the suitcase with the money, but she didn't say any of those things; she just said that she was glad and asked to be put to bed for she didn't feel right. She couldn't remember who she was or anything but kept repeating that she was glad.

Ernest and Henrietta put their grandmother to bed wrapped in a white cotton nightdress and bonnet and resting on a blanket of cotton wool. Her face was sunken and olive green, the black lines showed the coal grit of nearly a hundred years. She kept mumbling that she was glad and couldn't remember anything.

William took a load of cripples to Burnsall together with his brothers, and they swam in the Wharfe with the disabled on their backs. They climbed the fells with them on their shoulders and described what they could see to the blinded. Where the river widens and snakes through the village by the pub they paddled and drank ale, and the man with the terrible rotating eyeballs syndrome who couldn't focus on anything for more than a few seconds at a time disappeared his eyes into the top of his head and didn't frighten anyone anymore.

The following week he took the asthmatics to Ilkley Moor in the motor, the finest in Yorkshire, and in the heather heard them breathe more easily. Like Sidall Junkin, they wheezed and spat great gobbets of mucus black as printer's ink, all over the pink and violet heather; but there was a spring in their strides which they never displayed in the village. He took some heather home to his great-grandmother and noted that her skin colour was green as the plant and he told her of the trip to the moor. She said that she was glad, and with the cotton wool haloed about her head she looked like a dead angel. My father continued for as long as I can recall to take a car load of the less fortunate each week into Wharfedale.

The motor remained parked on the common at the side of Henrietta's laboratory and was washed twice a week. On only one occasion was it vandalized, and that was when a boy from another village stole a headlamp. It found its way to a pub at Middleton where the landlord, realizing what it was, returned it to William and apologized for the thief's bad behaviour. Such was the fame of the Jam Sahib's motor.

The imprisoned stones yielded little information to my demented great-aunt. At night they shone white and mauve from between their black neighbours, appearing a ghostly mosaic under the moon to those who viewed from across the common. During the day, however, the coating of soot which they quickly collected gave them a dull and grimy look, that is until it next rained, when they were again washed clean. Then they glistened as cold stone does and the moss beneath the coat of paint stretched itself. Seated in her striped deckchair Henrietta waited and prised time apart. She created a continuous present pulled high as the laboratory walls and from the safe limbo she was able to see that everything which had passed carried the historian's stamp of inevitability; yet there was nothing at all inevitable about that which was to come. Here in her waiting room, walled off from the world in both space and time, she would wait. Was she waiting to bring history to an end she wondered? Here in this super present would it all finish? Or was she waiting for some accidental happening to nudge events along? And what of God? Was she waiting for the Almighty to cause the unfolding of some great plan, or even perhaps for Him to tumble her Jericho there and then in her extended and stretched present just as He must have tumbled the dinosaur bones on to her father?

Hadn't Mr Darwin put an end to that nonsense though? Wasn't it now quite acceptable to see both history and nature travelling an unbroken line from their beginning and on into a never-ending and disappearing future? Ah, beginnings she thought. Where is the beginning of history then? Man's consciousness, she supposed. When nature was conscious enough to influence events, that's when history started. Isn't that what she had meant by her journal being a history, a book of causes? It was her own awakening consciousness that had first made her aware of the stones. But what had become of her since that first day, after the beginning of history? What line did she travel that old Dr Cartwright could not see the woman she so earnestly hoped would be found lodged between the stones in her journal? Her book of facts as the old doctor called it, her description of nature. Had she influenced the stones at all? She was beginning to doubt that she had; yet they had undoubtedly influenced the events in her life. Day by day by day, hadn't they? But what if the stones constituted an ever present even before the building of the laboratory, before the now. Perhaps they formed a present in which she had grown very old. Was her life to be but one day in the existence of the stones? Was the waiting room no more than a selfish indulgence which, like with her father, in the end would destroy her? Would she herself, too late, bring down the walls of Jericho? Too late because she had not even begun to do what she knew she must, and she returned again to thoughts of bringing the world to an end in the present. She must act, not wait. She didn't have to be the passive agent. Had she not acted, demonstrating her freedom of will only the other day in the scullery with Elyahou Tsiblitz? Had she there not changed the world?

If old Dr Cartwright was correct and it was the juices in nature which brought about biological change, then they managed things in a very slow manner, unlike historical change which came about much more quickly. And the agency through which that change came about was knowledge. Second-hand, third-hand knowledge passed from father to son, mother to daughter. This was the asset which progressed the historical world. Knowledge and reason both. Learned as much from our contemporaries as our fathers. Her grandmother had been correct when at Sidall Junkin's funeral service she had said that God was an engineer. God was a contemporary progressing the world through man's knowledge and man's reason and a whole new world was coming because of it, and she should act and be a part of it. So she decided she would be positive and brought the world to an end in that artificial present stretched and yawning between the walls of her strange laboratory.

But the idea of the end of history in the present is a nonsense, a lie, a fiction. The line which history travels doesn't stop, it just bends a little, loops perhaps, and the story becomes retold.

So Henrietta wrote in her journal for that day, 'My grandmother, who was born on the day of the battle of Waterloo, slowly climbed the slope of Hunger Hill.' She then went on to recount how her grandmother had encountered Duncan D'Arcy and Lady Annabelle Kerr and the coming to our village of a strange foreigner called Elyahou Tsiblitz. She wrote of John Tregus and a rape and so many other things filling a whole volume. Thus did my great-aunt's history become a literary fiction and in her mind stones became real people. Many years later, discovering these volumes in an old chest of drawers, I rewrote her story, changing the relationships between herself and her characters for those between myself and those same persons, and adding a few words of comment here and there.

16

Introducing Count Schubert and Rosanne

The year after they brought the water they brought the gas to our village. They didn't in that year bring it directly to the houses, but only to the few straggled and dirty streets in the form of gas lamps which stood upon tall cast-iron standards and the light which shone brightly from their glass housings. We had one such lamp directly beyond our door, the full length of which we were able to see through the gap in Henrietta's wall. It was situated about half-way across the common and quickly became the meeting place for the lovelorn. Emily looking from the pale glow of rooms still lit by candles was able to keep a mental note of who was courting whom and by noting the sad and prolonged waiting of solitary figures, who had been jilted by whom.

It was under this light that one night a large wagon pulled by a massive shire horse came to rest. It was far too late an hour to attract the attention of any would be poker-user, for the whole terrace was wrapped in a warm and magical slumber. As the giant horse stopped so too did the two small liberty horses who were tethered by short leads to the back of the wagon.

The man who held the reins, and who was seated with his two companions at the front, looked back and said, 'I think we must have taken a wrong turning back there, in the last village. This is just a dead end.'

'No wait,' said his male companion. 'I know this place.' And peering about the common he jumped down. He banged his heels into the turf with his heavy boots. 'I know this place. I helped lay pipes under this grass.' He smiled a dazzling white smile from his ebony black face. The man on the seat put his arm about the second companion, a small fair woman with turquoise eyes, and said squeezing her to him, 'Rosanne, we shall sleep here the night. Prince Ndolo knows the place.'

She smiled back at the man, her turquoise eyes full of wonder, and crawled through into the wagon behind followed immediately by the man. Prince Ndolo tethered the big horse to the lamp standard, then climbed into the wagon by way of the high step at the rear situated between the two liberty horses.

When the terrace awoke it was to see a crimson red wagon with beautifully scripted gold lettering on its side informing all that housed inside were the full contents of Schubert's circus. The occupants were awakened by Albert who had climbed aboard and, peering into the wagon from the seat up front, was somewhat surprised to see the three occupants sleeping side by side all under one beautifully woven Mexican blanket, with Mr Ndolo in the middle, sandwiched between a man with long waxed moustaches and the most beautiful lady he had ever set his eyes upon.

Resting upon one elbow but otherwise in repose, the man introduced himself as Count Schubert and introduced the others as his wife Rosanne, the granddaughter of Madame Saqui, the famous rope walker, and Prince Ndolo of fire-eating fame. Albert offered breakfast in the laboratory and on the way back to the house pondered the marvellous dual role of flame-eater and water engineer. He decided that the prince should be the subject of a portrait.

The three visitors quickly arose, jumped down into the salmon-pink dawn and entered my great-aunt's walled enclave, there to receive bread and raspberry jam and cups of tea from the lady herself. Henrietta busily explained that her grandmother, who was almost one hundred years of age, would ordinarily have attended the visitors but that unfortunately she had been laid upon a bed of cotton wool for some time now and, at least according to her doctor, had temporarily lost her sanity. But why the blessed Lord should keep her in this state, hovering between life and death, she couldn't imagine, she told her visitors.

'I too have a grandmother whom the gods have condemned to wander,' said the woman with the turquoise eyes, 'Madame Saqui, the rope walker at the court of Napoleon. She died a long time ago, many years before I was born, but it seems her soul is condemned to walk a line between earth and sky. It is said that she is sometimes seen, a small figure in black, climbing at the rainbow's edge.'

'I've not seen her,' Albert blurted out, not taking his eyes from the beautiful Rosanne.

'Nor I,' she answered him, smiling and causing a blush to creep at his neck, 'but an old medium told me that I must perform one of her tricks before she would ever find her way into heaven.' She looked at her husband whose moustaches dripped copious amounts of tea, '*Pauvre grand'maman!*' she sighed. 'I must jump through a hoop of flames while balanced on the rope,' she explained directly to Albert whose face registered only a growing admiration for the woman and an agony for the plight of her grand'maman's soul.

'Do you?' asked Albert. 'I mean can you? Can you jump through a hoop of flame?'

'Yes, I can leap through the hoop on the ground, but not yet while balanced on the rope.' She pouted her lower lip. 'Someday, perhaps.' She sighed again.

'Are you to perform your acts here, on the common,' Lancaster asked excitedly and suddenly aware of the enormous potential of Schubert's circus.

Schubert pulled a quizzical face. 'I don't know,' he said. 'We are only here because we lost our way. We are on our way to Roundhay Park in Leeds.'

'But now you are here, you must perform at least once, Mr Ndolo.' Henrietta appealed musically to the one she had known before, hoping this familiarity might influence Schubert's decision.

'Yes, we could spread the word that you are here,' said Lancaster.

'Bring in the crowds from Castleford and Kippax,' added Albert, his eyes not leaving the face of the rope walker whose long hair now glistened gold in the weak morning sun. Such was his stare into her turquoise eye, that his artist's brain split her face asunder, and he saw her turn a fragmented joy and grief towards her husband. Like so many other artists of the day, working alone and unknown to each other, he committed her disassembled beauty to the canvas in his mind, struggling with notions of mass and space and the architecture of people.

'*Chéri,*' she pouted at her husband, 'perhaps just the once.'

Count Schubert, feeling now the intense pressure being exerted through both of his companions, agreed to a single performance to commence that evening at seven o'clock. Much work was to be done, he told the small crowd which was beginning to assemble in the laboratory, and quickly led the way back to the wagon, squeezing the tea from his facial hair with a flourish at the ends of each moustache.

While Mr Ndolo instructed the helpers in the erection of the square tent, Rosanne strung a rope between the side arm of the gas lamp and the roof of our terrace, Charley Gill securing it to our chimney pot. Our roof of course was higher than the gas lamp's side arm but because of the distance, when pulled taut, the rope showed nothing more than a slight but steady incline. Meanwhile Schubert prepared leaflets, using a John Bull printing set, and gave them to my father and the twins, and asked for them to be distributed as Albert had suggested in Castleford and Kippax.

All that afternoon Rosanne, dressed in sequinned tights and with ostrich plumes on her head walked, like her grandmother, between earth and sky, practising and preparing for the day when she would speed her antecedent's soul upon its journey to heaven. The square tent, striped like seaside rock, slowly unfurled then rose, a magic castle slap bang out of the middle of our common. By six o'clock the tent had been erected and people were pouring from far and near on to the green area beyond the terraced houses.

At a flap in the tent wall Count Schubert admitted the customers one at a time jangling their silvery sixpences in a cocoa tin. At seven o'clock with much embarrassment he had to explain to the many still outside that the tent was full, not another person could he admit to stand about the small ring inside. He had to concede that my father and his brothers had done an excellent job and promised there and then that there would be another performance at the same time the following evening. He then explained that as a consolation to the disappointed if they bought their tickets now he would only charge them half price. The offer satisfied most, the few complainants seemingly having just arrived the worse for drink, but Charley Gill who had assumed the role of policeman cracked a few heads together and quickly dispatched them noisily back to the pub.

The show began with Rosanne, still dressed in her sequinned tights, riding around the ring astride the two liberty horses. She performed somersaults and various acrobatic tricks to thunderous applause and deafening whistles. Her husband then came into the ring and demonstrated his amazing teeth using them to dismantle an orange box. Having pulled out the nails with his teeth, he then demonstrated his amazing feet by reassembling the box using his toes to hammer back in the nails.

The famous fire eater, Prince Ndolo, was then introduced. In a hushed silence the African doused flames, breathed flames, ate flames and then, quite accidentally, set himself alight. Rosanne standing by with a bucket of water had thrown the contents, within a second, over his head. The Prince, unharmed, then demanded to know where the water had come from before he could continue with his act. Schubert, uncertain of the relevance of his demands, accused the fire eater of time wasting and insisted that he continue to give the public their money's-worth. Before the argument could get too far out of hand, Mrs Henderson had shouted up from the audience that there was no need for Mr Ndolo to worry for she had drawn the water herself from the new tap in her scullery. The prince smiled at her and waved. Mrs Henderson smiled back. Emily glared at Mrs Henderson, then at the prince. Bill Pettit glared even harder at Mr Ndolo. The act continued. Amid wild cheering the popular black-man eventually left the arena to be replaced by the husband and wife in Red Indian costume. Firstly he threw knives at her then, with the aid of a whiplash, he removed cigarettes from her mouth. Albert winced each time the angry leather passed within an inch of her pretty mouth. While everyone else applauded, Albert quietly felt the pain. Albert was in love. But why did Mr Ndolo sleep in the middle, he asked himself. Why didn't she sleep next to her husband?

Count Schubert then introduced Princess Ndolo, the famous her-maphrodite, and Albert, because he didn't understand the word, still didn't know why. In fact it's doubtful if any of those present in the audience knew the meaning of the word hermaphrodite when Count Schubert introduced the princess, but they certainly knew when she removed her golden cloak, for Mr Ndolo had breasts. Tits as big as watermelons, yet from the great bulge in his pouch they all knew he had male parts as well. The ladies hid their eyes, the men hooted and whistled. Mr Pettit called him a black pervert. Albert now knew why Mr Ndolo slept in the middle and his love became an angry love. He refused to clap the act from the arena.

Rosanne then walked a short rope in her ostrich plumes and danced back and forth ten feet from the ground. The entertainments ended with Schubert challenging for a fight. Any man who could last three minutes would be given a golden guinea. Albert, incensed by the way in which the count treated his wife, stepped forward before anyone could stop him. The boy shaped up, southpaw, to the circus owner, received a single blow to the side of the head and was carried off unconscious amid laughter. Mr Pettit, who wished to demonstrate his anger against the employment of black perverts, then stepped forward but a right cross followed by a left uppercut sent him quickly to the same place as Albert. When Charlie Gill was floored and at the count of ten was still found to be wandering about on his knees, the audience knew that they were in the presence of a true champion and all volunteering ceased.

The wild applause which greeted the trio of performers when they came to take their final bows suggested to Count Schubert that this little backwater with its wide common might indeed be a place for future performances.

17
Tsiblitz cruising

Cissy Tsiblitz awakened her husband who was sleeping in the lower berth. She spoke in Italian softly tugging at his silk pyjama jacket.

'Wake up, darling. Wake up, the engines have stopped.'

Elyahou sat up in bed very slowly rubbing the sleep from his eyes and yawning deeply. He looked at his watch. They had retired to their cabin only forty minutes ago.

'What? What is it?' he asked.

'The engines.' She spoke softly but exaggerated each syllable as one does when speaking to a foreigner.

'What about them?' he asked scratching his head.

'They've stopped.'

Elyahou sat there concentrating his attention on his bottom. Sure enough the gentle throbbing which had accompanied them the four days since leaving Southampton was no longer pulsing through the sprung mattress. He swung his legs out of the bed and noted the lack of vibration on his long toes when they met the floor. He wiggled them a moment hoping that this might get the ship moving, but felt nothing either on the soles of his feet.

'What do you want me to do?' he asked.

'Go and see,' she said quietly in the same exaggerated way as before. Without expression he stood up, put on his dressing gown and slippers and left the cabin. At the end of the corridor by the stairs he found a steward.

'Why did we stop?' he asked.

'Dunno, sir. I expect it's nothing.'

Several people, warmly clad, hurried past them and up the stairs. Elyahou allowed his gaze to follow them until they had turned the corner and disappeared from his view.

'I'll go and see,' he said, nodding after them.

'Expect it's nothing much, sir,' the steward repeated.

He climbed three flights to the sun deck. Several people stood about quietly talking in small groups. The night air was cool, the sea dark. The sky dazzled with bright stars clearer than he could ever remember seeing them, but the strange lack of moon lent a darkness to the night. He looked again to the black sea. Without seeing it, but from the total lack of movement of the ship, he knew it to be very still. As a crew member scurried by, Elyahou grabbed the seaman's arm.

'What's happened?' he asked.

'Nothing for concern, sir,' the sailor assured and pushed past continuing his urgent journey along the well-lighted deck. He then overheard an old man telling a lady wrapped in several furs how he was sure that the engines had started up again. Elyahou peered over the side of the ship and noted the tell-tale thin white line of foam which told him that the old man's statement was correct. The ship was moving again. He made his way back to the cabins to assure Cissy that all was well. She was already waiting for him, fully dressed and in the corridor.

'Get dressed,' she instructed, following him into the cabin.

'Now don't upset yourself, dear,' he said, 'it was probably some small mechanical fault. Everything's all right now. We're moving again.'

. 'Elyahou,' she said, braving herself to break bad news, 'Elyahou, the ship has hit an iceberg.' Her lower lip started to tremble.

'An iceberg?' he said, turning and taking her by the shoulders.

Cissy nodded. 'A steward told me.'

'Oh, nonsense,' he said, hugging her to him. 'But even if it were true, this ship's unsinkable, remember.'

'Yes,' she smiled, pulling away and looking into his eyes. 'You and your stories. You'd tell me anything,' she added good-naturedly, and sniffed back the tears.

'That's because I'll believe anything myself,' he answered her laughing. Nevertheless, he was beginning to wish that he'd never agreed to the voyage. It had been his wife's idea. He'd been working too hard at the factory in Berlin, she said, and needed a holiday. Anyway she wished to see her family in Paterson, New Jersey. She'd not seen Mama in years. So when she'd learnt of the *Titanic*'s maiden voyage to New York she'd pressed him to buy tickets; after all they could afford it now, he being one of the largest manufacturers of motor car tyres in the world. An Atlantic crossing with *hoi polloi* on the world's finest liner would be eminently suitable to solve both problems, she had said. He'd get away for a while and she'd see Mama. He wished now that he'd never agreed to it, but he kept reassuring his wife all the same.

'It is unsinkable, dear. It is, I assure you,' he said, as if he believed it, and started to dress. 'And even if we have scraped an iceberg little damage will have been done, I assure you. I've been on deck and there's no sign of damage. All is very quiet.'

Cissy helped him on with his jacket and overcoat and, when a steward knocked at their door and asked them to go up on deck with their lifebelts on, they'd joined a throng of passengers in the corridor. On the stairs he still insisted that it was only a precaution because the *Titanic* was unsinkable. And everyone about them agreed that the ship couldn't sink for it had been designed not to sink. Why, boats like that, with libraries aboard and salons and cocktail bars, lounges and grand bedrooms, tennis courts and swimming pools, they didn't sink. It was like imagining a grand hotel sinking. Impossible. And even when on deck for the second time Elyahou noted how the bows were now tilted downward ever so slightly he reasoned that Marconigrams would have been sent to every ship in the neighbourhood, and he told people how they'd be afloat all right when the rescue ships came to take them all off. So when an officer arrived and asked the women and the children to go down to the deck below and there take to the boats while the men stayed where they were, Cissy said, 'No, I'll stay with my husband. I'll go in his boat.'

'No, madame,' said the officer, tugging her arm. 'Please go to the boats on the deck below.'

'No,' said Cissy, shaking her arm free, 'I'll be rescued together with my husband.'

'As you wish,' the officer consented and moved along the deck issuing his instruction.

Then curiously the band appeared on the upper deck and played waltzes and hymns, and Elyahou felt more cheerful and, while still wishing that he had not come, he told his neighbours that he wouldn't have missed the experience for all the world, and people about him laughed, and his wife told them how her husband was such a joker, and they roared all the more heartily, slapping his back for appearing such a good egg.

They were able to see the boatloads of women and children, each with a few crew members, being filled and lowered from the deck below into the dark sea. They saw each one rowed off into the night and clearly felt the continual slow slippage of the ship's front end into the water. They looked about continually but never could they see any evidence of the offending iceberg. Looking out from the deck beyond the small boats, the only visible thing was a continuous line at which the sky would meet the sea, slowly dumping its load of stars from one into the other as the earth turned, and somewhere out there the inevitable sun to greet tomorrow whatever might then be left of SS *Titanic*.

There was no panic. As the band continued to play and the crew worked non-stop to release the final few boats, the realization quickly spread that for the remaining male passengers, plus the few wives who like Cissy had insisted on staying with their men, there would be no place in the boats. The music stopped. Elyahou turned to see each of the bandsmen disappear into an icy sea, all upright, still attempting to produce music from their waterlogged instruments. Other passengers followed, walking off into the deep end. The last boat left, the ship tilted at an ever steeper angle and Cissy watched the ship's deck, miraculously still well-lit, as people swam about as if in a pool.

'Dive, Cissy, dive!' Elyahou shouted, grabbing his wife's hand and pulling her with him through the cold air to splash into the iciness seventy feet below. He hung on to her as they went down under the calm surface, held her hand as they swam like fish, then felt a short tug and she was gone, and he was rising upwards in the darkness. He broke the surface only two or three feet from a collapsible raft manned by crew members who, even before he could look about and shout for his wife, had hauled him aboard. 'My wife,' he protested. 'My wife is here somewhere.' But they were busy sailors and hauled another three men aboard. Then a stoker, dressed only in a singlet and shorts who had been appointed captain for the occasion, instructed his men to row like hell away from the black stern of the ship which now pointed like an accidentally hammered finger into the sky.

Elyahou remained both physically and mentally numbed until the dawn came, painting a line of hitherto invisible bergs a rosy hue, like pink champagne which had frozen in the chilled wind. There was excitement in the raft. They were to be rescued, he learned. Rowing around a large iceberg they came upon their rescue ship and joined the queue of boats waiting in the still, calm waters to be emptied of their cold and hungry loads.

Once aboard the rescue ship he found it to be a cruise ship, SS *Carpathia*, which had been bound for the Mediterranean. A passenger called McDevitt kindly lent him a spare set of clothing and he quickly sent a Marconigram to Berlin informing the factory of his own safety but of the fact that Mrs Tsiblitz had gone missing. The *Carpathia* changed its course for New York.

In New York Mama Bresci greeted him with wet kisses and wept like she'd not wept since the death of her Gaetano. At the factory they waved flags, German, Italian, American and British, and wore black armbands. He told Mr Meyer, his secretary, that it had been a cock-up. A typical English upper-class, fucking cock-up. Only enough lifeboat capacity for one-third of the persons on board, he said.

'For a few pennies more, sir,' said Meyer stiffly.

'It's not the pennies, Mr Meyer,' said Elyahou, 'it's the lack of foresight and that bloody certainty the English have. Certainty that no one's to blame, not on their side anyway. Even the bloody passengers left behind couldn't believe they'd been let down. It was all so good-natured, Mr Meyer, as if they were practising – teaching us all a bloody good lesson and practising for something.'

18

Albert learns of lies and truths and
Elyahou finds a partner

On the day of the second performance of Schubert's circus the village awoke to a grey dawn. A heavy cloud of steam hung about the winding-engine shed, disappearing it from view. The morning air, pregnant with its own moisture, fell in upon the white cloud rounding it, even kneading it a little but emphatically not allowing it to rise to reveal the hidden structures at the pit head. The villagers, who knew their weather only too well, told Count Schubert that the warm steamy object would probably remain most of the day but by nightfall would have dissipated as if it had never been. But, he was told, if he was in need of warmth during the day, there was no better place to be. It was the villagers' very own Turkish bath he was informed.

'A *Schwitz*,' he said.

'Yes, a *Schwitz*,' Lancaster answered, setting down his kinematographic camera upon its tripod and not understanding a word of German.

So it was, with a large white ball settling about the pit like dough, circus performers emerging from their red and gold wagon and Lancaster preparing to film that strange troupe, that Elyahou Tsiblitz drove a white Rolls Royce on to the common, parked it alongside the Jam Sahib's motor car and asked Albert, seated at his easel in Henrietta's laboratory, if he may see my great-great-grandmother. Flustered by the rubber man's sudden appearance, my uncle asked him to wait and went selfconsciously into the house. Left alone in the walled enclave, the Transylvanian studied the work on the easel. What appeared to be two pierrots, one black-skinned, the other white with a single large turquoise eye, stared back at him. The whole composition was made up of simple geometric shapes, triangles, cubes and circles, each weighted differently with various colours. He slung his gaze to Hunger Hill and noted how in the grey light definition had gone. The mountain's sombre face climbed bleakly to an angular peak. The dim-toned sky hemmed in the brooding rock. How clever, he thought, looking back to the canvas stretched on the easel. Clever and sad, for he saw how the turquoise eye shed what could only be a small white tear, as if the moon were tumbling from out of the sky.

'These are shattered worlds,' he told my uncle when he returned. 'How come a boy like you can paint such a tableau of destruction?'

They both looked to Hunger Hill, hearing the whirr of Lancaster's camera from beyond the wall.

'That camera can never capture what's behind the peak, Mr Tsiblitz. Lancaster films only what the camera sees, the reality of the circus in this instance.'

'And what about you, Albert, what do you paint?'

'The same thing, Mr Tsiblitz.'

'The reality of the circus?'

'Yes, but from a different perspective. I shall call it *The Water Engineer and the Lady with the Turquoise Eye*.'

'I see. You paint with much love, Albert, but you must learn to distinguish between what you see now and what you think will come. Don't confuse your tenses, Albert, not even on canvas.'

There was satisfaction in his voice, and assurance. The tones one hears from a man who has just learned a secret. A mystery solved although the suspicion had been held a long time.

Albert searched the foreigner's face for what seemed an age, then he said, 'I nearly died once, but it's the same me as here and now.'

'Yes, that's all very well. The past and the present are one, Albert; the sum total of you, Albert Brightside is your past right up to this very second. But it was the future I referred to, don't confuse what you now see with that which it will become.'

'But you stand there now, Mr Tsiblitz. You bring the future. I've heard you say it. I've heard you promise to bring the future. How can you do that if you are not confusing tenses?'

'Someone has to invent the future, Albert,' the rubber man shrugged.

'But aren't we all inventing a future, all of the time? What's so special about your future?'

'Yes, we all invent a kind of future; we all go about inventing the inevitable future. Like wars. It seems to be very easy to invent the destructive future. Dissipation is the way of the world, Albert. But someone has to invent the constructive and useful too. It's like extracting beautiful lies from a terrible matrix of truth. It's like taking one of these coloured stones from out of the black wall.'

Albert stared at his aunt's laboratory walls. He had never considered destruction as being an inevitable thing before, nor had he considered destruction as truth, but Elyahou Tsiblitz was making him see, by omission if by no other means, that there was nothing inevitable about the safekeeping of the world. It would have to be invented. It would have to come as a fiction, written out of the dark.

'And what lies did you bring with you today?' he asked of Elyahou, not in the least bit cynically.

'Come,' said the foreigner, casting his eyes to the gap in the wall. Albert followed him to the white Rolls Royce. Elyahou opened the rear door and motioned for the boy to step inside. Albert was immediately aware of a sharp drop in temperature, particularly about his feet and legs. A metal box, about one and a half foot cube, stood in the middle of the floor in front of the rear seats on which they now sat.

'Do you see that?' said Elyahou.

'What is it?'

'It's a cold box. It works off the battery.'

'What's it for?'

'It refrigerates things, keeps them cold.' Elyahou opened the lid and put his hand into a smoking iciness. He withdrew a small glass container which appeared to be empty and handed it to my uncle. 'Do you know what that is?'

'Ice,' Albert said, turning the container in his fingers, and peering hard at the opaque fuzziness within.

'Good boy. Yes, ice. But it's a very special ice.' Albert looked at him questioning the speciality of the ice.

'It's from an iceberg,' Elyahou explained.

'An iceberg?'

'Yes, and not any old iceberg. It's from the iceberg which sank the *Titanic*.'

My uncle's eyes opened wide as saucers.

'You can have it,' Elyahou told him, dismissing those big hungry eyes with a wave of his hand. 'A present.' Albert was too thrilled to say anything but the saucers had indicated his appreciation of the gift.

As they left the motor and re-entered the laboratory through the hole in the wall, Elyahou said, 'I have also brought something to aid your manhood.'

'What's that about manhood?' It was Henrietta who spoke. She was standing by our door and the words caused Mr Tsiblitz to blush upwards from his neck to his forehead. Albert never would have believed it possible for anybody to turn so red. 'I believe you wish to see my grandmother,' she said, ignoring her visitor's rubrication but inwardly congratulating herself on being able to bring about such changes in his blood supply. She had embarrassed him; that gave her a power she had not felt before. 'My grandmother is unwell,' she went on before he could answer. 'She has lost her memory, but as you must be counted a special friend of hers I can hardly deny your request. Please come in,' she invited, ignoring his smile. Henrietta led him through the empty parlour and up the rickety stairs to the bedroom. Her grandmother was still lying upon a bed of cotton wool and the Transylvanian was shocked to see how green and wizened was his elderly friend.

'Emily and I bathe her daily, but we don't seem able to rid her of the black lines on her face. No sooner do we wipe off the soot than it returns. It's like it were coming from within; a hundred years of coal dust oozing out.' Henrietta then bent close to the old woman.

'Wake up, grandmother, there's someone to see you,' she said. ruffling the sleeve of her nightdress. The old eyelids flickered upwards, like shades at the windows, to reveal eyes as mischievous as he would ever remember them.

'It's Mr Tsiblitz, grandmother,' Henrietta shouted.

'I can see that, girl,' said the old woman, startling her grand-daughter for a moment. Henrietta looked to Elyahou a second in panic, then composing herself said, 'It's the first time she's recognized anyone for months. Please don't tire her with bothersome questions.'

'Hold tha tongue, lass, and get downstairs,' ordered the old woman and, with her newfound confidence fully recovered, my great-aunt descended to the parlour below. Elyahou sat upon the bed and told the old woman that a war was coming and he felt powerless to prevent it.

'This country and Germany too – they are both full of hate for one another. Filled with people like your Mr Pettit, it will be impossible to avert a war. They call themselves socialists but they're not. They're working class, they're trade unionists but they're not socialists.'

'What are they then?'

'I don't know. They're not liberals either. They have an almost pathological hatred of everything that's not of themselves.'

'They're called nationals, luv. They believe in their country and their king, right or wrong.'

'But they're nothing more than cannon fodder for the capitalist wars.'

'What do you expect? If the state has a cannon, it's got to have an army.'

'And if it's got an army it has to have an enemy,' he suggested to her.

'That's right, luv. It's the way of the world.'

Elyahou suddenly saw that the small square window had been filled with massive sequinned thighs which disappeared as abruptly as they had arisen. He noted too that they took themselves off heavenward. The strange noises from the roof suggested that they had been safely there received.

'Pigeons,' the old woman muttered. 'Ernest should do summat about the pigeons.' She seemed to turn more green as the bile rose in her blood. 'Did tha steal the Ascot Gold Cup?' she suddenly asked him. Elyahou stood and watched expectantly, then the small window filled with soft sequinned buttocks rubbing worlds together. He watched them recede from view as the taut wire which supported them sprang to life in a strange twangy harmony.

'No, but I know who did,' he said, turning from his view of the common to the old woman. 'He was an over-exuberant lieutenant to the cause. The cause needed money but some things are beyond destruction. It was senseless to steal a thing like that.'

'And the hat?'

'My brother-in-law. It was his hat. I found it among my things. I had to be rid of it, but I was too sentimental. You saved it for me.'

'*Giaconda?*'

'I returned it to Paris,' he said, turning again just in time to see the window filling once more with the sequinned thighs. My great-great-grandmother started to laugh loud enough to bring Henrietta up the stairs. By the time she had reached the top step her grandmother was rambling on about being glad, and then complained of feeling unwell and of not knowing who she was. Henrietta asked Elyahou to leave as she tucked up the wizened old woman with the olive green skin. He went, but not before he had seen the small square window fill again with sequinned buttocks, bringing worlds into being and shattering others in hopeless collision.

By the time Elyahou had returned to his motor, word had spread that the rubber man had come again to the village. Despite the counter-attraction of the circus performers at practice, the enthusiastic greetings of the gathering crowd of women and children showed that the Transylvanian had lost none of his magical attraction. They wanted to touch him. They wanted to touch his motor. And more than anything else they wished for the inflatable suits. And the sale of course – what had he got for them this time? What wonders from an inventive world would he cast among them today?

'But first, the suits, ladies and gentlemen' – his eyes twinkled at the children – 'and I have a real surprise. At my factory I have perfected the flying suits. There will be no more bouncing around, no more earthbound children; today you shall all fly. Eagle, osprey, bee and bat, gulls and tits, parrot, pig and pterodon – dozens of them. Here you shall all fly today.'

'Pig?' shouted Bill Pettit from out of the crowd. 'Pigs can't fly.'

'Today my friend, pigs shall have wings,' the foreigner called back. 'You'll see.'

'Stuff you, Tsiblitz,' Bill bawled back. 'Stuff you and your kind.' He spoke a clear king's English, lapsing out of his regional accent.

'My kind, Mr Pettit. Whatever is my kind, please tell,' the Transylvanian answered elevated now on the running board of his motor.

'Jews, anarchists, blackies, Germans. I dunno but damn you, Tsiblitz, and all like you.'

'Don't be such a killjoy, Mr Pettit,' Mrs Henderson called out as the collier pushed his way rudely out of the crowd and towards the house in which he lodged.

'Come' – Elyahou jovially coaxed the audience – 'forget the interruption. Here, there are even large size suits for those adults who wish to savour the wonder of flight.' Then, taking up in his hands a suit of green rubber, he pushed his way out of the throng to where Lancaster stood alone filming the proceedings. Looking directly into the lens he confronted my uncle.

'Come, Lancaster, show them. Show them that there is no need to be afraid.'

'Yes,' said Lancaster in a muffled voice from out of the black box and still turning the film, 'I'll show them.' Elyahou disappeared from my uncle's view but he could soon feel the familiar hands dextrously dressing him from behind. The bitter smell of the rubber product came again to his nostrils and then with a greater inrush of air than ever before, Lancaster inflated and sailed majestically into the air still clutching the camera to his eye. The tripod fell away landing harmlessly but with a clatter on the ground, and all the while Lancaster committed the expressions on the receding upturned faces to the recording eye of his machine. It was the very first aerial photography attempted with a hand-held camera, and it worked.

With more great inrushes of air others sailed into the grey skies until the air in our village was filled with floating people – perhaps twenty children and maybe a dozen adults, including Mrs Henderson and Charlie Gill who took off from earth like rockets holding hands all the way. Unfortunately, as they approached the rooftops they accidentally nudged Rosanne's rope where the walker was still at practice. The lady held her balance awhile, almost fell, regained her balance momentarily then, unable any longer to connect feet with line, tumbled into space all the while watched from immediately beneath by my uncle Albert. The twin, attentive, indeed expectant of the exotic lady's soft flesh about to pour itself into his clutching fingers, was somewhat surprised to receive a heavy blow which flattened him much as a falling tree might have done. For the second time in only two days Rosanne was to be the cause of my uncle's loss of consciousness. He was unable to hear therefore the many apologies shouted from above as both adults, still with hands held, probably more out of fear than affection, flew off towards the steam cloud and the pit head. Meanwhile Albert, amid heady perfumes, came to tucked under the Mexican blanket in Schubert's wagon. His hand was held and patted by the rope walker who, as she leaned over him repeating, *'Pauvre garçon, pauvre garçon'* many times, almost poured her burgeoning bosoms over him in much the same way as she so recently had cast her whole self upon him. Realizing with sudden alarm that he was occupying the approximate position that Mr Ndolo had so recently taken up, the boy quickly made his apologies and ran from the makeshift bed, still only semi-conscious.

It was with the memory of Rosanne's breasts falling to meet him that Albert stumbled back to the crowd to see Elyahou Tsiblitz stretching a rubber object about six or seven inches long between his fingers and thumbs.

'It's called a sheath,' he heard him say. 'It stretches over the penis and enables one to have sexual intercourse without fear of babies.' Albert sensed the embarrassment of the audience, but probably because the recent accident had played havoc with the zone of inhibition in his own brain, found himself asking if the sheath was washable.

'Yes, young man, quite washable, and you can peg it up with your underpants and shirts to dry on the line.'

'I'll have one then,' Albert said, amid a mixture of gasps and laughter from the onlookers.

Well, if Albert Brightside could have one so too could anybody else, thought the crowd, and within minutes practically everybody in the village was equipped with a washable, reusable condom. Only just in time, thought Henrietta, who was one of the few not to purchase a sheath, for she knew that the blue bottle on the scullery shelf revealed how near to extinction was her grandmother's female mixture. It was down to the last quarter inch and with the old woman in her present state there looked to be no hope of replenishment. Looking to Elyahou, she thought what a madman he really was and, looking to the sky, thought what a mad world he was bringing them. Mrs Henderson and Charlie Gill seemed to be mighty close to the ball of steam at the pit head, she observed.

All afternoon, Count Schubert practised alone in the tent. He put his rocklike body through crushing pain but as always emerged intact. His muscles rippling with sweat, he poked his nose outside the tent, immediately felt the chill and decided to partake of the *Schwitz* as Lancaster had advised. A quick look told him that the steam hadn't budged from its original location, so with head bowed (he was the shy, retiring sort) he made his way to the pit head. Once within the hot mass of vapour he realized how variable its temperature was, but nonetheless removed his leopard skin leotard. Some pockets were more dense than others, in fact certain areas were free of steam altogether. The lack of uniformity surprised him and he was grateful too to stumble across a small patch which appeared ideally suited in which to both relax and to bathe. The only problem was that it was already occupied by two small boys who were quite unsuccessfully trying to inflate a rubber object. He watched their pathetic attempts a while then offered his services. The boys smiled as wispy trails drifted before their faces. Although the sheaths had thick rubber walls it was no problem for the strong-man to inflate them, the inspiration coming from deep within his soma in short bursts. The more of the objects he blew into white balloons, the more the children seemed to produce. He let them rise into what seemed to be a chimney of clear air cleaving upward within the steam ball.

Meanwhile, on the common, fears were growing for the safety of Mrs Henderson and Charlie Gill. They were now dangerously near to the steam cloud at the pit head. If they were to fly into it there was no telling what might happen; a fearful accident with the winding wheel perhaps or landing amongst the belting machinery seemed favourite conjectures. Others thought they might be scalded alive in the hotter upper reaches of the ball. The temperature was unknown; nobody had ever entered from that end before. The crowd hushed as the two ballooning adults, hands locked more firmly than before, tried to fight back the approaching cloud, but the more they struggled the more perilous their situation became. With one last sad kick of their legs the two neighbours disappeared completely into the hot white steam, leaving the many onlookers both on earth and above to pray that nothing untoward should befall them. Lancaster, filming the whole sorry episode, was probably the first to see what happened next and certainly it is there preserved on film. The unfortunate pair came shooting out of the centre of the steam ball with a great whoosh at about a hundred miles an hour, supported and pushed by dozens of inflated white balloons. They were directed so far and so straight that Lancaster had to learn quickly to float upon his back to be able to film the ascent. Viewed from ground level it seemed that they almost disappeared altogether, showing in the sky as two blackbirds might on any old grey day. Then the terrifying plummeting as the two blackbirds grew bigger and the crowd realized that they had long since lost their supports. Vertically down they fell straight into the white steam ball – this bit of course is not on film – to land by the side of the now naked bather with the waxed moustaches. Now this is the truly incredible part of the story and perhaps, as Ernest later pointed out, gives credence to the power of prayer, for as all those villagers prayed for their safe landing it appears that on their way down through the steamball Mrs Henderson and Charlie Gill came across several inflated contraceptives rising to meet them, thus periodically breaking their fall finally to land on a cushion of the things which littered the ground three or four deep, these having failed to rise at all. There was, as they struck base, an almighty explosion of contraceptives, the energy from which caused the cloud to move from the centre outwards. As the steam lifted in wisps and drapes it was eventually revealed how close Count Schubert had come to being totally flattened. Charlie Gill, with Mrs Henderson on his knee and travelling in excess of one hundred miles per hour, would have been resisted by nobody, not even Charlie's conqueror of the last evening. Charlie, however, didn't hang around to find out what was happening. Believing as he did that there had been an explosion at the pit face, he tucked Mrs Henderson under his arm as if she were a rugby ball and hared off to the common as fast as he could. The count, dazed and covering his modesty with a condom, a fully blown one that is, walked back to his wagon with as much dignity as he could muster for the occasion. It was then that the shy man – looking at the ground under such circumstances no longer helped one's dignity – saw the open sky for the first time since the rubber man's arrival in the village and realized that people were actually sailing about the air above our terraced houses. Being first and foremost a man of business, the count dressed quickly and then sought out the person who was able to effect such a wondrous trick. Elyahou Tsiblitz was introduced to him as the owner of the manufactory where the flying suits had been produced. No, Elyahou would not sell his suits to Schubert's Circus. Nor would he rent them, nor make others even for £1000 each. What need had he of money? What he needed was a new life. A life which would provide him with a few comforts and an access to ordinary people whom he could entertain and service with his own peculiar brand of magic. He was still distributing condoms like seed corn to chickens when Schubert offered him partnership, a life in the circus, Rosanne, Ndolo. It would be a hard life teeming with joy and service. Would he take it? More condoms, more seed corn. Yes, he would take up the offer. He shook the hand of his new partner.

'Good. We are leaving tonight. We pack up straight after the show,' said Schubert.

The flying villagers came to land one at a time. The suits were deflated and stored away in the white Rolls Royce. The first condoms were pegged on to washing lines in those houses where occupants had been quick off the mark and by seven o'clock the steam had dispersed from around the winding-engine shed. The circus performers went through their acts as they had done the previous evening to applause as thunderous as any to be heard at the scoring of a try by the home team at the rugby ground. By the early hours of the next day, the loaded wagon pulled away, the big shire horse at last having something to do. The liberty horses trotted after it and between them the white Rolls Royce idled along, driven by Elyahou and with Rosanne and Mr Ndolo sitting in the back one at either side of the cold box.

Albert looked again at the bottle containing the iceberg but saw only water and marvelled at the sadness in science. Dissipation would be forever the way of the world.

'It were only a bit of ice, lad. 'Ow could it 'ave been from the *Titanic?* 'Ow could 'e 'ave brung it all this way, all this time. It 'd've melted lad. 'E were lyin' to thee, like 'e allus does,' said Bill Pettit.

Albert thought about the coloured bricks in the laboratory wall – inventing things from out of the darkness, like a cold box. He thought of Rosanne and grand'maman's tormented soul. Henrietta thought of Elyahou and wondered sadly if she'd driven him out forever. When the terrace awoke the next morning it was to find that the laboratory wall had been painted yellow. Outside and inside all the bricks were painted yellow. Albert would admit to nothing and swore that he'd been asleep the whole night. Some folk said that it was the work of a boy from Castleford, Henry Moore, who had visited the circus that evening. Meanwhile the flakes of paint beneath Henrietta's nails wore slowly away.

19

Revelation in the dark

The cinema at which Lancaster worked the projector was a poky fleapit of a place called the Royal. There was nothing regal about it, however, and the regular patrons, a hard-nosed bunch of realists, preferred to call it the Pigsty after the name of the owner of the establishment, Mr Pinkofsky. It was a small building tucked between a public wash-house and the smithy. The former was responsible for the building's distinctive odour, it being carried on the clothes of the washerwomen who, in the afternoon certainly, formed about half the audience. The second neighbour ensured that the afternoon performances were accompanied by the continual clanking of metal as the farrier brayed and brayed again the objects upon his anvil.

Although it was a filthy place in which to operate, and even though Lancaster knew that he could have got a similar job at one of the many picture palaces which were mushrooming in the area, my uncle stayed at the Pigsty. For one reason Mr Pinkofsky shared his enthusiasm for film and often developed free of charge the celluloid products of Lancaster's fingers turning usually with great appreciation for the results. Of course, these short, experimental films were not shown to the fee-paying audience but Mr Pinkofsky would at odd hours make the cinema available for private showings and here was a very good second reason for staying on. Lancaster was able to view the fruits of his labour and even allowed to use the projection room for the editing of his film. Mr Pinkofsky hoped that one day they would be able to produce a commercial film together.

My uncle worked six days a week, operating the projector for two and sometimes three performances each day. Since the onset of my great-great-grandmother's illness Emily had assumed the responsibility of accompanying the family on their weekly cinema treats. It was only natural once her son had landed the job at the Royal (she never could bring herself to call it anything else) that support for the establishment should be seen to come from the family. It was a loyalty which Mr Pinkofsky could appreciate and prompted him to allow them in without payment. So it was that every Saturday afternoon the family would accompany Lancaster to work, take up their seats in an audience composed roughly half of washerwomen smelling deeply of chlorine and half of urchins who scratched and passed their fleas, and wait, with breath held to conceal their rising excitement, for their family member to load the spools and get the show underway.

One Saturday, due to a mix-up with the spools, Lancaster accidentally loaded the projector with the film he had himself made during the time in which he had been flying in a rubber suit. The audience, unsure of what they were viewing (Lancaster too was unsure, for Mr Pinkofsky had only just handed him the recently developed spool), patiently waited for the action to commence. The opening unsteady shots of a crowd receding and filmed from above was novelty enough to keep them quiet. Then a short sequence in which a dumpy lady in tights and with ostrich plumes on her head fell upon a frail youth brought whoops of laughter from the washerwomen and a deep unseen blush from Albert. People dressed in animal costumes and floating in space caused uncomfortable speculation about the nature of trick photography. The sequence was met by a stony silence. There are some things that an audience would not accept even in the make-believe world of cinema. After a short interlude in which the camera seemed unable to decide where to deliver itself, the lens finally homed in on my family's earth closets and the surrounding ash-pits. A man was seen to walk along the path leading to the toilet, enter and, because the closets were devoid of roofs, was seen to drop his trousers and to sit upon our toilet seat. Why on earth Lancaster should have wished to film a man upon the toilet God alone knows, but there the camera lingered for a full five minutes amid howls of sheer pleasure from the cinema audience. It wasn't rude, don't get me wrong now, for the film was taken from almost directly above and the man's shirt tails adequately hid those bits which otherwise should have been censored out. But the audience rolled about clutching their sides and laughed at the little things people do when sitting upon a toilet. The man scratched his head right on the bald spot at the back. People fell out of their seats as he leaned forward to read the scraps of newspaper, probably the *Mercury*, strung behind the wooden door. Then as the man cricked his neck to view the sky and the unseen camera caught a face of desolate boredom the audience shrieked uncontrollably. As always when laughter becomes uncontrollable the pain came too. Oh, it hurts – it hurts, they shouted, seeking to fill their collapsed lungs with good air, most of which was outside the cinema. The man scratched his nose and twizzled his feet in the folds of trouser leg which hid them. From behind the screen the farrier rang his empty metallic sounds, braying the metal, and with tears streaming down their dirty faces they shouted stop, oh stop. Some just doubled up and keeled right over, but the film didn't stop; it kept right on running, and the farrier kept on banging. The man continued to sit and scratch and twizzle and read, then he suddenly stood up, a fragment of *Leeds Mercury* in his hand, lifted his long grey shirt tails and wiped his bottom.

'Cut, cut!' shouted Mr Pinkofsky, waving his arms frantically to the projection room, for he took seriously his duty to protect the public from such sights, but on this occasion the projectionist was unable to help. The public would have to suffer the crudity of the flickering images on the screen. Either that or hide its eyes; Lancaster was asleep. Hysteria mounted as the bottom on the screen wriggled. And what a dirty bottom it was too, a black bottom. The ghost of the closets came back to haunt William, and he thought what a dirty bottom Mr Tsiblitz has.

The urchin audience gesticulated, the washerwomen rolled in their seats and cried, and Henrietta, her heart leaden, her head stilled amidst all that simple joy, knew the cause of that bottom's blackness. Nobody could possibly read it but she knew her name was there, repeated many times. She beamed into the dark, hearing the torrents of hidden laughter then, carried on the bier of pointing fingers, she too began to howl until the stitch in her side pulled tight and thankfully at last sewed up the organ of mirth.

20

Thwaite, and how I came to possess a strange birthright

It's time now that I told you something of Thwaite. Thwaite circles the time of my family compressing the volumes of their history like grotesque bookends. At one end, in the beginning, sat Thwaite the family friend. For it was Thwaite, the mate of John Brightside who, at the very outset of my great-aunt Henrietta's chronicle, would tease my youthful forebear about his love for Jane Moore. Swallow him up boots and all, he'd said, and he was right. She did. It was Thwaite, the young mate who entered the darkness of the pit for the first time on the exact same day as John Brightside. Novices with only candles to relieve their gloom, they trapped the ventilation doors huddled together with rats for company. Eight years old, alone for ten hours at a stretch, they learned to amuse one another, learned to laugh together in an eerie darkness. Then as youths on to the tubs, chasing the lasses in their grubby skirts, chasing them and catching them in a torrid blackness that only those who'd been to hell could describe. And the two mates grew and learned to love. To love the women, to love one another as only best mates can. Then into their twenties and manhood, the one married, the other single but still in that stinking hole, the best of friends, trusting, trusting. For a hewer on his side, working an eighteen-inch seam, had to learn trust, and as the coal chipped away the trust grew and entwined them like trails of stonecrop growing from the crevices in search of the sun. The sun had to be there somewhere; even under the rotten earth they had to believe they'd find the sun. Trust in each other's ability to find the sun.

So, how come Thwaite ends up a coal owner and succeeding generations of Brightside finish up digging coal? I'll tell you, I'll tell you. The land all around both in our village and miles away in the village where Thwaite and John Brightside lived and worked was owned by one family. The Phillipses had owned the land for centuries and there were good Phillipses and bad Phillipses, but at about the time of John Brightside's marriage Snotnose Phillips took up his inheritance and moved into the manor house. It was Thwaite who christened him Snotnose on account of the fact that, unlike his father, he could never demean himself to speak with anybody who lived on his land. It seemed that they were only to dig out his coal, fatten his cows and sheep and pay him rent for the privilege of doing so.

But Snotnose had a weakness; he liked a gamble. He was particularly keen on the cards and would spend weeks on end at his London club dissipating his fortune. So it shouldn't have come as a surprise to find that one day he'd suffered too heavy a loss and as part payment of his debt he had to sign over the deeds of some of his land to Viscount Fitzroy somebody or other, a man who had never travelled north of Grantham and frankly never had any wish to do so. The land which had changed hands wasn't worth much; it was poor land, and extended to a total of less than fifty acres. It didn't include the pit or the village where Thwaite and Brightside lived, but it did include an old disused pit and a few small farms and it was a shock to those people to find that the landowner was quite prepared to gamble away their houses and their stock at the turn of a card. But it must have been even more of a shock for them to learn that the Viscount didn't want the land or the stock, or their rents for that matter. To him, Yorkshire might have been as distant and as inhospitable as the North Pole for he immediately issued an offer (probably to rub old Snotnose's face in it a little harder, for he wasn't liked at his club either) to all tenants on the Phillips estates. He offered to give to the first person who could provide him with four winners in a day's racing at an Ascot meeting title to the land which he'd recently won. Notices were posted on the farms which he then rightfully owned and soon the news had reached the ears of all who dwelt on the Phillips estates.

Thwaite at first suggested that he and John Brightside should offer a combined entry choosing two possible winners apiece, but my great-great-grandfather protested that because his wife disapproved of gambling he could not lend his name in entry to such a competition. Thwaite thought about it carefully but his tendril was already trailing far ahead of that of John Brightside in search of the sun. He put forward an entry in his own name for the final day's racing at the summer meeting and his four choices came in. It was rumoured that another collier had provided the Viscount with four winners on the first day of the same meeting, but as the gentleman hadn't taken advantage of the tips given, choosing a different entry for that day, the form was declared void. I have no idea if there ever was truth in that rumour but the Viscount certainly used the Thwaite entry and accumulated a small fortune on the day, for all four horses were rank outsiders, and being the gentleman that he was he coughed up the title deeds.

On taking possession of the title (he was made to receive the documents at the London Club), Thwaite suggested that the Viscount should give him a percentage of his winnings from the final day's racing; after all, he told him, his winnings surely were much in excess of the value of the land. The Viscount was so taken with the cheek of the collier that he gave him £1000 on the spot. So Thwaite was learning the rudiments of capitalism even before he'd come into his property. Then on returning to Yorkshire, he sold the livestock, sacked the tenants and moved into the big house. He sank a pit on the land and built our village of terrace houses, then he invited the labour in, and one of the first to come up from the village where until so recently Thwaite himself had been living was the youthful James Brightside with his new wife Aggie. And they moved into our quiet house that first day to watch the teeming rain.

Then at the other end of our history, much older and fatter and with his top hat and cane, sits Thwaite the relative, my other great-grandfather. About nine months after Elyahou Tsiblitz's last visit our village experienced a baby boom; his condoms developed holes, I'm afraid. They appeared to be excellent on first using but reuse wore the fabric thin; eventually they burst, every single one of them. And there was no more of great-great-grandmother's female mixture to see the lasses all right. Well, as I say, there was Thwaite the bookend holding back the final volume for all he was worth and there was me bursting at his granddaughter's belly. And with John and James and Ernest and William right behind me, Thwaite couldn't hold it any more and I came tumbling into the world with waters and words and all ready to write more volumes. Old Dr Cartwright said I had eyes like my mother who in turn had inherited hers from the coal owner. A lively blue and forever searching he said they were, and told us all that it was a Thwaite characteristic and carried in the genes. He'd at last identified his vital spirits and his language had moved smoothly from one jargon to another. To Henrietta he confidently expounded a scientific explanation, a genetic explanation for the Brightside melancholia, but she turned away from the old doctor telling him that the stones no longer spoke to her. Then she explained that she didn't mourn the loss of what had been a very special ability.

'I'm pleased to hear of it,' he told her long and elegant back, and quietly to Emily and out of Henrietta's hearing he advised that the best thing for her would be to find herself a husband and settle down to child-rearing.

On first hearing of the pregnancy, Thwaite refused to speak to his granddaughter and threatened to cut her off without a penny but she said that she didn't care, for she loved William Brightside and he loved her too, and to prove it they were soon married at the church in the next village. But Thwaite stayed away from the wedding. Then came the birth and Thwaite stubbornly refused to have anything to do with my mother. On hearing that the child looked like himself, however, his attitude softened, and then when he learned that I should be given his name, Donald, he at last decided to pay me a visit. (I think, too, the name Westminster must have aroused curiosity.) When he saw me he cried, blubbered like a child on his granddaughter's shoulder and called my father Willie.

It was an extraordinary thing for the hardened coal owner to have done and Emily said that it was all the bad coming out of the man brought on by the sight of the angel in the cot. Then he took some documents from his inside breast pocket, signed them with Henrietta's pen which still resided with the rent book on the mantelshelf, and handed them to my mother. It was my birth-right he told her. I had become the owner simultaneously of a coalmine, a cemetery and a museum, for he had assigned me the title to the disused pit at the bottom of Hunger Hill. We didn't see a lot of him after that, but Ernest still paid him three shillings and five pence rent each week, certainly until the week Thwaite died.

EPILOGUE

After the departure of Schubert's circus, Albert fell into a morose silence. It lasted until well after my christening and nobody in the family was sure whether it might have been because he had not had opportunity to use his condom (considering the population explosion, if it were so, then he must have been the only one not to), but Albert knew the reason for his mood only too well. For it was in his heart. Within its slowed beatings there was a pining for the woman he loved. Rosanne the rope walker, she of the sequinned thighs and the falling breasts, she with a grandmother crawling towards God along the outer edge of the rainbow (what colour lane would that be) who had first quickened and then, on leaving, slowed his heart to a drawl. Lub! Lub! Worst of all, was the uncertainty. Who was her lover? Schubert? Ndolo? Tsiblitz? All three perhaps? Albert had to find out. But to find out would take money and they were probably somewhere on the continent by now. Who knows, France, Germany, Spain? He decided to sell his few possessions. He received four guineas for the *Blue Boy* (an inferior copy) and three guineas for the *Mona Lisa* (an even more inferior copy). An assortment of other paintings brought him another twelve pounds ten shillings. Less than twenty pounds was hardly enough with which to be planning a trip to Europe. Albert's dejection worsened.

One day he found some undeveloped photographic plates. They were the ones he had used years ago when photographing his great-grandmother the morning of his illness. An idle curiosity caused him to have them developed and when he received them back he saw that he had been filming his great-grandmother at the Roman Wall. On her head she wore a cap and she held an old suitcase in both hands, cuddling it beneath her ugly grin as she would a small child. Now Albert of course had heard stories of the old woman's fortune and so set off immediately for Hunger Hill using his shovel as a walking stick. Albert dug earth from around the base of at least half the circumference of the wall but found nothing. He went back to the house and complained to the old woman that he couldn't find her money. He asked her where she'd hidden it, but she only reflected back his solitude by failing even to open her eyes. She breathed quick shallow breaths waiting for him to depart and he knew she wished him to leave her to whatever it was which she did when alone.

He dug more holes and found nothing. He sank holes on my land which that winter quickly filled when it rained and when Aggie came to visit towards the end of 1913 she commented how the village was beginning to revert to what it had been when she and James had first come there. Puddles were everywhere, and soft mud oozed through the very best leather squelching into the socks, but Albert found nothing and remained silent.

Then one summer night when the moon and stars were lined up, it seemed queueing above the pit head waiting to be cycled into the earth and shown the blackness of the mine below, and the dark stinking galleries would in magical turn accept the shining heavenly bodies and be cleansed for ever by their radiance, a big horse pulled a red wagon on to the common jolting the occupants over the uneven ground and caused them to wake from their slumbers beneath a comforting Mexican blanket. Schubert's circus came to rest once more beneath the gas lamp beyond our door. Mr Ndolo jumped from the small steps at the rear of the wagon and tethered the horse to the lamp standard. My great-aunt Henrietta on seeing that the circus had returned ran immediately from the house inquiring if Mr Tsiblitz was well and still with them.

'He's in the wagon,' Ndolo answered her.

She thrust her face between the canvas drapes at the rear to see Elyahou sitting up between the prone figures of Rosanne and Count Schubert who were still snuggled in the warmth of the blanket. A hurricane lamp hung above their heads.

'Mr Tsiblitz, I know what you have on your bottom,' she declared. The Transylvanian who had shaved all hair completely from his face and head coloured significantly, all but a healing scar on his crown that is, which remained stubbornly white. He had recently been fired from a cannon.

'I have a headache, Miss Brightside. Can it not wait until some other time?' he said.

'It certainly may not, Mr Tsiblitz. I have seen your bottom on kinematographic film and I know it has my name on it,' she insisted.

Count Schubert leaned across and tapped Rosanne. 'This must be Henrietta Brightside,' he advised. His wife opened one eye, sat up in bed clutching the blanket to her beautiful neck. 'Not the Henrietta Brightside, child of charm, poetry and love,' she said with a snigger.

'What is it that you want?' moaned Elyahou, still nursing his head.

'I want what's mine, that which I stamped.'

'My bottom? You want my bottom?' He stood up in the wagon revealing himself completely to my great-aunt – and to my uncle Albert who had now joined her. Her initial reaction was to recoil, withdraw from the sight of the naked man, but she stood her ground.

'Yes. That and the other bits,' she said.

The count and Rosanne started to laugh and playfully rolled about in the makeshift bed.

'Leave her be,' shouted Albert angrily from beside his aunt.

The count looked up, an expression of concern clouding his normally happy countenance. As Mr Ndolo somersaulted into the bed from the front end of the wagon, Schubert spoke: 'There's an awful lot of instruction being passed here, but I can't see any generals,' he said.

'I want what's mine,' my great-aunt repeated.

'And so do I,' sang Albert in the chorus of her conviction.

'Now look here,' Schubert said, allowing the blanket to fall from his shoulders and revealing his massive chest and rippling biceps, 'there's nothing that belongs to either of you in here, so please leave before I throw you out.'

'*Chéri, chéri,*' Rosanne said sulkily. She blew Albert a kiss and settled herself back into the bed.

My two relatives climbed down from the steps and walked back in that punctured night to our house, where smoke as always curled from the chimney.

Hours later war was declared on Germany. The news came hurtling from the other side of Hunger Hill and Albert went to the police station in Castleford. He told them that there were enemy aliens camped outside his house. An inspector and a platoon of infantry men were dispatched back with him and Schubert was arrested immediately. The inspector didn't like Austrians and Bill Pettit cheered the news from the window. After the inspector had consulted his map and found Transylvania to be a part of the Austro-Hungarian empire Elyahou too was arrested. When Bill Pettit told him that Transylvania was the place where Dracula came from, the inspector declared his aversion to vampires and decided that he didn't like Transylvanians either. He instructed the sergeant in charge to see that they were put on a train to France and then sent on to Vienna. Henrietta said that she would go too, for she was to marry Mr Tsiblitz. The inspector looked doubtful until she told him that he could take down the Transylvanian's trousers if he wished and would find her name imprinted on the man's bottom. The inspector allowed her to go, reasoning that there was no place for a woman of such doubtful moral worth in Britain at such a time of crisis anyway. Rosanne, however, was allowed to stay for she had such a lovely smile and the French too were our allies.

Bill Pettit argued that Mr Ndolo too should be arrested, but the inspector pointed out that the man was a citizen of the colonies. Mr Ndolo agreed and informed the inspector that he would like to join the British army, but on learning that he was hermaphrodite the inspector couldn't decide where to send him, so he put him in jail instead.

Albert moved in with Rosanne and lived in the wagon on the common for the duration of the war. He got a job in the pit but still had to pay my great-grandfather three shillings and five pence rent each week for the space the wagon occupied under the gas lamp. Nonetheless by the time war had ended Rosanne could leap through a hoop of flame while on the aerial wire and her grandmother was never seen again in anybody's rainbow.

My great-aunt and Mr Tsiblitz were married in Vienna and Count Schubert was their best man. Henrietta was settled with some friends of Schubert in a classy Viennese suburb and the two men went off to war. They both joined the Austrian army as privates and quickly fell in with another soldier Ludwig Wittgenstein, the philosopher. They became an inseparable threesome, at least until Schubert bought one at Cettinje. It was soon after the death of Schubert that

Tsiblitz confided to Wittgenstein the passion which his new wife had for thinking while immersing her hands and arms in water.

Meanwhile at home, Lancaster joined the Royal Flying Corps and Bill Pettit became an infantryman. Army life agreed with Bill; the regimentation of men was no different to the regimentation of the stacks in his head. He'd be a socialist when the bloody war was over, he told everybody; it was the death of anarchy. He hated bloody anarchy, he told them. He'd even been won over to the cinema. Watching a good story, with a beginning, a middle and an end from the rows and rows of seats in a darkened theatre; it was ordered. He'd learned to love the cinema, the death of anarchy. Bill died with a metal filing cabinet. It was painted battledress green and had louvred doors. The company was retreating, not very far; nobody went very far in that war – just to get there was a long way – but after that nobody went any distance. They were retreating only a few yards – from one hole to another. He and another man had been detailed to carry the filing cabinet. It was bitterly cold. He'd got his greatcoat buttoned to the neck and he'd been advised to wear his respirator; there was a possibility of gas attack. A bullet struck him and another hit the metal filing cabinet. He heard the ping as the bullet smacked into the metal. His tin helmet was still on his head and his respirator was in place as he fell back into the hole. He and the filing cabinet fell into the hole. Bill fell on top of the filing cabinet with its louvred doors. His greatcoat caught on some wire so he didn't fall all the way into the hole, just part way down the slope, and the filing cabinet which lay on its back looking up at the bleached sky prevented him falling any further too. It started to rain but it didn't prevent the gas from wafting across from one muddy hole to the next. Bill cursed everybody as he lay dying. Nobody came. Just the rain. It rusted the filing cabinet. Bill's flesh soon rotted. Even beneath the respirator the flesh disappeared. Bill became a skeleton with its feet resting on the rusted metal. The slats in the louvred door looked like rows of sandwiches, their brown crusts exposed. The pipe from the charcoal box to the mouth remained intact, like a short cable connecting nothing to nothing. Charcoal had spilled from the box, though. It was as if things had all poured out of his head, just like when he lived, but there was nobody there to rearrange the stacks. It was the kind of confusion Bill hated and he would have been glad not to be there.

GRANDMOTHER, GRANDMOTHER, COME AND SEE

To my mother

How my uncle Lancaster Brightside and Charlie o' the Terrus End came back from the War

Let me tell you about my uncle Lancaster and of the day that he came home from the Great War – that was the day on which I had been made to return to school following a nasty attack of the whooping cough.

Uncle Lancaster is my father's younger brother, a twin to my uncle Albert. When they were born, Albert was so much bigger than Lancaster that their mother, Emily Brightside, thought that the one would fit quite snugly inside the other – just like Russian dolls. Consequently, during their early years my poor grandmother lived with the perpetual fear that Lancaster might one day be gobbled into the belly of his larger brother. Old Doctor Cartwright, who knew the family's pipes as well as any water engineer would have known the layout of our drains, was unable to explain such a variation in sibling size but his son, the young Doctor Cartwright who continued in the practice of his father after the old man's retirement, considered that a battle had been going on and that the larger of the twins had been stealing all the nourishment from the smaller; he named their period of gestation as the War of Emily Brightside's Womb and he wrote a paper about it which was to have been published in a distinguished medical journal. The editor's secretary, on seeing the title, however, imagined that the piece of writing was destined for a history magazine which happened to be published by the same organization. The consequence is that the young Doctor Cartwright's observations constitute the only gynaecological tract ever to have appeared in the *Journal of World History*. It was published complete with diagrams and bibliography and it completely mystified the historians.

Young Doctor Cartwright was unable to explain exactly what had happened but I think there was a notion that Albert had been sitting on his brother's umbilical cord, perhaps even giving it a nasty nip with his transparent embryonic fingers and causing a kind of back pressure to be built up, so diverting most of the available nourishment down his own tube. Their two volumes were soon to even up, however, when in early childhood Albert suffered a terrible illness from which he almost died and during which time Lancaster decided that it was time to inflate. Again, nobody was very sure as to what exactly had taken place, but by the time that Albert had recovered from his illness, the two were as alike as two peas. Young Doctor Cartwright saw it as an extension of the War in Emily Brightside's Womb – the weaker hitting back at the stronger, but being very careful in choosing his moment, so to speak.

By the time that I was born, early in 1913, it was almost impossible to tell them apart. By then the two brothers were both accomplished artists; Albert had already completed some of the world's most famous one hundred paintings, copied from a book which Great Great Grandmother had bought, and Lancaster had photographed several reels of kinematographic film – experimental kinema he called it. Before he had gone off to join the Flying Corps, my uncle Lancaster had been employed as the projectionist at the Royal Picture Palace in Kippax and due to the kindliness of the owner, Mr Pinkofsky, he was able to view his own experimental films during those hours in which the establishment was not being used by the general public. Albert never went to war, choosing instead to go down the pit with my father. He lived in a gaily painted wagon which was parked beneath the village gas lamp. He shared it with a French rope walker called Rosanne and they had a child called Clarrie who was a couple of years younger than myself. My grandfather, Ernest Brightside, as he bounced Clarrie upon his knee said that she had a skin like porcelain. As the only other porcelain figure which I knew of was a pot spaniel which stood on our mantelshelf, it wasn't until I was about ten years old that I realized Clarrie to be human. Until then I somehow imagined her to be a dog.

Clarrie and I were struck down with whooping cough at about the same time and young Doctor Cartwright had advised our parents that we should be taken to sit by the gas works. My father and uncle Albert, each carrying a chair from around our dining table, walked the two of us into Castleford, a journey of several miles. When we arrived at the gas works there were already dozens of children sitting in the hazy sunshine forming a circle about the small gasometer. They were tied down to their chairs with white cord and each was coughing his guts up. Both Clarrie and I were admitted to the circle like children get absorbed into a game of ring o' roses except that we were unable to hold hands for we too were tied down to our chairs. Then we were left to breathe the foul air whilst our fathers went off to the pub. Clarrie started to bark and I watched her porcelain face and thought, poor little spaniel. Then I looked about me at all the other barking children and wondered which of them had skins of porcelain. Which of them are dogs, I wondered? I started to cough. The spasm was uncontrollable and the wooden dining chair jumped up and down to the sound of my coughing and with me still firmly strapped to it. The air was foul, like one of my grandfather's farts. I could hardly breathe. Then in one of those rare periods when I was able to stop the whoop I saw that everyone else was in spasm, spittle smearing their red cheeks and full wet lips. Although I'm sure that they would have wanted to weep, there was no time for crying – there was hardly time for breathing. I thought to myself as I watched their dancing chairs and bloated faces, I thought, why am I the only one out of step, so I threw myself wholeheartedly into tune and coughed my little guts up until the chair fell over with me still strapped to it. Then Clarrie started to laugh and she was laughing and coughing so much that she too managed to tumble over her chair. The smell was now quite vile and causing some to vomit. Eventually they too toppled one by one choking in the hazy sunshine. When our fathers had returned from the pub we were mostly on the ground staring up at the sun as if it was an unexpected alien and totally exhausted from the rigours of our treatment. There was hardly a sound or a contortion from any of us; the small gasometer, a metallic sentinel, watched over us in silvery solitude. My father righted my dining chair and untying me he said to uncle Albert, 'Good stuff, this gas.' My uncle, surveying the silent children like so many dead soldiers bogging up a stinking trench in that peculiar afternoon's heat, nodded his agreement. 'Must be,' he told my father; then he untied Clarrie whose porcelain cheeks flamed as angrily as the fire in our parlour.

As I told you, by the time that uncle Lancaster came from the

War I had recovered sufficiently from my illness to have returned to school. It was my first day back. I was six years old and in Standard One and my teacher's name was Wenceslas Piggott. Senseless Spiggot is what most folk called him but my great great grandmother, Jane Brightside, who had been the kindliest of women found no exception in Wenceslas and had called him the Good King, for he had educated my father and his twin brothers way beyond what might have been expected only a few years before. He was still a young man when he started upon my own education – in his early forties, I suppose – and he had a heavy black tash. The schoolroom was painted two-tone green. There was a thin brown line which had been painted half-way up the walls and which encircled the room, with a couple of breaks only for the windows. The line however did cross the door. Anything above that line was painted a pale green colour and anything below the line was painted the colour of the muddy grass of the winter common. My uncle Albert had been invited in to brighten up the place and he had painted a couple of Turners and a Constable into the walls of the classroom. There was an unfinished Rubens at the back of the room. An outline of two full female bodies had started to appear and there was endless speculation amongst the children as to whether the ladies would be given their painted clothes or not. In their incomplete state it was difficult to imagine them one way or another for I had not so far laid eyes upon the naked female form and had no real image of what lay beneath a lady's heaving and bumping clothes, yet it was equally difficult for me to visualize two colliers' wives sprawled across that sumptuous bed in full black skirts, laced-up boots and shawled heads. In any event what they might be doing with each other in such a situation remained a complete mystery.

Wenceslas Piggott sat at his desk at the head of the class facing forty noisy children and he threw a yellow rag at me.

'Come on, Donald, lad. Tha can clean this rubbish off the board,' he said referring to the words which he had chalked on to the blackboard when teaching us about gold mining in Africa. I began to clean the board and as I watched the half white words disappearing and tried to comprehend the other half white words which remained at each arced wipe, Billy o' the Terrus End who sat by the window said, 'Please sir, there's two puppets attached to a biplane in the sky.'

Mr Piggott rose up from his desk, ambled to the open window and stuck his head into daylight. Sticking one's head into daylight from the gloom of our schoolroom was not just moving it from one abstract intensity of light to another, it was more like thrusting the head from one medium to another. Like shoving it 'twixt air and strawberry jam. Schoolroom windows were a painful reminder of the other world.

'That's not puppets, son,' he said excitedly, pulling his head back into the room. 'Them's men. Men on parachutes coming down from the sky.' And he rushed back to his desk. I felt the heat of his enthusiasm as he opened up the lid close by my face. Now here is education, I thought as I continued to wipe the zebra-striped words from the blackboard, for until that day I had learned only of how to keep myself clean at all ends and how to open a door for a lady – a category which I became surprised to know included *both* the coal owner's wife and my grandmother. I'd also learned of wool and sheep and had just started to learn something of gold; unfortunately the whooping cough had deprived me of lessons in leather and silverware. But the look on Wenceslas Piggott's face as he grabbed his spy glasses from deep within the black well of his desk, and from right in front of my nose, told me that parachutes, whatever they were, were far more interesting than anything which we had tackled thus far. I needed to know about parachutes, I thought as I watched him race back to the open window. Our schoolteacher thrust his head into the day again, this time ogling through his spy glasses.

'Well, that's odd,' he said, bringing his head back in again and looking directly at me. 'They've got no bloody trousers on.' Now parachutes sounded interesting, but parachutes without trousers sounded even better. I needed to know more and ran from the schoolroom as quickly as my small legs would take me.

'Grandmother, Grandmother,' I was shouting, 'there are parachutes coming from out of the sky and they don't have any trousers on.'

'Donald, come back, lad,' the schoolteacher shouted from the open window as I whizzed along the strip of grass at the front of our school. 'Come back, Donald, where does tha think tha's off to?'

I turned my head just for a moment, sufficient to see Billy o' the Terrus End drop from the window and attempt to race after me.

'Wait, Donald. Wait for me,' he was shouting, with Mr Wenceslas Piggott hanging half out of the window to keep a firm grip on the young lad's breeches.

It was only then that I realized that I hadn't the faintest idea of what I was doing. What is a parachute? Where am I going? Why am I running from Wenceslas Piggott? What is it that I wish to tell my grandmother? Is this really what education is all about? I looked into the sky. Two men were floating like thistledown. They seemed to be miles above me but I could clearly see that they were men and they floated like the seeds of a plant on a warm summer's day. Yes, I confirmed excitedly to myself, this is education; this is schooling worth having. I seemed to collect myself together and ran off with the bits gathering in my head and I was again shouting, 'Grandmother, Grandmother, come and see. Come and look. There are men like parachutes coming out of the sky and they haven't any trousers on.' With my eyes firmly on the men in the sky I ran slap bang into my grandmother who had wandered on to the common beyond our front door.

'What is it, Donald? What is it?' she asked, trying to still my shaking head held between her gentle hands.

I pointed into the sky. 'It's men, Grandmother. Men like parachutes. Mr Piggott says they haven't any trousers on.' My grandmother raised her eyes to heaven and we both watched the biplane trailing smoke and phut-phutting away to disappear behind Hunger Hill. Then we ran together to stand directly beneath the falling men. I gawped at the spidery trouserless legs above me as they fell through the dry still air. Then with a little drift sideways they started to climb again and we watched the parachutes going up into the blue.

'They're not supposed to do that.' It was Wenceslas Piggott's voice shouting behind us. He had brought out the whole class to observe like he did sometimes when we were on a nature ramble. 'I can't understand that,' he said, looking into his spy glasses.

The parachutes then continued in their descent until there was another small sideways movement and the men started to ascend again.

'They've got some peculiar undergarments on,' said the schoolteacher, tearing his eyes from the lenses. 'And they're bloody going up again.'

'Mr Piggott!' warned my grandmother heavily on hearing the teacher's bad language.

'Ay. I beg tha pardon, Mrs Brightside. But I never saw owt like this afore.' He looked through the glasses again. 'They've got knickers on. Great big knickers.'

My grandmother smiled as the men started to descend again. 'It must be Lancaster,' she told me excitedly. 'It's our Lancaster,' and she gave me a hug. They were now no more than fifty feet above our upturned faces and we saw how their large knickers seemed to billow out as, caught in the updraught, they filled with air and again shifted the trajectory of the parachutists' fall.

'They've bloody double gussets in 'em and they're made of silk I think,' I heard our schoolteacher telling the class.

'Well, they would have,' said my grandmother to the excited schoolteacher, 'and there's no need for such language,' she chastised. 'It was I who made them, tha naws, Mr Piggott. I allus let in a double gusset. An' now the War's over I can tell thee another thing,' she went on. 'I made the parachutes too.'

'Now, Mrs Brightside, there's no need for stories,' the schoolteacher advised.

'I did,' she protested but Mr Piggott wouldn't hear of it and concentrated his attention through the spy glasses and on to the billowing knickers of the ascending men. How strange, thought my grandmother, that men who saw themselves as educators had themselves so little stomach for the stuff of it, for what my grandmother had been telling him was perfectly true. For a period of three years now, she had been employed at Mr Gaylord's knicker factory which was situated just outside the village and on the road out to the next village – that's the village where we have our church. About two years back a man from the Ministry had paid a top secret visit to Mr Gaylord and the factory had been commissioned to make parachutes to a stolen German design. Mr Gaylord had said that it was essential war work and Emily Brightside had been entrusted, along with two other women, to cut out and stitch up the silken canopies on a special machine that had been pinched and shipped out very daringly from right under German noses at a factory in Berlin.

Now, not only was my grandmother an excellent seamstress, but she was also a designer with a most economical turn of mind. 'Waste

199

not, want not' was her motto. So when she found a way of cutting out the silk and at the same time saving an extra piece of material she thought it only right that the offcut should be put to good use and so she ran up a pair of French knickers with double gusset. She saw to it that each parachute pack when folded away also included a pair of knickers for the airmen – after all, someone was paying for the silk, so why shouldn't our brave lads have the use of it? That's why she was so certain that one of the two men falling out of our sky was her son Lancaster and she was able to make a pretty good guess that the other body dangling now almost to the ground was that of Charlie o' the Terrus End whose brother Billy was my classmate in Standard One. After all, she argued, Charlie was the only other village boy who had joined the Flying Corps. Wouldn't he be surprised to know that Mrs Brightside had made his knickers for him?

It had been an educated guess, she thought, still observing our village educator playing around with his spy glasses and wondering when he was going to teach the children something of that at which they gawped. But the view in the sky was an education in itself, really. One didn't need the comments of a schoolmaster. Wenceslas Piggott was defunct in such a situation and he probably knew it. As I had thought before even leaving the classroom – parachutes were likely to be educative. So much of an education, in fact, that even before my grandmother had mentioned his name, I knew that one of the two falling men was my uncle Lancaster. I had hardly any recollection of the man at all yet from the mythology constructed within the Brightside home I had reasoned that if a man was to fall from the sky then it would be Lancaster. It was Lancaster who had donned the flying suits of uncle Elyahou Tsiblitz and crashed to the ground on a number of occasions. It had been Lancaster who had taken the balloon ride from London together with Great Great Grandmother and who had been tipped arse over tip to the ground, with the balloon hovering only feet above the hedgerows near our home. It had been Lancaster, the pioneer of aerial photography, who had taken film of our villagers roaming about the sky like lost planets and dressed in the strangest of costumes – everything from pterodon to pig. If a man was to fall from the heavens, then why shouldn't it be my uncle Lancaster?

My grandmother had first to find him among the billowing silkiness and when he had uncoupled his harness she hugged him. She cuddled and loved him for her Lancaster had come out of the sky without trousers and displaying the jap silk knickers which she had run up and double-stitched for the entire squadron. The trouserless hero stood in the middle of our common kissed by his adoring mother and surrounded by schoolchildren. Charlie, to avoid the same treatment, quickly gathered up Billy o' the Terrus End as if he had been a dropped parcel and ran off with him to find Mrs Terrus End. Mr Wenceslas Piggott, spy glasses strapped about his neck and with drops of sweat on the ends of his heavy black tash, at last turned his attention to the education of the children in his care.

'What happened to tha trousers?' he asked my uncle plain enough for all to hear.

'Our aeroplane was stolen,' Lancaster said sheepishly.

'Gerraway. Tha's 'avin' me on, Lancaster. How does anyone come to steal an aeroplane?'

'We was just sitting there, me and Charlie. Sitting in a field near Lincoln and talking about coming home when this man climbs on to the wing, pokes a revolver at us and tells us to take off our trousers.'

'What sort of man?' asked the educator.

'He was a foreigner. A German, I should think. Perhaps he doesn't realize that the War is over, maybe he intends to fly back to Germany in our biplane. He was very pleasant but very firm and he kept on poking the gun at us. He'd obviously been listening to our conversation, because he asked us where home happened to be and when we told him he said he knew the place very well and told me to take the machine home. I think that perhaps he was some kind of spy. Once we were in the air he flung out our trousers, they're somewhere in Doncaster I think.' He seemed aggrieved that his trousers were in Doncaster. 'Then when we got here he had us bale out and took the controls himself. He's no fool, an accomplished aviator I should say.'

'Ay up,' said Mr Piggott with his glasses pointing towards Hunger Hill. ''E's bloody comin' back again.'

We tipped our gaze to the sky and saw the smoke and heard the little phut-phut as the engine almost stalled directly above our heads. Then a large object was hurtling down towards us.

'Come on, gerrout a road,' the schoolteacher advised as we all turned and fled from the falling object. It was falling so fast that we thought it was going to make a large crater in the centre of our common, so it was with great surprise that, when a safe distance from the thing, we turned just in time to see it hit the ground, bounce about twenty feet into the air and bounce again this time to a height of only about ten feet. It bounced and bobbled about for a few moments and then came to a complete standstill without causing so much as a dent in the grass. It looked peculiarly like an armchair and we approached it with caution.

'Careful,' said Mr Piggott, 'it might be a bomb.'

It *was* an armchair and my grandmother, the excitement of the day catching up with her, threw caution to the wind and sat in it. It didn't explode. She said that it was the most comfortable seat which she ever had the pleasure to sit upon for it was made completely of a bouncy rubbery material which seemed to flow and mould itself to the body. There was a note attached to the back of the object and it was addressed to the Brightside family. My grandmother read it whilst the biplane phut-phutted in a circle above. She then waved her arm at the aviator who waved back, or so we were told by Mr Piggott, who had caught the foreigner in his spy glasses.

'It's from your uncle Elyahou Tsiblitz. He says that the armchair is his latest invention and that your aunt Henrietta is well and has made a complete recovery from her madness.'

'Uncle Elyahou Tsiblitz!' Lancaster exclaimed.

'Uncle Elyahou Tsiblitz?' I chorused. That was the second piece of Brightside mythology to be introduced to my eager young ears in no time at all and I stared longingly after the aviator and the machine which was disappearing once more behind the dark slopes of Hunger Hill. 'Education,' I thought, watching the final lingerings of the smoke in the blue sky.

'Elyahou Tsiblitz,' said all of Standard One in an astonished tone, recalling their own versions of village mythology.

'Tha didn't recognize him?' Emily asked her son.

'No, Mother.'

'Lancaster. Tha's taken pictures of the man's bottom and tha didn't recognize him?'

'Be fair, Mother. He had on his goggles and a flying cap. How was I to know who he was?'

'Ay, but he weren't wearin' 'em on his backside.'

'No, Mother, but he had his trousers on.'

'Unlike some,' she said and then she sighed. 'E' tha's a great puddin', Lancaster. Come on, let's get some tea.'

We walked off between the walls of my aunt Henrietta's yellow laboratory, a rough stone structure which she had tacked on to the front of our house during the final phases of her madness. I looked back to see that Standard One was being given a lesson in physical exercises; seeing how far each child could bounce off the rubber chair. Most of the children seemed to catapult off it to a height of about twenty feet but Wenceslas Piggott, his black tash drooping in the heat of the afternoon, shot off to at least double that distance and landed in a pile of horse muck – then he took the class back to the schoolhouse, brushing down his dark waistcoat with limp-wristed hands and explaining that perhaps it was more important for them to learn about gold.

My grandmother led us into the house and she filled the kettle with water from our tap in the scullery and brought the kettle back into the parlour and placed it on the roaring fire.

'Where shall I sleep, Mother?' Lancaster asked.

'Tha'll sleep down 'ere in Sidall Junkin's wide winged chair. Mr Brown's in t'other one. The one that Bill Pettit used to have. Did tha know that Bill Pettit were dead?'

Lancaster shook his head. 'I suppose some of us had to go,' he said.

Emily thrust her hands deep into her pinafore pocket as she sat by the fire. 'Maybe,' she said, looking into the coals. 'I miss Sidall Junkin spittin' on the coals, tha naws.' She was talking of an old miner who had dossed in our parlour for years and who had died when he choked on his new set of teeth. 'Tha father and myself are in the room above like we allus was. William and Mary and little Donald are in tha great grandmother's old room at the front here. Tha naws she's gone too, does thee?'

'Ay, I heard something of it.'

'Ay. I went up to bathe 'er one day and all the green had gone from her skin. All the black, all that coal dust had gone too and she had the skin of an angel, white as Christmas buttons, and she suddenly opened her eyes and she smiled at me like she were a babe, like she smiled at thee when tha was born, Lancaster, and I thought it were all going round in a big circle and she just passed away the next minute while I was bathing her face and I were thinking how it all comes around in a big circle.'

Lancaster's lip trembled for an instant and I thought that he was about to cry. Then he said, 'Where's my camera, Mother?'

'It's under her bed,' she said. 'Tha camera's safe enough.'

My grandmother mashed the tea then she said to me, 'Go get Rosanne and Clarrie, love. Tell 'em that Lancaster's come 'ome.' Then to Lancaster she said, 'Albert's still with Rosanne in the wagon – they've a little girl now, Clarrie they call 'er.'

'Goodness,' I thought, 'today must be a very special day for my grandmother is making tea and having visits out of turn.' For unlike when my great great grandmother was alive and had run the house, Emily had a time for everything. Our parlour was a dining-room and a kitchen and a bakery and a playroom and a bathroom, a study and an artist's studio, and when the old woman had been alive it had been a laboratory and a pharmacy too and more importantly it had been all those things at one and the same time. While some had eaten, the children had played beneath the table, Henrietta had baked and Albert had painted, old Jane had made her potions and the world had passed in a mad whirl of activity. Just like it did in the Terrus End house where me and Billy played under the table whilst the rest of his large family got on with whatever it was they had to do. But Billy played in our house only at playtime – half past four till five and never beneath the table. Then the props were changed and new actors were shoved in to get on with the next activity – baking till six. Then it was bath time and the water was poured into the tin tub. Then it was meal time. Then it was time to read or study and possibly time for a little idle chatter before it was bedtime and the lodgers flew off on their dreams in the wide winged chairs like demented voyagers in the fairy stories sail away on the backs of the flying swans. Emily, unlike Jane, had got it organized and what an extraordinary display of precision clockwork it was. But today, because of the return of her son, she was letting time scramble itself – whatever would the neighbours say, Rosanne was to visit and it was still the cooking time. Tea would be taken in the kitchen and not in the dayroom.

'Mother, I'll not take tea,' Lancaster said moodily and he suddenly stood up. 'I'll just go and pack up the parachute.'

'No tea, son? Why ever not?'

'Don't fuss, Mother. I'll be happier packing up the parachute.'

'Is something wrong, Lancaster?'

'No. I don't think so, it's just that I never returned home from a war before.'

'Not since tha was born anyroad,' his mother answered him. 'Go on then, son. Pack up tha things. Tha'll see Rosanne and Clarrie later.'

My uncle went back to the common where Charlie, alone, had already started to pack away his parachute. The two didn't talk, they seemed to be each one stuck with the memories of his jerking and silent family like a film running in his head. Lancaster walked around his parachute straightening out a billow of silk here and a knotted cord there. Then I watched him folding it ever so slowly, and ever so carefully away. Bit by bit, segment by silken segment the parachutes disappeared into their packages and the two aviators, without so much as a glance at one another, carried them off to their respective homes.

'Tha can get Rosanne and Clarrie now,' my grandmother told me as she was putting away the baking trays – the tin tubs would be out soon, steaming before the roaring fire. Visitors at bathtime, I thought. Crikey, even old Jane Brightside wouldn't have allowed visitors at bathtime. I fetched them from the wagon, holding my cousin's hand all the way. She was still whooping and her porcelain cheeks were all aflame. Rosanne gave Lancaster a big kiss upon his forehead and told him that she was pleased to see him home. Then, as Clarrie and I played beneath the table, the three adults chatted about Lancaster's adventures in the Flying Corps and eventually I heard them leaving the house as they went outside to greet the menfolk coming home from the pit. The two of us still beneath the table, I showed the neatly packed parachute to Clarrie and she tugged at a corner of silken white which peeped invitingly from within. It immediately doubled to two corners of silken white. Then just as quickly doubled again to four. The canopy seemed to have a life of its own and as Clarrie undid a button and I tried cramming back a full billow of silk, a second wave of material found its way into the room. I imagined that this was how a many-headed monster might behave when the knight had lopped off a head. I was telling the material to get back into the canvas pack but Clarrie had now undone another button and there seemed to be no room left beneath my grandmother's dining table.

I scampered out from under and stood up. I tried rolling the segments as I had seen my uncle doing but I only succeeded in bringing more of the soft material into the room. Clarrie was completely hidden beneath the canopy but even worse she had the still mostly buttoned up pack with her. I was painfully aware that there were still many more buttons to be undone. The amount of free material suddenly doubled in size. It undulated to the window. I tried kicking it back beneath the table but only succeeded this time in getting it to mount half-way up the stairs. I heard Clarrie coughing and then being sick. She was vomiting in my uncle's parachute. Then there was a sudden draught and the white folds opened a little. The silk had blown into the scullery and a little had crept to the top of the stairs. Clarrie, completely unseen, was undoing more buttons. In fact by this time I couldn't really see anything other than the billowing silk which floated about me in a quiet diffused light. I remember hoping that the door to my father's bedroom would be closed and then from somewhere came the answer that it wasn't for I heard my father's voice asking, 'Whatever's that at bedroom winder?'

Then there were noisy footsteps and angry voices raising the wind and, unfortunately, the canopy too. The parachute blew itself more deeply into my family's little home. Water was being chucked on to the fire and I heard the sizzling of the wet coals and they spoke to me like many things in our village would speak to a six-year-old but the coals were talking through a silken muffle of whiteness and I hoped it might be God telling me that this wasn't my fault. I could hear the other children's voices and whoops of laughter. People were running up our steps to the bedrooms and Albert was shouting for Clarrie.

'She's under the table,' I managed to say.

'What bloody table?' came back my uncle's response and I decided that it might have been more prudent for me to have kept my mouth shut for in raising my voice I realized that I had given my position away. I was yanked up into the air though still completely surrounded by billowing silk and passed through a window. Moving from the diffused light and into the bright blue day made me blink. Then suddenly I was on the grass next to Clarrie and surrounded by adults all shouting at me.

'What's tha think tha's bin playin' at?' my father asked.

'Leave the lad alone,' my grandmother said. 'He doesn't understand.'

Not understand, I thought. Whatever does she think it is that I don't understand? I wanted to tell her that parachutes were pure education – now I knew all there was to know about the bloody things. They brought men from the sky, they nestled into small homes. I understood everything.

'Well, there's no watter and there's no fire and the house is full of parachute,' my father said, glaring at Mr Brown, our lodger, 'so there'll be no baths, not for any of us,' and he fetched me one around the ear. Then my father turned to the house with such a disbelieving look on his face. Billy o' the Terrus End had just slid down a piece of canopy which was pushing its way from our bedroom window and which had almost found its way to the ground. The parachute, working from the inside, was now beginning to wrap itself about the outside of the house. Here was more education. This was mathematics at its most interesting. Parachutes could both wrap around and themselves be wrapped up at one and the same time. Here was the geometry of surfaces at its most baffling best – topological nightmare. Billy was quickly followed down the slide by Danny Pratt and he by little Jackie Henderson. My father was gobstruck as he watched the three of them re-entering the house, finding their way blindly to our rickety stairs and obviously preparing for a second go.

'Where's tha think tha's going?' asked my father, trying to find his way into the house once more but being beaten back by the flapping of the silk. Emily collapsed to the ground, clutching at her side with the pain of laughter. Ernest and Albert had to support one another for fear of falling in their merriment and Mr Brown had eventually to come to their rescue by supporting the pair of them until eventually all three tumbled over. The neighbours too, who had all come to watch the antics in our house, sank to their knees in fits of the giggles. Eventually Lancaster's dam burst too as the sepia memories ran momentarily from his head and he saw my father trying to do battle with no more than a posh woman's frock. 'My parachute's done for,' he told his mother with tears of laughter streaming down his cheeks.

His mother looked at him for what seemed to be a full minute hardly able to control the speech which she wished to deliver over the tide of laughter which broke at her tongue. Then very quietly and with a control that could push back waves she said, 'No matter, Lancaster love. I'll be able to make dozens of pairs of French knickers for all the little lads in t'village.'

2

The Bellman, the Schoolman and the fire brigade

Ah'll tell thee a riddle.

Ay. Tell me.

I'm tellin' thee. I'm tellin. Listen. What is it that binds the Bellman, the schoolteacher and the lads in t'fire brigade?

Nobody was speaking. They were just disembodied voices. In our village sometimes you could hear the stranded voices. There was a voice in the winding wheel as it cycled endlessly through the drizzle. There was another in the metal-tasting rain which spattered the roof of the terrace. And yet another which spoke from the cold stone in the walls of our house. Aunt Henrietta had known that voice. A sad melancholic voice in the old stone which spoke to her of its history – that was an unhappy voice which in its turn created madness. But these were neutral voices speaking to me now. The tones were soft and clear like someone telling a story to the hushed children sitting cross-legged on the floor in Standard One.

'I don't know,' I said aloud and my mother stirred in her sleep. I had my small hands gripped about the silken crook of her arm as she slept. She faced my father clothed in his fancy striped pyjamas; her back to me. The collar of her rough nightdress scratched at my face as she turned from a disturbed dream.

Doesn't tha know? Doesn't tha know what gives 'em a voice?

'No.' That was my voice again. 'What's tha riddle?'

I'll tell thee, shall I? Shall I tell thee?

'Ay, tell,' and my mother shifted again making me move away from her to avoid being suffocated beneath the beached body tossed up from her dream.

It's bell, lad. They all share the same bell.

'Oh yes, the bell,' I said. 'They all have the same bell.'

'Shh, Donald,' said my mother. 'Go back to sleep, son,' and she put her arm about me.

The Bellman is a sort of town crier, except that in a village like ours he doesn't need such a big voice and he doesn't shout *Oyez* or *Hear ye* or anything like that. He just says *Sithee* in an ordinary quiet way and he rings his bell in the rain; then he tells you things. Things about other people or about other villages. During the War he had stood in the rain dressed in his oilskin cape and his black fisherman's hat. He has a silken white beard which hugs the lines on his face and he told us what was happening in the War. How many had been killed or who from the surrounding villages and pits had died or been maimed. Things like that.

Our Bellman is called Jacky Jellis and he has an old dog called Bruno. My father had known Bruno when he had been courting my mother, that's how ancient the dog is. He's called Bruno only when he's with the Bellman, but when he plays cricket with the lads on the common he's called Percy Holmes and can catch a cork ball in his mouth. I always feel so sorry for Bruno. He has no teeth, but that isn't the reason why I feel sorry for him. Not exactly. I feel sorry for Bruno because he has such intelligent eyes. Bruno is so intelligent that he actually knows that he's a dog, that's why I feel sorry for him. All the other dogs in our village don't know the difference between a dog and next Thursday, but Bruno does and it creases me up that I know that he knows. You see, if Bruno knows that he's a dog, then Bruno knows that I'm a human and he can see the difference and I'm sure that Bruno would like to be human too, just like me. He looks at me with his sad brown eyes and I know that he's asking why he can't be just like me and why he has to walk about on all fours and catch cork balls in his toothless mouth. Why he can't eat at table instead of scavenging about with all those other dogs looking for scraps of food.

'I don't know, Bruno,' and I give a little whimper and my mother tightens her arm about me in her sleep and I wish that I could turn a key and unlock the human in Bruno. Release him from his canine imprisonment, either that or I wish that somebody would take him away so that I didn't have to see his intelligent sad eyes any more.

The bell is kept in a little wooden box on the outside wall between the two windows of our schoolroom. Wenceslas Piggott sometimes rings the bell to call us to school on a morning or after the break for dinner and Marlene Jellis, the Bellman's daughter, who teaches Standard Two rings it to call an end to lessons. She sometimes calls us to school too, as does Miss Fountaine, the headmistress. Marlene Jellis has long ginger hair which she can sit on but she ties it in a bun at the back of her head and my grandmother says that she's a loose woman and that she is having an affair with Mr Piggott. She says that Marlene goes into the pub with him and unlike the other women she doesn't sit in the snug but she sits in the bar with the menfolk and drinks with them and listens to their foul language and that's no way for a schoolmistress to behave. She's a loose woman? But her hair is scraped back in this bun with not a strand out of place. Perhaps she's only loose when she is sitting on her hair, when her red hair falls over her face and touches her bottom and all over.

'Perhaps that's when she's loose,' I murmur and my mother edges closer to me and away from my snoring father and his fancy pyjamas. I turn my head to avoid the roughness of her garment again.

When there is a fire anyone can ring the bell and the fire brigade come running with their buckets of water and their ladder; when the Bellman comes he just carries the bell off with him, clanking it and shouting *Sithee* until somebody has the time or the inclination to hear what he has to say. Then he returns the bell to its little wooden box in the wall and walks off to the next village to tell them things. Things about us. I suppose that he's already told them about my uncle Lancaster and Charlie o' the Terrus End coming out of the sky and about how wicked Clarrie and I were when we undid the parachute.

It weren't tha fault.

'I'm sorry.'

'Shh. Go back to sleep, Donald,' says my mother. 'God's already forgiven thee.'

Wenceslas Piggott was a bachelor, his mother and father were both no longer alive and because he wasn't a pitman himself he never had colliers lodging with him. He lived alone and ate his breakfast alone. He never knew what it was like to live in our village, not to truly live with others in our village. The jam in his sandwich was making his tash tacky and he ran his tongue over it tasting the sweet sticky edge of hair. He gulped from his mug washing the hot tea back on to his lips to dissolve the strawberry jam which had stuck there and his tash dripped tea on to the tablecloth. He heard the ringing of the school bell, picked a book that he would need from his bookshelf and dashed from the house which was just around the corner from the school. Actually, everybody's house was just around the corner from the school, it was just that Mr Piggott lived nearer to the corner than most. He said good morning to Mr Clayton, the caretaker, who stood in the yard. Mr Clayton was thin and wiry like a piece of ivy in a waistcoat and a flat cap. The schoolteacher went into his classroom and sat at his desk. He put his head in his hands and with elbows resting on his desk he stared at the wall at the back of the classroom, wondering when our Albert would complete the Rubens and whether the ladies might get some clothes. Then he looked at the forty empty desks before him. The schoolbell rang again.

'Oh, Christ,' he said without shifting his hands from his head. 'It's Saturday.' He rose up slowly and walked out of the school and into the small yard. Mr Clayton was ringing the bell.

'What is it, Mr Clayton?'

'There's a fire, Mr Piggott,' the caretaker answered, removing his flat cap and scratching at his balding head.

'A fire?'

'Yes, Mr Piggott. You can see the smoke on't terrace by t'common,' and he pointed a nicotine-stained finger towards our house.

'Yes. Oh, yes Mr Clayton. Right,' said the schoolteacher, following the direction of the accusatory finger. 'I'll do summat about it, right away,' and he went back into the school to get his spy glasses.

'Shouldn't tha be gettin' t'others?' Mr Clayton shouted at him from outside and rapping at the closed window.

'Yes, Mr Clayton. Right away,' Piggott shouted back through the dirty glass whilst strapping the glasses about his neck.

There was a team of six local fire fighters. Mr Piggott, Mr Hardwick the owner of the pub and Charlie Gill our nextdoor neighbour who had been invalided out of the army – they formed one half of the team. The other half were all colliers and because it was Saturday morning Wenceslas Piggott knew that they would be down the pit. He ran to the pub and hammered on the door turning his spy glasses every once in a while on to our terrace. A wisp of smoke came from one of the downstairs windows.

*

I could hear the tap-tappings from way below ground. The men were at work and there were disembodied voices there too.

Why isn't tha father in t'pit, this mornin'?

He's in 'is striped pyjamas.

And what of Mr Brown, the inventor of brown paper? He's not shouted up the steps yet.

He must be off to somewhere in his wide winged chair.

Where Donald where? The question was tapped hard into the dark shining coal.

'China,' I said.

And tha grandfather? Where's tha grandfather?

'My grandfather's bent in two, almost clapped out from tapping tha two foot seam, tha bastard.'

Tha grandfather must go to work, Donald.

'We had a party for my uncle Lancaster coming from the War and we had beer and Scotch whisky to celebrate his homecoming. That was unusual because my grandfather normally won't allow alcohol into our house.'

He's temperance tha naws and like Winston Churchill he's been brung up to have the utmost contempt for people who get drunk.

'I saw them curl and pack away the ripped parachute, even the bit with Clarrie's vomit on it. Then they went and got ale and whisky from the pub and they all got drunk, all except my grandfather and my grandmother. Nobody had a bath and they all went to bed when it was light outside and the dawn was touching at their black faces.' I opened my eyes and looked upon my mother's sooty face. I glanced across at my father's blackened face too. The sun's rays streamed through the window.

I could hear Charlie Gill at the other side of the bricked-up hole in our bedroom. He was making a strange noise like he was being sick whilst hopping about on his one leg. The Bellman seemed to know that Charlie had only one leg even before Charlie himself knew it. One day he had stood there with Bruno sitting on his foot, the rain was lashing at his cape and he was making his proclamation. He seemed to be so ancient that the Gods had to hold him up with strings like a celestial puppet who they kept on sending back down to talk with us. *Sithee*, he said and rang the bell. It was like the fanfare which heralds the coming of the narrator in a play.

He introduced the one-legged Charlie Gill who hadn't yet come home, but Jacky Jellis knew all about Charlie's other leg – the Bellman knew where it was. It's funny how the narrators always know what's going on. I don't know why they bother to have scenes and acts and all those actors when all that's needed is a good narrator who can remember the story. Perhaps that's the reason, perhaps they can't always rely on the narrator to get it right and they need the actors to nudge his memory. Perhaps that's what actors are – just scraps of memory in the narrator's head. Perhaps that's why the narrator only appears on odd occasions – the rest of the time he's thinking and all those actors are only a playing-out of his wild thoughts. So Charlie came home as Jacky Jellis told he would and he went to live with his mother. There was no more rugby, no more fooling about. Life was for real now. Now that the stinking war was over for him and they'd grabbed his leg from him, life was for real. And Charlie couldn't face too much of that reality so he started to drink – drink more then he used to do, that is – and Charlie bloated up like a balloon so that his one leg couldn't support the massive gut which he had and he kept on falling over. I could hear him vomiting up my grandfather's beer and his Scotch whisky whilst trying to stand on his one leg.

'Poor Charlie.'

'It's too early, Donald, go back to sleep.'

There's smoke, can tha see the smoke?

Ay.

Can tha smell it? Can tha smell?

'I can smell smoke, Mother.'

Wenceslas Piggott was hammering at the door of the pub. 'Wake up, Rube Hardwick,' he was shouting. 'There's a fire.'

Rube put his head out of the upstairs window. 'What's up, Mr Piggott?' he asked, scratching at his vest.

'There's a fire, Rube,' said the schoolmaster and he pointed in the direction of our house.

'Ay. I can see t'smoke,' Rube said as he looked over at our terrace. 'I'll be down soon. I'll meet thee over yon.'

Wenceslas ran aimlessly back towards the schoolhouse where Mr Clayton was still ringing the bell.

'Why don't tha get buckets?' the caretaker asked as our school-master went by.

'Ay, that's a good idea. Right,' and he turned and went back into the school to get the buckets from the cupboard in which they were kept. He reappeared moments later without the buckets. 'Where's the key?' he asked Mr Clayton.

'Charlie Gill's got key, Mr Piggott.' He removed his cap and scratched his balding head again.

'Right,' said Mr Piggott, racing off to the Gill house. When he got there he was surprised to find that it was the very house from which the smoke poured.

'Charlie, Charlie Gill, is thee up?'

Charlie was hopping about on his one leg, groaning.

'Mrs Gill. Ay up, Mrs Gill.'

'Go back to sleep, lad,' my mother murmured.

'Mother, I can smell smoke.'

'What's that smell?' It was my father in his striped pyjamas sitting up in bed. 'Come on gerrup everybody.'

'Charlie. Mrs Gill. For God's sake rouse thasens.' That's Mr Piggott's voice.

My father was thrusting a leg madly into his trousers and hopping about just like Charlie Gill would do. 'Mother, Father, gerrup,' he shouted.

'Oh, my God, is it our house?' my mother shouted. 'Come on, Donald, don't just lie there. Get up.'

'Charlie, 'as tha got the key to the bucket cupboard?'

'It's next door. There's smoke pouring from the window at Mrs Gill's.' It was Mr Brown's voice calling up the rickety stairs.

I can still hear Charlie hopping about on his one leg and vomiting in his room behind the bricks, then I heard my grandmother say, 'Never mind the buckets, Wenceslas Piggott, tha puddin'. Smash the window and get the slops,' and she rushed down the stairs with her chamber pot shouting for my father to bring ours too. I heard the smashing of the glass and the hopping of Mr Gill as he descended the stairs and by the time that I had reached the street there was a whole queue of neighbours filing in through the Gills' front door each with a potty full of pee and other stuff. Emily was orchestrating the lines and to avoid congestion she was directing people through the house and out of the back scullery door. Wenceslas Piggott sat on the grass, hearing Mr Clayton still ringing the bell, and he marvelled at my grandmother's organizational abilities. The fire was soon put out and the helpful neighbours dispersed back to their homes each having deposited his slops in Charlie Gill's parlour. If only Wenceslas Piggott had lived in our village, truly lived in our village, he would have known what was to be done.

In the area built on to the front of our house and which had become known to the family as aunt Henrietta's laboratory we kept a duck. Other folk kept pigeons and ferrets and Mr Henderson, Oliver's father, had a greyhound and a whippet. There was a whole arkful of lively animals, but we had a duck. He was just a plain ordinary duck that waddled about and swam in the water which was trapped in a cut-down rain barrel. He was far too lazy to fly though, and to get him to do something, mostly one would have to pick him up and throw him into the rain water where he would quickly settle and float about on the still surface until boredom struck. Then he would turn himself upside down and let his arse float about for a while, presumably until he became equally bored with life that road up, and then he would revert to his former position. So like some great philosophers, his day would alternate between the two worldly positions until, uncomprehending and absolutely fed up with it all, he would close his duck's eyes and go to sleep. It was whilst I was watching the duck in one of his bottom-up phases of life that Jacky Jellis rang his bell. He stood on the common in front of our house letting the rain spatter his oilskin cape, then he sat in the rubber armchair which had fallen out of the sky on the previous day and with Bruno curled at his feet he said *Sithee*. My uncle Lancaster came out of the house, grabbed me up under his arm and walked out of the walled area to face the seated Bellman. The Bellman rang the bell and said *Sithee* again but nobody else came out to listen.

'My lad Archie's come 'ome, too,' he said at last, realizing an audience of two was all that he was going to get, 'but there's nowt to keep 'im here. Nowt but pit and Hunger Hill.' He looked very comfortable in the chair. 'He's one of them hintellectuals, is my Archie. He should go. Better gone and be done with it.'

'Ay. He was always the cleverest in the class, him and your Marlene. What'll he do, now he's back from the War?' my uncle asked.

'He'll be a doctor, that's what,' Jacky Jellis responded. 'I'll give 'im ten pund and he can tek the dog too and 'e'll be off to London, I expect. He'll mek 'is fortune in healing, I know that.'

'But he'll have to go to a medical school, Mr Jellis. Ten pund won't see him very far.'

'Ay, that's why he'll be taking the dog.' The rain pattered on his fisherman's hat and he roughly stroked the black dog beneath the chin. Bruno looked at me with his sad brown eyes and I said, 'I'm glad you're going, Bruno, perhaps things might be better for you in London,' and I turned my attention from the animal to concentrate on the man sitting in the armchair. He was relaxed as if nobody was holding up his old bones any more.

All the intellectuals had gone from our house too. Sidall Junkin had not been what you would have called an intellectual but he was politically aware, as was his friend, my great grandfather, James Brightside, but they'd both gone. Ernest was a church-goer, but he wasn't political. His sister, Henrietta, had been an intellectual, but her intellect had been supported by madness and when the madness went I suppose her enthusiasm for things, particularly for the love of history and for the love of nature, well, they just died too. My great great grandmother, although lacking any kind of formal education, had in some ways been the most astute of all. If it hadn't been for her none of us would have survived, so she must have had a social awareness even if she couldn't turn it to political action. Even Bill Pettit had been aware, though it was only with the intelligence of a computing engine. Like the Babbage machine, Bill had been born into the wrong era. His head filled with fact had been forever breaking down beneath the weight of his knowledge. He needed some other means of storage but it hadn't even been invented yet.

But what were we left with now? After the War, what came home? Ernest was religious and Emily was organizational, but there was little intellect. Albert painted and my father worked, but they were not political. And Lancaster, who flew aeroplanes and made moving pictures with a hand-held camera, what was he?

'Mr Winston Churchill will win the day, Lancaster,' Jacky Jellis was telling him. 'Social reform won't lead to any freedoms – it will only bind us closer to the State. The State might organize us but it won't bring us owt. Authority and History are the same thing, Lancaster. They've both got big mouths and they've got to gobble to keep going, but be careful, Lancaster, because keep going they will. If nowt else History has to keep going. Be careful of them socialists, lad.'

'What are you saying, Mr Jellis?'

'I'm saying get out while tha can, lad. Go off with my Archie, piss off quick cos there's nowt 'ere for thee. Join 'em in their Empire building, lad. Theres nowt in t'pit.'

'But what'll I do, Mr Jellis? I'd be no good at doctoring or owt like that.'

'Moving pictures, lad, isn't that what's in tha bones? That and aviation. Tek the plunge, lad, and use tha gifts in the coming world. Don't be fearful of tha gifts and don't swallow all that stuff from the hot 'eads in't pits. They've seen nowt of future and they know nowt of History. They think that History is a snake whose head can be turned but it can't, I tell thee. The best tha can do is divert its head into a sack for a while, while tha teks a runnin' jump and tha hopes it hasn't seen thee. That's the best tha can hope for, understand.'

Two weeks later I saw Archie Jellis winding up the road away from our village. He had on his Sunday suit but it was a Friday and he held Bruno at the end of a piece of string and the dog was leading him over by the big house to the crossroads. That was a place where the world began, the crossroads – you could go anywhere from there, anywhere in the whole world, yet it was amazing how often people came sliding back down the hill unsure of what lay down the paths of the other three roads. Archie didn't come back, though. He and Bruno just kept on going down one of those roads.

There was the smell of creosote coming from next door as Mrs Gill was painting the floor in their parlour. She put her nose to the window and watched Archie climbing away. Then I caught sight of Lancaster with his head pressed to the window in our parlour and he too was watching the Bellman's son leaving with the dog. Lancaster shut his eyes. When he opened them again, Archie had gone.

I saw Charlie Gill hopping on his one leg and leaning on his wooden crutch. He had dragged the urine-soaked pegged rug from out of the house and on to the common. Then his mother came outside and poured turpentine on to the smelly old rug and Charlie lit a Swan Vesta and hobbled away as the flames erupted with a whoosh. The bell rang immediately. Since the morning of that fire in the Gills' living-room, observers had been posted everywhere. Within moments the fire had been extinguished by a brigade of men drilled to perfection by a smarting Wenceslas Piggott. Charlie gave a short cry like I've seen the other invalids sometimes make and he hobbled away, not looking at anyone, until his mother went to fetch him from the far side of the common and she led him into the house. Wenceslas Piggott stood on the grass apologizing to the closed door as Mrs Gill drew the black curtains over the window in their living-room, just like she used to do for the rugby team when they came to her house for a bath after the match. But I don't suppose that Charlie would have wanted to be reminded of that.

Lancaster, incorporeal behind the window in our house, suddenly materialized himself on the common. He walked down by Bottom Boat, by that part of the river where his aunt Henrietta had first descried the stones with which she had eventually built her laboratory. He brushed the aerial spiders from his face and, with his airman's head thrust back, he watched the lapwings passing over. By the river bank there was frog spawn and caddis-worm and he saw the chasing sticklebacks. He wandered into Kippax. At the Royal Picture Palace he asked Mr Pinkofsky if he could have his old job back.

'It's nice to see you back, Lancaster. It's good to see you, boy,' said the proprietor.

'How about the job, Mr Pinkofsky?'

'Are you still making those wonderful pictures?'

'I've not been back for long. I haven't had the camera out yet.'

'Such an eye. You've such a wonderful eye, Lancaster. You must take your pictures.'

'What about the job, the projectionist's job? Can I have it back?' He heard the farrier next door hammering his metal. The noise rang uselessly throughout the empty cinema.

'There's someone else, Lancaster. You didn't expect me to wait for four years, did you?'

Lancaster looked away from the owner's wrinkled-up face and contemplated the upturned orange boxes which passed for the seating for most of the would-be audience.

'She's a nice girl, Lancaster. Come tonight, come. I'll see what we can arrange. Maybe we can organize something even if it's only part time.'

'Thanks, Mr Pinkofsky.'

'That's all right. You're a good boy, Lancaster. You come back tonight, we'll see what we can arrange.' He squeezed my uncle's arm.

3

Mr Brown, the inventor of brown paper

It is often said that the Great War changed everything which it touched. Well, it didn't change our village. It changed the people all right – some of them, like those it butchered at the Somme. Bill Pettit and Oliver Henderson, they got changed in that way. It altered my uncle Lancaster. He had always been a distant child, my grandmother said, but the War seemed to have gifted him with a vagueness which was even beyond her fathoming. It blinded some and it created a lot of cripples, too, like Charlie Gill who lived next door and Mr Doyle who kept the pigs. Mr Doyle came home with only one arm and he couldn't cut up his bacon any more. But the pit could do that too, the pit could change you in those ways too. The War changed Danny Pratt's father as well; made him so he couldn't breathe. I saw him every day shuffling slowly off to the pub and gasping at every step. But the pit could even reproduce that effect in men. Who needed wars?

As I already told you, Henrietta had gone from my family – she'd not been killed or anything, she'd just run off with Elyahou Tsiblitz. He'd fought with the Germans. My great great grandmother had died and Mrs Henderson, Oliver's mother, had gone in her sleep. The other Gill boys had taken themselves off to the colonies and old Thwaite, the coal owner, had died in an armchair at the big house. My maternal grandfather, Joseph Thwaite, was now our landlord, but he wanted nothing to do with the likes of us. But you expect with all that dying, the geography of the living changes about you, you expect that. Even the massive shire horse which had pulled the wagon on to the village common, bringing Rosanne to our Albert, even he'd been put in the pit with the ponies but the darkness had scared him and he'd galloped off into the galleries making a hell of a clatter and nobody ever saw him again.

As I say, you expect the living to change but the thing which failed to change in those years was the village itself, all the inanimate stuff. The Jam Sahib's motor car remained parked at the side of aunt Henrietta's laboratory and my father cleaned it regularly and kept it in good running order and he regularly took the crippled and the daft off to the dales in it, just like he used to do. Hunger Hill still brooded at one end of the village and the big house with its sad trees still guarded the other. In our house, the bible remained shut at the centre of the sideboard beneath the rickety stairs, emphatically closed with a large brass clasp like the golden brooch on her dress locked away Marlene Jellis's lumpy body. The bookshelf had the same few books leaning one on the other and they were still mostly unread. Aunt Henrietta's volumes, the natural history which she had written whilst at Bottom Boat, had, however, disappeared. From the window, one could still see the gas lamp but the gas company had never brought the gas into our homes and we still read and ate at night by the light of the candle. The remnants of my great great grandmother's dispensary of bottled herbal remedies collected dust and cobwebs on the shelving in the scullery and the view of the ashpits from the scullery window remained very much the same. Sidall Junkin had gone, Bill Pettit had gone too and now it was Mr Brown who raked out the earth closet each morning and tipped the contents of the ash bucket on to the smelly heap. I suppose Mr Brown was the only thing which had really changed. The War brought Mr Brown to us. It took others away but it brought us Mr Brown.

Mr Brown described himself variously to me as the inventor of brown sauce, brown chocolate and brown paper. I knew that brown sauce came only from Hammonds sauce works and I wasn't taken in by his claim on the chocolate either, because I had already learned that it came from the Rowntree factory in York, a place where they had a church as large as a battleship, my grandfather said. On the question of his claim to brown paper, however, I was unsure, or more accurately I felt that he might have had a claim on the invention of brown paper bags. He had thousands of them, thousands and thousands. He would suddenly produce a brown paper bag from his trouser pocket or from his waistcoat and he would blow into it and then with a rising excitement I would watch wide-eyed and full of smiles; at the appropriate moment I would blink, just as he banged the extended bag between his large hands.

And in that twinkling of an eye the paper bag would be no more and I would be left attentive of an empty report which he now encased in those same hands. *Wonderful*, *wonderful*, he would say and who was I to disbelieve him?

He was a typical dossing collier, thin and consumptive with baggy trousers and a dirty striped shirt. He had a brass collar stud at the back but he never wore a collar with that shirt; he had lively blue eyes and very unusually he had a Sunday suit. I never knew him go to church but on a Sunday he would dress up in his suit and walk about the village with a brass-topped cane in his hand and whistle the tune of one of the hymns. Or sometimes he would even go off to the next village and walk back with those who had observed the Lord, but he would never pretend that he had been to church when he hadn't. If anyone asked if he had been to church he would say, 'No. I've no time for that stuff. God and all that stuff, it gives me the pip,' but he would always make polite conversation to those with whom he walked. My grandmother thought that he looked very smart in his Sunday best and said that he was a man with a lot of pride for his suit gave him the appearance of a person with financial security. He's a man who knows how to be respectable, she said.

''Ow can 'e? 'Ow can 'e be respectable if the man won't go to church and kneel to the Lord?' my grandfather asked.

'His Sunday suit has nothing to do with God,' she told my grandfather who couldn't understand why he wore it. 'Doesn't thee understand, it's what keeps him from the poor house. His suit is the covering which keeps him from being destitute – it's his esteem. Surely tha can see that much, Ernest. It's the poor man's second skin and without it he's as helpless as a babe.' But I doubt that my grandfather could see anything of the kind.

Yes, I suppose it was Mr Brown who brought a small element of change into the village during the war years. It was those paper bags which fascinated me.

'Where's tha get all them paper bags?' I would ask.

'I telled thee, I invented 'em.'

'Tha didn't really. Not really.'

'Ay, ah did.'

'Did thee, honest? Cross tha heart and 'ope to die?'

'Ay,' and he would cross himself.

Then I would lie awake at night worrying that if he'd not told me the truth the Lord would strike him down, and when Mr Brown shouted up them stairs in the morning and I knew that he'd not been taken off in the night I'd think, well, it must be, it must be that he is the inventor of brown paper and I'd give our important lodger an extra special smile when I saw him on that day.

'I med a lotta money,' he said to me once. 'I got a penny for a dozen bags.' It was the first occasion on which I was given to consider that Mr Brown's paper bags might be worth something. In fact it was probably the first occasion on which I ever considered anything as having a monetary value. All of life is not dross, I must then have thought to myself for I suddenly had the urge to collect and save paper bags but with a definite view to one day realizing their true worth and selling them on for a penny to the dozen.

'Tha must be worth a lotta money, Mr Brown,' I told him whilst imagining possession of all those paper bags.

'Ay,' he said, coughing a little and twinkling his eyes at me.

'I'll bet people believe tha's very rich.'

'Ay.'

Well, I suppose that was the small change which Mr Brown was able to bring about in me if you'll forgive the pun. But it wasn't until after the War that the inanimate things started to change and it all started on that day when my uncle Lancaster came home on his parachute. The day that the rubber armchair fell from the biplane; that, at least, changed the family's view from our living-room window. It was only brought indoors many years afterwards and it remained for the rest of my childhood, a piece of solid geometry in an alien and messy landscape.

Now I look back upon that time, it was all so obvious, wasn't it? If anyone was going to change the way things looked in our village then it would be Elyahou Tsiblitz. Look back at the mythology, look back on the reality. Either set of references would tell you – find Tsiblitz, walking, pedalling his tricycle, motoring or flying, it didn't matter, find Tsiblitz and you will get changes. Some men act as History's messengers, God knows why – I doubt if they know why themselves.

Looking beyond the village, however, beyond the deep slope of

Hunger Hill which even on a sunny summer's day manages to hide its true contours in a secret shade of purple treachery, one could discern the changes which the War had ravaged. The new militancy of the working class was evident over there, beyond that hill. The War had given them a self-assertion if nothing else. There was a huge increase in trades unionism and interest in the organized labour movement and particularly among the women. Wars are sudden great explosions of power and they have the habit of awakening little eruptions, little wars in all of those involved. There had been a longing for the War to finish, for an end to come to the beastliness which mangled a loved one's body. There was an anger developed which moulded the working class from the huddled protective groups which they had been and made them into cohesive forces of resistance which demonstrated a strength and a backbone. It was like God creating Adam from his clay – they became real people, upright and able to stand on their own feet without falling over. They were organizing now not just against low pay and overwork but against lack of investment and poor housing and ill health and things which nobody but the capitalists had thought about before. And not merely those things; the vomit of the trenches made them wish for better things like music and books and education – somebody called it culture. But above all, the government, by asserting the social control of armaments production during the War, had shown the feasibility of the alternative to private ownership to working people. The miners wanted a nationalization of the mines and they wanted national pay agreements too.

My grandmother ran up jap silk knickers for all the urchins of the village using Gaylord's machines. It was more or less her last act at the factory before she handed in her notice. Now that the men were home from the War she mustn't be occupying a scarce job which some man might need in order to feed his family. She believed that ours was a land fit for heroes and it was they, the lads who had returned, who would make it so.

Not many of the boys wore their knickers but the girls wore theirs and I was made to wear mine by an angry grandmother. Most of the lads ripped them up into handkerchiefs and bulged their grimy trouser pockets with them. Some cut holes about their edges and attached strings to them, turning them back into small parachutes. My grandmother wrote to Henrietta thanking her for the chair. She told her of Lancaster's homecoming and of the incident with the parachute. She also told her about the fire at the Gill house. Jacky Jellis came over and rang the bell and sat in the chair and told everyone about the contents of Emily's letter to Henrietta. It was amazing how he knew everybody's business.

'Archie's gone,' he then told his audience.

'Ay, we saw him leave,' said Mrs Gill.

'There were nowt for 'im here,' he told them.

'Ay, 'e was a clever lad.'

'Village is like a flower, tha naws. It's been in t'bloody bud all this time and it teks a stinking war to bring it to flower. It suddenly opens up and spits out its kids, tha naws. Spits 'em out o'er yon.' He nodded towards Hunger Hill. 'But it's for t'best.'

'Did tha hear from 'im?'

'Ay, ah heard. He walked to London and he's a place at Kink's Cross.'

'He's a railway porter, then?' Lancaster asked.

'Naw. I told thee, Lancaster, he'll be a doctor.'

'Then what's he doing at King's Cross?'

'Studyin'. What else?'

'At King's Cross?'

'Ay, at Kink's Cross Medical School.'

'Is tha certain it's not Charing Cross, where he's studying?'

'Oh ay. Tha's reet, Lancaster. Charink Cross Medical School. Tha wants to get thasen off, lad, afore it's too late. Remember, like I told thee afore.'

'But how is he managing to live, Mr Jellis? It costs to go to a medical college.'

'Ay, well 'e'll live all right. 'E's resourceful lad is my Archie and 'e's got the dog.'

That was the second occasion on which I had heard Jacky Jellis mention how having Bruno would help Archie to overcome his poverty and it set in train marvellous thoughts of how the dog would earn the money whilst his master went on with his studying. Perhaps Bruno was a human being after all and once in London would slip out of his doggy skin and go off to work washing dishes in a swank restaurant. Or perhaps he would retain his doggy skin and astound packed audiences at the theatre as he recited poems and computed mathematical sums in his human head. Or perhaps he would just stand in the rain with Archie, like Archie's father did, and stare at the passers-by with his sad brown eyes, and people would stare back and feel as if they wanted to cry for Bruno because he knew who he was. And they would be moved so deeply that they would put money into Archie's cap which he held in his outstretched palm. Knowing who you are like that, knowing your place like that – that must be the saddest thing in the whole world, I thought.

When Lancaster went back to see Mr Pinkofsky, the cinema owner introduced him to Mrs Cushman. She was about the same age as my uncle and her husband had not come back from the War. She didn't know for sure if he was dead because nobody had told her but he just never came home. She didn't like to call herself a widow, not until someone told her that she was.

Lancaster said hello but she was very shy and kept her eyes on the running spool in the darkness of the projection room. Mr Pinkofsky explained that my uncle had been the projectionist before she ever came to the Royal and explained a little indelicately that he had just returned from the War and needed his old job back. She had a face like a pixie and wispy brown hair which gave off the blue smoke from Mr Pinkofsky's cigarette. She sat on a little wooden chair, silhouetted in the darkness with smoke rising from her head, and said nothing. Then Lancaster said that it was all right and that he didn't need the job all that much. He told them that he could always get a job in the pit. Then she looked at him over the winding spool and the flickering images from the cinema screen reflected back on her small face and Mary Pickford and Douglas Fairbanks dazzled there, stars in her dark eyes.

'No. You have the job,' she said. 'I'll manage.'

'No, I wouldn't hear of it, missus.'

'Well, perhaps we could share the job,' she told Mr Pinkofsky, who nodded his approval of her suggestion. 'We could work on alternate days.'

'No,' said Lancaster. 'You must have a rent to pay. You need the money for food and such. I can live at home with my mother.'

She looked away again, embarrassed by their situation.

'Well, I'll be off then,' he told them, anxious to sever himself from her awkwardness.

'You may as well watch the film,' Mr Pinkofsky said. He was disappointed that my uncle would not be working for him.

'Ay. I'll go down and watch if it's all right with you.'

Lancaster sat at the back of the cinema where there were three rows of seats of red crushed velvet. Sitting right at the back he could hear the kissing and the cuddling of the couple next to him. He'd been through a bloody war and now he had no job. He didn't know whether to take Jacky Jellis's advice and follow Archie to London. He could see that the man next to him had his hand right up the skirts of the woman he was with. She moaned softly and he wished that films had a sound to go with those talking but silent heads on the screen. Her moaning got louder and Lancaster became more embarrassed. The woman was now fumbling with the man's trouser buttons and he grunted as she revealed his erect penis. Thankfully the piano started to play. Their mouths locked together she began to masturbate the man in tune to the piano player's music. The scenes changed on the screen, the piano was played faster – a more exciting theme. The farrier next door began to bray his metal and his heavy thumpings reverberated about the cinema. Lancaster was just about to move to an empty seat at the end of the row when several people entered the auditorium and took up all of the remaining seats locking him into position beside the loving couple. He contemplated going out past the couple but decided that it probably wasn't the wisest thing to do. He continued to sit firm and thought of Mrs Cushman and her pixie face as the man next to him ejaculated to a selection of music from *Lilac Time*. The man sat back groaning for a moment as the woman buttoned up his trousers for him. Then he took a comb from his pocket and began to comb his hair watching the screen.

'What's going on?' he heard the woman whispering.

'I dunno.'

She took his hand and rubbed it on her covered breast. The screen suddenly went blank. The film had ended.

'What was all that about?' the woman asked.

'I dunno,' the man said again and put his comb away. The lights came on.

'Excuse me,' Lancaster said as he stood up. He looked at the couple. 'Oh. Hello, Mr Piggott. Hello, Marlene,' he said as he pushed his way past them. Marlene had her hair down, it was flowing past the golden brooch which pinned her together and kept her in one piece. Lancaster went back up to the projection room and sat with Mrs Cushman as she changed the spools.

'All right,' he said. 'We'll share the job, but we both work at all performances.'

'But he's not going to pay two wages, is he?' she said without looking at him.

'No. You get the wage, the full wage. I'll be all right. I'll just come in to help.'

'But why?'

'I told you, I'll manage. You need the money more than me.'

Lancaster walked home with Mrs Cushman that night after the Picture Palace had closed. She lived in Kippax and he slept the night in her bed. He was twenty-two years old and a virgin and she helped him all she knew how. He lay awake most of the night waiting for the ghost of her dead husband. Nobody came. Then he felt really dreadful because he imagined that the ghost hadn't put in an appearance simply because the man wasn't dead after all. He didn't tell that to Mrs Cushman in the morning after she kissed him on the lips and told him that he couldn't go, not until he'd done it again anyway. So he did it again then he lay on his back and felt the welcome draught blowing in at her window and fluttering up her blue curtains. They were fancy curtains, he thought, women's curtains. He watched them gently billowing in the breeze. Then he looked back to Mrs Cushman's ceiling and eventually he said, 'It can't be too difficult to make pictures talk, can it?'

Mrs Cushman didn't reply but stroked his nipple with the tip of her finger, then she wound the hair on his chest in her hand. He gazed at her pixie face and the wispy hair on her head moved in the breeze from the open window. 'I was wondering, that's all. Maybe you could record the voices as they speak and then somehow fit the film with the sound. That wouldn't be so difficult, would it?'

After a week or two he brought Mrs Cushman home and introduced her to everyone. Her name was Millie and most of us liked her. Albert didn't like her very much but my father thought that his reaction might have had something to do with the War in Emily Brightside's Womb. Lancaster never had any money but nobody knew the true reason why. His mother thought that he must have been spending it all on Mrs Cushman, which in a way he was, and she grew to dislike her because of it. She told Ernest that Lancaster was spending too much time with that married woman. Ernest corrected her, saying that Mrs Cushman was a widow woman, but Emily refused to have it, not until there was proof. It's odd how women think alike on this issue; they have to know where the other bits have got to before they can change – officially change. Men aren't like that. When Mrs Doyle went off because she couldn't stand to be living with a one-armed man and a dozen pigs any longer, Mr Doyle pronounced her dead straight away and married a young lass from the next village. Anyway, Lancaster continued to see Millie Cushman, though he didn't bring her home very often and he never had any money.

Eventually he moved in with her and they would both go off to work together and they would come home together. Her window was always open and the cool draught always blew in her room, disturbing her curtains and swirling the dust and the soft wispy hair from her brush which she pulled out and dropped on to the linoed floor. Lancaster asked her to marry him but she couldn't do that, not without knowing what had happened to Mr Cushman. He lay awake at night thinking about pictures which talked and writing imaginary scripts for the film stars of the day. Then Mrs Cushman would wake up and make him do it and then she would turn over on her stomach and make him do it that way as well. Then one night Lancaster failed to respond. When Millie Cushman woke him up in the middle of the night and grabbed him by his soft genitals he just lay there and counted the frames in a sequence of film that ran through his head. She spread her legs and took hold of his hand and made his fingers disappear into her warm blackness but he turned his back on her and went to sleep. After that, they slept with their backs to one another every night. They went off to work together and they would come home together and they slept in the same bed but always with their backs to each other until one day Mr Cushman appeared and Lancaster came back to our house. He continued to work at the Royal but Millie Cushman moved off to another village with her husband.

4

Aken Jugs, Owler Crimble and the latest German fire-fighting equipment

Throughout the next twelve months I worried about the acquisition of paper bags. If something as ordinary as one of Mr Brown's paper bags had such a value then what price should one put on my duck or on the French knickers which crept tell-tale fashion beneath the hem of my trouser leg? Through the changing school programme I pecked from Wenceslas Piggott's handfuls of education – I knew a fish from a flower and a leaf and I could name all the pink bits on the globe in the schoolroom by heart. Yet I had learned nothing of the value of possession. Indeed I had no true knowledge of the value of anything but for a brown paper bag which in my little head was costed at twelve to a penny piece.

Standard Two, if anything, proved to be even more disappointing than Standard One. Marlene Jellis spent most of her time reading from the works of H. G. Wells. She was obsessed with Wells. *The Time Machine, Doctor Moreau, The Invisible Man, The First Men in the Moon, The War of the Worlds.* She read them over and over again. Billy o' the Terrus End loved it – he knew all there was to know about aliens from strange planets. For me, however, education was proving to be a terrible disappointment. And whilst for those unlike Billy – those who didn't care much for Mr Wells's futurology – there was always the opportunity to educate oneself on Marlene Jellis's lumpy clothes or to ponder how my uncle's unfinished picture back in Standard One might look if only he could be persuaded to stroke a camel hair brush between the nooks and crannies of the female form, I thought only of the respectability conferred by possession.

We were an odd couple, then, were Billy and I. He thought only of Martians, I thought of acquisition and most of the other boys in the class dreamed of ... Well, I was unsure of what it was which caused their world to move. However, my grandmother's analysis of

Mr Brown's Sunday suit, though perhaps wasted on Ernest, was not wasted on me. Respectability was a consequence of acquisition. Collection seemed to be the only answer, but what was I to collect and from where? The answer when it came was beautifully simple and I was sure it had been sent by God. It was a coat hanger and He left it hanging in a tree.

Billy o' the Terrus End and I had skipped school one day and taken a walk down to a field called Aken Jugs – there are a lot of fields round here called Jugs. Jugs is an old word for a field and it was called Aken, I suppose, because this field was full of oak trees. We sometimes went down to Aken Jugs to collect acorns and we sometimes went just to swing on the branches or to watch the birds. It wasn't strange to find things hanging in the trees. I can remember once finding a kite all bashed up and unable to fly. Someone had left it fluttering there and knocking against the wood as the wind moved it. The kite clapped itself silly in that tree for months then one day it fell to the ground and Billy's brother picked it up and took it home; he used the string to tie up Mrs Doyle whilst he robbed the house of a side of bacon. Billy's brother's in the prison now. Another time Billy and I had found a dead fox in a tree at Aken Jugs and I said that the poor thing must have climbed up and couldn't get down, but Billy said that the cats had dragged it up there and were living off its blood. Then when we learned about lions in school I guessed that Billy had probably been right after all, and that we had a lion living just beyond the village. After that Billy and I went about with sticks for a while just in case we met the beast, but after a time we forgot about the lion and got on with our games. Anyway, on this particular day we were up in a tree and swinging on the branches when I looked across to another tree and at about my eye's level I could see a coat hanger hooked on to a small branch.

'Ay up. What's that in tree?' I said.

Billy stopped his swinging and looked across to where my nodding head was indicating.

'There's another one up there.' Billy nodded back and I followed his gaze.

'Ay, and another,' I said.

We swung ourselves to the ground and climbed the other tree to retrieve the coat hangers which hung from the branches like some strange triangular fruit. We combed the branches and as we discovered each one among the leaves we tossed it to the ground, then we came down and counted our coat hangers. We had forty-one of them and each was marked with the name of the Savoy Hotel, London W. They were lovely coat hangers, solid and shiny with varnish and polished up like my grandmother's table and the metal hooks were brand spanking new too. We looked about to see if there were more in the other trees but we couldn't find any. It seemed that there was just the one tree on which the coat hangers grew and at first we thought that we would ask Marlene Jellis how a tree could grow coat hangers, but on reflection I decided against asking Marlene anything.

'They'll only tek 'em from us,' I told Billy.

Billy gave a sigh, indicating his resigned agreement at the way in which the adult world behaved, and I told him that we would have to find somewhere to hide the coat hangers because these were going to be our acquisitions and nobody was going to take them from us. We made a pile of the hangers and covered it with leaves and grass and a few dead branches that were lying about and we set off to look for a more permanent home for our find.

There's another field close by Aken Jugs which is called Owler Crimble – Crimble because it has crooked hedges and Owler because of the elder tree which grows up from its middle like a turned-out belly button. When we approached there was a boy swinging on the gate and he had a clapper in his hand.

'Is tha clapper boy?' Billy asked him.

'Ay. My father told me to chase away sparrers.'

'Ain't no sparrers 'ere,' Billy observed.

'No. Chased 'em off,' the boy sniffed.

'What's tha name?' I asked him.

'Isaac.'

'I'm Donald and this is Billy o' the Terrus End. Hello, Isaac.'

'Hello. Is tha from t'village?' He nodded towards our village.

'Ay.'

'Ah'm from t'next village,' he told us. 'My father's got corn in this field. It's just bin drilled.' He waved his clapper in our faces and Billy stepped back, away from the raucous noise. I watched a disturbed rook flying off to Hunger Hill and we were all three silent for a moment.

'What's tha want?' Isaac asked presently. He was probably no older than Billy and I but he seemed to have the confidence of an older boy.

'Secret,' said Billy.

'What's secret?'

'What we want, daft. It's secret.'

Isaac, still on the gate, looked up at the sky and watched the clouds float by.

'What's tha do all day, Isaac?' I asked.

'Frit birds,' he answered still looking into the arched sky.

'Is that all?'

'Ay. My father says I must. I must keep birds off so I walk about whirling my wooden clapper till my arm aches or sometimes I shout at 'em. Gerron, yer bastard, I shout at the top of my voice. That scares 'em.' Another rook took off into the wash blue sky. 'Sometimes I whittle a bit of wood or sometimes I just go to sleep.' I thought of my duck sleeping on the water in the rain barrel and I felt sorry for Isaac.

'Shall we tell 'im?' I asked Billy.

Billy was silent for a while, watching the stranger carefully. 'When tha falls asleep in t'crimble who wakes thee up, Isaac?' he asked after a while.

'Spiders.'

'Spiders?'

'Ay, spiders tickle me ears. That wakens us.'

Billy looked at me. 'Ay, we'll tell 'im, Donald,' he said. For some reason the spiders had made up his mind for him. For me it was the duck, for Billy it was spiders.

'We're looking for somewhere to keep us coat hangers,' Billy told him.

'Where'd tha get coat hangers?'

'From tree that grows 'em, daft.'

Isaac swung on the gate watching the sky again and I looked up at it too but I wasn't used to the vast sky like Isaac was and it frightened me. Strange that, how in only a matter of a few hundred yards the community's make-up can change. The miner never sees the sky, so there's an inborn fear of it, whereas the farmer works in the sky. So, to the farmer's lad who lies on his back and stares at it all day, the sky presents no threat at all. Young Doctor Cartwright would have said that it was genetic. I looked away from the feathery clouds.

'I know a place,' Isaac told us.

'Where?'

'O'er yon.'

'What sort of place?' I asked.

'It's a hut. An old wood hut, o'er yon.'

'Will tha tek us?'

'Ay. Come on, I'll tek thee.'

Isaac led us over the fields to the river bank. The woody nightshade and the dog-rose were in flower and bent men were sowing turnips silently in another field. Then we passed Simmonds's dye works, where the river smelled of marzipan and where my aunt Henrietta had found all the red fishes floating upside down, and beyond the dye works we came upon Isaac's wooden hut. There were hearts carved all over it. Hearts with arrows through them and with initials carved at each end of the arrow. The boy untied a bit of string on the door and we followed him inside.

'It smells,' I said.

'It smells of women,' Isaac told us.

'Women?' Billy asked whilst poking about in a dark corner. 'Tha means women?' he then said, unable to find another way of describing them.

'Ay, tha naws, rumpin'.'

We looked at him blankly though I had an inkling of what he was getting at. I'd heard about farmers' boys. They watched cows and lambs being born. They knew a thing or two, did farmers' boys.

'Tha means rumpin',' I said, also bereft of synonym.

'Ay. It smells of cunt.'

Billy and I looked at one another again. We were unsure whether we wished to keep our coat hangers anywhere near to women, irrespective of how they smelled.

'Well, tha'd better get tha coat hangers and bring 'em afore someone pinches 'em,' Isaac said, hurrying our decision. 'Shall I help thee to carry 'em?'

'Ay.' We ran off to Aken Jugs and uncovered the stash of coat hangers. Then we carried them as quickly as we could to the hut and laid them in a sloppy pile in the corner where Billy had been searching about.

'What's tha want them for?' Isaac asked.

'Respectability,' I told the clapper boy and Billy looked at me hard wondering if that was the reason he wanted them too. I swore the other two to absolute secrecy and took one of the hangers from its pile and stuffed it in my trousers.

'They'll see that,' Billy said, referring to the beady-eyed members of my family. 'They'll see that, then what use is us secret?'

'What's tha want it for, anyroad?' Isaac asked.

'It's for Mr Brown,' I answered. 'We can trust 'im. I need it to try summat out.'

'What summat?'

'I can't tell thee, not yet.'

The other two looked at one another, wondering how far they might trust me.

'Alreet,' Isaac said, 'tek off tha shirt.' I removed my coarse wool jersey revealing my pale skinny body to the two boys in the gloom of the wooden hut. Isaac took the shirt from me and put the hanger inside like he was going to hang it up in a posh shop. 'Reet, put it on again,' he instructed.

I put my head through the hole and pulled myself into the uncomfortable contraption which Isaac had just prepared. He walked around me once or twice then he said, 'Alreet, tha can go home like that. Nobody'll notice owt.' I walked home with Billy, unable to put my arms straight at my sides and with a wire hook digging uncomfortably into the back of my head. My mother wanted to know why I appeared to walk in such a peculiar manner. I told her that I had become musclebound with swinging on too many branches at Aken Jugs.

The following day when nobody else was about I gave the coat hanger to Mr Brown.

'It's for tha Sunday suit,' I said.

'By, it's grand,' he commented. 'Very posh, the Savoy, eh? That's real posh.'

'I found it for thee, Mr Brown. It's for tha Sunday suit.'

'Well, I thank thee, lad. Thank thee,' he said and I stared into his sky blue eyes begging him.

'Tha wants summat?' he asked.

I nodded.

'Oh, ay,' he said and produced a bag from his waistcoat pocket and wheezed into it. He exploded it at me but he could see by my face that it wasn't yet another demonstration of his *Wonderful, wonderful* that I needed. The lodger then stood up, put his hand into his trouser pocket and rattled the loose change which lay in a heavy lump on his thigh. He gave me a threepenny piece.

'Is it worth thruppence?' I asked excitedly.

'Ay, lad, all of that.'

I showed him the shiny silver coin. 'How many of tha paper bags will this buy?' I asked him.

'Thirty-six.'

'Reet, Mr Brown. I'll have thirty-six of tha paper bags then,' and I pressed the money back into the lodger's hand.

'Well, I can't right now,' he said, 'but I'll get 'em for thee, lad, don't tha worry, I'll have 'em for thee. Now thee put tha money aways and don't spend owt, mind, and I'll get the bags from my factory. Will that be satisfactory?' He smiled at me, his prospective buyer, with his blue eyes and I nodded excitedly as my grandmother came through the door dressed in her outdoor coat and with an enormous parcel in her outstretched hands. She seemed to have it balanced at the back edge with the tip of her nose though the heavy parcel rose way above her head. She slammed it down on to the dining table, like a seal ridding itself of a tiresome object.

'What's tha got there, Grandmother?'

'It's a parcel, lad. From th'aunt Henrietta Tsiblitz.'

'Well, what's in it?' I asked, noting the large amount of Mr Brown's paper that it had taken to wrap it.

'I don't know, puddin', tha'll 'ave to wait till it's open.' She tugged at the layers of paper.

'I'll bet tha med a lotta money from the Germans when tha sold 'em that,' I told our lodger. He smiled at my grandmother as she continued to unwrap the parcel.

'What's tha bin tellin' him now?' she asked but the lodger only continued to smile.

237

Lancaster came into the room and, sniffing the air, said, 'Rubber. I know that smell, Mother, it's them suits that Mr Tsiblitz used to bring with him.'

Sure enough, my grandmother had unwrapped a neatly folded pile of rubber clothing and was now reading an accompanying letter from the sender which she had found at the bottom of the parcel.

'Ay, it's them smelly rubber suits. I remember the feel of that stuff,' Lancaster told us as he let his fingers ripple through the cold and folded garments while his mother's eyes scanned what had been written in the correspondence.

'Not exactly,' said Emily.

'No?' asked Mr Brown, eager for an explanation.

'No. It's Mr Tsiblitz's latest invention to help fight fires.'

Lancaster had by now removed several articles of rubber from the neat pile and was looking critically at them. 'Can't see how this will fight a fire, Mother,' he said.

His mother slapped his hand and told him to stop playing about with the clothing then she read aloud from the letter. 'They are fire-fighting suits,' she explained, 'and they come in three parts. There's a cape . . .' Here Lancaster, disobeying his mother, grabbed the rubber cape and put it about his shoulders. It was very long like a policeman's cape and it almost touched the floor. 'Then there is the helmet,' my grandmother continued. My uncle slipped the helmet over his head but in truth it was more of a hood than a helmet. It too was made from rubber and it had a visor through which one could see, though the material clearly wasn't made of glass, and there was a peculiar metal disc which had holes all around its edge and which lay flat on the top of my uncle's head; the hood was long and met the cape at the shoulders, completely hiding his clothes. A piece of rubber hose trailed from the back of the hood. The third and final part of the uniform was a pair of rubber trousers which Lancaster pulled over his ordinary clothes and snapped to his waist beneath the cape with strong elastic. They were much too long for him and for a minute or two he stomped about our parlour like a Martian in flippers. Eventually he sat down on one of the dining chairs and he removed the hood to reveal his red and sweating face.

'By, it's hot in here,' he said, blowing out his cheeks, 'and that helmet thing weighs a ton.'

'What's that tube for?' I asked, pointing to the length of hose which hung at the back of the hood and which my uncle now held in his hands.

'Dunno,' he said.

'Watter,' said our lodger. The engineer in Mr Brown was now coming out.

'Watter?' I asked.

'Ay. Watter. It's fire-fighting equipment, isn't it? What else will tha fight the fire with if it's not water?'

'Tha'll get some strange things from my Lancaster's head, Mr Brown, but tha'll not get watter from it,' my grandmother said defensively.

'No, look at it t'other end, Mrs Brightside. Tha fixes loose end of hose to watter tap.'

'And fills my Lancaster's head with watter?' My grandmother was quite indignant at the thought of it, but Mr Brown was a patient man.

'Ay, in a manner of speaking. Look, watter will come out of this 'ere disc, them's 'oles in it, sithee,' he said, pointing to the disc which had been laid flat on my uncle's head and which presumably was responsible for the helmet weighing the ton.

'And then what?'

'Then tha can put out fire. The disc will spin round, throwing out the watter and putting out the fire.'

'Well, why not just have a length of tube? Why tek watter through the fireman's head?' my grandmother asked with exasperation.

'So he can rescue them who's caught up in flames, Mrs Brightside. If I see it correctly, the fireman can wander into the heat of the conflagration with his own watter all about and keeping down the flames, and at the same time have his hands free to make his rescue and keep the poor soul free from further burns, too, while the watter whizzes o'er him.'

'Brilliant,' said Lancaster.

'Mr Brown, tha's a genius,' I said.

'Ay, well, I suppose it's Mr Tsiblitz who'll be the genius,' Mr Brown said uncomfortably. 'He invented it.'

'How many suits are there, Mother?' Lancaster asked.

'There's six, one for each of the members of the fire-fighting team.

Your aunt says that she was sorry to learn of the fire at the Gills' house and Mr Tsiblitz thought that a present of half a dozen suits would prevent anything like that from happening again. Buckets is past, she says, we must progress with the world, tha naws.' Then she said, 'Tha'd better go and get Wenceslas Piggott, it's him who'll be wanting them.'

Lancaster went off to get the schoolteacher and brought him to our house a few minutes later. My grandmother showed Wenceslas Piggott the suits and Mr Brown explained how he thought they might work.

'Ay, that's all very well, Mr Brown,' he said, 'but where does tha find six watter taps, eh?'

'I can see tha's not an educator for nothin',' Mr Brown told him. 'Tha leave that with me, lad. I'm no schoolteacher but I've bin a fine engineer in my time and I should think I could rig up summat for thee. Tha naws, a single hose feeding all six fire fighters, sithee.'

During the following week Mr Brown turned out a modification to the original design and built the suits into a single fire-fighting unit, but he made it so that each suit was detachable and the end product was a fire-fighting unit of anything from one to six men. The main thing was that no matter how many men there were in the team, they were plugged into a single water point. Wenceslas Piggott was so impressed that he invited Mr Brown to join the brigade and our lodger then officially replaced the one-legged Charlie Gill. At first Charlie objected but Mr Piggott, to demonstrate the futility of Charlie's membership, made him put on one of the suits and connected it to the tap in our scullery and every time the disc on his head spun round, flinging out its water, the one-legged Charlie spun round too. Then finally he fell over and every time he tried to stand up the disc, which continued its dizzy spinning, flung him over again. All that water was making the ground very muddy anyway and Charlie couldn't find any purchase on the common. He ended up scrabbling in a sea of mud and he started to cry. Mrs Gill had to come and get him and take him indoors and Wenceslas stood on the common apologizing to their closed door again whilst Charlie's mother gave her son a bath in the tin tub in front of their fire.

Seeing Charlie Gill's performance wasn't enough; Billy and I couldn't wait for the brigade to demonstrate the true value of El-yahou Tsiblitz's latest invention, not to mention the genius of Mr Brown's modification. Time passed without fires and we became impatient. One day Mr Brown called me to him and slipped me thirty-six paper bags with a blue-eyed wink. I handed him his silver threepenny piece and asked him how many bags he would exchange for another forty Savoy hangers each as pristine as the one which he had received from me before. One thousand and summat seemed to be so many that I wondered if they might not fill the whole of the wooden hut. Billy and I ran off there to stash away the paper bags and to assess our storage space. As we crossed the fields – jugs and crimbles – we could see the small figure of Isaac standing on an upturned bucket and peering into the hut through a small window. The window was high up near the roof and no bigger than the thickness of a miner's forearm.

'What's up, Isaac?' I called.

'Shh. It's rumpin'. They're rumpin' in there,' he told us.

'Women?' Billy asked in a knowing kind of way.

'Ay. What else?' The clapper boy looked puzzled.

'Tha never naws,' Billy said. 'How many?'

'How many what, Billy?'

'How many women's rumpin' in there, daft?'

'Just one, like allus.'

Billy couldn't see why so much fuss was being created over a single rumpin' woman and I couldn't understand what they were on about anyway. I climbed on to the bucket and peered in through the dirty window expecting to see a rumpin' woman and was surprised to see in the gloom of the hut a man without his trousers. He seemed to be rolling madly about the floor and possessed by demons. My grandfather might have said that he was a man struggling with his soul and I was about to impart this nugget of wisdom to my companions when I put my foot through the rusting base of the bucket and my leg started to bleed.

'It's nowt,' I told the others whilst we all sat on the grass. Interest in the activities in the hut had ceased. I tore a piece from my silk French knickers and tied a bandage round my leg.

'Well, bucket's burst,' Isaac told us and he lay on the grass and watched the sky. Billy and I lay on our stomachs, our noses only inches from the ground. We had a genetic propensity to lie in an eighteen-inch seam, that's what Doctor Cartwright was later to tell our mothers. 'We could smoke buggers out, like ratten',' Isaac said to a passing cloud.

'Ay, that'd do it,' Billy said and with a sudden flurry of activity we had collected sufficient wood and twigs to make a small fire in front of the hut. We tried to waft the smoke under the tight-fitting door. From the lack of response within we concluded that the smoke was not getting through. Then with the sudden realization that here was the ideal opportunity to call the newly equipped fire fighters into operation, I said, 'I'll run and ring t'bell,' and I hared off to the schoolhouse. Mr Brown and Rube Hardwick came from the pub and the three strapping miners dashed up from the pit and congregated in the school yard. Carrying their suits, they followed me across the fields in the direction of the wispy smoke. When we arrived the door was just about scorching and Isaac said to Mr Brown, 'Tha'd better get in quick, there's two people in there,' and I said, 'Never mind people, Mr Brown, us forty Savoy hangers are in there.'

Mr Brown instructed the other four to put on their suits.

'Where's Mr Piggott?' asked one of the miners. 'He should be instructin', not thee.'

'Bugger Mr Piggott,' said Mr Brown. 'Come on, we've important work to do, get tha bloody suits on.' He ran off to Simmonds's dye works with a long length of hose, presumably looking for a water tap. When the brigade had got their suits on Billy went to tell Mr Brown to turn on the tap and Isaac and I could hear the water as it ran, picking up speed in the pipe, but when it finally arrived at our lodger's contraption the water seemed to take the line of least resistance and come only through one of the discs, flinging the unfortunate miner to the ground and dragging the other three bodies on top of him like collapsing cards.

'Turn the bloody thing off,' I heard him shout from under the pile of bodies. 'Tha's connected it to hot watter tap.'

He lay on his back with the disc whizzing round on top of his head but the spray was not falling anywhere near to the flames. The other men were trying to disentangle themselves, but every time they scrambled up, the force of the water away from them kept dragging them back on to the yelling miner. Isaac then showed what a bright lad he was by standing on the main pipe, thus cutting off the water supply and giving all four men the opportunity to get to their feet. He then took his foot from the hose and the water this time found itself in the helmet of the man at the other end. He screamed, tried to escape from the hot water by running away, fell over and dragged the others on top of him. Now it was his turn to lie on his back with his disc spinning dizzily, unable to raise himself from the ground.

The door now appeared to be fully alight but there were no screams from within the hut, just a few grunts like Mr Doyle's pigs might make. Suddenly the flow of water stopped; Mr Brown must have got the message and turned off the tap. Then with all four men standing upright the water was switched on again and now it was cold water that whizzed and swirled from the discs on the top of each man's head. This was what we had wanted to see – the new German fire-fighting force – and how magnificent they were, too, as in no time at all they put out the fire. Rube Hardwick was battering at the smoking door with his shoulder when his disc stopped its spinning altogether and his share of the water for some reason channelled internally rather than through the equipment on the top of his head. A steady stream of cold water flowed from the bottom of his rubber trousers. The discs belonging to the two men on either side of him were working perfectly, though, and the circling tensions of the water seemed to ripple a strange torsion into the innkeeper and his rubber equipment, lifting him some nine or ten inches from the ground between his two larger companions. The water continued to trickle from his trousers: from behind he appeared to be taking a leak whilst suspended in mid-air. In this hovering, almost angel-like posture, Rube managed to rip the door from its hinges and flung it, still smouldering, to the ground. As Mr Brown dashed back up from the dye works he saw his team disappear through the dark doorway to reappear moments later. One man carried the naked Wenceslas Piggott over his shoulder. His moustache drooped in a bedraggled silence and water whizzed about his befuddled brain. A second man had grabbed up the curved and white nakedness of Marlene Jellis, whose beautiful red hair managed to cover all those bits in which we boys at last showed mild interest and which might have given Billy and me insight into how the

243

unfinished portrait at the back of the classroom in Standard One might one day appear.

Fortunately the hangers were safe. Billy and I stashed our bags in a dry corner and the following day Isaac brought his father to the damaged hut. He was a man much older than I thought he would be, perhaps as old as my grandfather. He carried a shotgun over his shoulder like an old soldier and he leaned it against the side of the hut whilst he set about rehanging the scorched door.

Mr Brown improved his original design of the fire-fighting equipment by incorporating valves in the six individual hoses. Each man was then able to control the flow to his own disc, thereby putting rationality as well as water into the system. We had a few fires after that but none ended in the chaos that Mr Brown had promoted that day.

5

The flower opens to take in the news

Prior to my being ten years old, Jacky Jellis brought the news. Apart from the Bellman we didn't have a lot of visitors to the village. There were one or two travelling salesmen, that's all. In the old days long before I was born, there had of course been Elyahou Tsiblitz. Then there was the tailor with the tape measure around his neck who sold us our suits on the drip, then the man who sold us our spectacles from his tray of lenses; though he was long-sighted and she was short-sighted, my grandparents shared their glasses and couldn't imagine there would be anything wrong in the practice. After all, they were married, she told those who bothered to inquire. There had even been a man who brought around window frames which he carried on his back as if it was about to break and there was the midden man who shovelled the shit from the ash heaps and carted it away in his wagon, but none of these people brought us news. Only Jacky Jellis brought the news. Then when I was ten years old, that will have been in 1923, three things happened, all of which opened up the trumpet of the flower which Jacky said that our village was – suddenly, very suddenly the village didn't seem to be as remote and as cut off from civilization as it had been.

Firstly, in the spring some men came and planted a signpost at the crossroads beyond the big house. The signpost had three white arms, all at right angles to each other; they pointed in the directions of Leeds, Castleford and Wakefield and were intended to be for the assistance of the motorists. Needless to say, the fourth road, the one which led down to our village and to nowhere else except to Hunger Hill, didn't warrant a positional arm on the post. On a spring day from the village you could distantly hear the traffic at the crossroads, the honking of horns and the rub of tyres on the rutted road. It was all mixed in with the calls of the willow wren and the chiff-chaff and the buzzing of the insects and the cycling of the wheel at the pit head, but you couldn't see it. Nothing came down our way.

During that spring the ground ivy grew up the post, almost obliterating the signs, and a family of thrushes built their nest right at the top of the pole. It wore the nest like a hat and we lads had to be careful when cutting back the green tangle of leaves so that the goggled motorists wouldn't have any difficulty in finding their ways. Then one day as Billy and I sat in the dust watching the Hillmans, the Calcotts and the Model T Fords chugging by or turning at the intersection, we had a brainwave. We turned the post through an angle of ninety degrees and directed all the Leeds-bound traffic down to our village. Consequently we had a steady stream of traffic tootling past the terrace, digging up the common and coming to an abrupt stop where the track petered out at the foot of Hunger Hill. The traffic would then have to swing round in an arc and head back the way it had come. Sometimes a motorist would ask, 'Can I get to Leeds up here?' and point up the dangerous slope of Hunger Hill and Billy would say, 'Ay. Just keep going',' and invite the poor man to take his motor on the precipitous journey.

When it rained the ground would become extremely boggy at that end of the village and the motors would get themselves embedded in the mud. Billy and I – and sometimes Isaac if he could get away from Owler Crimble – would, for a penny each, offer to help get the car out from where it had stuck. We once got a posh yellow Napier stuck half-way up Hunger Hill and nobody could budge it, not even the colliers could budge it, so the motorist left it there rusting on the hill, until all its bits and pieces had been stolen by other motorists who broke it up piece by piece. Eventually everything went, except the four wheels, that is, which remained firmly embedded in the mud and are there to this day. One day a motorist, having climbed Hunger Hill and given Billy and me two pence each to help him carry down one of the doors from the Napier, spied the Jam Sahib's motor car parked outside our house. He was just about to rip off one of the lights from the front of the motor when my father came from the house and beat the man to the ground – he drove away with the yellow door but I don't think that he ever came back.

The new influx of traffic brought more strangers into our village in a single day than it had received in a hundred years. And these were people only too eager to speak, to tell not internalized salesmen's stories like yarns told by characters in a book – no, like the Bellman, they wanted to tell you things, real things about the outside world.

Did tha naw that the Duke of York had married Lady Elizabeth Bowes Lyon? Did tha naw that there was a Cup Final at London? Wembley? Did tha naw that Bolton Wanderers had won the Cup, my team tha naws? Fancy, Billy and I had met a man from Bolton Wanderers. He might as well have been from the other side of the planet, so strange and wonderful was he. Did tha naw that Mr Baldwin had become Prime Minister? Did tha naw that we'd signed a peace treaty with Turkey? I didn't naw that we was at war with Turkey, I told Billy. Did tha naw that Mount Etna had erupted? Did tha naw that there had been an earthquake in Japan? There were a million questions, a million pieces of information all from the men who had lost their ways in the motors. Now, here was education. Cubitt, Buick, Calthorpe, Lagonda, Riley, Vulcan, Austin, Clyno, Humber, Jowett. Now, here was education, being driven at breakneck speed down the hill and into our village.

It was a glorious summer's day when they brought the electricity. It slipped silently in the soft mosses at the summit of Hunger Hill. It crept noiselessly among the flowers. It got in the yellow rattle and the common veronica, it stepped quietly over rock rose and gromwell and the great stitchwort. It got entangled in the bindweed and the woodbine and among the red poppies. The cherries were ripe and it shook them from the trees. Nothing could stop it and it came right into the house. Nobody knew what to make of it, not really. Ernest said that you could see the water and taste it, it wasn't like water. Nor was it like the gas. Although the gas had never actually been taken into the house, you knew the gas at the lamp standard. You could smell the gas – like when Clarrie and I had whooping cough we could certainly smell the gas. But the electricity didn't have a smell and it came in wires and it brought us something which we knew very well. It brought us light. That's how it was, completely alien yet bringing us something as commonplace as light. It was difficult to make much of that. Yet it was fitting that I should have thought it to be travelling in the flowers. All those Latin names which nobody understood; but it was those same flowers described by such

247

lack of understanding which gave us the commonplace too. They gave us the colours – red and rose and yellow and blue. Sometimes at night it was silent no more, probably because the flowers had gone to sleep, and it hummed in its wires and I would lie awake listening to the owls and the electricity and the severed voices. When it rained, it hummed all the more and the metal in the rain turned to acid and that was a new taste for us to experience. It was than that I knew that this stuff was different. It had a power. It could kill you. It came from a long way off and it came right into our house.

One day in the autumn, Mr Brown arrived home with a large cardboard box full of bits of wire and wood and string and raspberries. He gave the fruit to my mother, telling her that he had found them on the bushes down by Bottom Boat as he walked back from Kippax.

'Why did you go to Kippax, Mr Brown?' she asked him.

'To get this lot, love,' he told her and waved his hand like a magician over the boxful of wonderful things.

'What is it?'

'It's stuff to make a crystal set.'

'What's a crystal set?' I asked.

'A wireless, lad, a wireless,' he said excitedly.

I watched Mr Brown constructing his wireless. He made a wooden base for it. Then he wound some copper wire on to a cardboard tube and he called this the inductance. He mounted it on to the wooden base with some brass screws and fitted some slider bars on to it. He then showed me a bornite crystal and told me that he was going to bring voices out of the other side of Hunger Hill and make the voices speak through the crystal. I asked if it would be like the voices I could hear caught up in the winding wheel or like those I heard at night whilst lying in my bed with my mother and he told me that they would be just the same. He set the crystal into a brass cup, using some molten metal to hold it there, and when it was ready he set that into the wooden base too. This he called the detector. Then he fixed down a thing which he called a condenser. He took a length of wire through our window and attached one end to a screw on the inductance and walked with the other end all the way to the gas lamp on the common. He shinned up the pole like a monkey and tied the wire to the very top, then he slid down and came back to the house. He told me that this was an aerial. He then took a second length of wire and attached it to another screw on the inductance. He tied the other end of this wire to the cold tap in our scullery sink. He called this length of wire the earth. Then he asked me to place a pair of headphones over my ears and he moved the sliders on the inductance. I heard a high pitched squeak which then disappeared as he continued to move the slider, then the set blew up in our faces as we sat there looking at it. After the initial bang I sadly watched one of the wires burning weakly then give out, and Mr Brown said, 'Bugger it. I'll have to insert a switch.'

He then put a switch into the circuit, fixed up the burned wires and asked me to put on the headphones again. For a second or two I could hear people talking then the voices went. I hadn't heard what had been said. Mr Brown looked with a screwed-up eye at the ticking clock which sat on the centre of our mantelshelf. Then he looked at me thoughtfully. 'It's nearly six o'clock,' he told me with a nod and with his eye still screwed. 'Go get Rosanne. She should hear this. I'm going to get the time signal from Paris. Go on, lad, go get her.'

I went over to the wagon and asked Rosanne to come and see Mr Brown's new invention and she came back to the house with me and put on the headphones. At six o'clock precisely Mr Brown put the slider to a wavelength of 2600 metres and Rosanne heard some pips. They weren't English pips, they were French pips and Mr Brown was satisfied for he had thought that it was only right that a French person should be the first to hear the broadcast from France in our house. Rosanne danced from the house as happy as if her own father had been talking to her from Paris. The fact that she had only heard a time signal made not the slightest difference, France had spoken with one of her daughters not just across Hunger Hill but across hundreds and hundreds of miles. And she'd spoken in our house.

After that a whole web of wires spread from the houses in our terrace. They came out of windows and were fixed to the gas lamp on the common. The aerial wires gradually became more sophisticated than that which Mr Brown had strung up. Some were slung from chimney pot to pole and these Rosanne used to walk over, practising her high wire tricks and teaching Clarrie to do the same. They were both dressed in sequinned tights and had ostrich feathers in their hair. I was ten years old, Clarrie was eight, and I realized at last that she was no longer a pot dog. I think that I was in love with her.

Gradually, as more crystal sets grew in our houses and as outside the web of wiring became more complex, we heard less and less from the broadcasters and more and more of what was going on in each other's homes. For a time, eavesdropping became a popular pastime, all information being relayed via the gas lamp on the common. Then one day Mr Archbold bought a commercial wireless set with knobs and dials and a plug to go in an electric socket. We could see through his window and watched him and his whole family bathed in yellow light, sitting there in their parlour and listening to the world together. Gradually we all got them and tuned into the world. The aerials stayed up though and Rosanne and Clarrie were often seen dancing at night on the web of wires beneath the diamond cold stars.

6

'Say nowt 'bout us poverty, it's a bloody secret'

The immediate post-war mood of confidence and militancy among the miners didn't last long. Fear for the future once again took a hold as trade became depressed and the labour market declined with it. The government had taken control of the mines during the War but in 1921 Lloyd George gave control back to the owners. That happened to coincide with falling markets, falling prices and reduced profits. At the same time as asking his men to take a cut in wages, my maternal grandfather, like all other coal owners, took the opportunity of ridding his pits of the most troublesome men. The hotheads were booted out – and good riddance, said Jacky Jellis who thought he knew what was going on.

There was no peace of mind in our household despite the familial ties; Ernest was bent up with his arthritis and Mr Brown was beginning to spit up great black gobbets of muck, just like Sidall Junkin had once done. Neither of them could count on a secure wage, even a reduced one. Young Doctor Cartwright told them both that it would be only a matter of time before they would be forced to pack in their work. But Ernest said that he wasn't about to retire and that he would be hewing the coal until he dropped; then Mr Brown told him that the doctor hadn't quite meant it in the way in which it was put. No. What the doctor meant was that he and Ernest, because of their poor health, would be the next to be made to leave the pit. If they were lucky they might be given light jobs grading the coal at the surface but their wages would be halved if they did that.

'Well, I'll not do it,' Ernest told him. 'They'll not 'ave me sorting coal till it's time.'

'Oh, ay, they will,' said Mr Brown. 'And I'll tell thee why, Ernest. It's because tha's got no political clout, lad, that's why.'

'No clout!' exclaimed my shocked grandfather. 'What's tha think the union is? It's a funny sort of no clout is that.'

'No, Ernest, tha's not hearing me. I said no *political* clout. Oh, ay, the union can mek a noise, it can mek a noise as far as Barnsley and I grant thee that's a long road. But the capitalists can mek a commotion a lot further than that, lad. They can mek a row all o'er bloody country and that's political clout, that is.' My grandfather looked glum. 'The only hope is to support the Labour Party and try to organize us selves into a political force – that's what we must hope for Ernest, sithee.'

Mr Brown was right. The Labour Party was just that – a band of hope. That was the weakness of the Labour Party; it was no more than a rag-bag of supporting voices of working people and most of them were saying, 'I want to work' and 'I want a decent living wage' and 'I want decent working conditions.' But there was no ideology because those same voices had no time for ideology. They were just stranded voices like those I heard every night when I lay there in my mother's bed.

I want a job.

My family needs a living wage.

I need to cough this shit out of my lungs.

When Ramsay MacDonald in 1921 was moved to tell that the weakness of the party was the 'fault of the minds of the people' that's what he meant. They had no ideology, they had no theory, they knew where they wanted to be but they hadn't a clue how they should get there. Billy and me though – we knew how to get there. It needed inspiration like the turning of the signpost. And so did Mr Brown – he knew how to get there, that was his genius.

Early in 1924 there was a lock-out at the pit. Trouble had been rumbling on for years, ever since Thwaite had taken back control. There had been a lock-out in 1921 culminating in the miners' capitulation on Black Friday. There had been lock-outs in each subsequent year, a week here and a week there. The miners never won anything. The coal price fell and so did wages. Then in 1924 Thwaite asked the men to accept another cut. He wandered on the common in his silk top hat and frock coat, walking amongst the young lads and a few dogs who played cricket with a real cork ball. Then he sat like a king in the rubber chair holding his cane like a sceptre and he shouted to the assembled pitmen, 'If tha won't see sense and tek a cut in wages then I'll close up pit,' and he got up and walked back to the big house jeered all the way by the colliers.

After a few days we knew that the lock-out was going to last and our house was running out of money. My grandfather called a meeting of the family and all who lived at the house. There was Grandmother and Grandfather and William and my mother; Lancaster and Albert were there and so were Rosanne and Mr Brown. They all sat around the dining table in the parlour and tried to work out a strategy for survival whilst Clarrie and I sat on the pegged rug in front of the fire. My grandmother who was a proud, proud woman said that she wasn't about to fall back on the parish and told us that anyone who wanted to live on charity had better leave right away. She wasn't going to ask the local shopkeepers for extended credit either; tick was for those without self-respect, she said, cutting down our options at a stroke.

'But if tha rules out charity and tha rules out local credit, Mother, what's left?' Albert asked.

'Sell up,' said Lancaster glumly. He still worried about following Archie Jellis down to London and agreement to sell up would have eased his own difficult paths to decision.

'There's nowt to sell, lad,' my grandfather said, poking a matchstick in his ears and scraping the wax on to the side of his matchbox.

'That's typical, isn't it, all tha's got is a box of Vestas and a bit of wax and tha tells us to say nowt 'bout us poverty as if it's all a bloody secret.' My father scorned his parents.

'Now, William, careful 'ow tha speaks to tha mother,' Ernest warned and my father sat back angrily in his chair.

'Pawnbroker.' Mr Brown spoke suddenly and emphatically and they all turned to look at him. 'Will tha stand for t'pawnbroker, Mrs Brightside?' he asked my grandmother. She was unsure if falling back on the pawnbroker demonstrated a loss of self-respect or not and was unable to answer the lodger. 'I go to pawnbroker regular,' he confided to his stunned audience. 'Nowt wrong in that. I pawn my Sunday suit on a Monday if I'm stuck for a few bob and I reclaims it of a Saturday when I gets my wage. Now tell me, what if anything is wrong in that?'

'Like my husband says, we've nowt to sell,' my grandmother told him coldly. 'If we've nowt to sell then we've nowt to pawn.' She sat with her hands hidden in her pinafore pocket and stared poker-faced at the lodger. 'And I'll not pawn the furniture,' she told him. 'Now that is a lack of self-respect, Mr Brown, pawning the furniture brings nowt but shame.'

'What about tha Sunday best?' Mr Brown asked.

'I'll not have us going off to church in rags,' she said and my grandfather nodded in agreement. 'I'd have thought tha would understand that, Mr Brown.'

'Oh, I do, I do,' he concurred.

'The Brightside family has a respect in this community, Mr Brown,' she went on, 'and it'll stay that way. We may be destitute but by God we'll not show it,' she told the lodger, and my grandfather murmured his approval of her bold statement whilst my father squirmed in his chair. There was a long silence which was only broken by Mr Brown's voice once again.

'Tell me, Mrs Brightside, if tha'd got two Sunday best, if each of the members of tha family had two sets of Sunday best, would that give thee more or less respect?'

'Why, more of course,' she answered.

'And if tha'd got two sets each would tha have any objection to the pawning of one of them sets?'

'None, Mr Brown. Of course I wouldn't. But we don't have two sets of best, do we? We have only the one.'

The lodger turned to Albert and all were attentive of what he was about to say. 'Tha naws that chap who comes o'er from Leeds, the tailor with the tape around 'is neck?'

'Ay.'

'Well, 'e'll mek up clothes on drip, won't 'e?'

'Ay.'

My grandmother put on the shared glasses, hoping, I think, that she might be able to hear better the gem of an idea that was about to fall from Mr Brown's lips. However, she couldn't see anything through them at such short distance and took them off, turning her ear to him instead.

'Now suppose we instruct him to mek a set of best for each of us. Mek 'em quick and payment on the drip. Then we teks 'em straight o'er to the pawnshop, how's that sound?'

'Brilliant,' said Albert.

'Ay, it's an idea,' said Ernest, though looking cautiously for my grandmother's reaction. 'What's tha think, luv?'

My grandmother was silent, mulling over Mr Brown's suggestion. 'Well, I can't see owt wrong in that,' she said at last. 'Not yet, anyroad.'

'It'll bring in some money. Quite a bit of money, Mrs Brightside,' the lodger encouraged her.

'Ay, but will it be enough to see us through this 'ere lock-out?' Ernest asked.

'Well, it won't last more than a month, will it?'

'Probably not, but will it bring in enough to see us through the month?'

'I should think so,' said the lodger. 'Sithee, there's summat I've not telled thee.'

'What's that, Mr Brown?' my grandmother asked suspiciously.

'Well, it happened a bit since did this, but tha Donald is sittin' on the key to a fortune.' My ears pricked up at the mention of my name. 'The little lad comes to me and 'e brings with 'im a clothes hanger. A fancy clothes hanger from the Savoy Hotel in London.' I felt the discomfort at the back of my neck as all eyes fell upon me. 'Now, don't go on at lad,' said the lodger, ''e did the right thing, did the little lad. Like I say, 'e brung me this 'ere coat hanger and I hung my Sunday best on it. That's what the lad said it was for anyroad. Am I right, Donald?' I nodded. 'Well, when I next took my suit to the pawnshop, it were on this 'ere coat hanger, sithee, and Mr Partridge, instead of giving me five shillings like he normally did, he gives us ten. Ten bob for a Sunday best. Well, at first I thought there must be some mistake but I says nowt, like. Then next time I takes my suit in to him, I gets ten bob again. So I says nowt again like and I thinks, well, must be, but just to test I take it the next time without the hanger and guess what?'

'Tha gets five bob for it,' Ernest said.

'That's right, Ernest, five bob. So I sticks it back on the coat hanger and I tek it down to Mr Zermansky over in Leeds after that and guess what?'

'Tha gets ten bob again,' Ernest said.

'No. I don't Ernest. I don't get ten bob at all. Mr Zermansky gives us fifteen.'

'Fifteen shillings?' my grandmother said disbelievingly.

'Ay.'

'For a Sunday best?'

'Ay. I tell thee them coat hangers is worth a fortune and tha little lad 'as gotten forty of the buggers.' He winked at my father. 'So what I have to suggest is this. We get tailor in to mek us suits and dresses. Even the two young uns. That'll be ten lots of clothes and we put 'em all on the lad's hangers, then we teks 'em round to different pawnshops – spread it about a bit like, so none of 'em get to askin' questions. We puts us other Sunday best on when we do it, like, then we'll look posh and the Savoy hangers won't appear to be out of place. Tha naws, we can put on a bit of a show, posh up the accents, that kind of thing. Then we let the word out a bit, tell one or two of the neighbours, them with a bit of brass tucked away like Mr Doyle, and we offer to sell 'em one of the surplus hangers, say for two and sixpence – that way they'll be able to get an extra five bob from the pawnbroker if they come to pawn owt. It'll be an investment for a man like Doyle. What's tha say?'

'Mr Brown, tha's a genius,' I told him from my perch on the rug.

The others remained non-committal, looking from one to the other.

'We'll still 'ave us self-respect,' Ernest told my grandmother.

'And going out of a weekday in us Sunday best will be a right treat for the neighbours,' my father then told her.

'Not to mention pawning tha Sunday best whilst all got up in a second best,' reminded Mr Brown. 'That's real posh, that is.'

'But what of the expense of the new clothes?' my grandmother asked.

'It's on drip,' Mr Brown said.

'Ay, but it'll still cost in time.'

'We're still paying for the last lot, luv,' Ernest said, 'and we had them afore the War. Spread o'er time we'll not notice it.'

Listening to that conversation in our parlour taught me a lot about pride and about respectability and about the self-esteem of our class. But it also taught me about fear. The fear of the dispossessed. There was no way that my grandmother would have pawned the furniture because, exactly as she had explained to Ernest about Mr Brown's suit, it would have left her family naked and she wasn't having that. Possession and fear were intertwined in a working class community and the fear of nakedness was the worst fear of all. A naked house was just as fearful as a naked body. That's why we had the pot spaniel on the mantelshelf and the two flying ducks on the wall – it dispelled our fears and what is more because they were on display it showed our neighbours that they had been dispelled. In effect it gave us our self-esteem. Lack of fear and our self-esteem were the same thing and it was conferred on us by our neighbours. It was probably for the same reason that Mr Brown had his paper bags; because apart from what he stood in of a Sunday plus a spare brass collar stud, he had nothing. But my knowing of the paper bags, that gave him his self-esteem. And that was probably why I longed to acquire paper bags for myself and why I prized those coat hangers. But *they* had turned out to be something quite different, hadn't they? They were investment. Fancy that. Forty of the buggers at two and six apiece. Like the man said, I was sitting on a fortune and I didn't care that nobody would see them stashed away in a mucky hut. It was like having pound notes in a bank, you put them away and you didn't tell, but you knew where they were and you could afford to smile.

'Well, where's tha coat hangers, lad?' my father said.

I looked at Mr Brown, pleading telepathically, and eventually a liveliness found its way into his blue eyes and he said, 'Don't tha worry 'bout that, William. I've got 'em stashed.' Mr Brown was like lightning.

The following day it rained and Mr Brown came trampling over the wet grass at Owler Crimble and approached Billy, Isaac and me at the hut.

'Expect tha wants paper bags then?' he said, standing at the door with the rain drizzling down on him.

'Don't think much of paper bags. Can't do owt with 'em,' Isaac told him, whirling his clapper at knee height. Mr Brown did a little skip in his baggy trousers like he would have done to avoid a whizzing cricket ball smashing into his shins.

'Can't 'urt thee, daft,' Billy told him.

'What, lad? What's that?'

'Clapper can't 'urt thee, Mr Brown.'

'No, lad, no.' Then after a while he said, 'What's tha want for 'em then?'

The rain was bouncing off his head and small rivulets were running over his nose and down his cheeks and dripping from his chin.

'Tha'd better come in,' I offered and the man came into the hut and sat on some dry potato sacks which Isaac's father had given us for our den.

'We want to sell 'em to thee,' I told him.

'Sell!' exclaimed Mr Brown. Then, rubbing his palm on the wet stubble on his chin, he said, 'Well, I don't know about that. I hadn't expected we should 'ave to buy 'em. Tha naws how tight money is at the moment.' Then he began to cough and he caught one of the great gobbets of muck in his mouth, went to the doorway and spat the black gob as far from the hut as he could manage. Then he came back and sat on the sacks, shaking his head. 'Sell, eh! I'd not considered having to buy 'em,' he said again.

'Well, tha can owe us money, Mr Brown,' Isaac said, looking at the stack of hangers in the corner of the hut, where they had been since that day we had brought them from Aken Jugs.

'Ay, that's a possibility,' the lodger acknowledged more brightly.

'Not for too long, mind,' Billy said.

'Well, 'ow much then?' Mr Brown asked. 'What about sixpence each, that'd be generous?'

'Nivver.' Isaac laughed, scorning the ludicrous offer.

'Two and sixpence,' I said.

'Three shillings,' Isaac topped me quick. 'Three bob or nowt.'

Mr Brown looked stunned. The rain still ran slowly from his hair. 'That's a lot of money, lads. Where shall I find three bob a hanger from?'

'From the pawnshop,' I told him. 'Tha said that Zermansky would give thee ten bob a hanger. Even Partridge gave thee five, tha said so thasen.'

'Ay, but it's not hangers we're pawnin', lad, is it? It's suits we're pawnin'. Hangers are just a way of gettin' more for a suit like I explained to tha grandmother yesterday.'

'Same difference,' Isaac interrupted. For a lad without schooling he was sharp as a tack and from the look in Mr Brown's eye, the lodger knew it.

'Tha's reet, lad,' he said and coughed a little. 'Look tha three, I'll tell thee what'll do. We need one another, us lot, I'm no use without the hangers and tha's got hangers. But tha hangers no good without clothes to hang on 'em, and I'll have the clothes, reet?'

'Reet.'

'So I'll tek ten hangers now and I'll owe thee fifteen bob. One and sixpence per hanger for thee and I get the other one and sixpence for my trouble.'

'Trouble? What trouble would that be, Mr Brown?' Billy asked.

'Negotiation trouble, lad. I'll be the one put out with the pawning of the bloody suits, tha naws. That's trouble.' And he slipped us an enormous blue wink from under his wet forehead.

We nodded our agreement to the deal, each of us appreciative of the trouble to which we were putting the man. Then the four of us spat on our palms and shook hands all round, concluding the transaction.

Mr Doyle had a washable condom which he hung out on the line every morning and, he had to admit, he was ever surprised to find it still there at night when he needed it. Why he imagined that anybody should want to steal his condom was a complete mystery. His new wife, the lass from the next village, was pretty enough but there had always been a suspicion about the pigs. People stayed away from Mr Doyle's condom waving on the line in his small garden at the back of the terrace. It was the last of the condoms brought to our village by Elyahou Tsiblitz. It was a complete rogue – it hadn't developed holes like all the others had. Mr Doyle didn't have unexpected children, he just had pigs. And chickens. Mr Doyle kept chickens as well as pigs, he kept them in a run in the garden too and they were the fattest chickens in Yorkshire. It was fairly common knowledge among the colliers that the reason why his chickens were so fat and healthy was because Mr Doyle fed them with the contents of his condom after it had been used.

Now for sure, one person who did not share this gem of information worthy of a note in the manual of animal husbandry was my grandmother, Emily Brightside. If she had known anything of it, she would not have eaten his chickens and, come to think of it, if she had harboured a suspicion about the other she would never have

259

eaten his pigs either. Yet, had my grandmother been told of it and had she been able to come to terms with the awfulness of Mr Doyle's habit and of course with the chickens' predilection too, then she really would have appreciated the practice as an exercise in masterly economy. Remember 'Waste not, want not' – presumably her motto would have intellectually extended to the use of semen as a protein source for chickens. I only tell you this because during the four weeks of lock-out Mr Brown and Albert stole chickens from Mr Doyle's run on three separate occasions and they gave them to my grandmother to supplement our meagre table rations. Mr Brown lied that he had been able to exchange them for paper bags at Leeds covered market and my grandmother chose not to disbelieve his explanation.

I don't know if the parson knew of Mr Doyle's practice and, if he did, what he might have made of it, but it was he who on one occasion got most of my share of the chicken. Sitting beneath the table, staring at the black gaiters of the man who had been invited to tea, I could only hope that the extra protein might choke him. When you are starving you don't care much for God and his preachermen. Mr Brown didn't care much for them even when he wasn't starving. They gave him the pip and on that occasion, Mr Brown kept on handing me down scraps of food which he took from the plate of the parson, who was sitting next to him. He stole it from his plate when the minister wasn't looking, which was usually when he was busy trying to hide a belch – something he often did. 'Pardon,' he would say with closed eyes and Mr Brown would pass me down another scrap like he would feed a dog out of the sight of the Lord.

Mr Goldenberger came over from Leeds with the tape around his neck and spent a full afternoon measuring each of us up for our new Sunday best. Mr Goldenberger's father was a rabbi and I could never understand how a Jew was able to make Sunday best for a gentile, but he seemed to manage it without complaint so I thought that it must be all right with his Lord. He ran his tape quickly over our bodies a bit at a time and jotted his numbers down in a grubby blue notebook and did a lot of additions sitting on a chair in the parlour with his head in one of his bony hands. He had a dreamy quality about him, as if he might go off to sleep if we were to leave him alone. He reminded me of my duck and of Isaac and I felt sorry for him. After measuring each person he would stop a while, add up his figures and drink deeply from the mugs of tea with which my grandmother plied him. The tea would sometimes drip into his beard and he would suck it from his moustache with nicotine-stained teeth. After all the additions he would then ask us to choose a cloth from a sample book which he carried in his case, but we had already decided that we wanted the most expensive. Then he would give us a price for the job and then another price because we wanted the clothes to be made in a rush. We had rehearsed what we had to say. Then Mr Brown would haggle and usually get ten per cent knocked off the price. When he went away, walking up the hill past the big house, all alone and with his brown case and long beard, it was with the biggest order that Mr Goldenberger had ever received, even if it was to be paid for on the drip.

When the clothes were delivered after only a few days and we had all been fitted we were amazed and delighted at how grand everyone looked. It was a credit to Mr Goldenberger's ability to measure his bits and of course to those whom he employed to follow his instructions. The clothes had been snipped to near perfection and we told the tailor so. He went off again, hundreds of shining pins stuck into his lapels and sucking my grandmother's tea from his moustache. I watched him winding up towards the crossroads and then I watched my duck sleeping on the still skin of water in his rain barrel. Life's diverse philosophies were coming together in my young brain.

My grandfather said that because he was such a clever devil, Mr Brown could do the pawning alone, which of course was a development which the lodger was fully expecting. I guess that he earned his one and sixpence per hanger. He got his usual ten shillings from Mr Partridge at Partridge, Peardorp and Treene in Castleford and he got the fifteen bob from Mr Zermansky. He was dressed in his Sunday best and carried his brass-topped cane like a gentleman. In each shop he visited he passed some comment about not having much time for God, because all that stuff gave him the pip. It seems that it was the only thing he could say in a posh accent but it didn't do his cause much harm because he managed to raise between ten and fifteen shillings in each establishment, and at one in Wakefield –

unfortunately it was the last place that he had to go for he would have tried it a second time – he got seventeen and sixpence for Clarrie's dress.

Mr Brown was a real gentleman, there was no messing about. He came straight out to the hut after he had given my grandmother the money he had raised – after deductions that is, but she knew nothing about them.

'There's the fifteen bob, like I said.' He gave us six shiny half-crowns – two apiece – and said, 'It's been nice doin' business with you,' like a real businessman would.

'It's been nice doin' business with you,' we each said in turn and shook the gentleman's hand.

When the policeman came our parlour was in playtime – quarter to five of an evening – and Billy and I were doing a jigsaw puzzle on the parlour table. The policeman said that he wanted to see Mr Brown and my grandmother fetched him from Mr Doyle's piggery.

'It's about some suits which tha's pawned in Castleford,' the policeman said, holding his helmet under his arm. He was only a young constable and he shuffled uncomfortably at what he was about to say. 'Savoy Hotel, eh?' He looked at Mr Brown's shabby trousers and at his dirty striped shirt. 'When was thee ever at the Savoy Hotel in London?'

'About ten years sin',' Mr Brown answered. 'I used to go regular when I was sellin' me paper bags.' He winked at Billy and me.

'Tha's sure tha's not bin more recent?'

'No.' Our lodger shook his head.

'Then how come tha's pawning clothes with Savoy hangers on 'em?'

'What's this all about?' asked Mr Brown. 'I'll not answer any more of tha questions unless th' explains thasen.'

'Just answer my question, please,' said the constable.

'No. What's going on? What's tha suggestin'?'

'There's been a theft, Mr Brown. Someone cleaned out the ward-robes from a number of rooms at the Savoy Hotel in London a few years since and tha's got spankin' new clothes pawned on Savoy hangers. How does th' explain that?'

'They was my suit and others' Sunday best who live 'ere and I found the hangers, that's how I explain it, constable. Now if tha'll excuse me I'll get back to t' pigs.'

'Well, where d'tha find the hangers, Mr Brown?'

The lodger looked at Billy and me for a moment then he coughed loudly and spat a black gobbet on the fire. When he turned he continued to look at Billy then he said, 'Found 'em on a tree.'

'Where?' said the policeman.

Mr Brown looked now at me concentrating his eyes on my lips. I was mouthing the words silently, willing him to understand.

'Aken Jugs,' he eventually said.

'Tha expects me to believe that tha found coat hangers from the Savoy Hotel in London on a tree at Aken Jugs?'

'Ay, I do,' he said.

'Yes, he does,' I piped up.

'Now, son, no need to go tellin' stories for the likes of Mr Brown. We know all about Mr Brown in Castleford, don't we, Mr Brown?'

'What's tha mean?' my grandmother asked.

'Nothing, Mrs Brightside. Just that we know all about Mr Brown's previous activities. Now, come on, Mr Brown, tha'd better come down to the police station with me and tha can mek a statement there.'

We watched with horror as the policeman slapped handcuffs on to Mr Brown's wrists and frog-marched him out of the house. Billy and I ran after them as my grandmother plonked herself heavily into a chair.

'It weren't him. It was Billy and me. We took the hangers,' I shouted.

The constable smiled as he escorted our lodger over the common, leading him by the arm. Mr Brown looked at me and he said, 'Best say nowt, lad. Go back home. I'll see thee soon.' He didn't come home that night.

I lay awake hearing the voices thrown up by the dark tide of night which had engulfed us. I no longer slept in my parents' bed but alone in a small bed at their side.

Get tha bloody foot off my pipe.

It's not on tha pipe.

It is, tha's not letting watter thru.

I'm not on tha bloody pipe. Tha must be standing on th' own bloody pipe.

'Rube Hardwick,' I said. 'Rube, tha's standing on his pipe.'

It's not Rube, it's me.

'Who? Mr Brown?'

No, Mr Brown's in jail. It's me.

'Who's me when tha's at home?'

It's me, tha brother, daft.

'I haven't got a brother,' I said aloud and I sat up in my bed, sweat pouring from my brow. The stones were speaking, bringing the madness which they had inflicted upon my great aunt Henrietta – or so I thought.

7

My mother, Mary Brightside, and the moment she knew who she was

My mother's story cannot be told without also revealing the conflict which circled within her, which was eventually to eddy up in me, which there was in our family after her marriage to William Brightside and which remained a constancy in daily village life. In its widest dimension it was the struggle between capital and labour, the coal owner and the pitmen. With regard to myself, it was typified by the opposing views I had of my two grandfathers: Ernest, the one with whom I lived and loved, and Joseph Thwaite, the one who lived at the big house less than a mile away yet was as remote as the King of England. As for my mother, it was the tension created in being both the daughter of the coal owner and the wife of a collier – and it was a tension which, no matter how it may appear to have been controlled, was constantly revolving within her slender frame.

Don't get me wrong, after her marriage and following my birth my mother had no loyalty to the Thwaites – her loyalties lay squarely with the Brightsides and in the Brightside home. It was other people who shifted the focus of her tensions, circling it about at their pleasure as if it was a wheel fixed to the cam which they controlled. They could poke it at her as they would a stick and my mother's wheel would find itself elsewhere, somewhere she never intended it to be, and as with all things poked at the ends of sticks she suffered a mixture of anger and fear. It was the geography of the place to which she was pushed that frightened her, for it was always that she found herself on the edge. She was never pushed over the edge, never banished properly, she was just kept at bay and found herself walking the dangerous perimeters of circles.

She had been brought up to be a lady, the granddaughter of old Thwaite, the one who had sunk the shaft and built the terrace of houses long, long ago. Old Thwaite, because at a time even before the sinking of the shaft he had been a pitman, had some sympathy with the miners – he knew their needs and though he had a reputation for being a hard man he wouldn't often see his workers starve. He knew the politics of the pit instinctively and he would always skilfully negotiate to firstly keep the pit productive, that was paramount – if he wasn't producing coal nobody won. But secondly he would negotiate production at a rate which gave employment to a maximum number of bodies at a wage where the least number might starve. He was a hard man but he wasn't a wicked man. Not like his son, Joseph, who locked out the men whenever the fancy took him.

Mary was brought up at the big house and as a child had played in the gardens among the warm sad trees. The gardens were bounded by a high wall which had a single set of gates. They had big stone pillars at either side and there were great stone pineapples on top of the pillars which everyone thought were just fancy balls until the coming of the cinema – then after seeing the film about East Africa we all learned that they were pineapples. I suppose that my mother knew they were pineapples long before my father did. He had to wait for the cinema, she had a governess. So my mother from an early age knew all sorts of things and spoke properly. She was pretty too. My father told me that she was the prettiest thing that he had ever seen. When he first set eyes on her she was playing on the red painted swing, in the gardens at the big house with her brothers and her sisters. They were both then fifteen years old. He had heard about her – he had heard about all of the Thwaite children – but he had not seen them until that day. Mary had a straw boater on her head like the one which Henrietta sometimes wore and she had on a long blue dress with something shiny threaded into the material and it shone and dazzled him in the sunshine.

'What do you want?' one of her brothers asked as William walked down the path among the weeping trees. The foliage pressed upon him causing an unease never expressed in nature beyond that walled place.

'Ah've come to see Mr Thwaite. I brought 'im summat from my father.'

'Oh, well, I suppose you'd better go knock on the door then, but go around the back, don't go to the front door for heaven's sake.'

William knew that the girl on the swing was staring at him but when he turned his face to hers she looked away from his dirty and torn breeches at which she had been staring. My mother gazed without concern into the sun and my father continued on his uncertain path to the house. He had never seen it before, not close up. He counted fifteen windows on the flat-fronted façade. Three rows of five windows – and he wondered which one would belong to the room of the pretty girl on the swing. In fact it was none of them; Mary slept at the back of the house which had just as many windows set into its dismal stone. As he approached within feet of the front door looking for a path which might take him round to the back of the house as the boy had suggested, the door opened and Thwaite came out with two dogs heaving at chokers about their heavy throats. William was frightened.

'What's tha want, lad?'

'Ah wants Mr Thwaite, sir.'

'Well, tha's got 'im. Stand still and the dogs'll not harm thee.'

'My father asked me to give thee this, Mr Thwaite.'

'Oh, ay. Who's tha father, when he's at 'ome?' he said, taking the package from William.

'Mr Brightside.'

'Ernest Brightside?'

'Ay.'

'I knew tha great grandfather, lad. John. John, wasn't it?'

'Yes.'

'Ay. John. I knew John. I worked in pit with John and tha great grandmother, Jane.'

'Yes, Mr Thwaite.'

'Worked with 'er, too. Still here, isn't she?' And whilst William nodded he said, 'Give tha great grandmother my regards, lad.'

'Yes, sir.'

'Tell tha father,' he said and he raised in the air the parcel which William had given him and waved it above the silk hat on his head, but he never said what it was that he should tell his father. Just 'Tell tha father,' that's all he said, waving the parcel about. As the dogs barked my father watched the sky turning blue all about the head of the black-clad coal owner.

'Yes, Mr Thwaite.'

As he turned to leave, the dogs growled angrily at his movement and strained all the more to be free of the leash. Old Thwaite said, 'It's all right, lad, I've got 'em. Tha'd better run whilst tha can,' and my father hared off as quickly as he could go, back through the green pressing trees to the other side of the gates with the pineapple balls.

He went back every day to see the girl on the red swing but usually she wasn't about. Once or twice he caught sight of her playing in the gardens and he would creep into the bushes and watch her from the sadness of the lush leaves. He would never reveal himself, though, not because he was uncertain of what she might say or because he was ashamed of his dirty dress but out of fear of the dogs. One of those dogs might have taken a piece out of his arse as large as a rich man's dinner. Then one day my father had the idea of taking Bruno, the Bellman's dog, with him on one of his visits to the big house. It was with blind faith that he said to Bruno, 'Now look, Bruno, we're off to seek the lass who lives with Mr Thwaite and if we can find her tha's got to help me. There's two big brutes who live up there in the big house and I know tha's not a lass thasen, Bruno, but does tha think tha could tek 'em off somewheres whilst I talk to the girl? Does tha think tha can find some way of occupying their attention or summat?'

Bruno just looked at my father with his intelligent brown eyes and whilst Bruno didn't have the same effect on William as he would later have on me, he knew that Bruno had understood and that he would help my father if he could. They went up to the big house and hid in the bushes together and waited for the girl to eventually appear. She sat alone on the red swing lazily twisting and untwisting in the heat and my father asked Bruno to go into the gardens and find the two big dogs and to take them off as he had agreed he would.

Bruno ambled on to the lawns and barked at the girl on the swing. She took no notice of him. So Bruno sat on the lawn shuffling his bottom on the grass and barked at the house with his black back to the girl. There was a barked response from within and soon the two great brutes came flying from the front door and raced up to the Bellman's dog, growling and barking as if they intended to tear off his head. Bruno sat becalmed in the centre of the lawn and barked at the sky, ignoring the two who had just appeared. Then they both sniffed at him but he refused to budge and remained sitting on his bottom. One of them had his nose rooted beneath Bruno's tail but the black dog still refused to budge; he continued to bark into the sky as if he were telling it to come down and do something. But the sky just sat up there and Bruno continued pluckily to sit on the lawn, now with both the coal owner's dogs rooting together and trying to lift him out of the ground like a claw hammer eases an old nail from a bit of wood. But Bruno had his solid tail anchored firmly to the lawn and still refused to budge. By now the others had ceased their barking and alternated their attention between Bruno's seated rear end and his barking head which was still fixed on the sky. Suddenly the black dog got up and walked off down the path, the others docilely following him, and my father saw him take them out beyond the gates and into the world of the miners. Then my father shouted, 'Ay up' and he threw a small stone at my mother which hit her on the ankle. She turned to see the boy who had delivered the parcel to her grandfather two weeks before. He was half submerged in the bushes and he made gestures with his hands calling her to him. She left the swing twirling in the lazy afternoon light and approached the boy.

'What's tha name?' he asked her, bending down so that he was out of sight of anyone at the house.

'Mary. What's yours?'

'William.' He didn't know what else to say and became embarrassed. 'Tha grandfather and my great grandfather were friends,' he told her eventually in an uncertain voice. She looked at him, smiling but unable to think of how she should reply. 'Can we be friends like them?' he eventually asked her.

'I don't know,' she told him.

'Well, can I come here again just to see thee, like? Can I see thee here in t' garden again?'

'I suppose it will be all right.'

The front door to the big house opened and somebody whistled for the dogs. Then, when they hadn't responded, the person in the doorway started shouting Mary's name over and over again and she told my father that she had to go indoors but that she would like to see him again sometime, just to say hello in the garden like they did now, and she left him alone in the warm secret of the bushes. He returned home in a daze, his heart thumping and the blood flushing up his cheeks. The dogs too returned to the big house. They went home each with several teeth missing. Bruno had been showing them how to play cricket on the common with the lads.

My father and Bruno went back to the big house on many occasions after that and Bruno always took the dogs off to some exciting new place. He taught them to swim down at Bottom Boat and he showed them the old mine where my great grandfather had found the dinosaur and where he was buried under the collapsed skeleton. He led them to the church in the next village to show them where God was and he showed them the ashpits behind our terrace of smoking houses. They were never the same after that – Bruno had brought down the sky and civilized them. The world was now a smaller, more friendly place and they weren't brutes any longer; after a time my father had no need to take Bruno with him when he went up to the big house for the two dogs became his friends. Whenever he rustled in the bushes they would bark and someone would let them out of the house and they would come lolloping over to him and lick his face with a true affection.

Then one day old Thwaite discovered him sitting in the bushes with his granddaughter; the two dogs were lying beside them flicking flies with their lazy tails and watching them kiss. The mine owner raved and ranted and chased my father from his property and threatened to have the Brightside family evicted from their home, because that was his property as well. Then he had the dogs put down and replaced them with two more brutes who tore up rabbits and even sheep with their big jaws. Mary began to dislike her grandfather after that and sometimes, not very often, but sometimes when it was possible for her to get away she met William under the gas lamp on the common and they would go over to Hunger Hill to do their courting. Then when Elyahou Tsiblitz brought the washable condoms to our village, like so many other curious couples married or not, they made love in a starry haze of coal dust which on some nights had the habit of glittering the air like green diamonds causing babies to come from nowhere, penetrate the rubber sheaths and swell the bellies of the leggy lasses.

That was how I came to be and how my mother and father came

to be married. Old Thwaite didn't like it but when they named me Donald after him, and when he learned that I had his same mischievous blue eyes, he relented and at last he came to see me and cried on my mother's shoulder. Grandfather Joseph, however, didn't have his father's softness and he cut my mother from the family without a penny. Her father had not spoken to her since before I was born. It was harsh, then, that some of our neighbours would not speak with her either. As I said, they held her at arm's length with sticks as if she was a different animal, and she didn't know where she belonged. Emily knew though, Emily quite rightly said that she belonged with the Brightsides, and that's where she stayed till she died. But she did walk those outer circles when she wasn't at home – the suspicion of some of the less pleasant of our neighbours pushing her there.

I can't remember exactly when it was, but there was a time after the bringing of the electricity that I heard it gather momentum on Hunger Hill. It ran ever so fast in the wires, scorching the moss and burning up the grass. It hummed very loudly at night. The extra surge caused our parlours to glow with so much candle power that when viewed from across the common the rooms seemed to be bathed in a startling brightness. We sat for a time in a kind of naked explosion, listening to our electric wirelesses and ironing our long johns. It disturbed us. It made the women self-conscious and brought a variety of shades to cover the neat bulbs and a selection of curtains to drape across the windows of the terrace, but even then the sheen glowed through. It was on such an evening during this period that young Doctor Cartwright informed my mother that she was having twins and he told her not to be so surprised because twin births ran in the family. It was at that moment that my mother learned for sure that she was a Brightside for the Thwaites had nothing like that to offer to the world. They had only dogs which didn't know where the sky was and a head of family so cruel that he didn't need to sleep. They didn't have twins or anything as human as that.

8

The rediscovery of Bresci's hat

Ernest's condition worsened; he got himself all bent up and had difficulty in straightening his back, besides which the joints of his fingers swelled up and he could hardly move his hands. Young Doctor Cartwright advised him to go to bed, lie flat on his stomach and have weights applied to his spine and to the backs of his hands in an attempt to unbend them. He lay on his bed, naked to the waist, with a flat iron in the middle of his back and with weights from our baking scales holding down his fingers. Also, because young Doctor Cartwright had suggested that the presence of copper might help, Emily had piled pennies, halfpennies and farthing pieces along his spine and Lancaster had unwound the inductance from Mr Brown's crystal set and turned the copper wire about my grandfather's wrists. He was given an aspirin tablet with a glass of water every three hours. After a day or two of such treatment Ernest told Emily that his back felt a lot better and she removed the weights. She also took the weights from his hands but she left the copper wire binding up his wrists and rewound it a little around his fingers too. There were great swellings on his joints. It was just as well that he was locked out, she told him, for with his hands in such a state he would never have been able to have held the pick.

He heard the Bellman come to the village and climbed clumsily from his bed. He thrust up the window in my parents' bedroom using the backs of his hands and he put his greying head into the dull day. A crowd larger than normal had assembled to hear the Bellman's news – everyone was waiting on news of Mr Brown.

'They've gone and stuck him away for six months,' Jacky told us.

'But 'e didn't do owt,' Ernest said from the window. Billy and I had told my grandfather what we knew about the hangers.

'Oh, ay, 'e did,' said Jacky.

'What?' said my grandfather. 'What did he do?' The eyes of the crowd were on my grandfather leaning painfully from the window.

' 'E stole 'em.'

'What? I don't believe it,' said my grandfather. 'Why should he go and steal a load of coat hangers?'

'Not the hangers. It weren't the hangers he was done for – it was the paper bags.'

'What! All them paper bags he was forever blowin' into?'

'Ay. 'E stole 'em from the bag factory in York, tha naws.'

'When was this?' asked my grandfather, who liked to know the sequence of things before he could accept a judgement.

' 'E stole some only last week. Apparently 'e were allus doin' it. Compulsive, the magistrate said 'e was. A compulsive thiever of paper bags. Brown ones. Like 'is name.'

I couldn't believe what we were being told. 'No,' I shouted up, 'Mr Brown had his own factory. He made his own paper bags, Mr Jellis.'

'Oh, ay, an' I got a place making jam sandwiches,' said Mr Archbold, who had slung up his bedroom window only a short distance from where my grandfather's naked torso leaned into the daylight. Everyone laughed. I felt ashamed that I had piped up when I had.

'Never mind, son,' Jacky said kindly. 'We all get took in from time to time.' Then to all the others he said, 'It weren't his first conviction for it. It was third time 'e'd bin copped for stealing paper bags. Police'll be comin' o'er to tha 'ouse, Ernest,' he then called up to my grandfather. ' 'Appen they'll be searchin' for the bags.'

I broke into a cold sweat and saw that Billy had turned bright pink.

'We'll 'ave to be rid of 'em,' my friend informed me in a quiet voice.

We went down to Owler Crimble to find Isaac. He would know what to do. When we found him the lad was sitting on a log and had fallen asleep with the wooden clapper across his knee.

'We'll 'ave to burn 'em,' Billy told him when the boy had woken up and we had told him of the stolen loot which was stashed in our hut.

'I'n't no point in doin' that,' he said. 'Tha's just mekin' a panic for nowt. We can tek 'em o'er to my father. They'll hide in his desk until it's forgotten, nobody ever think of lookin' there.' Isaac was ice cool. A welcome influence on our overheating brains.

'Come on,' he said. 'We'll go get 'em now.'

We walked across to the hut and Isaac stuffed the bags down his trousers and told us that he would take them to his father's house.

The following day the lock-out ended. Thwaite had sold all his coal to a gentleman in India and informed us that we didn't have to take a cut in wages after all. In fact he gave each man another sixpence per shift and my family went back to the pit tapping out a little more than normal. Emily bought more pot ducks for the wall in the parlour to show the neighbours how affluent we were.

Of the few visitors who regularly came to our house the one I didn't tell you about was the man from the Burial Society. He came every Tuesday evening. His name was Mr Willmott and he came on a bicycle. His tash grew so low over his mouth that when he spoke you couldn't see his lips moving and I used to wonder if it was he who had spoken at all. The words didn't even come from his direction. He would sit very still at the parlour table with a money bag in his hands and with cycle clips about the bottoms of his trousers. He was only animated when it was time to drop the pennies which my grandfather had just given him into the bag. Then he would nod his long head for a moment or two and stare at my grandfather with dark smouldering eyes. Billy said that he was a Martian and that his eyes were capable of emitting a ray that could pierce metal. He always wore a neat collar which was buttoned down with little brass studs and he had a red tie. Throughout the time of his visit he would just sit and apparently not say anything. Ernest always looked as if he was having a conversation with someone else when Mr Willmott came. It was as if there were three people in the room – Mr Willmott, my grandfather and a third person. Someone over there, whom you never saw.

Ernest paid into the Burial Society because Emily insisted that he should. He paid the insurance for all of us, even for Mr Brown and even during the six-month period the lodger spent in jail. The money, though it wasn't a lot, could have been used for the purchase of food but Emily insisted that when the time came we all had to be decently put away. A pauper's grave would have been ignominious and she would never have had the neighbours see us in such a disgrace. Our deaths, like our Sunday suits, were going to confer a respect upon us. We could walk tall, happy in the knowledge that self-esteem would follow even after the destruction of self. The effect of such tortuous thought was to give me a headache. Such questions needed the mind of a philosopher, so I went outside and asked my duck if self-esteem was practised by the spirits. He promptly turned himself upside down and showed me his arse. He refused to reappear until I had gone back indoors and seated myself with my grandfather, who as always was admiring the strange ventriloquism of Mr Willmott. I looked back out of the parlour window. My duck was asleep on the still surface of his rain barrel water.

When my great great grandmother died she had a grand funeral. There were four black horses, each with red and white plumes, which dragged her carriage away from the dark stone of the terrace house and up the hill to the church in the next village. There were motor cars and carriages following and my father started up the Jam Sahib's motor and I rode with him and my mother among the cortège. I remember looking back. 'Don't look back,' my mother said. 'It's unlucky.' But I looked back and saw hundreds of people in their best clothes all following the coffin up the hill, their flat caps jostling under a thin rain. Then my father looked back with tears in his eyes and eventually my mother turned her head too. She never instructed me not to look back again.

When she went, my great great grandmother had left a fortune hidden somewhere. It was the fortune which she was reputed to have brought with her after her husband had died and when she came to live at our house. Some of it had been spent – the cameras which she had bought for Lancaster and Albert and all of those painting materials which she had given them to launch their artists' careers. That must have cost. There had been many other presents, too, not to mention the money she had handed over in payment of the Jam Sahib's motor. But the general feeling was that there was more, much more – but nobody knew where it was. There is a photograph in our family album which had been taken by Albert. It is a photograph of the old woman standing on Hunger Hill and she is seen to be nursing a large suitcase in her arms. She has a cap on her head. The cap is commonly believed to be that of Bresci, the man who assassinated the King of Italy and the brother-in-law of Uncle Elyahou Tsiblitz. His former wife's brother's hat, that is. The

275

suitcase is commonly believed to contain the missing fortune but, as I told you, nobody knows where it is. Albert spent a lot of effort digging about the summit of Hunger Hill, which is where the photograph was taken, but he didn't find anything. Then he just dug holes at random all about the village but he only succeeded in creating puddles of metal-tasting rain. Earlier still, the five Gill boys who had been our next-door neighbours had dug up the inside of our house when no one was at home, but they had found nothing either. So when my uncle Albert was found dead down the pit with Bresci's hat on his head it was assumed that he must have found the missing fortune. Of course, we didn't know that it was Bresci's hat, not at first anyway.

Ernest came home with his mates, he was all doubled up with his arthritis and he was crying. He opened the street door and came into the parlour, letting the yellow electric light escape from the house a little, and his mates waited outside huddled in its paleness. He explained to my grandmother that Albert was dead and that he didn't know how it had happened and she ran off upstairs to consider her grief. My mother went after her. It didn't do to be alone with grief; like a man from the asylum, there was no telling what it might do. Ernest dispatched Lancaster to go and tell Rosanne what had happened and to fetch her to the house because that's where they would bring the body when it was taken from the pit. My father was sent to get young Doctor Cartwright.

When the doctor arrived, Albert's body was already laid out on the parlour table. Rosanne had been taken off to join my grandmother in the bedroom and Clarrie sat on her grandfather's knee, unable to understand why her father wouldn't wake up. It was a reasonable lack of understanding, Albert did appear to be asleep. Asleep in his grimy clothes and with a dirty face and with a flat cap on his head. Lancaster was trying to remove the cap from his dead brother's head but it wouldn't come off. He complained immediately and somewhat vaguely to Doctor Cartwright that he was unable to remove the cap from Albert's head and the doctor concluded that Lancaster was in a state of shock and made him sit down. Mrs Gill, who had come from next door, gave him some strong tea. The doctor then tried to remove it but he too was unable to wrench the cap away. Our neighbours, some of whom were staring in at the window, were now shouting advice on how best to be rid of the hat, advocating in turn the use of Mr Doyle's lard and a good lathering of glycerine of soap on the forehead of the deceased.

Then my grandfather, handing Clarrie on to me, said 'Give it 'ere,' and tried to get his fingers under the cap so that he could lift it from his son's head, but he couldn't control his arthritic fingers. His swollen nodules were too large and too painful to allow him to get his fingers between the cap and Albert's head and the neighbours then advised smearing his fingers with Vaseline. Ernest put his head into his curled-up hands and wept with frustration.

Finally, Emily came down the rickety stairs, my mother hanging on to her elbow. My grandmother immediately closed the curtain across the window and over the startled faces of the onlookers. She kissed her son's dirty face and asked my mother to put some hot water into a bowl and to bring her a rag. Whilst all about hopelessly watched she took a pair of scissors from the drawer directly beneath the bible in the sideboard and cut the cap at the side of Albert's head, close by his dead ear. The cap then came away and she handed it to Ernest. There was a clean white ring about my uncle's forehead. Then she bathed his face whilst my mother knelt beside her holding the bowl of steaming water. She washed away all the coal dust and kissed him again, this time on both cheeks. Then she straightened up and faced my grandfather.

'How did it happen?' she asked her husband almost as if it was he who had been responsible.

'I dunno,' Ernest shrugged whilst squeezing the cap in his two arthritic hands. 'Archbold comes to me just before the end of the shift and 'e says, "It's tha lad, Ernest. Tha'd better go and see." And 'e was there in the gallery lying on 'is face when I went to look.' His chest trembled and wheezed and I saw my grandfather's face all screwed up and tears squeezed from his eyes. Then he stood for ages, trembling and looking at his dead son laid on the table, and nobody seemed to know what to do.

'Stinking pit,' was all that my grandmother said and she sat heavily down into a wide winged chair.

The doctor started to examine the body. Then Rosanne came downstairs and clutched Clarrie to her. After his examination the doctor said, 'I can't find anything wrong. Seems like natural causes.'

'What tha mean, like his heart or summat?' Ernest asked.

'Maybe,' said the doctor and he watched Ernest turning the hat in his hands. 'Had he complained of feeling ill?' he asked Rosanne and she shook her fair head.

Then quite suddenly my grandfather, who had been turning the hat inside out and back again several times, said, 'Hang on. This is my cap. This is the cap that grandmother gave me, the one which Bill Pettit told us had belonged to the man who killed the King of Italy.'

Everyone then seemed to lose interest in the corpse.

'Give it 'ere, Father,' said William. 'Ay. 'Tis,' he said. 'Look 'ere, it's got 'is name in it. Gaetano Bresci,' he told all who were assembled in the parlour.

'Well I nivver,' said my grandfather, as if now nothing had happened to his son other than that he had found a long-lost hat.

'Tha naws what this means, doesn't tha, Father?' Lancaster said, dashing to the bookshelf and turning up the photograph which Albert had taken. 'There,' he said, pointing to the hat which Great Great Grandmother had worn on that day. 'It's the same hat.'

'Albert found the bloody fortune,' William told my grandfather, light dawning all over his face.

Rosanne insisted that the wagon be used as a funeral carriage. She wished that she had still got the shire horse to pull it – Albert would have liked that, she said – but she was more than satisfied when the Burial Society offered the four black horses with the red and white plumes to pull the wagon. We all went in a procession up the hill to the church in the next village.

Ernest ranted. He was a lay preacher and he had picked up the ranter's ways. My great great grandmother would have hated it, having to listen to her Ernest going on about poverty and punishment and how we all should behave ourselves and accept what the Lord sends us or we would be packed off to everlasting damnation. He went on about resurrections as if it was Easter and at one time seemed to be talking about the resurrection of his son. It became all too much for my grandmother.

'Ernest,' she told him, 'sit thasen down. Stop frightenin' thasen and everyone else with tha nonsense. Albert's gone and tha'll not bring him home with that sort of talk. Why he died God alone knows, but it's all to do with the grim funny business of life, Ernest, and it's about time tha learned such a thing. The grim funny business of life will get us all in the end. So don't go mekin' such a fuss, luv.' Then she sat down and sniffed into her handkerchief. The congregation sat for a while in stunned silence whilst the four plumed horses stood quietly in the warm sunshine beyond the open door, not doing much other than occasionally move their legs away from the blowflies. They made distinct clopping noises that echoed in the silent pews. One of them did his droppings on the path in front of the doors. Then we all went out and buried our Albert. We had a tea at our house and people kept coming in and they said how sorry they were that Albert had gone whilst they ate my grandmother's jam tarts. 'Yes, I'm sorry he's gone too, luv,' is just about all she would say to anybody.

At about six o'clock somebody asked where Rosanne and Clarrie were and though we searched about we couldn't find them. Then Billy o' the Terrus End pointed out that the wagon had gone. We all ran outside. I could never remember before having seen the gas lamp without the red and gold wagon parked under it. I felt that something had gone from my life. Then Mr Piggott came over and told my grandfather that he had seen the wagon being pulled by the four plumed horses on the Wakefield road. He had passed them in his car only half an hour before. He said that Rosanne was up at the front and that she had a long whip with which she lashed the horses like a madwoman.

'Never mind,' my grandfather said. 'She has her own grief to live with.'

It wasn't until a couple of days later that we realized that she had gone off with the Burial Society's prize horses.

'Well, somebody's at last got more than a burial out of 'em,' my father commented sarcastically.

A few days after that we realized that Rosanne had probably scarpered with Great Great Grandmother's fortune too.

It wasn't long before we had another funeral to attend. It was the burial of my little brother who had to be put into a pauper's grave as no one had ever paid subscriptions into a Burial Society for the little fellow. My grandmother told Mr Willmott that it was all a piece of nonsense, since no one would ever think about someone being dead before they were born. Mr Willmott didn't say anything, at least I don't think that he said anything, he just continued to stare at her with his piercing eyes and she asked him if it was possible to transfer payments from one name to another. But the insurance man was adamant that burial insurance could only be for named individuals in the policy, unless you were to take out another policy to cover those persons who might not have a name. He explained that if the family had taken out such a policy then my brother would have most certainly been covered – providing my mother's pregnancy had gone full term. If it hadn't, then there would have had to have been a third policy to cover him because he wouldn't have been classed as a person – just an embryo or something.

The twins had been born. There was a boy and a girl but the boy had been born dead. He was tiny, like Lancaster had been when he was born. The girl was a great bouncy thing and Doctor Cartwright said that it was probable that, just as was the case with Lancaster and Albert, the girl had been standing on the boy's umbilical and had cut off his nourishment; but where Lancaster had survived, my brother unfortunately had not. Mr Brown returned just in time to attend the funeral. My sister was christened Irene Rose and Henrietta sent her a rubber cot sheet from Berlin.

9

Significant events inside an onion

In 1919 Lloyd George set up a Royal Commission of Enquiry into the state of the mining industry, telling the miners that he would implement whatever recommendations were made, but at the same time assuring his cabinet that the Commission wasn't likely to suggest any radical changes. He told his colleagues that even if the Commission were to recommend nationalization, a very radical change but a most unlikely proposal, then he would not be prepared to pass the necessary legislation. Well, the Royal Commission went and recommended nationalization, didn't it, and old Lloyd George had to break his pledge to the miners. Of course, Lloyd George said that there never had been such a pledge; the implementation of their recommendations had been dependent on the Royal Commission's unanimity, he said, and as they were not unanimous there could be no nationalization – the majority decision was neither here nor there.

The rumbling trouble in our village over the next twenty years had its roots in Lloyd George's broken pledge. All those strikes and lock-outs, ostensibly about rises in wages and cuts in wages and increased working hours, were really about the broken pledge. It was a measure of the miners' dislike for a man who had shown himself at some time a hero only to settle to being a plain cheat. Everyone got very confused about the issues after that and even the union lost sight of what the discontent was about. At one time it had been about 'Mines for the Nation' and then suddenly it was about wages and working conditions. But it wasn't, it wasn't about wages and conditions at all. In our village it was about being rid of Thwaite. As long as Thwaite remained the coal owner the troubles would rumble on.

Working people had talked about a General Strike for a century or more but when it came it really was a non-event. It lasted only nine days, yet fifty years later people spoke of it as if it was the most significant thing in modern British history. In the first place our village had been locked out for months before the event – it was called in our support anyway – and we were to be strike-bound for many months after it was all over. So for us it was nine days of nothing in the middle of a much greater period of inaction. The year was like an onion, it had layers. At either end was a month or so of work. The rest of the months were either locked out or strike-bound and in the dead centre were those nine days in May when the nation stood still. It was during that period of doing nowt in 1926 that significant things happened in our village.

Lancaster, going on seven years home from the War, had still not managed to shake himself free from the past. The war years tugged at him, pulling him continually back to the terror of the skies. His dead comrades limped by. His dead relatives and friends, those whom he hadn't properly mourned, constantly called him. He wanted to go. He wanted to follow Archie Jellis and Bruno down to London but ghosts kept on calling him back. Then one day in the middle of the General Strike Lancaster got up from the chair in which he slept and shaved as always in the scullery. In the small mirror which hung on a piece of bent wire and dangled from the window frame behind the sink he saw the street door closing behind him. There was only himself imaged in the glass and he started to whistle an old song. He took himself off to the schoolhouse. On the way he could hear Isaac's father potting at the pigeons and the rooks with his shotgun. At the school he asked Wenceslas Piggott if he could finish off Albert's painting on the wall at the back of Standard One.

Slowly, and disappointingly for the children, the two shadowy figures seated on the bed were transformed from curved, full-breasted symbols of sketchy voluptuousness into a likeness of the craggy and handsome reality of my twin uncles attired in a strange Sunday best. Flights of fancy gave them neat clean collars and striped ties and brought to one of them a pair of angel's wings. The one without the wings unaccountably wore my grandparents' glasses and held a white cane like a blind man might have done. The two figures perched at the edge of the bed dressed in their electric blue best appeared to be slightly nervous of their surroundings in a very ordinary room. I guessed that the one with the wings was my uncle Albert but Lancaster would never tell which was whom.

Mr Brown said that in finishing Albert's painting, Lancaster had taken on his twinly duty of having to tie up his brother's loose ends. Settling his estate, he called it. Young Doctor Cartwright, looking into the schoolroom through the closed dirty window and seeing Lancaster sitting on the top of Mr Clayton's steps at the back of Standard One, agreed that he was certainly tying up loose ends for he saw it that my uncle was knotting the umbilical.

'Surely tha does that after a man's birth, not after his death,' Mr Brown told him uncertainly, for he didn't like to be questioning the doctor's province: Doctor Cartwright delivered most of the babies born into our village these days.

'Not necessarily,' the doctor pontificated. 'In the case of twins, twins like these two, there is a second umbilical which needs attention. The rope which ties them together throughout their lives needs attention too. There comes a time when that must be severed, you see. Lancaster hardly wants to be dragging his brother's corpse about with him for the rest of his life, does he? So he tidies up the estate like you say, Mr Brown, and then he snips the cord and lets his brother sail free.'

Mr Brown looked into the sky as if at any moment Doctor Cartwright might have Albert floating there. 'What of Irene Rose?' he then asked the doctor, bringing his lonely gaze back to earth.

'The lad had no estate, Mr Brown,' the doctor reminded him and left hurriedly to call on his next patient.

The day that H. G. Wells stole Marlene Jellis from the pub, my uncle Lancaster, having tidied up his brother's estate spoke to Mr Brown of talking pictures.

First things first. A turned signpost brought what little traffic there was down to the village. Most of it wandered about the common a while and then Billy o' the Terrus End directed the cars back up the hill from where they had come down, telling the motorists that they must be daft if they imagined that here was the way to Leeds. We watched them disappear into the distance by the big house, each motor giving a tired honk as it negotiated the steep rise. Then at about four o'clock a bull-nosed Morris arrived and the motorist dismounted at the far end of the terrace. He was dressed in a neat but very lengthy overcoat and he wore a trilby on his head. The man was all muffled up with a scarf so that one couldn't see his face. He smoked a Turkish cigarette which disappeared into the folds of material and presumably from there on into his mouth, which was completely hidden from view. The yellow smoke which curled from the lighted end of the cigarette hung about his head like an extra garment.

'Is there a public bar in the village?' he asked us without removing the cigarette. We could see now that he wore goggles beneath the scarf but we were unable to see the man's eyes.

Billy pointed. 'O'er yon,' he said and when the man had walked off in the direction of the pub he said excitedly, 'That's the invisible man, Donald. Did tha see?'

I watched the man walking away from us and heard his shoes squeaking. 'I'n't no such thing,' I told my friend, convinced somehow that squeaky shoes were something which one could only attribute to the material.

'He's a friend of Mr Willmott's,' Billy said, undeterred by my scepticism. 'He's been to Mars, tha naws, 'as the invisible man. Probably brought Willmott back with him, last time he went.' Then with a last edgy glance at the departing stranger he sneered, 'Who'd buy insurance from a Martian?'

I suddenly felt guilty for my family's support of the man from another planet. Commission for aliens was not something in which we were now encouraged to indulge. Things weren't like they had been in the days of Great Great Grandmother. She had encouraged a warmth for Elyahou Tsiblitz and it hadn't been difficult for our neighbours to respond – most of them. Strangers, though distrusted, were eventually taken in to the hearts of the people. Even Mr Ndolo, the first black man to come to the village, had been accepted warmly after he had demonstrated how he could eat fire and then turn himself into a beautiful princess. I suppose it was the War that must have started it – this dislike of strangers. It hadn't been like that before the War – there had been distrust but not dislike. Bill Pettit maybe, perhaps Bill had hated, but not the others. But I expect that it's normal to hate if you happen to be born before your time like Bill had been. The world must be a strange and frightening place if you can mislay things in your head.

Then when old Thwaite died along came Joseph Thwaite and we all saw the terrible way that he and those strangers at the big house would treat the colliers – there was a real hatred of Thwaite and what he represented for he was at the dead centre of our misery, or so we told ourselves. Looking back on it, perhaps it was the War which after all taught us to hate and the coal owner just happened to become a convenient focus for our feelings.

Thwaite was at the dead centre of those nine days, too, at the dead centre of an inactive ten months. He was at the centre of 1926 and at the centre of what seemed to be years of Brightside troubles on either side of the strike. We were inside that dark shell, he and I. My maternal grandfather and I were in the centre of a dark egg, pressed in; it was a struggle within the coal, a struggle within the living history of the stone, as my great aunt Henrietta might have said. Many years later Henry Moore, who came from just down the road, would show me that struggle in his gravid, sculpted forms and he would show me the road out through the hole in my mother's belly. But for the time being I was locked tight within the coal, an embryo being brought to term for a delivery into the stinking pit.

'Shall we go and see?' I asked Billy as the stranger went from our view.

We followed him over to the pub and from the open doorway watched Rube Hardwick draw half a pint of beer which he set down in front of the man who even on his rough stool at the small iron table retained his invisibility. Although the Turkish cigarette was now much shorter, the yellow smoke still hung about his clothes. He began to unwind the scarf from about his head and we each shivered a little, anticipating the horribleness of the man's lack of substance. I'm not sure why – perhaps when he sat down the man's shoes had ceased their squeaking – but I was beginning to sympathize with Billy's wild fantasy.

The only other people in the pub at that time were Mr Piggott and Marlene, who were engaged in conversation at a table next to the newcomer. Marlene rocked her buttocks on the small stool, her red hair done up in its neat bun. She seemed to stop in mid-sentence, her fascination for the stranger's revealing of himself equal to our own. The scarf continued to unwind. Were we to see bandages about an incorporeal mummy? It was with great disappointment that we learned that the man had eyes beneath his motoring goggles and that he had moustaches as bushy as any which we had yet seen.

He saw Marlene's fascination with his extra-long scarf and we heard him introduce himself first to Wenceslas and then to Marlene, at whom he twinkled. He called himself Sosthenes Smith. Marlene caught her breath. Billy and I could see her holding it in and we thought that she might be counting to see if she could beat some kind of record for not breathing. Her face reddened. The stranger said that he was a futurologist and told Marlene that she was going to get a big surprise because she was going on a journey. Wenceslas looked very unhappy. Marlene was breathing again now but her face was still very red. The stranger hoped that he wasn't being too indelicate when he told her that she had a liking for older men. The stranger sipped his beer and Mr Piggott, painfully aware of his greying head, seemed to grow more gloomy. His tash drooped and Marlene told him to remove the beer from it as it was dripping on her arm. He gloomily sucked at his tash. Then the stranger asked Wenceslas Piggott how he didn't know that there were men on Mars and Billy gave me a nudge under the ribs with his bony elbow. Wenceslas said that he didn't know, he couldn't know for sure, and the man called him a ditherer. Marlene beamed at the stranger and Mr Piggott fell into an even deeper depression. Then the man said that we should all in years to come probably end up looking like Martians; without any legs because we drove about in motors and with great big heads because our brains were bound to expand with all the knowledge that we should have to fill them with. Wenceslas started to say that he was a schoolteacher and that in his opinion there wasn't so much knowledge about that it could make heads grow and anyway in his experience most people weren't very much interested in education. Most boys spent the day dreaming about lasses, he said, and Billy, whose brain was by now large enough to accommodate both Martians and women, gave me another dig in the ribs. Marlene looked angrily at Wenceslas for having raised such a matter in front of a total stranger. The schoolteacher looked positively suicidal after that and drank down his beer as if it were some painful toxic potion.

Then Sosthenes Smith, seeing the look which had passed between the lovers, begged his leave of them and apologized, hoping that he hadn't caused a row or anything, and he got up to go, beaming at the red-faced Marlene. He slipped on his goggles and wound the lengthy scarf back around his head, then he pushed his way roughly between Billy and me; we were still standing at the door. Marlene, making a lightning decision, came hustling by and she caught up with him by the motor. He invited her to hop into his bull-nosed Morris and Sosthenes Smith drove her away. He shouted back to Billy and me, 'Which is the way to Leeds, boys?' and Billy and I both pointed over to Hunger Hill, but Sosthenes Smith was more than a match for the likes of us for he turned the car round and headed out the way he had come in. Marlene was already letting her hair fall over her golden brooch even before they had got as far as the big house.

You know, there are some mornings when the sun has risen a deep red colour over the river at Bottom Boat. It catches in the waving poplars down by the river bank and it casts tinted shadows in the fields and on the hill and across the village. The particles of coal dust which fill the air get tinged purple and deep violet and they scatter the dark light like little prisms. Everything is given an edge of the rose-red hues, even the transparent wings of insects which bustle in the pink air. Dragonflies and bees, mayflies, tree wasps and beetles take in the redness. Gromwell, holly, ribwort and sorrel are touched by it and the little forget-me-not flowers and sauce-alone turn magenta. At Aken Jugs the oaks seem to be aflame and in the crimble, the elder bursting alone from the red mother earth takes a fire to its berries and leaves. Hunger Hill hides behind its treacherous purple veil and you can hear the songs of the corn-crake and the redpoll. The bean begins to flower and the larks sing miles above the land. In this May morning the lime and the sycamore and the beech trees start to leaf. And in the blood-red grass the drunks who have slept the night in the fields like fallen scarecrows rouse themselves, perhaps trailing a last note or two of the carousal with which they had sung themselves to sleep – a long-gone cadence slipping easily on the mind. Lullabies. Lullaby Danny Pratt's father, who had limped breathless from the pub the night before, pulls his cap over his eyes so as not to see the yellow Haltica beetle creeping orange on his dirty sleeve. Then up, up in a windmill, whirl-arms wheeling towards the village and his irate wife.

It had been Danny Pratt's father who had one such morning smashed his way through our scullery door and slithered to the floor by our white sink, with several bottles of Great Great Grandmother's herbal mixtures which he had grabbed from the rows of dusty shelving. Drunk and drugged on Ipomoea and Arnica nut he slumped there; a bag of warped dreams. Young Doctor Cartwright had said that he should be sent to the asylum at Wakefield where he would have his brains wrung out but Mrs Pratt wouldn't allow it. So she just took him back to the field and left him among the thorns and the crowfoot. She left him there for days sleeping off his poisoned intoxication while the larks twittered morning and night. Then, another red morn he had picked himself up and dragged himself faltering of both step and breath back to the house which huddled somewhere in the middle of our terrace. The smoke curled from the chimney pot, the fire roared, the bread fried in the pan, his sons took themselves off to the pit. In his parlour Danny Pratt's father imagined the corpses in the trenches, imagined the gas wafting through, imagined the command to fix bayonets and he charged the stairs. Then he fell asleep in his own bed until Mrs Pratt came to wake him in the afternoon with a pot of tea and a kiss.

So this red morn too, Danny Pratt's father, with his cap over his eyes, stands uncertainly up, wheezing in the field of flowering beans. He thrashes about with his legs, he whirls his arms with purpose and finds somehow the direction he must travel to find his wife. 'Coming home,' he's saying. 'I'm coming home.' At the same moment Isaac's father, ever ready to protect his crop, beans as well as corn, fires the shotgun which he holds. He fires the gun only, I am sure, to frighten him but he puts a hole clean through the poor man's pickled head. The rooks lift off in a dust, clattering into the blazing red sky.

Mr Clayton discovered the body the following day and he got Wenceslas Piggott and my uncle to help him carry it home to Mrs Pratt. And we all had to troop off to bury Lullaby Danny Pratt's father and sing him to sleep forever in the far corner of the graveyard at the church in the next village.

My uncle Lancaster and Mr Brown, standing outside the walls of

Henrietta's laboratory, saw Marlene Jellis speeding off in the stranger's motor but thought nothing of it. Emily had told them Marlene was always speeding off with somebody, as long as he had trousers. They didn't doubt that the muffled man also wore trousers.

'There must be some way of getting them to talk,' my uncle said. Ever since he had first voiced his thought of talking pictures whilst lying in Mrs Cushman's bed he had dreamed of the possibility, but Lancaster was no engineer and could find no way of theorizing the technicalities which the problem presented, besides which he had been bound up with thoughts of other things. The past hadn't until that morning, when he looked in his shaving mirror and saw it departing behind him, let him go. At last he was able to bring his thought to the inventor of the brown paper bag.

'Synchronicity. That's what tha wants,' Mr Brown told him.

'What's that?'

'It's the exact marriage of sight and sound. Tha's being synchronous when tha's talking, like. Watch my lips move, see. I can't help it, can I – it's reality.'

'So what?'

'So the only true method would be for us to put the sound on to the film.'

'I don't understand.'

'Well, if tha could get the wave pattern of the sound on to the film and have it read and translated back into sound as the film is being shown on the screen and if tha could at the same time amplify the sound, then the picture would be synchronous with the sound and the bloody thing would look like it's talking to thee, see.'

'Is that possible?'

'Ay. Nowt's impossible. It'd just cost a bloody fortune, that's all.'

'So what else?'

'Well, t'other way would be two separate systems. Tha meks tha picture and tha records tha sound on a wax disc and tha marries 'em up like.'

'Would that be expensive?'

'Naw, not really. Tha's got camera, I could knock summat up for sound.'

Before the General Strike was finished we had all piled into the Royal Picture Palace to watch the very first talking picture ever seen in England. The film makers synchronized their machines and a picture of Mr Brown appeared rather shakily on the screen. There was no amplification of the sound so we had to be very quiet to hear the man, dressed up in his Sunday best, saying rather scratchily and in a very posh squeak, 'I'm sovvy, I have no tile for God and all that stun. It give me the bib.' Then Mr Brown smiled, eyes twinkling, from the white flickering screen and his tash drooped at us for what seemed an eternity. We clapped and cheered and stamped our feet and the urchins whistled enthusiastically at the marvel which we had just witnessed, then the figure on the screen bowed like a real gentleman would and he waved at us like royalty.

'How did tha know to bow, Mr Brown?' I asked him as I stood by the man in the darkened auditorium. 'How did tha know tha'd get all them people clapping thee?'

'I just knew it, son, just knew that if I could be heard then I'd 'ave 'em clappin' me.'

'Mr Brown, tha's a genius,' I told the lodger, not for the first time.

Word soon got about that there was a minor miracle to be heard at the Royal. People came from miles about and paid good money to see Mr Brown talking on film. The sequence was so short that Mr Pinkofsky could have filled his cinema a dozen times a night but he showed it only twice nightly, choosing to incorporate the film into the regular programme. That way, he argued, the miracle had an even greater impact on those who saw it.

On the day that we buried Danny Pratt's father, the police arrested Isaac's father for his murder. I didn't see much of Isaac after that. It seemed that it was all right to mix with thieves like Mr Brown but one shouldn't become involved with those who are themselves tainted with the most unforgivable of sins. Even when it's a terrible accident, as Isaac's father always pleaded it was. That didn't save him, though, and they hanged him at Leeds jail the following year. Sometimes I used to wonder whatever happened to my brown paper bags but I never could find the right reason to go up to the farmhouse and ask for them back – it just didn't seem to be right to be finding reasons in such circumstances. Gradually I just forgot about the bags, as I forgot about Isaac too. I used to see him occasionally in the crimble, asleep with the clapper across his knee, but I didn't bother to waken him. I sometimes used to see his mother too, policing the beanfield with the shotgun beneath her arm and keeping it clear of the rooks and the pigeons. The killing hadn't deterred the drunks, though. They still flopped in the fields at night and woke up like scarecrows on rosy mornings.

The funeral brought its change in me, too. I stood about the graveside with all the others, hearing the wail of little Danny above the singing, and I thought of how beautiful was that word lullaby. I said it over to myself time and again until it became a foreign word devoid of any meaning. I broke the word into its three syllables and slowly repeated the three syllables to myself until it was all as incomprehensible as my uncle's painting at the back of Standard One. One could now only guess at the meaning. Then I suddenly said aloud, 'Lullaby Danny Pratt's father,' as if I had unlocked a door with a key which I didn't know that I possessed and all of the syllables lined up in tidy meaning and I knew that some day I should have to go through that door like a schoolteacher ushering in the kids and find me and Danny and his father and Isaac and his father, all there in a kind of book or something and I should have to explain the way in which Mr Pratt had died.

When I came back from the funeral Lancaster and Mr Brown and Mr Pinkofsky from the Royal were talking about making a film. They sat around our parlour table. Mr Pinkofsky had decided that the little sequence which had proved to be so popular at his cinema deserved to be extended. Therefore he had put up the money to make a film incorporating the process of vocalization as he called it. He had decided that what the public really needed was a curious amalgam of both silence and speech. He had hit on the idea of making a silent film in the usual manner but whereas the traditional film would have showed captions indicating something of what had just been uttered by the actors the revolutionary film would be intercut with a vision of Mr Brown speaking the words.

When they had explained to me what they intended to do I said, 'Tha means like the Bellman.'

'What about Bellman?' Mr Brown sounded mystified.

'Oh, it's nowt,' I said. 'It's just that I used to imagine the Bellman as a kind of narrator in a play. I used to think that the actors were nowt but bits and pieces in the head of the story-teller. I think I had the idea that we were nowt but bits and pieces in Jacky Jellis's head, that's how he knew what was goin' on.'

'That's brilliant,' Lancaster said. 'We'll use the Bellman.'

Mr Brown was overjoyed – I think more at not having to appear in any more of Lancaster's experimental works rather than with my idea – but he twinkled at me nonetheless and he said, 'Tha's a genius, lad,' and I suddenly felt incredibly important.

The three film makers set about producing their talking picture with the help of Jacky Jellis. The Bellman was a most unlikely film star. Though the sun shone he insisted upon wearing his oilskin cape and fisherman's hat. He persisted too in sitting in the rubber chair to speak his lines and in holding the bell on his knee. Each of his short speeches was preceded by a loud ringing noise and it was only because of Lancaster that he didn't introduce each of his lines with the word *sithee*.

'It's sithee this and sithee that,' Lancaster told him, 'tha'll have to stop it, Jacky, or we'll get another for the part.'

The Bellman, who had seen Mr Brown's masterly performance in the first short sequence which was packing them in at the Royal, eyed our lodger with some concern and obviously decided there and then that he had better take direction from my uncle if he wasn't to lose his part to the most famous talking star of them all. But let me come back to the film later on – it's time now to close the nine days.

We are now into the final day of the General Strike, the signpost up at the crossroads is still turned so that the Leeds-bound traffic is directed into the village. H. G. Wells has taken off Marlene Jellis to God knows where, we've buried Danny Pratt's father and Marlene's father is about to star in the most important film ever in the history of the cinema. At about eleven o'clock that morning a pair of camels led by a couple of bedouin gentlemen appeared on the rise up by the big house and proceeded sure of foot down into the village. Behind them was a whole ordered zoo of other circus animals. There were horses and giraffes, vicuna and goats. There were lions and tigers locked in their cages, safely stowed on the backs of giant lorries which puffed smoke like loosed railway engines. There were dozens of caravans housing all of the circus performers who waved from behind the windows as the procession went by. Bringing up the rear were a dozen elephants. As the two bedouins approached one of them asked if this was the way to Leeds and Billy, with eyes as wide as those he would produce to greet a Martian, said, 'Ay. Keep straight on,' and the camels led off, drawing the circus up Hunger Hill.

We watched spellbound as the troupe went by and Billy asked me if I hadn't recognized Rosanne and Clarrie in one of the caravans. I shook my head – a youth who imagined insurance salesmen to be from Mars might see anything. Lancaster was filming everything and his lens followed the circus as it left us, negotiating the slope of Hunger Hill without too much difficulty. As the last elephant's bottom disappeared from view over the purple summit of the hill I knew that the strike was over. I knew that out there beyond Hunger Hill the strike was finished. The elephants would herald a new dawn for them o'er yonder. An elephant's bottom symbolized too the closing of an age in our village – a different age. It was a last bottom wedged in that trapdoor in the sky to the east of our village. In the morning it would blot out the rising sun.

Seeing the Bellman still sitting in the chair, I thought that perhaps he might have said that it was the end of the age of the open flower. I could sense the flower closing again. It had spat out its kids – Lancaster hadn't been one of them. The open flower had also taken in the outside world but not any more. A policeman would watch the crossroads from now on. That was the last procession. That elephant's rump was the rear-end view of the last visitor from an ancient time. There was electricity and wireless but they weren't quite the marvels that they had been. We were growing old, were Billy and I. As I told you, I was locked in the coal and nearly ready for the pit.

10

The rubber woman

After the departure of Marlene Jellis the schoolmaster became more morose. He could hardly manage to take himself off to school on a morning. He would sit at his little table, breakfasting on jam and bread and sucking the sweetness out of his tash with copious back-washings of tea. He always ate Mrs Gill's strawberry jam at breakfast time – it was sweeter than most, for Mrs Gill added the extra sugar which crystallized in his facial hair. And it was more red; Mrs Gill also added cochineal, a dye made from the squashed bodies of a silvery Mexican insect. It imparted the colour of the fresh wild fruit to her confection.

It was usually whilst he washed his plate and his chipped mug that Miss Fountaine would ring the school bell. He hoped that it would be Marlene ringing the bell but he knew that it never was. He could tell the difference between the noises the bell made when it was shaken by Marlene and by Miss Fountaine. The head-mistress's ringing was tuneful, she taught the children to sing, you know, whereas the bell in Marlene's hands was less melodic – more of a clang than a ring. Despite his love for the woman, he knew her to be a dull ringer of bells. On the other hand she held the bell in such a manner that it excited him. He liked to watch Marlene holding the bell. After Miss Fountaine had called the children to school he would sit a while, trying to shake the images of Marlene from his grieving head and listen to the footsteps scurrying past his door.

On one such morning, whilst he was still eating his jam and bread and before the bell had been rung, there was a knock at his door. It startled him for a moment. There were very few knocks on Mr Piggott's door. Sometimes a mischievous child might bang on it as he went by, but Wenceslas would always hear the running steps fading quickly away on such occasions. He waited at his table and heard nothing more than the knocking. Then he waited some more and there was another knock.

'Who is it?' he called, without bothering to get up from the table.

'It's Lancaster Brightside, Mr Piggott. Does thee have a moment?'

The schoolteacher got up and let in my uncle. He was initially surprised to see that he was accompanied by a bald woman whom he'd not seen before, but failed to give the woman a second look before he took his depression back to the breakfast table.

'What is it, Lancaster?' he asked gloomil · as he sat down.

'It's a rubber woman, Mr Piggott.'

'What?' said the schoolteacher. He still hadn't yet given of his time to cast the woman a second look.

'Ay. It were sent to me by Mr Tsiblitz. It's another of his inventions.'

'What's tha talkin' about, Lancaster?' Wenceslas asked with his head held in his hand and his elbow on the table.

'This, Mr Piggott. She's made of rubber.'

Mr Piggott looked more carefully at the person who had come through the door with my uncle. Besides being bald, she had the face of a young woman with perhaps a touch too much rouge, but wearing an older person's coat. In fact he thought it was the coat of Mrs Brightside, Lancaster's mother.

'Rubber?' he suddenly asked.

'Ay, she's not real. She's rubber, like the flying suits.'

The schoolteacher got up from his seat and touched the object about its face. He smiled. 'By, it's a good likeness, is that.'

'Ay, well it would be, if Mr Tsiblitz invented it. He sent it for me but my mother has told me to be rid of it.'

'Why?'

'Well, tha can hardly keep summat like this in the house, when there's all them others livin' there. Children and women and such.'

'What's tha talkin' about, Lancaster?' Mr Piggott asked again.

Lancaster looked embarrassed. 'Well, tha naws, tha can't go rumpin' and stuff with a house full of people.'

'Rumpin'?'

'Ay.'

Mr Piggott sat back into his chair and put his head in his hand again. Lancaster always had been a bit of a dream but the schoolteacher was now totally unable to comprehend what his former pupil was talking about.

295

'What's tha mean, rumpin', lad?' he asked slowly.

'Doin' it?' my uncle said. He couldn't be more specific than that and he pointed to the thing in his mother's coat.

'Doin' it with that?' Mr Piggott's voice rose an octave. He was not quite believing of the fact that he had asked the question.

'Ay.'

Lancaster undid the coat and let it drop from about the object's shoulders to reveal to the schoolmaster a body every bit as curved and creamy as that of Marlene Jellis. The breasts were full, the nipples large and pink; those of a young woman. The skin was white as milk and appeared to have a silken softness. There was a brush of pubic hair covering a thrusting mound, the belly was white and flat and the button like a vortex screwed his gaze into the model's femininity. Hair grew freely from the armpits just as it did from beneath Marlene's arms. Wenceslas was just beginning to contemplate the silken thighs when the bell rang. He knew instinctively that it was not the hand of Miss Fountaine for there was no music in the noise. Perhaps it was Marlene clasping the bell. Mr Piggott got an erection.

'Is thee all right?' my uncle asked, noting the painful and awkward way in which the schoolteacher had risen up quickly from his seat.

'Well, what's tha want to bring it here for?' Mr Piggott asked, ignoring my uncle's concern, and, grabbing a book from his shelf, he limped out of the door.

When he had turned the corner and seen that it was not Marlene but Mr Clayton who was ringing the bell, the schoolmaster stopped in his tracks, but the caretaker had already spotted him approaching the school yard.

'Miss Fountaine's ill today,' he called out.

'Is Miss Jellis at school yet?' Mr Piggott called back.

'Not seen 'er.'

'Well, there's something which I have to do, Mr Clayton, so will tha put all the children together in one classroom and take the first lesson.'

'Me?'

'Yes, you, Mr Clayton. Tell the girls to get on with their sewing and read the boys a story or something.'

'Can't read, Mr Piggott,' the caretaker told him, removing his flat cap and scratching his bald head with his little finger and the one next to it; it was more a tickle than a scratch. Seeing the caretaker's hairless head reminded Wenceslas of where he must go and he quickly turned on his heels and headed back for his home just around the corner shouting angrily, 'Well, make one up, Mr Clayton, it's not that difficult.' He turned the corner in time to see Lancaster leaving the house. He lugged the object in his mother's coat after him.

'Lancaster, don't go,' he shouted. 'Don't leave just yet.'

My uncle turned and walked slowly back to Mr Piggott. 'Let's go back inside,' the schoolmaster said, anxious to usher him into the house again. 'Now, as I was askin' thee, why me, Lancaster?'

'Well, it'd be a shame to destroy it, Mr Piggott. But I got to thinking who might tek it and I thought, well, it would have to be a bachelor and one who lives alone at that.'

'But why, lad? I don't understand. Why a bachelor?'

'Like I telled thee, Mr Piggott. Because of rumpin'.'

'Rumpin', Lancaster? Tha keeps telling me about the rumpin' but tha's not explaining thaself too well. What's tha mean?'

My uncle shuffled and then he said, 'Well, I thought with Marlene going off like that tha'd be lonely, Mr Piggott. I thought she might cheer thee up.' He patted the arm of the rubber woman. Then it suddenly occurred to Lancaster that perhaps Mr Piggott hadn't quite understood the function of the object which he had brought for him. 'It's not just a good likeness, Mr Piggott,' he said, 'it's more than that, it's got 'oles.'

''Oles?'

'Ay, 'oles. In the right places, Mr Piggott. There's 'oles.' Light then dawned on the face of the schoolteacher and he quickly undid the coat and gave the specimen a thorough investigation. When my uncle left, Mr Piggott's erection had returned.

The first thing which Wenceslas did was to buy his rubber woman a ginger wig. He let the hair hang loose and he tucked her up in his bed and let the hair flow over the silken milky white body and touch her bottom. Then after a couple of days he went to see Jacky Jellis and told him that Marlene had come home and that she was moving into his house with him and that she had sent him to get some of her clothes. Jacky gave him Marlene's dresses and her underclothes and stockings and he took some of her perfume and her jewellery too. Her father asked if he could come down to see Marlene but Wenceslas told him that she didn't want to see her father, not just yet, but that he would send her to see him as soon as she felt better about it. That really upset Jacky because his children had never stopped loving their father, they were always pleased to see him and he couldn't understand what had gotten into his daughter to make her not want to see her father.

Wenceslas took the clothes home with him and dressed up the rubber woman and had her sit with him in the parlour. He put her right by the window so that people could see in and note that Marlene was back and was living in the house of a man who wasn't her husband. Which of course wasn't untrue. He'd show them, her and that H. G. Wells. The clothes were slightly too big for the rubber woman so Wenceslas spent several days making alterations. He sat at his parlour table each morning before school started, cutting and sewing and stitching and eating his strawberry jam and drinking his tea. The tea would drip from his tash, and once or twice it dripped on to Marlene's dresses but he didn't care, he was too obsessed with his new toy to worry about tea stains on her clothing. He went into Leeds and bought a golden brooch like the one which she had always worn, the one which held her together, and he clipped it to her dress.

Then one day he did her hair up in a bun, dressed her in her altered clothes and took her for a spin in his car. He drove past our terrace and waved and we all commented how well Marlene looked after her time with the futurologist: even Lancaster was taken in by it all. Mr Clayton asked when Marlene would be going back to school and Wenceslas said that she wouldn't be going back because she was pregnant. That shocked Miss Fountaine and it shocked my grandmother too – despite the fact that my cousin Clarrie was illegitimate. Schoolteachers are different, she said, which was just what Wenceslas Piggott had wished her to say. He was making sure that if she ever truly came back, Marlene would never work at the school again.

He drove her about all over the place. The policeman at the crossroads saw them regularly and each time they passed Wenceslas would make certain that he was seen to be engrossed in conversation with his companion. He would lean towards her and sometimes nudge her, saying things like 'You women, you're all alike. Always going on about something or other.' Then the policeman would smile and think how those two were always going on at each other. Lovers' tiffs!

Whenever he bought his strawberry jam from Mrs Gill she would ask after Marlene and he would say that she was doing very well.

'Is she getting bigger?' Mrs Gill would ask.

'Oh ay. Much,' he would answer. 'Gettin' bigger every day. We think it might be twins.' And Mrs Gill would pass on the good news to my grandmother and soon everyone in the village would know how well Marlene was doing. It was the one thing which Jacky Jellis seemed not to know, for whenever he came to give us the news we would first of all have to give him ours.

'Tha Marlene's doing fine.' He had to know that first then he would ring his bell and get on with telling us what he knew.

One day Wenceslas took her up to the crossroads. Waiting to turn right on to the Wakefield road, he noticed the policeman sitting by the signpost eating his sandwiches and he said loudly, 'Look, dear, bobby's havin' 'is lunch,' but the policeman was too busy reading his newspaper to notice them. As he made the turn another car smashed right into them and there was a terrible explosion. The policeman, when he described it, said that it was just as if a bomb had gone off. The second motorist fainted and had to spend a week in the hospital. He was unable to remember anything about the crash and had a permanent tremor for the rest of his life. When the policeman ambled over to see what had happened, Wenceslas was already gathering together the pile of clothes from the front seat and was tucking them under his arm. The policeman asked the schoolteacher what had happened and Wenceslas, seeing that the other motorist was unconscious, blamed the poor fellow completely. He was unable to account for the explosion, he said, but he was sure that the report had originated in the other person's car. He left his own vehicle parked up by the crossroads and wandered down to the village with Marlene's clothes bundled in his arms.

'Is Marlene getting any bigger?' our neighbour asked as the schoolteacher passed.

'She's exploded, Mrs Gill,' he answered and, mildly concussed, he wandered on his way, arms filled with her voluminous clothing. Of course my grandmother soon got to know of this and eventually it came to the ears of the Bellman too. Jacky Jellis wasn't going to let it rest at that; he wanted to know what had happened to his daughter. He went round to see Wenceslas Piggott, together with my grandmother. At first the schoolmaster wasn't going to let them in but Jacky threatened him with the police and he finally opened the door.

'Where's my Marlene?' the Bellman asked.

'She ran off with Mr Wells.'

'Ay, but she cem back. Tha took her clothes, Wenceslas. Now where is she?'

'She's gone back to Mr Wells, I'm tellin' thee.'

'But tha's still got her clothes. No woman would go off without her clothes,' my grandmother told him.

'I haven't, I haven't got her clothes at all,' Wenceslas said.

'Don't lie. It only makes it worse. Mrs Gill saw thee with her clothes when tha came into the village t'other day. Now where is she, lad?' my grandmother persisted.

'I've told thee, she's gone off with H. G. Wells.'

'Right,' said Jacky, 'I'm going for bobbies,' and he went off and brought a policeman from the station at Castleford. The policeman searched through the house and found Marlene's clothes stuffed under Mr Piggott's bed. There was a nasty hole right through the dress and just about where her heart would have been. And the hole was bang in the centre of a nasty red sticky patch with looked suspiciously like blood.

'No, it's not,' said Wenceslas when challenged. 'It's strawberry jam and tea which has dripped from my tash.'

But the policeman wouldn't hear of it and arrested the schoolteacher. He took him off to the station and cautioned him, which prompted Mr Piggott to partially tell the truth. He told his interrogators that Marlene had met with an accident whilst in his car. He explained that was how there came to be a hole in the dress but the admission only got him into deeper trouble. The police could find no blood in the car. And of course neither the policeman at the crossroads nor the second motorist could remember seeing a woman in the car at the time of the accident.

'He just seemed to be keen to be off. And off with the lady's clothes which were on the front seat,' said the policeman, imparting a significance to the event which it didn't have.

When they had submitted the clothing to some tests, however, and found that the red stains were not bloodstains an even greater confusion found its way into the case.

In the meantime the village children were without a schoolteacher, for Miss Fountaine, who had been nicely on her way to recovery, suffered a relapse of her illness when she heard that Mr Piggott had been arrested on suspicion of murdering Miss Jellis. Each day all the children went up to the crossroads to look for the clues which might lead to an explanation for Marlene's sudden disappearance. Then one day a small boy turned up a piece of something which when he handed it to Billy and me had us both quaking in our shoes. We were thirteen years old now and knew what it was immediately. It was a rubbery piece of skin with a hole in it and the whole thing was surmounted by a mass of curly hair.

'Is it what I think it is?' I asked.

'Cunt, daft.'

'By gow. He's cut her up into little bits,' I told him and he nodded gravely, then we solemnly went off to the police station in Castleford to show them our find.

The detectives were mystified as they stretched the material this way and that. They turned it over and did the same, causing the occasional hair to fall out.

'What is it?' asked one of the detectives, handing it back to Billy.

'Don't tha want it?' he asked back.

'Not particularly. What is it?'

'Cunt,' Billy told him in a whisper.

'It's what?'

'Cunt,' I said as softly as I could manage. We were promptly ejected together with our evidence.

The case of the missing schoolteacher made the local papers. The police, puzzled by the lack of a body, began to suspect that Wenceslas might have got rid of Marlene by dissolving her in acid. An examination of his home however showed that there were no traces of either blood or acid, even in the drains. Suspicion then turned to burial as a means of disposal and the police began to look for freshly dug earth in and around the village. They found a recently dug patch by the Roman wall at the summit of Hunger Hill. The disturbed soil went down about as far as one might stick a corpse but there was no body. In fact there was nothing buried in the patch at all and that puzzled the police too. Then one day when Mr Brown overheard two policemen talking about the recently dug hole on Hunger Hill – he had been taken to the station on suspicion of having stolen more bags – he suddenly realized that it must have been the spot where Great Great Grandmother had hidden her loot. Nobody had buried anything on the hill, he said to my father, but Albert had certainly dug up something from there. Meanwhile all that Wenceslas Piggott would say was that Marlene had gone off with Mr Wells.

Archie Jellis, Bruno and Bottom Boat Beauty

During that period of his sister's disappearance and the detainment of Mr Piggott, Archie Jellis was in his final year at Charing Cross Medical School. He never wore the tie and could never have afforded to buy the blazer. He had a doctor's white coat and a stethoscope, both of which he had been able to purchase out of the ten pounds which his father had given him. He always borrowed the books he needed for his studies from the other students. They mostly thought him an odd ball and they didn't care for him very much. He was not of their kind. To pay his fees he picked up work in restaurants, washing dishes here and there. After midnight he would then take home the scrapings from the customers' returned plates and share his one meal a day with Bruno. Sometimes he was unable to find work and he and Bruno would have to resort to some other means of feeding themselves.

One day, at a time when he was unable to find work to support himself, he received a letter from his father and slipped it neatly folded into his pocket without opening it, thinking that he would read it whilst he had his meal. He had eaten in a different place on each of the last dozen nights. He left his cold flat, holding Bruno at the end of a bit of rope, to look for yet a different eating house. He took the dog up the Strand past all the swank restaurants, passing by Covent Garden where he had savoured the fare in most of the smaller places during the last few weeks and went further afield and into Holborn. There he found a pie shop. He tied Bruno's rope to the leg of the chair on which he sat and asked the dog to lie down. Bruno obediently curled at Archie's feet and sniffed the cooking smells out of the warm air. A waiter dressed in a starched white apron came to his table and Archie ordered a large eel pie with mash and peas. He read his father's letter with tears in his eyes for he learned that his sister had disappeared and that Mr Piggott, the schoolteacher, had been arrested on suspicion of having murdered her. His father wanted him to go home for a while; until all this muddle has been sorted, he wrote. Bruno could see the emotional struggle which the letter had triggered in his master's head and he stared at Archie with big brown eyes. Then very suddenly tears flowed over his snout and on to the floor where he was lying. He didn't make a sound. He just let the tears flow silently, wetting the pale linoleum. Archie continued his meal in thoughtful silence. When he had eaten a little more than half of his dinner he called the waiter to his table and asked him if he would put the rest of the food into a bag so that he could take it home for his dog. The waiter took the food back to the kitchen and returned a minute later with the remainder of the meal neatly packaged up. Archie slipped the packet into his jacket pocket – he still wore his Sunday best – and asked the waiter if he could direct him to a toilet. The man showed him out through the tiny kitchen to a red brick toilet in the yard at the back of the shop. When the waiter had returned to the kitchen Archie heaved himself over a wall and ran off.

Naturally the waiter assumed that Archie would be returning even when it was apparent that he was no longer in the toilet – after all, he had left his dog who lay down in a small pool of tears and was still tethered to the chair. It is curious that the waiter in the starched apron should not have assumed the wet to be something other, but he knew it to be a puddle of tears thus he never scolded the dog. He just patted him and said, 'There, there. Has your master gone and left you? It's a shame. Isn't it a shame? He'll be back, I expect, just you wait and see. There there.' Then he went off to the kitchen to bake more pies.

Bruno patiently waited for Archie to return. Bruno was a good actor and he knew exactly what he had to do. He waited. As only a dog can wait, he waited. Then at about midnight with the moon up and bright in the sky, Bruno was kicked out with a curse and sent off to stray about the Inns of Court. But Bruno knew his way home from almost anywhere in London. Back at the cold flat he received his share of the meal, barked softly at the moon and the stars and then curled up with Archie he fell into a deep slumber.

In his time as a schoolteacher, Wenceslas Piggott had three pupils of whom he could be justly proud – four if you count Marlene, but I think that Wenceslas stopped counting Marlene when all this muddle was over.

There was my uncle Lancaster, the famous film maker and aerial photographer. There was myself, the literary prize winner and curator of the strange museum – I didn't tell you about that yet. Then there was Archie Jellis who after qualifying as a doctor went on to become the president of the Royal College of Physicians, a man with rooms in Harley Street. Of the three it was Archie of whom Mr Piggott would have been the most proud. Archie's achievement was nothing short of a miracle. He had got the brains, that was never in dispute. But his ability to overcome adversity, to take on the establishment and play them at their own game and to win – to win right through to the very pinnacle of his profession – that was Archie's achievement. And for Mr Piggott it was a miracle. It was the miracle which he would have liked to have quoted to succeeding generations of pupils had he been allowed – take heart, he would have said, look at the miracle of Archie Jellis, old boy of this school.

You see, Lancaster never had to overcome adversity. In his early years he had the backing of my great great grandmother's fortune; she got him started. Then Mr Tsiblitz had moulded the fear out of him – as a boy he had overcome his fear of flying. And Pinkofsky too – he had provided encouragement and finance in the early years. Brains were something with which my uncle was never blessed, nor, as it turned out, did he need them.

As for me, like I have said elsewhere, I just fell from my mother's womb spouting water and words – neither of which has much to do with being brainy. A parrot in the rain can manage the same. The museum was a mixture of luck and acquisition, the latter a notion learned from Mr Brown and a paper bag. No, Lancaster's mastery of his craft and my eventual rise to success had nothing whatsoever to do with the miraculous. Archie, though, Archie was a miracle.

The first that I knew of Archie's return was when, looking from the window, I saw Bruno wandering into the yellow laboratory and sniffing at my duck. I left the house and said, 'Hello, Bruno. Did they teach thee to be human down in London?' The old dog just stared at me with his intelligent eyes and all of those old feelings

305

started to flow back into my head. 'I don't know, Bruno,' I told him. 'I don't know why it's like that, but we must be thankful for what we are and that we're alive, that's what my grandmother says and I think she must be right. So stop looking at me that way, will thee? Why don't thee just go off and behave like other dogs?'

I watched Bruno sneak off with his tail between his legs and as he left the laboratory Archie appeared at the entrance.

'Hello, young 'un,' he said. 'How are you getting on?'

'I'm alreet, Archie. Is tha doctoring now?'

'Not yet. Not properly. I'll soon be qualified though.' He smiled at me.

I picked up my duck and threw him into his rain barrel. He promptly turned himself upside down and we both watched him floating about like that.

'Can I ask thee summat?'

'What is it, Donald? What do you want to know?'

'What's tha Bruno been up to?'

'Oh, his usual tricks, you know. He likes it in London.'

'No, Archie. I mean, will tha tell me how come Bruno saw thee through tha studying?'

'Well, he just looked after me like he always did.'

'Tha father told us tha wouldn't starve, not with Bruno. Did tha beg in t'streets or do a turn or summat?'

'Oh, that. Well, we sort of did a turn and it was a kind of begging I suppose.' Archie then told me the story of how when he had no money he would take Bruno to a restaurant and tie him to a chair. He told me the whole tale of how he managed to eat and get food for the dog too.

When he had finished I said, 'That's not begging, that's thieving. Tha means tha's a thief, Archie.'

'No, Donald. I'm a student doctor.'

'Ay, well, tha's a thief as well, then.'

'Let's say that I could never have become a doctor, if I hadn't learned a bit of thieving first, then.'

'Ay, alreet, we'll say that then.'

Archie wandered off, whistling for his dog. I saw Bruno come hurtling past me, chasing after his master with feathers falling from his jaws, and I ran as quickly as I could to the laboratory. There were a few brown feathers floating on the skin of water. There were feathers on the grass close by the rain barrel. I ran back on to the common.

'Tha bastard, Bruno,' I shouted after the disappearing figures. 'Tha's eaten up my fuckin' duck.' I watched them now very small walking away from me. I was crying my heart out and the world was changing about me. I had no idea how to prevent it from changing.

When Mr Piggott saw Archie at the police station in Castleford he burst into tears too.

'Where's my sister, Mr Piggott?' Archie asked gently.

'She's with Mr Wells, Archie. I swear to God, she's with Mr Wells.'

'That'll do for me, Mr Piggott, but nobody else seems to believe you. Did anyone try contacting Mr Wells to see if your story was true?'

'I don't know, Archie. Thank God tha's here, lad, thank God.' Then the schoolteacher broke down, warbling great incoherent sobs. Archie waited for the man to cry himself out. Then in the relative calm which followed he asked Wenceslas Piggott to tell him all about it. Archie listened patiently as the schoolteacher spoke. At last, a real doctor had come to our village, even if he was a thief.

'I fell in love with a rubber doll, Archie. I dressed her up in Marlene's clothing. I just wanted to show 'em. Show all the villagers and Marlene and Mr Wells. I wanted to show 'em that I could be just as good as them. Have my respect. I wanted to show 'em all, so I dressed the doll in Marlene's clothes. I took her to my bed at night and I took her out in the car during the day and told 'em she was pregnant. She was beautiful, Archie, every bit as lovely as tha sister. Then when the bloody thing exploded I didn't know what to do. I couldn't tell anyone, not really, because I had their respect now and I wasn't going to lose it, Archie. I'm not going to lose that respect now. But nobody's hurt. There was no murder or owt like that, it was a doll, Archie, a bloody doll and I loved her. Marlene went off with Mr Wells, I swear to God she did and she's not been back.'

Archie went back down to London and found his sister living with Mr Wells under the assumed name of Sosthenes Smith and he

307

took her to the police station and had her identify herself. Archie was never short of money after that. His sister and Mr Wells always saw that he was properly housed and fed until he had qualified in medicine. After finding his sister he came back to the village immediately and took Doctor Cartwright down to the police station with him and he asked Mr Piggott to repeat his story to the doctor. The schoolteacher told his story again, explaining his love for a rubber doll which had long since exploded, and they both certified him and had him put in Wakefield asylum.

When all this muddle was over and Archie was about to go down to London to finish his studying he came round to our house with Bruno.

'I'll be living with my sister from now on,' he told us, 'so I'll not be having any need of the dog. I thought Donald might like to have him. He's not got much time left and I think he would be happy to finish his old days with your Donald.'

'Bruno, why'd th'eat my duck?' was the very first thing that I asked him when Archie had gone. He stared at the sky. Then he barked and the sky began to rain great drops; as blue as distant hills.

I never let him forget that he had eaten the duck. Sometimes he would climb into the rain barrel and just sit. He couldn't help it – Doctor Cartwright said that it was obsessive behaviour but it was odd to see a black dog half submerged in the rain-water like that. Sometimes when the barrel was a bit more full he would duck his head for a few moments, then lift it out and shake off the water with a few strong shakes of his ears and he would fling the water in the pattern of stars in a spiralling galaxy sometimes as far as the window. My father, sitting in a wide winged chair and reading his newspaper beneath the electric light, would lift his head and ask, 'Hello, is it raining again?'

Bruno died the following year and I buried him in the laboratory and inscribed his name on one of the yellow stones. 'Bruno and duck,' it read, 'who died with all the sadness of knowing exactly who he was and of who he might have been.'

The coal owners mourned the passing of our country's greatness. Britain wasn't paying her way in the world, which to them was another way of saying that we were not exporting a sufficient quantity of coal. World markets were expanding and we were selling less, that was why we had so much unemployment – that's what they told us. Then they told us that the only way to reduce unemployment was to export more coal. To export more coal they would have to reduce the selling price and the reduction in price was dependent on the miners accepting a cut in wages.

Of course this kind of logic didn't just apply to coal, it applied to everything. We had to pay our way in the world. Nobody seemed to be asking why the government didn't stimulate demand at home. Nobody seemed to be advocating higher wages and making things for home consumption to take up the extra spending power. Mr Piggott, he once mentioned it. He told my grandmother that there should be factories all over the country churning out pot ducks for the walls in people's parlours and that the coal owners should be giving each collier an extra sixpence per shift so that they could buy them. That would provide employment and step up the demand for more coal, he said. He was the only one I ever heard mention such a thing and look where he ended up. No, the conventional wisdom was that we should accept less pay to make the country great again and the amazing thing is that we did.

It was also amazing that we survived the strikes and lock-outs of 1926. We were paid benefit by the union but by July the fund was exhausted. Then other trade unions sent donations and there were many fund-raising activities organized by the church and by local people. But Emily wouldn't have that – despite the fact that we were all in the same boat and self-respect had given way to a communal concern for survival. My grandmother was made of a different material to the others. Her pride was her pride and she needn't follow the sheep. It confounded us all and had us thinking of other means by which we could be supported.

Mr Henderson had a greyhound. She was a cross-eyed brindle bitch who slept in one of his armchairs and she could run like the wind, especially if he had lathered her backside with turpentine. Her name was Bottom Boat Beauty but she was anything but beautiful. Mr Brown preferred to call her Bottom Boat Wonder because with those cross eyes, he said, when she raced it was a wonder that she could see the hare at all. She snoozed all day in her armchair and rarely took exercise but Mr Henderson used to take her all over Yorkshire and have her race against other pitmen's greyhounds. Bottom Boat Beauty rarely lost a race. Now Mr Brown saw in this squint-eyed, lazy good-for-nothing a way of making money. Not in backing her to win – the odds were far too short even if you could find someone to accept your bet – but in backing her to lose. To effect such a phenomenon he had to bring Bottom Boat Beauty together with yet another marvel of technology – a wonder of an ancient technology. My grandmother's dumplings. Emily Brightside's dumplings were in their way just as famous as the brindle bitch. Ernest maintained that a dozen were sufficient to sink a battleship. And Mr Brown thought quite rightly that three or four would be enough to sink Bottom Boat Beauty.

Twice a week he would go to some far-flung pit village together with old man Henderson. The racing bitch had already been weighted with my grandmother's dumplings and trotted lithely along at the end of a stout rope. The wily villagers, remembering the pasting which had been meted out to their local champion only a short while before, would put all of their available cash on the visiting dog whilst Mr Brown would back the recently defeated local. He always got good odds and usually managed to clean up. Then the three of them would return triumphant to our village, the brindle bitch still springy of step and trotting along between the two smiling men. Mr Brown would then divide the winnings between the two households. My grandmother, although she never approved of gambling, accepted that in the special circumstances it was a legitimate source of income and a good deal better than falling back on charity. She never knew why Mr Brown was so keen on her dumplings but was flattered that he should eat so many of them and her pride was maintained.

I2

'Grandmother, Grandmother, come and see'

The project which saved the whole village from starvation in the
latter period of the strike, though, was Lancaster's talking picture.
The film was finished late in August and had an immediate showing
at the Royal Picture Palace. Lancaster received a commission of a
penny a seat from Mr Pinkofsky – a penny per arse as the proprietor
put it – and it brought about five pounds a day into the village.
That was just about enough to feed everyone. The film showing
opened on a bright gusty day when the local farmers were sheaving
the crop and we walked in twos from the village, like they did when
Mr Piggott had the smaller children out for a nature ramble. Filled
with gossip we trudged across fields and counted the twisted trees
which grew from the coal-cut land. Those who had trained their
ears to recognize a pitman's tappings in the earth had no difficulty
in hearing the slugs slurp at the ripe corn. The wind's bluster tossed
black dust from our village into the warm air and birds fell among
it, blotting out the sun. I saw Isaac racing through a hail of sparrows,
whirling his wooden clapper at them and causing the storm to take
back to the skies as suddenly as it had arrived and miraculously the
birds lifted the coal dust with them. For a time it was dark in
heaven whilst below in the bright stage-set world Isaac's mother
thonged a yellowed sheaf. I waved and Isaac waved back but we
didn't speak.

We took a short cut through Mouldy Orchard where the plums
were ripe and falling from the trees. The blackberries were large and
several people stopped to pick them and when we came from the
Orchard and entered Aken Jugs those who had taken the berries all
had blue tongues and lips. There were earwigs carried on the wind
and every so often somebody would fall out of line to brush them
from their hair or from the hair of their companions. It was that
kind of gusty day.

*

It has been said of the motion picture industry that its problem was that it could talk before it could think. Well, my sister Irene Rose went one better: as you know, she could talk before she was born. Lancaster's film opened with a grey shot of my sister. She was sitting on the grass on the common outside our house. She had on a dress which I think used to be my own and she showed the dimples in her chubby knees and thighs, pumping her elbows excitedly. These were the bellows which fanned the flames of our enthusiasm; we were alive to the picture maker's illusions. It was a picture of an ordinary babe with fair hair who wore a quizzical expression. You could see the smoke curling from the chimney behind her. It wound into a cheerless sky, curling and questioning. Irene Rose was talking. Mouthing baby words to the silent camera before her.

The scene faded to a flickering dark. There were white spots flashing on and off the screen. An image was trying to find its way to the hushed audience. The whirring noise of the projector, even though it was in a separate room, was getting into the auditorium. We held our breath, trying to make out the voice above the whirring projector. The image on the screen was still trying to put itself together – then suddenly the Bellman appeared; he looked like the man on the matchbox. Then it dawned on me. Jacky Jellis was the man on the matchbox. Jacky Jellis was the pilot, guiding us on a ship so vast that we couldn't see the sides. He was sitting in the rubber chair. He held the bell like the pilot grabs the wheel, then he shook the bell and whilst we still held our breath we could faintly discern the bell's ringing. We stared at his whiskery lips and saw him say in the same squeaky voice as that of Mr Brown on the first film, 'Granmovver, Granmovver, come an' see. There's unter Lancaster with a camera.' The image of the Bellman held and then he said, 'There's a whole world out there, Granmovver,' and I thought, that's odd, because I hadn't thought that Irene Rose had said anything of the sort. The Bellman continued with his monologue. 'Come an' see. Come an' see,' he seemed to be saying over and over again in a thin squeaky voice. The audience was spellbound. The shot of the Bellman slowly faded and another image formed on the screen. We watched the circus passing through the village and climbing Hunger Hill. There were the camels led by the two bedouins and the goats and the lions and all the rest. Then as the caravans passed and one took account of all those frozen faces, I distinctly saw Rosanne and Clarrie smiling from a small window and I thought, Billy, Billy – tha's got it right, Billy. Why did I ever doubt thee? Willmott is a Martian after all – a Martian and an earthling. There is no difference between Mars and Earth. They're interchangeable.

The Bellman was still talking, talking over the pictures. 'It's a fantastic world, if you will only give it a chance to come to you. Look at that elephant, look at the way its bottom moves as it climbs into the sky. Look at the way it starts to fill the door in the sky up there.' The scene slowly faded with the elephant's bottom wedged at the top of Hunger Hill exactly as I had remembered it and filling up most of the screen and I thought, Jacky, how's tha know these things? How's tha know what we're thinking? 'Don't let it go from you. You have to know when to hold. When to drop anchor and say this must be the place. Yes, look, I recognize it – even though it's only a patch of sea in an even greater ocean – you have to be able to recognize it.' The audience was gripped by a view of the water in the rain barrel outside our house. There was no duck, no movement. Just Jacky talking over the image of the still water. 'Let it come, let it come and see it for what it is,' the Bellman's voice said.

'That's right,' I said to myself. 'I'll not let it go. That's why I remember it like I do. Like the camera does too. It's stuck there, in that hole in the sky and it'll not go.'

The hushed audience were hypnotized by the succession of images. People whom they all knew appeared one at a time. They were persons who, if on some other occasion the audience had seen them on film, they might have laughed at, they might even have jeered at.

Charlie Gill stood in his doorway with his arm about his mother. He stood quite still, balanced on his one leg, and he smiled for the camera. Mr Doyle appeared in his piggery and he slapped a pig on the rump with his one big hand and the pig ran off and we had to imagine the squealing because Jacky was saying, 'Faces, faces,' over and over again and the portraits lingered in their sombre tones – one after the other – like the sepia images which ran in Lancaster's head. Then there was film of Mr Pinkofsky sitting in my aunt Henrietta's striped deckchair in the laboratory. He has a neat tash and his hair parted in the middle and greased back with cream. He looks just like my grandfather. Mr Pinkofsky smiles and nods at the camera, then by means of some cinematographic deception we see that it isn't Mr Pinkofsky at all, but my grandfather himself who smiles from the deckchair. Mr Brown appeared in his Sunday suit and everybody thought that he was going to say that stuff about God, but he didn't – he linked his arm into that of my mother and they both walked off on the common and the camera lingered after their back view as they went away like two people at the tail end of an old book. Then the scenes faded again and the Bellman was trying to form himself from out of the dark and finally he was there in the chair again and he said, 'Friends. And now, old friends,' and he faded again.

Now we saw film of the flying animals. Lancaster had edited in bits from some of his early experimental films, the ones he had made from a time before he had gone off to the War. You could sense a kind of fear in the audience. On the one and only previous occasion when the flying animal sequence had been shown to the public – it had been an accident – the audience had greeted it rather coldly. They had believed it to be trick photography but it hadn't excited them. This audience was not as cynical – they believed in what they saw and their belief filled them with a kind of dread. 'Don't be afraid,' the Bellman said, anticipating their reaction. 'This also is a part of the coming world. Open up your hearts and let it be. You will be surprised at the wonders that will come. Grandmother, Grandmother, grab your spectacles – those which you share will do – and come and see.'

There's Mrs Henderson; she's dead now. And Charlie is there with his two legs. There's Albert – and he's gone – and William who now has children. There's Bill Pettit who was blown away at the Somme and Oliver who had a similar fate and look, there's Rosanne falling from her rope and Albert catching her, or was she catching Albert? Can you see Clarrie in her belly? Is the daughter in Albert's eye? Look. *Albert's dead in Bresci's hat.* I look about. Who said that? Was it merely whirring of the projector or was it yet another disembodied voice?

'Time's passing,' the Bellman told the silent audience. You could have heard a pin drop. 'Time, that's what it's all about. Follow that road, stay on it. It's all there is for you, but stay on the road. Fight

314

for what's right – but don't get greedy or too curious, don't wander. Wandering's what'll get you in the end. So stay on the road and recognize when to drop anchor.'

The screen was now showing bits of film which Lancaster had taken here and there since he had returned from the War. Emily in the church at his brother's funeral. 'That's the grim funny business, that is, that wandering, that's the grim funny business,' Jacky said and I felt my grandmother shuffling on her orange box as she sat next to me in the quietened cinema. Then came an image of Lullaby Danny Pratt's father lying in a field. *Lancaster, how could you? How could you have filmed the poor man dead like that?* Then the shocked audience gasps as the corpse struggles upright, whirling in the grey-filmed sequence, arms circling pell-mell, and the drunken man shambles off like a broken windmill. It wasn't *that* morning, the audience realizes, and there is a huge sigh of relief breathed into the hot air of the cinema. Lancaster had just spotted him on any old morning. It had been Lullaby Danny Pratt's father drunk in the black and white fields like it always was – there was no blood, no red day.

There was film of the stars and of the moon which we could hardly tell from the blank and flickering screen which we received between sequences. There was film of Bruno barking at the sky and of Mr Brown blowing into a paper bag – only he seemed to be breathing from it. Lancaster had set up a reversal of reality and Mr Brown was taking from the bag as if it contained life-giving oxygen and one wanted almost to shout, don't take tha lips away, Mr Brown, don't present thaself to the rarefied atmosphere of the moon. I could hear Mr Brown wheezing away at the other side of my grandmother and the Bellman's squeaky voice was saying, 'Come and see the wonders of science. There's time. Don't be afraid. There's time because that is all there is. Do you understand? Do you see?' And as the voice finished its speaking the photograph of my great great grandmother was held on the screen. The photograph which Albert had taken of the old woman with Bresci's hat on her head and hugging the suitcase to her. Then she slowly faded away and the lights came up.

For about a full minute the audience stayed wrapped in a silence of their own thought. They were truly spellbound. Gradually they began to stir like dazed insects shaking off the effects of a freezing night. Then there was a sudden great clapping of hands. The volume was enough to hurt the ears as the applause turned to cheers and there were great stampings on the wooden floor. The Bellman was brought to the front of the cinema and asked to take a bow. The farrier next door, who had been told to remain silent throughout the performance, brayed on his metal. Lancaster was brought forward and he too took a bow. Mr Pinkofsky stood between the star and the film maker and the three of them were cheered for a full half an hour until everyone was so tired and hoarse that they could neither shout nor clap nor stamp any more. So they just filed up from the upturned orange boxes and they touched the three of them in a loving kind of way as if they were just-born babies or something.

The film ran for months and people came from all over the country, and even from abroad, to see Lancaster's talking picture. Then one day Mr Pinkofsky said that we needed to transfer to a larger cinema because so many people wanted still to see the creation. And he said that if we were to show the film in another place it might as well be somewhere in which there was a decent amplification system. He looked about for the right theatre or hall but soon realized that the only places suitable were in London and nobody wanted to transfer the showing of the film down to London. Lancaster said that it wasn't because people down there didn't want to see the film, because they most certainly did, but he said that if it was shown in London nobody would understand it. He said that the only way in which the people from the south could understand was for them to come up and see the film in the coalfields. They should have to suffer the glitter of a diamond-hard night and listen to the squeaking of the wheel to understand what was in his film and you didn't get that sort of thing in London. Then Mr Brown suggested that we build a cinema in the village. One to house a thousand people and to have the best sound system in the world, and he asked Mr Pinkofsky if he could raise the money for such a venture. The proprietor imagined that there would be no difficulty in getting hold of the capital needed but after discussions with Joseph Thwaite he learned that the coal owner was demanding a rent equivalent to fifty per cent of the audience receipts. After all, the village belonged to Thwaite, he told us – Mr Brown then remembered my birthright.

13

Coming in on the wings of socialism, going out touched by the world

Some of you might know about my birthright; I wrote of it in another place. Didn't I already tell you that when I was born my maternal great grandfather, old man Thwaite, came to see me? Didn't I tell you that? That was the time when he cried on my mother's shoulder and called my father Willie. Well, on that occasion he brought some papers with him and he signed them with my great aunt Henrietta's pen which was kept on the mantelshelf and he gave the papers to my mother. This was my birthright – it was the title deeds to the old disused pit and a little of the land surrounding it at the bottom of Hunger Hill. The disused pit is the one in which my great grandfather, James Brightside, is buried; the one in which he found the dinosaur and in which he's buried because the bones tumbled down on top of him.

It was common knowledge that I was the owner of this bit of land. It hardly made me a capitalist – a clapped-out pit filled with foul water and a pile of dinosaur bones – but whilst the rest of us were discussing where best to locate the proposed new cinema it was Mr Brown who remembered the birthright. That was the genius of Mr Brown; he always could be relied on to find a solution to our problems. They were never long-term solutions, but they directed us away from the immediate crisis and if it was straight into another one, well, that didn't matter. Mr Brown could always find a way out of that one, too. He always saw the simple way through the webs which we wove about ourselves. He was a guide, I suppose, taking us from one marvellous bit of the woods to the next but never wholly outside them – never beyond the trees – that was dangerous and he respected our rights to see the world only a bit at a time.

'Of course,' said my father after Mr Brown had told him that we could build on my land and that there would be absolutely nothing Joseph Thwaite could do about it. 'Why didn't I think of that?'

That was the genius of Mr Brown. He could always make people say those very words.

Wagons brought the wood in the snow and the carpenters from the pit knocked up the shell in a week. Thwaite came down to make sure that we weren't using his nails and his tools to execute the job. He had three inches of snow on top of his hat. Pinkofsky had been extra careful about his sourcing of materials and had bought everything needed from reputable suppliers in Leeds. It was all itemized on the invoices and the cinema owner took great pleasure in showing them to my grandfather. Everything down to the last tack had been paid for. Thwaite trudged back up the hill, slipping in his galoshes as he climbed and with an extra inch of snow on his hat.

Then they brought the bricks and everyone got on with the building under the direction of Charlie Gill, who because he had only the one leg didn't seem to suffer from the cold like everyone else. He said that having only one foot in contact with the freezing ground made him only half as cold as the rest of us. He was planted like a scarecrow in the middle of the shell after they had put a floor down and he shouted his directions all about as the four walls were erected simultaneously.

They brought slates from Wales and tarpaulin from Dorset and they made pitch which smelled like cough drops right there in great vats and the roofers got to work and had a top on the building by the following week. Then the electricians came in and fixed the sound system which had come from America. It was called Movietone and in America it told you the news – it was a sort of American version of Jacky Jellis, I suppose. A bit flash compared with the Bellman but unlike Jacky it never knew what you were thinking. Whilst the electricians worked on the sound the carpets came and then the swank seating. There were no orange boxes now; only the best crushed velvet chairs. Rows and rows of them.

Before the strike ended the council sent some workmen to add a fourth arm to the signpost at the crossroads. The white finger pointed down the hill to New Royal Cinema – our village apparently still didn't warrant a name. Every evening hundreds of cars honked their way to the disused pit and Billy o' the Terrus End, wearing a peaked hat, directed the motorists to park in orderly fashion, in neat rows one behind the other. They were real nobs from London and places like that who had come to see the wonderful talking picture which like the village didn't even have a name. But the nobs weren't disappointed – they were processed with the courtesy they might have expected. Billy passed them on to Charlie Gill who wore a red commissionaire's uniform which displayed a dozen shining medals across his massive chest. He leaned on a crutch outside the cinema doors and all that brass and silver on his chest rattled as he hopped about directing the customers to the ticket office where his ancient mother dispensed tickets. Whilst the world gawped at the giant screen Billy and I would sit in one of the splendid motors lined up in the stillness of the car-park and listen to the voice of Jacky Jellis booming into the night through the windowless walls. Across at the terrace we could see our fathers and our neighbours sitting in their chairs and reading in parlours full of electric light. They were like wax figures at a sideshow. Beads of sweat stood out on their foreheads and one could only hope that the electric wasn't about to melt them down. Above us the canvas roof of the motor held back the moon and the falling stars and before long we knew Jacky's script by heart and could talk along with the Bellman. 'Grandmother, Grand-mother, come and see.' We would always stop our conversation at that point. No matter what we were discussing, no matter how important it might have been, we stopped and waited and all three of us, Jacky, Billy and I, would shout into the night, 'Grandmother, Grandmother, grab your spectacles and come and see.'

Then as the performance closed to rapturous applause, Billy and I would scoot from the motor in which we happened to be sitting and the nobs would suddenly appear all at the same time and climb into their motors. But there was no orderly way of leaving, not like there had been an orderly way of arrival. Mr Brown said that they were only mirroring the way it was in life. He said that we came into this world in sequence – that we all had a number – but that the scramble out wasn't like that at all. It should have been but it wasn't. Apparently people, after they were born, couldn't be bothered to queue. We came in, ordered and socialist, but went out something else. Consequently we exited in a terrible mêlée, he told me. Billy and I would watch the motorists every night going forward, going back, unable to wait their turns, bumping and scratching, shouting dreadful obscenities at one another just like colliers in the drunken pub. Where's the difference? Billy asked. The nobs and the colliers – where's the difference? Every night we were treated to this messy exit from the village and every morning we would have a team of panel beaters bashing out the bumps in the bodywork and demanding payment from the owners who had been unable to leave and who had stayed the night in one of Rube Hardwick's done-up rooms above the pub.

It was because he had so many visitors that Rube needed the salmon. My father knew of a secret river tucked away in a green dale. It was a place where he took the blind and the daft in the Jam Sahib's motor. He had taken the blind and the daft up there for as long as I could remember – ever since my great great grandmother had bought the motor from Elyahou Tsiblitz. It was a secret place and because he only ever took the blind and the daft up there, it remained that way. When he heard of Rube's need he drove out alone one foggy morning and arrived back that same evening with sixty pounds of silver salmon piled on the back seat of the car. He charged Rube three shillings a pound plus his petrol money and an industry was suddenly born in our village. The second Mrs Doyle was a French chef of some distinction and turned out *darne de saumon du gave grillée au beurre blanc béarnaise* and *auguillettes de saumon Turenne* and even *escalopes de saumon à l'oseille*. The food went down a treat at the pub and those who ate it always insisted on complimenting the chef, so at the end of the evening Rube Hardwick would produce Mrs Doyle from the kitchen and the lady would give a coy little curtsy and scurry back across the common to her husband where they would then feed the pigs with the fish heads and unpeg the condom from the washing line.

It was because Mr Doyle's piggery began to smell of fish that his neighbours complained. There was the permanent smell of fish in the air which when mixed with the natural smell of pigs produces something all the more disgusting for the olfactory lobes to cope with. He didn't do anything about it though – not until we all stopped buying his bacon because that had a fishy smell too. Then, of course, Mrs Doyle had a load of spare fish heads on her hands but my grandmother, suddenly aware of boundless opportunities, bought them from her for a penny each and produced masses of fish head pie which was just as legendary as her dumplings. At first, Rube Hardwick wasn't so very keen on offering it on his menu but was eventually persuaded to give it a try. The result was amazing. Not only did Rube now have to feed those who must spend the night waiting for the repair of their motors, but suddenly the cinema-goers were including a visit to the pub in their itinerary merely to sample the local fare before leaving the village. He served it like fish and chips, wrapped in newspaper. The nobs would take it back and eat it with their fingers in their motors or quite often they would stroll about the village staring in at the wax-like figures who read their newspapers in yellow rooms and deposit their own grubby newspapers outside our front doors for our mothers to sweep away in the mornings. My father tutted that the nobs had no manners.

For a time fish head pie became the most popular dish even among theatre-goers in the metropolis. Fish head pie restaurants sprang up in the West End of London and one or two of the more discerning proprietors paid my grandmother handsomely for her recipe and featured the authentic preparation on their menus – à la Emily Brightside. The second Mrs Doyle wasn't pleased. My grandmother was stealing her thunder and a great row was brewing. Mrs Doyle refused to sell her the fish heads any longer. A silly thing not to do, as my father was the one who controlled the supply, anyway. He simply lopped off the head and the tail of the salmon before he sold them to Rube and from then on the main ingredient didn't cost my grandmother anything at all. We were all learning the rudiments of capitalism and it was a relief to many when a halt was called to the strike and we could all go back to the mucky pit and forget our schemes for making ends meet.

All except me, that is. I had no wish to go into the pit. When we knew of the capitulation and that the strike had ended my father said, 'Time for the pit, Donald, tha'd better go and see deputy.' That's all he said to me. I shouldn't have expected more but I had kept alive a tired hope that he would ask me if there might be something else I would like to do with my life. He might have said, how about farming like Isaac's father or keeping pigs like Mr Doyle? What about the cinema like my uncle or doctoring like Archie Jellis? School-teaching, Simmonds's dye works, Gaylord's knicker factory, the church, the pub, the shops? Motor mechanic or water engineer?

What about the police force or working at the gas works? But he didn't say any of that. Time for the pit, Donald. Time for the pit, son.

The deputy is a man in a strange position. He talks to everyone. He talks with the coal owner and with the manager and with the colliers, but nobody talks to him. Not unless they want something, then they talk with him. I needed something, or so my father told me. I needed to work in his stinking pit. So I had to go and see him.

His name was George Smart and he had a nose like a half-open knife blade. He was captain of the football team but after a game he would never take a drink at the pub with his team mates. Instead he would always go off and have a drink with the opposing side. Win or lose, it made no difference. He took his drink with the opposition. It wasn't that he didn't like the men in his team, it was just that he suffered the penalty of being deputy. That was the fate of a deputy. You drank with the opposition because none of your own would sup with you.

Of a morning, George Smart gave you eighty yards in which to discuss what you had to say. Take it or leave it. He lived in a neat cottage up by the big house and if you got out early enough you would stand outside George Smart's door and wait for him to begin his walk to the pit. If you were second in line, you stood by the way eighty yards from George Smart's door and on the path that you knew he would follow to work. If you were third in line, you stood a further eighty yards down the road. If you got as far as the pit and still had not found a place in the queue you had to wait until the following day before you could discuss matters with Mr Smart and you made sure that you got out early. Some people queued all night for Mr Smart. He called it the eighty-yard rule; others called it the eight-hour wait. He was a man of few words which was just as well, otherwise eighty yards would probably have been quite insufficient in which to settle matters.

'What's up, lad?' he said to me as the previous interviewee fell by the wayside.

'Start in t'pit, Mr Smart.'

'Name?'

'Tha knows me, Mr Smart. I sometimes come to training sessions for the football.'

'Name, lad?'

'Donald Brightside, Mr Smart.'

'Start tonight, lad.'

'But can't I start dayshift, Mr Smart? Go down with my father?'

'Start tonight, lad.'

'Yessir.'

'Report at pit head, we'll have thee sorted.'

'Right, Mr Smart.'

I fell back and saw Billy o' the Terrus End take my place a little further down the road.

14

Events leading to the foundation of the museum

On the nights which follow the bright red days, with the coal dust particles still floating in the air at suppertime, the village takes on green hues. When the purple has finally faded from Hunger Hill and the ditchwater colours are trying to sort themselves into the children's paint-boxes for the night, the cats appear. They walk in a dim spectrum on the fences down by the pit head, their fur slowly turning to shades of myrtle and olive, and one tom cat in particular sings love songs to his many mates; then he sprays the wood with the secretions from his sex glands. He heralds the night as surely as the cockerel foreshadows the day and the menfolk in our houses begin to fidget in their armchairs. And maybe once a year, coincidentally when the moon is full and casting opal beams into the scattering dust, even the dark stones of the terrace suddenly begin to sparkle like emeralds. It's then that those who are able take to their beds or to the bushes, wrap themselves tightly in their partners' arms and stay that way exploring and re-exploring orifice and mucosa until the dawn wakes them with a bang. The winding wheel squeaks, the semen hangs like spittle and the men dress for another day's toil. That's what they don't understand in London, that's what they have to come and see for themselves if ever they are to realize what a differing people we are.

In the years following the strike there were two such nights that I can recall. The first was soon after I had started working in the pit. I walked home with Billy. The moon was up. The furze growing about the rat-ridden land at the pit head was green as the grass, the cats screamed at one another, fur frozen on arched backs, and the stone twinkled at first like broken glass then with a fresh input of moondust, like freshly cut emeralds. And on the wires slung from chimney pot to gas lamp two exotic figures moved among the stars. Rosanne and Clarrie had returned to our village.

'What are they doin' 'ere?' Billy asked in a gruff voice which I ignored.

I stared at Clarrie a few feet above my head. She had taken on a new shape in her absence. She curved at the thigh and at the waist, she had developed breasts. I gazed at the pale full moon. It looked like a hole in the sky and I imagined that I could see clean through it. I then stared at the slumbering terrace of houses. There wasn't an electric light to be seen. Somewhere a lass giggled and I felt suddenly discomforted in my baggy trousers held at the middle with a bit of old cord.

'Doesn't tha naw?' I asked.

'Naw they's bloody hoss thieves,' Billy answered.

I looked about the common and heard the lass giggle again but this time from further away as if she'd somewhere been lifted into the sky.

'Better go back to H. G. Wells, Billy,' I advised my friend, knowing that the magic was not for him.

'Naw she nicked tha family's fortune,' Billy told me as he turned to go. He shouted good-night and ambled off to the terrace end and I heard him close the door. I looked up to the two figures on the wire. They knew that I was there watching them but they hadn't yet acknowledged me. They had ostrich feathers in their hair which took on the colour of the sea and their sequinned thighs shone a strange subdued silver. I sat in the rubber armchair and watched them for a time. They were the colour of pixies. Then without my knowing how she had got there, Rosanne was naked astride me and thrusting herself onto my erect penis. My trousers were about my ankles. Her young daughter was removing my shirt and moving her tongue over my back and my nipples. The girl in the sky giggled from much further off than before. Then the three of us, naked, were walking as if we were pushing through water towards the wagon which was submerged only a short distance away. We lay wrapped together beneath a Mexican blanket until, like all the others who had succumbed to the magic of the green night, dawn woke us with a bang. I quietly left the wagon and went back towards the house, stopping to struggle up with the armchair which I carried with me and manoeuvred carefully through the door. From now on I was to sleep with Lancaster and Mr Brown in the parlour.

*

325

Nobody from the family was too pleased to see Rosanne and Ernest accused her directly of stealing the family fortune, but she denied it emphatically. Yes, in a moment of grief she had gone off with the plumed horses and she regretted it but she had never even had a sight of Great Great Grandmother's nest egg. As far as she was aware, Albert had dug up the suitcase from around the Roman wall on Hunger Hill and had immediately reburied it elsewhere for safe-keeping. When she was pressed by my father she admitted that Albert might have hidden it in the pit – which would explain how he came to be wearing Bresci's hat when he died. Ernest, my father and I then spent some time searching about the pit for Albert's new hiding place. Word soon got about and others joined in the search. Before long nobody was hewing coal any more, but everyone was digging in the most unlikely places in an attempt to find the missing money.

The brass was never uncovered though some amazing things were turned up in the scramble to find it. In the first instance, three more rubber women were found buried in the galleries, the last one causing a terrible fright as a collier put his pick through the doll's head. It produced an almighty explosion which most thought was due to fire damp and led to a panic in which Billy broke his leg. It seems that Elyahou Tsiblitz had sent his latest invention to a number of other bachelors besides our Lancaster. Then one day a stash of false teeth and rubber legs was found together with a whole sheaf of my aunt Henrietta's poetry. We could only conclude that she and Mr Tsiblitz had been down the pit one day to hide unwanted property but nobody could imagine when such an excursion had taken place. When the Ascot Gold Cup turned up nobody said anything. My father just took it into Leeds as he had done twenty years before but this time made certain that it was melted down. He put the money that he received for it into the miners' welfare fund.

The find which gave me the most pleasure, however, was the skeleton of a horse. It was found complete and wedged in a fissure leading off one of the galleries. It belonged to the massive shire horse which used to pull Rosanne's wagon – the one which had galloped off when it was brought into the pit because it had been frightened of the dark. Mr Brown and I took it up to the surface a bit at a time and rebuilt it, hitched in its harness in front of the wagon.

Then, because of all that extra digging in unlikely places, the pit roof began to crumble and it finally collapsed, killing two men. Everyone blamed Rosanne. If she hadn't returned to the village none of this would ever have happened. Billy, still with a broken leg, threw stones at the wagon and daubed slogans on the side suggesting that we were better off without the French. My father defended her for a time until Billy told him that I didn't always sleep in my armchair but sometimes was to be seen creeping across the common to spend the night in the arms of the two lasses. My father removed his belt and leathered me then he too threw stones at the wagon until one muddy morning having had enough, Rosanne unhitched the skeleton horse and replaced it with a pit pony. She blew me a kiss, Clarrie swore that she would love me to her death and they went away in the thin drizzle.

Throughout this time, of course, Jacky Jellis's voice had continued to boom from the walls of the New Royal Cinema. The nobs continued to pour in from London and my grandmother was approaching her second ton of fish head pie. Then one day nobody came. And nobody came the next day either. The wind of change was about to blow itself through the cinema on my land. *The Jazz Singer* had opened up in London. The cinema audience could see real talking pictures with real film stars now. Lancaster took his film spool home. Two weeks later he was on a boat bound for America. One might have understood if Mr Pinkofsky had been bitter but he showed no unkindness, he had no regrets. He had made his money just as Rube Hardwick and Emily Brightside had made theirs. They had made it whilst the talking picture had boomed. It was a blip in their careers. Just as the film itself had been a blip in the career of Lancaster Brightside – now he was on his way to America to show the world what a great film maker he could be.

Mr Brown's consumption got worse and he decided to leave the pit. He had a little tucked away, mostly earned from his winnings when betting against Bottom Boat Beauty. He continued to live in our house though. Then one day I saw my future come together with my past. I told George Smart to stick his stinking coal pit. I sat on the common with Mr Brown with the skeleton of a horse grazing before us. Between its ribs we could see the pit and the cinema at

Hunger Hill. The wind whistled through the old bones causing doors to bang.

'All them seats,' I said. 'It's like a bloody church.'

'Nay, it's nowt like a church, lad. Tha doesn't want to 'ave owt to do with that stuff.'

'Well, it's like a museum then.'

'Ay. It'll be like a museum,' he said. 'Take out them seats and it'll be just like a museum.'

I was squinting between the horse's bones. Marvelling at the way one could see the cinema right through where the flesh had been, and suddenly the bones and the building were one. The skeleton was inside the fabric of the building.

'How long did it take to put that thing together?' I asked.

'About six weeks, I think. Must've been a bloody record.'

'No. Not the cinema. The horse. How long did it take to build the skeleton?'

'A week maybe. Don't really remember.'

'And how long does tha think it'll take to put the dinosaur to-gether?'

'A year perhaps.'

'Ay. That's what I was thinking.'

'Come on, lad,' said Mr Brown. 'Let's go and see.' He stood up and spat a black gobbet of muck into the ground.

Gradually throughout the next year we cleared the cinema of its seats and brought the bones from the disused pit. We borrowed books from the libraries and made a trip to the Natural History Museum in London to see the iguanodons. Slowly we put the skeleton together inside the building and we had expert palaeontologists come to view it. Nobody said anything but we knew that it couldn't have been quite right. My great grandfather's bones were in there somewhere but it didn't matter – the skeleton looked just like the pictures in the books.

Mr Brown had Jacky Ellis impersonate a dinosaur's roar and when he played it over Movietone it sounded to be the most ferocious thing that anyone had ever heard. Here was my museum. The schools brought their children from far and wide to see the only complete dinosaur skeleton in the North of England and to hear the only authentic dinosaur roar that was left in the whole of the world.

15

How Mr Brown came to lead the blind

The Jam Sahib's motor was a twenty-eight horsepower Lanchester which had been built in about 1907. It was a massive vehicle and could accommodate ten persons quite comfortably. My great great grandmother had bought it from Elyahou Tsiblitz soon after it had been built. Since almost the first week of its being in our family my father had taken the less privileged in the car, on trips to places where they might breathe more easily and look at hills and rivers without having to see them through the filter of coal dust which nearly always hung in the village air. Such trips for these people had been the dearest wish of my great great grandmother and there was talk at the time that it was the sole reason for her purchase.

One bright red morning, my father asked Mr Brown if he would drive the blinded up into the dales as had been promised them. Unfortunately my father had come down with the chickenpox and was unable to go. Mr Brown agreed that he would stand in for my father and asked me if I would like to accompany him on the trip as he was uncertain that he could handle all of those blind people on his own. At that time Mr Brown and I looked after the museum together but after discussion we decided not to open up for that day, packed our sandwiches and set off in the motor with half a dozen men who couldn't see the end of a nose between them. Mr Brown took the car through Ilkley and Skipton to Settle where he turned off the main road and followed a path to the foot of a mountain.

'That's Pen-y-ghent,' our lodger told me. I looked at the sunny hill and was immediately reminded of a loaf browning in the oven. 'We'll tek 'em up that path,' he said.

'What, tha means tha's going to tek this lot up there?'

'Ay. Why not?'

'But they're blind, Mr Brown,' I confided, trying to keep my voice down.

329

'That's nowt,' he said. 'Come on. Give us a hand.'

We helped the men from the motor and had them sit in a circle on the grass, then Mr Brown lifted out the back seat and produced an enormous coil of rope.

'Now, we're off for a little walk up this 'ere 'ill,' he told the men on the grass. 'Don't tha worry 'bout nowt. There's a rope.'

'Will we 'ave to tie it round us middles?' asked a man who had no eyes and who until this moment thought that he had banished mountain climbing from his list of allowed activities.

Mr Brown stared at the empty sockets for a moment and said, 'No. Nowt like that. Rope's fixed. Tha just feel for t'rope. It goes from 'ere right the way to top. It'll be like walking up steps with tha hand on a banister rail.' Then he helped the man up and made him hold the rope for a few seconds. 'Can tha feel it?' he asked.

'Ay.'

'Well, it's a bit slack just 'ere but tha'll get more confidence further up the hill where it tightens up a bit.'

I took our lodger to one side and said, 'Mr Brown, tha can't be serious about this. They'll never mek it to the top. They'll never mek it fifty yards without falling over the edge.'

'It'll be all right, lad, tha'll see,' he tried assuring me.

'But Mr Brown, I don't like this. It's having a bit of fun at their expense. It's not right.'

'Fun, lad, tha calls it fun? It's not fun, lad. It's deadly serious is this. It's giving these people back their self-respect is this. It's not fun. Nobody will be laughing, lad, least of all yours truly. Now come on, get thasen moving, we don't want to be bringing them down in the dark.' He started to cough and I watched this man who was already talking about bringing half a dozen blind men down a mountain even before we had got them up there, and God alone knew how we were going to achieve that. I watched the muck coughed from his lungs as it caught in the wind-whipped blades of grass. It nestled there like cuckoo spit. 'Now, tha get hold of back end of rope and I'll tek lead,' he said. 'And for God's sake keep it taut.'

'I thought tha didn't believe in God?' I chided, unable to disguise the sneer in my voice.

'Not believe? I never said owt like that, lad. I believe all right.

330

Believe more than most,' he told me. 'Just can't stand all this prayin' and praisin', that's all. God don't listen, lad, and why should he, so what's the point in talkin' and singin' to him?' He looked over to the six blind men. 'Ask them,' he said. 'Ask them how much he listens.' I watched a lark twittering high above the summit of the hill. 'Too busy, lad. Too busy to listen to all that stuff is God. But he's there all right. I believe that. Anyroad, who the fuck do you think is going to get us up to the top of this 'ere mountain, eh?' I couldn't reply as I struggled with such an irrational chastisement. 'Come on, get a hold of the rope end and like I said keep it taut.'

'I'll keep it taut, Mr Brown, tha worry about t'other end,' and I sniffed back a tear.

'Good lad,' he said, then he led the blind men one at a time and stood them, spaced several yards apart from each other, on the right hand side of the rope telling each one not to move. Our lodger then went to the head of the line which he had formed, picked up the other end of the rope, slung it over his shoulder and set off up the hill tugging it tight.

'Right, stick out tha left hands,' he called, then after a moment he asked, ''As tha got it? 'As tha got the rope?' From where I was at the rear of the line I could see that each man had a grip on the rope and I called up that everyone had got a hold on the rope. 'Right, keep on walking and keep on feeling for the rope. Like I said it goes right to the bloody top so there's no need to worry.' Then he turned round and shouted, 'And for God's sake keep tha bloody feet up. Lift tha knees and tha'll 'ave nowt to worry about, does thee understand?'

'Ay,' all the blind men chorused and we set off at a slow march up the path which would take us all the way to the summit. After we had gone about fifteen yards the six men started to bunch up towards Mr Brown who then shouted for us to stop exactly where we were. He instructed the men to leave go of the rope, something which they were hesitant in doing.

'Trust me,' he shouted, 'and if tha can't trust me then trust in God, all right?' The men let go of the rope. He then walked about fifteen to twenty yards up the path taking the rope and I at the end of it with him and causing me almost to bump into the man at the back of the line. Then he shouted, 'Right, stick out tha left hands

331

again,' and once more the group of men took up the rope and walked a little further towards the peak. In this stop and start fashion and with several stumbles along the way the men climbed to the top of Pen-y-ghent.

We sat about the cairn and ate our sandwiches and Mr Brown told the men how he could see the sea in directions both east and west. He said that he could see the seagulls flying over Scarborough and told them how he could see the anglers who were landing dolphins and sharks from off the pier at Blackpool. And when one of the men asked me if Mr Brown was right and was it possible to really see such things I remained silent for ages pretending not to have heard the question until a bird's feather came spinning out of the sky and landed on my jam sandwich shaft first, and as I picked it off and put the feather in my pocket I said, 'Ay. Of course it is. True as God's my judge, there's dolphins and sharks and there's a man riding out to sea on the back of a turtle.' And the blind man smiled and told us all that this was the best day of his life and of how he'd always believed that one day he would marry a mermaid, at which news Mr Brown couldn't stop laughing. Not until it was time to come down the mountain.

'Right,' he shouted. 'We'll be turning round, remember, so tha'll be needing to hold the rope with tha right hands this time. Is that all right? Is there anyone who isn't comfy with the thought of changing hands?'

'I'm not,' said the man with no eyes. 'I've got arthritis in my right hand. I'll not grip right.'

'Well, that's no problem,' Mr Brown told him and went through the charade of passing the man under the rope and have him grip it with his left hand. Then we came down the mountain in the same fashion as we had gone up it.

I don't think that anyone knows why Wenceslas Piggott's motor was never removed from the crossroads after he had the accident. But it never was. A family of mice had made their home from the upholstery on the front passenger seat, and what they didn't live in they lived on. They had eaten most of it. A family of thrushes had made their nest in the driving seat and the back seat was given over to various activities. The young ones, during the day, used it as a hiding place or as a place for setting up house. The older ones did a spot of courting in the back at night but until Mr Brown drove the Jam Sahib's motor into the back of it nobody had any idea that the policeman ate his sandwiches there too. It was one of those nights when the world turns sparkling green and how Mr Brown didn't see it I shall never know but there you are, he didn't, and the policeman who had just climbed into the back of the stationary motor and was about to start on his cold bacon sandwich was given a real jolt.

Oddly enough, one of the blind men said that he saw Marlene Jellis standing in the road just before the accident and that gave everybody the creeps. It also initiated a whole set of new rumours – there were many prepared to believe in the ghost of Marlene Jellis. It was put about that she wasn't living with Sosthenes Smith after all, that there had been collusion between Archie and Mr Piggott, though nobody could imagine why. Perhaps Archie had just become one of those wishy-washy liberal doctors who saw murderers as being sick in the head and in need of care. That's why he's in the asylum, they said. But it was spooky, wasn't it? Who better than a blind man to see a ghost up at the spot where the woman's clothes were known to have been found? The poor soul was only looking for her bloomers, Mrs Gill told my grandmother.

The policeman was badly shaken, having his back banged like that, but at least he was on hand when we had calmed him sufficiently to investigate the accident and make a few notes with his blue pencil.

Mr Willmott sat in our parlour and brought a fart from the direction of my grandmother who, when all eyes fell upon her, reddened considerably. She looked at the corpse on the table hoping that some of us at least might think the noise had come from there. Mr Willmott remained impassive, his long black tash hiding his ventriloquist lips. He too looked at the corpse, thinking that perhaps he had not thrown his voice far enough. Mr Brown, dressed in his Sunday suit, was the third corpse which I had seen. The first, that of my great great grandmother, had appeared to be very dead. She looked like a pickled walnut despite the fact that Emily had washed the coal dust from her skin. I tell you, she was like a pickled walnut. That of my uncle Albert had seemed to be asleep. Mr Brown, though, looked to be wide awake. His alert blue eyes were open, drinking in the surrounding room despite the fact that there was a hole right through his middle where the steering column had penetrated. The room itself was quiet and appeared to be the dead thing in our midst. I looked about me at the others present. The parson, my grandfather, my parents – they were unmoving. Mr Brown's blue eyes and my grandmother's red cheeks – at that moment it was they who gave our parlour its liveliness. My father and the parson put him in a coffin and nailed down the lid after throwing in our lodger's extra collar stud. We took him to the crematorium in Wakefield and Mr Willmott remained outside watching over his plumed horses. He didn't want a repetition of what happened on the last occasion our family had to draw on the services of the Burial Society.

My grandfather stood up and made a short speech explaining how it was only fitting that a man like Brown should be cremated for he claimed that cremation somehow went along with the man's anonymity. He came from nowhere and nobody knew very much about him. We'll scatter the ashes, he told the small congregation, and send him back to wherever he arrived from – that's about the best we can do for the man.

'There's more to it than that, grandfather,' I said, 'he had a spirit did Mr Brown, a real spirit. Cremation will release that much from the old bones. His spirit will find its way back to where it needs to be. That's why he preferred cremation, he didn't want that spirit locked in no more, and as for the ashes, well, if nobody objects I think I would rather keep them at the museum. He doesn't need no scattering.'

Nobody seemed to object so I took the urn back to the village and set in on a plinth next to the iguanodon. He had been the last of the dossing colliers which my family had known. There were no others after Mr Brown. If, as I have said before, Bill Pettit was born before his time then I reckon that Mr Brown had come in right on cue. He made up his life on the run, so to speak, and he painted us like he wanted, right into his own and the world's fabric of being. After his funeral my father took the wide winged chairs from our parlour and burned them on the common. He bought a couch which converted at night into a bed and for a time that's where I laid my head.

334

THE BRIGHTSIDE DINOSAUR

To Stephanie

1931

I

In the beginning – Squire Potterton

On the far side of Hunger Hill there is a bowl-shaped hollow called Kettle Flatt. The coarse English grasses growing around its rim have been brought to a sheen by the constant brush of wind. Harebell and scarlet poppies grow there. Grasses of a differing variety (perhaps Spanish), bitten short by the sheep which graze, grow in the deep and darker parts of the bowl. These grasses are stained evergreen by a light which cracks through a fine haze of coal dust. Here also five-foot teasels spring. Squire Potterton, whose family has owned the land since a time even before the sinking of the pits, walks in the hollow of the Flatt where once an airship crashed, tumbling its two occupants almost on top of my great great grand-mother. There is no sign of that incident now – just the grass and the warm and the quiet occasionally broken by the song of the peewit; the lark rises way above the land.

The red dogs trailing in the squire's shadow raise their silken ears. A large bird has suddenly appeared in the sky. A rush of blue, the squire has not seen anything quite like it. He sniffs, causing his moustaches the colour of weak milk-tea to twitch. He raises his gun and lets blast at the bird. Miles above, too far even for the attentive red dogs to see, the lark falls out of the sky. The man has no idea whether or not he has hit the giant bird. He slowly lowers both gun and eyes and instructs his dogs to go fetch, though he knows it will be more of a 'going to see'. But he has never been able to find those words, 'Go see.' Not even in these lately years of failing sight. Always it has been, 'Go fetch, go fetch,' instructed with all the sureness of his class. With a careless disregard for frailty which is so much a part of their naïve philosophy. The ridiculous posture that wealth will somehow shore up decaying structures: that a bankful of brass can face out time.

The dogs lope up the steep side of the hollow, trampling poppies like steeplechasers, their soft mouths already practising the formation of cradles in which to deliver back the game – cradles made safe by years of practice carrying Squire Potterton's well-fed grandchildren through a maze of corridors and rooms at the manor house to be eventually deposited dazed and wondering in yet another un-explored corner of their land. And by years of breeding too, for the dogs are descended from a line of bitches one of which was drilled in the art of lifting in her mouth none other than the baby squire himself; both into and out of his lace-lined cot.

The dogs lope madly back. One of them has the dead lark on his tongue. The squire takes the soft ball of feathers which the red dog has presented. He sniffs again, so setting the milk-tea mous-taches atwitch once more. With a puzzled stare he turns the warm belly-of-a-bird in his hand, noting the bloody wound. He offers a pat to the head of the gun dog which surpasses all understanding, for who anyway can understand that quite by accident he has brought the wrong world to its end? The squire allows his fingers to slowly uncurl letting the bird fall; *his* secret among the grasses.

The tale begins perhaps with that airship and its two occupants falling almost on top of my great great grandmother, the gentle-man in silk, the lady in chiffon and in lace. Perhaps it begins with that tumbling mad world in which Great Great Grand-mother, disturbed whilst collecting herbs for her basket, learned of machines which might fly. It begins perhaps with her confusion about a world made suddenly unfamiliar, for she told herself then, if people can live in the sky which is up and where was down? And if it were so, if indeed there was no 'perhaps' about it and the tale did begin right here at Kettle Flatt, with an old woman's musings on the up and downness of the world, then the tale would be imbued with reason (reason beyond the meaning) for it would be charged with symmetry. The story, complete, would breathe pattern into myth; the reason of the ring, the reason for the dark cycle of birth and rebirth. If it were so and myth understood, then reason would be satisfied and nothing should surprise. The beginning would be no different from the end and it ends, I have no doubt now that it ends, with Squire Potterton on his daily walk in that same flat bowl. But, enough of lazy conjecture, for the moment let us construct a beginning.

2

In the beginning – Salon Marguerite

When cousin Clarrie and her mother, Rosanne the French rope walker, left our village for the second time they went to Manchester where the older woman assumed a title – Madame it was, in a city brothel. They worked in a dilapidated Georgian house: two top-floor rooms covered in chintz and dust. They had bedrooms too on the floor below, cosy rooms divorced from unsavoury business, to which the clients were never invited. (Rosanne circled such perimeters about her separate lives and times. She had a geometer's regulatory expertise which, as you will learn, like the ruling queen she passed to the only daughter of the lineage.)

The brothel was known as Salon Marguerite. The house was overlooked by the city's black, brooding cathedral and was only a stone's throw from the Medical School's Department of Anaesthesiology. There was a pet shop filled with sad animals on the corner below.

The pet shop was a typical Northern corner shop. The previous occupant had been an apothecary who had whisked his ailing business to Altrincham, a town, he said, where the sick could afford to pay for their medicines. He had however left behind his glass-fronted cabinets and rich mahogany shelving. The cabinets ran the length of two adjacent walls and the present tenant had filled them with small animals bedded on straw. Guinea pigs and mice, hamsters and gerbils peered with eyes sharp as sewed diamonds from narrow confines behind the glass. It was not difficult to imagine them a myopic display of jewels in a posh London shop.

The stone floor was overrun by pups and kittens forever chasing and tying each other in balls of coloured wool. Suddenly, amid the ceaseless play, a pup deciding on more urgent needs might sit and pee; then raising her floppy ears as a lass might ease up her drawers she gathers her immodesty to continue with the chase. Not surprising then, the floor was always wet and the place stank of urine.

The low, wood ceiling was dimly hung with dozens of crowding cages which swung back and forth to the rhythm of the noisy, swaying captives within. Each barred, bamboo cage housed a blue and green parakeet or perhaps a scarlet macaw. There were the odd love-birds and rhinoceros hornbills. Humming birds hummed. Above the raucous din one might hear a canary sing – alone.

In charge of this rowdy menagerie was Bagshaw Moralee, an ancient adventurer and sometime proprietor of zoological gardens at both Arundel and Southport. He had spent the mid-years of Victoria's reign, hardly more than a boy, adventuring in Java and in South America. He had then called himself a field naturalist and hunted new species which, by sailing ship, he sent back to England for dissection and classification. Such operations were performed by a group of lugubrious men who chopped things up in dark closets subjecting the bits to scrutiny under their microscopes. Not for nothing were they known as the 'closet men'.

Bagshaw Moralee claimed to have been the first European ever to have set eyes upon the beautiful Charlotta Bird of Paradise and indeed it was he who named it for the royal princess of that name. For those who might not know, I must tell that Charlotta was the fifth illegitimate daughter of the King of Sweden, remembered now only from entries in rarely consulted editions of the Scandinavian equivalent of *Debrett's Peerage*, where on drear buff pages she is described as having been born without kneecaps. At her birth, the attendant midwife realized how the princess's femurs and fibulas had suffered congenital malformation by fusing into single longbones for she saw that the baby failed to draw up her knees when having her belly tickled. Tragically the legs continued to grow in the normal manner through childhood and adolescence. The court doctors had periodically discussed the possibility of breaking the bones at the approximate position of the knee but had always refrained from carrying out the operation, fearing it unlikely that improvement would follow. Indeed, it seemed very likely that the situation might be made much worse, for as the princess grew who was to say where the 'knees' might end. The doctors also advised, from time to time, that the legs be surgically removed but the king would never hear of it. Consequently, the princess spent most of her short, wretched life unable to geniculate and stiffly bumping about in a rough wooden wheelchair hewn from the forest by the good but sombre people of Norkopping.

In a box, put together with equally rough timbers, Mr Moralee sent that first specimen of the bird named for her to Joseph Quekett. The latter was the famous Leeds closet man, a nephew of Edwin and Thomas Quekett who were founder members of the Microscopical Society. His wife had been a distant relative to Buckland, the geologist. It had been Buckland who, for the amusement of his students at Oxford, would hang on to his coat-tails and gallivant about the lecture theatre imitating what he thought might be the grotesque flight of the pterodactyl.

Quekett, coincidentally, was a person to have known my great great grandmother. The two had a passing acquaintanceship through a shared interest in the compounding of medicines from plant materials. She too had sometimes sent specimens to him. Small world.

In order to successfully package the bird with all its brilliant black and crimson plumage intact, Bagshaw Moralee had severed the spindly legs from the unusually plump body. He was only following local native habit, much practised by the women to facilitate the stuffing of a bird into the standard-sized stew-pot, but unfortunately he forgot to include the severed legs when packing the bird destined for Quekett. For a time, to the distress of the princess, whose legs must have extended from that wheelchair like a couple of battleship gun barrels, and to the embarrassment of the scientific establishment, the specimen received in the wood box at Leeds became known as 'the legless bird of paradise'. More of this later.

Above the pet shop the clients at Salon Marguerite frittered their brass on the thin sickly girls; the sweet smell of ether wafted up from the Department of Anaesthesiology and hung heavily in the drab drapes shushing some to sleep. Others, not overcome by the whiff of anaesthetic, lay partnered in their cots, listening to the hush from the locked-in animals below – that hush of nature which anticipates the dawn. It's a prophetic silence which warns of the sun soon to come over the soot-black roof of the cathedral opposite. A silence of the night which is understood only by those who are themselves caged, or by those fearful of irrational spaces swirling about them.

342

3

Rosanne and Clarrie

Rosanne the rope walker with the yellow hair and turquoise eyes, with breasts like water-wings, had first sailed upon our village the year before the commencement of the Great War. She lived in a wagon which was painted red; from the golden lettering curlicued on the sides one read of its occupancy – *The Count Schubert Circus*. The wagon was parked beneath the village gas lamp on the common in front of our terrace of smoky houses.

At the outbreak of war the alien Count Schubert had been packed off to Austria together with two others – Elyahou Tsiblitz, the rubber salesman, and my mad great-aunt, Henrietta Brightside, who had relentlessly pursued the favours of Mr Tsiblitz. They were all three considered undesirable in a time of national emergency.

Schubert had been Rosanne's husband. He wore a leopard-skin leotard, had a waxed moustache with curled ends and was able to pull nails from blocks of wood with his teeth. He was reputed to be one of the strongest men in the world but that didn't stop a stray Greek bullet from exploding in his chest during a spying mission at Cettinje. The force of the explosion blew him into the sea where he drowned like a sackful of very expensive potatoes. So much for strong men.

After the deportation of Schubert, the rope walker chose to remain in the village. She continued to live alone in the wagon. It was then that Uncle Albert, who was infatuated (like so many others) from the moment he first cast eyes upon that yellow hair, decided not to enlist. He spent the war years down the pit and quickly moved into the wagon with Rosanne. They soon had a child, Clarrie, a few years my junior. Since being ten years of age I have been hopelessly, and I had thought secretly, in love with my cousin for I had never told of my passion to a soul. But it seems a passion like mine finds other means by which to reveal itself.

When Uncle Albert died in mysterious circumstances the coffin was carried to his funeral at the church in the next village stowed in the back of the painted wagon. The wagon was pulled by four plumed horses which had been loaned to the family for the occasion by the local Burial Society, yet immediately after the funeral Rosanne decided not to return the horses but took it into her head to abscond with them – taking Clarrie with her. That was the first occasion on which they left the village.

Now, it's known that for a time they joined another circus (the evidence for it is overwhelming for they were caught on film when their caravan unexpectedly passed through the village at a time when my Uncle Lancaster was shooting the first talking picture) and it has been suggested that the Burial Society's horses provided meat to nourish the lions and tigers, but I doubt it. Rosanne loved horses, as she loved all else in life, and she will have given them freedom one place or another where the travelling circus happened to stop for a night.

Eventually Rosanne and Clarrie returned to the village. I found them one night, pink ostrich plumes adorning their hair; sequinned tights dazzling their muscular thighs. They were walking the wireless aerials which crawled in beneath our windows bringing voices and music to our houses, filling the empty stone with sound. The aerials stretched from the gas lamp on the common. Although both mother and daughter were by now proficient rope walkers our neighbours couldn't get it out of their heads that we gave hospitality to a couple of horse thieves.

I was seventeen at the time of their return and Clarrie must have been about fourteen, going on fifteen. Billy o' the Terrus End, who had been my best friend until then, told my father that I was spending my nights not at home sleeping in the armchair in the parlour as I should have been, but that I was sleeping in the wagon beneath the gas lamp. He implied that I was sleeping with Clarrie, which simply wasn't true.

I was sleeping with Rosanne.

I loved Clarrie but I had quite unaccountably become a fumbling lover captured in one of her mother's drawn circles. It was Billy's stories which finally drove the two of them from the village. That and the dislike of foreigners which had suddenly found its way into the hearts of the village folk. They went off for the second time in the wagon, pulled now by a pony that had been brought from the pit – thus lending a truth to the conviction that Rosanne had been nothing but a horse thief all along. And a whore. 'Whoring bloody hoss thieves,' Billy called them.

I suppose being Madame at Salon Marguerite lent a truth to the whoring bit too, but Rosanne had never been a whore with me. Never. We just made love among the crystal scatterings of coal dust which on some nights caused the dark to sparkle green – often with Clarrie pale and naked in the moon's light, lying beside us in a circle of her own, hardly covered by the Mexican blanket.

4

Mr Sligh and his barrel

At the brothel Clarrie shared her room with a lodger – a man who exposed himself from a barrel. His name was Montague Sligh and he had a permanent erection. The only way he could gain sexual satisfaction was for him to climb into a barrel where he would kneel and thrust his erection through a carefully prepared and very circular hole. The circumference of the hole had been lined with crimson velvet, thickly padded with a wadding, and tacked to the wood by means of tiny gold-headed pins. There was a tumescence about the padded velvet much in keeping with the unusual condition of Mr Sligh.

Clarrie found her attention being drawn and drawn again to that red-lined hole and to the golden pin-heads which arced like stars about its circumference, as if the hole might be the earth itself floating lazily in the white universality of space and she were seeing it projected negatively, from some other planetary aspect. During the quiet hours of the day she would place her eye to the hole and peer into the darkness. And here she sensed the discomfort of one intrusive upon the messy moments of birth; unable to dam back the genesis of shoals of bivalves and jellyfish and whatever else she imagined to flow there, she settled to being the reluctant midwife at the belly of Mr Sligh's barrel.

The Professor of Oleopharmocognosy, at the time of one of his frequent visits to see Rosanne, tried to allay the mother's fears for the sanity of her child. 'Clarrie is like an early pioneer of photography, interested only in sharing with others the images she has seen. It isn't her fault we are unable to see what she sees. Things come forth. I have spent my life studying the endosperms of oily seeds. New seeds spring forth. I cannot see them there in the old seed but I know for sure, as night follows day, seeds will follow seeds. The barrel is not just her seed of study, but her camera obscura; she sees therein history and time. Her frustration is that she is unable to share with us the evolution she sees. I think this is not madness, merely a groping towards maturity. Like all else, it will wilt and sadly it will pass. Then, in adulthood, and like the rest of us, she will be satisfied with only the knowing of what she has seen. She will know that seed follows seed and live with the knowing, she will settle to living in a world made mad with reproduction; the repetition of image and photograph. For the moment though she is fortunate to have the innocence of a pioneer, a frontierswoman. As a parent you should have no fears, there is no cause for concern, none whatsoever.'

Each evening, the lid was placed in position on the barrel and it was stood in a corner of the brothel's fussy parlour. There, Montague Sligh would summon whatever satisfaction he could, exposing himself to the girls as they went about their nightly duties. As they toyed with their clients in the dim glow from turned-down gas lamps, thrust from anaglypta walls in the outstretched hands of bronze nymphs, Mr Sligh sighed from his barrel.

One night the brothel was raided by the police and the large, uniformed officer sent along to arrest those present asked Rosanne what it was which she stored in the barrel standing in the corner.

'It's a pickle barrel,' Rosanne lied.

'For what?' he asked. The room was gloomy. Dark suffocating drapes hung about the windows and the door.

'Cucumbers, of course,' she said in mock surprise.

'Well, let's take a little peek, shall we?' he suggested disbelievingly and with his gloved hand he gripped what he took to be a broken handle sticking out from the side of the barrel and dragged it uneasily into the centre of the room. Rosanne heard the cucumbers groan. The officer was trying clumsily to lift the lid with his leather-gloved hands when Clarrie, clad in an expensive silk nightdress, rushed across the room and threw herself on top of the barrel. Kicking out her legs and waving her arms about in the most alarming manner, she looked as if she was taking her first swimming lesson whilst drowning on top of that barrel. Her small silken posterior was wriggling shockingly only inches from the policeman's nose.

'Oh, here's Clarrie,' Rosanne said, introducing her daughter to the policeman as if she had been the tardy maid at last arriving with the tea. Rosanne appeared to have completely forgotten about the man groaning in the barrel though in truth she hadn't forgotten about him at all, for she was just now thinking how his experience so far might have cured Mr Sligh of his uncomfortable permanent erection and she was hoping that the officer wouldn't want to take up the handle once again for he might be surprised to find that it was no longer there.

Clarrie smiled up at the policeman from her prone position and Rosanne then invited the officer to take her daughter into the adjacent room.

'Are you offering me a bribe, madame?' he asked, walking about the barrel and viewing the wood with doubting curiosity. 'The bribe of such a young thing?' he muttered more to himself than to Rosanne, but Clarrie had not failed to note and be afeared of the wicked glint in the policeman's eye. Then he dipped his toe at the barrel as if testing the temperature of the water in which my cousin was surely now drowning. Decisively he went into action. He picked up Clarrie and dumped her heavily on the brown velvet couch. A cloud of dust rose like the seeds from a puff-ball towards the ceiling. The policeman peeled off his leather gloves, aggressively slapped them once on the top of the barrel and threw them after the girl, then turning his attention back to the barrel he managed with difficulty to get his large fingertips under the lid and started to lift. It was at that moment that the house began to shake. Down the road at the Department of Anaesthesiology primates with electrodes implanted in their brains leapt from the operating tables and shrieked as if they were back in their jungle homes and the blue and green parakeets caged in the pet shop on the corner below squawked as if it was the end of the world. At Salon Marguerite one might have been forgiven for believing at that moment that the brothel was situated in a tree house deep in the South American rain forest.

But only for a moment. Within seconds civilization would waft in with the drapes of anaesthetic. The gin and tonics which had been poured for the clients developed turbulent surfaces and sloshed wave-like over the sides of the glasses without anyone touching them. The lights came up and went down a dozen times, in turn illuminating and dousing the bronze nymphs in a secret coppery darkness – the uneven light eventually dying to a dim flicker. The policeman stumbled and fell over as the barrel started to gyrate. He too heard the cucumbers groan within. Rosanne ran to the window to see what all the commotion was about and as she drew back the dusty drapes, exposing the black cathedral in all of its sullen glory, the front side of the house fell away and she too disappeared with the heavy curtains and the falling rubble. The girls started to scream. Clarrie, petrified, clung to the couch which was inching its way towards the eerie blue-black night and the brooding cathedral. The barrel continued to gyrate, then it suddenly shattered. The hoops broke first and then the staves slowly peeled away, revealing to an astonished policeman the squatting figure of a naked man who slowly began to rise with the lid of the barrel balanced on his head, like the hat of a Chinese coolie.

Mr Sligh, eyeing up the situation in a second, leapt to make a grab for the brown velvet couch which was taking Clarrie towards a tumble into the street below. He was a tall ex-guardsman with a sad moustache and despite his nasty affliction, which one could now see hadn't in the least bit been affected by the night's experience, had no difficulty in displaying his athleticism. Unfortunately, because of the man's quick movement, the hefty policeman thought the naked man was making his dash for freedom and from his position on the floor he made a surprisingly agile leap for Mr Sligh. The officer had anticipated too much and too far, however, and leapt into nowhere as the naked man, still standing with his feet on the base of the barrel, managed with sinewy arms to haul the couch and Clarrie back towards the safety of the doorway and the stairs. The unfortunate police officer, though, with one piercing scream had thrown himself heavily into the night – after Rosanne.

Clarrie dressed hurriedly in her bedroom below and made off towards Oldham where she was relieved to read the following day in the newspaper that her mother had sustained no more serious injury than a broken leg in her fall. It seems that the single fatality in what is, I think, known as Manchester's only earthquake was a police officer who fell to his death within sight of the dark cathedral. That had occurred on 3rd May, 1931, and three days later, Clarrie was wandering about the Millstone Grit in a curious area which straggles the dark and light border between the warring counties of Lancashire and Yorkshire.

5
The village

Our few houses smoke in a bowl cut from the surrounding hills. To the west is a road – the only road out of the village. It climbs steeply past the big house in its grey-walled garden where the coal owner lives. He is my maternal grandparent but he has nothing to do with the likes of us – he hasn't spoken with my mother since before she was married. It had been her grandfather who sank the pit and who built the terrace of smoky houses which tottered the village out of its random sticks and into order, inserting a pitman in every doorway. They brought the water, they brought the gas and finally they brought light; for a time the village burned, radiant as an expanded sun in a defiant but ultimate glow. We live in the middle of that terrace. You can spot our house easily. It's the one with the Jam Sahib's motor parked outside. Mr Tsiblitz, the rubber salesman, sold it to my great great grandmother years ago, and ever since it has been used to cart the disabled to the seaside and into the dales to show them that there are other places on earth, places where you can breathe without gasping and where you can see for miles without grit hurting the eyes.

To the east is Hunger Hill and the museum of which I am both owner and curator. The museum is a converted cinema, famous for being the picture house where the first talking film – made even before *The Jazz Singer* – was shown. The film had been made by my Uncle Lancaster before he emigrated, lugging his special sadness to Hollywood, and paradoxically becoming assistant cameraman on the set of that hilariously funny film, *Cocoanuts*, which starred the Marx Brothers. It is one of life's ironies that a man as sad as Uncle Lancaster should eventually have taken a hand in the direction of their latest film, *Monkey Business*, a film which when they saw it caused his mother to split her corsets laughing and had his father coughing out teeth. Lancaster was a glum twin to Clarrie's father, my Uncle Albert.

Hunger Hill dominates our village.

Beneath the hill the houses are strung like a row of fairylights fronted by a grassy common, beyond which are more hills – the slag heaps which hide the pit. But you know it's there. You can hear the perpetual creak of the rusting wheel, fetching up the tubs fifty times to the hour, birth and rebirth in the thin drizzle. You can hear the tapping of the men, golems returned to the cloying earth. You can hear the tiresome braying of the smith, shoeing fatigued ponies.

A path winds away somewhere over there too – the way out to the next village – and in the valley beyond is that part of the river which snakes, the place we call Bottom Boat. Perhaps this is where I should have started my tale. Not that what I have already told you is irrelevant – all that stuff about Clarrie and Rosanne. All that *is* relevant. It's just that there are two beginnings, I suppose. Give me time and I shall explain.

6

Field and closet

At night the bowl sculpted from out of these hills receives a lid of stars. It comes like a priest's blessing, snapping off the light.

Standing on the common, the wagon now gone from beneath the lamp, the lamp unlit, its glass covers cracked, one can arch back one's head and count forever in the dark sky. One can count – and there are some too who can name. They are men and women without education, but they have made it their life's work to name. Sirius, Betelgeuse, Geminorum. They are old men with grizzled beards and women without teeth and they can name Alpha Centauri and Beta Centauri and with their heads flung back exhaling hot breaths into a freezing winter's night they look like crazed hags screaming a nomenclature at the cold heavens, yet they are anything but mad. They are desperately, naïvely, magically, exhilaratingly, incandescently human – counting and naming the stars away and giving their all, everything with the fire of their lives. They are the descendants of those who founded the Philosophical Societies and the Temperance Societies and the Mechanics Institute – places of learning, where knowledge still doesn't peer too easily from grimed windows – yet it wasn't until I found myself the curator of a museum, looking for objects with which to fill spaces, that I began to realize just how persistent they were in their pursuit of education and order. How they followed their instinct for making a sense of senseless existence thrust upon them in a stinking pit.

But theirs was an understanding, like a directory, put together from facts. They had no understanding of deduction or of analysis, of dissection and design. Through fact-driven messages they came to the peculiar and startling belief that the progress of science and the development of socialism were one. Of course they were no such thing. It was only the yearning for scientific fact and the longing for the achievement of the Utopian socialist state which were one. Need naïvely interlocked them, and it was the teaching of each which was so well satisfied by the Workers' Educational Association and the Labour Colleges that they came to be accepted as the same.

In our part of the world, for nearly a century the colliers had been encouraged to study natural history. The open air was uplifting and good for the health. The educationalists pointed out that the naturalists, those famous ones whom some had heard about, lived for ages. The study itself seemed to promote longevity. They said it was a virtuous study, a learned one too; though the main advantage, the coal owners cannily perceived, was to prevent insurrection.

A bracing walk among fields kept the working people from drinking themselves to stupefaction in the pubs. There was less brawling in the streets; the danger of a march on the big house in drunken frenzy was reduced. And the Church, ever ready to back the land owner and the coal owner, also encouraged the activity. The clergy taught that a study of nature would bring the student closer to God, and they were right.

God the designer, I mean, not that peculiar invention, God the all-seeing, the Lord of fact.

'Tha can't get too excited by God the all-seeing,' Mr Brown had told me on his last fateful day. We had just brought a group of blind men down from the mountain. They were in the rear of the Jam Sahib's motor and Mr Brown was driving us home to the village. 'He's as blind as these buggers in the rear of the motor. Misses everythin'. That's why the world's in such a bloody state. He gets his facts wrong, history's all muddled,' he moaned. 'We should be leadin', not Him. Like it was us what led the blind buggers up and down the mountain. Ay, tha's got to have faith, but in the end it's us what does it, not Him. Mind, tha can feel the Designer's presence when handlin' a dog violet picked from the bit of scrub; or when tha scoops a whirligig beetle from the pond. I reckon anyone who's taken the trouble to study the dog violet and the whirligig beetle will have invented their God, they'll have had to.' Then with his nose pressed hard up to the windscreen he speculated, 'I'll bet my God's got pebble glasses, like one of them bloody Swiss watch-makers, short on sight from all that close work.' I'll come back to Mr Brown. It's always a pleasure to come back to Mr Brown.

The study of natural history was split into two camps. There were the field naturalists and there were those who came to be called the 'closet men'. The field study was undertaken by the amateur naturalists, men like Bagshaw Moralee who walked for miles and observed the live world dance in a kaleidoscope of its own invention and they derived from this dance the facts about life. On the other hand the closet naturalists were the professionals and they hardly ever left their stuffy rooms. They received their samples from the field naturalists and those which were not dead on arrival were soon done away with. Then the closet men could set about carving up the samples, classifying them and handing them names. It was a lonely obsessive business conducted solely by gentlemen. It was secretive work and sadly the men were mostly crass. Too insensitive to know what it was which they held in their hands.

There had been a crass closet man living in Leeds. His name was Thomas Quekett. He was already an old man when Bagshaw Moralee sent him the bird of paradise from Java. When Quekett received the boxed bird which had no legs, he truly thought that it was a legless species. He wrote a letter to an ornithological journal speculating on how this wonderful bird would have to spend the whole of its existence on the wing. 'Eating, mating or sleeping, because it has no legs, it will always have to be on the wing,' he wrote. Other closet men corresponded, congratulating the journal, congratulating Quekett and eventually congratulating God Himself on this creation of such breathtaking beauty; such a strange addition to all of His diversity. One of them went so far as to send a drawing, which the editor stupidly published, illustrating how the beautiful crimson and black bird would have looked whilst suspended without his legs, forever shimmering his feathers in the hot Javanese air.

Yet, undeterred Quekett and the other closet naturalists, living off private incomes, beavered away hoarding their collections of forms and design. Some of them wrote books. And some of the field men wrote books too. They published their articles and pamphlets describing the appearance and the behaviour of the animals and plants which inhabited the countryside which proved to be popular with all classes. Who wanted to read an account of a post mortem or to peruse a list of Latin names? Facts were everywhere strewn in the fields at God's feet for it was known that if He lived anywhere then He lived in a fresh field; you could hardly expect to find Him

354

hovering on a pickle in a smelly closet. But fact and truth here diverged, for the truth, all too often, was in the pickle – bottled and ignored in the rare collections of design. Very few knew and almost nobody cared. The fact market was to propel us forward. There was to be a fact-driven progress of science towards Utopia.

7

The pressures to classify and to collect

It is going to take time to explain how a man of little learning came to have proprietorship of a museum set down in the middle of nowhere, but permit me to make a start by introducing you to Great-aunt Henrietta. She's the one deported to Austria at the outbreak of the Great War, along with Schubert and Tsiblitz.

As a young woman she wrote a natural history, describing a small group of stones which formed a crossing place down by the river at Bottom Boat. Each day she described the stones and the gradual changes in the plant and animal lives found there. It was nothing unusual; young ladies then were given to the study of botany. Although in Henrietta's case her study was augmented by a little entomology and some ichthyology and of course with a smattering of geology too – for I stress, and you will soon learn, her prime interest was in the stones. In retrospect, I suppose it was a true natural history which she studied – natural history as it used to be, before the coming of Darwin and the specialists. Natural history as it had been studied by that great network of pre-Darwinian families, who chased butterflies up hill and down dale. Who picked shells and flowers as well as pockets. Who hoarded birds' eggs and insects as well as gold. Families which founded the societies of the Aurelians and the Microscope as well as banks. There weren't many of them, but they were a truly intellectual aristocracy.

In those times the study of natural history had included the learning of geology and of palaeontology too. It was only in the late nineteenth century that men and women began to hug specialities to their breasts, as children in uncertain darkness hugged bedtime toys. Yet Henrietta, secure in a kind of madness, sailed on; skirts billowing in the changed wind she described her true natural history. For others, though, speciality became a symbol of learning and independence; a token of power in a tiny pool.

And this was true not only for individuals but also for groups. Each study became the preserve of a different group.

For example, entomology was for the poor. You didn't have to travel far to study the bugs and the beetles and no special equipment was required. The bugs lived right there with you; in the house, in the bed even. The working-class naturalist was ever looking for bugs – bugs as big as grapefruit. Of course he rarely found one. It was usually those rich enough to get themselves to the jungles of South America who were able to find such things but that was another preserve and another group – the idle rich wandering abroad.

Then there were the ornithologists. Only the gentry could afford to have a go at ornithology. You needed a gun like Squire Potterton and his forebears. With a gun you could blast the birds out of their nests, stuff and classify them and steal their eggs – what was left of them – right into the bargain. That, it seems, was a job for a gentleman.

But it was the women, rich and poor alike, who took to botany. It didn't demand any cruelty or nastiness. (Despite her brutish appearance and her early life pulling the coal tubs, my great great grandmother had taken to botany because there was no call for violence and male-dominated games. And the step from flower to physic was a natural one too.) There was a second group however which claimed the botany: the clergy. It is said they claimed the botany for the same reasons that it was claimed by the women but my great great grandmother doubted the truth of it. The clergy took to botany, she said, simply so as the churchmen (a group for which she had little time) could be close to the girls. Pretty things, like my great-aunt Henrietta who wore a straw boater and a billowed dress and who dreamily sailed the wind, sitting by the river with her long legs drawn beneath her chin. Henrietta, whose mind much of the time too was on men. And whose mind, like the snake in the river, was to take a very strange contortion.

How strange? Well, one can tell of her strangeness by for a moment considering her beliefs. The belief, for example, that the stones forming the crossing place at Bottom Boat, which she eventually had brought by the barrowload to the common and with which she built a wall outside the house, should suddenly come to life. The belief that some of the stones, which she painted yellow, were representations of members of her family – dead and alive. That's how strange.

It was with such beliefs that she abruptly changed her natural history for a family biography and began her story one day either when she went mad or when she became sane – nobody knows for sure which it was – with the words: *'My grandmother, who was born on the day of the battle of Waterloo, slowly climbed the slope of Hunger Hill.'*

And what a contorted yet lucid tale it was which she had to tell. A duality which makes me ponder that perhaps she had suddenly regained her sanity and was then describing the period of madness from which she had only just emerged. On the other hand, who but a mad person could have experienced inanimate stones drawing human breath in the first instance and then, as if to confirm the lunacy, committed such thoughts to paper? That is the argument for the second theory: that she was perfectly sane when she wrote the natural history but took on her madness when translating it to read as a history of her family.

Old Doctor Cartwright, the father of young Doctor Cartwright who wore the half-glasses and who always seemed to be looking at two things at the same time because of them, reckoned there was a third explanation. He thought Henrietta had been quite mad for most of her life, both before and after the writing of her book. He thought madness spanned both the natural history and the family biography and it wasn't until she found the love of her good man, Mr Tsiblitz, that she discovered her sanity. (Did the young doctor need his optical aid, I have often wondered, in order to develop his father's compromising skill?)

What has any of this to do with my ownership of a museum? you may ask. Well, I'll tell you this. From her grandmother Henrietta had been handed the genes for an urge to collect. I too have those genes. It seems the urge to classify and to collect are represented by a tough old gene and I tell you, from my own experience, I have detected a granny knot in that chromosome which no amount of boyscouting will untie.

But let me not wander from Henrietta just yet. It was in 1936 that I happened to discover the manuscript of her family biography which she had stuffed away in an old chest of drawers. It was I who rewrote it, changing relationships and altering a few words and phrases here and there. It described the period up to the time of her leaving the country at the outbreak of the Great War and since her going it is I alone who has described subsequent events.

You can now see why in the present tale there are two beginnings. My great-aunt's tale is concerned with the family and the village and their history and has an origin in stones which predate even the elder growing blood-red from out of the crimble. (In village lore that elder is a kind of tree of life. An Eden elder. The *Eldest* Elder. Touched red at dawn, it acts as the sun's messenger spurting life-giving blood around the village and bringing the world each day into new being.) I have to be true to my great-aunt and her project – whatever that project might have been, and I admit that I am still uncertain as to the purpose of her abrupt change in style and content. But I have my own passions too. They are with myself, with the museum, with Clarrie and Rosanne and they too must have my attention. That's why there are two beginnings and perhaps why you may feel a slight unease when reading these accounts. In effect there are two authors. Both young persons, but bearing their youth in differing generations – in a sense this makes them young and old. They are male and female, sane and perhaps mad. Mad and perhaps sane. I'll dwell on it no more.

Collecting of course can be a cultural pastime, as well as an inherited bent – nurture as well as nature in the language of our time. This cultural basis for collection became apparent to me when I advertised for the antiquities and curiosities with which I was to fill my museum space. At the time I had only three exhibits. Pride of place went to the dinosaur.

That was the dinosaur which had been dug from the disused pit. Old Doctor Cartwright had identified the skeleton as that of an iguanodon when it was hewn from the rock by my great grandfather James Brightside and his friend Sidall Junkin but the family have no love for such a thing. It was so old it had petrified and it all fell on top of him when James Brightside blasted it to bits so that Thwaite the coal owner shouldn't have it. But I'll not bore you with the tale, all of this was documented by his daughter, Henrietta, in those early writings. I should add however that I contemplate the beast. I am continually pondering the significance of James Brightside's find.

Years later we brought out the bones and Mr Brown and I rebuilt the skeleton in the museum. In truth James Brightside's skeleton is also in there somewhere – all but the skull, which we were never able to locate. We were never able to identify exactly which bits belonged to him either and which bits to the iguanodon. I expect the members of the local palaeontological society are aware, but we don't ask. It's enough that the palaeontologists call the skeleton the Brightside Dinosaur; it's a well-known object in some circles and though it doesn't carry the family name as far and wide as does Lancaster Brightside, the famous Hollywood film-maker, it lends a little local flavour to our optimistic patronym.

Then there's the skeleton of a horse – of a giant horse which carted the wagon bringing Rosanne to our village for the first time. That was when Uncle Albert fell in love with her yellow hair. In their haste to have things working the colliers had dispatched the massive shire horse (like the sun he was a mechanism, therefore why wasn't he going up and down, back and forth, round and round) down the pit where the dark frightened him and he ran off down the galleries making a hell of a clatter and was never seen again. At least, not until many years later, when Mr Brown and I found him wedged in a fissure and we had to chip out the bones from where he had got himself stuck.

And lastly, there were the ashes of Mr Brown.

You will have already noted how Mr Brown's name recurs in describing all three of the original exhibits and it has to be said, if there is another reason why I should find myself lumbered with an urge to collect, besides the nature and the nurture, more important still is Mr Brown. He was a small man with a big compulsion. He had a mad urge to acquire paper bags and, it seems, sometimes he would be not totally honest in the means by which he came by them. All the same, from my being a small child he had been a guide along collecting byways. As a youngster I had coveted his thousands upon thousands of paper bags, gasped delightedly at his blowing up and bursting of the occasional one and wondered (as only the fertile surface of a child's uncluttered brain has room enough to grow a wonder) at the startled silence which followed such a report. I had longed secretly – and as it happens in vain – to discover the store-house of so much childhood brown paper. Was it any wonder, then, that when Mr Brown and I together conceived of the plan to convert the decaying picture palace to a museum, I immediately saw how I might emulate my mentor and satisfy acquisitive need?

When he died he was still lodging at our house – the last of the dossing colliers. For as long as I could recall he had slept in one of the wide winged chairs which we used to have in the parlour. His ashes are kept at the museum, housed in a small urn of red cedarwood. There was nowhere else for him to go, unless, as my grandfather wanted, we were to cast him to the wind.

He was a strange man, was Mr Brown. He had a Sunday suit and on the Sabbath he would dress up and strut about the village, walking with a brass-topped cane casually resting on his shoulder, but he never went to church. 'No time for that stuff,' he would say. 'God and all that stuff, it gives me the pip,' he would tell those he met on his stroll. My grandfather said that the man was a heathen, but it wasn't until the day Mr Brown died that I discovered my grandfather's assessment of him to be way off beam. For it was on that day that I witnessed his true faith. 'Course I believe,' he told me. 'No time for that prayin' and praisin', that's all. But I believe all right.' That's what he told me before leading a group of blind men safely up and down the mountain with me alone as witness to the faith of the man. That's why I took the ashes. We weren't going to scatter them. They needed to be on show did those old ashes. Close by. No prayin'. No praisin'. Just there – like he had been. Not a saint, merely a curiosity. A man true to himself was Mr Brown, and those contained ashes are a symbol of his solid faith – most curiously too, their dusty formlessness is an indication of the awesome intent in the design he so dearly acknowledged. I sometimes imagine him, a miniature version of what had been, reinvented and hunched like a homunculus in the cedarwood urn. I love you, Mr Brown.

8

Bringing in the collections

As I said, I only began to realize how these village folk worked so persistently to make a sense of their nonsense world when I advertised for exhibits to go with the three items I already had, and I realized too the deep cultural root tapping away in the drive to collect and to classify.

'Will this do?' asked Mr Whinny, bringing me a home-made frame displaying the complete Lepidoptera from the North of England. 'It's not very old,' he began to apologize. He held his tall, willowy body painfully erect and he coughed quietly and continuously like a machine, labouring. Sixty years of dust had overgrown his lungs and replaced the airy moist linings with a choking cement.

'No, Mr Whinny, don't go on. It will look fine on that wall over there.'

'What about this?' asked Mrs Tarbutt and she unwrapped a book from a rough black shawl which had been tightly bound about it. I took the large gloomy tome in my hand and turned the flimsy blue pages. The woman had compiled a list of place names running into many thousands, all of which she had found mentioned in her bible. There, in the neatest script, she had written down the place names, drawn maps, created cross-indexed references. The book could have been a motorists' guide to the Bible scrolled in Stephenson's ink. The completing of it must have taken her years. I turned the pages. Here was the geography of imagination detailing trips from Jericho to Gethsemane; trips from the Temple to the corner shop for salt hacked from the torso of the wife of Lot.

'That'll be fine, Mrs Tarbutt. We'll display it on the table over here, shall we?' I said and carefully laid the book to rest on the tiny marble-topped table. She stooped and kissed her book, turned and smiled lopsidedly and went from my life forever, wrapping the black shawl about her head as carefully as she had wrapped her book. She died the following day, old and alone in the house with lace curtains next to Billy's at the terrace end.

Then they brought the boxes of spiders and the harvestmen. And the cases of birds' eggs. Then drawers filled with insects, and sea shells nestling in beds of cotton wool. There were volumes of pressed wild flowers and pads of drawings which detailed the village and its buildings from all angles. But everything was neat and it was labelled. Everything had been named.

Somebody brought twelve hundredweight of plaster of Paris and another brought twenty-five tons of raw sugar in hessian sacks which my grandfather thought must have been stolen and insisted we bury beneath the stage where the cinema screen used to be.

And don't get the idea that they brought only the past and the dead. They brought the live things too. There were birds in cages and newts in jars. Cicadas and crane flies, whirligig beetles with their two pairs of eyes like young Doctor Cartwright with his glasses perched on the end of his nose seeing two things at once. They brought a water boatman who swims on his back and dives in a pickle jar. And the flightless saucer bug who walks like a packman on stilts between one stretch of water and another. And a pondskater who rows up and down the surface of the water in a Hammonds sauce bottle placed on its side. There were geometer moths and swallowtailed butterflies; squashbugs and damsel flies. I gave over a small corner of the museum to them. We called it the entomological section. The insects lived in tins and boxes and in bottles and jars and the schoolchildren came in daily to watch them crawl.

And to multiply. The ladybirds and the sugar bugs increased in number almost daily and the children never tired of counting the spots on the ladybirds' backs. That's how some of them learned their multiplication tables.

'How many three-spots?'

'I can count seven.'

'Then how many spots all together?'

'Twenty-one,' shouts an excited mathematician convinced of the magic of numbers, a superstitious belief he will carry with him all his life and when his time comes take into the dark pit, knees knocking on ill-numbered days.

The sugar bugs were foreigners. They hailed from the Caribbean and I was never sure how they arrived at the museum. It seemed that they just happened there one day but somebody must have brought them in. The colony lived at first in a Sunlight soap box and each week I had to feed it a cupful of sugar from the hidden source beneath the stage; every few months I had to find a bigger box. Many years later, Bagshaw Moralee would tell me how the sugar bug was related to the Colorado beetle, that it didn't live on potatoes, but on sugar. They just ate and ate and never seemed to stop, not even to take a breath.

9

Arkwright and his rotating eyeballs

On a dull October morning Mr Arkwright arrived with a boxful of rubbish. It had been only a few days since the death of Thomas Edison. Arkwright told me that he could no longer accept responsible guardianship for his own treasures. Now that Edison had gone he realized more than ever the mortality of the inventor, yet the durability of his invention. He told me what history was, and what it was not. 'It's not a stream of the natural and all that evolution stuff. It's not that. It's a record of artefact and invention. It's his invention what needs the passing, not the man. The man will disintegrate like all else what's bin alive, but not the idea. Invention can be passed along like heirlooms,' he said. 'Like heirlooms is passed in important families. An' aren't we an important family? Aren't we?'

'They need a home for displayin' 'em in,' he added. He had a shock of long white hair which gave him an eccentric look, reminiscent of some mad mid-European composers. But, more seriously, he had the terrible rotating eyeballs syndrome. Without warning, whilst in mid-sentence, his eyes would sometimes roam off to the top of his head, leaving his interlocutor staring into two white holes, until the eyes decided to return.

'But what are they?' I asked.

'They're my inventions,' he said guardedly. I noted that he had soft brown eyes. They were eyes filled with care, yet a certain mischief danced there too, at the pointed ends of brown almonds. I looked into the box. It was stuffed full with bits of rusting metal twisted into odd shapes. As I rummaged among the bits and pieces a spark flew out, landing on my jacket sleeve above the elbow, where it burned brightly for a second or two, then it died. It left a smouldering hole. I said nothing.

'Tha's got to be careful how tha treats an invention,' he warned me as the mischief danced. 'They have a habit of goin' off when tha doesn't treat 'em right.'

'But what are they?' I asked again.

'Mostly new-fangled stuff,' he said modestly. 'A utensil for eating jelly and an egg warmer. There's a thing what cuts keys, too. Stuff like that.' Then he fell silent and I saw his eyes wander. I waited patiently for them to return but I raged within, cursing the dark of the foul pit which could do such a thing to a man. When the eyes fell back into their orbits I pressed him.

'Ay and what else?' I asked.

'Well, the main thing is a device for mekin' thee invisible,' he said, shuffling a bit. He put the box down at his feet.

'Oh ay, that sounds promising,' I said and immediately wanted to apologize for having patronized him, but he seemed not to notice my tone. He was bent double, rummaging in the box from which he dragged a metal helmet which trailed a mass of copper wires squeezed up and squashed like a concertina. It was a soldier's helmet. Perhaps Arkwright himself had worn it at the Somme. Tommy Arkwright? (I never did know his Christian name. He was always Arkwright or Mr Arkwright to me.) The wires flowed away from two electrodes which had been soldered to the top. Arkwright, who was a tall fellow, brought himself to attention stamping his foot, then he plonked the helmet on top of the shock of white hair. He gave a neat salute, and handed me a two-pin plug which was fitted to the end of one of the wires.

'Just connect up and I'll show thee.'

I inserted the plug into a wall socket. The helmet made a buzzing noise and a blue spark jumped across the wires.

'Can tha still see me?' Arkwright asked, raising his voice above the noise. I decided to ignore him. I thought that if I ignored the old man he might take it that he had become inaudible as well as being invisible. That would have given me the excuse for not having to say anything which might disappoint him.

'Can tha see?' he asked again, the spark still dancing over the electrodes. I stared at the old buffer, white hair flowing from under the hat. I saw that the tin had a dent in it and imagined that his helmet had at some time saved the old man's life. Deflected a bullet perhaps and brought him this far – to this absurd moment. I turned off the current.

'Did tha see?' he asked when the helmet had ceased to buzz.

'Ay, I saw, Mr Arkwright,' I said.

'Will tha put it in't museum then?'

'Ay, I'll strap it up just there. Just at the height of a man when he comes into the museum so as he can render hisself invisible.'

'Good lad,' Arkwright commended and he gave my arm a friendly squeeze. 'Tha may as well have the rest,' he said picking up the box of metal scraps. He placed it on the marble-topped table next to Mrs Tarbutt's book which was open at a page labelled 'The road to Damascus'. It looked much like a map of the road out of the village where it goes up past the big house and joins the crossroads. That would be the road to Wakefield, or to Castleford, or to Leeds.

Naming more names

After Arkwright had gone I shut up the museum for the day. It was still only morning and it had started to snow. My experience with the old inventor had upset me. His eccentricity was something with which I could cope well enough, but the disappearing eyeballs were an affliction with which it was difficult for the observer to come to terms. Cursing the cruelty of the pit was something which we all did from time to time, but it only led to a bitter frustration. I closed my mouth and bit back the anger and the cold.

Because of his arthritis, my grandfather had recently left the pit. He was no longer able to hold his pick and Thwaite the coal owner – my other grandfather – had told him that he was neither use nor ornament. But illness is something my pasty-faced grandparents don't talk about. They display a white-faced approval and disapproval of the world about them, but there is no talk of frailty. My grandfather sometimes talks to God. My grandmother lets him. It's their answer to the posturings of the Pottertons of this world; their answer to what they perceive as the dullness of brass.

My father had recently gone too, but that was because of redundancy. Ever since the General Strike Thwaite had been whittling away at the labour force. My father's redundancy then was no surprise. It had been bound to come sooner or later. He took my mother and my small sister, Irene Rose, to South Yorkshire. He wanted me to go with them but I wished to stay on at the museum with the dinosaur. I didn't want to leave my grandparents' house either, the house in which I had been born. My father despaired of my ever growing up.

'Unless tha gets thasen down t'pit and stops fartin' about with that bloody dinosaur thing like a bloody fairy tha'll nivver come to owt,' were his last words to me before he went. My mother carried a suitcase, my sister had a bucket and spade. They strode off up the hill as if seeking digs at Bridlington. I watched them go as far as the crossroads. My father had never understood the nature of the

Brightside Dinosaur. I'm not sure that I understood it myself at that time. True, it's a unique family possession but it's more than that. The iguanodon has a significance beyond the musty museum.

I walked now towards my grandfather's house. The elm leaves were falling out of the ice air. I could hear a redwing somewhere, lost in the white sky. As he called, fern fronds curled and blackened in the cold. Through the falling snow I witnessed the smoke come as a ghost from the chimney pot of the house in the middle of a robust and friendly terrace and I began to name the names.

The Terrus End. Billy o' the Terrus End and his brother Charlie just out of prison. Mr and Mrs Terrus End.

Mrs Tarbutt's house with the lace curtains now lived in by the Pole, Mr Smircz, who is built like a brick shithouse. His wife, the former Edith Juvelah, and their twin babies, Mildred and Alexander. It had been Smircz who walked one day into the village with a canvas knapsack on his back. The knapsack had something tucked inside which moved like the tiny feet and fists of an unborn child kicking at his mother's innards. He drank a pint of ale at the pub and told Rube Hardwick, the landlord, that our village was the nearest thing he had yet seen in England to his sooty home village in Silesia. He said that he had peered in at the window of the little house with the lace curtains and seen it was empty. Then he said that he would like to settle there. Rube watched the uterine contractions within the sack for a moment and told the Pole to go up to the big house and see Mr Thwaite. He finished his ale and went off, the undulating humps fighting fiercely on his back. In the gardens at the big house, Mr Smircz came across Edith Juvelah, a local girl, who was in service to Thwaite. The cook had sent her off with a shopping basket over her arm and she was walking towards him. They met almost at the gates. Smircz wriggled the knapsack from his back and placed it on the ground where it continued to writhe, then he dragged Edith off into the bushes, in the process scratching her legs and her backside on the brambles. Edith didn't resist much. She never had resisted very much whenever lads had dragged her off into other bushes, either. But here were the moments in which Mildred and Alexander were conceived. The lovers sat on the grass a while and she told him that she was sure to be pregnant, telescoping the whole of their dynastic selves into a few seconds. Smircz returned with her to the big house where he demanded to speak with the coal owner. Thwaite saw him at the door – nobody was ever invited into the big house. There, Smircz told him that he wished to marry the kitchen maid and live with her in the empty house with the lace curtains. He casually wore the bulging knapsack with one strap slung over his shoulder. He offered the coal owner fifteen shillings which he expected would cover the rent for a month. And when the startled Thwaite didn't take the money the Pole pressed it into his palm, then he heaved Edith across his shoulders with a massive free arm and began to walk up the path away from the house.

'Hang on, lad,' said Thwaite, 'tha can't tek her just yet, she's notice to work out.'

The Pole dropped the girl heavily on the grass and the coal owner wandered across to retrieve his final pennies-worth of service. He walked slowly, distrusting the foreigner's motives and methods. Smircz shuffled the knapsack from his shoulder. He undid the two brass buckles and the coal owner, deciding caution to be his best policy, stopped. Smircz turned the knapsack upside down letting the air breeze in. A dozen week-old chicks tumbled to the ground chirping wildly as if the blue sky above had painted them a voice. One of them fluttered in the white pinafore on the dazed girl's lap, her backside now bruised as well as scratched. 'Is this how marriage will be, all bargaining and hurt?' she wondered rubbing her hand across the painful area.

'Twelve chicks,' said the Pole humourlessly, 'that will be a merry Christmas, sir.'

'Ay, well, I suppose it may.'

'And for me some work in the pit, yes.'

'By, tha's a cheeky young bugger but I suppose it may well bring that too, ay.'

'Good.' Smircz yanked up his bride-to-be from the place where she sat on the grass. The chick fell from her lap with a squawk. Then in both arms he carried her up the path to the gates leaving the coal owner to collect up the chicks into Edith's discarded basket.

*

Mr Arkwright with a yardful of cement and rotting machinery.

Jacky Jellis, the Bellman, who once recorded his impression of a roaring dinosaur, which when we amplified it through the Movietone system at the cinema sounded just like the real thing. Jacky lives alone now that his daughter, Marlene Jellis, has gone off with H. G. Wells.

Doyle, with one arm, who used to keep the pigs and his second wife to whom he isn't really married. There was a lot of trouble over the pigs. Nasty tales flew about concerning Mr Doyle's washable condom and the use he made of it with a dozen pigs. The pigs were kept in his garden at the back of the house and the tales were probably untrue, but you know how it is in a small place like this. Mr Doyle grows vegetables now. 'Nobody will ever accuse him of stuffing a lettuce,' said the lady who lived with him when the pigs went off to the bacon factory. The condom is pegged to the washing line, freezing brittle in the falling snow.

The Pymonts' house where the panharmonicon fills the parlour with its colourful fairground pipes. The panharmonicon is massive and painted up like a steam organ at the fair. But there is no steam. It's a sort of combined barrel and church organ and imitates a full symphony orchestra. It has a giant handle which must be cranked continuously to work the bellows and it has keyboards too. The hundreds of wooden pipes, Mr Pymont tells us, were whittled by seven thousand Frenchmen with nothing to do; all of them prisoners of war in a camp at Norman Cross. A seaman taken at Trafalgar, a man who loved the music of Mozart and knew scores by heart, had apparently directed the operation together with the famous toy-maker Père Cruchet, who was taken at the Nile.

The automaton, which had been in the possession of the family of the camp commander, found its way to the Great Exhibition at the Crystal Palace only, one night, to be stolen from its stand. It turned up years later on a Birmingham rubbish tip, infested with wood-worm. Old man Pymont spent the next half-century restoring it. He and his wife perform the duet. He grinds and she sits on the built-in lovers' seat and depresses the keys forcing the Prague Symphony from the pipes, spilling it out on to wet pavements on Sunday afternoons. They syncopate breathlessly, bringing to Mozart the quickened noise of a fun-fair.

Then it's us, Ernest and Emily Brightside and myself, in the house with the strange wall, painted yellow, which my mad great-aunt Henrietta had built on to the front. The wall shines and crackles like lightning into the dark night and makes a rectangle at the front of our house. We call the rectangle Aunt Henrietta's laboratory. I can see my grandparents staring from the parlour window, their faces as white as the falling snow. Always white, yet instead of expressed sickness, a bright-eyed approval for their odd grandchild and most of his collection of knick-knacks.

Then the Gills: Mrs Gill, who must be a hundred and two, and Charlie, her son with the one leg which the Germans grabbed and failed to give him back. Charlie is nightwatchman at the marshalling yard. You can throw stones in the dark and get him out of the tin hut where he usually sits. He holds the lantern aloft, peering into the rain with screwed eyes, and stands on his one leg. With the waterproof cape about his shoulders he looks like a Christmas tree.

Old Henderson alone with his greyhound and his memories.

Danny Pratt and his mam and all the other Pratts whose dad was accidentally shot by Isaac's father when I was a child. Shot when he played scarecrow in the drunken bean fields, turned blood-red by the elder and the sun scattering the coal dust. They hanged Isaac's father at Leeds jail.

The Archbolds, who sit in an electric light which for some reason seems to be brighter than anyone else's. My grandfather says that it's because the Archbolds have bulbs of a greater wattage than anyone else but I doubt that it's true – they get them from the store just like we do. I think that it's some magic in their house which makes the light shine brighter than the others. Cheeky Archbold sits in the yellow window blowing into his tuba, the snow falling thicker as I watch.

Then it's Edith Juvelah's mother and Edith's daft brother. He has soft blond curls and keeps a toad on his head. It makes his hat wobble. He is an ageless child. It's anybody's guess how old he is, but he might be thirty-something. Grandma Dolly Juvelah who reads the tea-leaves and smokes them in her stone pipe. My grandmother thinks it a despicable habit, like burning babies she says it is.

Then the Bowens and the Westermans who, now Doyle doesn't, keep the pigs. My hands and ears are numb with the cold. In biting back my anger and the freezing wind I find that I have severely bitten my tongue but I feel no pain. The cold is numbing. So is the repetitious naming. I watch the terrace stretching endlessly away into the white blizzard. Everything. Everything is named I think. All except the village that is. The village and the pit. They have no name.

A broken leg

In the confused moments when he was heaving the velvet couch back to safety, Mr Sligh was unsure what had become of the policeman. He had neither seen the man leap nor witnessed him fall.

He accompanied my cousin to their bedroom on the floor below where they hurriedly dressed. He rushed into his old guardsman's uniform, not bothering to button up the tunic. It remained untidily open displaying his naked chest, though he took the trouble to brush dust from the gold epaulettes and from where it sometimes gathered on the braid on his sleeves. He laced up his shoes and raced down the stairs and out of the building in search of Rosanne.

He was surprised then to find the officer lying in the rubble. His lips were parted and bruised the colour of bilberries. The eyes were open. Rosanne, beside him, sat uncomfortably on a pile of rocks. She had one of the heavy curtains draped about her shoulders; leaning forward, she cupped a shapely calf in both hands.

'I don't seem able to move it,' she whined. Her voice sounded foreign. Although she spoke her English with almost no trace of accent, sometimes when agitated, or when preparing herself to tell a story, the Gallic origin of her tongue might show. At such times she whined. The whine was accompanied by a pout – as if the pout itself closed off the palate and forced air down her nose.

Mr Sligh picked his way carefully over the rubble, causing dust to rise. As he took Rosanne's stockinged foot in his hands his scarlet tunic fell completely open. He gave the foot a gentle twist. She let forth a short cry.

'Perhaps it's broken?' he inquired quietly.

'That would be an assumption reasonable, *mon chéri*,' she said with a little exasperation. Her lodger's slowness of wit irritated her.

The man looked again to the corpse. The eyes reflected the darkness of the sky. He took the curtain from about his landlady, exposing

374

her bare shoulders, and cast it over the face of the dead officer, then he helped up Rosanne, leaning her against a wall of red brick. She remained balanced, stable as the circus performer she was, on her one good leg. Sligh turned his attention hesitantly into the street in search of assistance and was surprised to see that his actions had been observed by the old man from the pet shop.

'Do you need help?' Bagshaw Moralee asked of the ex-guardsman once he knew that he had been spotted, at the same time trying to create an impression that he had only just arrived on the scene.

'I think we should get her to a doctor.'

'Well, there's the Anaesthetics Department down the road.'

'Will there be a doctor?'

'They are doctors, aren't they? Anaesthetists, they are doctors.'

Mr Sligh had never given it much thought, but now it was mentioned he supposed those who worked there would probably be medics.

'But, I mean, isn't it a bit late for anyone to be there at all?'

'Always there,' Bagshaw grumbled. 'Always someone there, torturing the animals,' he added. 'Day and night.' At such a late hour, he was at a loss to suggest an alternative. Even though he knew the seamy side of the city as well as anybody, for he could often be found working late into the night huddled beneath the cries and snorts which emanated from the rooms above at the brothel, he could think of no one else who might receive the woman. There were only the anaesthetists.

The reason for his late hours was always the same: to collect more of the viscid extract from the sperm sacs of his scarlet macaws. Like most men he gave hours easily to his interests, though – as it is with most men too – interests and needs happened to coincide.

As soon as he had felt the first tremor, Bagshaw had known the disturbance for what it was. He had spent too many of his eighty-odd years in exotic locations not to recognize a natural catastrophe when his feet became planted uncertainly upon one. At that initial tremor he had dashed into the street, a needle full of juice from the sperm sac in his hands. He had been too late to see Rosanne more swing than tumble from the building for she had fallen still clutching the large curtains and had for a time appeared as a gradually lengthening pendulum inside a capacious clock until, exhausted, she had dropped on to the pile of masonry. He had however been just in time to witness the police officer hurtling down and had seen him land awkwardly, emitting a little dry-powder cough.

'Well, there appears to be no choice. We had better get her down the road to the Anaesthetics Department then,' Mr Sligh said ponderously. 'Come on, give us a hand. We can give her a basket lift,' and he held out his crossed hands for the elderly pet shop owner to grab a hold. With a nod of his head he then invited Rosanne to sit on their hands. 'Come on, *madame*. Let's see if we can't find an anaesthetist capable of attending to your leg.'

I 2

Dibden Dawson and his baboons

Dibden Dawson, meanwhile, had been experimenting on two baboons when the earthquake struck and he was now having a terrible job coaxing the animals back to the operating tables. They had electrodes implanted in their brains. At the first rumble they had leapt from the tables screeching fearfully. Now from their position by the fanlight window on the upper floor they trailed a mass of wiring back as far as the doctor's electrical equipment, ends coiled in chaos on a console between the two tables. The baboons stared from the window, their grey washed nightdresses filled with holes. One of them had a comfort blanket clutched in his paws. The animal nervously rubbed it back and forth with hurried jerky movements across his face. They both jumped excitedly up and down when Mr Moralee pulled the bell-rope at the door in the street causing two bells to jangle rustily in a corner of the laboratory.

Rosanne and her two companions could see the white-coated doctor remonstrating with what they took to be his patients at the illuminated window above. They received quite a shock when a few moments later they were in Dibden Dawson's laboratory and learned that what they had assumed to be geriatric patients were in fact young baboons whom the doctor was trying to persuade to remount the operating tables.

Were they to have their brains removed? pondered Mr Sligh, who had taken note of the metal electrodes which protruded from between their ears.

'Here, Parsifal,' the rotund doctor was shouting, it seemed drunkenly. He stood between the tables twiddling the dials on his console. 'Come along, Gwenda, old thing, back to bed now.' He turned back a white cotton sheet which was already splashed with the old blood of the two frightened animals. This he did apparently in an attempt to show them how cosy it was in there. Mr Sligh turned away his head on a wave of nausea and nervously buttoned up his tunic.

Bagshaw Moralee, who in his old field days had developed a way with animals which had never been forgotten, approached the baboons. He held out his hand and first the female and then the male came to him, dragging their masses of wiring just as he had once seen the brides of Count Dracula hump chains dustily behind them in a silent film.

'There we are. There we are,' he repeated several times in a trilling voice as he carried them, one on each arm, to the tables. He laid them down gently, as he might have put his grandchildren off to bed. Dibden Dawson however wasn't one to waste a moment. As soon as it was apparent the baboons were becalmed he applied a pad of ether across the nose and mouth of each animal, pressing powerfully down on their contorting faces.

'All in a day's work,' he explained to his alarmed guests whilst he continued to apply the ether pads. His speech, though slurred, had a distinct military note; it was an ordering voice, thought Rosanne.

When the baboons were immobile he chucked one of the pads into a metal waste bin where it landed with a startling zing and then, more alarming still, he applied the second pad to his own face for a few moments. He inhaled deeply. He shook his head, screwed up the smaller of his two eyes and his face crumpled to what the others took to be a grin though none of them could be certain what the expression might have truly signified. A single eye in the head of an ether addict is able to convey more than the summated expression in the two eyes of any other individual, but it is unwise to trust initial impressions. Such a concentrate is usually the random distillation from a headful of muddle and often viewed out of context, hence the alarm of Rosanne and her companions at that moment. Why should the man be grinning?

'Which of you did you say had the broken leg?' the doctor ordered.

The two men were quick to indicate Rosanne as the needful one and before she could utter a word of protest, she had been grabbed by Dibden Dawson and laid out next to Gwenda, the ether pad pressed firmly to her own face. Dibden Dawson then set the broken limb in a plaster cast.

When she opened her eyes Rosanne was peering into a silver haze.

She could see three men sitting about a round mahogany table; two baboons, wires connected to their heads, were interspersed between them. All five appeared to be drinking ale. Smoke curled lazily from a cigarette which dangled from the lips of one of the apes and, if she wasn't mistaken, wasn't that the sad face of her lodger, Mr Sligh? She at first couldn't think where she was. A commotion in the streets brought her thoughts back to the house tumbling down and she lying amid the fallen masonry. She raised her head and peered to the end of the green velour-covered couch on which she was stretched. The silvery haze was slowly dissolving. She saw the white plaster cast which covered her leg from toe to thigh; the smell of ether hung heavily in the air. She then imagined the whole thing to be an awful dream and felt certain that she would wake at any moment and find that she was performing no greater task than drawing the curtains at Salon Marguerite.

'Drat,' she saw the funny old man from the pet shop saying as if he was an Alice in Wonderland character scurrying by. 'Looks as if the meal's on me.'

She watched the rounded figure of a man in a white coat rise up from the group; his movements were shambolic. He gathered the two baboons to him and took them back to the tables, which she now realized also happened to be their beds, where he carefully removed metal plates from between their ears. He tucked them up and gave each animal a kiss on the cheek. Rosanne thought that surely now, now at a time of such happy ending, wasn't this the moment to wake; then before she could explain why, she was being lifted down the stairs in the basket chair formed by the clasped hands of the two men, in much the same way as they had carried her there. The round figure of Dibden Dawson hobbled behind, an ether pad pressed firmly to his nose, a single eye glaring an intoxicated warning that nobody must approach. Normally at such a late hour there would have been nobody about, but news of an earthquake was attracting quite a gathering to its epicentre. To avoid the throng the strange huddle had to weave this way and that in the cobbled street, eventually reaching the pet shop which though surrounded by rubble was still miraculously standing in one piece. It was only then, for sure, Rosanne knew herself not to be dreaming.

The sad animals were screeching within. Bagshaw explained to the policeman who was posted in the doorway that he and his friends had come to calm the animals, having only just learned of the freak accident which had beset them. No, he said, he had no idea where the ladies from the brothel had gone but good riddance.

'Ay, good riddance,' said the policeman speaking for the upright people of his city and watching an ambulance cart away the body of the officer who had tumbled from the building.

'There we are. There we are,' Bagshaw trilled repeatedly as he led the way through the smelly shop, toe-ending pups and kittens out of his way. Much of the raucous noise ceased immediately. He continued his odd comforting trill throughout the hour it took for him to prepare the food. By the time two birds had gone into the oven there was hardly a squawk from any of the closely barred bamboo cages.

13
Zoophagia

Bagshaw Moralee suffered from zoophagia. It isn't normally a disease, in fact nobody had ever suffered from it before, at least not in Dibden Dawson's recollections. One normally practised zoophagia – the eating of exotic animals – if one could afford to do so. One didn't suffer from it – unless it was from the flatulent after-effects. To Bagshaw Moralee, however, zoophagia was a sickness and after Doctor Dawson had made his diagnosis it found its way, as almost the last thing, into the indices of the medical textbooks.

While Bagshaw Moralee cooked his companions an odd brace – a peach-faced lovebird and a bloodstained cockatoo – stewed in red wine with carrots and potatoes, he told Dibden Dawson (between frequent trills of 'there we are, there we are') about his zoophagia.

It was in the closing years of the last century when the man ate his way through two zoos. He had opened zoological gardens first at Arundel on the south coast when, having cooked and eaten most of the quadrupeds, he was chased down the High Street by furious parishioners led by the Duchess wielding a shillelagh. He had been forced to move his bird house together with the few remaining four-legged beasts to Southport on the Lancashire coast where he again set up shop. And it was here, whilst intensively breeding for the restocking of the mammals, that he developed his taste for exotic birds.

To his perpetual shame, in the time spent at Arundel he had eaten two quagga – two of the last in existence. He had since suffered regular bouts of remorse accompanied by suffocating guilt for having brought the species to final extinction – something reported in the learned journals soon afterwards. But as Dibden Dawson tried to explain, the old adventurer couldn't shoulder total responsibility himself. After all, had he not been egged on by the famous and the wealthy who had lived down there, by the salty sea? Nobody would ever believe, for instance, that he had managed to eat his way through a pair of quagga alone. He would certainly have needed help and as he continued with his tale, which was gradually becoming more of a confession, this became evidently so.

Hadn't it been the crinolined ladies who had brought their spouses and friends regularly to Bagshaw Moralee's dinner parties, chomping their way through giraffe meat and elephant steaks, zebra and rhinoceros and God knows what else to satisfy their peculiar lust for the novel and the meaty? He told of the titled lady who started a fashion for teeth, which soon caught on in that particular geriatric wonderland by the sea. She had evidently commanded her dental surgeon to remove her teeth and replace them with a false set of gnashers having a more tenacious bite so as to satisfy her liking for lion steaks – an apparently extremely tough animal at the best of times, but even more so because of Bagshaw Moralee's choice of elderly beasts, who were supposed to laze away their days at the zoological gardens. He felt sorry for the old and, somewhat ironically, for the toothless ones.

Bagshaw's strange affliction, though, was made even more odd, some may say evil, by the curious habit he had of naming his animals. I must say that when I first learned of it I couldn't help comparing his habit with the ways of the Namers of Names. Then, after more careful consideration, I realized that it had been wrong to draw such comparisons for the two practices were quite dissimilar, though it might be argued that Bagshaw's habit was nothing more than an extension of the other. But, whilst it was certainly in order for the Namers of Names to identify the classes of things, was it correct for Bagshaw Moralee to take individuals out of the class and by the magic of words bring them into the particular?

'Here is Isaiah the camel, tomorrow he shall be roasted and eaten. There is Trixie, the pretty zebra with a vertical stripe – she goes into the pot a week on Saturday. Can you suggest a sauce with which she might be served, my lady?' It was ghoulish. Yet Bagshaw was honouring them with a notion of individuality. He was conferring upon the animals the magic of the word and I was unable to decide whether it was a correct thing for him to have done or not.

I was in the museum when, years later, Mr Moralee told me of what had been his strange habit and my attention fell, as it often did, upon the red cedarwood urn. I imagined I heard the homunculus within. 'God meks it so far and no further. He meks the designs. All them animals, them's 'is creatures. Them's 'is and they can get on with their prayin' and praisin' if they wants to. But not us. Not us 'umans. We're past all that. We've got us own systems. We've got words, lad; words with which to build us systems. But Bagshaw Moralee, he misuses words, sithee? It's a common fault though, the misuse of words. Dead common. We'll gobble up everythin' in the end, by the time we've named it all. Name it and eat it – like a bloody catalogue of extinction in old library drawers, tha naws. Words? They'll drown us in the end, will words, less we conserve 'em and use 'em well.' That's what Mr Brown, himself a man of startlingly few words, might have said.

14

In which the idea of a circus unfolds

The Second Count Schubert Circus enjoyed an even greater reputation than the first of the same name. Excitement and fantasy were its hallmarks. The acts were exotic, like jungle blossoms. They displayed the ecstasies of birds and of madness. The circus lasted eighteen years, folding up only after the death of Bagshaw Moralee who was then over one hundred years of age. In its heyday the circus played to full audiences across the length and breadth of the country, but for much of the time it found a permanent home in the tower at Blackpool.

An idea that she should revive the circus came to her on the night Rosanne broke her leg. She was nibbling meat from a bone, part of the meal which had been cooked in the oven at the rear of Bagshaw Moralee's shop. The peach-faced lovebird and the white cockatoo with chest of crimson feathers (had its markings been no more than lifelong seepage from a fatal wound?) were eaten moodily. Dibden Dawson persevered with his efforts to placate the old zoophagist who, now he had told the full story of the quagga, was waterlogged in grief.

'Good heavens, man,' the doctor bellowed at him in his army captain's voice, 'when will you realize that you are not to blame? As you have already told us, you were only fulfilling a demand created by those gentrified neighbours of yours whilst you lived at Arundel. Market forces and all that. Good heavens, you weren't to know that the shelves were almost empty, man. That there were no quagga left!' The doctor appeared to be less drunk than he had been. The effects of the ether were wearing thin, though his smell still pervaded the air.

'Yes, but it was me what butchered them – slit their pretty throats,' the old man said emptily, echoing words which must have occurred to him a million times before.

Dibden queried him with a round eye. Rosanne put down the drumstick on which she had been nibbling and pushed her plate away. The last time she had seen that look was when the doctor had grabbed her struggling body and pressed an ether pad to her nose. She was still suffering the after-effect of a sickly headache.

'Good heavens, man, we're always slitting throats down at the department, pretty ones too,' Dibden answered and then quickly apologized as he caught sight of Rosanne pushing away the plate.

'No. It's nothing,' said the rope walker, thinking it hardly worth informing the doctor that she felt out of sorts. He didn't seem to be doing a lot to improve the condition of Bagshaw Moralee.

Mr Sligh was not hearing the conversation, or if he was then the talk of throat-slitting hadn't seemed to disturb his appetite, for he quickly tucked into the meat left on Rosanne's discarded drumstick. That was the fourth leg he had eaten, she noted – in fact most of the smaller bones were on his plate too. The ex-guardsman appeared ravenous. She thought that it must be all the energy expended when giving her the chair-lift through the street. (Of course, it was due more to the energy used when heroically rescuing my beautiful cousin, but Rosanne hadn't known of the incident with the couch.)

'I think I prefer this one,' Sligh commented, holding up the drumstick and tactlessly waving it about like a small flag in the hand of a child, in order to gain the old man's attention. 'Is it the lovebird?' he asked.

'No. That's Captain Blood, the cockatoo,' Bagshaw answered gloomily. Then with sudden uncontrollable rushes of air to the lungs, blood to the face and bile to the lips, he wailed for a time, disconsolately.

Mr Sligh looked away, embarrassed at what he had brought about, and let his eyes dally on the pile of feathers which Bagshaw had plucked from the birds during the preparation of the meal. They were piled at his corner of the table. Feathers of pure pleasure, some were crimson, others peach; many were of a dairy cream colour and those which were white had the nacre of pearls as if grown in an ocean. There was a single iridescent green feather no longer than his little finger which, before being ripped from her body, had clutched at Lola Lamonde's tiny twirtle like a G-string covers the last of a stripper's virtues. Mr Sligh lifted it lightly from amongst the pile of soft feathers. He brought it to his nose and sniffed gingerly. Then he shifted his bottom uncomfortably on the chair – he had become aware for the first time in several hours of his erection and fell into gloomy silence remembering how his barrel had been violently split asunder.

'Oh come along, Mr Moralee,' he heard Rosanne saying to the old man, 'we are all friends here. We hold you no malice for the quagga or whatever it was you ate. Clarrie's father's family uncovered a dinosaur, an iguanodon I think it's called. Albert's grandfather found it down the pit and that has been extinct a damn sight longer than your quagga, but we don't cry about it, you know.'

'No, but he didn't kill it, did he? He wasn't responsible for bringing about the extinction of the whole species.'

'No, but he blew it to bits.' (Rosanne had left the village before Mr Brown and I had rebuilt the beast.) 'Exploded the skeleton when it was still in one piece so that the coal owner couldn't have it.' She rapped the cast on her leg with her knuckles, disturbing Mr Sligh's reflections upon the barrel. He glanced at the pot hoping that it too was not about to disintegrate. He let the green feather fall.

'Good Lord, that's worse,' the round doctor said, winking at Rosanne to let her know that with her assistance he would soon have old Bagshaw lifted from his depression.

'Why? Why is it worse?' Bagshaw Moralee demanded to know.

'My dear chap, consider the matter, for heaven's sake. Once in fifty million years. Once in fifty million years the compete skeleton of an iguanodon comes along and Albert's grandad blasts it to kingdom come with a stick of miner's gelly. Good heavens, what sadness. Fifty million years. And here's you, my dear chap, grieving over the quagga who disappeared, in geological time, only yesterday. Good heavens, they'd be digging up quagga skeletons for evermore if Rosanne's family were ever to know of its passing.'

'It's not my family,' Rosanne corrected him in a second of bemused silence. 'It's my daughter's family.'

'Then it must be your family, if it's your husband's family,' Dibden insisted. He was a little put out that he had been sidetracked, annoyed that Rosanne was directing her effort into family tittle-tattle and not into the lifting of Bagshaw's mood.

'No. We weren't married. Albert and I were not wedded,' she went on.

'Not wedded?' Dibden Dawson screwed up his eye again.

'But I thought you had been wedded?' Montague Sligh dreamily interjected.

'I was married, once,' Rosanne replied quickly, though from her tone it was apparent that she wished Sligh had not been so slack as to allow his dreamy thoughts to mould so easily on the lubricant of his tongue. Then, deciding that now the cat was out of the bag she may as well continue, she said, 'I was Mrs Schubert. Still am for that matter. My husband was Count Schubert of circus fame. He was the strongest man in the world, you know.' She began to pout. 'Ah, *chèris*, he was so strong. *Trop fort*,' she whined.

'And you, Madame, if you don't mind my asking, what part did you play in this circus? I couldn't help but note the magnificent musculature of your legs when I was given the task of setting the break – the legs of an athelete, I remember thinking at the time.' Rosanne twinkled her turquoise eyes but before she could answer, Mr Sligh had said with resigned gloominess:

'She was just a rope walker.'

Rosanne glared at her lodger for he had made it sound as if there was no difference between her former and her present occupations. He made it sound as if rope walking and street walking were the same thing.

'I was queen of the high wire,' she said stonily to Sligh. That was the last of her he had seen, when viewed from the inside of a barrel, she thought haughtily. She pouted again at Dibden Dawson, who screwed up his eye and smiled. She was becoming quite used to Doctor Dawson's peculiar facial expressions. 'Dressed in ostrich plumes and sequinned tights,' she added and raised her brows, offering a wide-eyed invitation for him to inquire further.

'I once cooked an ostrich,' Bagshaw Moralee chipped in. His elbow rested on the small table, the palm of his hand supporting his ancient head. He surprised the others with his comment. 'It was eaten at one of my dinner parties. He was served up on an enormous platter of ice borrowed from the Duchess's kitchen, his neck was wound around a golden sceptre and he had a grapefruit stuffed in his beak. I recall that it wasn't very nice.' The others looked at him, each wondering who was to ask why the ostrich had not been nice. 'Made you fart,' Mr Moralee went on, much to everybody's relief. He pulled a face. 'A table full of crinolined ladies farting like a bloody symphony orchestra. Not very nice. They blew out the bloody dining-room candles, I recall.' The others laughed and eventually Bagshaw laughed a little with them. Dibden Dawson winked at Rosanne again.

'And tell me, dear lady,' the doctor asked, turning his full attention now to Rosanne, who had managed to maintain the saucer-like quality of her eyes during what she thought had been the old man's time-wasting interruption. 'How on earth did you manage to get yourself involved on the high wire?'

'Ah, that was Grand'maman,' Rosanne pouted. 'Grand'maman was the famous Madame Saqui, rope walker to ze court of Napoleon.'

'Ah, so it is in the family.'

'*Oui*, my daughter too, she is accomplished on ze high wire.'

Well, I must say that is interesting. I do admire you circus people. Always fancied it myself to be honest, somehow got stuck on doctoring though.'

'You?' Mr Sligh condemned (would nobody allow her to develop a conversation with this fellow?), allowing his eyes to roam around the circularity of Dibden Dawson and at the same time blessing himself for having, despite the blemish of his erection, a physique worthy of at least an athlete.

'Yes, I, Mr Sligh. I can see what you are thinking but one doesn't need the body of Adonis to take part in a circus performance, old chap. Heavens, no. Just look at the clowns and some of those blokes with the animal acts. No, always fancied myself as having a way with the animals, you know.'

'You?' This time it was Bagshaw Moralee's turn to condemn whilst Rosanne's mouth practised the pout and her eyes registered boredom.

'Yes, me. Good heavens, look at the way I taught the baboons to play a hand of poker. Took your money from you, right enough, old man. Seem to remember that's the reason why we're here, isn't it? Wasn't this splendid meal in lieu of stake money, eh?'

Bagshaw nodded at the pile of small bones on Mr Sligh's plate which was surmounted by the iridescent green feather where he had let it fall. Bagshaw had to concede that perhaps the doctor did have a way with animals.

'Yes, looks to be cruel, I know. But a little surge of current and the blighters soon know what to do,' the doctor added, bragging a little.

'Do you mean to say that those monkeys were actually playing cards?' Rosanne asked, the severe quality of tone in her voice surprising even herself. She had not yet had time to reflect on the night's events. In fact as the card-playing baboons were the first thing she had observed when coming round from the effects of the anaesthetic, she was still unsure if she had truly witnessed the happening at all.

'Oh yes, Madame. Your companions here didn't believe me when I told them we had time for a few hands of poker with the baboons in the time it would take for you to recover fully from the effects of the ether. They're not fantastic, you understand, but then of course the baboon is not a fantastic bluffer in the wild – comes with not having too many predators, you know. Perhaps they might be better suited to rummy.'

'No, they aren't intelligent enough for rummy. Trick-making would be beyond them,' Bagshaw commented unexpectedly again. 'Pontoon's their game. I seen them in Somaliland where as many as a hundred individual males will join in a game.'

'What, a card game? You'll be telling us next that they have casinos with baize tables,' scoffed Sligh, fiddling with the tassels on his epaulettes.

'No. It's a game which the baboons have invented themselves,' said Bagshaw, ignoring the sarcasm. 'A game in which they're dealt leaves. The member of the troupe holding the leaf with the largest number of serrations on the margin wins the game. In order to play such a game they have to be able to count without question, way beyond twenty-one, I can tell you, and I suspect that some of them have learned to cheat too. I heard it said that a few have learned when foraging to hang on to the odd leaf they come across simply because it has an unusually large number of teeth on the saw edges. During the game they are cunning enough to swap leaves just as a card-sharp gives hisself an advantage with an ace up the sleeve. They play for the odd scorpion which the chief of the troupe comes across.

The winner gets the scorpion, shows the rest of the troupe his colourful bum and wanders off with the spoils.'

'I don't believe a word of it,' said Mr Sligh.

'Believe it or not, I seen it with my own eyes,' insisted Bagshaw.

'Amazing, absolutely amazing. You know, I never thought of pontoon,' Dibden Dawson said.

'Well, zere we are. Get your act togezzer, Doctor Dawson, and perhaps you will get to appear at ze circus after all.' Rosanne took her opportunity to get in another pout.

'Madame, I most certainly will. I shall start teaching them pontoon tomorrow,' he answered perkily. 'And what of you, Mr Moralee, did you never have a wish to perform at the circus? Surely having led a life dedicated, in one way or another, to the beasts, the idea must have crossed your mind? Lion taming or something?'

'No, can't say it did,' said the old man, whose acute attack of depression seemed to have passed. 'But let me show you something.' He rose from his chair whistling tunelessly. The shop beyond the kitchen fell into deep hush. 'Give me a hand, will you? I'd like you to go in there, go around the shop and release the birds from their cages, will you? Go on, don't be afraid, they'll not harm you.' Bagshaw started again to whistle the same tuneless song. The others wandered into the shop and gazed up at the cages swaying on the low wood ceiling. With a cold eye, a macaw watched Rosanne untie the string which held his bamboo cage shut. When freed the macaw headed straight for the noise and settled on Bagshaw's head. She let another macaw free. At the same moment Dibden Dawson unknotted the tie on a third cage. The two birds made straight for Bagshaw and they too settled on his head. The tall Mr Sligh lifted his hands just above his own head and with nimble fingers unknotted the strings on two more cage doors. Again the birds made for the tuneless whistling. They continued to set free the birds and watched with a mixture of horror and amusement as the old man's head became covered in a bush of silent feathers.

'Good heavens,' Dibden Dawson exclaimed. 'What a wheeze,' and he burst out laughing, his eye almost popping from his head. Bagshaw's head and shoulders had disappeared completely. The birds which perched there remained silent. An occasional one ruffled his colourful feathers.

'Good heavens,' Dibden Dawson said again. 'He looks like a bloody parasol down at Epsom on Derby Day.'

'Like at the seaside,' Sligh said, unaware of where Epsom might be but fascinated at the ruffling quietude which reminded him of the sea at Bognor where he had spent his childhood.

'What a wonderful act,' shouted Rosanne. 'Bagshaw Moralee and his birds of a colourful feather. What a wonderful performance,' she whined, rapidly knocking the heels of her palms together in joyous applause. '*Peut-être* we can begin tomorrow with our rehearsals. This is so fabulous, *mes chéris*.'

'I say, old boy, you've made me quite envious.' The doctor spoke to the umbrella-shaped mass of birds as they clung to Bagshaw's head. The old man shifted himself sideways, lugging the enormous weight of bird, and felt for the back of his chair with both hands. He guided himself, like a blind person, into the seat he had occupied before. 'This really is most extraordinary. I simply can't wait to get cracking with my own rehearsals tomorrow morning,' Dibden Dawson continued enthusiastically.

Bagshaw held up a hand, cutting short the doctor's excitement. The others watched, hardly daring to breathe. The birds remained silent. Rosanne was reminded of the fearful silence at the brothel before the sun peeps over the black roof of the brooding cathedral. Suddenly, the old man clapped his hands once and the birds flew back to their cages in a clatter, the occasional feather drifting on to the table-top and to the floor. The old man then went round locking the birds into their bamboo cages. He continued to whistle his tuneless song.

'Amazing,' said Dibden Dawson as dawn broke weakly through the small window at the back of the pet shop and the pale light fell directly upon the face of Mr Sligh. 'And what is it that you are able to do?' asked the doctor of the ex-guardsman. The gold braid on his tunic shone as if the touch of sun had only just brought Mr Sligh to life.

'He can expose his penis from a barrel,' answered the lady. She had not yet forgiven Sligh his reference to her as merely a rope walker as if she had been two a penny, common as muck. 'Our friend here spends much of his time kneeling in a barrel, you know, with his prick thrust through a hole in the wood.' Then for good measure she added, 'He has a permanent erection.'

'Really?' Dibden Dawson displayed a doctor's concern for the man's affliction. 'This is turning out to be quite an evening.'

'Yes, isn't it? said Sligh with sarcasm, exaggeratedly wafting away ether fumes which had been delivered on the doctor's breath.

'Oh, come now, Mr Sligh, don't be so disingenuous. Yes, I have a problem and I admit it, but come along, you must tell us about yours.'

Sligh was uncomfortable. He crossed and uncrossed his legs, acutely aware of his problem. The eyes of his companions followed the movement of his legs – all but Rosanne's. She had seen the problem more than enough and if a policeman almost yanking it off hadn't cured him, then she despaired of his ever being rid of it. Sligh was a reticent man – he was a good fellow too – but he didn't wish to discuss his erection. Not even with a doctor.

'Look, I'm a damned good athlete, I can tell you. In much better shape than either of you two, anyway.' He spoke to the men.

'Well, of course, we had rather gathered that,' Dibden Dawson said. 'Built for distance rather than for sprint, wouldn't you have said, Mr Moralee?'

'More's the pity,' concurred Bagshaw. 'A sprint man would probably have welcomed having the extra inches in a dash to the tape.' Then the zoophagist burst into a fit of uncontrollable laughter and had to be slapped on the back several times by the doctor to prevent him from choking.

'As a matter of fact, living so much of my time in a barrel has given me certain gifts you know,' the ex-guardsman bragged offensively when Bagshaw had completed his bout of coughing. 'For instance, I can curl up inside one and get around a bit, you know.' He was indignant but eager to inform.

'Can you really?' asked a surprised Rosanne.

'Yes, I can. You don't know everything. You have seen me only in the evenings. During the days I have spent much time at practice.'

'You mean all that noise from your room wasn't just humping in the barrel?'

'It most certainly was not, Madame. Your daughter is still as pure as the driven snow. All that noise was merely practice for what eventually will be a soldier's life in permanent quarters.'

Sligh's retort set the old man off again. He laughed and spluttered quite uncontrollably and though the doctor did what he could to relieve him, this time he too succumbed to the mirth. Soon Rosanne had joined in. The two men found themselves stumbling about the wet pet-shop floor hanging on to their bellies whilst pups and kittens clawed at their trouser legs. Rosanne slithered from her chair and came to rest with a bump, her legs splayed in the most undignified way. Tears rolled down her cheeks and she slapped her plastered leg continually and noisily with an open palm. They were all gesticulating wildly at the unfortunate Sligh who would choose to spend his time in a barrel. Sligh for the life of him was unable to see the funny side of things, his face a knot of hard guardsman muscles, each drawn to attention around his sad moustache.

Dibden Dawson struggled back to the kitchen clutching at his splitting sides. He sat in a chair, took several deep breaths and waited for his companions to make their own ease with the merriment. Eventually he spoke into Sligh's soldierly features. 'Good heavens Sligh,' he bellowed, 'I shouldn't have thought so up until this very moment, but you really are a bloody barrel-load of laughs, aren't you?'

'There's nothing amusing about thrusting his prick through a hole in a lump of wood,' Rosanne said, drawing the doctor's thoughts back to her earlier display of anger. '*Mon dieu*, when I think of the things I've done for you whilst you were kneeling in that barrel. You have no gratitude. I feel you have cheated me, Mr Sligh.'

'Done?' shouted Sligh as Dibden Dawson helped Rosanne up off the floor and seated her back in her chair. 'But I don't understand. There is no need for you to have done anything. It is I who was supposed to be doing the doing. It is I who exposed myself, not you. Do you mean to say that you were doing things whilst I was kneeling unseen in my barrel? If so, then it is I who am cheated, Madame.'

Mon dieu, thought Rosanne, the penny having dropped, there was no need for me to have performed at all. Nor for the other girls to have put on their special performances for the pleasing of this ridiculous pervert. It now seemed the ex-guardsman was actually complaining to Rosanne because she had paid insufficient attention to his flashy exhibitionism when kneeling in his barrel; moaning, because she had occupied her time with other matters, even though, as she had thought at the time, the performance was arranged for his benefit. What ingratitude.

The doctor understood at once what must have been the man's situation whilst kneeling in the barrel. 'You were both unseen and unseeing, were you not, Mr Sligh?'

'I most certainly was,' Sligh responded, his face now lit by the sun.

'It's quite strange, isn't it, how we treat the priapist as if he is nothing but a peeper,' the doctor told Rosanne, 'but I think you now see he is no such thing.' She had to admit that she had for much time carried somewhere in her mind the peculiar idea that Sligh had observed the antics of her chums at the brothel through a rudimentary eye embedded at the end of his penis. 'It is strange, isn't it, how we treat him as a pervert and think he needs only a thumping great dose of the same thing to satisfy his affliction,' the doctor summarized.

'And is that not the case?' asked Sligh.

'Good heavens, no. His priapism must be examined thoroughly and the cause of this unfortunate malady expunged. Though I admit, it is perhaps more difficult than it sounds. The cause very often cannot be found and, sad to say, the condition is very often irreversible but I stress that the erection and the perversion are in no way connected except that occasionally the perversion is perhaps a false consequence of the erection and no more.'

Sligh turned his face into shadow. He looked glum.

'Bet my extracts would cure his condition,' Bagshaw Moralee butted in. As the night had passed it had become increasingly apparent that the old man's interjections, though each time quite unexpected, had a pertinence that couldn't be ignored.

'Well, tell us, old chap,' the doctor invited with an accommodating gesture of the hand.

'My extract from the sperm sac of the scarlet macaw. That'll sort him out. Sorts out most problems of a sexual nature, you know.'

'Oh, really?'

'Yes. First experienced it long ago in Java where it was used for all sorts of things. Those who couldn't get it up, those who couldn't get it down.' (He makes it sound like a faulty gamp, Rosanne thought haughtily and not without some discomfort at the notion of

394

it.) 'Infertility in the women. Frigidity. Loose moral worth. It was used for the lot, a sort of hormonal regulator for sexual practice. It gave rise to a healthy lusting once a day. Both man and woman thrived on it, I can tell you. I've used it every day for more than sixty years and never had an erection out of place, a dirty thought or a stray ejaculation.'

'Well, that sounds just what the doctor ordered,' said Dibden Dawson admiring such tidy and persistent drug usage in a notoriously error-prone area of therapeutic care.

'It certainly does,' commented Rosanne having caught the unmistakable glint in the eye of the old man.

'Not only might it cure his priapism,' the doctor continued, 'but it may also regulate his sexual rhythm so that satisfaction may be found in something other than exhibition from a barrel,' concluded Dibden Dawson flatly. He appeared suddenly tired.

'He lectures me with boredom, as he would a dull student,' Rosanne complained sulkily to herself. It was true, the doctor's eye had suddenly lost its glint and now registered a veiled boredom. A flaccidity had settled upon his roundness. Where before he had displayed the stored energy of a stilled rubber ball he was now dough-like.

'Shall we give it a go, then?' suggested Bagshaw.

'I'm game for anything,' Rosanne sighed, her attention diverted from the deflating doctor.

Quite without warning, the old man thrust a needle painfully through the material at the seat of Sligh's pants and into his slim buttocks, causing him to yell out loud. 'What the bloody hell are you doing?'

'Sorry, I thought you said that you was game.'

'That wasn't me. It was her, you idiot.'

'Heavens, come now, gentlemen. Let's not quarrel,' advised Dibden Dawson stifling a yawn. 'The injection will have done no harm, you have my word on it. Come along, Mr Sligh, calm yourself. Let's see what tomorrow brings and let us hope it may be an easing of your symptom, old chap. In the mean time I promise to begin teaching my baboons the rudiments of the game of pontoon as soon as I possibly can. I trust you good people will start a little practice of your own.' Then with shaking hands the doctor heaved himself from his chair. The dust in the shaft of light from the window was swimming about him. He shambled unsteadily from the table, staggering away through the pups and kittens to the shop door. 'Time for my sniff, you understand,' he explained. 'I shall be back to see how you are getting along sometime tomorrow.'

When he returned Rosanne had already decided to resurrect the circus.

15

Clarrie meets the laundry master

Whilst her mother imagined circuses, Clarrie wandered the moors. She walked among the black stones, here and there, like exotic fruits, cleft to reveal glittering golden interiors. The clouds gathered and darkened above, yet on valley slopes, only a little way off, the sun shone, touching the wind-blown grass. It lit up the heather and exploded off the yellow gorse. Factories poked chimneys into the sky and smiled darkly in their own small bowls below. There the river snaked and the occasional barge, no bigger than the nail on her finger, quietly tipped coal.

She was hardly dressed for moorland walking. In their hurry to escape the crumbling brothel, Mr Sligh had rushed her into the first clothes available – an expensive black strapless evening dress with a pink taffeta rose displayed at the bosom. In her haste she had forgotten to put on her underwear. She had stepped into high-heeled alligator-skin shoes which she now held one in each hand. She trod gingerly from one clump of rushes to the next trying to avoid the mud.

Of course, she had not intended to be walking on the moors but in travelling away from the catastrophe (I like to think that she was heading towards me) and after reading of the accident in the newspaper she concluded that it would be safer than travelling the roads. She had a feeling that the police would be looking for her – perhaps wish to question her about the death of the officer who had flown straight past her nose as Mr Sligh was hauling her and the couch in the opposite direction.

She could hear the continual overpouring of water on the stones as she passed from one tinkling stream to the next. The sky grew black. The waters caught the light cast by a stray beam thrust like a biblical ladder through clouds. It painted a touch of gold into the dark grasses about her.

She had no idea where she was but when near to Luddenden (she later learned) she saw a man exercising his dog. At first she thought him to be a boy; she judged him to be almost a foot shorter than herself. When he came close she saw that his clothes were ragged. His coat appeared to be made from clippings like the pegged rug which occupied the space before the fire in our parlour – the one on which Clarrie and I had sat as children to be seen and not heard. He puffed a short pipe. It jutted from his jaw like the steam valve from an old engine. Without removing the pipe he called to the mongrel which Clarrie could now hear rustling in the heather.

'C'mon, Shep. Gerronya,' he called gruffly, over and over again without easing the pipe from between clenched teeth.

He stopped a few feet short of her, waiting for the dog to wriggle its way from the vegetation. It was then she was sure that he was not a boy, but a man. He at last took the pipe from his mouth; Clarrie could see the end of the stem was so badly chewed that the wood had turned white and the hole through which he would have inhaled the smoke was almost closed. A brown mixture of spit and tobacco dangled from the end of the stem. The same strand of spittle dribbled unbroken from the man's pale lips, forming a viscid loop. It caught the lone sun's ray, reflecting a thin spectrum – a narrow bow in the angry sky.

'No place for a woman, these moors,' he told her, casting his puzzled eye over her expensive and unsuitable clothing. The rain began to fall in heavy droplets.

'I'm looking for somewhere to stay for a while,' she said hopefully. The cold raindrops spattered her bare shoulders.

'Tha wants work?'

'Yes, that too. I need a room though. Somewhere to stay.' She shifted the two shoes to a single hand, allowing them to dangle from the alligator skin straps.

'Shep. Gerronya, Shep,' he called, staring at the loosely hanging shoes. The top of his head was level with the artificial rose at her breasts. The rain now spotted her cleavage. She felt the tightening of her skin as goose bumps rose up. 'Luddenden Foot,' he said and pointed the chewed stem of the pipe down into the valley. 'There's rooms for rent in t'place where I stay. Tha can get work in t'mill.'

As he looked about she saw how wizened he was. His face was

tanned and weatherbeaten. She saw how he had the body of a normal man but his legs, which she at first thought might be sinking into the spongy ground, were supported by clogs which were clearly visible to her. He was even shorter than she had at first imagined. He was a dwarf. His legs were small and stumpy; his head too large, like caricatures she had seen drawn in books. The heavy lids dragged slowly over the eyes again. 'Summat's happened to t'stones,' he commented, still poking the air with the pipe stem. 'Nivver seen stones blasted open like that afore. Must have just happened. All that golden stuff'll be oxidized black in a couple of months.'

'It must be the earthquake,' Clarrie explained.

'What earthquake?' he asked.

'There was an earthquake in Manchester the other day.'

The eyes slowly closed their lids again, sleepily, like the eyes of a reptile. 'Gerronya, Shep,' he chided throatily.

'It's true. The stones must have been broken at the same time.'

'Gerronya, Shep.' He smiled for the first time, revealing his small brown-stained teeth, very even yet half eaten away by acid and nicotine. 'Earthquake eh! Summat's up wit' weather, then?'

He shook his large head and pointed the pipe down into the valley again. He set off, shouting all the while to his dog which was winding itself silkily this way and that between the dark green ferns and gorse bushes. She took the pointing to mean that she too should follow and, falling in step behind the dwarf and his dog, she trailed them down from the moors and eventually out of the rain. They walked mostly between high drystone walls of Millstone Grit and soon they were on the road which took them into the small town. The dwarf stopped before a house which seemed to be half submerged into the foot of the hill on which it had been built. Light green mosses grew on the roof, holding the slates together and tacking them to a steep inverted V. It was a grim place, built from the black stone which lay all around. The railway line ran close by and vibrations from the rumbling trains had caused the mullion stones to slip sideways. The windows stared from many angles.

'That's where I live,' the dwarf told her proudly. He pointed to the cellar door, the top of which was just visible above the ground. 'I get in through the window. C'mon.' He led her to a small window which was at the side of the cellar door. The sill was at ground level. There was no glass in this window and she could plainly hear the sound of running water rilling from within. It was the same noise she had heard on the moors where the streams tinkled over the stones. The dwarf had no difficulty in climbing in. He beckoned for her to follow, and Clarrie slipped over the sill with ease. Her wet dress rode up, almost to the waist – she could feel the damp mossy stone on her backside – and she let herself drop to the floor. She found herself in a cave which was hung about with white linen. There was no light other than the little which came from the window; even so the cellar was bathed in a blue glow enough to hurt the eyes. Now she had got up close to the linen and there was nothing more on which to settle her gaze she realized that it was the linen itself which reflected this cold light. She regarded the dirty dwarf in his rags for a second and had difficulty in comprehending what sort of place she had just dropped upon. The man, anticipating her confusion, explained.

'My name's Glynn, Harry Glynn. I'm the laundry master. I teks in the town's washing. Wash it with me blue powder – scrubbed by hand, mind – then I hang it here on the lines to dry.'

Clarrie looked to the corner of the cellar where the stream, flowing through, ran over some rocks. The stones glowed with a pale blue light too, presumably absorbed from Harry Glynn's powder which would have been used when he pummelled the collars and cuffs. She saw also how a weak glint was cast from a glass bottle which stood on the stone flags beside the rocks. It was a large round sweet jar closed with a grey tin lid and half filled with something slivered and silvery. Something which she thought would run like quicksilver if ever it was to be released on to an unprepared world.

The underground room was threaded with stout cords. They ran from the front wall, which housed the window through which they had just dropped, to the opposite wall where at its base the stream flowed. The linen was neatly arranged on these cords.

'My name's Clarrie,' she told, looking at the sheets.

'Pleased to meetcha, Clarrie,' the dwarf said and stuck out his open palm. She ignored the offer to shake his hand, preferring to consider the hanging linen. She ran the backs of her fingers up and down a bed sheet sensing the texture of the material.

'Do you live here, Mr Glynn?' she asked.

'Oh, ay.'

'You live above, do you? Up there?' and she pointed her index finger to the ceiling, the low height of which struck her when she allowed her eyes to follow the direction of her pointing, for until that moment she had felt she was in a more roomy place. There were several hooks secured there too, each with a hambone dangling from it. The dog sat on his haunches on the cold flags and stared longingly in the direction of her pointing finger.

'No. I live here in the laundry. Live down here. A troglodyte, that's me.' He smiled at her with eyes half covered by dozy lids and directed his own finger down into the earth. Then he offered his hand again. She declined the invitation a second time and returned her attention to the linen.

'Tha can live up there,' he told her, tilting his face to the hambones. 'The rooms is empty but the landlord lives right next door. Shall we go and see?'

She nodded a little uncertainly and, following the dwarf's courteous gesture for her to go first, she began to climb out of the window. It was whilst crawling on all fours, with the dwarf so close she could feel his hot breath on her, that she thought about her wet dress. It was riding to the waist again and she wished she had had sense enough to remember her underclothes.

16

Settling in with sweets

Clarrie, wet and uncomfortable, stood in the landlord's drawing-room where only the damp prevented sad paper peeling from the walls. Her body steamed beneath the black evening dress; it had acquired a halo in this dim light. She wore the alligator-skin shoes which raised her a good four inches taller than she had been and Harry Glynn sheltered beneath the wilted pink flower at her breasts: a gnome posed in the recovery of lush, tropical gardens after rain.

A long-haired, dark girl played the pianola behind a low mahogony screen.

The landlord's name was Agrelovitch. He also was standing in the middle of the drawing-room. He faced them, listening to both Clarrie and the music at the same time. He was a bear-like Russian with a fierce red beard. He had come to England from Omsk on the eve of the revolution accompanied by a minor princess, hidden in his baggage. The princess, who left her country crammed in a hide-covered shoe-box with ball claw feet (the one there in the corner of this depressing room) lived several summers in the Millstone Grit before running off to France with an Umbrian count whom the couple had met when on a boating weekend at Windsor. During her time at the house the princess had borne a daughter. It was the daughter who played the pianola half hidden by the mahogany screen. This fragment of no great significance was related by Harry Glynn as he and Clarrie crossed the shale-covered yard which separated the two houses. Agrelovitch had been amenable. She had explained that she had no money but intended getting work in the mill.

'Take, take. Sokay Sokay,' the landlord had said generously with an expansive wave of his large hand, then picking up the phrase he had been listening for he heartily sang along to his daughter's music. As Clarrie and the laundry master crunched away from the Russian's house, treading loose stones, they could hear him singing, unaware that they had left him.

Clarrie found employment at the weaving shed and was be-friended by a young girl who had started work on the same day as herself. The girl was called Daisy Miller. She had a face as white as a dish rag surmounted by a mop of curly black hair. Clarrie learned to read Daisy's painted lips, elastic as rubber sprung to arched bows of silken red. It was a silent accompaniment to the harsh racket of the looms. What she failed to realize, though, was that all the other mill lasses too could read the lips of those around them. The confi-dences she expressed to Daisy were rapidly picked up by the others. All the girls knew of Mr Sligh and his barrel and the slimy trail of evolutionary history she had seen born from it. They knew of the earthquake and of her mother's broken leg and of the death of the policeman who had gone into the night.

With her first month's wage she paid her rent and bought herself a pair of French knickers.

When Clarrie realized, too late, that her lips were being read by whoever cared to look – and some sweating, turbaned girl in a floral cotton pinafore dress always was looking – she took to confiding directly into Daisy's ear, hissing words through closed teeth and creating the noise of the sea as it circles in shells picked from the beach. Standing in that enormous hot shed, surrounded by clatter and bathed in a shafted, dusty light which filtered down from the huge glass roof above them – the room where, like in heaven, Clarrie imagined a quiet God would sit and judge – the girls spoke their words in classes of two. That way no secrets would be breached. Clarrie and Daisy could share their thoughts in the din of the weaving shed. Communication of another type was by way of their ruby red lips.

'How's your mother?'

'Did you see that chap last night?'

'I'm starved. Can't wait to get home for us tea.'

'Did you come on the rags yet?'

But Clarrie's thoughts which didn't seek answers – the desires and the fears – they were reserved for Daisy and for God; kissed away like pain into the warm secret of the friend's ear.

The room she lived in was long and draughty. The walls were pannelled in oak which had been coated with a heavy brown varnish.

Everything was cast in a gloom from the tiny bulb at the centre of the ceiling rose. The bulb was covered by a ridiculously small shade which sported a half-dozen lengthy toffee-coloured silk tassels. Light filtered through the silk as a creeping stain.

The room's feature, however, was a magnificent Jacobean oak fireplace which at some time had acquired an iron surround. This addition was blackleaded regularly by the landlord. Apparently, before application, the blacking was mixed with a portion of cold tea, which was kept in a samovar. It was Agrelovitch's belief that the practice led to a better finish, not a trick he had brought with him from Omsk but a little home economics he had learned, amongst other things, during a liaison with a deacon's wife in Brontë country.

Clarrie soon discovered that by keeping a fire roaring in the grate, and in not using the electric light, the illumination so cast gave the room a glow of shadows which she had not predicted – the warmth of the flames charged the varnish with a palette of healthy reds. The crackling logs gave her room the sound and the smell too of rosy splendour.

Harry came from his cellar each night accompanied by Shep. He brought mint imperials and lemon sherbets, sometimes he arrived with chocolates individually wrapped in coloured ribbons, and he sat like a rag child in a large armchair. Their talk was small. They might discuss the weather or Harry might complain about the never-ending flow of bed sheets which he was asked to launder. With hooded lids he offered his confectionery. He sucked on his old pipe whilst watching her untie the bows of blue and red ribbon wrapped about the chocolates. He sucked on the lemon sherbets with the pipe clenched in his teeth, causing the enamel to rot away like the disappearing sherbet itself. And like the disappearing sherbet, too, his talk ended in nothing.

Sometimes in the long silences he stared into the fire which always blazed in the grate causing the walls to dance like a shadow rumba band.

Sometimes a train might rumble by shaking the old house.

Then, when the night's supply of sweets and chocolate had been exhausted, the dwarf slid from the giant chair, turning himself around so that his back was to Clarrie as he did so, and returned to his cellar and to his work. Sometimes she sensed that he wished to offer his hand before they finally parted but she was glad that he never did. She felt like the child reader of the fairy stories eager to follow the adventure yet unable to extend herself when she discovered that she had been miraculously transported into the pages of the book. She stayed on the outside looking in, but she knew full well that there was already a part of herself which had crossed the perimeters of drawn circles. She could see a part of herself on the inside looking out like she had seen those things in the dark of the barrel's belly. She knew that history was thrusting her towards maturity and as her mother's friend, the Professor of Oleopharmacognosy, had predicted she knew that she would have to let the past times go.

17

Bargaining with knickers

They talked little. Over a period of several weeks Clarrie learned that Harry Glynn was descended from the great Porsini, the Punch and Judy man.

'When ah was a youngster, ah used to perform on the sands at Southport and at Blackpool. Used to stand on an orange box hidden behind a Union flag with me father. I've still got family over there carrying on the tradition and performing on the sands,' he once told her, and on another occasion he squawked, 'Love thee, Clarrie, love thee,' in the raucous voice of Mr Punch. Then he spat something into his fist like a man delicately spitting orange pips. Clarrie was frightened. 'Don't be afeared,' the dwarf said, 'it's only the squeaker.' Shadows danced in the red room.

'The what?'

'The squeaker. It's what gives Mr Punch his voice sithee.' He held out his hand and opened his palm.

'What is it?' she asked. The logs crackled in the hearth.

'It's a threepenny piece. A silver bit all bent up,' he said knowingly. 'There's not many what knows that.' Then he winked at her conspiratorially.

She told him nothing of herself.

One night, having finished his chores, Harry came to Clarrie's room as usual. He had the sweet jar tucked beneath his arm. It was the sweet jar which contained the silvery stuff – the one she had noticed by the rocks in the corner of the cellar when she had first been invited into the laundry master's room. The flames licked up the large grate. In the red glow Harry wriggled himself comfortable into the armchair. He looked into her pretty face. Lids slowly closed over his eyes, then lifted just as slowly.

'Know about thee,' he told her.

'Know what about me?' she asked.

'Know about tha being a prostitute and about tha mom.'

Clarrie was embarrassed and frightened. She didn't know what to say. She looked away, into the fire. 'Know about the policeman,' he then told her.

'It wasn't my fault,' she blurted directly at him.

'Didn't say it was. But the law might not think so.'

'You won't say anything?' She was alarmed.

'Might do. Might not.' His lids blinked slowly again. 'Depends.'

'Depends on what?'

'On thee.' He drummed his fingers on the tin lid of the sweet jar which was still tightly held in the crook of his arm. The nicotine stains on his stubby fingers appeared magenta in the room's red light. She didn't like those disproportionate fingers. They appeared boneless like blood sausage with a life of their own; they rapped out that terrible drumming noise on the lid of the sweet jar. She summoned bravura and allowed her eyes to roam over the man's small body.

'You look lost in that chair, Harry,' she told him confidently.

'Ay, well, tha'll find me. If tha wants to,' he said, dismissing her display of bravado. He drummed his fingers again. *Rat a tat-tat.* 'Depends.'

'Yes. You said. Depends on me, you said.'

'That's right, missy. Depends on thee.' She stood up and went over to the Jacobean fireplace where she turned her back on the blazing logs.

'Depends on thee, missy,' he told her again, watching. He was always watching, she thought.

'I don't understand,' she suddenly said. 'What am I supposed to do, Harry?' She gathered her long skirt in her hands and raised the hem an inch or two from behind. She let the flames warm her bare calves, enjoying the moment.

Harry drummed on the lid of the big round jar. 'Tha can tek that off for a start.' He nodded towards her skirt. She ignored him for several seconds, enjoying the warmth on the back of her legs.

'What's in the jar?' she suddenly found the courage to ask.

'It's me threepenny pieces.'

'It'll cost you one of them,' she told him with a calculated smile.

'Ay up, missy. I'll want more than a look for me threepence.'

'Then I'll touch you. I'll touch you for threepence and you'll not tell the police?' she suggested – but she knew that she was instructing. She knew that somewhere she was bargaining with her future.

The dwarf nodded and hurriedly began to unbutton his trousers. 'I'd like the money first, Harry,' she told him.

Harry ceased the unbuttoning and unscrewed the grey lid of the jar. He thrust his arm into the silver threepenny pieces. He grabbed up a clumsy handful then let them run tinkling through his fingers back into the bottle. Finally he fished out a single coin.

'Doesn't tha trust me?' he asked, holding up the coin, which reflected the light weakly back at her.

'Prostitutes never trust anyone,' she told him and she could see that he winced as if she had fetched him a blow to the side of his head in that spiked red room. She took the silver piece and removed her skirt. She stood before the fire still enjoying the warmth from the flames on her body.

'And tha knickers,' he said.

'That'll cost another threepence,' she told him.

'Naw. Tha's agreed.'

'No. I agreed to take off my skirt and to touch for threepence. Knickers is extra, Harry.'

The dwarf pulled another coin happily from the jar. 'Cheap at twice the price,' he said. He handed over the money, then still lost in the depths of the chair he rolled down his trousers as Clarrie removed her recently purchased French knickers. For a time, he watched her strong dark thighs before the dancing flames.

'Come here,' he said. She knew from the tone of his voice that he was trying to be gentle with her but she was afraid again. Her bravura had died. She hated those sausage-shaped fingers, the rotted teeth, his filthy jacket and pipe. The smell of nicotine and laundry smell and dog pee smell. She was shaking within, hardly able to control herself, but she knew that to survive she must find new strategies; as her mother was able, she must draw new circles. 'Come here,' he said again gently.

She went across to his chair and stood over him. She smiled letting her falling hair touch his face. She caressed his penis with the tips of her fingers. In her other hand she clenched the two silver coins.

*

That's how it was every night. It went on for years. Sometimes he brought chocolate, sometimes lemon sherbets and mint imperials. He always brought the dog and he always brought the sweet jar. They chatted and ate sweets, sometimes he smoked his pipe. He taught her to make puppet clothing, cut from animal hides sewn together with a large steel needle. At some point in the evening Harry fished two coins from the jar and Clarrie stripped. Never above the waist and always before the burning logs in the magnificent Jacobean fireplace. She would touch him, allowing her shadow and her hair to fall on his freakishness. Sometimes the train rumbled by, shaking the old place to its foundations, dislodging more mullion stones and sending the windows ever more crazy but she never commented, she just enjoyed the warmth of the fire on her legs and on her back in that red room and she saved the threepenny pieces in a sweet jar of her own.

1936

18

An inspector means-tests the Archbolds

Redundancy was always symbolic of the coal owners' power, but after the General Strike it was a power which burned with frightening intensity. Thwaite used it like a branding iron, scorching despair into the rump of our community. And with despair came degradation for the collier and a splintering of the union.

The secretary of the miners' federation was Ebby Edwards. He fought hard for a strengthening of ties at national level but the federation was slowly fragmenting and, though he couldn't prevent the process from continuing, he was hell-bent on one day amalgamating the federation into a single union. Ebby had this dream, you see, he had this perverse dream of unity. He was laughed at, but nobody could take away his dream.

In 1935, after a massive vote in favour of national strike action, many districts had ignored the call and negotiated their own pitiful deals with the coal owners. The men accepted any insult to stay in work. That's how it was in our village. Thwaite sacked dozens, he stretched working hours as if they were made from knicker elastic, he cut wages; and because his actions had brutalized unremittingly for so long, it seemed quite natural for him to have acted as he did. It took the Second World War to change things.

One of Thwaite's more cruel tricks was to sack the sons whilst keeping their fathers in work. In more recent years he hadn't bothered to employ the young at all. That was his policy; no work for the under-thirties. It drove away the young family men and it left us an ageing, dying community. Thwaite's policy was designed to keep the hotheads from the pit. It resulted in elderly bones rattling in cramped seams. They were living coffins in Thwaite's dank pit and the young men who stayed on in the village had to endure the humiliation of living like limpets on their parents' cramped backs.

Archbold's was such a family.

The old man had started down the pit in the same year as my grandfather. He had a fucked back but had to keep on, breaking himself in two because Thwaite's policy shut out his sons.

The lads were musicians, gentle boys, hardly the material from which the hothcads were made, but Thwaite wouldn't break policy. He wouldn't break wind if he thought somebody might gain from it. Cheeky, the younger of the two lads, had won prizes in national competitions. Miss Fountaine, the headmistress, claimed him to be the only truly gifted musician she ever had at the school. All the other kids loved to go into the Archbold house, explosive in its electric glare, brighter than anyone else's, and watch Cheeky playing his tuba. Since leaving the school he had regularly played with a local pit band and because he never worked he was able to devote a lot of his time to practice, sometimes coached by Miss Fountaine herself who visited the house after hours. You could always hear his practising down our terrace. Sometimes he played the Sousaphone on the bandstand at Roundhay Park in Leeds – but he could play anything; anything you had to blow into. He could play the kettle by puffing into its spout, regulating the notes using the lid as he might have used the mute in the bell of a trumpet. He had so much puff, he once played the fire brigade's hose pipe and Rube Hardwick, the landlord at the pub who then acted as commander of our fire brigade, was so engrossed he let Mr Henderson's allotment hut burn down rather than disturb the performance.

Cheeky sat for hours in the parlour window polishing his tuba with a soft brown rag until it glowed like a giant Aladdin's lamp. The children on the common often stopped their games and edged closer to the window just to watch him taking the shining instrument into his large hands. Then he would blow, a long sorrowful note like the barge slowly caught in the settled dusk and dust, scraping too close to the bank at Bottom Boat. There was a regular disappointment that a genie was never pushed all crumpled and sleepy from the bell as Cheeky thrust his massive breaths into the glinting metal body beneath the startling electric glare. 'What is it, O master?' he might have said, coming as a great bubble in silken purple pantaloons from the bell.

'Get us a job, lad, get us summat to do in t'pit. Me and me brother. Get us summat to do in t'pit,' Cheeky might have pleaded. Then cheeks puffed up once more he might have blasted out the sorrowful note before running into his practice.

Um-pa-pa, um-pa-pa. The kids from the common, their arms about one another's skinny waists like a line of underfed chorus girls, kicked their legs in time to Cheeky's wonderful huffings and puffings. *Um-pa-pa, um-pa-pa.*

The brothers went on the dole, but dole money was only paid out for a short time. One day, during her visit, Miss Fountaine suggested their father should have the boys mean-tested to see if the family could get a little extra to help with the food.

They sent an inspector who wandered about the terrace house like a rat in a bowler hat casting the point at the end of his brolly into the soft centre of family possession. The father and his two sons watched the man prodding in a corner of the parlour.

'What's that?'

'It's my wireless set.'

'Tha'll have to be rid of that.'

'But I were first in terrace to get a wireless set.'

'It's a luxury is that, tha'll have to be rid.'

'But it's got a walnut cabinet.'

'Ay. That's what I mean. It's a luxury is that. Tha'll have to be rid of it.' The inspector screwed up his eyes. 'By, it's bright in here,' he said.

'It's the electric.'

'I know what it is.' He pointed the end of his brolly to the bulb hanging from the ceiling. 'Tha's not mekin' much effort to save with bulbs like that.'

'It's same bulbs like anyone else's.'

'Tha doesn't need all that bright. Tha'll have to start savin'. Get a smaller bulb like.' He sniffed and poked about some more. 'What's them then?'

413

'It's my lad's instruments.'

'What, for music?' His tone rang harshly.

'Ay.'

'By, them's bright too.'

'It's because the lad's forever cleaning 'em.'

The inspector looked at Archbold doubtfully. 'It's a bright house is this, Mr Archbold. I'm not sure we can give thee owt, livin' in such a bright house.'

'Think we should move ourselves to a mucky house, then?' Archbold asked.

'Tha'll have to be rid. It's luxury is that,' the inspector told him, ignoring Archbold's remark.

'I'll not sell me instruments,' Cheeky piped up.

'Tha will, lad. If tha wants chitty for more food tha'll have to be rid. It's luxury is that,' the inspector told him.

Cheeky looked to his father. 'I'll not be rid of the tuba, father,' he said.

'It's extravagant is music,' the inspector said and lifted his bowler hat for a second to scratch at his head.

The following night the children playing football on the common saw Cheeky sitting in the parlour window, the room as always bathed in its powerful electric light. He had the bell of the tuba over his head. The boys laughed and wandered close to the window. They saw that Cheeky had buffed up the instrument. It was brighter than they had ever seen it before. They could read 'Hartmann, Königsberg', quite clearly on the side and there was a little crest with lions and a crown on it. They formed the chorus line and kicked out their legs waiting for the *um-pa-pa* to begin and then with a slow dawning of the dreadful truth they stopped kicking their legs and uncoupled their arms from about their partners' waists. The game broke up and the children went home to their mothers.

Cheeky had stuffed a cork into the mouthpiece and wrapped an old jumper about his neck, before jamming his head into the bell and going off to sleep with the genie in the purple pantaloons. At his funeral, brother Bob played the Sousaphone but it wasn't the same as if Cheeky had been playing it. It wasn't the same *um-pa-pa*. And much of that night, a barge adrift on the bank at Bottom Boat moaned low.

Miss Fountaine never interfered again, not with anyone. She continued to teach at the school but she never visited any other house in the village, nor in the next village. She just scuttled there and back, from home to school and back again. That's all.

19
The Brightside Dinosaur

In this year events which would alter my perception of the dinosaur were going to occur, so it is perhaps only right that here I should break to describe him to you and tell of the museum which housed him.

The museum wasn't anything like you might expect it to be. After all, it had been a picture palace – purpose-built like a tomb to retain darkness as long as the main attraction was showing. The illumination came by way of a crop of milky light bulbs which straggled from the high roof, eyes at the ends of raw optic nerves, and made intermittent noises, as if the messages flowing in them were leaking away, dripping like rain-water into a zinc bucket.

The floor sloped away from the glass-panelled doors through which hoards of picture-goers had flowed to see Uncle Lancaster's first talking film. It sloped at an acute angle, thus the legs on the display cabinets and tables were not of uniform length but were built so that those legs nearer to the doors were always shorter than the ones further away. The glass shelves within the cabinets, though, were naturally flat in order to safely house and display the exhibits. The cabinets then were blocks, like the cinema itself, made up not of rectangles as those in any other museum might have been, but of trapezoids and other geometrical freaks. Freaks to house freaks – a rag-bag of acquisition and curiosity.

The light bulbs blinked incomprehensive of the muddle, the messages leaked away.

The iguanodon filled a large central area and faced that end of the building where the cinema screen had at one time exploded out its images, flanked by two sentinel speakers – the Movietone system. Though the screen had gone, the speakers remained in place, often blaring out Jacky Jellis's imitation of a dinosaur roar. Standing down at that end of the building and looking back at the skeleton one felt that at any moment one was about to be leapt upon. He

416

reared up on massive hind legs and had many times the bulk of a rhinoceros.

It was difficult to know what was keeping him back – the big square-headed steel bolts with which Mr Brown had secured the giant tarsals and metatarsals to the floor and which he had covered in a black pitch seemed quite inadequate. All else was the old dosser's magical threading of the bones with a silver wire. Wire difficult to see unless you looked for it.

The enormous teeth, inches long, flashed from the jaw. The stone bones which had supported the hunched and springy shoulders and shortened forelegs moved slightly with the dead weight of fossilized material pushing from behind. The ribs occasionally made a noise as two of them turned on silver threads perhaps touching softly in a sudden draught. *Clink clonk*. Then they would drift slowly away from one another in the musty air.

I go to the museum at night and sit. With the aid of the beam from my electric torch I pick into the darkness. *Clink clonk*. Then from elsewhere the ghosts of the picture palace whisper gently. I shift my torch, casting a circle of light which dances on the butterflies or on the shushing sea shells. *Clink clonk* again but this time more harshly and I swing back my torch to the dinosaur. The ribs tremble. The beam searches the walls again, back to the butterflies and the shells, the spiders and the birds' eggs. I can hear the ruffling of the pages in Mrs Tarbutt's book still alone on the marble table. I can hear the sugar bugs munching their sweet ways through life and multiplying in their new box.

Stuffed birds and sketches now all in wall frames. The circlet of light catches Arkwright's helmet, suspended it seems from the mile-high ceiling. The light shines up and up the thread which holds it, up to the milky light bulbs. What is that noise which leaks from their wires? I swing my torch in a short arc. A bat squeaks, caught in the thin light. *Clink clonk*. The beam drives back to the ribs which are quiet and still. Must be a spider hanging on its thread, I think. *Clink clonk*. The gossamer thread turns in the lisped draught spinning the small creature this way then that, like a toy in a child's hand. Yes, that one there, that spider twisting on her thread.

A photograph of my great great grandmother gazes sternly at me from the wall where she hangs. *Clink clonk*. What is it which holds up the dinosaur? What is it which holds him so far from the ground? I look for the spider's thread. Nothing. I look for the bones of James Brightside. Nothing. The beam searches out the wooden urn which contains the ashes of Mr Brown. Nothing. Then the skeleton of the horse.

The display cabinet boasting lumps of coal with black leaf and ammonite fossils patterning dark interiors; the miners' lamps. Snap boxes and boots. Rubber boots supplied by the rubber salesman, Mr Tsiblitz, which failed to protect the toes of every miner who ever wore them. A set of rubber teeth. Are they the ones bought by Sidall Junkin when Mr Tsiblitz first came to the village? Golf balls and enough knicker elastic to stretch four times around our terrace. A collection of miscellaneous curiosities. Nothing. *Clink clonk*. The air is cool. I direct the beam towards the iguanodon. His teeth flash like iron. The stone bones in the deep rib cage are moving gently up and down now, as if the animal is laughing at dead images still projecting on to the cinema screen. Charlie Chaplin. Buster Keaton. Stan Laurel. Oliver Hardy. The Marx Brothers accepting my Uncle Lancaster's sad Hollywood directions. I smile with the beast. We have developed the ability to laugh at ourselves and are grateful for it we two, for how else would we deal with our peculiar constructs? But I am angered too. And I am saddened. Saddened with the tragedy of the last one hundred years. Those with the ability rarely have the means, I think. I pick out in bright circles a rag-bag of curiosity but I know that elsewhere are hidden designs and ideas as bright as souls, and I ponder how those with the means rarely display the ability. I hurry with my torch, cutting a path away from the rag-bag of fact and freak which we have come to call working-class culture. Baggy-pants culture.

20

A village dawn

The village wakes to a silver dawn. The poplars down at Bottom
Boat are stiff in a cold mist jacketed about them. The wheel creaks
at the pit head shaking off ice. The drunks in the bean fields stir
in their dewy bedlam, taste their tongues and put them away wanting nothing to do with their mouths or their families for at least
an hour more. In some homes there is bread sizzling in the pan,
in others there is nothing. The sun looking like a bloody orange
breaks light over the poplars, touching frozen tops. The river
water rills icily over ten-spined sticklebacks. In the crimble the
elder is still wrapped in dark ice and the mist begins to lift a
revealing hem, an inch at a time. The grass turns green. A
meadow vole scuttles by. The tops of the poplars are now pink,
the weak sun warms the upper layers of icy air. The summit of
Hunger Hill is purple and treacherous. In the hedges the thorn is
in flower. The drunks stir again in the bean field. Wakened, they
remember yesterday as the day of Cheeky Archbold's funeral, put
their hands to their ears to drive out the noise of Bob's Sousaphone
and the sad wail of the vessel banked at Bottom Boat. They fall
barmy among the beans, breaking wind. A dog-rose blooms. The
mist is lifting faster now, the sun not quite so red. Soon there is a
band of fog, a Saturnine ring, undulating about the elder. A ray
falls through a hole in the sky tickling the still-cold trunk and the
tree in the crimble suddenly bursts from its ice house and is
aflame. At Aken Jugs the oaks take their cue and creak and
breathe. A cat climbs on a far limb of oak, its ginger stripes caught
now in opening warmth. The drunks stir a third time, dust themselves off and begin to make their unsteady ways home: to their
wives, to their breakfasts, some to the pit.

The drunks, staggering a ragged line, file by Billy o' the Terrus
End who winds his way up the path to the next village. Sacked by
Thwaite only a week since, here he is eagerly walking to his new
employment – not the brightest man in the world but a lucky one.

Billy walks the old path to the next village where he will start today as lather boy to Mr Beresford, the barber. It's mornings only, but it's better than nothing. Beresford, bald as a crown green bowl, is far too canny ever to allow Billy to cut hair or even to shave the clients – that would be too much like apprenticeship and would give Billy a learning of the trade. Beresford doesn't want competition.

It was rumoured that Beresford had brought the baldness upon himself, only because he then didn't have to consider the possibility of anyone else cutting hair – not even his own. In truth, because of a nervous disorder when young, all his ash blond curls had fallen out and had never grown back again. So, despite a surface brashness, Beresford is a sensitive soul who ponders his shop floor at the end of each day, not without a twist of bitterness. For the shop floor is deep in a useless commodity which nobody wants but which he himself would pay dearly to have grown in the natural way. It is this same wryness which prevents him being a stylist; one received a curt nod and a short back and sides at Beresford's, and nothing more.

Nonetheless, the barber always has a queue of likely beards to shave, and some braver heads of hair to deal with too. But most go to Beresford for a shave. Some of the colliers, those in regular work, go every day. They reckon that it's cheaper than buying blades. Beresford needs a lad like Billy – a none-too-bright lad, who can walk across the silver dawn and not question the elder flaming from the crimble. The barber needs just such a lather boy.

The two jobs of Billy o' the Terrus End

Beresford made his own lather out of large blocks of grey soap which he bought direct from the general wholesaler in Wakefield – it was cut with the same wire as he used to cut the wedges of cheese and Billy thought it gave the lather a slight whiff of sweaty feet but it didn't seem to deter the customers, who lined up a half-dozen at a time. Billy sat them on short wooden chairs which had been bought from Miss Fountaine at the schoolroom when Beresford discovered she had spares. He lined them up in front of a long mirror which ran horizontally along the length of the wall above the zinc sinks. Then he shrouded the men in white sheets. They looked as surplus furniture would look in the spare rooms at the big house.

As lather boy, Billy's main task was to mix the shaving cream in a mug which had been issued to celebrate the old Queen's Golden Jubilee – and to slap it on the thrusting chins of the clients who sat patiently in the school chairs. They stared at their redundant reflections whilst Billy painted their chins, using a brush made from badger bristles.

'What you doin' on that telephone thing?' The question came spookily through the wall and mirror at which they stared. 'I wanted a criminal lawyer for a son and I gets a bookie.' The second statement came through the same wall and mirror.

The barber's shop was next to the bookmaker's. The small red and white pole in the street outside marked the common wall separating the two dwellings. The bookmaker's name was Huddy Greenblatt and he lived in the back-to-back house with his parents. He was the first person around these parts to have a telephone. Nobody was supposed to know that Huddy was a bookmaker, gambling was quite illegal, but most people had an occasional flutter and everyone knew what went on at the house adjoining the barber's shop. Even the police knew that Huddy was the local bookie. Sometimes Billy could hear him speaking on the telephone, taking in his bets and laying them off too, I suppose. But it was his father who did the shouting. 'What you doin' with that telephone thing, boy?'

Huddy's father was Jewish. He had married one of the local girls and settled to live in the village years since. Huddy was brought up not knowing what religion he had. Nor did his father much care, but they were both seen in the church most Sundays. The old man knew he wanted his son to be a lawyer, though. He was always scolding Huddy, telling him what a lazy good-for-nothing son he was. He wanted to know why his son was forever receiving bets over the telephone from twopence-ha'penny shysters when he should be conversing with the bigwigs at Lincolns Inn, the finest criminal lawyer in the country. The customers at Beresford's often heard him berating his son through the adjoining wall and those passing in the street outside at such moments would have seen the red and white pole vibrating between the dwellings.

It was whilst the clients ghostly sat, hearing the disembodied voice of Huddy's father coming from their own soaped-up reflections in the long mirror above the zinc sinks, that Beresford made his entrance. He appeared like a stage magician from behind the black curtain which divided the shop from his living quarters and he gave the faces a quick scrape with his cut-throat razor. He held their upturned noses (Billy wondered if it was to hide the smell of the cheese) and gave each client six strokes of the blade. It was always six strokes. It was said that he was the most efficient razor man in the business. And just to practise his good judgement, at the end of each morning session, he shaved a balloon which had been lathered up by Billy. The lather boy even took to drawing a face on the balloon and sometimes going so far as to place a collier's cap on the top of it, but it never deterred the barber. His performance always earned him a little extra cash as the few clients who hung about to view the proceedings could be guaranteed to slip a wager of a penny or two on the possibility of the balloon going off with a bang.

'Does thee never bust 'em?' Billy once asked.

'Nivver,' said Beresford, wiping the soap, which had collected between thumb and forefinger, on his starched white apron. 'Now get on and sweep floor, lad. And no more damn fool questions.' Billy was never very smart, but it was in studying the barber's quick wipe

422

of the foam on to his apron that he learned balloons do not have noses. He wasn't quick but he made connections.

The none-too-bright Billy found himself a second job. Whilst most youngsters were hanging about doing nothing, unable to find employment at all, Billy got himself his second job. He spent his afternoons pedalling around the villages on a rusting tricycle which had ugly black tyres as thick as those on some motors. The contraption had a straw basket filled with ice-cream fitted to the handle bars.

The ice-cream was made by an Italian whom we called Mr Gelatini although we knew full well that his real name was Franco Luciano and that he had lived the whole of his life in Kippax. Gelatini sounded much better than Luciano; the name was more redolent of ice-cream, even to us non-linguists. In fact Gelatini – the name Gelatini not the man – positively smelled of ice-cream. The ice-cream however smelled of nothing. It was made mostly with water and although it was frozen solid when it left the factory by the time Billy had delivered it to you, it was hardly ice any more.

Billy made further connections following which it occurred to him that he should steal Beresford's shaving cream. Thereafter, at the finish of each morning session, when the balloon had been wiped clean and retied on string to the arm of the chair where it lived and when Beresford, having polished his head to a shine with a stiff brush and ointment of mercury had gone off for a pee, the lad filled a small cocoa tin with lather and slipped it into his jacket pocket. Beresford knew of the tin's existence and believed it to be the tin in which the lad kept the money from the ice-cream sales. Gelatini, who knew of it too, believed it to be the tin in which Billy kept the meagre tips he earned whilst working at the barber's shop. The fact that the tin was empty as the grave when rattled by both employers (an action they each undertook with heartless glee at unobserved moments) only served to convince them how idle Billy happened to be when at his other place of work.

After the morning sessions at Beresford's, Billy walked the few miles to the back of the coal yard in Kippax where the ice-cream was made. The first thing he always did was to take the tin from his jacket pocket and stow it in the basket. When it was time for his round Gelatini himself loaded the basket with a huge block of ice-cream. He was quite aware that each block was equivalent to sixty scoopfuls (Billy was given an iron implement with which to measure exactly the standard scoop) and therefore expected to receive payment for sixty ice-creams on Billy's return. The Italian always loaded him with sixty-six cornets to the block and Billy was never sure if that was Gelantini's way of saying, in his phoney Italian accent, 'Hey, have a one on me, kid,' or if it was merely the employer's recognition of the poor-quality biscuit from which the cornets were manufactured – an acknowledgement that a few might crumble in the process of preparation. It was usually with thoughts of his employer's meanness that Billy pedalled off on the old bike with the fat tyres, waved away by Gelatini as he logged the load in a red ledger book.

Billy stopped beneath the same copper beech tree each day. That's where he mixed the contents of the cocoa tin with Gelatini's ice-cream. It had the effect of increasing the volume of product in his basket. This extra volume was of course profit for Billy and one might think at this point in the tale that the fellow was a damned sight brighter than he allowed others to think.

Unfortunately, the process of dilution carried with it the disadvantage of turning Gelatini's watery ice into a nasty-tasting mush which caused the consumer to exhale endless streams of bitter bubbles. For a short time, it was possible when going about our part of West Yorkshire to know, merely by a casual glance at the sky, if Billy had paid a recent visit.

It was strange to see bubbles hanging unexpectedly in the air. Often there were no people, only bubbles in that hazy summer, observant as the orbs of interplanetary angels.

In the fields, the jugs and the crimbles which were farmed between pits, you would come across bubbles. They floated above the falls. They got caught in the trees. The tell-tale bubbles became markers, buoys displaced from a mysterious inland sea. It was recognition that one was about to stumble upon children enjoying an ice-cream. Boys and girls making conversation to the accompaniment of a stream of bubbles. Laughter brought the most. A laughing child was bound to produce more bubbles than a sullen one. For a time laughter rang in the coalfield.

Not surprisingly then, when a complaint came it wasn't from the children. They were quite happy blowing their bubbles at the sky whilst the larks hovered and the peewits twittered and they ran this way and that to float their blue kites. It was Jacky Jellis, our Bellman – he was the one who complained. Publicly too, right in the middle of the common. But that was the function of the Bellman. He was a sort of town crier with a bell and a grizzled beard like the pilot on the matchbox. He was there to tell us things. He got a lot of his thoughts from Grandma Dolly, the clairvoyant, which explains what we sometimes took to be his own spookiness – like how he knew about the Germans pinching Charlie Gill's leg even before Charlie knew of it himself. It also explains how he knew what was in my grandmother's letters to Henrietta even though she hadn't shown what was written or even told what was in the letters to anyone.

On this particular day, the day of complaint, Jacky Jellis stood on the common dressed in his fisherman's hat and cape and he watched the village kids running about, floating their blue kites and blowing streams of bubbles at the sun. He rang his bell. The stilled silence which followed was broken only by the sound of Squire Potterton's gun firing off at the other side of Hunger Hill and the occasional bark from his bounding gundogs.

The Bellman moaned on about the poor quality of Gelatini's Neapolitan ice-cream. The children continued to run into the light breeze with open mouths. Mildred and Alexander Smircz ran right up to and about him reciting their Polish nursery rhymes and tying him over with a string of bubbles all the colours of the rainbow. Alexander couldn't stop. The child was unable to open his mouth without it giving rise to an arc of coloured balls which swam like a migraine headache about his small head.

The Bellman's complaint hadn't originated with Grandma Dolly though. This wasn't the supernatural. Here he was talking from experience. He had always been partial to a bit of ice-cream. He knew about ice-cream and he knew that the Neapolitan was a songster with a cornet in his hand, not a sleek salesman with a pack of suds like the bloke in the newspaper advertisements. He spoke up passionately for a better-quality product, bubbles popping gone on him when they finally came to nothing on his old cap and cape, and the children's flashing blue kites lost themselves in the glare of the high sun.

Naturally, when Gelatini got to hear of Billy's deceit he took away the tricycle and threatened to sue the family at the terrace end. Not that he would have received a penny; the Terrus Ends were poor as church mice. Nonetheless, Billy lost his job. Then Beresford, learning of the theft of his shaving cream, gave Billy the push too, but the boy had no regrets. He walked brazenly from the barber's shop and straight into the bookie's. Billy got himself involved with Huddy Greenblatt. I think he just placed a few bets, probably trying to earn himself a bob or two to supplement his lost income, but he found that he was soon obliged to act as Huddy's runner.

22

A village dusk

Billy walks back from the next village. Late afternoon light skewers off the coal dust patterning the air with subdued gleamings. Ice begins to form in the many puddles about the pit head where a white goose waddles in search of food, the feathers on his underside caked in mud. He grunts at his reflection in one of the pools, the pale yellow clouds behind. He cracks the transparent skin of ice with his beak and gobbles up some water.

Billy heads for the pub where the men crowd in the noisy tap room, black and unwashed, downing three or four pints to put piss back into their aching bodies. They raise heads from their draughts boards and fall silent when he enters, suspicious of one who is no longer one of them. Billy has a fancy waistcoat and he wears a trilby hat like Huddy Greenblatt. He no longer looks like one of them. When he moves on, to the best room, the chatter starts up again.

The best room is where the customers are fewer – men who don't work in the pit. Some are strangers, travelling men who tell stories continuously. Billy buys a pint of ale and sits at the same rough table with the pit deputy, who rests his boots on the wrought iron cross support, picks his teeth with a matchstick and speaks to nobody. They both listen to the singing from the next room. Some of the men are already getting drunk. Billy peers from the window into the now darker yellow sky. The top of Hunger Hill has disappeared in a haze. The cats are beginning to creep across the common. The odd house has the electric switched on. He watches a blue van moving slowly past the big house. It takes the steep descent, down the hill towards the village.

23

The arrival of the Beanlanders

It was almost dark when the blue van trundled to a stop outside Arkwright's house in the middle of our terrace. The van had the word 'Uproot' painted in large white letters on the side. It was owned by Mr Uproot from Kippax. After Thwaite had made him redundant, Uproot contemplated his few assets and concluded his surname alone to be a thing of value. Having little else to do with it, he gave it to a company engaged in the haulage of family possessions.

Nobody had seen a vanful of furniture arrive in our village before. If you came or went it was usually with a hand-pulled cart, occasionally it was a horse-drawn cart and sometimes (as was the case with my own parents) it was with a suitcase and a bucket and spade. The idea of a whole van laden with belongings was so novel that when Billy spread the word, the pub emptied. All the colliers stood about on the common, pots of ale in hand, gawping at the two men who had been hired to bring Mrs Beanlander and her five children from the other side of Wakefield to live at her father's house. Her husband had been a scrap dealer. It was rumoured he had links with the Mafia. One morning he had got out of bed, washed and dressed and gone downstairs to the kitchen. He had pushed open the door, taken a lingering look at his wife and five children through a three-inch crack and then walked into the street. And he had continued to walk – apparently until he had disappeared. There had been sightings of him as he had covered the miles of road all that day and on the days which followed but he seems to have disappeared somewhere around Newark – and nobody ever knew, for sure, what had become of him. Arkwright never spoke of his son-in-law and Brenda Beanlander, who had the shape of a prop forward with a frizz of marmalade hair, became quite flustered if her husband's name was ever mentioned. It was assumed, however, that the man had been done away with in true Mafia style and that Brenda was fully aware of her husband's fate, for soon after moving to our terrace she had let my grandmother know of her intention to marry her boyfriend. The boyfriend's name was Clyde Wimpey: he was the police constable who manned the crossroads up by the big house. In fact the employment of PC Wimpey in the village was the main reason for Mrs Beanlander coming to live at her father's house. Brenda was herself employed at the police station in Castleford. She had been secretary for many years to Mr Sumner, an accountant whose task it was to save public funds. It was through her work that she had come to know Wimpey in the first place. They had been acquainted with one another for a long time but it was only since the disappearance of her husband that friendship had blossomed. She now felt the need to be close to her man, measured as much in leagues and yards as by extra beats fathomed in a butterfly heart.

Uproot's men climbed from the cab, two round fellows with balding heads. Their white shirt-sleeves were rolled to the elbows and each had a felt-backed brown mat tied with white tape about his beer gut over which was a blue and white striped butcher's apron. One of the men opened the doors at the back of the blue van. The five Beanlander children stepped into the evening light and one wondered for a second if Uproot had been clever enough to have given his name to a second company. This was not Uproot the haulage contractor, but perhaps Uproot the market gardener, I thought? For by the look of them the young Beanlanders might recently have been plucked from the ground. Walter, the eldest, if inverted would have the appearance of a mandrake. His hair stood from his head, forked in great roots. As he pushed by me I couldn't help but note the mixture of intelligence and mischief which danced in the boy's eyes. Them's brown almonds like his grandfather's, I thought. His siblings had hair not nearly so unruly but tending to grow in the same direction and they were all of them grubby as a stone of King Edward potatoes. The children silently followed their grandfather into the house. Their mother, the ugliest woman he ever saw, said Billy o' the Terrus End, brought up the rear.

'It's no wonder bugger disappeared,' Billy whispered rather unkindly into his glass of ale.

The Uproot men carried in the furniture, so much of it that we wondered if the little house was not about to burst its walls. There were huge *fauteuils* and mahogany armchairs of the George IV period, there were dining chairs with short backs which made the over-large seats look pregnant and there was a sufficient number of tables to have had a banquet. Secretaires and knee-hole desks. There was the biggest bed you ever saw (for the sleeping of the young Beanlanders) and one almost as big, presumably for the sleeping of the mother. There were cupboards and tallboys, sideboards and dressers and tea-chests stacked high with bric-à-brac.

When they had emptied the van the two men, puffed and sweaty, sat on the grass and had a smoke. We watched, somehow unable to dislocate this side show from the main event, as if the two men's idling was a part of the process of removal and included in the service for which presumably a fee had been paid. We gawped at the men smoking their Woodbine as if the fag was as rare as a William and Mary gilt-gesso and it too had never been seen before.

It wasn't until they had climbed back into the cab and trundled off up the hill past the big house that we split up and went about our business, most to return to the pub where the van, the men, Uproot, the Beanlanders and the furniture were discussed endlessly until Rube Hardwick, the landlord, chucked the stragglers into the night.

The topic most favoured for discussion (Brenda Beanlander, both her shape and her marmalade hair, ran it a close second) was the furniture and what was to be done with it. By the time Rube Hardwick had ejected the last man, the furniture had been brought into and out of the house a hundred times, rearranged every which way in all of the rooms (there were only four of them, two up and two down, and the scullery would have been full once Mrs Beanlander had squeezed herself to the sink) when it was concluded that the drinkers had earlier witnessed an optical illusion. Arkwright, besides being an inventor, was a bloody magician. It was an impossibility to have got all of that furniture into the house, they had concluded.

Of course, I could have told them how the trick had been performed, in rather simple fashion as it turned out, but coming the clever dick with Rube Hardwick's late drinkers would only have invited trouble so I left it for them to discover the truth for themselves.

When the van had gone off up the hill I returned to my grandfather's house and an hour later, on my way to the closets (out back through the scullery door), saw the furniture towering over the fence in Arkwright's garden. Uproot's men had been directed straight through the house with most of it.

The Beanlander children grinned at me from where they rested in a Louis-Philippe giltwood canapé balanced precariously on a stack of large oak tables. Later in the year when the snows came the kids were there still, eyes like those of animals peering from the dark of their shelter where they had inverted the seat. That winter, the carved cabriole legs terminating in scrolled feet kicked sedately at the sky.

24

Arkwright and his apprentice

When Uproot's blue van brought Walter Beanlander to our village he was fifteen years old. He had finished his schooling the summer before his arrival but because of Thwaite's policy of not employing the young he was unable to get work in the pit. So his mother sold off some of the furniture in Arkwright's back yard to a dealer in Harrogate and paid for her son to be sent to the technical college at Leeds where he studied engineering. He travelled to school and back on Fox's green bus, caught at the corner of Kippax main street.

At weekends he visited me in the museum. He had a keen mind and developed an interest in most of the things he saw. He particularly liked the dinosaur. One day I told him that if he was interested in prehistoric animals, he should come with me to the Mechanics Institute in the next village where in a few weeks' time there would be an evening devoted to the dinosaurs – we had been fortunate to get a world expert along to talk to the group, I said. He nodded his unusual head of hair, indicating his eagerness.

Walter had a notion that like his grandfather he should be an inventor. In the evenings Arkwright was happy to have Walter help him with his own crazy invention.

Arkwright, of course had been a collier until his eyes began to rotate. It was a rare condition he had, but he wasn't unique. The rotating eyeballs syndrome had visited other pitmen. It was usual that the oscillation of the eyeballs occurred laterally but in Arkwright's case (almost unheard of, said young Doctor Cartwright, peering over his half-glasses and looking ever more like the water boatman in the jar at the museum) they jumped in the vertical plane. At first his eyeballs disappeared for just a second or two and then came back again. That's how it was when I first saw the affliction, but gradually it took more time for the eyes to reappear. And as the length of time of each episode extended so too did the concern which crystallized out of it – the concern of those who must live with the fright of staring into white sockets, wondering if sight would ever return.

Each night when the boy arrived late, back from Leeds, his grandfather sat with him at the parlour table whilst Walter alone ate his tea – the rest of the family having been fed hours before. The old man questioned him on everything he had learned at the college that day and Arkwright gave whatever advice he could, adding to the gaps in the boy's knowledge and polishing his understanding of the world of machines. However, one night when Walter explained that he had received lectures on rheology at the college, the old man was dumbfounded.

'Whatever's that?' asked Arkwright.

'Tha'd better learn it for thasen, Grandad,' advised the boy, digging a crumpled printed pamphlet from his canvas satchel. 'Tha can read it, if tha wants to.'

After reading the pamphlet Arkwright fancied himself as a rheologist. His interest was turned to the flow and deformation of matter. He became interested in the setting properties of jellies and cements. In the spreadability of paints, jams and boot polishes, in the drying times of varnishes and the icing on cakes. He studied the flow of water in pipes of many diameters. The information supplied by one of Walter's teachers had provided the old man, fed up with the metaphysics of invisibility, with new direction at just the right moment. He was to use rheology – perhaps the first man in the world to do so – as a tool in the development of his inventions.

'Why, it's nobut a science of the scullery and the home,' my grandfather observed disappointedly when rheology was explained to him. He expected his science, both the practical and the metaphysical, to lift him away from this small disappointing world and dump him on the moon.

Arkwright's house, which was a few doors away from my grandfather's, was no different from anybody else's. A parlour, a back scullery. The outside toilets and the ash pits. Rickety stairs to a couple of bedrooms. They were all much the same. Mrs Beanlander slept in a bed in the back bedroom and the children slept in the huge bed at the front. Arkwright slept in a chair in the parlour.

The old man, in a conversation shouted over the fences one evening, informed my grandfather that he was working on his latest project – the development of a burglar-catcher.

'What's that got to do with rheology?' my grandfather wanted to know. He was holding a bouquet of dandelion heads weeded from his rose bed; he cast a hopeful glance at the stars.

'I grant thee, it's not immediately obvious,' Arkwright shouted back. 'If I say quick-drying cement, does that help?' He noted my grandfather's blank expression which only served to augment the pastiness of his face, the crippling decay which nobody talked about. 'No, I don't suppose it does,' he answered himself. 'Did thee ever get cramp in a calf muscle?' he tried asking after a moment's thought and when my grandfather had nodded enthusiastically he went on, 'Ay, well, it's like that, sithee. The muscle's perfectly all right one moment, then it's rigid as buggery. Tha can feel it on the turn, like the sudden souring of milk when some po-faced bugger looks on it. Clotted milk in the calf muscle. Are thee beginning to see it?' The stars whizzed and fizzled in the sky.

'Well, it's like that with some cements. Free-flowing and fluid one moment then summat 'appens to mek it set. It's all to do with energy. Put energy into it and it'll turn just like milk curdles or tha calf muscle cramps up. Put a stick in it and the cement'll set, just like that. Set bloody solid. Got it?

'Well, I mean it's ideal stuff for catchin' thieves. Put a tray of that stuff beneath tha windows at night and any bugger thinking of breaking in soon finds he's set rigid up to the ankles in a cement block. Sithee.'

'Ay. I see, Arkwright,' my grandfather told him. He looked critically at the yellow heads of the weeds he had been holding then in quite deliberate manner slung them on to the pile of rubbish at the bottom of the garden, as if, for the moment anyway, he had made the decision to part with his ignorance and follow Mr Arkwright into the new temple of home science.

The day he thought he had the cement preparation right for its intended purpose I heard Arkwright shout Walter down from the canapé where he and the other children still played. I was in our garden, flitting rose-bushes. I had heard Arkwright labouring for much of the afternoon, turning his cement mix with heavy snorts. Walter, hair rooting exotically and ever deeper into the air, climbed down from the den where he had been eyeing me over the fences with those brown almonds. He became lost in Arkwright's garden. (I keep referring to it as a garden but that isn't strictly true. I call the space at the back of Arkwright's house a garden simply because it occupies the equivalent area in our plot which we call a garden. We have roses and chrysanthemums and a neat bit of grass but Arkwright has all that furniture piled up to heaven and cement bags and bits of rusting machinery. It's surrounded by a wooden fence on three sides and there's a rotten gate down at the end which leads to the brick closets and the ash pits. It stinks over there and breeds flies. Perhaps we should call Arkwright's garden a compound. But come to think of it, Arkwright himself still refers to it as the garden.)

'What's up, Grandad?' asked Walter.

Arkwright, who had been doubled over, turning the muddy mixture with his shovel, pulled himself painfully upright. His white mane was splattered here and there with flecks of dried cement. 'I think it's ready, lad,' he told his grandson. 'I'll want thee to help me set the trap. Better tell one of tha brothers to give us a hand.' The old man treated Walter as if he was the foreman when they handled the inventions.

Walter put his fingers in his mouth and whistled up the pile of tables. I turned my head from the roses at the sudden shrill noise. My hands froze in the piston position, flitting the greenfly. I saw brother Tarty drop like the giant-killer to the ground. He too had been eyeing me from the canapé in the sky. Tarty Beanlander was almost the double of his brother except that he was about three inches shorter and two years his junior. In fact the Beanlanders, all looking alike, scaled down in years of two and inches of three right the way to baby Annie who lingered shortly at the end of the queue. Such a progression, moving constantly through juvenile time as it did, was an authentication of the constancy of Mr Beanlander's virile parental gametes; one in the eye for that monk Mendel and his variously heighted pea stalks, for it was certain that all the Beanlanders would find themselves, in adult life, all of a level.

My grandmother reckoned the two-year gaps between the children's births was sure confirmation of Mr Beanlander's involvement with the Mafia. 'Two years inside, followed by a week or two with poor Mrs Beanlander will be just about right for a bootlegging henchman of Al Capone,' she once told us though she had little idea what a bootlegger might be. When we pressed her she explained that he might be something like a footman – an Italian toady of the coal-owning classes, she speculated.

'Right, it's ready,' I heard the old man say again as I continued to flit greenfly, freezing them to the pink and red flowers.

'What does tha want us to do, Grandad?' asked Tarty.

'We'll fill it in two troughs. One for each side of house. We'll put one of them under scullery window just'ere and we'll tek t'other through the house and put it beneath the window at the front.' The boys looked blankly at him. 'Go get troughs. There's two at end of garden. Don't look so bloody gormless, there's two wooden troughs up there if tha go and look.' His eyes were dancing.

The boys went to the far railings and discovered two rotting wooden troughs stacked one inside the other by the gate. The wood was black with age and when moved the troughs shed dozens of damp splinters. They had at one time been used to hold the feed of Mr Doyle's pigs, before he had sent them off to the bacon factory and gone in for vegetables. The boys carried them one at a time to their grandfather and his mound of sloppy cement.

'Here, tha can shovel it in,' he told Walter, handing the boy the implement.

Walter began to fill one of the troughs with the cement mix and when it was about six inches deep Arkwright said, 'Right, tha can start filling t'other,' and Walter set to, filling the second trough.

'Don't be so bloody rough,' Arkwright scolded him. 'Don't go putting all that energy into it, lad, remember what tha was telled at technical school. We want it just at the point where it's on the turn, but where it'll not go till it's disturbed. Be gentle, son – be gentle, sithee.'

When the second trough was filled he instructed the boys to place it beneath the scullery window. Then he told them to go back and fetch the other trough. They carried it through the house and put it directly under the parlour window – the one which looked out on to the common.

25
Catching burglars

That night Arkwright left open the windows in both the scullery and the parlour, inviting the burglars in. He drew the curtains closed and went upstairs to the room in which the children slept and snored beneath a silken, black and white patchwork quilt. He sat on the bed and waited. He knew to the inch, exactly where to place himself without disturbing the children for they slept in their order of both age and height with Walter at one end and Annie at the other.

After several hours he heard the window in the room below being pushed upwards and he heard no more but for an occasional yelping like the complaint of a bitch who has lost her whelps. He also heard the owl hooting on the roof. The old man curled on his side in the legless silk triangle bequeathed by children who had been ordered like a set of snoring organ pipes, and he fell asleep, eyes dancing behind closed lids.

In the morning he was first downstairs as always and without drawing back the curtains he laid the parlour table. He fried the bread and singed the toast at the end of a long fork held on bent tines to the fire. He made strong tea and put out the jam in its stone pot, accompanied by the little silver-plated spoon. He called up the rickety stairs for his family to join him and when they were all seated around the parlour table, spreading raspberry jam and sipping tea, Mrs Beanlander said, 'By, Father, it's dark in here. Whyever haven't you drawn back the curtains?' and leaning across little Annie who sat with her back to the window she drew the curtains with her big hands. Billy o' the Terrus End stared in. The children stared back, the silence broken only when their mother shouted up, 'What is it, Billy? Is there something you were wanting?'

Billy didn't reply. His eyes were all aglaze.

'Do you think there's something the matter with him?' she asked her father who continued to ignore the neighbour whilst cutting portions of fried bread into soldiers for the younger children.

'Nowt much,' he said at last.

'Well, it looks like something's wrong to me,' she said with a questioning look around her brood and hoping for a confirmatory response. They continued to stare uncomprehendingly at the man at the window.

'It's his legs,' Arkwright eventually told her wheezily, still busy with the knife.

'What about his legs?'

'They're stuck.' He looked up from his task. 'Aren't they, Billy?' he shouted. 'Tha legs is stuck, aren't they?'

The bookie's runner still said nothing.

'Well, does he need some help?' asked Mrs Beanlander, herself beginning to feel quite helpless.

Arkwright put down the knife and fork. He went out through the street door. The children continued to stare at Billy with silent concern.

'It's a burglar. Copped red-handed,' they heard their grandfather say with a little whoop of laughter. He knelt to test the solidity of his cement mix. 'Copped red-handed, Billy,' he confirmed tapping the block with his hardened knuckles. The old man stood up unsteadily, ran his fingers through his mane of white hair and stuck his head in at the open window. 'Tha'd better go and get Clyde Wimpey, love,' he said and Mrs Beanlander, grateful for the opportunity to have unscheduled moments with her man, slipped on her coat and ran off to the crossroads. She brought Wimpey hurrying back. The policeman looked at the thief who had his feet set in concrete and he didn't know what to do.

'Can't understand why he should want to break into the house when there's all that expensive furniture out there to nick,' Wimpey commented.

'Daft. We invited him. Daft,' said Arkwright.

Wimpey was uncertain if the old man had offered an explanation for the thief's behaviour or passed comment on his own, perhaps foolish, question. As the remark had been made by his prospective father-in-law he decided it prudent not to inquire. Arkwright nodded at the policeman.

'Is he dangerous?' the constable asked.

'Shouldn't think so,' Arkwright answered. 'He's only bookie's runner.'

'Well, we'd better chip him out then.'

Walter was dispatched to get a hammer and chisel from the house and soon broke Billy free. The burglar promptly fell over, his legs as stiff as two pit props.

'I can't move my legs,' Billy complained.

'We'd better get him inside,' the policeman advised and they carried him stiffly, head first through to the scullery. Walter was sent off to find young Doctor Cartwright.

Then the old man's eyes went.

Mrs Beanlander leaned her father against the wall in the parlour out of harm's way for the children had burst suddenly into a commotion of curious activity.

Tarty, who didn't have his brother's intelligent eyes, persuaded his milling siblings that they should put Billy in the oven to warm his legs through. The younger ones brought buckets of coal from the garden and banked up the fire until it was roaring away and then, all lending a hand, the children dragged Billy by the arms to the chair by the range. He was filled with weak protestation when they slumped him in it. They bundled his legs into the oven. The constable was having reservations about what the children were up to, but imagined that he had a duty to remain at the side of Mrs Beanlander until her father had recovered his eyes. Billy's legs went in up to the knees.

When young Doctor Cartwright arrived at the house with Walter, they were horrified at the sight of Billy sitting in a chair with his legs in the oven. The doctor shouted 'Stop!' which had the startling effect of causing Arkwright's eyes to fall back into place, welcome to Wimpey as a couple of aniseed balls dropping from the dispenser at the funfair. On occasions, such is the power of the healer.

But not for all persons. Alas, the order was issued too late to save Billy. His feet had been baked black and he had lost the little toe from his right foot. Before Wimpey was able to arrest him, caught (literally) in the act of burglary, Billy spent a week in the workhouse infirmary, his feet smeared in foul unguent.

*

The policeman sat in the parlour writing his report. He was a middle-aged man with rosy cheeks and a little on the stoutish side. Mrs Beanlander fussed about him until it was time for her to go off to work. She put her arm about his shoulder and pecked at his cheek. His own arm searched half-way round the woman's plump waist and, deciding there was no end to the sailing of this particular world, the hand suddenly grabbed at the woman's floral belt catching the roll of surplus flesh too, as if it was a life saver. The little ones watched, dirty-faced, in sullen apprehension. Walter turned his chair from the table and contemplated the empty common beyond the window. He didn't care for Wimpey.

Eventually, the constable left. He was followed up the hill. He led the children past the shiny-leafed briony twining about the hawthorn in the hedgerows. He led them past the biting stonecrop and the pink pellitory, secreted in the stone walls at the big house. They watched him enter the blue police box which had recently been installed next to the white-armed direction sign. They saw him telephone his report through to the station at Castleford. He bent uncomfortably in the confined space, knocking his helmet askew, and took a large ledger from a cupboard which he placed on the chrome arm rest at the side of the telephone. He opened the ledger, turning the pages carefully until he came to the place where he wished to make an entry. He straightened his helmet, loosening the strap beneath his perspiring chin. He took a pencil from his breast pocket, wet the point – twizzling it between his lips – and wrote slowly in the ledger with a little black lead circling its unfolding pattern in his spittle. When he had made his entry he pulled his head back a fraction, cocked it to one side and checked the work with a satisfied look which was not meant to hide a hint of smugness. He looked very important, the children thought, as he stowed the ledger back into the cupboard under the arm rest. Walter again turned from him – this time to watch the thrushes rebuilding their nest on top of the direction sign. The nest had the appearance of a fashionable hat on the head of a tall woman.

26

Grandma Dolly Juvelah and her prediction

Grandma Dolly Juvelah was a fortune teller. She read the future from tea-leaves which muddied the bottoms of breakfast cups. We often saw her a few doors down, sitting like an old sea captain on the steps outside her house, smoking wet leaves in her stone pipe and surveying the lonely common as if it was a great ocean. Then she would spit great gobs of muck and tannin the ten feet or so to the idle grass. Her fleshy arms were always bare and the fat hanging from them wobbled when she took the pipe from her mouth to gob out and when she popped the pipe back in again. Most people thought her a charlatan and shunned her. My grandmother, who thought the smoking of the leaves a despicable habit, was, nonetheless, one of the few who gave the fortune teller her support.

My grandfather said she approved of Grandma Dolly and her crackpot ideas because she was an optimist.

Like all optimists, though, my grandmother was in constant need of having her optimism approved in case the shaky infrastructure of hope and myth might collapse to nothing, like a bag of dreams on the sleeper's wakening, and leave her with only the taste of disappointment on her early morning tongue. So she put it on show. She showed her optimism like some show tall sunflowers in vases on window-sills. Folk walking by our window would self-consciously glance in hoping to glimpse my grandmother, and when they had sight of her hopeful, smiling face and those brave square shoulders they would nod approvingly. Her pride at such moments made her every bit as upstanding as those tall sunflowers in vases at others' windows.

Yet she was perfectly aware of the future not happening as a wild flower bursts from bud. She knew that if there was to be a blossoming of predicted event then the gardener might have to prepare the ground. And, what is more, such an intervention had to be subtle, unlike my grandfather's overmulching which could easily drown the world in a fall of horseshit. (Yet she loved him nonetheless for his clumsiness and his lack of understanding and when he once said from his armchair, 'There's some in this 'ouse what holds a healthy load of pessimism agin tha pan o' good on the daft side of life's scales,' I saw her sit on his knees and kiss him in the way young people do, then they stood up together and he patted her large rump and led her uncertainly up the rickety stairs to their bedroom. I listened, shocked, all afternoon to the arthritic creaking from their bed. When they came down from the bedroom she got on with the tidying of our healthily balanced household, and he asked her to name the three kings crowned since they had last done such a thing.)

Nor was she alone in her support for the fortune teller. There were others in our village who felt exactly as she did and consulted Grandma Dolly regularly. Not too many but there were some.

When Grandma Dolly stared into Mrs Beanlander's Coalport teacup – the one with the gold rim which when she drank from it deposited gold dust all about her waxed lips – and predicted a future of disgrace for Clyde Wimpey, Brenda couldn't believe it. (There was no optimism expressed here.)

'Nowt'll come of tha relationship with that'un. He's a bad lot,' Grandma Dolly concluded unhappily, whilst prospecting the gold on her client's trembling mouth and accepting the few coppers which passed in payment for her peculiar service. Walter, however, who was present at the occasion was only too eager to believe. After all, as Grandma Dolly well knew, any woman's tragedy would more than likely turn out to be some man's triumph. That was the way of the world. And exactly as it was understood by my grandmother, Walter was aware too of prediction becoming reality only if the gardener lent a hand. Weeding had to be done. Weeding in, not weeding out.

27
Walter learns to use a telephone

He must weed himself into the life of the rosy-cheeked policeman. Walter had to befriend PC Wimpey, he knew that he could no longer afford to spurn him. The policeman soon found that he was accompanied everywhere by the lad and he welcomed it, assuming his headlong rush to friendship to be a part of the youth's growing pains. One day at the crossroads, with the policeman about to enter his box, Walter asked:

'Can I come into t'box with thee?'

'Ay, come on. I shouldn't allow it but tha can come and see.'

The policeman opened the door with a key on a copper chain which was attached to the belt about his spreading gut.

'Can I see all tha keys?' Walter asked.

'Ay. But don't go tekin 'em off the chain,' the policeman warned as they squeezed into the box together. The constable uncoupled the chain from his trousers and handed Walter the bunch of keys.

'What's that?' Walter asked, nodding towards the ledger which Wimpey had just lifted on to the chrome arm rest at the side of the telephone.

'It's me book. Me book for reporting me telephone conversations.'

'Who does tha telephone, PC Wimpey?' the lad asked.

'Station, lad. I have to telephone station.'

'Will tha do it now?'

'Ay.'

'Go on then. Let's see thee. I never saw a telephone afore.'

'Nowt to it, lad,' the policeman bragged breezily. 'Just watch this.' He unhooked the earpiece from its cradle with thumb and two fingers and held it to his ear. As the constable whistled softly to himself Walter watched the hot breath curling into the mouthpiece.

'What's tha doin?' Walter asked, fingering the keys which he had been given and seeing the policeman tap at the cradle.

'I'm getting to speak with the operator, lad.'

'What for?'

'To connect us up to the police station, lad.'

'Well, how does the operator know how to connect thee to police station and not to anywhere else?'

'By, tha's askin' a lot of questions.'

'Well, how? How does the operator know?' Walter insisted.

'Because there's a number, that's how. Each telephone has its own number.'

'Each one has its own number, does it?'

'Ay.'

Walter suddenly heard the female operator's squeaky voice, though he was unable to hear what she was saying.

'Ay, it's PC Wimpey. Can tha connect me with 222, love?'

'Is that number of police station at Castleford?' Walter asked.

The policeman nodded as he lolled on the side of the box, the earpiece still between thumb and two fingers and pressed close to the side of his head. He patiently waited for his connection. Walter then heard a man's voice talking and as Wimpey spoke, he made a note of his conversation in the ledger. Walter was surprised to see that the policeman wrote everything down in shaky capital letters. The policeman continued to speak and the boy fiddled with the keys. Unseen, he took a moulding of the key which had opened the police box, pressing it on to a lump of Plasticine which he had hidden in his trouser pocket.

28

The Mechanics Institute

The Mechanics Institute is in the next village. It's a single-storey shed of stick and stone built on to the chapel and it has a corrugated tin roof. The rain-water, in tiny rivulets flows in the folds of tin and pools in the guttering from where it forever drips through a bit of rusty piping into a wooden barrel. Tadpoles live in the barrel, moss grows on its side. A green slime mould crawls up the stone wall where the water drips.

The next village is not unlike our village except that it has the church. The church was built there because the people wanted it. At the time of its building nobody in our village wanted a church; they were not then a God-fearing lot. The next village is built on a hill whereas our village is in the valley. That's the only other difference.

Sitting in the schoolroom at the Mechanics Institute one can look out from the window on to the cemetery. The headstones slope away from you, down the hill towards our village. There are discs of white lichen eating on the ancient sandstone which in time change the names of the dead who are buried there. The day is bright - there is rain in the air but the day is bright. I sit with Walter Beanlander at the back of the room, come to hear a lecture about the dinosaurs. This is the first time that Walter has attended such a meeting.

It's a small gathering - few of the chairs are occupied. In their neat rows, high-backed, they stiffly face the front. There's Arkwright and Whinny. I nod to Archie Jellis, now doctoring in Wakefield, who sits on a chair in the front row. His legs are crossed, one knee lazily slung over the other, his free foot wags. I have not seen Archie for years, not since he gave me his old dog Bruno who lived out his last days at my grandfather's house and who swallowed my duck. Archie smiles at me.

'What's tha doin' over these parts, Archie?' I ask across the rows of empty chairs.

445

'Looking for a wife, lad,' he answers. 'London lasses . . .' he adds and pulls a face, then he turns away, uncrosses and recrosses legs in their fancy tweed trousers and settles to read his newspaper, flapping it open noisily.

There are a few others, faces I know but to which I cannot put a name. And, yes, somewhat surprisingly, sitting alone, directly in front of me, wrapped in a large overcoat and with a brown trilby on his head, is Huddy Greenblatt. I was unsure at first if it was Huddy but Walter, who can see the man's profile very clearly, suddenly asks him for his telephone number. As he slowly recites the numbers I recognize that it's Huddy who is sitting there in the stiff-backed chair. The boy stands and writes on the back of a tram ticket with the blunt tip of a pencil. He does this whilst leaning over the vacant chair at Huddy's side, his hot breath blowing in the bookie's face.

'I didn't know you was interested in natural history?' I say to the back of Huddy's head.

'I'm not,' he answers, leaning back in his chair, his head turned slightly yet still facing towards the front. He watches the speaker enter the room. He claps lightly along with the rest of us whilst the speaker takes up a position at the wooden lectern, polished up like my grandmother's table. The newcomer is an old man with a long grey beard. He is tall and dressed in black. I hear Walter gasp at my side, I imagine because of the strange appearance of the speaker. He is so very tall and so very thin - I imagine Walter to be gasping because of this.

'It's Skymuffin Stiltwalker,' the boy says. He doesn't mean for others to hear him but he has said the words aloud. I give him a curious look. The audience of naturalists turns to stare at him as if he had just had the audacity to name a species. He hurriedly sits up straight and concentrates his eyes on the numbers he has just written at the back of the tram ticket. It is a blue halfpenny fare. He goes over one or two of the digits with the blunt pencil making the numbers unreadable. He tries to ignore the cold stares of the others. He listens for the ruffling of coats which will indicate to him that people have turned away their eyes and he hears also the light scraping of the chair legs on the wooden floor. They raise dust into the air. You can taste it.

'Hope you're not going to be taking up the horses,' I whisper to the boy, wishing to make him feel more at ease.

Walter looks at me and smiles. 'It's Skymuffin Stiltwalker,' he whispers back excitedly. I haven't the faintest idea what he is talking about unless it's the name of a horse.

'It's not a horse,' Huddy whispers, it seems telepathically, from around the corner of his hat. Then Walter pulls a comic from down the front of his trousers and hands it to me, indicating the front page with his finger. I scan the story of Skymuffin Stiltwalker, the space adventurer with stick-like legs.

A man in a waistcoat and wearing gold wire-framed spectacles gets up from his chair in the centre of the front row. He tells us how honoured we should be to have such a distinguished guest speak to us today. I can hear Archie turning the pages of his newspaper and the man stops talking for a moment to glare at the doctor. I hand the comic back to Walter and stare from the window at the head-stones. Someone has left a bunch of violets by a freshly dug grave, so fresh it has not yet received a headstone. The plot is on the far side of the low church wall, next to Cheeky Archbold's grave. A black goat which has been munching the yellow rattle which grows all about the cemetery crunches into the violets. I screw my eyes at the pall of smoke which hangs over our village a mile or two below. The mere sight of the smoke stings my eyes, causing a tear to be squeezed. *'The speaker knows things about dinosaurs which no other man has known. He has spent years in the Gobi desert where he found a nest of Protoceratops eggs.'* I watch the goat return to the yellow rattle, tearing it from the earth. I wonder about the yellow rattle. It binds under the grass. It has suckers which bind to the roots of grass. I wonder about the bodies here in the cemetery. Do they know about the yellow rattle? *'I leave you in the hands of Mr Tsiblitz,'* says the man with the gold wire-framed spectacles.

29

How Mr Tsiblitz and Great-Aunt Henrietta
came from Berlin

Elyahou Tsiblitz, Transylvanian Jew, manufacturer of rubber goods, great-uncle by marriage, anarchist, business partner to Ludwig Wittgenstein the Cambridge philosopher, sometime friend to the Sultan of Turkey from whom he learned to speak English, and to the Jam Sahib of Nawangar for whom he had built the famous motor car which eventually killed Mr Brown, had in recent years become an expert on dinosaur remains. In the years before the Great War he had been a frequent visitor to our village, bringing with him the wonders of a new materials technology. He brought cycle tyres and golf balls, waterproofs and ladies' girdles, spare anatomical parts including sets of rubber teeth, and he was the first man to introduce the rubber sheath into our village, of which Mr Doyle's is the only surviving example. But he was best remembered for his flying suits.

The flying suit was a magical concept. He dressed the children in smelly rubber outfits which when inflated took on the appearance of some or other beast. Thus attired the children would roll about the common. But the suits which were fashioned in the guise of birds did more than roll – they soared away. Literally, dressed as an overfed sparrow or some other flying creature, a child might fly. My Uncle Lancaster, the film maker, in the costume of a bee was on several occasions seen to float to the sky and tearfully hang about the village.

Mr Tsiblitz eventually was to perfect the flying suit at his factory in Berlin. On one occasion, retold so often that it had passed into legend, he had dozens of villagers floating about at the same time – children and adults alike. They roamed the sky like planets and Uncle Lancaster filmed the whole thing. Unfortunately, the film was lost along with that other important piece of cinematographic history, the first talking picture. They went down with his baggage when the liner taking him to America sank as it approached Ellis

Island. Nobody was drowned, and nobody got their luggage back. It's been twelve or thirteen years now and is still the subject of an insurance claim.

After the Great War Mr Tsiblitz returned to Berlin where he continued to turn out tyres every bit as famous as those of Mr Dunlop and Mr Goodyear. He also manufactured a range of general rubber goods and we received many products drawn from the man's extraordinary imagination during the inter-war years – rubber furniture, rubber clothing, cot sheets and even rubber women having holes in the right places. They were all sent for our sampling.

It was in 1936, at about the time I happened across Aunt (you don't mind if I call her just plain aunt, do you?) Henrietta's manuscripts, that she and Mr Tsiblitz decided upon leaving Germany. He had by then been replaced at the factory in Berlin. The state had taken over the running of the plant and my uncle (let us give him the title of one who is married to an aunt) had been set to work in the German museums; it was apparently only his usefulness as an expert on Protoceratops eggs which prevented the administration packing him off to a concentration camp. (Hitler had some crazy idea that Protoceratops eggs were in no way related to the dinosaurs but were the rotted eggs of Indian myth – the *hiranyagarbha* – and might be turned back to gold in an alembic which had been built to his instruction in the Chemistry School at the University of Heidelberg.)

Henrietta suffered much abuse from the neighbours and hardly dared leave her home. If the Nazis had ever discovered that Tsiblitz had her name stamped on his bottom many times in indelible ink (something which I was to learn from the reading of her manuscript, rather curiously, at the very moment their neighbour Dora Koch was directing opera glasses to my relatives' bedroom window) God knows what would have become of them.

Perhaps Miss Koch, an elderly spinster with a calcifying liver, had on that occasion spied what she shouldn't and had imparted such information to the secret police, for the next day they called to the house and confiscated my uncle's identity papers. Mr Tsiblitz was however convinced of her treachery, for when he was closing the door quietly behind the departing policemen, he happened to catch a glimpse of his neighbour rooted in her room, spyglasses raised, and beaming like a lighthouse. 'Ach, it is so,' he reported to my aunt on returning to the living-room, 'Miss Koch, the neighbour with the terrible calcifications, I have just seen her – sadly the poor woman has already turned to stone.' They had to act quickly.

As I read and re-read Henrietta's manuscripts and learned the amazing history of my family (even the account of my own birth when apparently wet and squawky I tumbled from my mother's womb), she and her husband were already journeying to the airport. There, they purchased tickets for the flight to Hamburg. Arms linked as old lovers they casually strolled over the damp tarmac. Rain was spitting from a lead sky. He held a valise in his free hand – he allowed it to swing back and forth at the end of his lengthy arm. The engines coughed once as they approached the aeroplane and they felt the draught when the propellors slowly began their silvery rotation. My aunt wore a felt hat. It had a black net veil on which odd sequins had been sewn and which sparkled when caught in the light – it gave her an air of mystery like the *femme fatale* in the American pictures which my Uncle Lancaster was directing in Hollywood at about this time.

The plane's three propellers turned faster as they boarded. With bony fingers Mr Tsiblitz gently nudged my aunt up the steps ahead of him. They were the first passengers to board and he asked the stewardess who greeted them if they could sit at the front. She smiled and showed them to the two seats immediately behind the cockpit which was curtained off from the cabin. She sat by the window, he in the aisle seat. He hugged the valise between his knees.

As the other passengers boarded, they each gave my aunt and uncle a firm but polite nod and some mumbled '*Heil Hitler*' as they pushed past, laden with their heavy baggage. My uncle nodded courteously back but said nothing. A young man dressed in the Nazi uniform and with a swastika wrapped about the upper arm of his brown shirt raised his hand in salute. '*Heil Hitler*,' he said demonstratively as he stood before my relatives. Mr Tsiblitz and my aunt remained silent, looking upon the terminal building which they could see swimming through the cabin window. It was raining heavily now and Mr Tsiblitz saw the droplets whisked by the

450

rotating propellers, streaking at the glass. The young man gave them a stony stare. He was a small man with a short scar on the temple above his left eye, he had a Hitler-style moustache pinching like a little crab at the base of his nose. My aunt from behind her black veil turned her attention to him. He was dark, not at all like an Aryan, and he was spotted where the occasional sequin fell upon his face. She struck up conversation in English with Mr Tsiblitz deliberately to annoy the young man.

'Heil Hitler,' he said again, raising his hand and flexing back his wrist in a double-jointed manner. The gentleman standing immediately behind him was eagerly peering over the young man's shoulder. He was anxious to find himself a seat and attempted to respond in similar vein but dropped the parcels he had been carrying. This caused a blockage as they both scrambled around on their knees in the aisle, collecting up the packages and shouting 'Heil Hitler' whenever they came close to butting heads. They were like cockroaches, Tsiblitz thought – cockroaches scuttering, feeling with their antennae in a nervous sort of way and identifying only by accident. They made the noise too of the insects rustling shinily on themselves, smooth, clean, living on dirt; they had elytra black and shiny, polished to a perfection yet unable to perform their design purpose – unable to get their lives to soar. He watched the shiny black backs of chitin rustling Heil Hitler as they scuttered about retrieving dropped parcels and he laughed to himself. National Socialism despite its slickness would never be able to fly, he thought. He laughed again and shook his head. Why was it that governments never sought the opinion of the inventor, or even the biologist, when tinkering with their social engineering? My aunt gave his arm an affectionate squeeze.

Others behind the young man were now pushing aboard eager to take up their seats. The gentleman who had now retrieved his parcels was trying to squeeze by and find a seat of his own. Eventually the young man had to give way and he passed menacingly by my uncle and took a seat a couple of rows behind him. After a few minutes the full complement of sixteen passengers had boarded and the door was closed.

The aeroplane taxied along the runway and my aunt watched the lit-up terminal swim by before the aeroplane rose slowly and shakily into the sky which through the veil she saw to be shining with black stars. After gaining a little more height, the plane banked and turned, then set its heavy nose for Hamburg and rattled off into the rain.

The young man in the Nazi uniform rose from his seat, brushed roughly past Mr Tsiblitz and gave my aunt's veil another stony stare before going into the toilet. He locked the door with an authoritative click. Mr Tsiblitz leaned his long body into the aisle, glanced idly over his shoulder and noted how most of the passengers were quietly reading; how a few of them had already nodded off to sleep. He turned his face to the black curtain ahead of him and released the strong grip which his knees had exerted on the sides of the valise. He slid it on to his lap. He turned the case around so that the locks were towards himself and he opened the case with two clicks loud enough to awaken the sleepers. They had even more authority than the one which had just closed the toilet door.

Terror bound the stewardess immobile. She was standing between Mr Tsiblitz and the curtained-off cockpit from which position she had a view of the whole cabin. She watched as the cabin space started to fill with the soft plastic form of a green alligator. It rapidly expanded displaying a yellow underside, its awful eyes needlessly made to look more friendly by the incorporation of black lashes as long as any displayed by the cinema stars. The rubber alligator, which continued to hiss as it grew from the valise in my uncle's lap, eventually filled most of the cabin.

The stewardess, who was now pressed up to the separating curtain by the tip of the alligator's nose but who had also recovered sufficiently from her initial shock to know that the thing had ceased its growing, asked:

'Is there something wrong, sir?' and Mr Tsiblitz, taking a pin from my aunt's hat answered:

'If you don't take us to England, I shall blow up the plane.'

He held the pin point close to the ballooning alligator. She saw that the pin had a large black bobble on the end and how the point almost touched the contraption which had miraculously found its way into the aeroplane. She noted how taut the skin was stretched.

'Just a moment sir,' she said with a courtesy not quite appropriate to the situation, stooped beneath the head of the rubber animal and found her way under the separating curtain and into the cockpit with the pilot.

Meanwhile the young Nazi had completed his ablutions and he clicked back the lock of the toilet door. He opened it to be faced by a solid wall of green.

'What is this?' he asked.

'Don't do anything stupid.' An elderly man's infirm voice wailed up from behind my aunt. 'He will blow up the plane.'

'Rubbish,' shouted the unseen Nazi. 'Remove this immediately. Do you hear?'

My uncle allowed the balloon to grow a little bigger, hemming the man more firmly into the toilet area.

The separating curtain was drawn back from behind the cockpit, the metal hooks jangling on the brass rail, and the pilot peered from around the front end of the alligator. He wore a flying cap and goggles.

'What's going on?' he asked my uncle.

'I wish you to take my wife and me to England.'

'Well, you may wish that, my friend, but I am afraid it's impossible,' he said jovially.

'Impossible? Why?'

'Because we have insufficient fuel. That's why.'

'Then you will take us over the Dutch border into Holland,' Mr Tsiblitz instructed.

'And if I don't?'

'Then I shall simply blow up the plane,' and my uncle showed the pilot the hat-pin with the large black bobble on the end.

'Is that possible?' my uncle heard the pilot asking the navigator, who was sitting unseen behind the curtain.

'Search me,' the navigator responded.

'He is bluffing,' came a voice from the toilet.

'No, he's not,' the elderly infirm voice piped up from behind.

The pilot ran his fingers along the alligator's snout. 'What is this stuff, anyway?' he asked.

'It's a new material,' Mr Tsiblitz replied. 'One prick and the whole thing will explode. In this confined space it will probably blow out all of your windows and might well take off a head or two. You will probably lose most of your passengers before reaching the ground.'

The toilet door closed with a bang shaking the green and yellow alligator as if it was a giant jelly at a Christmas party.

'Including yourself and your wife?' the pilot reminded him.

'Of course. We are prepared for that eventuality. I am seventy-eight years of age. My wife and I are quite prepared to go wherever you decide to take us, be it heaven or Holland.' He gestured out of the window pointing out both places, up and down a violent sky.

'What do you think?' the pilot was heard to consult with the navigator once more.

'Search me,' the unseen navigator said again.

'Take them. Take them,' two or three voices shouted. 'They will kill us, they will kill us all.'

'OK,' the pilot said, 'I'll take you across the border.' Some of the passengers were heard to cheer.

'Good. You do that and everyone will be quite safe. You have my promise.' Tsiblitz showed the pilot the pin once more.

The toilet door opened again. 'He is lying. If he bursts this thing, there will just be a small explosion like a balloon bursting. That's all,' the Nazi was heard to say from behind the wall of green. 'Look, I'll burst it myself.'

'No, no,' shouted several of the passengers all of a panic. 'Let them go. Good riddance. Let the pilot take them to Holland.'

My uncle let the alligator grow a little more and the hissing set in a new silence among the frightened passengers. The plane banked and changed course, throwing the Nazi back on to the toilet seat.

'When are you going to come out of there, anyway?' a young woman asked. 'There are others who wish to use the toilet, you know.'

'Fräulein, I wish that I could get out of here,' replied the man, trying to struggle up from the toilet.

'Can't you climb underneath?' the lady responded.

The Nazi tried to scramble out by going under the alligator but Mr Tsiblitz caused his contraption to let out a warning hiss and the young man withdrew. 'The Fatherland will destroy you for this,' he let my uncle know when he had finally scrambled back to his feet.

'Fatherland!' my uncle exclaimed. 'What do you know of fathers, you in your little nappy with a wet willy? What do you know of land? Tramp tramp. Is that what your land is for? To put on your big boots and go tramp tramp? Is that all you can think of doing with your land, you poor wretch? Fatherland? Little boys with wet willies going tramp tramp.' He looked at his wife's veiled face and laughed. She noticed that his old hands shook a little and she stilled them with her fingertips then they settled into their seats, he with his hat-pin poised.

The young man retreated back into the toilet and locked the door again. The aeroplane droned and rattled towards the Dutch border and the passengers fell into hushed silence. Soon, the curtain was drawn back again and the stewardess peered from around the front of the alligator's nose.

'We shall be crossing the Dutch border in about five minutes,' she said. 'Please prepare for your descent.'

The toilet door clicked open again. The young Nazi spoke unseen. 'You are fools. You give into this Jew's threats. It is a bluff, I tell you. This child's toy cannot harm us.'

'Don't do anything stupid,' the old man sitting behind my aunt called out.

'Weaklings. The Fatherland will be rid of you, all of you. And the crew, I tell you. When we are back in Berlin, I shall make a complaint myself. This jellyfish of a pilot will never fly again. *Heil Hitler.*' And with his salutation he sank his crazed teeth into my uncle's plastic alligator.

The balloon disappeared in a deafening roar. The explosion was blinding. The wind whipped through the cabin as the windows shattered. The passengers screamed, holding tight to their seats. The pilot was unable to hold the aeroplane on a straight course for long and the wings dipped madly one way and then the other. Eventually the plane rolled right over, and over again flinging everyone about the cabin in frightful turmoil.

At the initial explosion the young Nazi, a large piece of green rubber clenched between his teeth, was blown backwards into the toilet. He landed head first in the bowl, his legs kicking hopelessly as new pressures sucked his body further into the plumbing.

Although not at a great height, nor travelling now at great speed, the terrified passengers clutched at anything they could to save themselves from toppling out of the craft. Gradually the pilot was able to bring the plane under control and the bruised and dazed people found ways back to their seats. The legs of the Nazi had given up their obscene struggle with the plumbing; the body, quite upright, was plonked like a plant in a pot. The toilet door moved back and forth, opening and closing to the now gentle swaying of the aircraft. The breeze blew softly on the faces of the passengers. The craft was hardly moving. After a few moments of this blessed quiet, my aunt and uncle were able to clamber through a window, out on to the wing of the aeroplane. They perched unsteadily on their hands and knees looking in. Then they disrobed and to relieved cheers, they crawled off into the sky.

The suits which they were wearing beneath their street clothes inflated with a magical inrush of air and a deep crimson turkey sporting a black veiled hat and a blue pterodactyl, ancient as the Jurassic, floated in heaven's realm above the mother earth. A whole rounded birth away in our village I was re-reading my aunt's account of how James Brightside came to dig the dinosaur from the disused pit.

30

Huddy Greenblatt's need for prayer

I sat spellbound as Elyahou Tsiblitz told of his adventures with the dinosaurs. He began his talk by telling us how useful dinosaur skeletons are for filling large spaces in empty museums. It was meant as a joke; he was flattering me with humour before my companions. They turned to stare, and then they smiled. The speaker stopped and smiled too, then he asked if we had ever thought to question their world? What were things like when they were young? How was the world when they were young?

Had we ever stopped to consider their behaviour? Or how they looked and what it was which they lived on? He went on to reconstruct a world from a few old bones which he pulled from a Gladstone bag. From his knowledge of the musculature of the crocodile and of the birds he was able to guess at the size and shape of the dinosaur's muscles using the few bones he had produced as a guide. He had models, brought like a magician brings large objects from a bag too small to house them. He drew chalk pictures squeakily on the blackboard. From fossils found with the bones he had reconstructed the flora of the time. He knew the shape and the height of trees and bushes. He knew of the dinosaur diseases – of their arthritis, their rheumatism. He gave us another world to consider. He told us that the dinosaurs were not stupid. Not as daft as we would like to believe such great lumbering beasts might be. He asked us to consider brain/body size ratios and compare them with the brain/body size ratios of other animals. He concluded that the dinosaurs will have been about as intelligent as the elephant – and as hairless. He could not speculate on how or why they had died out. Their extinction though was what one might have expected.

'Is that not the lot of all species?' he asked.

They had lumbered around for a hundred million years. 'Shouldn't we see that as a sign of their intelligence?' he asked. 'Do you think that *Homo sapiens* will manage a hundred million years?'

he concluded and then he sat in the chair which was placed at the side of the lectern.

As we clapped politely the man in the waistcoat, wearing the gold wire-framed spectacles, stood and thanked the speaker. Then he asked if we had any questions to put to our guest. Huddy Greenblatt said that he had a question for Mr Tsiblitz and stumbled uncomfortably to his feet.

'Can you say the Kaddish, Mr Tsiblitz?' he asked.

'The what?' asked the man in the waistcoat.

'It's all right,' Tsiblitz said, 'I know the Kaddish. It's the Jewish prayer for peace to be said by those mourning the dead.'

'Yes,' said Huddy. 'Can you say it?'

'Please?' said the man in the waistcoat quite reasonably and directing his plea to everyone in the room. 'Can we please limit our questioning to the relevance of the talk? Do you have a question about the dinosaurs?' he asked Huddy.

'No,' Huddy answered and he sat down.

'Why do you ask?' Tsiblitz inquired, staring through the man in the waistcoat.

'Please?' the man appealed again as he turned to the speaker. He pushed the spectacles more firmly on to his face. Huddy stumbled to his feet again.

'My father is out there,' he nodded through the window. 'We buried him yesterday. He has scented violets on his grave. Nobody has said the Kaddish.'

'Not any more he hasn't. The violets went,' I muttered to Walter Beanlander.

'Was your father a Jew?' Tsiblitz asked.

'Yes.'

'Please,' said the man in the waistcoat. It was less of an appeal than it had been before. I watched the goat pulling more of the yellow rattle from the grass around the freshly dug plot. The man in the waistcoat sat down.

'He was not a religious man,' Huddy continued, still on his feet, 'but he paid into the local burial club. He went to the chapel more often than he went to the synagogue. He's buried out there in the unconsecrated ground. Someone should say the Kaddish for him, you know. That's only right.'

'And you can't say the Kaddish?' Tsiblitz asked.

'No, sir.'

'You cannot read Hebrew?'

'No, sir.'

Tsiblitz was silent for a time. The others present were bemused by his silence and by the nature of Huddy's request.

'I shall make a pact with you,' the old man said eventually. 'I shall say the Kaddish for your father if you will say the Kaddish for me.'

'But I told you, I am unable to read the Hebrew.'

'Then you will have to learn,' Tsiblitz said quietly.

'That seems fair enough,' said old Arkwright, turning to look at the bookie.

'When my turn comes, you will reciprocate,' Tsiblitz repeated more forcefully. 'Who else will say the prayer for me?' He looked about the room searching for takers. Feet shuffled uncomfortably.

'It all seems very fair, does this,' Whinny commented.

'Ay. It's right enough, is that,' said another.

'But what about the dinosaurs?' pleaded the man in the waistcoat.

'Bugger bloody dinosaurs,' came a response from the floor.

We all followed Huddy from the room. We went in single file past the tub where the tadpoles swam and we heard the rain dripping into the water. The slime mould stank. We congregated, forming a small circle about the grave of Huddy's father. Mr Tsiblitz borrowed Whinny's cap and covered his head. We listened to him reciting in Hebrew the Jewish prayer for the peace of the dead man's soul whilst the black goat munched at the yellow rattle in the bright bright air.

Receive we beseech thee in thy great loving kindness the soul of Huddy's father who hath been gathered unto his people. Have mercy upon him. Shelter his soul in the shadow of thy wings. The sun was shining, the wind rippled Arkwright's hair. *How great is thy goodness? The sun shall no more go down.* I watched the sun dappling the face of the inventor who stood beside me. His eyes hovered for a moment, wavering on the freshly dug mound.

'Hold on, Mr Arkwright,' I whispered.

'Ay, I'm holdin',' he smiled. 'I'm holdin'.'

May there be abundant peace from heaven and life for us and for all Israel. Amen.

'Amen,' we all said instinctively and whilst Huddy shook Mr Tsiblitz by the hand we washed our own hands, in the time-honoured way, in the forever dripping water at the rain barrel. Then we all trooped back to the Mechanics Institute to ask our questions about the dinosaurs. I thought I heard laughter as if coming from distant rooms and wondered about the yellow rattle.

31

Considering Mr Tsiblitz's talk

It confounded me that I had been chosen to play a major role in the reconstruction of the skeleton. I had no grasp of the purpose.

'Why us, Mr Brown? Why us?' I asked of the red cedarwood urn. There was no reply.

I thought about the talk which Elyahou Tsiblitz had given at the Mechanics Institute. I moved my chair about the museum viewing the skeleton from different angles, hoping it might inspire some new insight. I sat hidden behind the cabinet which houses the fossils and studied the bones through the glass. I watched him reflected in the frame of Whinny's lepidoptera – in the still of tortoiseshell and fritillary. I sat where the cinema screen had been and faced him square on. He charged but failed to move. Once or twice I thought he laughed. I moved the chair about him, stopping to sit at many loci, until I had completed the circle; at each pause studying monumental pre-history and quite unable to come to any conclusion as to its purpose. I began to know every bone, every piece of wire. I climbed the high ladders brought from the pit and stared down upon his silent spine. I took a brush and cleaned the bat crap from the top of the skull and thought how the occasional spatter there might account for the noise which sounded like the drip into a zinc bucket. I thought long and hard about Mr Tsiblitz's talk. I went over the questions he had asked.

How had the world looked when the dinosaur was young?

What did they eat? What were their illnesses?

How did they look fully clothed? How was the world when they were young?

I thought of the strange interlude when we had gone out to the cemetery to say a prayer for Huddy's father. That had been a great act of faith, I thought. A symbolic act. We had sent off Huddy's father, with a prayer, a gush of words born out of nothing. Is that what Mr Brown and I had done, followed blindly in an act of faith?

461

Were they really as intelligent as the elephants?

What was the flora at the time? Where did they frolic?

Why did they not have hairy bodies and was this a reason for their eventual extinction? Hypothermia?

How was the world when they were young? Tsiblitz had asked.

How was the world when we were young?

Did he mean a world of children? A different time? Is that what he had meant?

Was Tsiblitz saying look here, look how an age separates him from us. It's a different time. A child's time. Time lived in a different bubble. How was the world when they were young? And suddenly, I knew what I had to do. I had to recreate that bubble. I had to build an environment for the iguanodon. I had to construct an environment in which he might breathe.

There he was in the museum, 'nowt but a bloody skeleton,' my father had said, and my father in his clumsy way had been right. The skeleton was subject to draughts which might blow ribs together, it was subject to the slow drip of bat crap on the skull. It had been subject to the ravage of time. But only since its unearthing by my great grandfather. Until then it had avoided time. Now, exhibited here in the museum, it had been named. It had become yet another of time's great captives. It was no wonder he looked ready to run, to escape from the bondage of so much wire, the restrictiveness of giant bolts which held him to the floor of the museum which had given him a name.

It had been my great grandfather and his friend Sidall Junkin who had with pick and shovel dug back the clock, unearthing more time. But it had been a time ticking in a different bubble. And God had made payment for the intrusion, blindly thrusting the moment forward and demolishing fifty million years in a solitary exploding second. He had taken James Brightside from the face of the planet and swapped him – left us with a pile of iguanodon bones turned to stone. Then along had come Mr Brown, a man of different mettle; a collector, a hoarder, a man of infinite patience, one who appreciated above all else the grand design. He did what he had to do, he put the model together again, and I had been his willing apprentice. And despite his emphasis on design, even Mr Brown had fallen into the trap and named him, the

Brightside Dinosaur. Even Mr Brown had failed to avoid becoming a Namer of Names.

'Christ, Mr Brown,' I spoke to the cedarwood urn, 'why me? Why me who has to find a way through to purpose? Mr Brown, do you hear, you certainly have something to answer for, for Christ's sake.' I pointed my finger accusingly at the urn and found myself becoming angry. 'I'll build a bubble, Mr Brown, but I can't do more.' My voice wavered. 'I'm not a bloody alchemist, Mr Brown. I can't breathe life into the bugger. Christ! Rebirth and soul, they were more in your line than mine. You were the one with all the faith, not me Chrissake.' Tears were pouring down my cheeks. My shouted words echoed in the space above the milky light bulbs. I picked up the red urn and was about to dash it to the floor when out of resounding silence came the advice, 'Don't do that.'

It took a few moments for me to realize that I had said the words myself. 'Don't do that,' I said again to prove to myself that I had made the utterance in the first place. 'Christ, Mr Brown, a bubble of breath?' I asked, temper subsiding. I sat a long while in the darkening museum. 'I love you, Mr Brown,' I eventually said.

I knew what I had to build but I needed help. I had to have the help of a fit young man. An intelligent man who had an interest in the dinosaur, one who had insight. One who might understand obsession and know the need for a new environment. I went over to Arkwright's house to find Walter Beanlander.

1940

32
Of war and the pits

The Germans invaded Poland and took the Silesian coal-fields. The country went to war and Mr Smircz got drunk in the pub and smashed up the snug. He hurled a three-legged stool through the smoky glassed window and refused to be arrested when they sent an officer from the police station. Rube Hardwick, the landlord, had to spend the night in the hospital having the slivers of glass removed from his face. The Pole walked in the warm rain to Castleford where he attended the Catholic church and lit a candle. Father Silvert heard his confession. When he left the church, Mr Smircz went across to the police station and gave himself up. Clyde Wimpey was on night duty behind the desk. Wimpey was expecting promotion. Mrs Beanlander had more or less forgotten Grandma Dolly's prediction. Walter Beanlander had forgotten about it for a few years, then one day at the museum he recalled it as being unfinished business..

The British government didn't like the idea of the Germans having so much coal. Along with the coal from their own pits the enemy could now mine almost as much fuel as all the allied European countries put together, including Britain. War was going to increase the demand for coal. The British government reckoned another forty million tons per year would be needed. The ministers wanted to know where it was going to come from.

Ebby Edwards, the secretary of the Mining Federation, immediately saw the opportunity to unite the fragmented unions. He was unsure how it was to be done, but the mere fact that the country – not the mine owners but the government – required the colliers to make more sacrifices gave the window through which his dream, like a mist-veiled moon, might peer.

The coal owners' association and the unions were invited to sit together and talk. The coal owners hadn't negotiated with the Federation since the General Strike thirteen years since. Ebby took his opportunity and said that if the two bodies were to sit together then they would have to negotiate more than just increased production. He knew that if he could sit at the same table with the mine owners' representatives and ask for a wage increase then he would have destroyed the owners' purpose for those wasted years. There he would be – doing what the coal owners had vowed he would never do. He would be negotiating a wage demand with them on behalf of all the members. At a stroke it would reverse the procedure which had favoured the coal owners. District negotiations would be rendered meaningless and he would be in a position to reunite the union into a strengthened federation.

He was invited to sit and talk of increased production. He asked for a shilling a shift for the men and sixpence for the boys. He got eightpence and fourpence and rejoiced. Ebby was a far-seeing man.

The government prated about increased production but continued to recruit the miners from the pits into the armed services.

'How can thee expect increased production if tha keep taking away the fittest of the colliers?' asked my grandfather.

The Ministries of Mines and Wars then decided on a common policy – there would be no more recruitment from the pits and where possible the government would return the colliers who had been enlisted.

'Nowt much'll change. Tha'll see,' said my grandfather.

Nothing changed.

In our village hardly anyone went to war. The men were mostly too old or too knackered. Some of the younger ones went off to fight. Bob Archbold went off blowing his brother's shining Sousaphone all the way to the railway station in Wakefield but the sergeant wouldn't let him take the instrument on board train so Bob gave it to the station-master for safe-keeping. Bob never had the opportunity to claim it back. It's still there in that dusty ticket office, the golden glow spent. You can purchase a ticket to almost anywhere in Britain from the man at the tiny window and look in at that reminder of our village's dull war.

Billy o' the Terrus End went back into the pit. So did I. I didn't fancy all that soldiering. My father went. He wrote us from Barnsley to say that he was joining up. He asked if I would be going; wanted to know if I was to become a man. I wrote back and told him that I'd gone into the pit and wasn't that man enough for him? He didn't reply. Lancaster wrote my grandmother from Hollywood and told her that he was coming home. He went straight into the Air Force as he had done during the Great War, only then it was called the Flying Corps. Now, my grandmother had two sons in the forces. She wept buckets when she learned they had gone to war.

Then we heard France had fallen. So had Holland and Belgium and Denmark and Norway. That gave the Germans more coalfields to work and it effectively reduced the coal owners' export markets. We couldn't sell our coal abroad, not into countries occupied by the enemy. As the coal owners understood it, that meant less coal and therefore fewer jobs but the government wanted more coal for the war effort. The coal owners laid men off, including myself. I felt like a yo-yo. Muddle?

There were few enough colliers even if one included the ones who were doing nowt, but nobody sent the soldiers home.

'Why should they?' my grandfather asked. 'We've enough buggers hangin' around doin' nowt.'

Then the government decided that it needed more enlisted men so they took some of the unemployed. There were even fewer potential colliers now. But the government wanted more coal for the war effort too. Everyone was confused. Everyone but Ebby Edwards, who sat by the window of opportunity and stared on to a bright new day. He reflected so much dazzle that even Winston Churchill could see nothing in seeking to look back through the same window.

'Good old Ebby,' my grandfather cried. "'E's not only put pits into public ownership but 'e's so dazzled Mr Churchill that the Labour's slid in whilst bugger's bin blinded from t' glare.' But that was later, much later: after the War.

33
Of war and flowers

What more can I tell you about the war? Do you want me to tell you about the flowers? About the way in which they send men home without their legs?

They send men home in blue flannel suits with the trouser leg pinned beneath the stump; a large silver safety pin defines the limit of the limb. They have crimson poppies stuck in their lapels like medals.

A man is taken from the train at Wakefield in a wheel-chair. He will never walk again and in his one hand he holds a bunch of forget-me-nots the colour of sky after rain. Some of them are still in bud, tight buds of pink. The man's wife, crying, wheels him past the ticket office where Bob Archbold's Sousaphone gathers dust. The man grips the tiny bouquet, hanging on to it as if he is clinging to life itself. The chair wheels creak from the dark iron of the station into the sunlight and the buds open. There is not a hint of pink in the blue blossoms.

Danny Pratt's brother Frog lost his legs. He was called Frog before he went off to war and had his legs blown off. People who hadn't known him that long thought it was cruel that we should call him Frog simply because he had no legs. It was irony, that's all. But you can't tell people that it's only irony. They don't believe you. They don't understand it anyway. They don't understand and they don't believe you, in that order. That's the trouble with irony. Irony is no less cruel than the lads in the pit, as if it had a tongue which clacked away, mocking everything because it had nothing better to do.

He sits on the corner of the street in the next village, opposite the barber's shop and the bookie's, and he sells wild flowers from a tray. His mother goes out every morning and picks them fresh. So early they still have the dew on their petals. She packs his tray with little watered bunches and Danny and his other brothers carry Frog to his pitch in the next village. Look out of the parlour window any morning early and there they are winding away on the path over there carrying their brother like a prince from his palace in a sedan chair. They set him down at the pavement on the corner and wave goodbye. The others go off to the pit leaving him to his life among the flowers.

Cow wheat. Yellow loose strife. Melancholy thistle. Fumitory. Devil's-bit. Asphodel. Foxglove. Nodding thistle. Frog goes to sleep and people bring him pennies. When he wakes his tray is empty. There is a pile of pennies in his lap or in what used to be his lap. Is it necessary to have legs to have a lap? Huddy Greenblatt and Mr Beresford display the colours for a day. Then they toss them into the dustbin to be replaced the next day and the next and the next and always a pile of pennies in Frog's lap.

Sometimes I walk up to the next village myself and I watch them. I watch Frog asleep on the pavement. I see Huddy in his overcoat and trilby, I watch Beresford with his head bald as a crown green bowl. They exchange their pennies for the small bunch of flowers. I see the pennies in Frog's lap and I think it's like a Chinese puzzle. The Chinese would have an ideograph for a lap without fucking legs, I think. I want to scream.

34

The Wardian case

I was advised to read the book *On the Growth of Plants in Closely Glazed Containers*. It had been written about a hundred years since by the man who invented the aquarium, Nathanial Bagshaw Ward (yes, he was an uncle to Bagshaw Moralee, illustrating yet again how the study of natural history circled like wealth in families).

Ward discovered the very simple principle that plants will flourish in airtight containers providing there is moisture in the soil in which they are grown. The leaves transpire, water condenses on the glass walls of the case and either runs in rivulets or drips back to the soil. Consequently the plants have all they need to flourish. They have their water and naturally, living in such open glass spaces, they have an abundance of sunlight. Usefully too, pollution and disease are shut out.

Ward made a present of several such cases to his nephew which he took with him on his first field trip to South America. Bagshaw Moralee had been one of the first to send species and varieties of orchid and aspidistra, fully grown in their Wardian cases, back to England. He had more sense however than to send them to Quekett and the closet men. Bagshaw had sent his samples to the London nurserymen who had an eye for a commercial opening. Soon, ships laden with cargoes of pitcher plants and other exotic meat-eaters, nibbling in their glass cages, were on the high seas bound for Southampton and Liverpool. The nurserymen were quite unable to satisfy the demand for the colourful plants of the Amazon, it seemed from every middle-class home. I suppose Bagshaw Moralee had done as much as anyone to help develop the idea of an aspidistra growing in the living-room or tiled hall of the Victorian family house. He made a fortune out of it too, sufficient to finance trips further afield and eventually to open his zoological gardens.

By strange coincidence, it was Squire Potterton's family who, along with others, used the Wardian case to best advantage: to create the Empire's greatest achievement.

Tea. The Pottertons had tea plants shipped from China to their plantations in India, which were able to survive the journey only because they had been packed in the glazed containers. There might have been a lot wrong with the Pottertons but they always sold their tea at a price the collier might afford and in our part of West Yorkshire Potterton's Tea was on day-long standby, brewing in every home.

. Tea in its pot, I suppose, was our aspidistra.

The most common use to which the Wardian case was put, however, was for the growing of ferns. One hundred years ago, they had been used to house enormous ferneries. Fern-growing became a compulsive habit; it even had a name – pteridomania. As with most acquisitive habits, though, ferns had only reflected fashion and after a few years these extraordinary collections, built painstakingly by the pteridomaniacs, were dumped to make way for the newer fashion in fish.

After reading the book, I soon realized that the Wardian case was hardly going to make the skeleton thrive but my advisers had been right to draw my attention to Bagshaw's uncle's book. Here was at least a beginning in my search for the correct bubble, for hadn't Mr Tsiblitz told how ferns and conifers had formed a large part of the flora during the dinosaur period? Was this not the natural environment of the iguanodon?

Inside the museum, Walter Beanlander and I constructed a Victorian conservatory based on a model of the central section at the Crystal Palace. It had a cast iron base and we used a wrought iron framework. Walter secured the skeleton to the base re-using the giant pitch-covered bolts which Mr Brown had originally employed. We spread five tons of well-watered topsoil about him and planted ferns and conifers and dug in lots of fertilizer which we brought by the barrowload from the crimble. We put rats and voles in among the vegetation. I chucked in a load of rocks; they fell upon the soil displaying shiny ammonites and prehistoric leaves. Finally we set the huge glazed plates in place. Then we knocked holes in the museum walls and fitted windows, making the milky bulbs redundant, and flooding the place with natural sunlight.

The ferns grew rapidly within the warm enclosed space, pushing at the glass sides, seeking escape. They meandered lushly through the bones in the way that saplings push through tumbled walls in a derelict house. They fanned up and the frond tips tapped at the arched glass roof. The skeleton soon became difficult to spot. By the time war had been declared he was a ruined Mayan temple, overgrown with time. We had to open up the case to cut back the foliage. At the same time Walter thought it would be an opportunity to add a prehistoric bird to the scene.

'Did he make thee look?' Walter asked whilst at the top of the high ladders, pinning silver wire to suspend a cardboard pterodactyl from somewhere among the redundant light bulbs. The boy's head of forked hair had disappeared from my view in the void below the ceiling.

'Did who make me look?' I asked.

'M'grandad,' he said, ducking his head back beneath the bulbs. Walter was pointing across to the suspended tin helmet. 'Did 'e mek tha test it?'

'Ay,' I smiled up at him.

'And did he? Did he disappear?'

'No,' I said emphatically.

'No, my mother says she never saw him go either, but he believes it, tha naws. He believes he goes off, somewheres.'

'Yes, I know.'

'Funny how he believes that. It must be 'cos all the other stuff works. The egg warmer really warms up the eggs, tha naws. Tha can have 'em soft boiled, hard boiled, how tha likes and all without watter. He's bloody marvellous really, is me grandad.'

'Yes.'

Walter struggled with the wire at the top of his narrow perch shoving his head into the void again while I thought about mandragora and the way the roots were meant to shriek when pulled from the ground. Would Walter shriek if I pulled him now, yanking his head from out of the void in which it was planted, I wondered? I heard him bang pins dully into the wood. When he ducked his head out again he casually shouted down:

'Me grandad wants us to cut him a key, tha naws.'

'The key cutter's over there,' I shouted back.

'I'll come down now,' he said, teetering on the top step.

'Go ahead. Do you know how to use it?'

He began to descend the ladder. 'Ay, me grandad showed us how when I was little,' he told me and when at the bottom of the ladder he produced a piece of steel plate and a plaster cast from his pockets. He cut the new key as I watched him. It was good to see one of the old man's inventions working so well.

When he had finished he said, 'I'll have to be off now. I've got to meet Clyde Wimpey up at box and give him a message from me mother.' I walked with him up to the crossroads and left him there, outside the blue police box awaiting his mother's boyfriend.

35

Crossed telephone wires

When he was sure nobody was watching he let himself into the box with the replica key he had cut at the museum. He picked the earpiece from the cradle with thumb and index finger as he had seen the constable do. He wouldn't have known that Miss Pickles, the operator, was having a terrible day.

She sat on a wooden swivel stool surrounded by wires and plugs. Her switchboard appeared to have an insufficient number of sockets. She looked with frustration at the three wires in her hands, unable to insert them anywhere within her system. Lights flashed on the board before her. She sighed 'Dear oh dear' into the dark cone-shaped mouthpiece which sprang erect and perky between her sagging breasts. Her hand-knitted cardigan had the colour of wine. The last mother-of-pearl button was missing which caused the bottom of the garment to splay out in an inverted V as she sat, revealing a roll of middle-aged fat gathered over the elasticated waistband of her tweed skirt. 'Dear oh dear,' she said again and, with mild anger, pulled a wire from the board. She then inserted one of those which she had been holding.

'Dear oh dear,' Walter heard her say.

'Can tha connect me with Huddy Greenblatt, please?' he asked hurriedly.

'Who is this?'

'It's Clyde Wimpey here, love,' he lied.

'Oh, good afternoon, Constable. Do you want the police station?'

'No, I want to speak with Huddy Greenblatt, love. Can tha connect me up please?'

'Do you have the number?'

'Oh, ay, sorry.' He leaned on the side of the box trying to be breezy as he had seen the policeman behave. He took an old blue tram ticket from his trouser pocket, unfolded it and read out the smudged and creased numbers, having to rely on memory for what had been written there.

474

'One moment please, PC Wimpey.'

There was a low hissing noise which continued for several seconds. It was followed by a few bars of music which appeared to have been played by a full symphony orchestra. He heard Miss Pickles humming the melody, then she said 'Dear oh dear' a time or two. A conversation, spoken in German, came down the wires. The voices were very tinny and he couldn't understand anything of what he was listening to. The words rushed and faded like waves breaking on a rocky shore.

'Are you sure that's the number?' Miss Pickles asked, her voice quite plain as if she had spoken directly to him from a deckchair at the side of the ocean.

'Ay. That's it, love,' Walter said and he repeated the number which he had previously given her, trying desperately to read from the back of the halfpenny fare.

'Well, we seem to be connected to the German War Office in Berlin,' she said. Then she said 'Dear oh dear' twice more and hummed a little more of the melody which they both before had been hearing.

Walter was so panicked at being in the presence of the Nazi High Command that he let slip the earpiece without replacing it on the cradle and ran from the box slamming the door behind him.

The connection remained live for the next three days, unfortunately coinciding with the constable's period of leave. It was also Miss Pickles's period of menstruation, a time when it was usual for the wires at her exchange to be jumbled as an Italian spaghetti. The connection was discovered only when Wimpey next went into his police box. That was the day he returned to duty. He put the earpiece back on its hook and thought no more about it, convinced that he himself must have replaced it incorrectly when he had last telephoned his report to the station.

Eventually, the police department received a massive bill from the Post Office and Mr Sumner the accountant at Castleford police station (and Mrs Beanlander's boss) was moved to begin an investigation into unnecessary expenditure incurred in the use of telephone time. It was during this investigation that Brenda Beanlander discovered a call to have been made from the blue box up at the crossroads, via Miss Pickles, to the German War Office. She kept the knowledge to herself but she couldn't prevent a suspicion which questioned the loyalty of her boyfriend from growing like a lily in her head.

A journey to Luddenden Foot

When they had jumped from the aeroplane's wing, coming eventually to earth in their rubber flying suits, Elyahou Tsiblitz and my aunt Henrietta made their way to Rotterdam where they caught a fishing vessel bound for the Humber. They disembarked at Goole and eventually settled into a farm labourer's cottage on Squire Potterton's estate over by Kettle Flatt.

My aunt illustrated children's books in the style of Kate Greenaway (one should be careful when comparing their works for it is difficult to tell them apart, but for those speculators who consider art to be a suitable form of currency I offer the following advice: note Henrietta's use of the colour green. My aunt, influenced by the iridescence of grasses brushed flat about the hollow, has reproduced on her paper a glittering verdure obtained by dilution of an antiseptic powder, normally painted on to the heads of infectious spots, which she buys from the chemist's shop in Kippax).

Mr Tsiblitz gave the occasional talk about dinosaurs to interested parties. He was also appointed consultant to the Kensington Museum of Natural History and travelled widely, confirming whether or not uncovered egg clusters found about the planet's crust were those of Protoceratops. He took an interest in my museum too and came occasionally to cast his eye over the skeleton in its Wardian case, but he never advised.

One day he brought my aunt to visit with my grandparents. He left her at the house and walked to the museum alone. He told me of a man he had met whilst shopping for my aunt's sable paintbrushes in Halifax. The man was a Russian with a fierce red beard. His name was Agrelovitch. He had a daughter with long dark hair which she was able to sit on when she played at the pianola that stood in the corner of the Russian's gloomy shop. A hide-covered shoebox with claw feet stood next to it.

It emerged in conversation, as it often must when fellow *émigrés* come upon one another, that Mr Tsiblitz was married to an English-woman. Her name before marriage had been Henrietta Brightside, he told the Russian, whereupon Agrelovitch mentioned that he had at one time owned property in Luddenden Foot, a town not many miles distant. He explained that rooms had been rented there to a girl calling herself Clarrie Schubert Brightside and he wondered if there might have been a connection between the girl and my aunt. Mr Tsiblitz knew only too well of the connection, for not only had he intimate knowledge of the girl's mother but, through the correspondence of my grandmother sent to his wife whilst she had lived abroad, he had learned of the birth of Clarrie – a child fathered by his wife's nephew, Albert Brightside. Knowing of my own fondness for Clarrie (learned of course through that same correspondence), Mr Tsiblitz wondered if I might be interested in a trip to Luddenden Foot to see if the girl could be found.

My reaction was one of profound embarrassment. That my grandmother should think such tittle-tattle worthy of a place in her foreign correspondence filled my head with blood and the idea of her letters travelling abroad, suggesting that God knows who in the wide world might know of my affection for Clarrie, set my heart racing. Finally, and much the worst, the possibility that Clarrie herself might have got wind of my feelings for her caused a reversal of flow (no doubt stopping my heart completely at the point of switch) which carried blood to my toes and left my face as pasty as that of my grandfather's.

'Well, that's settled then,' said Mr Tsiblitz to my white face. 'I'll arrange the visit immediately.' I was too sickly to protest.

The following day, together with my aunt, we called upon Mr Agrelovitch at his shop in Halifax. He expressed delight when Tsiblitz suggested he should accompany us to Luddenden Foot to indicate the house where he knew Clarrie to have stayed. The long-haired daughter remained behind to look after the shop which, it turned out, specialized in the sale of artists' materials – at the time being one of only a handful of outlets for such things in Yorkshire. (Another was in Leeds close by the College of Art where Henry Moore, who lived just down our road, had attended and felt the need to reproduce the dark enclosing spaces of our village.) We set off crammed into Mr Tsiblitz's dull black Austin Seven.

When we arrived in Luddenden Foot, a journey of not many miles, Agrelovitch asked Mr Tsiblitz to stop the car in front of the house with the lop-sided windows.

'That's where she lives,' he said, huddled up to the car's rear window which he had to wipe clear of condensate with the back of his gloved hand before we were able to see out.

I peered through the misty hole he had created. I saw the house. I had the feeling that it was staring back. 'She is in the rooms there on the ground floor. Up the steps. The mullioned windows on either side of the door are hers,' Agrelovitch informed us.

We got out of the car and approached the house. We ascended the few steps slowly and my aunt knocked at the door. There was no reply. She tried the large brass knob. It turned easily, surprising us all. We entered the house. The Russian led us to Clarrie's sitting-room. There were the grey ashes from a fire which had very recently been allowed to die in the grate.

'This needs some tea,' the Russian told us cryptically, running his gloved palms lovingly over the iron surround of the Jacobean fire-place (recalling warm nights in the arms of a deacon's wife).

The room was dark but I was instantly able to recognize a number of distinctive small red and white wrapping papers strewn about the floor – Mintoe sweet papers carelessly dropped to the rugs. They are like clothes scattered in a hurry, I thought glumly. The trail led across a draughty hall to another room. Here was a bed and more sweet wrappings. I felt the cold gloom and the sink of betrayal.

'Hello,' the Russian called several times. There was no reply. I could see nothing in either room which I might associate with Clarrie; in fact we were each of us unsure that Agrelovitch was calling out for the Clarrie Schubert Brightside who used to sit upon my grandmother's pegged rug before the roaring fire. These thoughts cheered me a little for a short time, until I remembered that I hadn't seen Clarrie since she left the village for the second time with her mother and I knew nothing of her present life and situation. What on earth should there be for me to recognize or associate? Gloom settled upon me once more.

We went outside.

'There is a man, a dwarf,' the Russian recalled when on the steps, 'who lives below. Come. We can ask him if he knows of the woman.' He led us to a window-sill almost at the ground level, where he bent his large frame and with his flaming red hair touching the ground he called in, upside down. I was reminded of the flamingo's head, feeding. There was no response. I thought I heard a dog yapping, but the others couldn't hear it. They could, however, hear the noise of running water. The Russian invited me to slip over the sill and seek out the dwarf who worked within. I dropped uncomfortably into the eerie cavern. There was a stout rope which stretched between the front and back walls. My vision was hindered by bed linen hanging on other lines close by and fluorescing an odd blue light. I noticed another line had been cut down and removed – the few inches of rope which remained were knotted to a rusting metal ring which was embedded in the wall. I tiptoed to the end of the full line of washing and turned to come back up the other side of the line. It was then I came face to face with him. I screamed, not very loud I think, for the others told me later that they didn't hear me. But I screamed. A short scream. The man was dangling from a rope which had been tied in a noose about his neck. His trousers were still wet, not allowed to dry out in the damp air, where he had pissed himself. The man was very short – so short that at first I thought it might be a dummy or an overstuffed doll which dangled there. His face was black, his tongue lolled from his mouth. He wore a jacket of the materials from which my grandmother pegged her rugs. The bowl of a pipe peeped like a flower head from the rough breast pocket. I looked to the ceiling. It was hung about with great hams. The rope was tied to one of the hooks. There was a dog beneath the hanged man. It gnawed, glassy-eyed, on a shank held between black paws. An empty glass sweet bottle lay on its side on the floor, close by. I turned and fled. When I had recovered sufficiently to relate what I had seen to the others, the Russian went into the cave to cut down the dwarf and my aunt went off to find a policeman.

The policeman whom my aunt brought back to the house with her thought that the death was probably a suicide but he also established from evidence given by her friend, Daisy Miller, that Clarrie had been living at the house right up to the time of the hanging. What's more, she had now gone missing. Daisy told the policeman that Clarrie hadn't been to the weaving shed for two or three days. And just in case there were any lingering doubts about the identity of the girl who had lived at the house, my aunt established with certainty that the girl was our Clarrie. It took only an answer to a simple question.

'Why yes, her mother was a rope walker, granddaughter of Madame Saqui, rope walker to the court of Napoleon. She told me so herself.'

I dipped my fingers into the cold grey ash in the grate and rubbed my thumb across the tips of my fingers.

The policeman also learned that a considerable amount of money had gone missing. It was apparently common knowledge (confirmed by Mr Agrelovitch, sitting uncomfortably beside me in the rear of the Austin Seven on the return journey to Halifax) that the dwarf had a fortune saved in silver threepenny pieces which he kept in a sweet jar. The jar was discovered (had I not seen it myself?) empty in the cellar with the hanged man. The policeman for the time being therefore considered the only crime here to have been one of theft, the thief having made off with easy pickings once she had discovered that the dwarf had hanged himself.

After our visit to Luddenden Foot, Mr Tsiblitz came over more often. To the village not to the museum. In fact his visits to the museum were fewer, but it was always on a Sunday that he came to the village. The panharmonicon was usually spilling out the Prague Symphony from the Pymont House and on each visit he brought with him the rubber suits which he and Henrietta had worn beneath their clothes on their escape from Berlin. As in the days before the Great War, he dressed the few village children who still lived there in the suits of smelly rubber, released the valves and after the magical inrushing of air the children lifted off. It happened about four or five times in that year. The blue pterodactyl and the red turkey took the children to the sky accompanied by Mozart's Prague on their ethereal journeys. It happened as many times a year as that – four or five – right up to the time of Tsiblitz's death.

37
To hear a nightingale

A nightingale hadn't been heard in our neck of the woods for fifteen years. When the Bellman told us that one had recently been heard piping away in the grounds of Stanley Wood Hall, my Aunt Henrietta asked if I should like to accompany her there to hear the bird sing. I accepted the invitation.

The following afternoon I walked over Hunger Hill to collect her from the cottage. She greeted me at the door wearing a lavender blue dress. The hem trailed on the floor, sweeping up dust as she walked; she had lace on her bosom and at her neck. To my unversed eye the dress looked to be of the Edwardian period. She gripped a furled parasol, tailored from the same material as the dress. She had me wait a moment or two in the timbered doorway whilst she collected her purse from the kitchen table. I saw her slip the leather thong over her wrist. Then she picked up a large book and put it beneath her arm. I read the gold-lettered spine: *War and Peace* by Leo Tolstoy.

We caught the bus in Kippax. It was crowded with soot-faced colliers returning home from the shift. As the bus swung about the winding lanes the pitmen steadied their snap boxes in their laps with tapping fingers, beating out tunes that must have been running through their heads in grotesque darkness all day. My aunt sat in a seat by the window, reading. I sat next to her and spent most of the journey looking past her bowed, but occasionally swinging, head. Through the glass I saw the horse chestnut and mezereon in leaf.

The bus driver put us down by the low stone wall which surrounds the manor house and we walked along a lane of sycamores to the wooden gates which had recently been painted white. There were several motors parked in the lane close by. The gates were open and we went through. The gateman nodded but he didn't speak. I noticed that we were followed by several pitmen who had got off the bus with us. They clutched their snap boxes in black curled fingers. I heard one of them draw a companion's attention to the fact that Goldilocks was in flower. We were heading now up the path towards the dilapidated Elizabethan manor house. Unlike the gates, the house was in need of a good lick of paint. On the approach we were prevented from going any further by a second gateman who silently directed us to turn off the path and walk to the right. We followed in the direction of his pointing finger. So too did the pitmen behind. We were now walking beside lawned gardens where a child flew a remote-controlled model Spitfire. It flew silently in a great circle marking out the boundary of the lawns. In the evening sun the metal plane flashed blue, then white, then blue again. Two red dogs loped beneath the model marking out the same great circle. Round and round like horses on a carousel.

We approached a man relaxed in twills, his backside on the seat of a shooting stick. A sporting gun rested at his thigh, the wooden butt on the ground. He poured tea into a cup from a Thermos flask. My aunt sauntered by, the closed parasol slung across her shoulder like a swagman's stick. She didn't speak to the man in twills but he knew her question. He stopped in mid-sup, displaying his mild milk-tea moustaches.

'Yes, keep on. It's in those woods over there,' he said.

She thanked him with a nod of her head and we walked towards the trees.

'That was Squire Potterton,' she told me. 'He owns Stanley Wood Hall. He owns everything around here right over to our cottage at Kettle Flatt.'

I could hear a chiff-chaff singing. There were several people whom we could see ahead of us now. We quickened our pace and passed a woman whose black shawl covered her head as my grandmother's still did whenever she left the house. The woman carried a small child which slept with its scabbed head on her shoulder. Nearby, a soldier, a private in uniform, had stopped to tie his shoelace, his booted foot resting on a rock. A second soldier held his cap for him, the cap badge gleaming in the last of the daylight. The second soldier wore his own cap at a jaunty angle on his head. We hurried past the soldiers and the path suddenly widened into a clearing where dozens of people had congregated. I recognized the man with the gold-framed spectacles who had spoken at the meeting on the dinosaurs which was held at the Mechanics Institute. He was talking with another soldier – a general. The two privates who had now caught up with us saluted the general as they went by, the capless one hurriedly covering his head with the cap which he carelessly grabbed from his friend. The general ignored them, engrossed in his conversation with the man in the gold-rimmed spectacles.

A woman in a long black skirt sitting on the grass accepted a glass of champagne from her companion who had pulled the cork from the magnum with a loud pop. The man, in a boating jacket, returned the opened bottle to a silver cooler which was in a hamper. My aunt told me that the woman was a film star. Several dirty boys sat on the grass close to her. They had holes in their shirts and in their trousers. One of them had a book in his hands. The others talked with him excitedly.

'What's tha book?' I found myself asking the boy, pointing it out with the toe end of my shoe. He lifted the book slightly, turning the dust cover towards me. It was titled *British Birds*. I thanked the boy and he acknowledged my thanks with a dip of the head.

My aunt walked on a little way with me trailing in her wake then, looking back to judge her distance from the bulk of the crowd, she selected a spot beneath an oak tree and sat down, resting her long back against the mossy bole. She opened her lavender blue parasol and shaded herself whilst preparing to read her book. It was almost dusk. I sat with her, my legs drawn up, and I allowed my arms to lazily encircle my knees. As she read in the thin light I heard people whispering about me. 'He's here. He's here,' someone said. The crowd hushed.

'Who's here?' I asked.

'I don't know.' My aunt looked gaunt.

'Not the nightingale. Surely he wouldn't announce himself?' I quipped and she smiled at me. The moon was up, full and casting everything in a green glow. My aunt returned to her book.

I saw a woman, a pitman's wife, make an exaggerated curtsy up by the trees where we had entered the clearing and I saw several well-dressed men, including the old squire, bowing stiffly as two more people, attired in white, drifted on to the grass. They were quickly engulfed by an encircling crowd. I got to my feet and walked across to the crowd to see what was going on. The crowd was about five or six persons deep and I was unable to see anything other than the occasional flash of the gentleman's white trousers through the scrum.

'Go round, son,' a flustered policeman advised.

'But I don't want to go round.'

'Then go back, son,' the policeman said.

'Why? What is it?'

'It's the Duke of Windsor,' said a man at the back of the crowd. The policeman was trying to prise him from the person in front.

'What, tha means Edward, bugger what abdicated?' asked a straggling collier.

'Yes, Edward. And Mrs Simpson.'

'Go round, lads,' I heard the policeman saying as I turned and headed back towards the oak under which my aunt sat reading.

'It's Edward. And Wallis Simpson.'

'There'll be quite a crowd expected then,' she said without raising her head from the book. I nodded, seeing the scrimmage like clouds slowly coming apart. Somebody produced chairs and the two important personages were invited to sit. The Duke sat with his gloved hands resting on the top of a cane. She sipped from a glass goblet. Perhaps it was champagne from the magnum in the film star's hamper.

The tree-tops began to shake in a sudden wind. I looked up. The moon was in among the branches.

The nightingale began to sing in the hushed air. He was in the tree directly above us, silhouetted against the moon. The eyes of the Duke and Mrs Simpson turned upon us. Others danced a mad dance about them, fawning. The bird fluted a rich blue note. Then another.

Two very short clear notes.

The bird then warbled and the song built to a great crescendo. It seemed that nothing breathed but the wind. The Duke moved his head forward allowing his chin to come to rest on the backs of his hands which covered the top of the cane. His eyes, which still looked in our direction, expressed boredom.

A man poured Mrs Simpson more champagne. My aunt returned to *War and Peace*, that mass of one man's word sprawled in the big book which she had placed back in her lap. She read in the green light as we waited for the song to fade. She looked up once more into the silence of the trees at Stanley Wood Hall, then she bowed her head like that of an automaton returning a dead gaze to the page. A little way off, a white doll in his wicker chair, the Duke acknowledged what he had perceived to be my aunt's obeisance with a dip of his own head – his eyes now closed.

'You know, some events are so little understood that they are in need of an environment to be created specially for them,' I told my aunt.

She stood, smoothing down her dress with one hand, the fingertips of her other hand searching out for support to the mossy oak. 'Like the dinosaur?'

'Yes, like the dinosaur. But Walter and I got it wrong. We got the environment right but our perception of the dinosaur is wrong, I mean. We have been treating him as an object, like any other exhibit in the museum, but he's not an exhibit, not an object in the same sense as the fossils or the birds' eggs.'

She secured the leather thong of her purse to her wrist, listening carefully. She handed me the book she had been reading without comment; her eyes revealed nothing.

'Don't you see? The dinosaur is an event, an occurrence like a nightingale's song is an occurence. He is not an object.'

We walked away from the tree in search of the bus which would return us to Kippax. As we passed the wicker chairs Wallis Simpson placed a brass trumpet to her ear, listening for the bird's song like a deaf woman. Some wag tossed an apple core into the bell and the policeman hared off up a grassy bank chasing the culprit.

'Come back here a second,' the policeman shouted.

'It's fifty million years of occurrence,' I told my aunt.

'So what will you do?' she asked.

'I have to make him move. I must create time for him.'

38

The Wardian case automated

Back at the museum Walter Beanlander creates a machine. A system of great iron cogs, teeth caked in grease, grind on each other turning out a different universe; a tortuous world which moves one tooth at a time, like a spool of one of Lancaster's films running the Marx Brothers, ever so slow. It's a world which turns on a cam shoved through glazed panels.

The iguanodon's head nods to the visitors, as the head of my aunt searching through Tolstoy's words, as the head of a mistaken king will slowly nod his satisfaction at another's submission.

In time the cut ferns will grow high in the Wardian case wrapping themselves about the iron, sapping at the machine's strength and energy and hiding it from view.

The metal rusts in the air sweated by the plants.

In Europe, the war rages. The iguanodon, too, is like a bombed city waiting to be rebuilt.

Walter and his brother Tarty sit in a hide, cranking up. Soon, their sister Annie will have to add her weight to the effort.

Automata? I know they are not enough.

39

I'll tell you what happened to Harry Glynn

The silver meniscus in Harry's jar plummeted as if recording fallen winter temperatures. The number of silver bits in Clarrie's jar increased. The exchange, two bits a time, was one way only. In increasingly hard times few people used his laundry service and the dwarf's meagre earnings were spent on chocolates with fancy ribbons, on lemon sherbets and on mint imperials, more recently on Mintoes too. The savings were taken nightly from the jar and handed to Clarrie two bits a time. There came a night when there were no more silver pieces in Harry's jar: that was the night when Clarrie's clothes stayed on and glad of it she was, too, for water was freezing in the pipes. Harry came from the cold to her rose-red room where the logs burned.

'The two silver bits, Harry, before we begin,' she demanded as she always did.

'Nowt left. I'll have to owe thee.'

'What? No more threepenny pieces in the jar?' This was the moment for which she had long waited. She could afford a wry smile.

'Tha's had the lot.' He held the jar with its mouth open towards her so that she could judge the emptiness.

'There'll be no tick, Harry.'

'Aw, come on, missy, tha can trust us.'

'No tick, Harry. I said.'

'But I've no money left.'

'No money, no play, Harry.'

'Well, tha's a right bitch. After all these years tha could trust us. Tha's a bitch, missy.'

'After all these years I've a right to be a bitch.'

'What's tha on about?'

'Blackmail, Harry, that's what I'm on about. You've· blackmailed me all these years with your threats of going to the police about the officer who fell from the brothel. Well, you'll not threaten me any

488

more.' Harry was surprised at the emergence of anger which had remained bottled for so long. She sighed quietly. 'Look, I'm making a bargain with you. I'll be more generous with you than most would. You can have one of the threepenny pieces back each night you stay away from my room. That way you'll have the opportunity to get your money back, do you understand? Threepence a night to stay away.'

Harry was destitute. He accepted the threepenny piece she offered him and agreed to stay in the laundry. But the following night he returned to the rose-red room.

'Tha's a drug, missy,' he shivered.

'Well, here's another silver bit,' she said when she had fished one from her jar which stood by the enamelled clock on the mantelshelf. 'Now, don't be difficult, Harry, we have a bargain. Go back to the laundry.' She caught sight of herself captured dimly behind the glass which covered the clock face, before she turned from it and offered the dwarf the money.

'Naw, I've got us own threepence, thanks very much.' He showed her the silver coin which she had given him the night before. 'Tha can tek off tha skirt.'

'But knickers stays on,' she said, letting the coin drop back in the jar.

'Don't much care for thee with knickers on,' Harry sulked.

'Well, that's the way it has to be, Harry. You only have the one coin. Take another one,' she said, trying to reason with him, 'and come back tomorrow night. That'll buy my knickers.'

'Naw, I want thee to touch me. I want thee to touch me now,' he shouted like a petulant child.

'All right. All right, if that's what you want, Harry. I'll touch you now if that's what you want,' and she accepted back the silver piece.

The following night she returned the coin to Harry (the same one, for there had been no need to return it to the jar) and the night after that he bought her caress with it. This sequence continued for several months, the same coin passing back and forth and my cousin never having to strip off her French knickers and touching the dwarf's penis only on alternate nights.

One evening she went down to the laundry to give Harry the

silver coin. She squeezed through the window and dropped over the sill into the eerie blue cellar. The dwarf was kneeling by the phosphorescent stones scrubbing a shirt collar. She tossed him the silver threepenny bit. The coin was spinning in the air and he grabbed at it like a man disturbed by flies. They were both silent a while hearing the water rill on the rocks. She observed his silent anger. She watched his powerful sausage-like fingers, icy blue in this light, bending the threepenny piece into the shape of a thimble. He put it into his mouth and in the rasping voice of Mr Punch he said, 'I love thee. Doesn't tha naw I love thee? I've always loved thee. I want thee, Clarrie.'

'Don't be silly,' she said, startled for the moment. Then, striving to retrieve mastery of the situation, she added, 'I'm saving myself.'

'What for?' asked Punch, puzzlement intermingling with his unhappiness.

(Oh, that here she had said, 'For my Donald,' but she didn't.) 'For my husband,' she said.

The dwarf spat out the squeaker as if the mention of a spouse disturbed his digestion. It landed in front of her and Clarrie bent to retrieve it. She slipped it, as would a seamstress, over her fingertip. 'What's tha mean, saving? Tha's bin a prostitute, working in a brothel. What's tha got to save?' he asked in his natural voice.

'I'm still a virgin, Harry,' she explained. 'You don't think that Mr Sligh had me, do you? That silly pervert – he was only interested in exposing himself from his barrel.' She giggled. 'There was only room for just the one in there, anyway,' she said as an afterthought.

'I'm going to have thee, Clarrie,' the dwarf warned.

'Don't be silly,' she said again and backed playfully from him.

'I am, Clarrie. I love thee.' He made a dive for her legs, hoping to bring her down in a rugby tackle, but Clarrie was far too nimble and with a single bounce she had landed with both feet on one of the washing lines. For a second she let herself spring on the rope feeling for balance, then, bent almost double, she passed hurriedly along and made her escape through the broken window.

She returned to her rooms to collect a few items of clothing which she squeezed into a small brown case. Then she grabbed up her sweet jar and she ran from the house, loose shale crunching beneath her tread.

*

We can only guess at what happened next. There is no human witness, only the dog was there. Harry must have heard her footfall on the shale. The dog probably whined.

'Is tha hungry, Shep? Hungry, boy?'

The dog barked. Harry cut down one of the lines with a blunt knife leaving the frayed end tied to the iron ring cemented into the wall. He stood on his empty sweet jar and reached for a hambone which he was able to unhook from the ceiling, standing tiptoed. He threw it to the dog.

As Shep settled with the shank between his paws, Harry tied the rope about the hook, stretching to his fingertips. Then, relaxing, he knotted the other end of the rope in a noose about his neck. He stood with one foot on the sweet jar, Eros denied. Then he kicked away the jar with his other foot. There was just time enough for him to see it slither on the stony floor; he swung into the blue. He wore the ragged coat. His pipe peeped like a flower head from the rough breast pocket. Nobody jeered. Nobody clapped. For a time nobody came, not until Mr Agrelovitch brought me to that subterranean room with its odd blue light.

40

Clarrie meets up with her mother

When she left the house Clarrie had little idea where she was headed and it's difficult to guess why she chose to go to Blackpool. Perhaps when she arrived at the station she discovered the Blackpool train to be the first to leave. It's difficult to say. Anyway, she caught a late train, endured a cold journey staring at two pictures of a frozen Lake Windermere hung beneath the luggage rack, and arrived at the seaside town in the middle of the night. She walked from the station to the promenade, and leaning with arms folded on the silver barrier rail she watched the dark swirling ocean for a long while.

She observed donkeys climbing unhappily from out of the sea. They plodded on to the sands, shaking water from their fur. Each of them had a white salt line around his bloated belly indicating both the depth to which the animal had waded and the amount of water which had been swallowed in the process. They tramped up the beach, away from her, snorting in a cloud of hot mingled breaths. Silver bells tinkled. At her back, the sky paled. As the waves caught the pink of the dawn she became aware of others, out of depth, swimming towards the shore. Their grey ears were laid back and edged with rose; their frightened lips drawn from gritted teeth. Black nostrils flared, pushing out the occasional plume of salt water.

Oyster-catchers waded on the wet sand picking the early soft molluscs leaving pearls to the brightening day. They flew into the air when startled by an old ass heaving himself from the sea then, more bravely, they circled the waves for a few moments. They were gone from my cousin's vision when their spiralling paths took them plummeting towards the water.

Immediately below the barrier rail, a wet Union flag covered an object. She imagined it to be a rock. The wet drape remained stiff, sculpted in the chill wind which hammered in short knocks off the sea.

When the weak sun broke and warmed them, her clothes began to steam.

She looked to the sweet jar tucked beneath her arm and rattled the threepenny bits enjoyably as a child enjoys the shaking of a noisy toy. She thought of the value of the jar's contents. Not since the very first night she had earned her two pieces had she thought of it as money. It had been a silvery stuff which moved (tracking rising and falling fortunes), a stuff which she received and which eventually she would use to bargain with the laundry master – to bargain, not to spend. That bargain had always been in her mind. But now the bargaining had been concluded it had left a hole somewhere. A hole in her mind which had suddenly materialized as the object held in the crook of her arm.

Two young boys are on the beach. In the rock pools they turn things over with sticks.

'It's mine.'

'No, I saw it first. Gis it 'ere.'

Then into the bag on the second boy's back.

'We'll eat it at that table o'er there.'

'Ay. Someone's set it for us, look.'

'Very kind of 'em, I'm sure.' They both laugh as one of them bows low to the other exaggerating a servile posture, his thin leg sticking out stiffly like that of a crane.

As the boys approach the flag spread upon their table in cold stiffness she senses that something isn't right. She wants to shout, 'No, don't. Don't do that,' but she doesn't.

'I'll shek off the crumbs,' says the first boy.

'No, allow me,' says the second boy and he grabs the wet flag and flaps it heavily in the air. He sees the first boy's face, the sudden absence of amusement, the chill of fear. He looks to what has been revealed from under the sopping flag.

Clarrie bought herself a ticket and hurried down the platform alongside which was the train for Leeds. Passengers were boarding. The train hissed quietly to itself. As she scurried along she stopped briefly before each dirty compartment window and peered in. She had no need for conversation but she realized from the movements within each carriage that the train was rapidly filling, so she quickly made

493

up her mind to take her place in a compartment occupied by a woman who she saw talking with three men. She reasoned that she would be quite safe if there was a second woman in the compartment with her. She opened the door and after stowing her case and her jar in the netted rack she took her seat in the near corner sitting with her back to the engine. She hadn't realized just how safe she would be, however.

The first face which she recognized was not that of her mother. It was the guardsman's face of Mr Sligh. The second face was that of her mother.

'Mr Sligh! Mother!' she cried.

'Clarrie, *chérie*?' her mother asked, 'Is it you?'

'Is it Clarrie?' echoed the man who had spent his life in a barrel whilst sharing Clarrie's room at Salon Marguerite. He stooped, bringing his face close to hers to give himself a clear view of my cousin.

Rosanne, who had been sitting in the seat opposite her daughter, stood up. She turned herself about, causing her dark skirts to rustle, and she allowed herself to drop into place next to Clarrie. She put her arms around her daughter and kissed her, watched by the three men who were standing, crowded about them. 'It most certainly is. It is Clarrie,' she told them, a hint of emotion catching in her throat. She choked it back. 'Come, *chérie*, let's have a good look at you,' she said and with lacy fingers she lifted Clarrie's chin for all to see. The white lace of her mother's glove irritated my cousin's skin.

The guard's whistle blew and with a great chug of smoke which drifted along the platform the train started smoothly forward. The occupants of the carriage watched the smoke float by the window.

'My, how beautiful you have grown,' Rosanne said, turning her attention again to Clarrie. 'Hasn't she grown into a beauty?' She sought confirmation from her silent companions, smiling proudly at them. Their faces were detached, like cherubim placed between earth and sky painted by an artist of the baroque. Then, of her daughter, Rosanne asked, 'Do you remember Mr Moralee, Clarrie? You must remember the pet shop on the corner?'

'Of course, Mother. The man at the pet shop,' she exclaimed, regarding the ancient adventurer who squeezed a smile from his leather face. She looked to the others. 'And Mr Sligh I know,' she said, pointing to the ex-guardsman, remembering the occasion she had seen him last, when hauling in the couch. He had reminded her then of a flower, sex parts risen from amidst fallen petals.

'Do you still have the barrel?' she asked.

'I have many barrels. Lots and lots,' he smiled.

Letting her inquiring gaze settle upon the corpulent third man she asked, 'But I don't think that we ever met, did we?'

'No,' said Rosanne as the train gathered speed out of the station. 'You won't have met my husband. This is Doctor Dawson, *chérie*. He used to work down at the Department of Anaesthesiology but I don't think that you will ever have met.' She looked out of the window for a moment noting the regular red brick backs of the boarding houses shooting by. 'How could you know him?' she asked suddenly. 'I didn't meet Doctor Dawson myself until that dreadful night when the house fell down. The night we formed the circus.'

'The circus?'

'Yes, my dear. We are the Count Schubert Circus. We are on our way to give a performance in Leeds. We have baboons and birds and lots of props, they are going by road in the red wagon. You must remember the red wagon.'

'Good heavens,' Doctor Dawson bellowed suddenly, emitting ether fumes and reminding Clarrie vividly of the smell of Salon Marguerite, 'now isn't that a strange thing. You two get parted at the time of a rare natural disaster, namely the Manchester earthquake, and nine years later you are thrown together on the day of a disaster of equal rarity. What happy coincidence.'

'And what disaster might that have been, Doctor Dawson?' my cousin asked.

'Why, my dear, the tidal wave last night. The tidal wave in Blackpool. You must have seen it. It almost washed away the promenade.'

41

Walter completes his plan

The lily growing in Mrs Beanlander's head managed not to disturb her frizz of marmalade hair. A coolness towards Wimpey, however, intensified and Walter sensed it. He was sufficiently encouraged to try again. In casually placing a bet with Billy he was able to ask confirmation of Huddy's number without arousing suspicion. He went back to the box and let himself in.

He impatiently rattled the cradle with his fingertips and held the earpiece to his head with his other hand.

'Number, please.' That was Miss Pickles's voice.

'It's Clyde Wimpey here, love,' Walter stammered.

'Do you want the police station, Constable?' She spoke over a quiet noise. She was knitting, needle points clacking away in tiny crossed circles over the mouth of the black cone which sprang from the top pearl button of her cardigan. A ball of white wool rested, caught between the edge of the cone and the slim depression between her small breasts.

'No, no. I want thee to get us a connection, love.' He recited Huddy's telephone number.

'One moment, please.'

'Hello.' That was Huddy Greenblatt's voice.

'Is tha there, Huddy?'

'Yes.'

'It's Clyde Wimpey here, Huddy.'

There was a long silence. Walter could hear the clacking of Miss Pickles's needles, wands waving across a cauldron of technology which bubbled voices out from the ether. He eventually said awkwardly, 'Well, I've some bets for thee, Huddy.'

There was another, even longer silence in which Huddy was thinking furiously.

'Hello?' Walter asked, panicked at the quiet.

'Hello,' Huddy responded suspiciously.

'Doesn't tha want me bets?'

'Don't know what you're on about, Constable.'

'Aw, come on, Huddy, don't play games, lad,' Walter cajoled with a growing confidence. 'I'm just trying to mek a little bit on the side, that's all. A policeman's wage won't keep such a large family when me and Mrs Beanlander's wed, tha naws.'

Silence.

'Well, look,' Walter sighed, understanding the awkwardness of the situation he had thrust upon the bookie. 'This conversation's not getting us very far, is it? Let me give thee the bets anyway and tha can write 'em up if tha likes. I'll mek a note 'ere in me book. If tha doesn't accept 'em, well, there'll not be a right lot I can do about it, will there?'

Silence. Walter wondered if one day Miss Pickles's magic cone might not throw out pictures as well as words, giving him a view of the silent bookie with the trilby on his head. Then a wave of panic when he realized how Huddy might also see that he wasn't having a conversation with the person he thought.

'Is thee listenin'?'

'I'm listenin',' Huddy answered a little impatiently.

The lad reeled off half a dozen bets, picking the names of horses at random from the race card at Ascot which was printed in the *Sporting Pink*.

'Is thee still there?' Walter asked.

'Yes.'

'Well, look, it's best we don't meet, like, so I'll leave stake money in t'cupboard in police box up at crossroads and I'll leave thee a key to t'box under the rock right outside. If there's owt to come tha can leave it in t'box, but don't forget to replace the key.'

Miss Pickles, an unlikely gatekeeper to the new world of sudden communication, said, 'Dear oh dear,' dropping a stitch. She picked up and continued to knit her universe, drawing wool and words from the space in and around the dark cone. 'Dear oh dear,' she said again.

'Well, I'll 'ave to get off now,' said Walter hurriedly, embarrassed to know the lady had heard his deception.

He connected the earpiece to its cradle and lifted the ledger from the cupboard and placed it on the chrome arm rest, allowing his fingers to run along the coloured pattern of the edge of the closed book. He debated for a moment with himself. Should he proceed? Eventually he opened the ledger. He took a sharpened pencil from his trouser pocket, licked the point as he had seen the constable do, and started to write on the next available clean page. In capital letters he shakily wrote down the date with the half-dozen bets printed beneath; he left the book open at the page and placed the few coppers to cover the bets in the cupboard. When he left the box he searched about for a large rock. He placed it by the door and slipped the key beneath. Then he went home.

42

The case against Clarrie

Inspector Lockhart sat round-shouldered at his desk. He removed his glasses and rubbed the lenses with a clean handkerchief, then he ran the handkerchief around the metal, studiously dislodging any grease which had collected on the wire frame. He carefully replaced the glasses, bending the soft wire around his ears. With a flourish he stuffed the handkerchief back into his top pocket where it spilled brightly. Like Buckland the geologist, who for the amusement of students had simulated the flight of the pterodactyl, the inspector wore dark coat-tails which he draped over the back of his chair. Lockhart was definitely an oddity.

There were several files on his desk. The folders were of a rough pulp board which had the colour of hay in the light cast through the dusty window.

A name had been typed on each folder. One of them bore the name Clarrie Schubert Brightside. The typed name was underlined in red ink – the line was straight and had been drawn parallel to the top edge of the folder. Close by on the desk was a six-inch wooden ruler: there were red marks on the edges and on the reverse side where the ink, over the years, had soaked into the soft wood. Tucked into the folder were several papers and there was also a cracked sepia photograph of Clarrie which had been snapped many years since. Lockhart carefully removed these things from the folder. In the photograph the child wore sequinned tights and she had an ostrich feather banded to her head in the manner of the Red Indian braves Lockhart had seen in the cowboy pictures Uncle Lancaster had been making in Hollywood.

The photograph had been neatly snipped from a larger photograph. A downy arm dangled from nowhere, the hand touching the girl's shoulder. Lockhart knew it to be the arm of the child's mother – it was, after all, he who had with rusting iron scissors cut up the photograph many years before.

The girl's face smiled out at the inspector with all the innocence of her ten or eleven years. He remembered her exactly as she looked – she had lived with her mother in a red wagon which had been parked beneath the gas lamp in a pit village near Kippax.

He squared up the papers on top of the folder with well-manicured fingertips and began to read what he had already read many times. The papers were mostly scrawled upon in black ink though the words were scribbled in different hands.

Years ago, the Chief Constable of Manchester had written to Inspector Lockhart informing him that Clarrie Schubert Brightside was wanted for questioning in connection with the death of a police officer who had possibly been pushed from a building on the night of the Manchester earthquake. It was a routine letter, the kind which circulated between forces, the main purpose of which was to eliminate people from an inquiry. The inspector rubbed the edge of his finger back and forth, brushing into his heavy black tash as he might have brushed his teeth. The Chief Constable had lamented the death of his officer but he made no accusations, commenting that accident was the most likely reason for the fall.

There was a second letter written only recently and received from a police inspector in Halifax. The letter told of a dwarf, a harmless soul calling himself the laundry master, who took in washing in the village of Luddenden Foot. He had been found hanging in a cellar. It also told of the theft of a considerable amount of money which had been the dwarf's savings. The money was saved as silver threepenny pieces and had been kept in a sweet jar. An empty sweet jar was found lying on its side close by the hanged man, wrote the Halifax inspector. Clarrie Schubert Brightside had lived for many years in the same house as the dwarf and whilst there was no evidence to connect her with his death the police had a sworn statement from a mill girl, Daisy Miller, that Clarrie had disappeared from the house on the night the dwarf had met his death.

Inspector Lockhart reached across his desk to take a cigar from a wooden box. He lit the cigar, puffed on it several times, and faded into a cloud of contemplative smoke. He considered Daisy Miller's statement. In itself it didn't seem to be particularly significant. For one thing, the time of death was not corroborated – the police surgeon apparently being too drunk to attend the scene when the body was discovered. (The body had been found by a relative of Clarrie's, Donald Brightside, it said in parentheses. Inspector Lockhart knew him, too, had been a schoolfriend to his uncle, Lancaster Brightside, the famous Hollywood film maker.)

There was a third letter, received by Lockhart only that morning. As he started to re-read it with beetled brows, Mrs Beanlander brought in his mid-morning tea. She made a wafting motion with her hand to indicate how excessively smoky was his environment and left. He thanked the closed door and returned to his task.

The third letter was from an officer in North Fylde. He explained that he too wished to question Clarrie Brightside – also in the process of elimination in connection with a death. The drowning of a youth, a Punch and Judy man. This death too had probably been an accident, for the fatality had occurred on the night the tidal wave had broken on Blackpool's shore – 'You must have heard about it,' wrote the officer with a flush of civic pride. He went on to suggest there may have been good reason for the youth being on the beach for it was rumoured that he slept there and, as the wave had arisen without warning, he may well have been asleep at the time and been freakishly swept out to sea and perished before realizing he wasn't dreaming of his drowning.

The unusual facts of the case however were, firstly, that the youth had died wrapped in a Union flag. Odd, but perhaps not inexplicable. The Fylde officer had a stab at explanation. He thought it quite possible that the flag had been a covering for the Punch and Judy stage, that it may also have been used as a night blanket and may well have been wrapped about him when the youth was so suddenly washed away.

But secondly, and so far without explanation, the boy had died with a bent threepenny piece in his throat. And here was the possible connection with Clarrie Schubert Brightside, for the Fylde police were well aware of the recent death and the theft of the threepenny pieces from the house in Luddenden Foot.

Tenuous? But there was more. The Fylde police had unearthed evidence that a woman had been seen with a jar filled with threepenny pieces whilst at the railway station in Blackpool. The man in the ticket office clearly recalled a woman having paid for her ticket with such coins which she had got from some sort of jar. What's more, they had a statement that the purchase of the ticket had been made at about the same time the police had become aware of the tragedy. The man in the ticket office could not remember, however, where the woman had wished to travel. From the approximate time of purchase and with regard to the train timetable for the day, it may have been to Wigan or to Leeds or to Leek in Staffordshire.

Furthermore, the body had been discovered by two boys and they too recalled a woman who had been watching them from the promenade directly above the spot where the body had been discovered. She had something which reflected the sun's rays nestling under her arm, one of the boys had recalled. When prompted he stated that it could have been a glass sweet jar.

Lockhart re-read the three reports together, alternately brushing his dark tash and puffing on his cigar. The statement from the boy on the beach of course meant the existence of two sweet jars, but why not? Why not two sweet jars? What would happen when the first sweet jar was filled with its silver bits? Wouldn't the dwarf begin to save in a second jar? But was it possible, he wondered whilst scrutinizing the photograph of Clarrie Schubert Brightside? He allowed his shoulders to slump even more roundly. He had known the girl's father, a twin to his childhood friend Lancaster. He knew her grandparents, good solid folk. He had known her mother, the rope walker (who hadn't?) – a thoroughly bad lot, he had always thought. He had known the girl too. Could that sweet tot have grown into a psychopath, he wondered? Was it possible?

He re-read the statement made by one of the girls who had worked at Salon Marguerite. 'Madame had just offered her daughter to the police officer when the house began to shake,' she had stated. A thoroughly bad lot, Lockhart said softly to himself.

He considered the flimsy connection between hanging and rope walking and wondered how adept Clarrie might have been in handling a rope.

43
Lockhart visits the police box

There was a knock at the inspector's door.

'Come,' he called out. Walter Beanlander put his nose around the door. The room was so smoky that they could hardly see each other. 'Who's that?' asked Lockhart.

'It's me. Walter.'

'Oh, Walter. Hello, son. Come to see your mother?'

'No, it's thee I want to see, Inspector Lockhart.'

'Oh, yes. Well, I'm rather busy at present, lad,' he said, squaring up the papers on his desk.

'Well, it's important, like.'

'Well, won't it wait?'

'No. I think it's summat tha should know.'

'You had better come on in, then. Close the door and sit down.' The boy came into the office and sat in the chair at the other side of Lockhart's desk.

The inspector noted how agitated Walter was. Not surprising since the boy had received little sleep the previous night. Last evening he had learned from the wireless that he had picked winners in two of the six races at Ascot. They had come home at long odds too. He calculated that the bookie would be owing Wimpey a few shillings. He was so excited that he had been unable to sleep.

As soon as the sun was up, warming the elder from its strait-jacket in the crimble, Walter had raced up to the box. His few coppers had gone, replaced by two shiny shillings and a halfpenny. He had been hanging about the crimble since early morning, giving Lockhart time to get to his desk.

'Well, what is it that's so urgent, lad?' Lockhart prompted, tapping the ash from his cigar.

'Its PC Wimpey, Inspector.'

'Well, what about him, lad?'

'He's placing bets with bookie, Inspector.'

'What?'

'Ay. He bets with Huddy Greenblatt.'

'Are you trying to tell me that one of my constables is acting as a runner for a bookie, lad?'

'Ay. PC Wimpey, he does. He placed bets yesterday, go and ask Miss Pickles if tha doesn't believe me. He uses telephone up at the crossroads.'

'Nonsense, lad. He was having a joke with you. Must have been. Wimpey would never do anything like that. He's in line, should receive his promotion any day. He wants to marry your mother.'

'No,' Walter said.

'No? But he does, lad, your mother said.'

'No. I mean he did. He does use the telephone. He had a key cut, Inspector. He leaves it under a stone and the bookie comes and lets hisself into the box.'

'What, lets himself on to police property?' Lockhart was now alarmed.

'Ay.'

'No. Can't be. Wimpey wouldn't do anything like that.'

'But he does. Come and see. Come and have a look, Inspector Lockhart.'

'Can't, lad,' the inspector answered, shuffling the files on his desk. 'I've too much to do.' Then, seeing the boy's disappointment, he asked, 'It's that important to you, is it, lad?'

'Of course it is. I don't want my mother married to a bent copper, Inspector Lockhart.'

'Well, I can understand that, Walter,' Lockhart answered and he sipped the lukewarm tea which Walter's mother had brought to him earlier. He flourished the handkerchief from his top pocket and wiped his mouth roughly, then he mopped his brow with it and stuffed the handkerchief untidily back where it had come from. 'Perhaps I'd better come and have a look, after all, eh? Come on, we'll go in the car, it won't take long and we'll get this business sorted. Only as it's you, mind. Like him near being your father, an' all.'

'Key's under the rock, Inspector,' said the lad as they got out of the motor. The inspector turned the rock with his shiny boot and was surprised to see the equally shiny key, solitary on the brown earth at the side of the moved rock. He stooped and picked up the key. He inserted it in the lock and was even more surprised when he saw how easily the key turned to open the door to the box. He looked at Walter, raising his beetle brows, and the two of them squeezed in. Inspector Lockhart removed his handkerchief again and cleaned his wire-framed spectacles, then with a sigh he studied the ledger still open at the page where Walter had left it. He read through the bets shaking his head with disbelief, his eyes widening as he read the comment which Huddy Greenblatt must have written there when leaving the winnings.

'PC Wimpey,' the bookie had incriminatingly addressed his remark, 'here is how your winnings is calculated.' There followed a neat sum, the answer underlined twice in red ink. Two shillings and a halfpenny. Both the boy and the inspector separately followed the arithmetic to confirm the bookie's workings. They arrived at their answers simultaneously, Inspector Lockhart with his index finger pointing at the underlined answer. He nodded. The boy nodded back gravely. The note was finished off with the comment that the money owed 'is herewith left in the cubbard below'. The inspector stooped to open the cupboard.

44
The Wardian case orchestrated

Old man Pymont died. It was our village's first trafficking fatality, if you exclude Mr Brown running the Jam Sahib's motor into the back of a parked vehicle and skewering his heart with the steering column. What I mean is that Mr Pymont was the first pedestrian to get himself run over in the village. It happened outside his house. Oddly enough it was a Sunday afternoon but it wasn't raining. If it had been raining Pymont wouldn't have been outside, but probably in the parlour cranking out the Prague Symphony. I bet his wife wished it had pissed down all day. I remember being in the church and thinking that. I looked at the widow's sad waxen face, revealed for a moment when she lifted her veil to blow her nose, and I thought, 'I'll bet you wish it had been pissing down all that day, love.' But then, as my grandfather said, 'When tha time's up, it's up. If it hadn't bin that stranger reversin' his van over 'im it would've bin somethin' else.' My grandfather was a fatalist. He believed we all had a deathday as well as a birthday. His pessimism was such that he would have sent us all deathday cards had he known the dates.

But I suppose my grandfather was in a sense correct. Old Pymont's death was something which was just waiting to happen. I don't mean that it 'had to happen', of course it had to happen sometime, but it was waiting to happen – perhaps more precisely the happening was watching, choosing its moment. Then, when the time was right – not a pre-ordained time but the random falling into place of other things' time – out he stepped. It happened.

The purpose for the stranger's visit was an episode more of the 'had to happen' type. He drove his van over to the museum. Nobody had ever seen him before but he demanded to speak to me. I wasn't around, so Walter directed him over to my grandfather's house. He can't have been too bright because he missed the house the first time round and he had to come back again when he got as far as the big house. He parked outside our house facing the museum and Hunger

Hill. I was out back tending the roses. My grandmother came out, her head covered in her black shawl, and she said: 'Donald, there's someone wants to sithee. It's a stranger and he's got summat fothee, for the museum he says.'

I went through the house to be greeted at the door by the stranger. He wore a deer-stalker hat and a shooting jacket. The bottoms of his trousers were stuffed untidily into his socks which was a bit of a shock, because in looking at him above the waist you would have thought he was a gentleman and put your money on him having worn plus-fours. From the waist down he looked ready to cycle to the pit. His heels were well down too.

'I've some things for your museum, if you'll take them,' he said and from his voice I knew he wasn't from around these parts. He sauntered to the back of his van and threw open the doors. The rear of the van was stuffed full with animal hides.

'There's also several heads up front. Mostly reindeer, an odd bull, some goats and sheep, they've all got full sets of horns and antlers though. Do you want them?'

'Got no money for stuff like that,' I said, putting on a miserable expression.

'That's all right. I don't want payment. Just take them if you want them.'

I had never been in the habit of turning down gifts when offered to the museum, no matter how odd they were, or how useless. My face brightened.

'OK. I'll get in the cab and you can drive us over to the museum. We can unload over there.'

He drove me to the museum and he helped Walter and me unload the skins and the heads, then he asked: 'Do you want me to drive you back to the house?' as if it was a hundred miles away. I got back into the cab anyway and in driving back, he did the same thing as he had done before. He missed the house, got as far as the big house and turned about. He dropped me at the door to my grandfather's house, said goodbye and started to reverse towards the terrace end. That's when he knocked down Pymont who had stepped out of his doorway only two seconds before. Bang.

The children playing on the common ran up to the crossroads

and brought back Wimpey's replacement, who arrested the stranger for careless driving. A police car came over from Castleford and the stranger was bundled into the back seat, protesting that he was a member of the Royal Family and shouldn't be treated in such a fashion. The new constable drove away the van, presumably to the police station. An ambulance came and took away the body.

It turned out that the man was a poacher. 'A bit puddled,' Mrs Beanlander told my grandmother, for Mrs Beanlander saw everything that went on at the station including the transcripts of interrogations. 'He shoots cows and such. Probably lock him up in the asylum at Wakefield.'

'Tha'd better say nowt about the reason for 'is visit, then,' my grandfather advised me. 'Tha'd get done for receivin' stolen property. Probably stick thee in't funny place with 'im, if they get a good look at that museum of tharn.'

I had to agree with my grandfather. I told the police I had no idea why the man had called at the Brightside home and I told Walter that if he breathed a word of it to anyone, including his mother, then he would end up in the funny place too. We hid the skins and the heads with the sugar sacks and the plaster of Paris under the stage.

My grandfather wouldn't let the matter drop. 'Tha'll 'ave to be rid of 'em. Tha doesn't want Lockhart nosing about, diggin' up them pelts,' he told me. I had to agree with him again. I suggested that we should either bury them on Hunger Hill or perhaps dump them in the deeper stretch of water down past Bottom Boat.

'Why don't we cover him in them?' Walter said.

'Who in them?'

'Him. The dinosaur. Why don't we clothe him in a skin? Mek him more appealing.'

'Ay, tha's right, Walter. Cover over the skeleton, I'd never thought of that.'

'Be more like the real thing, wouldn't it?'

We began immediately to sew the hides about the skeleton. At the same time we rid ourselves of the stuffed heads, hiding them in the deep hollow of the dinosaur's rib cage before we covered him over. It was several days before he was completely clothed. We stepped back to admire our handiwork. The skins wrinkled sadly. Gravity played its part, letting multifolds of skin drop to his ankles. He had the look of a young boy dressed in his father's Sunday suit. We congratulated one another, all the same, over a pint or two at the pub and were glad to be rid of the evidence.

The following day was Pymont's funeral and I thought, looking at Mrs Pymont, 'I bet you wish it had pissed down all that Sunday, love. I bet,' and walking back from the church in the next village Johnny Pymont ran ahead of his family to catch up with Walter and me.

'Do thee want the panharmonicon?' he asked.

'Why?'

'Me mother says we're gettin' rid, now me dad's gone.'

'Well, I don't know,' I said, breaking the habit of a lifetime.

'Could use the panharmonicon,' Walter commented.

'Could we?'

'Ay.'

'Ay. Well, me mother wants to know.' Johnny nodded back towards his mother walking with the other women. A net veil covered her face.

'Why's she want rid?' I asked.

'Mek room in the house, she says.'

'But if you don't mind me saying, Johnny, now tha dad's gone, tha needs less room.'

Johnny shrugged. 'She just wants rid,' he suddenly said.

We began our steep descent into the village. 'What we want with the bloody panharmonicon?' I asked Walter.

'Orchestrate the exhibition.'

'What, like a musical box?' I screwed my eyes into the sun.

'Ay. Now he's got his skin, he'll be able to feel the music. I'll get crackin' right away.'

'I think we'd better wait a day or two, Walter,' I felt bound to advise. 'We can't go tekin' Pymont's treasure before he's had time to go cold in the grave.'

'Tha can,' Johnny piped up. 'She wants rid now.'

'Now?'

'Ay, now, then we can get all us guests in the 'ouse.'

There were half a dozen of us who wheeled the automaton on bogies up to the museum whilst Mrs Pymont doled out sausage rolls and planned with the other women what she was to do with all that space in the parlour.

It was a sad week. The following day we heard that my Uncle Lancaster had been killed in the war. The bomber he had been flying had exploded into the sea. My grandmother was so overcome she had to sit, something which she didn't often do. She watched the pot of broth blackening on the coals for ages, then her eyes suddenly went up inside her head like Arkwright's did. Tears trickled from the two white holes.

''E were forever fallin', were the lad,' my grandfather said quietly.

Henrietta remembered how Lancaster had often flown about the village dressed in one of Mr Tsiblitz's suits.

'Ay, until gravity fulfilled its promise and felled him down again. Funny that, how he should die in a machine which had his name.'

My grandmother's eyes reappeared. 'Funny that.' She repeated my grandfather's words.

I had to go for a walk, get away from the grief and the wintergreen. I went up to the next village. Frog was at his usual pitch on the pavement. I bought a bunch of bog asphodel and another of foxgloves. I went across to the church and laid them on James Brightside's grave. There were men cutting down the iron railings from the wall around the churchyard. The saws they used made a noise like the butcher's saw when it cuts through the bone.

'What's tha doin'?'

'Tekin' railin's.'

'But why?'

'For tanks.'

'Fuck the fuckin' war,' I said and went back to Frog, asleep on the pavement. I took the only bunch of fumitory he had left in his tray and tossed a penny into his lap. He stirred and opened his eyes.

'Oh, hello, Donald.'

I turned my back, hiding anger and tears, and walked down the path to the village. I went to the museum and put the flowers in water in a stone pot. I stood the pot on the cold, marble-topped table next to Mrs Tarbutt's book.

Walter was well on with his project. He had coupled the Wardian case and the panharmonicon in series. They were linked like a trailer to its motor vehicle. The crank handle on the panharmonicon not only drove the music, it now worked the dinosaur's head. Tarty played the keyboards. The beast in baggy pants nodded his approval of the Prague.

Walter finished what he had to do then, like his father, he just walked away. I never saw him again, at least not in the flesh. It was in 1947 that I saw a photograph in a newspaper. A group of men at a Manchester laboratory, something to do with the University I think, had built an electrical computing device. Walter, wearing a laboratory coat several sizes too large, stood at the back, a little apart from the group of boffins. He had acquired spectacles but you couldn't mistake that strange hair.

1947

45
The return

Rain battered at the tin roof on the hut in the marshalling yard. Charlie Gill grabbed his crutch and his lantern and plopped out into the mud. He had heard an unfamiliar noise, as if somebody was driving a truck full of coal around the yard at this time of night. That couldn't be right. He held the lantern above his head and screwed his eyes into the rain which beat his face. He could hear the fairground noise of the Prague wafting from the museum on sheets of wind and ice.

'Oy,' he shouted, when he realized that there *was* a truck in the yard. Its engine idled. He could just make out the rectangular shape, darkly silhouetted against the slag, some way off. The headlamps, suddenly switched on, formed cones of light which pierced the driving rain. The square radiator steamed into the freezing air, sideways on to the night-watchman. The truck started to move. Charlie heard the wheels rolling stickily. Eight wheels he reckoned – it must be a big truck. He propelled himself forward to meet it, hurriedly thrusting his crutch into puddles of oozing mud which sucked at the rubber end.

'Oy,' he shouted. 'Oy, what's thee up to?'

The truck turned slowly. Charlie stopped, leaned on the crutch watching it turn. The light beams were now pointing directly at him, blinding. The truck inched forward; it appeared as if its driver was searching for something.

'Oy,' he shouted again, scuttering out of the dazzle. The end of his crutch plopped at each step. Charlie hopped to turn around and held the lantern aloft whilst he balanced himself. The truck rolled close by and he had a clear view of the mascot surmounting the hissing radiator. The truck was painted brightly in red and gold. The large tyres threw mud which spattered the watchman's cape.

'Oy,' he shouted, breathing heavily and leaning his full weight now on to the crutch. He watched the back of the truck moving away from him and in the light cast from his lantern he saw the huge bolts and brass padlock on the high doors which closed it. Charlie waited to see what the truck would do.

He listened carefully to the rain bouncing off his corrugated tin hut a few yards distant. The rain was falling faster now. A sudden gust of wind blew it in sheets across the marshalling yard as the truck turned again, rocking slightly; the cones of light revealed small mountains of shiny black coal. The truck edged slowly towards Charlie, the powerful engine idling. The noise was relentless, threatening to run on forever. He held up the lantern once more, higher this time, and he swung it in the rain, trying to attract the driver's attention. His arm ached. He could see the windscreen. The truck had no wiper blades. It came to him an inch at a time. When he realized it wasn't about to stop Charlie scuttled out of the way again, splashing his foot in freezing puddles and cursing the wet which had splashed inside his boot.

'Oy.'

The truck continued to roll. It was closer to him than before, when it passed by this second time. The enormous tyres chucked up mud as it went by. The night-watchman saw the truck demolish his hut. Then it stopped rolling. The engine was still idling when the driver jumped from the cab and squelched in the mud.

'Oy,' said Charlie, hopping about. 'What's tha doin'? Is tha tryin' to bloody well kill me?'

'Sorry.' It was a woman's voice. Charlie held the lantern to her face.

'Bit rum this. A bloody woman driver.'

'Sorry,' she repeated.

'Oy, don't I know thee?'

The driver looked him up and down then suddenly her white, wet face brightened. 'Why, it's Mr Gill, isn't it?'

'That's right. Charlie Gill. Who are thee when tha's at 'ome?'

'It is Rosanne, Mr Gill.'

'Rosanne who?'

She took off her cap and let her yellow hair spill across her shoulders.

'Bugger me, it's the rope walker,' Charlie said to the dark skyload of metal-tasting rain and leaned the relief for the knowing of it on to his crutch, where he lolled for a second or two. He chewed on his lower lip, thinking. 'Don't know there's many will want to see thee agin,' he said bluntly. Then he held the lantern away from her face so that he could see the side of the truck. He peered into the light cast, trying to read the golden lettering curling there. 'It's the circus wagon, isn't it? Big wagon what used to park under gas lamp?' The rain-spattered his face, wetting his lips, lubricating his words.

'That's right, it is. It's been given a motor, but you are right, it's the same wagon.' He saw another person climb down from the cab. 'Oh, here's Clarrie. Do you remember my daughter, Mr Gill?'

The man looked at my cousin. 'By, quite a young woman, eh? I'd never have recognized her.' Clarrie smiled at Charlie, the rain driving hard at her eyes which she had to close. He looked away into the blackness of the yard. 'Well, bugger me,' he said again.

Mozart wafted on the wind.

'What's that music?' Clarrie asked.

'It's young Brightside over at museum.'

'Donald?'

'Ay, Donald Brightside. Tha cousin, miss.'

'Sounds more like a fun-fair than a museum.'

'It's the dinosaur.'

'Well, what's he doing to it?'

'He's got it in a glass cage and he meks it nod its head in time to the music. It's a sort of living picture.'

'*Un tableau vivant?*' Rosanne told him.

'Ay, one of them.'

He chewed on his lip and was silent.

'I'm sorry about the hut,' Rosanne apologized again. The smashed hut lay on its side in the mud.

'Couldn't give a bugger,' Charlie said. 'Pit closes down next Monday.'

'The pit's closing down?'

'Ay. Thwaite's had enough. Nationalization, tha naws. He won't spend owt, so he's closin' up. Most of the men have found work at other pits.'

'You mean the village is empty?'

'Not so many left now. After they nationalized, most folk buggered off to find work in other pits. Thwaite's not interested in nationalizing. There's a few what still works there but like I told thee, he closes up on Monday. So couldn't give a bugger about hut.' He stared into the rain, tasting it. 'Soon be nowt left, nowt at all.'

The war left us first. After that the men went.

But the war went first – in a great Hurrah. We raided the workshops at the pit head and clattered trestles and boards on to the common. We erected long tables at which we sat in lines facing each other, struck dumb by a whiteness of tablecloths: linens taken from lavender-smelling chests, where they had remained folded for years, emitting their peculiar smell into the dark, storing it up for the special occasion when the boxes would eventually be opened and the rooms be overdressed with flowers and women.

The bereaved, the sad and the maimed sat in the sun shuffling their backsides on parlour chairs, wondering what might be expected of them; so they feigned the celebratory mood with the rest of us and tucked into Mr Westerman's pigs dressed up in different ways.

Rube Hardwick brought a barrel of beer from the pub which he mounted at one end of a long table. He acted the barman just as he did at the pub, allowing the ale to run through a brass tap into pint pots which were downed as quickly as he could fill them. Henrietta and my grandmother baked loaves. They were sliced into doorsteps and piled like the treads of a spiral staircase on to best china plates which were taken down from parlour walls where the sun had faded their colours. Or pulled from drawers which smelled of polish, where the colours had remained as fast as the days they were brightly painted.

The rooks came to peck at the crumbs then flew off, the wings of some catching in the bunting which was strung out above our heads. A rope of small paper flags of the allies fell on to the tablecloth and Mr Archbold tied them in a hat on the pig's head before him

Grandma Dolly predicted rain. The rooks, perching on the roof-tops, laughed.

After the meal was cleared away the trestles and the boards and those of us not too drunk to play enjoyed a game of cricket with some of the uniformed soldier boys who had come over from the next village. A dog ran off with the cork ball in his mouth. He ran towards the pit, where for once the wheel was silent, and was chased by hordes of children shouting. 'Len Hutton's nicked the ball, Len Hutton's nicked the ball.' The rooks returned whilst we argued what we should do. They pecked at the crumbs which had been shaken to the ground from the white tablecloths. We watched them for a while, until Billy o' the Terrus End appeared with a tennis ball and the game got restarted.

One of the soldiers immediately smashed the new ball for six over the roofs and the rooks took off in an hilarity.

We spent most of the remaining daylight hours searching the ash pits for the lost tennis ball. We didn't find it but managed to get in a couple of overs when Len Hutton returned, wagging his tail and with the cork ball still clamped in his jaws.

The bowler wiped the saliva on his khaki trousers. He thundered in on a long run up to the wicket, his shadow edged with the red of the late sun rolling across the common. Charlie Gill, who umpired whilst standing on his one leg, unaided by his crutch, shouted, 'Oy, no ball!': then the angry bowler hurled down another six deliveries with great exhalations and loud grunts of dissatisfaction. The bats-man swung the bat wildly, almost flinging himself off balance, and missed them all and each time Charlie Gill shouted, 'Oy, no ball!' as loudly as he could. It was as if he wanted for them over the hill in the next village to be aware that they had a son who couldn't get his run-up right. Cricket, even at this level, was a mean business to some.

Then, more quietly, Charlie told the soldier to bugger off and wouldn't let him bowl any more. From the other wicket Billy, who was playing for the soldiers' team to even up the numbers, bowled an assortment of Chinamen and googlies at my bemused grandfather who couldn't hold the bat too well because of his arthritis. When the sun went down it was declared that we had beaten the army by seven runs to six. There had been only the one scoring stroke during the whole of the match; that was when the soldier had smashed the tennis ball over the houses and lost it in the ash pits. Charlie Gill, saviour of the reputation of the village, was chaired from the common by a rabble of drunks and planted in the empty beer barrel which for some reason had been sawn in two. Charlie the Christmas tree?

It started to rain.

That night I asked my grandfather what we had celebrated. Was it the death of Lancaster? Or Frog losing his legs? Bob Archbold thirsting to death in a Burmese prisoner-of-war camp? What? What was it we had celebrated, today? He said he didn't really know, but it was important enough for him to break his teetotalism and down a half-bottle of whisky. The other half would be downed less than a year later.

In January 1945, four months before the war ended, Mr Foot, who was Chairman of the Mining Association and former General Manager of the Gas, Light and Coke Company, produced his plan for the future of the coal-mining industry. He proposed an association of companies – a cartel – in which all the mine owners would act with common purpose on prices, output and wages. He proposed a central board made up entirely of mine owners, the decisions of which would be binding on all members. Ebby Edwards didn't see how it was going to change anything.

That March Ebby issued his own pamphlet. He insisted on public ownership being the only way forward. It was the only way to protect the public interest, be rid of the hated coal owners like Mr Thwaite, bring new investment and efficiency, recreate the dignity of the collier and unify the industry.

Meanwhile the Minister of Fuel and Power had appointed a committee under the chairmanship of Mr Reid, a former director of the Fife Coal Company, to advise on technical changes necessary to bring the industry to full efficiency. Reid supported the coal owners to the hilt but his report damned an indolent industry which was creaking under the weight of its own putrefaction. The only thing the Reid report proved was the urgent need for the sweeping aside of the mine owner and putting the mines into public ownership.

The war ended and the Labour Party withdrew from the Coalition

Government. The Tory caretaker government, representing Squire Potterton and his kind, still postured the incredible, the wealthy were still going to face out time. They chose to support the Foot Plan for coal.

Mr Churchill called an election and was defeated. My grandfather leaned from the bedroom window and hollered and praised Mr Ebby Edwards until, hoarse of voice and fed up with crying, he took his tear-stained cheeks down to the parlour where he finished off the half-drunk bottle of whisky which, since the war ended, had been kept locked away in a sideboard cupboard with my grandmother's plates and linen.

The new Labour government pledged itself to the nationalization of the mines but ours was a dangerous pit. It would never have a daily output any greater than it now had; the roadways were too narrow ever to bring up an efficient amount of coal. The face was too distant from the knackered winding gear. The government didn't want it.

Thwaite didn't want them to have it anyway. So he made his decision to close it down and withdrew into his big house where, like an old sea captain having scuttled his ship, he allowed the oceans to close over him.

As soon as they were aware of Thwaite's intention most of the villagers went off and got themselves jobs in other pits; pits which the government was going to sink its brass into and turn (so the promise went) into places where men could work with dignity. Much of our terrace was already empty, when on a stormy night Rosanne and Clarrie returned to the village, hauling with them the madness of the Second Count Schubert Circus.

46

Tableaux vivants

The botanical name Sambucus has been given to the elder. The name is derived from the Greek word which describes a triangular-shaped musical instrument with strings, the *sambuca*. It's a happy word, a word one might dance with. Why then does the music fashioned from the elder come, not as plucked from a mandolin or a guitar, but blown from doleful pipes? The pith is easily removed from the insides of the green stems, hollowing the tubes. Most village boys at some time or another have made blow pipes and pea shooters from the stalks but occasionally an enterprising soul will come along and cut a set of pipes like those of Pan and fill the air with oppressive sounds when whispering up the sap.

When the village awoke to our red dawn, that redness which always follows a night of storm like the one which accompanied the circus to the village, fuddled brains slowly cleared to the sorrowful noise of distant piping. The few who then remained in the terrace flung back curtains to be greeted by the sight of a glittering circus wagon parked on the common beneath the gas lamp. For my grandmother it must have been an odd moment; she had been here before. The same wagon had been parked in exactly the same spot more than thirty years since. My grandmother on that morning too had been the one to draw back the curtains at our house. She saw then almost exactly what she sees now.

'Ernest, Ernest,' she calls with an element of wonder in her voice, 'come and see this, the wagon's back under the gas lamp.'

My grandfather puts his pasty face to the window; my heart leapt. We all three stared into the rose light, sad music thickening the tinct as we watched. I read aloud the golden words lettered on the side of the wagon. The music seemed to stir the air, causing clouds to coalesce.

'They're back,' said my grandmother flatly, the wonder having left her. I had no idea how she felt about Clarrie and Rosanne; she had rarely, if ever, expressed her feelings for them during their long absences. The enthusiasm she had just now shown in asking my grandfather to come and see and the subsequent dullness in her voice, like a butcher's hatchet hitting his block, suggested perhaps a final distancing. A cutting off. Their return was not a woman's business, but a matter with which my grandfather would have to deal. Then to me she said, 'They're back, Donald,' and this time there was, for my benefit alone, a returned excitement, even encouragement in her voice. 'Tha'd better go and see, lad. Go on, get gone and see them.'

'Yes, grandmother,' I said obediently and left the house. I walked towards the sound of doleful piping uncertain how I was to approach the woman whose very name had set my heart racing all those years.

She was sitting on a rock pursing her lips at the tubes she had cut from the elder, whispering as she and I had whispered when children. A wooden barrel stood beside her, upright on the grass. I knew her immediately. In our village the prettiness of girls was gone before they became women; the lasses humped wasted beauty in lumpy child-rearing years with displays of varicosities and piles. The pit matted their hair and greased their skins. Or sometimes it dried out their skins and put carbuncles and segs on their noses. But Clarrie had escaped early from the village; she was exactly as I remembered her and still, for me, a girl.

'Hello, Clarrie,' I greeted her quietly. I was surprised by my self-control despite the ticking pulse which was causing my shirt collar to throb.

She removed her pursed lips from the pipes. 'Who are you?' she asked, looking intently at me. I tried holding my breath in an effort to rein back my shirt.

'It's Donald, Clarrie.' I began to wonder if my own good looks might have been prematurely put to waste by the pit.

'Donald Brightside?'

I nodded.

'Hello. I should never have recognized you,' she smiled, confirming my fear. I had expected instant recognition and felt hurt. I searched my mind for something to say.

'You are in the circus now?'

'Yes. Mother and I walk the high wire.' She was vague yet assertive.

The barrel beside her suddenly moved, startling me. 'Don't be afraid, it's only Mr Sligh in his barrel. He has a nasty permanent erection, you know,' she informed me. Then she looked up at the gathering clouds. 'It's going to rain again.' I thought unhappily of Grandma Dolly. Would love end in the stale smell of smoked tea-leaves and a loose bagful of lard?

She arose from the rock on which she had been sitting and with two girl-guide fingers touched what I soon knew to be Mr Sligh's penis, which protruded from a hole in the side of the barrel. She touched it as she would have tickled a hamster at the back of its neck. 'He's quite harmless,' she informed me. I was uncertain if this had been an invitation for me to stroke Mr Sligh in similar fashion but declined anyway with a shake of my head. 'He has been with the circus since it was formed, you know.'

'Well, what does he do?' I heard myself asking and wondered if the conversation I was having was real. I looked back to my grandfather's house. Smoke curled from the chimney into the still-gathering clouds. The redness was drained from the morning. Soon we should receive the metal-tasting rain as Clarrie had assured. I could see my grandparents staring, still and white-faced, from their window. They displayed the pasty-faced stability which had gummed me together since childhood. The conversation was real, all right.

'He rolls around in a barrel. He can roll up an incline twenty yards long.'

'What! With that thing?' I was too embarrassed to use any of the village words for it. Here I was with the woman I loved, the love I had not clapped eyes on for more than fifteen years, and we were in our first conversation talking of another fellow's erection. I'd be damned if I was to use the words. Whatever it had been that I had felt for Clarrie since my tenth year was suddenly gone. She was not quite the erotic I had thought – she was a woman after all. The segs and the carbuncles, the piles and the eczema, they were all there, somewhere. 'How is he able to roll so far with that thing sticking out like Errol Flynn's sword?' I found myself wanting to know.

'Don't be silly,' she giggled. 'It doesn't have to protrude from the

522

hole. He sticky-tapes it to his belly before the performance.' I had an urge to return to the safety of my grandmother's apron; perhaps I had always had that urge when confronted with Clarrie. 'He hasn't always had the erection, you know,' she told me, wide-eyed.

'No?'

The desire to know more was strong enough to prevent my leaving. Clarrie went on to tell of Salon Marguerite and the earthquake and the separation from her mother. She told of how Rosanne had the idea for starting up the circus once more. She told me of Dibden Dawson, Rosanne's husband, who was at present asleep with her beneath the Mexican blanket in the back of the wagon, and of how he and Bagshaw Moralee had for a time cured Mr Sligh of his permanent erection and his habit in the barrel.

It appeared that Bagshaw's extracts had effected a cure for the priapism all right, but Dibden Dawson's analytical mind had soon deduced the extract to be the agent which also promoted Mr Moralee's zoophagia. 'Good heavens,' he had thundered triumphantly one night at dinner, 'the old man has a soluble problem.'

The doctor had been easily able to dissuade the old man from taking his regular dose of extract, for as Bagshaw had dashed from the table to the closet at the back of his kitchen after downing most of a particularly unhealthy-looking puffin, the doctor had mocked with his ether-round eye, 'Getting caught short in the middle of your act, old chap?' The ensuing illness only served to illustrate to the pet shop owner how much better he might be without his addiction, for even Rosanne took up Dawson's mocking tone, sickened from listening to Bagshaw's guts which rumbled constantly as if they were the work of a poor plumber. She accused the old boy in the first instance of talking through his hat and eventually complained of having to listen to the nonsense from his hat when it talked through his arse.

The old man ceased with the injections and was cured almost immediately. In the medical textbooks *Zoophagia, Dawsons* is described as being reversible. Unfortunately, though, the doctor was unable to prevent Mr Sligh from swapping one bout of outlandish misfortune for another.

Priapism or zoophagia? How is anyone to choose between such

heavenly gluttonies?' Sligh had demanded to know. The choosing had him nauseous, as if he had picked his way through the two layers in a boxful of rich chocolates.

The priapism was brought under control by regular treatment with the extract and life became somewhat easier when it was learned that a doubled oral dose gave a pharmacological response similar to that of Bagshaw's standard injection. Sligh took his medicine as an aperitif, served in a pewter wine goblet, before supper each evening. Unfortunately, though, he was rapidly becoming as big a menace to the birds as had been Bagshaw Moralee before him. Whilst rolling in a barrel in the cellars beneath the Department of Anaesthesiology, where the group rehearsed their acts, he was forced to consider an unlikely future catapulted between two whopping medical curios.

If he continued to devour the macaws he knew full well that he would shortly eat away the entire source of curative material. It would not be long before lack of treatment would swing him from the zoophagia back to being his old priapistic self. How many weeks were to pass before he would find himself one day consuming a pennyworth of chips and cutting a circlet of wood from the circus barrel? Or queuing at Kendall's store for a quantity of the best red velvet and going from there round the corner to purchase two pennyworth of golden tacks from the little ironmonger's shop in Princess Street? Not many, not many weeks, he thought.

He considered, as a consequence of his continuing zoophagia, the demolition of Bagshaw Moralee's act and with it the possible demise of the circus. Sligh was basically a good man, he couldn't let such a thing happen. He considered the alternative sources of supply which might be available to the zoophagist and wondered how difficult it was to obtain a regular supply of zoo animals from Regent's Park or have them sent to him from the Tower at Blackpool in the same way that his mother had received her hams in Bognor, delivered by motor and brought to the door by a little uniformed chauffeur from Fortnum and Mason's London store. He even considered the eating of domestic pets.

'Domestics is hardly satisfying,' Bagshaw warned him when asked. 'Same old stuff as farm animals, really. I suppose there ain't no substitute for the exotics but the zoo keepers ain't going to part with their beasts. The only way is to breed them yourself as I've had to do.'

'How about stealing them?' asked Mr Sligh who had ceased to roll in his barrel. He was resting, pinning the barrel to the floor with bony shoulder blades. He gazed up at the old man.

'That's hardly a practical proposition, is it?'

'Isn't it? Why?'

'Did you never think about stealing a lion or a tiger? Be a bit dangerous, wouldn't it?'

'Well, yes. I suppose it would, but I was thinking more of a zebra or a giraffe.'

'And how long do you think that will last you?' Bagshaw snapped back. 'Once you've slaughtered him how long do you think he will last before his meat gets high? Even if you kept the carcass cut up in a cold box, how long do you think it would last before the meat went off? You would have to pinch an animal every week to satisfy your lust and that whilst chucking the most part of what had been a perfectly good beast in the dustbin. How long do you think that you could live like that? Wouldn't conscience plague you after a time? Think about it, binfuls of sweet animal, putrid and useless, and all to satisfy your own lust.'

'Is that any different to the way we treat farm animals, cows and sheep and such?' Sligh asked.

'No. No, it isn't – not really.' The old man fell silent, assuming now the guilt for the world's carnivorous appetite.

'It has to be will-power,' Dibden Dawson interrupted. He had been listening carefully to their conversation and decided that he should here step in for he feared if such talk were to continue the old man might be cast into one of his sudden deep depressions.

'Well, you're a fine one to talk about will-power,' Sligh answered shirtily. He rolled in the barrel until he was comfortable on his stomach. His elbows rested on the floor, stabilizing. His head was cupped in his hands. 'You can never let a day go by without a whiff of the ether pads. Talk of will-power is a bit rich coming from you, isn't it? In fact, I'm sure the only reason you choose for us to rehearse in this airless cellar is so that you can pick up the odd wisp of anaesthetic which hangs forever in the awful air.'

'Oh, so you think that all this hard work is just so as I can top up my habit, do you, Mr Sligh?'

'Good heavens, yes,' Sligh mocked, still supporting his head in his hands.

'Good heavens, no,' the doctor answered him. 'No, no, no. Oh, for God's sake, let's not argue. Come along, the rehearsals are going splendidly. We shall soon be ready for the real thing, let's not spoil it by arguing.'

'Ready? However shall we be ready if I have eaten most of Mr Moralee's birds?' screeched back the ex-guardsman.

'But I repeat, it's only a matter of will-power, old chap,' the doctor said calmly, 'and please don't be upset that the advice comes from a man who hasn't any of his own. It doesn't make advice any less valid, does it?'

Mr Sligh stared up at the others. He considered Dawson's request seriously for a moment. 'No. Of course it doesn't. I'm sorry,' he had said.

Sorry as I saw him now, rising beside Clarrie, coming naked out of his barrel. I couldn't take my eyes from him. I searched for the marks the sticky tape would have made on his body.

'Come on, Donald,' said Clarrie, 'we don't want to be hanging about here.'

'But shouldn't I say hello to your mother?' I asked, unable to avert my eyes from Sligh's nakedness. He acknowledged my interest with a friendly nod and climbed a few wooden steps into the back of the wagon then suddenly disappeared into its blackness. I was reminded of a bather just come from the sea, returning to the bathing hut.

'She's asleep right now. She doesn't like to be disturbed. We can come back later and you can see her then. Take me to see the dinosaur.'

'How do you know about the dinosaur?'

'Oh, we met Mr Gill last night. Mother got us lost driving around the marshalling yard in the storm and she demolished his hut. He told us that you had a dinosaur which danced to music or something, we heard it playing.'

'No, he doesn't dance,' I laughed, 'but he nods his head.'

'OK. Will you take me to see him?'

'He's over at the museum.'

'Yes, Mr Gill mentioned that too. What is this museum?'

On the way over there, I told Clarrie of how Mr Brown and I had founded the museum and how Walter Beanlander and I had built the automaton. Since Walter's departure I had made one or two neat adjustments. The whole thing now was caused to begin its movement by the introduction of a penny piece into a slot on the side of the Wardian case. I had built a viewing gantry, too, so that a couple of dozen people were able to look upon the performance at about the level of the iguanodon's head. Many West Yorkshire schools had already organized visits.

I led Clarrie up the steps to the viewing platform, and left her up there while I returned to put a penny in the slot. The clockwork began to whirr, the music struck up and the head nodded among the growing ferns. I climbed back up the steps.

'He has baggy pants,' she said.

'That was Walter, sewing hides around the skeleton. He wasn't very good at it.'

'No. I can see that. I can sew hides, you know. When I lived at Luddenden Foot a dwarf showed me how to fit out Punch and Judy dolls in clothes made from hide but I expect it must be more difficult to fit clothing around a skeleton.'

'Yes. I'm not sure that it's possible to make clothes which will not hang loppy from a bag of old bones.'

'Oh, it is. It's possible but it's difficult. I think the secret is in filling out the bag.'

'Introducing muscle, you mean?'

'Yes, something which you can substitute for muscle. Coal dust, for example. If you shovelled coal dust from the slag heap into the bag it would fill out and take on the contours and the shape of what has been sewn.' I nodded, seeing her point. 'You would need tons and tons of it, mind.' she added.

'How about sugar?' I asked. 'There must be about twenty tons of sugar under the stage here. We are standing right over it.'

She shrugged. 'Sugar will do just as well, I'm sure.' The clockwork stopped, the dinosaur froze in mid-nod, the music ceased. 'You don't get very much for your pennyworth, do you?'

'Really? I thought I was being generous.'

'What? With a nod of the head?'

'No, with the time I allow.' She smiled at me. 'And with the music,' I stammered as an afterthought.

'He needs to be moving more than just his head. That's what people would want to see.'

'A live dinosaur?'

'Well, one which was as nearly alive as possible. People want to be frightened, have excitement like at the circus and at the cinema. Your dinosaur is no more fearsome than a crying dolly.' Then she seemed to be suddenly bored. 'Come on, let's go back to see if my mother is awake yet.'

We walked back towards the common. The drizzle had already begun. The wheel turned squeakily, slipping on the wet. She remarked that she could taste the metal in the rain, something she had not experienced since childhood. I looked at her face. The rain plastered back her hair. She was just an ordinary woman and I wondered how I had ever come to elevate her to the lofty place she had occupied in my head. She allowed me to take a hold of her hand. I felt as if I was making a new start, a fresh attempt at building images. 'Perhaps we could find a way of making him move together?' she said.

When we got back to the wagon, I followed Clarrie up the wooden steps and we too disappeared, as Mr Sligh had done, into the blackness. Once inside I soon realized that the darkness was caused by a pair of black-out curtains which covered the back of the wagon. From without the wagon had appeared impenetrable, but the interior was surprisingly well lit. A series of hurricane lamps hung from the roof. They burned brightly between bamboo cages filled with coloured birds. Many of the cages were open and the birds flew about quite freely. The shadows of the cages were thrust slantwise on to the walls and on to the floor of the wagon. The shadows of the bars were enormous, giving the interior the feel of a prison. The giant shadows of perched birds squawked incessantly. Occasionally one of the cages would swing, causing its shadow to move crazily. I saw the moving stripes fall across the two figures on the mattress which was laid out on the floor. The mattress was covered by a Mexican blanket. Rosanne stirred, her yellow hair falling heavily as she raised her head from the pillow.

'Oh, it is you, *chérie*,' she said. Her eyes were almost closed.

'Yes, Mother, but look who is with me.'

The woman raised her head again, higher this time, clutching the Mexican blanket modestly to her chin. 'Is it Donald?' she asked. 'Come, *chéri*, give your aunt a kiss.' She turned her cheek sleepily towards me.

Was that it? I thought as I bent awkwardly to kiss the cheek she had presented. Do old lovers have such recognition? Is it a smell? Perhaps a star, gazing from the eye? Are they always so formal? I looked at the man snoring heavily beside her and smelled his strange smell. Well, she wouldn't forget that one in a hurry, I thought. Of course, I suddenly realized, we were each in one of her drawn circles. He and I. He the lover, I the nephew. I had to play the part she now circumscribed – this was a new time, a new circle rapidly drawn.

'Hello, Aunt Rosanne,' I said.

'Hello, Donald. How are you?'

'Mother, Donald has a dinosaur,' Clarrie interrupted before I could answer. 'You should see it, it is wonderful. We shall make it move, shan't we, Donald?'

'Yes,' I nodded, wondering about the circle which my cousin was busily constructing for herself.

'A dinosaur? That would be quite a marvellous act, *mes chéris*.'

I looked to the corner beyond where Rosanne had been sleeping. Two apes of some sort sat, each in a captain's chair, and studiously picked fleas from one another's coats. One of them had a purple fez on his head. In the other corner were a stack of barrels, each with a circular hole cut in its side. The holes were surrounded by a bright red material which was tacked to the wood with tiny golden-headed pins.

'His wardrobe?' I whispered to Clarrie.

'More like his estate,' Clarrie answered. 'They are his residences, I suppose.' She laughed. It was loud enough to cause her mother to open her eyes fully.

'Yes, he likes to stick with the one design, like the collection of awful semis with the green drainpipes the council has built over in Leeds,' Rosanne said bitchily.

The man beside her turned open-mouthed in his sleep. A great raft of ether sailed off his breath.

'Oh, *mon dieu*,' Rosanne cried, wafting away the smell with one hand and clutching tight the blanket with the other, 'one day he will explode the hurricane lamps and have us all burned to death.' Then she flapped the invisible cloud of ether hurriedly with the backs of both hands, urging it towards the black curtaining to rid the wagon of the noxious fumes and panicking quietly at the thought of a fire.

And in her panic she had let the blanket slip, revealing her wonderful breasts which, I guessed from the placing of my drawn circle, I was not meant to see. Her amazing breasts, which had acted as stabilizers for much of her working life, were as beautiful as I ever remembered them. As anyone might have ever remembered them, for the sight of Rosanne in full flow on the wire above had been enough to stop children sucking sweets and produced cricks in the necks of colliers who had often attended one performance too many at the first Count Schubert Circus.

'Oh, *mon dieu*,' she said clutching back the Mexican blanket to her chin, 'this man is sometimes so *stupide*. We must be rid of this awful addiction. We have tried so many times and failed, yet in the beginning it was so different. How *stupide* I am, *mon dieu*, I thought once that I had actually succeeded, you know. I thought once that I had actually cured him of his addiction to the anaesthetic *dangereuse*.' Rosanne was pouting, and I knew that we were in for a story.

'You know, I have often thought of your ether as a kind of fuel,' Mr Sligh had confided one night at supper. In the early days following the earthquake and during the period of rehearsals the foursome had regularly taken their evening meal in the room at the rear of the pet shop and Mr Sligh had always dressed for the occasion. He was dressed in his scarlet mess jacket, ready for his soldier's life in the barrel. 'Much in the way petrol makes a motor work,' he continued. 'Without it I think that you would be incapable of carrying out the simplest of tasks.'

'That is probably true,' Dibden Dawson had conceded.

'So?' asked Rosanne of her lodger.

'So perhaps the doctor needs a different fuel, that's all. Maybe he should try gin or something.'

'But wouldn't that be merely replacing one addiction for another?' Rosanne asked Dibden Dawson.

The doctor sighed. 'Indeed it would, *madame*,' he said. 'I have tried alcohol and it only succeeded in putting me to sleep.'

'How about coffee?' asked Bagshaw Moralee.

'What sort of a fuel is coffee?' mocked Sligh irritably.

'You might scoff at the notion of using coffee as a fuel,' said the ancient adventurer, 'but did you know that in the old days the Brazilians used to run their ships on coffee beans? It's cheaper than coal over there and it also happens to be a useful way of creating a shortage, so keeping up the high price of the stuff, to be paid by them what drinks it.'

'Tried it already,' said Doctor Dawson dismissively. 'It only succeeded in keeping me awake.'

'Why don't we try him on petrol, then?' Mr Sligh asked his companions with a sudden flush of excitement as bright as his mess jacket. 'Did you never try petrol?'

'No, can't say I did,' the doctor answered cautiously but it seemed to him that, no matter how empirical the prescription, if he didn't give the suggestion his consideration, thereby setting a good example, there was no way that he was going to be allowed to solve Sligh's dilemma. This was in the days when Sligh was being treated with the extract from the macaws.

For a time the doctor became addicted to both ether and petrol, the latter also taken from a pewter wine goblet as an aperitif each evening. He represented such an explosive mixture that he was made to sleep with the baboons in a metal cage in the cellar under the Department of Anaesthesiology just in case he went off like a bomb. The fumes created in his sleep were constantly inducing the animals into a state of deep narcosis and they proved very difficult to arouse when Rosanne took his early morning tea to the baboonery each morning. Furthermore the fumes were affecting the animals' performances – they became sluggish at rehearsals. It was now a matter of some urgency that a cure be found for Dibden Dawson's ether addiction.

As is often the case in such situations, serendipity took a hand. It was purely accidental that the doctor received Mr Sligh's double dose of extract, his attention for a moment distracted by a pup tying his shoes around with blue wool. He absent-mindedly picked up the wrong goblet before supper one night and whilst Mr Sligh, with a buoyant 'Cheers,' downed the gobletful of petrol Dibden Dawson swallowed the extract meant for Sligh in a single gulp. The results were amazing and everyone was a little fortunate for them not to have been catastrophic. Mr Sligh, who had been smoking a cigarette at the time, set himself alight whilst Doctor Dawson immediately fell in love with Rosanne.

Whilst Bagshaw Moralee struggled with a one and threepenny soda syphon in an attempt to douse the blazing ex-guardsman, Dibden Dawson had quickly lifted Rosanne's dress and surprised the woman (and himself) on the dining table which she had just set for the meal. The macaws and parakeets began to squawk. Mr Sligh smouldered like a near-extinct volcano, crockery and glassware crashing all about him. Dogs barked and kittens meowed. The man and woman on the table thrust themselves this way and that in the wildest of ecstasies in full view of the mahogany shelving where myopic rodents strained to see down the lengths of their noses towards the commotion they could hear originating from the kitchen.

Bagshaw, seeking shelter from the flying plates, threw himself under the table with the pups and kittens. Unfortunately the table was unable to bear the weight of Dibden and Rosanne and only seconds after the old man had taken refuge the hefty pair had crashed through the wood and tumbled on top of him. Out ran the pups, squealing for their mother. The kittens remained, round-eyed, drinking in the scene before they too left, though with a dignity greater than that of their canine colleagues.

Mr Sligh sat and steamed. Half of his moustache had disappeared in the flame which had for a moment engulfed him. Strangely, he didn't look half so sad. He was however rendered senseless – amnesic, Doctor Dawson later said – and wandered about in a daze, still wearing his charred scarlet mess jacket, for a day or so. Poor Sligh now had to struggle on alone, soon to use will-power as the sole curative means for his new-found addiction for Doctor Dawson had discovered the reason for his own.

'At least he thought he had,' Rosanne concluded, 'but it didn't last, *mes chéris*. Ether addiction has a tenacious root, you know. It's too tough to succumb to a mere woman's pulling.' She looked at her sleeping husband and shook her head, I thought, a little ruefully.

47
Questions

Bright posters illustrating baboons, birds, barrels and rope walkers were pasted to the moss-encrusted walls in the next village. They were pinned to the iron-studded presbytery doors and to the rain barrel at the Mechanics Institute. They appeared on the oaks which crowded Aken Jugs, looking like 'reward notices' on the trees in cowboy films. The posters drew attention to the circus which was about to give its performance on the village common. (Our common, since the days of the original Count Schubert Circus, had been a regular spot on which to pitch a big top.) Indeed the flimsy red and white striped tent was already billowing out from the centre of the common, higher than the gas lamp.

Mr Sligh, who had been dispatched further afield to advertise, had tacked a poster, using his tiny gold-headed pins, to the door of the police station in Castleford. Inspector Lockhart wanted to know about it. It would have been an extraordinary coincidence of choice of title, he thought, for the Second Count Schubert Circus which was advertising itself not to have had connections with the first which he had known of the same name. He instructed Sergeant Potter to investigate. Lockhart wanted names. The sergeant went off in a car, seated beside a driver wearing a shiny peaked cap. The sergeant wore a trilby and a belted raincoat which was slightly too long for him. The length of the garment was accentuated by the high tying of the belt which centred the buckle way above the policeman's waist; only just beneath his sternum. As the car sped away, Sergeant Potter tugged the belt more securely about himself, as if tying his bulk into the car to prevent his ever falling out.

He returned an hour later with the names of the circus performers written on a sheet of paper which he handed to the inspector.

'Bingo,' said Lockhart when he had read through the list of names, puffing heartily at his cigar. 'We've got the lot this time, including Clarrie.' He looked at the youthful sergeant who didn't have a waist. 'You don't know what I'm on about, do you Potter?'

The sergeant shook his head. 'No, sir.'

'No. Well, you wouldn't remember the earthquake in Manchester back in nineteen hundred and thirty-one?'

'Pull the other one, sir.'

'No, seriously, Potter, there was an earthquake in Manchester back in May of nineteen hundred and thirty-one. You didn't know that, did you?' He brushed at his dark tash with his index finger thinking what an unbelievable occurrence it had been anyway.

'No, sir.' The sergeant watched smoke rising to the ceiling.

'And would you believe it, the only casualty in the catastrophe, Sergeant, was a policeman who at the time was about to make an arrest at a brothel. He fell from the building.' Lockhart paused, reading again the names which Potter had written on the sheet of paper. 'It's fascinating, don't you think, to speculate? Did he fall accidentally or was he helped on his way, so to speak?'

Potter was silent. The smoke curled into corners where it blindly turned, searching for ways from the room. He watched the inspector counting the names.

'The five names you have just handed me, written on this bit of paper,' he waved it at Sergeant Potter, 'are rather important, Potter.'

The sergeant remained silent, patiently awaiting explanation.

'You see, four of them were questioned by the Manchester CID at the time of the incident, but the other one has never been questioned about that death, or for that matter, about two other serious crimes in which she might have been involved. See, she was in the brothel at the time of the officer's falling, that's clearly established from statements made by the other four, but she ran off. Understand?'

'Yes, sir.'

'Yes,' said the inspector, stubbing out the cigar in a metal ashtray and tasting for a second the bitterness on his lips with a sensual flick of the tongue, 'it's about time we questioned this lass, don't you think? Come on, let's not waste the opportunity, eh? Back in the car, Potter, we'll get 'em at the wagon.'

'Or the tent, sir. They've already erected the tent.'

*

Clarrie brought the others to the museum to see the dinosaur. I was introduced officially to Mr Sligh, Dibden Dawson and Bagshaw Moralee. Bagshaw was feeling out of sorts, too feeble to climb the steps, but Clarrie led her mother and the others up to the viewing platform on the gantry. Bagshaw stayed below, wandering among the exhibits. I inserted a penny in the slot. The music started up and the iguanodon nodded. Rosanne clapped her hands enthusiastically.

'How wonderful, *chéri*. It is so amusing,' she called down when the performance was finished.

'But don't you think it could be so much better, Mother? So much better if we could fill him out and make the skins fit? If we could make the whole body move rather than just the head?'

'But how would you do that, *chérie?*'

'I don't know yet. But Donald thinks we might fill out the baggy skin with sugar.'

'I've about twenty tons of sugar down here under the stage,' I explained to the others. 'We might try it. Clarrie says she can sew the skins more tightly to make a better fit.'

'Yes, *chéri*, but how will you make him move?'

'Easy,' Bagshaw called up, 'you just chuck in the sugar bugs.'

'What sugar bugs?' called down Dibden Dawson.

'These here little bugs, there's loads of 'em all livin' off the sugar in this box down here.'

'Good heavens, yes. What a bloody wheeze,' called the doctor, who managed to see possibilities more quickly than the others, despite his often deceptively drunken appearance.

'If you put in enough sugar bugs, they'll move about, eating their food and bouncing against the skin. It would give the illusion of rippling muscles,' Bagshaw told us.

'Like a load of Mexican jumping beans,' the doctor explained. 'Bagshaw, you are a bloody genius.'

'Well, let's get cracking,' said Mr Sligh. 'The quicker we finish it, the quicker it gets a spot in the circus.'

'Now, hang on,' I shouted up to them. 'He's not for sale.'

'Not for sale, *chéri?* Who wants to buy him? We invite you to join the circus with your magnificent machine. You, Donald, it is you whom we buy, *chéri*.'

'But Aunt Rosanne, I have no intention of joining your circus.'

'Come, Donald. You mustn't be ungallant. You can't disappoint Clarrie. You two have been meant for one another since you were children, but we can't wait about with you. We must soon be on our way.' She looked from the gantry through the window opposite to the dead village. 'Who is waiting? Tell me, *chéri*? Who is waiting about in this God-forsaken place? Many have already left. When the pit finally closes tomorrow, the rest will be gone. We give a single performance tomorrow night and then we too are gone, leaving the place to the wind and the rain; all that it's good for, I think.

'Come on, Donald, this place is dead. As dead as the dinosaur before you. Bring him to life by all means, but bring yourself to life, also. Break away from this terrible place.'

Clarrie was silent, standing beside her mother. The four persons on the gantry above stared sternly down on me. I turned to Bagshaw Moralee, who shrugged his old shoulders and raised an ancient brow.

'How can you disappoint my daughter who has saved herself for you all these years? And don't think it won't be a disappointment for her to have to live with you in this foisty museum. With dead people? With dead things? With decay all around? She is alive, Donald. You must take. I am not asking you to come with us, but to take her. We invite you to take us all, take us after the performance, out of this dreadful place.

'Why do you think we are here, *chéri*? Did you think we came to give a performance? The finest circus in the whole of the land and do you think we came here merely to entertain a tentful of broken colliers, wheezing their early deaths at my breasts? Did you really think that? How dark. How black. How sooty. We are here because she chose for us to come, so that you might see her. How beautiful she is. Do you see that, Donald? And she has saved it all for you. Don't be ungrateful, Donald. Don't kick my daughter in the teeth. I beg you, don't run away from beauty.'

There followed only silence, in which I was judged by those above me. I had nothing to say.

'Don't be dumb, boy,' Bagshaw Moralee whispered into my ear. I felt his old warmth glowing at my side. 'Piss off quick, before you're gobbled into the dark. That's what I did. Java? South America? The circus? What's it matter? Just go and keep on going, boy. Live to a hundred and avoid the decay. Take her with you as I should have taken the princess I once knew. My only regret, boy, not taking my princess. Piss off quick, son.'

The silence from the gantry was broken by Mr Sligh, who again said, 'Let's get cracking then.'

'All right,' I relented, 'let's fill the sack. I want to think about what you have said, Aunt Rosanne, but let's make a start by shovelling the sugar into the bag. You lot get the hessian sacks from under the stage. There are ladders and buckets over there. Lean the ladders up against the glass case. I'll go and get the Beanlanders to come and help.'

'Yes, and I must go too. To find my sewing needles. They are special steel needles I was given for sewing the Punch and Judy clothes. They are in the wagon,' Clarrie said.

We left the museum together. Before we parted I asked, 'Is it true? Is it true that you have been saving yourself for me all this time?'

'Yes,' she whispered, 'it's true. I shall tell you about it sometime. I have done many things to save myself.' She kissed me on the mouth. I ran like the wind to Arkwright's house to find the Beanlanders, expectant of my next kiss.

Clarrie found Lockhart and Potter waiting for her in the wagon. The inspector invited her to sit in a captain's chair. He sat facing her in another, his coat-tails slung over the back of it.

'I have no idea,' she answered his question. 'I was on a couch about to tumble into the street below, when Mr Sligh pulled me back. I don't know what happened to the policeman.'

'Who is this man Sligh?' The light from the hurricane lamps glinted off the frames of Lockhart's spectacles. Clarrie saw a candle burning in the lenses.

'He was my mother's lodger. He lived in a barrel.'

'Why? Why did he live in a barrel?'

'It was something to do with his erection, I think.'

'I don't follow you, Clarrie.'

'He had a permanent erection. The barrel gave him satisfaction, I think.'

'You mean he was a pervert?'

'Perhaps.'

'And you say he prevented you from tumbling from the building at the time of the earthquake?'

'Yes. He rose up from his barrel like a flower and rescued me. I was on the couch which was being vibrated towards the void where the outside wall had been. People were screaming. My mother had already fallen out of the building.'

The cages above their heads were swinging gently, causing shadows to move. 'And the officer? Where was the officer at this time?'

'I told you. I don't know.'

'All right, all right, Clarrie. Take your time. Tell me why you ran away?'

'I don't know. I just ran. I hadn't been well. I was frightened.'

Lockhart was silent for a moment, thinking. Then he said, 'Tell me about the dwarf.'

'Which dwarf?'

'The dwarf at Luddenden Foot.'

'You mean Mr Glynn.'

'Yes. Harry Glynn.'

'What about him?'

'That's what I asked you. Tell me about the dwarf.'

'He threatened to go to the police.'

'About what?'

'About the officer who fell.'

'But how did he know that, Clarrie? How did Harry know about the officer who fell?'

'He must have heard.'

'But how? How did he hear of it, Clarrie? Did you tell anyone?'

'Yes. I told a friend.'

'Then how did you know, Clarrie? How did you know about the officer who fell?'

'Because I read it in a newspaper the day after the earthquake. I read of my mother's broken leg and of an officer who fell from the brothel.'

'Then if you had nothing to hide why be frightened of the dwarf going to the police?'

'I told you, I had been ill. I was frightened. I didn't want to be questioned.'

'All right, so you killed Harry Glynn because he threatened to go to the police? Is that it?'

'Killed him? No.'

'He threatened you a long while, love. Nine or ten years – that's a long time to endure a threat.'

'Yes, but the threat was softened by the game we played.'

'Ah, so it was a game? A hanging game? He was killed by accident?'

'What are you talking about? Nobody was killed. Harry's not dead.' She watched the candle flames burning in Lockhart's lenses. She was unable to see his eyes. The shadows of the bars moved back and forth across his face.

'Well, if you didn't kill Harry, who did?'

'I've no idea what you are talking about. Harry was alive and well when I last saw him, that's all I know. Is Harry dead?'

He ignored her question. 'Well, if you didn't kill him, Clarrie, you stole his threepenny pieces?'

'I did not.' She was indignant. 'I earned them. That was our game.'

'So you say that you won them from him?'

'In a manner of speaking, yes. I won them.'

'And the boy on the beach at Blackpool?'

'What of him?'

'Did you know him?'

'No.'

'What did you win from him, Clarrie?'

'Nothing. I told you I never knew him. I thought he was a rock.'

'You thought he was a rock?'

'Yes. I thought he was a rock.'

The Beanlanders, as had been predicted, became a credit to the constancy of their father's gametes. They not only looked alike but each child had grown to the same even height. They each entered adulthood, so far as I could judge, at the same height as Walter – a family of six-footers, as alike as the railings taken from the walls which had circled the churchyard.

I had made a large hole in the hides in the region of the skeleton's neck. It was big enough to allow the sugar to be poured in easily.

The Beanlanders humped the buckets up and down the ladders, pouring sugar from the filled ones and handing on the empties to Rosanne and the others who refilled them, shovelling sugar from the hessian sacks.

When after an hour Clarrie hadn't returned to the museum I began to get worried. Her mother was concerned too and Bagshaw Moralee and I were dispatched to see if we could find her.

We walked over to the wagon. We were some way off when I recognized the police car which was parked beside the gas lamp. As we approached I nodded to the driver in the peaked hat whom I knew slightly and I told Bagshaw of my fears that Clarrie might for some reason have been detained by the police. I climbed the few steps into the wagon, pushing aside the black-out curtain. I could see that the mattress had been stowed on its side at the back of the wagon where it had been covered by the Mexican blanket. Now that the big top was erected there was less clutter, giving the occupants more room in which to move around. The apes and the barrels had gone. The birds squawked in their cages, their barred shadows swinging back and forth across the two figures who occupied the central area. Clarrie and Lockhart were seated in chairs opposing one another. Sergeant Potter stood, slightly at ease (the way he wore his raincoat suggested that he could never be fully at his ease), with his back to us as we entered. Clarrie appeared to be washed out, energy drained by the ordeal of Lockhart's relentless questioning. A dusty quiet hung in the air, settling itself, as after an explosion.

'And you must be Mr Moralee?' Lockhart guessed when the old man had followed me through the black-out curtain.

'Yes. I'm Bagshaw Moralee.'

'You were in the street, outside the brothel, that night the earthquake hit Manchester, is that right?'

'Yes, that's right, but what you want to know for?'

'Never you mind what it's for, sir. Just answer the questions, please, there's a good chap.'

Bagshaw shrugged his narrow shoulders.

'Now, you saw the rope walker fall, is that right, Mr Moralee?'

'No, she was already lying there in the rubble when I got into the street. I saw him come hurtling down, though.'

'Who is him, Mr Moralee?'

'The police officer. Saw him falling from the brothel.'

'Think he might have been pushed?'

'Well, I can't say if he was pushed or not, can I? But he came over at some speed, I can tell you, like a cougar bounding over the falls at Niagara.'

'But you are certain the rope walker was in the street before the police officer came down?'

'Absolutely.'

'Well, that lets her off the hook, then, doesn't it?'

'Absolutely,' Bagshaw said again and smiled.

The inspector removed his spectacles and cleaned the lenses with a fresh white handkerchief. Then he replaced them carefully, hooking the soft frames over his ears. 'Miss Schubert Brightside has just told us that she was in the brothel at the time, but has no recollection of what happened to the officer. She does however recall being prevented from going the same way as her mother by a man who lived in a barrel. Montague Sligh. You know Mr Sligh?'

'Yes.'

'Bit rum, isn't it?'

'What is?'

'Him living in a barrel. Getting his pleasure from it, we understand.'

'Men get pleasure in all sorts of ways, Inspector.'

'Well, perhaps in your experience, eh? But not in mine.' He grimaced. 'I understand he was treated for it. Treated by this Doctor Dawson, who is also a member of your circus troupe. A medical doctor, is he?'

'That's right.'

'Now, I wouldn't have thought there was much could've been done for a complaint like that. Wouldn't have thought there was a tablet for treating a man of misplaced pleasure in a barrel. Would you have thought it, Sergeant?'

Potter laughed, playing with his fingers behind his back. He appeared to be counting them, over and over again, frightened perhaps that one of Lockhart's cutting questions might have lopped one off. 'I shouldn't have thought so, sir, no,' he said and started to whistle.

'Don't do that, Sergeant,' Bagshaw advised.

'Don't do what, sir?'

'Whistling. Don't do whistling like that, Sergeant.'

The policeman brought himself to attention, the buckle on his raincoat higher then ever. He stared through the old man and continued defiantly with his whistling. Why should an old fart like this tell him what he should or shouldn't be up to?

'I wouldn't whistle like that if I was you, Sergeant,' Bagshaw said again, as a red macaw flew from its open cage and landed on the policeman's head. Potter, who had unsuccessfully tried to take evasive action by ducking low, brought a confident full hand of digits from behind his back and carefully lifted the bird from his head. It ripped a sharp talon into his thumb. 'Christ. Tha little bugger,' he cried.

Half a dozen birds then flew from their cages and settled on Potter's head and shoulders.

'I wouldn't do that if I was you,' Lockhart warned his sergeant. 'I think the gentleman is trying to tell you that the whistling affects the birds. Is that not correct, Mr Moralee?'

Bagshaw nodded, but Lockhart's support had come too late. About twenty birds had now settled, causing the unfortunate Potter to have completely disappeared. He was stumbling drunkenly about the wagon, knocking into objects and causing them to fall over and all the while being joined by more of the quiet birds, who as a flock were intent upon sculpting their umbrella around him.

'Stand still, man,' Bagshaw called sternly. 'Stand still or they'll have your eyes out, do you hear?'

The policeman continued to stumble, muffled noises of protest coming from under the choking feathers.

'Or suffocated,' Bagshaw added quietly.

'Is there nothing you can do?' Lockhart asked, suddenly realizing the peril his sergeant was in. A deathly hush fell about Potter.

'What are you going to do about the little lass, Inspector?' Moralee asked, putting his hand upon my cousin who sat quietly in the captain's chair.

Potter fell to the floor under the sheer weight of feathers and lay on his back, arms flailing aimlessly at the dozens of congregating birds. Blood streaked on his hands.

'Now look, Moralee, if there's something you are able to do, then do it, for God's sake,' Lockhart said angrily. 'I've questioned the girl closely already. I don't think we have any reason to detain her. But I shall probably want another word with her, and with Mr Sligh and probably with the doctor chap too, before the circus leaves.'

'So the girl can go?'

'She can go for the time being, yes. Now, for God's sake do something about these bloody birds, will you?'

The old man clapped his hands once, the birds flew from the distressed policeman to reveal his florid gasping face. He had a mass of small cuts all over his head. He staggered down the wooden steps on to the grass, clutching at his collar, attempting to loosen it. There he spluttered and choked until, at last, he vomited.

Clarrie searched about for the sewing needles she had originally returned to get. Once outside the wagon, Lockhart drew me to him. We were under the gas lamp and he held open the heavy car door. I had the feeling he was trying to shield me in some way, putting himself and the car door between me and the others. 'I should be very careful, if I were you, son,' he said. Clarrie and I returned with Bagshaw Moralee to the museum.

48
The exhibition

The following night the dinosaur, wearing his new set of clothes, was put on public display. The glass case had been hitched to the wagon in the same way that the panharmonicon was still hitched to the case itself. They were towed from the museum after sunset and were now positioned behind the striped tent, out of the view of the audience.

We fixed up the Movietone sound system inside the big top. The iguanodon's introduction was preceded by several minutes of dinosaur roar, as a fanfare precedes the coming of the prize-fighter. The record which Jacky Jellis had made many years before blared from the speakers. We hoped that it would in some measure prepare the audience for what was to come. Children froze in their seats. Colliers, expectant of Rosanne, ceased to crick their necks and laughed and gossiped nervily. In near-darkness, the glass case was silently wheeled on its final journey to the centre of the sawdust ring. The lights were switched on.

The ferns had been cut back. As Bagshaw Moralee had predicted, the sugar bugs rippled the muscles. The effect had been achieved by inserting lumps of damp sugar just below the sewn hides and bunging a bug into each damp lump. As the bugs gobbled away, the lumps of sugar moved. The whole peripheral area was alive with the unseen, munching bugs. For added effect I had manacled the limbs to the four corners of the iron framework which supported the glass panels. The clockwork was dispensed with. The dinosaur's skin, so ably sewn together by Clarrie, rippled like a field of corn. The panharmonicon struck into the first movement of the symphony.

A silence fell about the audience. Having been quite unable to guess what it was which made the rattling noise whilst they sat in the dark, and now seeing that it was due to the chains, they became disquieted. Several children screamed and mothers ran with them from the tent. The muscles continued to ripple, causing the forelegs to tug at the manacles. A giant foot stamped, squashing a mouse. The organ pipes squeaked.

'Ooh!' they gasped.

The large spotlights played directly on him, and the hide and the area beneath the skins soon warmed, causing the bugs to become all the more active. The limbs tugged more fiercely at the chains. With a roar from Jacky Jellis a link snapped.

'Ooh!' they gasped some more.

A collier at the front of the audience, who thought he had come to see a woman with breasts like water-wings, panicked and shouted, 'Bloody thing's alive.' This brought several others racing from the tent. Another manacle snapped, and an even louder chorus of 'Oohs' went up. The forelegs were free. Half-way through the Prague's first movement his head began to shake from side to side and when he appeared to be beating at his chest in the manner of King Kong, the audience had had enough. Taking their cues from a collective memory of the film, they stampeded for the exit.

That night we needed police protection and a cordon of half a dozen bobbies was flung about the tent, which gave Lockhart his opportunity to interview Mr Sligh and Dibden Dawson.

The ex-guardsman was dressed in his new scarlet mess jacket. 'I have no idea,' he said. 'I was far too busy rescuing the girl. I don't know what became of the officer.'

'And the girl was on the couch the whole of the time?' Inspector Lockhart wanted to know. He was fascinated by the bobbling dinosaur which was in his glass case immediately behind Mr Sligh.

'Well, I am unsure when the officer disappeared, you understand. But yes, she appears to have been on the couch from a time before her mother fell to the time I lifted her from it myself.'

'And you saw her for the whole of the time, did you?'

'No, Inspector, you know very well that I was in a barrel.'

'So she could have pushed the officer sometime after her mother fell, but before the barrel broke, when you say you are able to verify that she was on the couch?'

'I shouldn't have thought so.'

'But it is possible?'

'Good heavens, no,' interrupted Dibden Dawson.

545

'Why not?' asked the inspector.

'If, as I am given to understand, the policeman weighed about three times as much as the girl, how on earth would she get him to move?'

Lockhart watched the dinosaur. 'How did you get him to move?' he asked.

'That's our secret, Inspector.'

'Then perhaps she has a secret, too.'

'Heavens, it's not very likely.'

'No, sir, it's not very likely, but not much about this case is very likely, is it?'

Doctor Dawson screwed an eye.

'It's not very likely she pushed him, Inspector,' Sligh said. 'In fact it's downright impossible for Clarrie to have pushed him, because although I couldn't see him, I could feel the policeman right up to the time when the barrel broke,' Sligh said.

'And what do you mean by that, sir? I thought you said you were in the barrel.'

'I was.'

'Then how were you able to feel him, as you say? You mean you could sense his presence or something?'

'Well, put more accurately, Inspector, he could feel my presence.'

'What do you mean, Mr Sligh? You'll have to explain.'

'Well, he had a hold of me.'

'But you were in the barrel?'

'Yes, I was.'

'Then how could he have had a hold of you?'

'He had a hold of my erection.'

'Your what?'

'My erection was poking out of the hole in the barrel and the policeman had a hold of me. Isn't that what a policeman should do when making his arrest? Shouldn't he take a hold of the culprit, Inspector? He had a hold of me, certainly from the time the girls began to scream, which is when Madame fell from the room, until the time when the barrel broke.'

'Are you sure?'

'Yes. I'm certain of the times.'

'I mean, are you sure it was the officer who was holding your whatsit?'

'It was him all right, I'll swear it.'

'Good Lord,' Lockhart said. 'What do you know? A bent copper.' Then with a quickness deserving of his position, the police inspector asked, 'Then how about you, Mr Sligh? Perhaps it was you what threw the officer from the building?'

'Good heavens, no,' Dibden Dawson interrupted again. 'How on earth could a person with a painful erection grapple with a man twice his weight and hurl him from a building, for God's sake? How would you fancy a brawl whilst handicapped with such an encumbrance, Inspector?'

'And you can verify he was in such a condition, can you, Doctor?' Lockhart snapped back.

'Yes, for heaven's sake. The fellow's a priapist. I treated the condition myself.'

'But might he not have been tricking you? After all, erections are quite commonplace. How do you know his was a permanence?'

'Mr Sligh, drop your pants,' the doctor instructed with a sigh.

Mr Sligh obliged.

'There you are, Inspector,' the doctor commented smugly. 'How many chaps do you know who might be turned on by your repetitive and, might I say, singularly unerotic questioning?'

49
The leaving

The bird cages were put back among the hurricane lamps, the baboons seated in the captain's chairs in a corner of the wagon. The barrels were stacked one on another in the opposite corner. The seating was dismantled and stowed in the wagon along with the ropes and other props. We lowered the striped tent and put that away too. The Wardian case was hitched again to the wagon, the dinosaur's muscles danced, the head nodded. The panharmonicon was once more hitched to the Wardian case. I overrode the triggering mechanism and Mozart spilled out continuously.

My grandparents left their window and came out to wish me luck. There would be no complaining about what was to become of them. I told them that I would send money. My grandfather mumbled, talking with God. My grandmother cast her disapproval on Clarrie and Rosanne and from the pasty-faced look I detected the duty I still must serve. I said again that I would send money as often as I could. She took his arm and turned with him, leading the way back to the house.

Arkwright came with his grandchildren. He shook my hand. I offered the keys to the museum and asked him to look after the rag-bag of acquisition I was leaving behind. He took the keys from me. His eyes danced.

Henrietta arrived. She apologized for the absence of Mr Tsiblitz. She explained that he couldn't be there to see us go, but he had promised a surprise going-away present. She told us to keep our eyes open and to be alert so that we shouldn't miss it.

Rosanne and Doctor Dawson climbed into the cab, Mr Sligh cranked up the engine which rumbled into life without fuss, then he joined the others in the cab. Bagshaw Moralee had previously been put into the Wardian case where he had gone to sleep stretched out among the ferns. Clarrie and I sat on the lovers' seat at the side of the panharmonicon. The wagon tugged us off, rattling the chains on the dinosaur's feet. The head nodded more fiercely as we rode up the bumpy road. The giant tail whipped lazily over the soil in the bottom of the case, sweeping the rats away. To hell with it, I thought, and began to mime the playing of the music on the keyboard. Clarrie soon picked it up and we provided a dumb duet to our leaving. The few who had turned out waved goodbye. We heard Westerman's pigs grunting among the butterbur. Doyle listened to his lettuce grow beside snoozing sallow. The wagon tugged us on up the hill. We passed the big house where deep in his home the drowned coal owner sat. The winding wheel was eerie quiet. We could hear Squire Potterton potting at the birds. It had turned out to be a bright day. I saw the breeze whip poppies and harebell as we gathered speed once over the rise.

Outside his cottage at Kettle Flatt, Mr Tsiblitz was preparing his surprise. He climbed into the rubber pterodactyl suit and opened the valve. The air rushed madly in, ballooning out the suit. Tsiblitz soared into the sky. A rush of blue, I saw him above us for a second or two then he was gone. Clarrie and I clapped heartily; distantly behind, we heard villagers cheering. The iguanodon had attracted a prehistoric bird to his leaving: nothing could have been more apt.

We hadn't got very far down the Wakefield road when Mr Gelatini came from behind, huffing and puffing on his tricycle with the fat black tyres. He caught up with us and asked us to return quickly.

'It's a gotta come back, boy, summat a terrible's happened.'

'I'm not going back to be questioned by that awful policeman, I'm not,' said Clarrie.

'No, it's a notta the police, it'sa Mr Tsiblitz.'

'What's up with Tsiblitz?' I asked.

'He's a bin and gotta shot. Squire Potterton's gone and shotta Mr Tsiblitz.'

We turned back.

There was a short inquest and the following day we took Mr Tsiblitz to his funeral at the church in the next village. There were a lot of mourners. The coffin lay on the grass next to the clay-red hole.

Nobody knew what to say. Henrietta wept, a black net veil covering her face. I thought about the inquest, how the coroner had acted in indecent haste, deciding the death to have been accidental. I thought how Isaac's father had been hanged for that, hanged at Leeds jail because he had accidentally shot somebody, but Potterton had got only a ticking off. 'Be more careful next time,' the coroner had said. Potterton had twitched his milk-tea moustaches, that gesture of little understanding. He had stumbled from the little court room in Castleford, bumping into a chair which was placed by the door to hold it open, letting air into the stifling room.

We waited by the open grave; no preacher came. At the other side of the hole, directly opposite me and standing shoulder to shoulder, were Mr Gelatini and his phoney Italian accent, Edith Juvelah's daft brother with a toad beneath his hat and Inspector Lockhart. I saw then what at some time my Uncle Lancaster must have seen, the prototype for the Marx Brothers. A grotesque triptych sculpted above the gaping hole. A cruel parody of the life we were about to bury and finish with, yet an accurate portrayal of life itself. The man who would choose to be the perpetual foreigner, the man who would choose to be stupid and the man who, in our stupidity, we would choose as being wise.

Lockhart, the wise one, flapped his coat-tails. 'Be careful, son.' He mouthed the words at me.

I looked about. Care and chance, I thought, and watched Charlie with his one leg, wringing his hat in his hands. Arkwright, with his mane of white hair blowing in the wind and his daughter with hers which frizzed and remained still. Rube Hardwick. Doyle and his woman, holding the lettuce sandwiches, for distribution after the burial, in a couple of brown paper bags.

My grandparents, and a host of others who could tell many a tale of having flown in those wonderful rubber suits. Old men and women, because that's all that was left, now the pit had closed for good. Old and knackered and not coming back. The wind blew over the grass. The surface of the water in the barrel stirred, the slime mould stank. I was wondering what we should do. We couldn't just bury him, not just put him there, in that red hole, without the words falling on him as well as the muck. I thought about Tsiblitz's inventiveness and about baggy pants culture. I thought about the atom bomb the Americans had dropped on Hiroshima and of the other, on Nagasaki. I thought how my Uncle Lancaster had lived long enough to make a film in Technicolor. I thought of Walter, whose photograph I had seen in a newspaper only days before, and of his computing machine with all those fancy valves. I thought of Edison and of Bell. I looked at Arkwright, hair to the wind. I thought about the telephone and about talking to our neighbours across the sea. I thought about invisibility machines and about cement which grabs burglars. It was all progress. If you accept evolution as progress, then it had all been progress. Blind alleys and false starts, but progress. It was all baggy pants culture. For us, there was no other. You picked up the ball and you ran with it, for that was the only ball there was. There was no other, not for us.

Clarrie was at my side. I loved Mr Brown. I thought about the love I had carried for Clarrie all those years and how I loved Mr Brown and I remembered then to collect his ashes from the museum before we left. Whatever Clarrie had seen at the barrel's belly had been progress too. Jellyfish and bivalve, she had told me. The Professor of Oleopharmacognosy had thought it was progress. Are we to argue with that seedsman, with that student of hope? Are we to argue with his science which one day, sure as seeds follow seeds, would dump my grandfather, pasty-faced, upon the moon? In this world of mutually agreed partition would the seedsman argue with our humour? With the Marx Brothers? Would he bother with the foreign and the mad? Would you expect him to take on Groucho, our spokesman, the one we have chosen to be wise?

I thought about the yellow rattle binding on the roots of grass and about laughter from distant rooms. Clarrie nuzzled her arm in mine. The wind rippled her hair. All was uncertainty. There is no certainty, I thought, watching her hair move. I thought of the clay hole. I thought of the earth and of the sky and I wondered where the preacher was.

'We can't just bury him. We can't just put him in there without the words,' I said aloud.

A long way off I heard wind caught in a wheel. Not our wheel, but the wheel at a distant pit, winding a new dark cycle of birth and rebirth. Then we heard a whistling and for a second my thoughts ceased. I stopped thinking long enough to listen and to understand.

The wind fell silent and above its silence, I heard. I looked about and I knew that they too had heard the whistling and they were silent, and thankful.

For up the hill comes Huddy Greenblatt. He is flanked by strong children and he is whistling. He comes carrying the lid of stars and whistling round the corner of his hat and I know in this bright day I shall move earth and I shall move sky, bringing together the two halves of the bivalve.